IRONBOUND

IRONBOUND BOOK ONE

ALSO BY ANDREW GIVLER

THE DEBT COLLECTION:
Soul Fraud
Dandelion Audit
Star Summit
Death Tax

————

Visit andrewgivler.com/books for more information
or to join my mailing list.

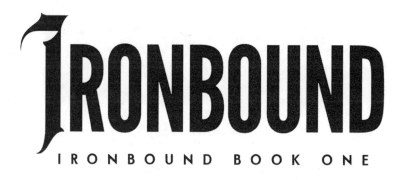

IRONBOUND

IRONBOUND BOOK ONE

ANDREW GIVLER

IRONBOUND
Published by Vault
In association with Aethon Books

ISBN 978-1-63849-304-4 (paperback)

First Aethon & Vault Edition: August 2025

Printed in the United States of America.
1st Printing.

Aethon Books
www.aethonbooks.com

Vault Storyworks
www.vaultstoryworks.com

Cover art by Matt Sellers. Cover typography by Steve Beaulieu.
Print formatting by Kevin G. Summers, Adam Cahoon, and Rikki Midnight.

*To my mortal rival: Brian J. Nordon,
I hope you choke on Quest Academy. (And caviar).*

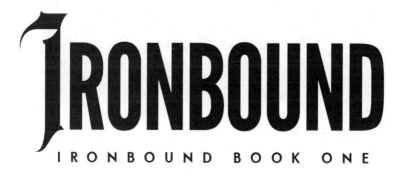

IRONBOUND

IRONBOUND BOOK ONE

PART 1

THE SENTENTIA

CHAPTER 1

agister Vellum's voice cracks like his whip overhead as he interrogates the student balancing on the undulating beam. "What are three congruencies of the Flame and the Ice?" he demands. I resist the urge to roll my eyes at how easy of a question that is. A light touch for one of the teacher's favorites.

The brawny teen boy is named Clintus, and he grimaces as he struggles to maintain his balance on the obstacle. He's not very good at theoretical questions while standing still, let alone while under duress. Vellum's whip flicks forward, popping in the air above the sturdy boy.

"They are both tied to temperature," the student mutters uncertainly, ducking under the threat of the magister. His widespread arms windmill, clawing the air like naked wings trying to help him find his equilibrium. "They both are deadly, and um—" Clintus's footing gives out, and he spills down to the sand pit a few paces below. Our teacher sighs in disappointment; Clintus is not one of his favorites because of his intellect. Vellum coils his whip as he turns to face the rest of our class with narrowed eyes.

We are the senior group of *discipuli*—students who will reach their majority before the end of the harvest season. All our lives, we have been weighed and measured, and we fifty have been chosen to stand before the Censors to be judged worthy. Like the wheat fields that grow in abundance around our town, we are here to be threshed. Only the best *discipuli* of our year will be chosen to receive the blessing of a *Cor* Heart from the Empress, and Clintus's poor showing is a good sign for me, as he is my competition.

"Castor, wipe that grin off your face and get on the machine," Vellum snaps, sharp as ever. His white toga shifts as he puts his hands on his hips, exposing the silver lines of metal running through the flesh of his arms like veins.

My heart skips a beat at his stern expression, but I nod and step out of line with the fifty other students. As I squeeze past my peers, someone sticks out their leg to trip me. Felix, I know without looking. I ignore him as I stumble, making my way to the narrow machine. It's crafted out of leather and articulating planks of wood tied together that make a wave when someone powers it. I settle my nerves as I climb up the front. This isn't my first time riding it. There's no reason to be scared.

"Let's see," Vellum muses, fixing me with his dark gaze. The magister has never liked me—which doesn't make me special. He doesn't seem to like most people. But he's especially never liked that I'm good at seeing similarities.

"Begin," he calls to me, nodding to one of his assistants to flip the lever on the machine. The relic within begins to move, and I ride the waves it makes easily. It takes a little while for it to build up momentum.

"What are three congruencies of the Sword and the Wind?" he asks, glaring at me, his brown eyes daring me to do something clever. I'm surprised but not shocked that he's chosen a Symbol that has at least five degrees of specificity. *Discipuli* are only expected to be proficient to the third degree before they come of age. The Wind is only two levels, but the Sword is much more complex.

"They both are sharp. They can cut a man or a crop," I answer without hesitating, cresting another swell. His eyes narrow, but he isn't bothered—finding one is easy; even Clintus *should* be able to do that. The motion beneath my feet begins to pick up, but I'm not off balance yet. My body follows the rhythm while my brain scrambles to find a solution to the puzzle.

On the surface, the Sword and the Wind are almost opposites. One is made of metal that has been refined and crafted into a specific shape by man. The other is a force of nature—it was here before us and will be here long after we are gone. But the art of finding the similar threads between things is to think beyond the surface. To find what a thing *is* and then what it has in common with the other.

Crack! The whip snaps just above my head. I flinch a little, but not much. The magister never hits a student until the third strike. A smile passes across my face as I realize that there is a congruence in what they cannot do. Negative congruencies can be just as important as positive ones.

"Both can be blocked by a shield or wall," I tell him, looking into his eyes. They narrow a little more, but he nods in acceptance. The tide beneath my feet has come in. I begin to dance a little to ride the crests of the waves.

I need one more, but I'm stumped. They're too different, or more correctly, the similarities are too subtle for my experience to detect.

There is always some sort of path to unite two elements. Excelling in the hunt for congruency requires the same sort of skill that makes an excellent sommelier, but a big part of it is simply instinct.

Then an idea takes hold, a candle burning in the otherwise empty darkness of my mind.

"Both—" Red-hot pain flares in my shoulder, and I lose the wave. My feet are swept out to sea, and I crash down on the wavemaker before being tossed down into the sand below.

Shocked that he struck me earlier than usual, I leap to my feet, spitting sand out of my mouth. But Vellum has already turned from me to pick on another member of the class. His negative attention is clear: my turn is at an end.

"Both dance," I mutter to myself, climbing out of the pit to rejoin my classmates. Marcus, my best friend, rolls his eyes at me as I slip back into the assembled students looking down on the training grounds. The dark-skinned young man is always telling me that trying to be clever only ever gets me in trouble.

That's easy for him to say. He'll probably be able to carry boulders on his back even without the aid of a *Cor* Heart once he finishes growing. Some of us don't have brute force as a backup to fall on if we don't make it through the *Sententia*—the Sentencing. Even if he is chosen, Marcus will probably join the legions anyway. Earning his Heart before enlisting will allow him to enter a more prestigious unit. It's been his dream since we were children. Not mine—I have a little more imagination and no desire to be prevented from Ascending.

The rest of the class goes in the same manner. Magister Vellum calls each student up to the wavemaker one by one. Everyone ends up in the sand eventually. No one else is asked about a Symbol with five layers of specificity.

I'd be more bothered if I wasn't used to it. My mother says that the teachers are here to push us. Since the Empress demands that the blessing of a *Cor* Heart only be given to her strongest citizens— especially in a drought year—he's only doing his duty.

Personally, I think it feels a little targeted.

When all fifty of us have failed, the crotchety old man turns, letting his whip drop to his feet. He crosses his arms and glares at us. My gaze is drawn once more to the metallic veins that course through his forearms and vanish up his shoulders. He is an *argentum*—a Silver-level *electus*. While I know that it is possible to become an *aurum*, that is Gold, I've never seen someone who has managed that task.

Old Magister Vellum is one of the most powerful *electii* in our town, and even though he doesn't like me, I still can't help but feel a little bit of awe every time I see the markings of his *Cor*. His eyes spear mine, and I feel certain that he knows exactly what I am staring at. A warmth spreads across my cheeks as I fight the urge not to blush.

"Right. Well, I can't say that I'm particularly impressed," Vellum sneers, turning his attention away from me to the class. "I've had word from the *Universitas*. The Empress's Censors are on their way. This was your last training session before the *Sententia* begins."

A low murmur of excitement runs through the room like a bolt of lightning. I feel an echoing surge in my chest as my own heart begins to race. So soon! In my head, I knew that it's almost harvest time. The wheat fields that surround our town have turned the rich gold color, which means they are ready to be reaped. But I thought that we still had a few more weeks before it would be our turn. Usually, we are one of the last places that the Censors visit on their route.

"I have informed the City Council to begin the preparations for the *Sententia*. This time next week, you will undertake your final tests. Until then, spend time reflecting on what I and the other teachers have attempted to teach you for these last few years. *Vale*," he dismisses us with a casual wave.

"Magister Vellum," I call without thinking. Surprised, the old man turns to fix me with an annoyed stare. "Did the *Universitas* say how many hearts they were bringing?" Annoyed scoffs echo from my fellow students. Of course they know I'm the one to ask. But despite the chuckles, my classmates all tense, most of them eager to know the answer too.

Vellum's eyes track over the room before his stern expression softens, and for a moment, he almost looks like a tired teacher who cares for his students. Then it passes, and his mask is back. "They did not. You'll have to find out at the end of the *Sententia* like every other *discipuli* in the empire. Now, get out of my sight."

We do as he commands, making our way out of the auditorium and into the main hallway of the *collegium*. Segesta is not one of the largest cities in the empire, but our rich farmland means that we have the money to afford a proper school. Ours has an auditorium, a library, *and* an arena.

Servants wait for us as we exit, each of them handing us a linen shirt and pair of pants that have been dyed a deep red. My heart skips a beat as I feel the cloth in my hands. For the next week, this is all I will wear when I am out of my father's house. It marks me as one coming of age, preparing to undertake the *Sententia*.

Around me, my classmates begin to shed their clothing, and eagerly, I follow suit. I'm too excited about the chance to finally wear my aspirant's uniform to realize that I'm changing around my peers. This is the beginning of the dream I've had ever since I was a boy. But today, I'm awake.

When I have finished, I tuck my old clothes under my arm and make my way to the entrance of the school, where Marcus and Valentina wait. They're wearing matching crimson outfits, and both of them smirk at the grin on my face.

Marcus is dark and striking. He's always been bigger than most of the boys our age. But he's not just brawn; a keen intelligence lurks in his brown eyes. It shows itself as a twinkle that always seems to be laughing at a joke no one else has heard. I said that my dreams are more imaginative than his, but that does not mean they are smarter.

Valentina, on the other hand, is shorter than me and thin. Her blonde hair is the same shade of gold as the wheat that surrounds our city. Large blue eyes burn with their own clever light. Her dreams are not subdued or gentle, but bold. Granted, since her father is the mayor of the town, she doesn't have to hide them.

The three of us have been friends since before we could walk. Our grandfathers were friends before we were born. Our fathers are all on the city council together, our mothers like sisters.

"Look at him," she chuckles to Marcus, waving a hand at me. "Our dear Castor looks as smug as a cat that has swallowed a nest of sparrows."

"He does seem remarkably pleased," Marcus agrees with a solemn nod. "Especially for someone who failed without completing their first congruency question during training."

"Hey," I splutter, feeling a little ganged up on. "No one else got asked about a Symbol that had five levels of specificity!"

"Five levels of specificity, was it?" Valentina mocks, turning to lead us away from the *collegium* and into the cobbled streets of the town. "I'm sure that was very scary for you. As if you don't dream in congruencies."

"I don't know why you're bullying me," I grumble, feeling a flush at the base of my neck. "You're at least *Tertius* in the class."

"Yes," she agrees languidly, glancing over her shoulder with a wink. "At least." She's right. The class rankings are a secret, but anyone with eyes can tell that Valentina is toward the top of the list. She excels at both the theory and the physical challenges that they use to separate the wheat from the chaff of our generation. She might even be *Secundus*. The only thing we know for sure is that she isn't *Primus*. The rankings may be a mystery, but Felix's place at the top is obvious.

"What about me?" Marcus asks in a mock-offended tone. "Do you have me ranked in the top decade, Castor?"

I narrow my eyes as I study my best friend, a hint of a smile tugging at the corner of my lips. Marcus is in the top ten and he knows it. "Eleventh, maybe," I suggest.

"How dare you?" The big boy draws himself up short and places his hand on his chest in pretend outrage. "After seventeen long years of friendship, I can't believe you would think so little of my abilities."

"Oh, spare me." I laugh, waving a hand to shoo his performance away. "Everyone knows that you're going to join the legions no matter what you place. You'll get a *Cor* Heart one way or another."

"True." A quick grin flashes across his face, then is gone.

"If there is anyone we should be worried for, it's you, Castor." Valentina stops and turns back to the two of us, a serious expression on her face.

"I'm not concerned," I lie, drawing myself up straight. "I'm probably *Sextus*. Sixth almost always gets a Heart."

"But there is a drought." Some of my good mood fades as I'm forced to acknowledge the dark truth that I spend a lot of my time deliberately not thinking about.

Cor is the conduit that allows a person to attune to a Symbol and channel its power. The mysterious metal is not from our world. Every year, it falls like rain, and the Empress's Censors recover it and refine it, preparing it into hearts for those coming of age.

No one knows—or if they do, they have not shared with me—where it comes from. The priests say that Prometheus stole the secret of its use from the gods before we killed them, but that story does not say where they found it. Whatever its source is, the empire treats it like rain and collects it. All *Cor* Hearts belong to the Empress, and she bestows them to her most worthy citizens as a blessing.

But like rain, sometimes the *Cor* harvest can be unpredictable. Most years, a town of our size and import receives ten hearts from the Censors. A full decade of our students can expect to be bound.

But this is not a normal year.

Even before the wheat began to sprout, rumors spread that the Censors were warning of a potential drought year. Most ignored it; everyone knew the heaviest *Cor* showers occur during the summer nights that had yet to come. There was no reason to be concerned. But summer came and went, and I only saw a handful of streaks in the sky, even though I kept watch every single night on my parents' roof.

The last drought was thirty years ago. According to the records in the *collegium*'s library, the Censors brought six hearts with them to the *Sententia*.

"I'm probably *Sextus*, right? If Magister Vellum is going to ask me for fifth-level Symbols…"

"You might be *Sextus*," Valentina agrees thoughtfully, but there is a troubled look in her eyes that I can't ignore.

"Didn't you say in the last drought that sixth got one?" Marcus asks, glancing back at me.

"Exactly." I smile, trying to dispel the bad feeling in my chest. "What are you both being so serious about? The *Sententia* is here! We're dressed in crimson. This is *finally* happening! Everything is going to be fine."

"Now you did it," Valentina groans with a smile that still doesn't quite touch her eyes.

CHAPTER 2

I'm alone by the time I reach the edge of our estate. My family's land begins at the very western edge of the town. Ripe wheat fields surround the marble home like an ocean, and for a moment, I pause to admire the glint of *Sol's* final rays on the golden sea as it sinks below the horizon. It is tranquil and beautiful, and some quiet part of my brain tells me that this is the only thing anyone should ever need.

But it's never been enough for me. Ever since I was a boy, I've dreamed of traveling the world and making my fortune. I want to see Forum, the seat that Empress Diana Agrippa rules from. I dream of watching the gladiator battles in Mars's Arena. I need to know if the mountains that make up the Northern Wall are as tall as they say.

When I have my Heart, I'll finally be free to find out.

Mons Olympus glides through the night sky above me, empty and forgotten. I barely notice its passage. It might as well be *Luna's* twin. Once, it meant something, but those days are long dead, like the gods who once lived in its halls.

As I step off the road, my tranquil moment is gone. The weight of the unfamiliar red uniform reminds me of my excitement. I break into a jog as I head down the cobbled path toward the front door, eager to show my parents. Agre, our family's faithful stonehound, barks in delight, sprinting to race with me as I head toward the house.

The large brown dog has bright copper lines running through his fur because he is a *mythus*, bound to a *Cor* of his own. Sometimes animals encounter bits of the transcendent metal in the wild, and bind it to themselves before the Censors can collect it, making them *electii* in their own right.

"After the *Sententia,* I will be just like you!" I promise the canine. He barks in delight. He does not understand my words, but he loves my joy.

The door swings open, and Gnaeus waits for me on the other side. He's dressed in the soft brown and gold of our livery. The aged servant has managed our house since my grandfather's time, and his eyes twinkle as he takes in my crimson clothes.

"Young *Dominus* Castor, welcome home," he drawls in his old voice. "It seems that you return to us with auspicious tidings."

"That's right, Gnaeus." I beam back at him. "Where are my mother and father?"

"Be welcome under this roof, young warrior." The old servant recites the traditional greeting. "May your feet be swift in the trials to come." I bow in appreciation of his greeting. Only my family is *expected* to greet me formally. But Gnaeus might as well be a member. He's been here longer than me.

"The *domina* is in her study. Your father has not yet returned from his workshop."

I pat the man on the shoulder in thanks and race into the house, heart hammering in my chest.

"Agre, you know there are no dogs allowed in the house," I hear him scold the stonehound behind me as I leave them behind. The canine whines plaintively, but my father's rules are firm. His *Cor* would let him tear up the stone floor with ease.

I chuckle at their conversation, caught up in my own excitement, feeling like a child rushing to his mother to show her a pretty stone that I found. In reality, that is not far from the truth. But this would be the last time that I did so as a boy. Soon I would be a man, and something told me that would be different. My step falters for a moment outside of my mother's study as my excitement dims. Why? I could not say. This is the day I had dreamed of since I could first remember my dreams.

And yet, suddenly, it has the feeling of death about it. The end of an age that I had not appreciated, only wanted to leave. I freeze before the door and look around my father's house, as if seeing it for the first time. Maybe for the last time.

"Come in," a warm voice calls from the other side of the door. My footsteps have not been missed. Swallowing a strange lump in my throat, I obey and step into the waiting study. My mother, Julia, is a beautiful woman, not just in her appearance but in the light and warmth that emanate from her like a hearth in winter. Her hair is a rich brown, with a white forelock that dangles from her right temple. She has deep green eyes that see all, and as they look up from her work, they see all of me.

Her expression clouds as she takes in my reds, and for a moment, there's a pained expression of sorrow. A tremor of disappointment runs through me to see my mother look so. Even under the heady influence of my excitement, I'm aware that this will affect everyone in my family.

Does she feel the same dread that I do? Like me, she must have thought that we still had weeks until the *Sententia*. Time has snuck a march on us.

Livia, my younger sister, turns to follow our mother's attention and gasps as she sees the crimson I'm wearing. There's no despair on her face, only unbridled excitement—and maybe a touch of jealousy. She's the younger version of our mother, and she leaps from her chair to tackle me in an excited hug.

"Be welcome under this roof, young warrior," Livia shouts into my chest since her face is still jammed against it. "May your arms be strong in the test to come." I kiss the top of my sister's head and grin before looking back up at our mother with hope.

Julia has composed herself, and her ever-present smile beams at me, burning with pride. Her eyes twinkle with a little moisture that I pretend not to notice. Crying is not something they teach us how to handle at the *collegium*.

"Be welcome under this roof, young warrior," she says softly. "May you come back to your mother in one piece." That is not one of the traditional phrases, but I do not complain. We embrace again, and for a little while, all the stress in my shoulders bleeds out as I find refuge in her arms one last time.

At last, my mother steps back, placing one of her hands on my cheek. "Your father needs to greet you," she orders. I can't tell if she's happy or sad. I can't tell if I am either.

At her urging, I sprint out of her study. From the patter of bare feet on stone, I know my mother and sister race in my shadow. I make my way downstairs, out the back, and across the fresh-cut grass to the long, low building that my father uses as a workshop.

When I spy him, my heart decides that I am excited. In some ways, this feels like the opposite of the death that I felt before seeing my mother. This was the last time I would greet her as a boy, but this is the first time I will greet my father as a man. Grandfather's *lumos* relics flare to life, glowing brightly as *Sol* finishes setting and night is upon us.

The wide barn doors are open, slid all the way to the opposite ends of their tracks to let fresh air into my father's nursery. Rows of waist-high planters fill the inside, perfectly lit as experimental crops grow in dirt bays under my father's watchful eyes.

Evander Castus turns from his crop beds at the sound of my approach. The copper veins of his *Cor* Heart glint as they catch the light. His brown eyes twinkle at the sight of me, but the expression fades as he takes in my crimson uniform.

My footsteps falter at the look in his eyes, but then the shadow is gone, and a proud smile spreads across his face like the dawn. "Finally, there's another man in my house!" his voice booms boldly. Something within me leaps for joy to be acknowledged so.

"Come here, my boy, and let me get a look at you," my father orders, gesturing for me to stand in front of him. I hear footsteps behind me as the women of our family catch up, hovering in the background of this moment.

Evander cups his clean-shaven chin with one hand, narrowing his eyes as he studies me as if for the first time. Heart racing, I stand up straight and do my best to hold his gaze. After a long moment, his grin grows even wider, and he steps forward to offer me his wrist.

"Be welcome under our roof, young warrior," he tells me as we clasp forearms. "May your wisdom never lead you into a fight you shouldn't have taken." Releasing his grip, he wraps me up in a fierce bear-hug, which I return, grateful for the chance to hide my own misty eyes.

"Gnaeus, let us have a feast! Tonight, we are joined by a new member of the family," my father roars as he releases me.

"Of course, *Dominus*, the cooks have already begun," the old man replies, materializing out of nowhere like a specter. Laughing, my entire family troops back into the house, celebrating together.

Despite the lack of warning, Gnaeus and the servants produce a feast that is delightful and speedy. Only a few hours later, we are gathered around the table, which my father insists upon. The *lecti*, the reclining eating couches used by most of the empire's elite, disgust him. They're only used when we have guests that would be offended by our familiarity—which is rare. There are not many palatines this far from the bigger cities.

I gorge myself on steaming slices of ham, fresh bread and butter, perfect potatoes, and more. It feels like it's my nameday. After we are served, the servants withdraw to partake in the feast too. Father will have it no other way; it seems only reasonable to me, although from conversations with my peers, I know that this is not always done in other patrician homes.

For a while, we eat in companionable silence, punctuated by beaming smiles and delighted sighs between bites. But after a few moments, I realize that my father isn't just chewing on his dinner, but on a thought.

Evander is the wisest man I've ever met. But with that wisdom comes a certain... ponderance. He likes to take his time to really dissect and digest something before he commits to it, and I've learned from experience what it looks like when he's working on something. Mother shoots him a knowing glance once or twice that tells me she already suspects what it is.

Finally, my father sets his cutlery down with a sigh and fixes me with an intense look. I swallow my ham, a task suddenly harder thanks to the lump in my throat. Instinct generated by a lifetime of being his son tells me that this will be a serious conversation.

"Castor, your mother and I are very proud of you," Evander begins. His rich brown eyes hold mine easily. I dare not look away even if I wanted to. "And we know that your dream is to earn your Heart"—he taps one of the copper veins running up his wrists—"but I want you to remember there's more to life than being an *electus*..."

"You are one," I interrupt, feeling defensive for some reason. Immediately, I feel like an idiot. He knows that. I may be close to becoming a man, but I still argue like a boy. Shame creeps a red on my cheeks to match the color of my uniform.

"I am," Evander allows patiently. "But I have never advanced beyond *cuprum*. Surely you've wondered why I am satisfied to remain a Copper?"

"Yes." I didn't just *wonder*. It is a question that has plagued my thoughts my entire life. My father has the thing that I want more than anything else, and he treats it like an unwanted pet. It is the only thing I have ever seen him do that felt ungrateful.

"Your grandfather was an *aurum*, and it consumed him."

I blink in surprise. I have only the faintest memories of my father's father. I was too young to notice or remember his markings. I had known that he was bound—the relics of his Heart still light our estate. But I always assumed that he was only a Copper or Silver *electus*—I would never have guessed that he had Ascended to Gold, the final tier.

"What do you mean?" I press, shocked at this revelation.

"He was never here. This land almost fell into ruin, and we almost lost everything."

"We would have if not for your father," Mother interjects from his side. For once, she is not smiling. It is strange to see both of my parents so serious. Our home has always been one of laughter.

"I don't understand."

"The Heart has needs," my father said slowly. "It has a hunger. It desires to feed—to grow. The more powerful you become, the stronger its demands will be on your mind and body. Additionally, the Symbol that you attune to will influence you; twist your thoughts."

"It has demands?" I arch an eyebrow in surprise. Magister Vellum and the other teachers have never told us about this. I want to be skeptical because it doesn't fit my vision of what it's like to be bound.

"It has expectations. Some pieces seem to want to grow more than others. Or perhaps their *electii* just have less self-control." My father shrugs as if slightly uncomfortable discussing this taboo subject. "If you're not careful, it can consume you like it did the *Ferrum Domini*."

A chill runs through me. The Iron Lords were the ones who founded our empire, who challenged *Mons* Olympus and killed the gods. That is something we have been told about. But they paid a price. Iron, more than any of the Symbols, corrupts. To protect us all, they placed restrictions on it and forbade regular people from ever attuning it again. Only the legions use it now.

"But Grandfather is the reason we have the life we do," I protest, changing tactics. "He built this home. Surely that was only possible because of his *Cor* Heart?"

"True," my father allows, and despite my sudden chill, I feel a burst of pride at his acknowledgment. Landing a point against my father in an argument feels like solving one of Vellum's impossible questions. "But what good is it to have everything if you throw it away?"

I have no good response. I rarely do. Evander excels at asking the kind of questions that only have answers I don't want to give. This is overwhelming. It is like waiting months to open a present on my nameday, only to discover it is full of poisonous adders.

"So you feel your *Cor*'s hunger…?"

"Every day," he tells me firmly. "A dull, gnawing pain in the back of my mind. I knew that if I advanced to become a Silver *electus*, the pressure of an *argentum* Heart would consume me and drive me to leave like it did my father."

"But wouldn't having a more powerful connection to your Symbol help you with the crops?" I protest.

"Yes, the Fertile Field is useful," my father admits. "But to advance, I would need to find places to cultivate a purer strain of essence than our farm generates. I could never do that here, and I fear once I left… I would never return."

"Why are you telling me this?" I demand in a defeated whisper, letting my head collapse into my hands. A warm hand settles on my wrist as my mother reaches to comfort me, but I don't move. I'm drowning.

"Because my father did not tell it to me," Evander says after a long time. There's an unusual note of heat in his voice. My father is slow to anger, but this has been burning inside of him for a long time. "Your mother and I love you, and we know what you want. It is what you have been raised to want because the Empress demands it—"

"Beloved," Mother's voice gently cuts him off midsentence. He is silent for a moment, composing himself before he continues.

"My dream for you, my son, is for you to be a builder and grower. This estate is your inheritance. It was almost lost once by the call of a *Cor* Heart. I have rebuilt it from the ashes, but you are smart and capable. You could nurture it into an empire of your own."

I'm silent, staring at the ham on my plate, which is beginning to grow cold. I don't have the heart to tell him that his blessing sounds like a curse to me. He seeks to give me a dream, but all I see are chains. I love my father, but I do not want to carry his burdens when he is done with them. I want to find my own.

"My son," Evander says softly after the silence grows too long. "If you are wise and wish to make your mother and me proud, do not win the *Sententia*. Do not seek a Heart and do not claim one."

I gape at him, unable to come up with words to respond. This entire conversation feels as if I am speaking to a stranger. I cannot fathom what he is asking of me, and the more I think about it, the more impossible it becomes to believe.

We speak no more of this. The rest of the feast is a more subdued affair. My dreams lie trampled on the table between my father and me. They're not quite dead but bleeding and broken. No one feels like celebrating anymore.

When we finish eating, I head to my room and bed. Angrily, I toss the crimson uniform over my chair and do my best to ignore it. When I finally climb into my bed, I lie on my back and stare at the ceiling for what feels like another seventeen years.

I don't know when sleep finds me, but my dreams are no refuge from my troubles.

CHAPTER 3

I spend the next week avoiding my parents. My feelings are confused and twisted. I'm angry that my celebration has this shadow cast over it. It's not my father's fault, but I can't help but blame him. As the *Sententia* approaches, the town begins to tear itself into a frenzy. The Censors arriving weeks early has thrown everyone off balance. It's as if Adventus was suddenly a different date after centuries of tradition. No one's ready, and everyone grows more frantic by the day.

I wander around with my friends in a daze. As one of the *discipuli* competing, I'm not expected to do anything. This is my last chance to be a child, and most of my peers spend it blowing off steam. There isn't a tavern in the city that isn't open by noon and full of red-clad adolescents.

Marcus and Valentina try to entice me to go out with them, and I do, but my heart's not in it. They can tell; they've known me far too long. Both seem to assume that my mood is because I'm worried about failing to earn the right to become an *electus*, and I don't correct their assumptions. The truth is much harder to explain.

"What do you think the final challenge will be?" Jasper asks the table of students, the fiftieth time I've heard the question in three days. He's a shorter kid with dark skin and a square jaw. I resist the urge to roll my eyes as I take a long pull of the ale in front of me. I've never found ale to be that interesting, but lately, I've noticed that it numbs the burrs in my mind until they are only little bumps.

I can't blame Jasper for the question, as unimaginative as it is. It's the one on the mind of every student in red. Throughout our entire childhoods, the magisters have tested us at the *collegium* to determine our ranking in our generation.

But there is always one final test, where everyone is given one last chance to prove themselves. The higher-ranked students are given some sort of advantage as a reward for their earlier success. But occasionally, some lower-ranked student surprises everyone and pulls off a miracle.

Jasper is certainly not in the top ten or even the top twenty of our class. He's too thin to excel at the physical challenges, and not smart enough to shine during the theory. He's hoping that the final test is something that will somehow favor him so that one of those miracles falls into his lap. I'd be more defensive if my head wasn't cloudy with life-changing truths.

I don't even know what I want. Would I be happy to be like my father, tending to the fields of our family estate for the rest of my life? I've always wanted to see the world. If the Heart drove me to explore it to sate its hunger, what of it? That sounds like the kind of adventure I am looking for.

"I bet it will be a duel," Marcus spouts. Everyone else at the table groans. "What better way to make sure that none of us become an *immundus* than by testing our ultimate strength?" I feel a shiver run down my spine at the thought of being one of the poor bastards who fails to fully bind their *Cor*. They are known as *immundus*—impure or unclean.

"When was the last time someone actually failed to bind their *Cor*?" someone else scoffs down the table. "That is the legend they tell to scare away the weak-willed. I've never seen a freak like that, have you? It doesn't actually happen."

"Then why do they wish to scare them away if there is no danger?" Marcus challenges.

"Go join the legions already," growls Cecilia, slamming her empty mug down on the table. "Leave the Heart to one of us who doesn't want to be an iron slave."

"Hear, hear," Aulus echoes from further down the table. He's a skinny kid like me. In fact, he's a lot like me. He's smart—done well in the congruencies and other intellectual tests but struggled in the physical ones against monsters like Marcus. If I'm *Sextus*, he could be *Septimus*, right behind me.

"Sorry." Marcus grins at them with a smile that's more teeth than it needs to be. "I'm off to join a prime Legion, not be a rank-and-file grunt."

"A prime Legion," Aulus breathes out in skepticism. "Remember us when you're a Praetorian, man."

"I won't," Marcus promises glibly. Everyone laughs as Aulus glowers. Even I chuckle, my maudlin mood lifted by my friends' banter.

"How about you, *domina*?" Aulus asks, turning his sarcasm to Valentina, who has been unusually quiet. "Has your *pater* whispered a clue in your ear?"

"No clues here," Valentina replies, looking bored. I don't blame her. There are still four days until the *Sententia* begins, and I'm ready for it to be over. Nervous tension fills my every waking hour and most of my sleeping ones too.

"*Salvete,* schemers," a voice behind us calls. As one, we turn to face the crimson-clad interloper. A sour pit opens up in my stomach at the sound of his voice. Felix needs no introduction to me.

Our class's *Primus* salutes us with a mocking smile and takes a long pull from the mug of ale he carries. Felix is everything I am, and more. He's fiendishly clever, skilled at congruencies and the theoretical craft of *Cor* Hearts. He's also big and strong. He stands well over six feet, with lean muscles rippling along his shoulders and arms. Whatever growth young men are supposed to get as they become men arrived early to this prick, and he knows it.

"What do you want, plebeian?" Valentina asks, her voice hooded. The same expression is on the faces of everyone at the table. The rest of our futures are in flux. No one knows who will end up earning the blessing of the Empress, but no one doubts that Felix will be one of the students to be bound at the end of the *Sententia*. It might as well be decided. If there really are only six Hearts this drought year, it would be better to assume there were only five, because one is his.

That only makes him more of an outsider to the rest of us. There's a resentment that we all carry for him. Most of it is misplaced because of his lesser social status. But I don't feel much guilt when he also acts like such an arrogant ass.

"Oh, I don't need anything from you, Valentina." Felix's smile is broad and genuine. He looks like he's greeting a group of beloved classmates, not mocking his lessers. "I was just curious what the field mice were getting up to before the big day. I do love watching a *Sextus* and *Septimus* squirm." He spares a glance for me and Aulus that is significantly less friendly.

Aulus and a couple of our fellow students shift uncomfortably. I roll my eyes because Felix has been lashing out at me since we were accepted into the *collegium*. I practically don't notice anymore. It's annoying rather than hurtful.

"Well, mostly, we're having a beer." I raise my glass in his direction. "Seems like the *Primus* has to drink the same swill as the rest of us." Chuckles run around the table as Felix glances at his drink with a skeptical eye.

"Ah well, it's always a pleasure to learn how my betters live," he says with a shrug, downing the rest of his beer like it's an adventure. Felix is the poorest student in the class by far. His family aren't patricians, like the rest of us. He's a plebeian who's managed to sneak into our *collegium*, and his lack of decorum rubs most of my peers the wrong way. My mother says it is my duty as someone who has been taught manners to extend grace to those who have not. But then, she's never had to deal with Felix.

"What do you think the challenge will be?" Crassus asks the interloper, as if his being the best student will mean that he has any special insight that we do not.

"Who cares?" Felix shrugs, tossing his empty mug on our table like discarded trash. "I'll win it no matter what it is." His warm smile flashes again, as if he's kidding. He's not.

With a sigh, Valentina rises to her feet, leaving her mug on the table. "As much fun as listening to you marvel at yourself is, Felix, I find myself in a mood for more *patrician* air." Felix's face drops into a dark scowl. A guilty bubble rises in my chest at my friend's barb. My mother would never forgive me for speaking like that. A silence as wide as the divide between our classes stretches across the table.

Valentina shoots a look at Marcus and me, and I realize that she wants us to go with her. Feeling a little dirty, I groan as I rise to my feet. Our big friend follows in my shadow as I nod farewell to the table. I even make an effort to make eye contact with Felix, who only rolls his own in response. I do not know why I bother. Together, the three of us wander out into the stone streets of Segesta.

It is midday, and the avenue is full of bustling servants and housewives out running their errands. Workers on ladders are hanging wreaths of wheat from the street poles, preparing for the harvest ceremony. It is ordered and beautiful to see the city so alive. I find pleasure in the peace of it all. The magisters teach us that this is what the Iron Empire brings—order and stability.

Down the street, a Heartsmith's foundry belches smoke as they turn the Hearts of dead wielders into relics to be used after their passing. My grandfather's Symbol was *Lumos*, something to do with light, so our inheritance of his *Cor* was self-sustaining lights for our home.

"What was that?" I ask Valentina as I catch up with her. She only gives me a dark glance before continuing on, leading us toward the edge of town. My heart skips a beat at the expression on her face. I know that look. She has a secret. Did her father tell her something? I doubt it's the same thing mine told me.

Valentina leads us away from the city center, until we're on the road to my home. We stop long before we make it to my family's fields, but after the cobbled road has turned to compact dirt. There's no one around for a mile in every direction. For the first time all day, we're away from the noise. We're alone.

"Val, what is it?" asks Marcus this time, a tense note in his voice. "Do you know something?" He's big but not slow. The mayor's daughter turns to face us, chewing on her lip, clearly torn over something. I'm shocked. I've never seen her like this before. Of the three of us, she is the one with the confidence, the one who does not hesitate.

"You don't have to share with us—" I start before I'm interrupted.

"He didn't tell me what the challenge will be," she blurts over me, giving me a glare. "But he did tell me something else." My heart is racing as she glances around the empty farmland, making sure we are truly alone. Cheating in the *Sententia* is encouraged. The Empress wants her Hearts to be given to her most resourceful and capable citizens. Getting caught is not.

"Is this worth it?" Marcus cuts her off with a serious expression on his face. It's a fair question. He has his eyes on a higher Legion.

"It's not against the rules," Valentina reassures him before looking at me. "Do you know how our fathers earned their Hearts?" Surprised, I shake my head. I hadn't thought to ask, which feels stupid in hindsight. I hadn't even realized that our fathers had been in the same *Sententia*.

"They had an alliance." There's a fire in her voice that isn't always there.

"What kind of alliance?" Marcus rumbles, scratching his chin in thought.

"They protected each other and worked together in the challenge. Together, they were *Primus* and *Secundus*." I blink in surprise again. I hadn't known my father had been ranked so highly. Suddenly, his advice seems even more unfair. I am only trying to follow in his footsteps.

"And you think that we should do the same?" Marcus asks, a spark of interest burning in his eyes.

"Of course," Valentina agrees. "It's a drought year, but the three of us *deserve* to be bound. Why not work together to make sure that we get what we want?"

"I'm in." The words come out without thinking, spoken by the part of me that knows what I really want. My father's warning is just that—a warning about something that could happen. He's lived his entire life as a Copper *electus*, and he was a great father. Why could I not be the same?

"Me too," Marcus says.

"Then we should take an oath," Valentina announces as she crouches on the dirt road. She picks up a stone the size of her palm and shows it to us. "Bound by blood, the three of us will be." Behind her, *Mons* Olympus, home of the dead gods, floats in the sky. It shines with a golden hue brightly, reflecting *Sol's* final rays. Once night falls, it will glow with a pale white, reflecting *Luna's* cooler light.

"An oath to do what?" A chill settles on me as I realize she's serious. The blonde girl pulls a knife from her crimson uniform and holds it to her own palm. This is a *votum*, an old, sacred thing that she invokes. A remnant from when the gods were alive. Marcus and I exchange nervous glances, but neither he nor I protest, caught up in her spell.

"I vow before gods and earth to protect my brothers in the *Sententia*," she intones, slashing her hand with the blade. Red blood wells up, matching our clothes. "Witness me: Mercury, Master of Deals; Mars, Lord of War; and Fortuna, Goddess of Fortune. Hear our oaths and honor our faithfulness. We will earn our *Cor* Hearts together, or not at all." Her blue eyes burn with a fanatical light as she passes the knife to me.

Apprehension grips me as I lower the edge to my own palm. The pain scares me, but that is only part of it. Oaths are things for heroes and foolish children, a thing to goad the gods into acting. Not only were there repercussions for breaking one—keeping one could be even worse. The priests warn us against doing things like this. The gods may be dead, but their bones are better left undisturbed. When I was a boy, my mother would strike me for swearing with their names.

Once, when I refused to listen to her, she dragged me and my sister out of the house and into the fields, where the family's marble mausoleum squats like a miniature temple. A piece of the everflame, a fire born of a powerful relic that has burned in the great Temple of Jupiter since the god's death, is kept outside in a brazier. There are no guardians left alive to guide our dead across the River Styx and into Hades when they cross over. So instead, we burn this never-ending fire as a beacon, trying to light their way home.

We stood outside for a long time. I remember feeling a sense of *something* bigger and unknowable. I wanted no part of it. At last, my mother grew tired of my hesitation and ordered me to go in. Only my grandfather is buried in there, but I did not dare disturb his bones.

"Dead things are still here," she told me that day.

Yet as I look into Valentina's eyes, I cannot tell her no. I am driftwood caught up in her waves, and the only way to go is with her. I hold her gaze and slice my own left palm, repeating her vow back to my friends.

I would do anything to earn my *Cor* Heart. That truth is written in my bones. My father made me question that desire for a moment. But as I stand on the dirt road in my crimson uniform, I know that when the day of the *Sententia* comes, there is only one outcome that will make me happy.

I will be bound.

Marcus hesitates even less than I do. Maybe he feels pressured since I went along with Valentina's scheme. Maybe he's not as worried about attracting the attention of the gods. But he speaks the same words, and one by one, we smear our blood on the oathstone that Val has made. When we've finished, she buries it off the road by a fence post.

There's an awkward release of tension after the oath is finished. Maybe we've heard too many stories. I don't feel any different having taken a *votum*. I thought there would be a tingle or something. Maybe a weight in my chest like a pair of chains. But the only thing that burns in my chest is the renewed flame demanding that I earn my Heart.

We don't tarry long in the dirt after we bury the stone. I think all of us were afraid of getting caught at the scene, as if a few droplets of our blood would cry out from the ground and condemn us. Marcus departs first; he has the farthest to walk to return to his family's estate to the north.

Valentina leaves shortly after him, but before she does, she takes my red-stained hand in hers again and kisses me on the cheek. Stunned, I stand alone above the site of our pact for a while, sorting through my emotions.

Understanding blooms in my heart as I watch her leave. We've been by each other's side our whole life. Yet as we've gotten older, there's been something different in the looks we share that I have not fully dissected. A heaviness to them that I do not experience with Marcus. I had assumed that is because we are smart in similar ways and share the same sense of humor.

Now, as my hand slowly rises to touch the spot on my cheek where her lips had just pressed, I realize that it is something else entirely. A flame bursts into light in my heart, a torch that I hadn't even realized I carried.

Already my mind craves the warmth and familiarity of that kiss the same way it demands food at the end of a long day. I have been starving my whole life, and I just hadn't realized. Somehow, I've been blind until this moment. I glance down at my bloody palm, and my spirits begin to rise, like a hawk caught on a thermal. Maybe there is one thing I want as much as a *Cor* Heart.

CHAPTER 4

The opening ceremony of the *Sententia* is as picturesque as it always was in my dreams. I stand with the rest of my crimson-clad peers on the left side of a raised dais in the center of the town square. Valentina's father, the mayor, waits in front of the council to receive the Empress' adjuncts. Marcus's father and mine are both there with him.

The people throng the sides of the street, pressed up against barriers, waiting to catch a glance of the Censors. My heart sings with joy while I simultaneously avoid glancing at my father. Seeing his disapproval would only ruin this experience. Today is about me, and I am going to enjoy it.

All I have to do is maintain my place in the rankings, and I will be bound to a *Cor* Heart before the end of the festival. Valentina, standing in the row in front of me, turns and catches my eye for a moment. A different flash runs through me as she winks at me before turning back to the front.

Today, I am invincible.

The crowd murmurs as a rhythmic stomping begins to echo off our stone streets. My heart skips a beat as the procession rounds the corner. A hundred legionnaires in purple armor march in lockstep, following the plumed helmet of a centurion. My eyes dart to the banner carried by the man in the first rank. It is a deep purple to match its soldiers, and it bears the golden imperial hawk with its wings stretched stitched into it.

Praetorians.

The Empress sends her elite soldiers, First Legion, her right hand with the Censors. Behind the century rolls a white carriage, worked in gold, drawn by two horses. I've never seen it escorted by legionnaires before. I've never seen a Praetorian before.

Whispers break out in our ranks, but they are silenced as Magister Vellum turns to survey us with a harsh glare. The old teacher's face is more severe than usual. I ignore his concern, caught up in the excitement of the moment.

Now that I look closer, I can see the *cuprum* veins running through their arms and the iron bands wrapped around each of their necks. The collars are some sort of hedge against their ascent. Every single one of them is Ironbound, attuned to the Symbol of Iron. A chill settles on me as I eye their power.

Several Legions march past Segesta every year. I've seen soldiers from Legions *V*, *VI*, and even *III*, once. But they pale in comparison to the splendor of the Empress's elite. Their purple uniforms are regal, their equipment pristine. If it were possible to be a Symbol of a legionnaire, it would be one of them.

"It's your future." I nudge Marcus, who's lurking next to me. The big boy is rigid, staring at the purple-clad soldiers with the hunger of a man long trapped in the desert. Not for the first time, I wonder why he's so fixated on becoming a legionnaire. It does not seem like a fun life.

"Look," he whispers back, nodding toward the five men in the front row of the formation. My jaw drops as I realize their veins are not Copper, but *Silver*.

"*Fidelis*," I murmur in awe. Only the most trusted—the most *faithful*—of legionnaires are allowed to Ascend to the second tier. They are said to be the most dangerous men in the empire, able to use their will to manipulate Iron like pale shadows of the Iron Lords who once killed the gods. These are the men that become heroes. I cannot believe they are *here*.

"I've got to win my Heart," Marcus breathes after a long moment. I give him a reassuring bump on the shoulder and settle in to watch the show.

The Praetorians march past the dais in perfect unison and draw to a halt without a command, stopping at the exact right spot to allow the white carriage to draw abreast of the dais. The door opens, and a man dressed in the white armor of a Censor steps out. It is made from a ceramic called *tellus*, a material that has no Symbol, said to be stronger than iron. A crimson cloak sweeps behind him, a match for our uniforms. The hilt of his dueling blade hovers at his hip, made from the same material. The long, partially curved blade is different from the straight *gladii* the legions carry.

He glances around the gathered crowd, and his narrow face pinches tighter. For a moment, I think it is scorn, but then his expression fades, and I wonder if it is something else. He has raven black hair that's been swept into a peak. His arms are bare, showing the Silver veins of an *argent Cor* Heart. I gape openly at that. He looks only a few years older than me! How has he already Ascended to Silver? Two more women in white follow him, capes fluttering behind them—they're only Coppers. All three of them bear the sharp cheekbones and strong nose of the palatine families. The horns continue to sound as they stride to the dais to greet Valentina's father and the council.

These are the Censors, the custodians of the Empress's *Cor* Hearts, her White Hand, who will decide who receives her blessing and who does not. Outside of senators and imperators, there is no one with more power in all the empire.

The council bows to the lead Censor, and he returns their greetings with a shallow nod. In front of the dais, his carriage departs, and without prompting, the Praetorian century marches backward, turning to face out toward the crowd, creating a barrier between us and the people.

For the first time, I begin to worry that something is wrong. No Censor has ever come to us escorted by a hundred legionnaires. Never have soldiers stood between the competitors and the people. I glance at the dark-haired man and evaluate the grim set of his mouth again. It's not condescension that lurks in his eyes, but something else—resolve. Something is about to happen.

I don't feel invincible anymore.

My own heart begins to race as I realize that the hand of the Empress is preparing for something. Murmurs run through the students and the crowd as the people around me react to the soldiers. How many see what I do and how many are just impressed by the precision of the elite troop's movement?

Despite my conflicted feelings, I glance at my father, trying to gauge his expression. But his face is the stern mask that he wears when dealing with palatines. It might as well be made of stone for all that it gives away. The other members of the council are equally blank-faced.

"Something is wrong," I murmur to my friends. Vellum's glare settles on me, and no one dares reply, but I can tell that the rest of us sense it too. Change is never a good sign during the *Sententia*. Not during a drought year. The lead Censor turns and faces the crowd. One of the women hands him a white scroll worked with gold. He unfurls it and begins to read in a clarion, clear voice.

"Empress Diana has spoken!" he declares, his voice echoing off the buildings of the square. "The *Sententia* of this year, the 573rd of our empire, is to be known as the Great Drought." My heart clenches as the confirmation of what the magisters predicted. "As such, only the strongest *discipuli* will be granted Hearts. The Empress commands that the *Sententia* shall be changed immediately. The town of Segesta and its fifty candidates shall be combined with the candidates of the town of Nicomedia for their trial."

A collection of outraged shouts breaks out from the student block. My voice might have been one of them; I don't know. Nicomedia is the closest town of similar size. They should have the same number of *discipuli* competing in their *Sententia* as we do. Instead of fifty competitors for ten hearts, we suddenly have a hundred.

The crowd is even more upset than we are. Dark murmurs run through the crowd like a rumor, and before my eyes, men begin to mass like waves preparing to crash on the dais. Many families have sacrificed much for their children to be in the *collegium*, hoping that they earn a Heart. This is the squashing of many dreams—not just the ones of the students in crimson.

As one, the Praetorians draw their swords. The iron blades glint in the sunlight as each legionnaire holds them toward the ground. A reminder that the Censor doesn't just speak with the Empress's voice but wields her strength too. The sound of a hundred weapons clearing their sheaths stops the crowd in their tracks.

In the distance, I'm dimly aware of the sound of footsteps as a group of people enters the town square, clothed in the same crimson that we are. They're escorted by even more Praetorians, who flank them on either side. These must be our new challengers.

"Furthermore," the Censor continues, ignoring the response to his news. "To accommodate this larger number of contestants, the final challenge of the *Sententia* shall consist of two parts. The first part shall be a melee between the students of each *collegium* until only fifty remain." Marcus lets out a thrilled hiss next to me, but I barely notice—I'm hanging on to the man's words. There are many different contests that the Censors use to make their choice—some would be better for me than others. "The second challenge shall be the *Labyrinthus*." Having finished his pronouncement, he lets the gilded scroll snap shut.

Jupiter's Dead Eyes, I cursed to myself, that's not good for me.

The *Labyrinthus* arena is one of the most physical challenges that the *collegium* uses to assess us. That's not to say that I'm weak—I'm not at all. But in terms of sheer physicality, I'm not one of the top members of my year. I would have done much better solving congruencies on the wavemachine or in one of the wargames. Marcus's odds, on the other hand, are looking much better. As if he senses my dark thoughts, my friend taps my shoulder with his fist.

"Allies," he whispers.

"Allies," I reply.

"My Lord Censor, this is highly irregular," Brontus Fluvius, Valentina's father, remarks, stepping close to the dark-haired man. His voice is low enough to not challenge the Empress's voice in front of the whole town, but I can hear him clearly.

"It is the will of the Empress, Governor," the man replies smoothly, his hand settling on the white hilt of his ceramic blade. "We must only hear and obey." The threat is obvious.

"Of course," Brontus agrees, bowing immediately. "I only wonder how the two classes will be combined, as they have been rated separately their whole lives. Is there perhaps not another way that would—"

"The head magister of each town will deliver their rankings unto us, and we shall determine the students' final placings, *as we have always done*." Ice enters the young man's voice as he glowers at the council. He's not hesitating anymore, not now that Legion I has drawn its steel.

"As the Empress commands." Brontus bows smoothly, his gaze fixed on the ground. The Censor grunts and turns, casting an appraising look over my classmates.

"Cheer up, Mayor," he says cavalierly. "I hear your daughter is an exceptional student. I'm sure she will rise to the occasion. We begin tomorrow."

CHAPTER 5

"How could they do this to us?" Valentina rages, pacing back and forth in front of Marcus and me. The three of us are in the corner of the room that they stuffed all fifty of the Segestan students into. The walls are made of limestone, and the floor is the same sand as the arena that waits for us beyond here. I want to join her in anger, but I only feel numb. The reality of my situation has begun to seep through my thick skull.

During the last drought, the Censors brought six *Cor* Hearts to Segesta for the *Sententia*. This one must be even more severe if they were combining our challenge with Nicomedia. I suspect that I am ranked *Sextus* in my year, which means that if I didn't mess anything up, it would have been very doable for me to secure the last Heart.

But with the added competition, I will need to be closer to *Tertius* to stand a chance, assuming their top students were of the same quality as our own. I am good, but I don't know if I am that good—especially not at the *Labyrinthus* arena. That would have been the worst possible challenge for me, even among my peers.

"We will be fine," Marcus asserts, trying to reassure both of us. The big boy has been more focused than ever on getting his Heart. Seeing the Praetorians has done something to him.

"Of course you think that," I snap at my friend. "These are the two best challenges for you."

"Good thing for you then that you have me as an ally." Marcus gives us both an insufferable grin. "Just stay behind me, and I will lead you to our Hearts."

Valentina and I both groan, but I can't deny that he had a point. At least for the melee. If the Censors intended to have us fight the other town for our spot in the final challenge, I would be more than happy to follow in his wake.

"I don't know how well that's going to work in the *Labyrinthus* arena," I point out. "We're going to be released at different times. How are we supposed to work together?" It's a question that kept me up most of last night, since the *Sententia* had been called.

"We have to qualify for the finals first," Marcus says, stretching his arms. "One thing at a time, Castor. Now, make sure you're limber."

Around us, the rest of our peers huddle in clusters, waiting for the summons to the melee. Something tells me that Valentina wasn't the only one to come up with the idea of an alliance. I see Jasper and Cecilia, our friends from the tavern, grouped with Petrus and Aulus.

A thought strikes me, inspired by the purple-clad Praetorians that lurk through our city.

Why should Nicodemia be given our hearts? They came to our *Sententia* to steal our blessing. It might be the will of the Empress that they compete, but that didn't mean it was her will that they *win*.

My heart begins to race as I eye the people around the room. I know all of them. I don't like all of them, but I know them. Thick-necked Clintus, whose plight on the wave machine I mocked, eyes me with distaste. The physicality of our challenges certainly works to his benefit. There's no love lost between us, yet I would rather see him bound than some *interloper*.

"Stay here," I whisper to my friends, leaping to my feet in a spray of sand. I hear them call after me, but I trot toward the nearest cluster of students. I hear their footsteps in the sand as they follow me. This isn't the first time I've charged off on some harebrained scheme.

"What do you want?" Aulus challenges me as I draw abreast of their group. His brown eyes are flat and unhappy, and I know he's done the same math that I have. The rest of his coterie turn to look at me, their expressions equally uninviting.

"Nothing really." I hold my hands open in a placating gesture. "I just had a thought that I wanted to share."

"This should be good," Cecilia mutters to a dark-haired girl sitting next to her. "Thoughts from Castor, something new and different."

"It's just that the way I see it, the Hearts the Censors brought to the *Sententia* were for *Segesta*." I emphasize the name of our town with an arched eyebrow. "Only fifty students can advance to the final challenge from the melee; there's no rule that says that they can't all be from our side." The hostile looks fade as the same greedy, thoughtful expression flickers across the five of them.

"What are you proposing?" Aulus demands, and I glance at my opposite, but the look in his eye is the same hope that I feel growing inside me.

"Simply that we watch each other's backs and make sure that only our town advances to the finals. We've worked hard our whole lives for this day. There's no reason that they should be allowed to come and take what we deserve." Heads slowly nod in the group as they process what I'm saying. Getting rid of the Nicodemians gets rid of their *Primus, Secundus,* et cetera.

"We're in," Aulus confirms after exchanging glances with his group. "But you'd better recruit the bigger guys."

"I'm working on it." I pat him on the shoulder and turn toward the next group.

It's shockingly easy to convince everyone to work together. It makes sense. On the one hand, we know each other's strengths and weaknesses—we've been competing against each other our whole lives, and familiarity breeds contempt. But the students from Nicodemia are an unknown quantity. Maybe they're better than us. More importantly, they're not from here. It's our *Corda* that they have come to steal.

I wait to approach Clintus and his group of cronies toward the end. I know that if anyone is going to give me trouble, it will be him. The big boy hasn't forgotten how I laughed at his failures. The three other thugs with him are brawlers who will likely do fine in the melee.

"Get lost, weasel," Clintus sneers as I approach. The thick-necked boy has watched me make my way from one cluster of students to the next like a vineyard worker. He knows I'm up to something, but I doubt he's figured out what. Haxus and red-headed Rufus chuckle at his challenge.

"Relax," I tell him, not letting him think that he intimidates me. He doesn't, but only an idiot would ignore the fact that his fists could be confused for decently sized boulders. "I'm here to help."

"Don't need your help or want it."

"Well, if you want to make it to the next round, you should listen," I snap, feeling a flush of annoyance. "The rest of us are forming an alliance against Nicodemia." Clintus's eyes narrow, but he glances past me to realize that the entire room is watching our exchange.

"Truth? That's what he's been fluttering about for?" he asks the nearest group of students. They all nod back.

"Cowards." He laughs, and his friends echo him. "Why should I ally with any of you?"

"Just making sure our people get all the Hearts," I tell him. "After the melee, everyone is free to do whatever they want."

"I think we'll take our chances," Clintus says, rising to his feet to tower over me. The boy has to be four inches over six feet, and I have to crane my neck to maintain eye contact. I resist the urge to sigh. I knew he was going to be difficult, but I already have the leverage. That's why I saved him for last—or close to it.

"If you're not with us, you're against us," I tell him softly and not in a whisper. Everyone can hear the threat. The attention of the room focuses on Clintus and his friends with hostile intent. He and his friends notice it, recoiling like it has physical pressure. The big boy sneers as he looks from me to the forty-five other pairs of eyes that are now glaring at him. He might not be bright, but he's not stupid. He knows that he has been outmaneuvered.

"Fine," he snaps, turning away from me in disgust. "We'll make sure none of the Nicodemian interlopers get one of our Hearts." Not satisfied, I stare at each of his cronies until they nod in agreement. Just like that, forty-nine of the students from our town are bound in agreement.

That leaves one on the outside.

For a moment, I stand and study the lean young man sitting by himself in the corner. He's playing with the sand, ignoring the rest of us. Felix has made no friends during our four years in the *collegium*. By being both plebeian and *Primus*, he has more than one target painted on his back.

A cold part of me, the part that would do anything to be bound, remembers that it is a drought year. If our *Primus* is eliminated, then I might be *Quintus*. All I have to do is turn away. I'm sure that any of our classmates would be more than happy to strike him from behind, taking him out before the melee even starts. I wouldn't even have to be the one to do it.

It is a good plan—a wise one even. But I can feel the disappointment of my mother and the judgment of my father burning like twin beacons in my chest. That was not how they taught me to treat others. I may be defying their wishes by trying to earn my own *Cor*, but that doesn't mean that I should flout all their lessons.

Gritting my teeth, I make my way toward Felix's corner, trying to convince myself that this isn't a mistake. It is. But anything else feels... manipulative and cowardly. I am going to get my Heart, and I am going to earn it fairly. Besides, if I left one person out of the alliance, who is to say someone else wouldn't want to cut out one of their own personal enemies? The whole house of cards could come crashing down in a matter of moments.

"What are you doing?" Valentina hisses as she cuts me off before I can reach the *Primus*. "He's not one of us."

"Yes, he is." I snort in irritation, stepping around her. I can't believe that *I'm* the one defending Felix. The world feels upside down. Maybe it is. That white-armored Censor flipped everything on its head, and this is the new normal.

"Leave him," Valentina insists, reaching out to grab my wrist. I stop and turn to stare at her, surprised by her tenacity. No one likes Felix, but I didn't think anyone hated him this much.

"We're Segesta, they're Nicodemia," I snap, frustration adding heat to my voice. We've gained an audience, but I don't care. Any moment now they will come to collect us, and I won't have our alliance frayed. If we don't go in as one, we won't come out as one either.

"But he's *plebeian*," she snarls, stepping between me and Felix. My eyebrows rise in surprise at her tone. Her cheeks turn a ruddy pink at my stare. She's not as pretty as she was on the road at sunset. Now she seems small and cruel.

"What are you worried about?" I demand. "You're practically guaranteed to earn your Heart."

"But you aren't," she replies softly, and my stomach drops a little. She doesn't think I can beat Felix. She doesn't think I'm going to get a Heart.

"I'll earn it," I shout in her face, tearing my wrist free of her grip and stepping around her. My vision is tinted red at the corners from anger and embarrassment. "I don't need to win that way." Valentina lets me go. I bear the eyes of all my classmates on my shoulders as I approach the *Primus*.

"What do you want, Castor?" he murmurs, not looking up from the castle he's building in the sand.

"We're making an alliance against the—"

"Obviously." He cuts me off with a small smirk but still doesn't look at me.

"Are you in or are you out?" The boy freezes at my question, long-fingered hands letting sand trickle out of his grasp.

"Am I in or out of what?" he asks quietly, looking up at me for the first time. There's no arrogant smirk on his face now. It almost makes me madder to see it gone.

"Join or die." I shrug, feeling dramatic as the irritation of the situation rages inside me.

"So, it's like that?"

"It's like that," I confirm.

"Very well." Felix pops up to his feet to look down on me. He speaks loud enough for everyone in the room to hear. "I accept your most generous offer of alliance." He holds out his hand, and after a second of hesitation, I clasp wrists with him.

It is done. Nicodemia will fall.

Behind us, a horn sounds in the arena. Magister Vellum appears as if summoned. His dour face is even more unhappy than usual. Silently, all of us rise to our feet and begin to drift to the center of the room, surrounding our teacher.

He eyes all of us, and for a moment, I think that he's about to tell us something important, but then he sighs and seems to deflate. Suddenly, he just looks like a tired old man instead of one of the most powerful *electii* in Segesta.

"It is time," he announces. Behind him, the gates to the arena begin to open. Fear spikes in my gut, despite our alliance. This is it. I will either walk out of that arena with the chance to earn my Heart or lose it forever.

CHAPTER 6

We clump together as Vellum leads us down the long hallway toward the arena. The floor is carpeted in the same thick sand. We walk past marble walls carved with the great deeds of warriors who have gone before us. Prometheus, who stole the secret of *Cor* from the gods. After him comes Titus and the six Iron Lords who ventured to the halls of *Mons* Olympus to kill them.

The final one is Perseus, the first Emperor, who conquered and founded the Iron Empire. I raise my left hand and brush the stone of his boot as I pass, hoping for a measure of his ferocity to pass to me. Today, I must prove that I am worthy.

As we draw close to the entrance, sound rolls in like a wave. With a start, I realize that the whole town has come to watch—probably both of them.

"What's the plan, Imperator?" Marcus nudges me out of my reverie.

"What do you mean?" I turn to him in a panic. I didn't have any *more* plans. I had already built us an alliance. What more was there to do?

"You marshaled us. Tell us what to do." Behind him, the faces of other classmates peer at us as they drew close to listen. Valentina rests a reassuring hand on my shoulder, our earlier fight forgotten.

"Okay," I manage through a sudden, terrified lump in my throat. I have no idea what I'm doing, but it is clear that everyone expects me to have a plan. "We're a legion now. Clintus, you and your boys take the center of the line. You're the anchor that holds us in place."

The big boy glowers at me, but his friends nod in agreement. I take that as good enough.

"Everyone else, form even sides off the center. I want us two lines deep." I raise my voice to try to reach the back of the group. I hear muted whispers as my classmates pass the instructions down the line. Vellum keeps walking toward the arena. He doesn't turn around, but his steps are suddenly slower. A savage smile spreads across my face. The old bastard wants his students to win too.

"Marcus, you pick three strong fighters and roam. Anywhere the line begins to sag, I want you to smash it."

"I'll go with you," Felix offers, appearing at my elbow. I glance at the tall boy. He's lean and strong, perfectly suited for fast attacks. I nod, and Marcus shrugs, unbothered.

"Where will you be?" Valentina asks, her hand still resting on my shoulder. It feels nice, grounding me from the panic that is trying to pull me up by the roots. I'm no commander. The only thing I know about tactics comes from playing soldier with Marcus when we were boys swinging sticks.

"Right in the center, where I can see what's going on," I promise. A good imperator leads from the front. That sounds like something one of the poets said once. I guess it is time to find out if they were telling the truth. We're drawing near the end of the tunnel. Not much time to give more orders. Not that I have any smarter ones to give.

"Any questions?" No one speaks up. It isn't that complicated of a plan. The silence mounts and I panic, trying to remember a quote worth sending my classmates into battle with. My mind is blank; all the poetry and literature Vellum made me read has fled. So instead, I make my own.

"When she lived, Fortuna favored the bold, so fight boldly, my friends, and you may find a *Cor* waiting for you on the other side of this field."

"Can't help but be dramatic, can you, *Sextus?*" Felix chuckles, moving past me to where Vellum waits for us. I sigh as I follow my personal bully. At least I tried.

The magister stands along a weapon rack that has been fitted with training *gladii* for the melee. Each one is made of hardwood, with a cloth-wrapped hilt. They're heavy enough to hurt but have no edge to cut one another with.

"Take your blade and get out there," he barks as we file past him. "No fighting 'til the Censor tells you."

I barely hear him over the rush of blood in my ears. The noise of the crowd waiting for us to emerge fades from my mind. There's only the roar of my own body as I reach out and grab my weapon. The weight feels comforting in my hand, like holding a lover I didn't know I was missing. No matter what happens, I won't be going into the arena alone. It will be the two of us together. Hefting the blade in my right hand, I follow the trail of my classmates out of the door and into chaos.

The Segesta arena is built in the style of the bigger ones throughout the empire. I've heard that the Mars Arena in Forum can hold fifty thousand people. Ours can hold a thousand. But even so, the noise is deafening. I spin as I walk toward the center of the ring with my classmates, marveling at the crowded stands full of the people of our town. Across the way are strangers who I assume are here with the Nicodemian students.

In the center of the ring of seats is a raised wooden box. I can just barely make out Valentina's parents and the rest of the council. Next to them, I spot the unmistakable white armor and red cloaks of the three Censors. The aristocratic young man stands at the front, watching us advance.

Across from us, the interlopers are spilling out of their gateway in mild disarray. Hope flares in my chest as I watch them scatter. They don't look like they've built the same trust we have. *We have a chance.*

"Form a line," I hiss at my classmates as we approach the middle of the ring. "Form up on Clintus." Slowly, our untrained mob settles into two ranks of twenty or so. I find myself standing right behind Clintus, just as I promised. Valentina hovers at my right like a shadow. Behind me, Marcus and his roamers lurk, waiting for their moment.

"Stop—er, halt!" I call, feeling more than a little ridiculous as we draw near to the halfway point. Sloppily, we come to a stop, our line leaning a little but still intact. The students from Nicodemia are watching us. I see surprise in some of the smarter ones' eyes as they realize we've unified.

The arena grows quiet as we wait, staring at the mob before us. I know this is not their fault, but I hate them. They have come from their homes to take something from me. It feels personal and violent, like I am staring at fifty thieves. My hand tightens its grip on the hilt of my wooden sword. A strange fire of rage begins to grow in my belly.

A trumpet sounds, and I glance at the box in time to see the lead Censor crouch and leap from it as if it weren't twenty paces in the air. He shoots through the air like an arrow and lands in the sand between us lightly, knees only slightly bent. His red cape billows behind him, making him look like he comes straight out of a myth.

My mouth gapes at his overt display of Silver power. He must be attuned to a Symbol of Air or Strength to let him soar like that. He rises to his full height, and his lips quirk in an amused smirk as he glances between our two groups.

"I am Atticus Augustus," he announces in a proud voice. His voice booms off the walls of the arena as if he is shouting, even though he seems to be speaking normally. I'm doubly certain that he is using a Symbol of Air to do it. "Censor to Empress Diana and Proctor of this final contest for her blessing. In accordance with Her Majesty's perfect decree, any *discipuli* from Segesta or Nicodemia seeking to earn a *Cor* Heart this *Sententia* shall engage in a melee."

He spares a glance at our battle lines, and his lips quirk again. I can't tell if he's impressed or mocking us. Maybe both. My cheeks flush as embarrassment runs through me. I feel like a boy playing at war—because I am. The *collegium* taught us the history of it, not battle formations.

"The melee will continue until there are only fifty students remaining. Although the weapons are made of wood, they will be treated as iron in this skirmish. Anyone struck on an appendage must cease to use it. Anyone dealt a killing blow must remove themselves from the field. We Censors will be watching to ensure that these rules are followed."

The two women in white armor also drop to the sands, although neither of them shoots across the arena as Atticus did. A body bound to a Silver Heart receives a lot of physical benefits, compared to even that of a Copper.

"When you hear the horn, you may begin," Atticus announces, turning to stride toward the sidelines where his fellow Censors wait. "You fight for the blessing of your Empress, young warriors! Do brave deeds and endure."

I barely have the chance to process that this is it when a long, low trumpet sounds. Its deep note rumbles in my stomach, bubbling with the rage that already burns there. The roars of the arena resume as our loved ones shout their support. The arena rumbles beneath us as the Censors activate some of the relics built into it. I spread my feet and share wide-eyed glances with the rest of my classmates. What is this?

"The ring! Look at the ring!" someone shouts in our formation, and I look to the edge of the arena in horror. The ground boils, falling away at a slow pace like a constricting serpent, forcing us toward the center. Sand pours into the opening hole like water, and I shudder at the thought of being sucked out. It won't kill me—that's not what the *Sententia* is for—but it certainly can't feel good.

The Censors' message is clear: you cannot hide on the edge of this melee and try to wait it out. Before I have the chance to shout encouragement to my troops, the Nicodemians lower their heads and charge.

The other students descend on us like a stampeding herd, coming in clumps of three and four. It seems that seeing our alliance has inspired the enemy to make one of their own. I curse myself for not ordering my classmates to wait until the horn was blown to reveal our hand. We gave them time to adapt, and now we pay for it.

Our line is set to meet them, but as they crash into my classmates, I learn my second lesson in as many seconds: shieldwalls without shields are not as effective as I would have hoped. Our line crumbles in an instant as a handful of Segestans go down, unable to dodge or block the enemy's attacks in the close quarters of our cramped line. I let out a yelp of pained surprise as Clintus steps on my foot, shoved back by the force of a Nicodemian's charge. They're close, and the big guy is locked in place, sword nowhere to be found, holding the wrists of two different *discipuli*, keeping them from stabbing him.

Spying an opportunity, I leap forward, slamming into Clintus and stabbing the top of my wooden sword forward into the guts of one of the Nicodemians. The boy lets out a surprised *whoof!* as all of the air rushes out of his lungs. He falls backward, stunned and effectively dead.

"Ninety," booms the Censor's voice, amplified by his air Symbol to drown out the cries of the spectators. Ten students are slain in the initial charge. The arena shakes again as the shrinking circle begins to increase its pace.

"Second line, attack!" I shout, hoping more of my soldiers take advantage of the Nicodemians being caught in our frontlines. I turn to stab the second girl who is terrorizing Clintus, but she wrenches her arm free and dances out of range, watching my weapon warily.

"Grab your sword!" I shout in the big boy's ear and pat him on the back, turning to inspect the line. My heart sinks as I see the right side buckle under the pressure of the enemy's furious charge. I watch Cecilia go down, struck by a savage slash across the chest.

We weren't close friends, but I still feel a pang of sadness for one fewer Segestan student surviving. The line bows and threatens to shatter. It has only been a matter of moments, and already we are undone. I am like some foolish imperator who led his troops into an ambush and got them killed.

Just as I think all hope is lost, Marcus and Felix appear, leading the reinforcement squad. My best friend is somehow wielding two swords and a savage grin of delight. This must be the best thing that's ever happened to him. Felix is in his shadow, his eyes glinting with a manic light. Together they slam into the Nicodemians like a battering ram, and the charge falters.

"Hold!" I scream, pointing at the left side. "Hold the line!"

"Eighty," calls Atticus.

The two juggernauts press their advantage, tearing into the Nicodemian students, halting their advance, and cutting them down. I whoop in support as I watch four more of the enemy trudge disappointedly out of the center of the arena.

This is actually working. I can't believe it. The melee stalls for a moment as our line holds and we repel the other class. A number of interlopers go down in the press as my peers work together.

"Seventy."

I sense a growing desperation in the Nicodemians. They were not fully prepared for our alliance, but they share the dream that we have. They want their Hearts as badly as we do. Their families and town are counting on them as much as ours are. Backed into a corner, they do what any animal would do—attack.

Our center finally splinters as they charge it together. I'm shoved to the side as three enemy students bowl through us by sheer force of will. I spin, catching the wild swing of a girl with bright red hair who follows her classmates through the gap.

She snarls and slices at me again, but Valentina slides in from the side and slams her blade into the side of the redhead's neck. My assailant collapses bonelessly, and I nod my thanks at Valentina. She gives me a tight grin and then is swept away.

"Sixty," the Censor calls. A thrill rushes through me as I realize I've survived more than half of the eliminations. Only ten left. We can do this. I can do this.

I rescue Clintus again, sliding the point of my blade into the ribcage of one of the boys attacking him. The Nicodemian glares at me with eyes full of tears as he slumps away from the melee. I almost wish I had killed him instead of his dreams—my conscience might be cleaner.

A blur of crimson in the corner of my eye warns me of an attack. I spin, awkwardly blocking a lunge that would have gone straight into my guts. I dance back a pace. There's space now that so many have been eliminated, and I realize with shock that I know this combatant.

It's Aulus.

The slim boy's teeth are locked in a grimace, and he won't look me in the eyes. They're fixed on the tip of my blade as we exchange blows. My heart sinks as I realize that he did the same math that I did. If I truly am *Sextus* to his *Septimus*, my falling in the skirmish makes a Heart that much more attainable for him.

He attacks relentlessly, and I fall back under the fury of his blows. Each step drives me out of the imperator melee and toward the shrinking edge. It also pushes me away from allies who would help me.

Panic shoves any tiredness from my limbs as I focus on matching his strokes. I am not a swordsman. They teach us the basics at the *collegium* as part of our physical tests, but it's never been a focus for me. Aulus has clearly been practicing on his own. He feints a low stab that I fall for. He steps back as my blocking slash swings by and lands a blow on my left arm. I grimace—by the rules of the melee, I'm not allowed to use it anymore.

I give more ground, afraid to cross blades with him. A quick glance over my shoulder is all I can risk to check how far I am from the shrinking edge of the arena. Far too close for comfort. The sand quakes under the soles of my sandals as we get closer to the part that rushes over the edge like a waterfall. As I dance, I seize on a hope to survive. Moments ago, there were only ten more eliminations left. I don't have to actually beat Aulus; just survive. My breath comes in ragged gasps. I had thought I was fit and hale, but this is a different sort of exertion.

Aulus still doesn't look at me—he just presses his attack. He knows the same thing I do. If he runs out of time, we both survive in the competition, and he needs me gone.

"Fifty-one," Atticus's voice rings out.

Around me, the arena has become very silent. I risk another glance over Aulus's shoulder and see that the fighting has ground to a halt. The few Nicodemian students that remain have all retreated and formed their own line, eager to survive.

The bulk of my army mills around in confusion. No one wants to risk themselves as the final elimination. Valentina and Marcus are arguing with Clintus and some of Aulus's other friends, who block their path to me, swords extended.

There is no waiting this out, I realize.

Throughout the entire arena, our duel is the only fight that still rages. The final elimination will be one of us. A chill settles on me as I realize that I am going to die. My body will live, but my dream, the thing that has fueled me since I was a child, is about to be murdered in front of two entire towns.

The rage, which had begun to sunset into fierce joy as our class's line crushed the battlefield, burst back into flame. Dead Mercury damn Aulus and his pinched face! He seeks to take my Heart from me? I think not.

Gritting my teeth, I sidestep his lunge and manage to score a blow on his left arm, matching the wound he gave me. His eyes flick up to mine as the hit registers, and I'm taken aback by the hate that simmers there. I've never considered the skinny boy a friend, but looking through the window of his soul, I see a resentment that has burned for years.

I return his sneer, our feelings as bare as our blades. This time, I press my own attack. My sword clacks against his with a heavy *crack* that echoes throughout the silent arena. As my rage builds, my fear flees and my exhaustion fades. My entire world narrows to the handful of paces between us as we duel. We dance along the edge of the arena, drowned by the roar of the falling sand that cascades into the darkness below.

Confidence grows as I learn his tendencies. He only has a few attacks that he's comfortable with. A thrust, a lunge, a horizontal slash, and a series of blows that he uses to set one of those up. Already I recognize that he's more limited than a real swordsman should be. He might know more than me, but it's not much more.

A cruel smile plays across my lips as I sidestep his lunge before he even starts it. But as my feet move, he reveals one of his own tricks. My heart skips a beat as I realize I've been fooled. Instead of a lunge, he strikes with the heavy slash. I twist my *gladius* to block it, but the angle is off, and the force of his blow sends my sword flying out of my hands and into the sandy abyss below.

My dreams go with it.

Quick as a viper, Aulus draws back for a real lunge that will finish me. I tense, ready to dive to the side, praying that I can avoid his strike. This can't be the end. I will not die here.

There's a thrumming sound, like the flapping of a bird's wings, and Aulus half-turns in time for a wooden gladius to slam into his head, hilt down. The skinny boy staggers, stunned by the blow. Sensing my chance, I explode forward in a tackle. He slams into the ground inches from the edge, his weapon tumbling from his grip.

I hold him down as I dive for the loose weapon. My hand wraps around its hilt, and my anger flares. My whole world is red. I raise the blade and slam it down with all my force. The blow lands on his face and he screams.

In my tremendous rage, I forget that this isn't a duel to the death, and I pull back my stolen sword to strike him again. For my dream's sake, I will take no chances. My swing is stopped in its tracks as something seizes the blade, wrenching me out of my fugue. Atticus stands above me, his hand wrapped around the blade of my practice sword.

"Fifty," he says softly, his blue eyes evaluating me with a cold stare. The arena grinds to a halt, and the roar of falling sands fade. I glance down to see that Aulus's head dangles off the edge—we are mere inches from toppling off together.

Awareness creeps back into me, and I scramble off Aulus, ashamed of the fury that had gripped me. I look back toward my friends to thank Marcus for the help, but the words die in surprise on my lips when I take in the scene. Marcus and Valentina are blocked off by Clintus and his friends. Both of them still have their swords.

It's Felix, the boy I almost left out of our alliance, who doesn't have a blade in his hands.

CHAPTER 7

"Fifty," Atticus repeats to the arena. The melee is officially at an end. Dimly, I'm aware of the roar of approval from the predominantly Segestan audience as my final victory is declared. It is over. I survived the first test of the *Sententia*. I've taken my first step to ascend the heights.

"The will of the Empress has been done!" the Censor proclaims as he launches into a speech. The *Labyrinthus* challenge will take place tomorrow. I barely hear him. The battle rage still surges in my chest as I walk away from Aulus's prone form in the sand. It's tempered some as I survey the makeup of the survivors before me. My plan was not perfect. Putting us into a line without shields was foolish; that's obvious to me now.

I should have formed several small squads and had them roam like packs of wolves, collapsing on each other's enemies, the way Marcus and Felix did. I won't make that mistake again.

Make that mistake again? I chuckle to myself in derision. I will never be in a situation like that again. The life of the legionnaire is not for me. Maybe I can use that piece of knowledge in a nice game of cards at a tavern in Forum or Antioch or some other exotic city.

Despite my questionable tactics, it is obvious that our coordination served us better than the Nicodemians. I scan the crimson-clad students who are still standing, looking for people I do not know. I only count twelve, which means that thirty-eight of us survived. A small fire of pride burns in my chest as I realize that I helped keep so many of my friends' dreams alive.

Valentina rushes to meet me as I approach and slams into me with an embrace that uses both her arms and legs. I stagger under the weight of her tackle but laugh as I wrap my arms around her. After a moment, she drops to the sand, and Marcus slams a heavy hand on my shoulder.

"You genius," he greets me warmly. "Your plan worked."

"Never doubted it," I lie, giving my best friend a broad grin. More of our classmates mill around us as I approach. For once, I'm not on the receiving end of a bunch of skeptical looks. Hands slap me on the shoulder as I pass. Even Clintus gives me a nod of acknowledgement. I don't think my feet are touching the ground when I walk. I am floating, high on the approval of a group of people who have never been wholly comfortable with me.

Magister Vellum emerges from our gate and gestures for us to come. Slowly, like a herd of cattle, we begin to drift toward him. Now that the heat of the skirmish has faded, my body craters. Even the approval of my peers cannot hold me up. My feet are leaden. My rage is gone, snuffed out like a candle. From the stunned looks on most of the other *discipuli's* faces, I can tell they feel the same.

The old teacher favors me with a tight smile as I pass. On his eternally irritated visage, it is like *Sol* rising over the horizon. It is the first time he's ever given me a look that isn't dour. I return it with an exhausted grin of my own as I pass by the murals of our ancestors. I brush the foot of Perseus again as I pass, thanking him for his help.

I spy Felix as I join the rest of our milling herd in the holding room that I forged our alliance in. The tall boy is in the corner again. I glance over my shoulder and jerk my head at Valentina and Marcus, telling them to follow me.

Valentina's lips compress, but she doesn't say anything. What could she? She didn't save me—the plebeian did. I feel Clintus and the rest of Aulus's friends' heavy gaze on me as I cross the room. I ignore them. If they choose to remain friends with a traitorous snake, that tells me all I need to know about them.

Felix looks up as we approach. His brown hair is full of sand, and his crimsons are similarly stained by the earth. To my surprise, he flinches a little, as if dreading our presence. But he has nothing to fear from me.

"You saved me." I have no problem admitting what I feel is an obvious truth. Aulus was more trained with the blade than I. Eventually, he would have cut me to ribbons—metaphorically anyway. "Why?" To me, that is the real question.

"You included me." Felix shrugs. His brown eyes flick from mine to look over my shoulder at Valentina. "No one ever includes me." Suddenly, I understand this rude boy in a way that I never have before. Maybe some of his lashing out wasn't derived from arrogance, but loneliness.

"Oh please." Valentina sighs. "It was a good throw, *Primus*, but Castor had it under control." Felix's gaze turns back to me, a guarded expression on his face. I shake my head silently, disagreeing. I know what he did for me. He kept my dream alive.

"Val, I was going to lose," I tell her without turning around. Marcus grunts in quiet agreement. I'm not offended. Well, I'm embarrassed. It's a blow to my pride that I am not better with the sword. I may not want to join the legions, but I should have taken my training more seriously. The girl scoffs softly, her voice indignant, but I cut her off. I need this to come to an end. An idea has formed in my mind, taking shape like my last battle plan did in this very room. The imperator alliance is over. But now every student knows that we can choose to work together. Tomorrow, there will be a dozen squads working together.

"I dropped my sword," I remind her, overriding her protests. "You and Marcus weren't going to be able to get to me in time, but he did."

"You saved us all. We're even." Felix's expression is guarded again. He's not used to being treated with respect by the rest of us patricians. I feel a small cut of shame at that. I've never been the cruelest to the boy, but I'm far from blameless.

"What do you say we make it a tradition?" I hold out my wrist to him. He stares at it like it's a viper coiling up at his feet. Valentina gasps, but Marcus watches silently. I've learned my lesson about allying with people I don't trust. Felix has earned mine.

"What do you mean?" he demands.

"The fifty of us are going to be back out in that arena tomorrow, and if we're lucky, six of us will come out with Hearts." Even Valentina doesn't have an objection to that point. Despite her bluster, she wants to be bound as much as I do. Having the best student in our school on our side can only help us—even if he isn't up to the social standards of the mayor's daughter.

"You're the *Primus*. She's *Secundus*." I tilt my head at Valentina. Felix arches an eyebrow but doesn't argue. "*Sextus*." I point at my own chest with my left hand. "Muscle." I jerk my thumb at Marcus. All four of us laugh. Marcus may not be a top student, but he was a monster in the arena today. In the *Labyrinthus*, he will be terrifying.

"There are four walls surrounding a fortress, four corners to a shield, we are four students, and we need four Hearts. The math demands it."

My right hand is still hovering in the space between us. I want him to take it. He's earned my trust, and tomorrow will be all about trust. He hesitates for another moment, his brown eyes flicking between the three of us as he tries to decide if we're setting him up.

Even Valentina must have convinced him because eventually he reaches out and clasps my wrist with his hand. We shake, and it is done. Our triumvirate has become a quartet. Together, the four of us will stand against forty-six of our peers to prove our worth to the Censors, who see with the Empress's eyes.

"He's gonna have to bleed on the rock," Marcus rumbles.

"Bleed on the what?"

"Oathstone," I explain.

"Jupiter's Ashes, you three swore a *votum*?" Felix's eyes go wide as if he's suddenly regretting joining us.

"What's the matter, Patrician? Scared?" Valentina's voice still has a hint of her bitterness. Felix considers her for a moment, then his wicked smile returns.

"No," he tells her. I believe him.

Vellum instructs us on when to arrive tomorrow and then dismisses us. The old magister might have a glimmer of a tear in the corner of his eye as he surveys us. "You did well. I am proud of you, my students. Tomorrow, you will prove your worth. *Valete discipuli.*"

The four of us make a journey to the buried oathstone, adding Felix's blood to the stained rock. There are grim smiles on all our faces as he swears the same vow. Vellum's words burn in my chest like a bonfire. My elation at surviving the melee is unwarranted. I haven't made it any closer toward earning my Heart. I was always going to be competing against fifty students for the Empress's favor. Today wasn't a test—it was the wheat being separated from the chaff. The next time we meet, we will be Sentenced for real.

Felix and Marcus leave first, but Valentina hangs back. Her blue eyes bore into mine. They're gentle but cold, like being prodded by two icicles. "I hope you know what you're doing," she says softly before she leaves.

She does not kiss me on the cheek before she goes.

CHAPTER 8

*C*enturies ago, the Censors in their white tower beside the Empress's palace decreed how the *Labyrinthus* is to be built and maintained. In the day since the melee, it has been assembled so that it now fills the empty bowl of our arena on four levels, with rooms that can be pieced together in any order.

Cor relics power different rooms, making them unpredictable. The entire contraption costs a fortune, yet in order for a city to be able to have a *collegium* and compete for the Empress's blessing, an arena must be raised. It is an investment, for how can any place flourish without access to power? It is why there are so few plebeians in the ranks of the *discipuli*.

As students, we've been through the *Labyrinthus* many times, but it never gets easier. There are a dozen paths that lead to the end or to nothing. It's never the same twice. My dreams last night were nightmares of twisting paths that I could not escape.

We're back in the sandy staging room, all fifty of us. As I expected, students sit in small clusters of three to five. The groups keep to themselves and eye each other with distrust. There are three that are made up of Nicodemians, but the rest are my own class. Any camaraderie we shared yesterday is now long gone.

I glance at Valentina, who's at my side, and try to catch her eye. She doesn't look up from the sand she's staring at until I poke her shoulder with my finger. Her eyes snap into focus, and she turns to me with a frustrated snarl. My heart, the one made of blood and tissue in my chest, stumbles at the anger in her. She sees the small grin on my face, and her expression softens, a ghost of a smile growing on her own.

Relief floods me as I realize that she's not angry at me, just tense. So am I. My entire life is waiting for me on the other side of this challenge. Once I have my Heart, I'll be free to explore the world, to find fame and fortune.

"What Symbol are you going to choose?" Felix asks the group suddenly. Our newest member is sitting with his head on his knees, as if he's cold.

"You can't *choose* your Symbol, idiot," Valentina snaps. "It chooses you."

Felix gives her a flat look that says, "*I'm the Primus, remember?*"

The blonde girl blushes slightly and looks away.

"Hmm, maybe Iron," Marcus muses as if it's a big decision. The three of us chuckle dryly.

"If you can't choose, how do they make sure that legionnaires all have the right one?" Felix points out with a small smirk. Valentina frowns as if she's never thought about it.

"I'm not sure," she confesses.

"You can't choose," I say slowly, considering his point, "but maybe you can sort of *guide* it. I know my father *wanted* some sort of Plant Symbol, and that is what he got."

"Then, for the sake of conversation, *what would you choose?*" The plebeian looks amused as he repeats his question. I exchange glances with him, and he tosses me the ghost of a wink. I know what he's doing. The four of us aren't truly allies. Marcus and Valentina might have followed my lead, but they both still don't trust Felix, *votum* or no *votum*. It is a dangerous position to be in before we go into the *Labyrinthus*.

"Maybe one of the fire ones," I offer. All three of them groan in disgust.

"Maybe he just likes how they dance," Marcus mocks, his fingers wiggling like tongues of flame.

"I don't know," I admit, feeling silly. "I just always thought that having control of fire would be useful."

"You and every boy under the age of twelve," Valentina scoffs.

"Well, if yours is so much better, what is it?" I laugh, eager to move the conversation along.

"Perfect Melody," she says after hesitating for a second. The three of us turn to stare at her in surprise. She blushes and looks back down at the sand. Felix lets out a low whistle, clearly impressed. A Symbol that is that abstract is *extremely* rare. Music is also forbidden.

"I just want to see what it would be like," she mutters defensively, her cheeks almost as red as her crimson uniform.

"It's a marvelous dream," Felix half-whispers reverently. Valentina's head snaps up to stare at the plebeian. She thinks he's mocking her, but he's serious. Something softens in the hard edges of her face. I resist the urge to smile, happy to see my friend opening up.

"What have you dragged me into, Castor?" Felix chuckles, looking between the three of us. "Fire, Iron, and Music—the three things banned by the gods."

"Well, what about you?" Marcus asks, looking at our *Primus*. "Planning on something meek and well-behaved?"

"Wheat." He grins.

"Wheat?" I sputter in surprise. It is such a boring choice for someone who is considered to be so promising. *Cor* Hearts have given men the ability to reshape the world. In all my life, I've never heard of anyone wish for wheat. Not even my plant-obsessed father would be satisfied with a single grain.

"I'm going to become a master baker and open my own bakeries." His teeth flash in a brilliant smile. He's enjoying seeing our reactions. "I'll sell the best bread in the empire until my family can afford to become patrician."

The three of us who are members of the higher class sit in stunned silence. I'm awed by the audaciousness of his plan. A plebeian family can buy their way into the higher rank, but it is not cheap. An uneasy feeling lurks in the back of my mind as I realize it is a dream my father would approve of. My own seems so much more selfish.

"Flour and Dough are congruent with Wheat?" I ask.

He nods, unsurprised that I'm following his plan. I'm one of the few students who might be better at those mental puzzles than him.

"Sourdough?" Valentina asks.

"What?"

"Will you sell sourdough?"

"Only the finest."

"I'll buy some," the mayor's daughter promises. Felix gives her a grateful look, and some of the weight slides off my shoulders. One good conversation hardly undoes four years of rivalry, but it is a solid first step. It will have to be good enough.

The low murmur of conversation vanishes as the Censors enter, followed by Magister Vellum and an *argentum* woman that I assume is the head of Nicodemia's *collegium*. Atticus and his two shadows are wearing their white *lorica*. Their red capes billow behind them. My eyes track the three Silvers among their party, sending a thrill running through me at seeing so much power accumulated in one place.

"*Discipuli,* your final task is at hand," Atticus rumbles, raising his hands as if to give us a blessing. Again, his voice is loud enough to be heard throughout the entire room, even though he is speaking at a normal volume. I'm more convinced than ever that he's some sort of airbound.

"You have all run through the *Labyrinthus* before," he continues in a bored, flat voice. He doesn't want to be here, dealing with children. "In this final *Sententia*, you will each be required to claim three ribbons: red, blue, and green."

Groans emerge around the room as students react to the colors that will be in play today. Every room of the *Labyrinthus* will give a reward to a student that defeats its challenge. Red is for strength; blue is for knowledge; but green... green is for resistance.

A smile spreads across my face as I realize that two of the challenges are to my strengths. Blue is easy for me. If the entire *Labyrinthus* was made of only it, I would have a chance at being *Primus* myself. Likewise, green is something that I am better at than most of my classmates. My mother calls me her stubborn child for a reason. All I have to do is prove my strength, and a *Cor* Heart will be mine. Joy blooms in my chest like a lily as I realize that I'm going to make it.

"As is the custom, you will be released into the *Labyrinthus* in the order of your final ranks. These have been merged by us according to the wisdom of your magisters." Atticus holds out his hand, and one of the raven-haired Censors passes him a scroll that I hadn't noticed before. The stern young man unfurls it and begins to read.

"*Primus*, Felix Pistor." I slap our new ally on the back. "*Secundus*, Patricia Candelarius." The room falls dangerously silent as we realize that one of the top-ranked Nicodemians is still in the running. My earlier confidence fades a little as I realize that there may be more people ahead of me than I considered.

"*Tertius*, Valentina Flavinius." I grin and squeeze her shoulder. She smiles at me and pats my hand, sending a different sort of thrill through me.. *Quartus* and *Quintus* are also Nicodemian survivors. *Sextus* is Antony Sutor, who used to be our *Quartus* before those thieves came.

I'm placed *Octavo*, two places down from where I was hoping to be. Marcus is *Decimus*, ten. Felix and Valentina give us sympathetic looks, but there's nothing to be done. As Atticus reads the rest of the list, I don't listen—I'm spiraling. In my head, I remind myself over and over that blue and green challenges are my strong points. It's an unceasing mantra that's part prayer, part lie.

I always knew that I would have to beat other students to earn my Heart. What does it matter if I have to catch two more in front of me? They probably are terrible at blue challenges. My heart rate begins to slow as false confidence buoys me. It is shakier and less sturdy than my earlier confidence, but it's all I have.

When the Censor finishes reciting our ranks, he commands us to line up. Silently, the fifty remaining students of two towns shuffle ourselves into the correct order. I glare at the three Nicodemians ahead of me. They don't look back.

Marcus taps me on the shoulder. I turn to look two spots down at my friend. Clearly, we had not given him enough credit as a student. He gives me a reassuring nod to remind me that he's still with me. A ghost of a grin splits across my face, and I tap my chest with my right fist in a lazy legionnaire salute. I am not alone. All three of my allies begin in the top ten. Together, we will be unstoppable.

Atticus roams up the line, followed by his fellow Censors, who are referencing the scroll, making sure that we are all in the correct place. When he is satisfied, he orders us to march, and we walk down the same sandy hallway that led us to the melee.

I brush the mural of Titus on the foot for luck this time. Perseus was a warrior, but the man who broke into *Mons* Olympus had to be clever. Today, I need to be like him.

We come to a halt in front of the closed gate that leads into the arena. My hands are sweaty and clammy. No matter how many times I wipe them on my crimson shirt, they stay the same. I'm shaking like a leaf in the wind. I glance at Flora, the new *Septimus*, glad that it is no longer Aulus lurking behind me. She's shivering too.

No matter how many times I have challenged the *Labyrinthus* before, it feels like this is my first time. There is a difference between practice and the real thing. Losing in practice matters only a little, but today, it means everything. As a boy of seventeen, I have only done one other thing where my failure or success would affect the rest of my life, and that was yesterday.

Atticus marches past me to the front of the line, where another Censor stands next to a hanging hourglass, filled with sand. The palatine looks down the line once and then waves at the gate. Slowly, it begins to creak open. The noise of the crowd begins to hammer us again, but it is muted by all the construction that has filled the arena. A curtain covers the exit, so I cannot divine much of what the first challenges are.

Magister Vellum comes down the line, passing out relic wristbands. I take the dark gray metal bracelet and lock it onto my right wrist. These simple *Cor* devices are the triggers that will activate challenge rooms when we enter them. Mine is marked with the numerals *VIII* so they can track my results.

"Each of you will get a thirty-second head-start over the *discipuli* ranked below you," the Censor's voice practically whispers in my ears, even though he is nowhere near me. I shiver, feeling almost violated by his simulated closeness.

"Return to the entrance once you have collected your three ribbons. Do whatever it takes to collect them." I shiver as his cold blue eyes measure us. There will be no rules inside the *Labyrinthus*.

"Today, some of you will earn the blessing of your Empress," he barks, some emotion finally bleeding into his face. "You begin today as *nil*, but tomorrow, if you can prove your strength, some of it will become *rasa*. *Ex nihilo omnia*, out of nothing comes everything."

He turns away from us and flips the hourglass over. Its sand begins to spill, and he watches it like a hawk. This is the final countdown. When he flips it again, the *Sententia* will begin. I forget to breathe, watching the little grains pour out of the top of the glass and into the bottom.

These might be the last moments that my dream lives.

"*Primus*," Atticus's voice booms. Felix lowers his head and sprints out the gate. The arena roars at the sight of him, knowing that the challenge has begun. The line shuffles forward as Valentina takes Felix's place. I try to catch her eye, but she does not look back. A true hunter, she gazes at her target before her.

"*Secundus*," the Censor shouts. She disappears in a flash of blonde hair. We take a step forward.

"*Tertius*."

Step.

"*Quartus*."

Step.

With each student getting a head-start, tension begins to build in me like a kettle about to boil. Every second feels like an hour. I half expect Felix to return before I'm even released.

"*Quintus*."

Step.

"*Sextus*."

My rage flares once more that my place was taken from me, but I take another step.

"*Septimus*."

Step.

I'm at the front of the line now. My heart is beating so fast that it feels like one continuous contraction. I'm panting like a rabid dog, begging to be released to chase its prey. Attius side-eyes me as the sand falls.

"*Octavo*."

I shoot out of the gate, dash through the tarp, and into the *Labyrinthus*. My *Sententia* has begun.

CHAPTER 9

The sound is overwhelming. The *Labyrinthus* fills every nook and cranny of the arena's sandy circle, and the roar of the crowd echoes through it, magnified a hundredfold. A few steps in, I encounter my first choice: three paths stand before me. The ones to my left and right are ramps, which will take me to higher levels of the *Labyrinthus*. The middle goes forward and turns.

There's no sign of any of the students who went before me. The biggest lesson I've learned from running the *Labyrinthus* before is that hesitation loses more races than wrong turns. Calling on long-dead Apollo to grant me speed, I dash to the right, my feet pounding on the wooden floor as I race up one, then two levels. I'm on the third floor, which means there's only one more level above me.

The path splits, curving to the left and right. Since I've already taken the right once, I do it again. Easier for me to remember the way back. I follow the hallway until it straightens out around the bend. It splinters, turning into a dozen paths. *Lumos* relics set in the ceiling light the otherwise enclosed space. Open bronze-rimmed doorways dot the walls to my right, but there are none on my left. I'm unsure why one side is blank. I've never seen anything like that before.

Now that I've been released, my quivering panic has faded. It bleeds out in my muscles as I race to make up for lost time. The *Sextus* is already a minute ahead of me. I cannot afford to take any false steps.

I skip the first door, and the second. It's superstition, but most of the *discipuli* think that the magisters put the hardest challenges closer to the beginning as a trap for lazy students. All of them are shrouded in a relic-manipulated darkness that hides the nature of their test until you enter the room.

I sprint down the straight path, choosing the last doorway before it begins to curve toward the left. It's not deep in the *Labyrinthus*, but right now, I only have to memorize two turns. Taking a little longer to beat a challenge is better than getting lost.

The door slides shut behind me as the room reacts to the relic on my wrist. The lights turn on, allowing me to see what I have chosen. I breathe a sigh of relief as I take in the small, rectangular space that I've been locked into. Thick panes of glass block my path to the other side. Looking through them, I can clearly see a blue flag on the wall. I've found a test of knowledge.

This one is easy. I've done it before. It's a congruency challenge. I turn to the left wall, where at the top is a picture of a Symbol. It is a simple line drawing of an uneven sphere. Four colored Symbols sit below it—red, blue, white, and brown. I snort in derision. This is the most basic level of congruency—even Clintus should be able to solve it.

My eyes narrow as I study the top Symbol. The hardest part of this test is figuring out *which* Symbol you're supposed to match it to. There are thousands of them, but they follow stylistic rules. I suspect that this is a variation of Stone. Perhaps the Resting Boulder, or the Round Pebble. But it doesn't matter, as all of them are in the family of *Terra*—Earth. I press the brown Symbol marker.

Before me, the first pane of glass ascends, triggered by the relics that control the room. I step forward into the new space and turn to the puzzle it revealed. The four base elemental answers remain the same, but this time, the sketch of the unknown Symbol is three wavy lines.

For a moment, I hesitate. It's always a little tricky to tell if something is the Wind or Wave. But as I study the drawing, I notice that the lines are mostly straight instead of cresting into surf. They are drawn from left to right. This is the Eastern Winds, unless I miss my guess. I tap the white Symbol for Air and grin as the next glass panel lifts. If Magister Vellum could see the questions I am being asked, he would scream like a boiling teakettle.

The third puzzle is more of the same. I quickly recognize the Symbol of Hearth and touch the red for *Ignis*—Fire. Immediately, the glass lifts to make way for me, bringing me one step closer to earning my blue flag.

Question number four is predictably tied to *Aqua*. I barely glance at it before I recognize the Symbol of Deep Water and press the blue marker. Once more, the next glass partition opens, and I feel a grin expand across my face as I realize there's only one left.

I turn to the final question and feel my blood run cold. Gone are the four elemental markers. Now there are only two choices. The drawing at the top depicts a sword with a slight curve. Below it are four wavy lines that are used to depict the Wind as a whole and the word *ferum* for Iron.

My mind races back to the final congruency question that Vellum had asked me on the wavemachine. Maybe he wouldn't be furious after all. For a moment, I sit frozen, shocked and upset at the intricacies of the question.

If the others were too easy—and they were—this one is too complex by half. No student is expected to be able to discern congruency at this level. This is what they teach in the *Universitas* in Forum! The Empress school's doors are open to only the most elite *electii*.

Aware that I am wasting precious time, I stretch my finger out toward the Symbol for Iron but hesitate. A failed room cannot be repeated. Squaring my shoulders, I take a deep breath and force myself to *think*. At the surface level, Iron seems like the most obvious answer. In fact, my biggest hesitation is that it seems *too* obvious. A Symbol with increased specificity should be most like the one that makes up its base material.

That's not even congruency, just basic logic.

But something tickles at the back of my mind, as I remember when Vellum had asked me to compare the sword to the wind. I managed to find three points of congruence, which is generally the minimum required for Symbols to cooperate. The strength of those bonds then affects how much the Symbols can manipulate each other.

But congruency is only necessary when the Symbol is not made from the same element as its base. When one thing is made from the other, that is the strongest possible bond. A sword is forged from Iron, the same way that Air is innately bound to Wind. My lips condense into a frown. What possible reason is there for the Wind Symbol to be one of the answers? It has to be Iron. Any other answer seems like lunacy. My attempts at congruency back in the *collegium* seem like grasping at straws.

Once more, my finger stretches toward the Iron Symbol. But before I press it, inspiration strikes me like lightning. I snatch my hand back and stare at the Symbol of the Sword again. I'm an idiot. I let out a soft curse at how close I came to ruin.

The Sword in the Symbol is not *gladius*, the iron sword of the legions. The slight curve toward the tip marks it as a dueling blade, like the one Atticus wears at his hip.

A sword that is usually made of *tellus*, not iron.

This is a trick. They want me to assume that the blade pictured is a simple weapon made of Iron instead of looking deeper. Those early easy questions were merely there to lull me into a false sense of ease.

There is no connection between Iron and *tellus*, which means the closest congruency is between the blade's ability to slice the air and wind. It is an incredibly weak one, but at least it exists. My body tenses as I press the button for Wind. *Here goes nothing.*

The final glass pane rises, and I let out a gasp of relief as my path to the blue flag is clear. Hurriedly, I step through to the final space. A box with a single ribbon sits on the ground. I grab it and tie it on my right wrist, twisting it through my relic bracelet to secure it. The box snaps shut like a turtle's mouth waiting for the next worthy student.

Satisfied that I will not lose my ribbon, I race out of the rectangular room. The door opens to allow me to exit, and I hear a clunk as the glass panes drop back down, sealing the blue flag for the next student who chooses to try their luck with the challenge.

Footsteps echo, and the *Labyrinthus* shakes lightly under the pressure of footfalls of all the competitors who are racing their way through the structure. There has to be at least twenty of us in here by now. I turn toward a flicker of motion at the curve of the hallway to see Clintus come barreling into view.

The big boy's eyes spark with a devilish light when he sees me. He still doesn't like me, despite our alliance yesterday. His gaze falls on the blue ribbon wrapped around my wrist, and it turns greedy. We all know that he is not as good at congruency as me. I do not think he would pass the final test in that room.

There are no rules on *how* you get a ribbon in the *Labyrinthus*.

"Dead gods!" I swear, spinning on my heel to rabbit before Clintus even starts moving. He's bigger and stronger than me, but it doesn't really matter if he can beat me or not. I can't afford to lose any time to him. Our feet thunder as we race down the hall and around the backside of the curved wall, heading deeper into the *Labyrinthus*.

Whatever the giant circle is for on the level above, it only takes up about half of the arena. As soon as I get behind it, the maze opens up into a dizzying series of hallways. I let out a groan as I realize that I'm going to get lost.

But there's no time to hesitate—the boy behind me is charging like a warhorse, and I have no interest in taking a hit from him. I dash into the rightmost tunnel, sticking with my pattern. When in doubt, turn right.

Clintus's footsteps stomp behind me, giving me wings. Other paths open to either side as I run, but I ignore them. The secret to the

Labyrinthus is to take the simplest path possible. Getting all three flags isn't the hard part; getting out with them first is.

I spot the bronze doors of a challenge room as I reach the end of the hall. I toss a glance over my shoulder in time to see my pursuer round the same corner I just did. With a cheerful wave, I step through the bronze doorway into the darkness.

The challenge seals itself shut behind me, locking the room. I hear Clintus pound the door in anger a few times before the sound fades. As much as he'd like to corner me, he'd be a fool to wait outside the room. I could fail and come out with only one ribbon, or sometimes there is more than one exit. The risk of not getting anything out of setting an ambush is too great.

In the *Labyrinthus*, wasted time is deadlier than a blade.

The lights turn on, and I groan as I take in the scene before me. The room is longer and narrower than the last one. At the far end of the challenge, a green flag rests on the wall. This is a test of endurance. I had hoped to do my test of strength—the red flag—before I took on the green, but here I am.

Enduring is not particularly difficult, but it is exhausting. For a moment, I consider failing and getting thrown out. But I reject that idea. Clintus should not wait for me, but if he is feeling particularly desperate to get his hands on a blue ribbon, he might tarry a few moments to see if I abort the test and come out. If I am going to hide in here, I might as well get my second flag.

Between me and my prize are four pulsing fields. Each glows with a different color and will deliver the pressure of a unique Symbol. All I have to do is get through them.

Simple enough, but not fun at all.

The first field is a light blue, and I steel myself as I step through the glowing border and into the Symbol's power. Frost winds hammer me instantly, and I'm driven to my knees as my breath shoots out of me. I felt like I had been punched in the gut. My lungs burn from the arctic air as I gasp. Snow swirls around me, and I have to lift my feet to clear the drifts that I am suddenly knee-deep in.

For a moment, I gape at my surroundings like a fish out of water. Why did it have to be Winter? I hate the cold. They must be using *somnium*—dream relics to change the world around me. I've never experienced one before—they're beyond priceless.

Ahead of me, glowing like the Northern Lights, is a shimmering wall. All I have to do is make it through. With each pace, the temperature plummets as if Aquilo, the Winter God himself, was back from the dead and intent on torturing me with his icy fury. Step by agonizing step, I carve a path through the bank of snow, keeping my eyes fixed on the glowing exit.

After what feels like an eternity, I emerge from the barrier and collapse to the floor in the gap between fields. I give up one precious minute to let my body soak up the warmth of the room. When feeling returns to my fingertips, I force myself off the ground, even though I'm still out of breath. The next field is red. I sigh in dread and step into its shimmering border. The only way out is forward.

I'm on the side of a volcano. Magma rushes by me in trenches, superheating the air with its molten fury. On the plus side, I'm no longer cold. The sky is nothing but ash, and I choke with every breath I take. Ahead of me, higher up on the mountain, is the shimmering border of my salvation.

Belatedly, I realize that I should not have waited to enter the second challenge. Being half-frozen would have been like wearing armor against this field's rage. I make a note of that, but this is no time for thinking. It is time for surviving.

I strip my crimson tunic off as I climb, desperate to lower my body's temperature. Sweat pours out of me like a river. I can feel my lips cracking, dehydrating in a matter of moments. I'm hunched forward, against wind and gravity as I make my way up the path to the exit. I'd give anything to be back in that icy wasteland for just a moment.

Steaming and partially cooked, I burst out the back of the field and into the gap of the Challenge Room. Feeling suddenly stupid, I put my shirt back on. The only part of the test that was real was the heat; the visual aspect was all implanted in my imagination. A shudder runs through me, but this time, I do not pause. Instead, I dive into the third field, hoping that being hot will somehow come in handy.

It doesn't.

I'm in the middle of a field of jagged rocks that stretches for miles. A hollow breeze swirls around me, tugging at my crimson uniform. It's as if I'm in the rolling hills of Segesta's wheat fields, but instead of grains, they grew sharp stones. I take my first step and learn that my boots have vanished. The soles of my feet bleed as the jagged edges of rock beneath me slice at them. There's no sign of the shimmering gray barrier that will deliver me from this place. Gritting my teeth, I set my eyes on the horizon and continue to walk.

The only path is forward.

My agony increases with each pace; I earn a new cut with every step. I leave a bright trail of blood behind me like a beacon. If this weren't a dream relic, my chances of finishing the *Labyrinthus* would be *nil* with the wounds this challenge inflicts on me. *This isn't real,* I tell myself over and over. The mantra gives me something to hang on to, to numb the pain.

Both this and the blue challenge have been elevated from the ones I've seen before. It seems that the *Labyrinthus* we used for practice was but a shadow of the one that the Censors brought with them. Is that always the case or is it yet another sign of it being a drought year?

I walk for what feels like hours, but time passes here like it does in a dream. It may have been no more than a moment. I'm withering under the pain and blood loss. Before me crests another mound of sharp rocks, like a dozen that I've already climbed.

I'm beginning to think that I've missed something in this challenge. It's trying my endurance, surely, but its size is becoming ridiculous. Surely there are limits.

Behind me, the breeze carries the low, mournful howl of a *lupus*—a wolf.

I glance over my shoulder, grimacing in pain and fear. There's no sign of the hunter, but my trail of blood could be followed by a child, let alone an apex predator. Fear adds a new resistance to pain, and my pace increases, despite the state of my tortured feet.

The stones crunch together as I race. As I crest the hill, I hear another howl answer the first. This one is off to my west. I feel a hint of despair in my heart as I hear it. I'm being hunted by a pack. On an open field like this, that can only mean death.

I'm running out of time. I need to escape this dream before they catch me. I don't know what will happen to me if I die here, but I cannot imagine that would earn me a pass. There is no time for failure in the waking world.

Another *lupus* howls, this one to my east. I suppress a shudder and keep up my brisk trot. They are circling me. The scent of my blood must be as enticing as the flame to a moth. But unlike fire, I can be devoured by the creatures that I tempt.

I'm not surprised when a howl sounds directly ahead of me, long and loud. It is the logic of nightmares that compels this. I was never going to be able to just escape. That is no test. Panting from exertion and pain, I stop running.

I took the dull gray of the field to symbolize the rocks that made up this dreamworld. But instinct told me that it was a different kind of gray that they wanted to see me endure. This is a test of my ability to survive the stalking death of predators. Gingerly, I crouch down and grab a handful of the sharp rocks in my hands. The wolves will never catch me, I realize now. They were there to see how long I would run instead of facing my predators.

Stamina is only one kind of endurance. They want to see if I will still fight even when I am weak and wounded. It is chilling to realize that this is a consideration the Empress's Censors make when evaluating someone's worth for a *Cor* Heart. A coward would never pass this challenge.

As I suspected, the Dream does not make me wait. Gray shadows slip among the rocks like phantoms. Out of the corner of my eye, I catch motion, but when I turn, it is gone. The *lupi* circle me, as if I were a fish and they sharks.

I shift my feet to get as solid of a footing as I can among the stones and turn my head, tracking the beasts. Slowly, like ghosts, they draw closer and closer. Trusting my new understanding of the test, I do not run. I endure the fear.

Finally, one emerges to challenge me. It is a *mythus*, like my family's faithful stonehound. Golden veins run through its fur, glinting even in the low light. I cannot imagine what kind of Symbol a creature like this would attune to. I hope it is not Fire. The massive wolf's head comes up to my chest. It slinks toward me with an unnervingly intelligent light in its eye. It does not fear me. Why should it? I am but one boy without anything other than some rocks. Even a fully armed legionnaire would respect a *mythus lupus*.

Fear rages like an unchecked inferno in my chest as the creature slinks closer. I hold my stones like daggers, hoping their sharp edges will cut through my enemy's thick coat and into its flesh as easily as they have my callused feet. The *lupus* stops ten paces short of me, and we stare at each other. I forget to breathe; I'm so focused on its paws, watching for a sign that it is about to leap.

I nearly die of a heart attack when a second *mythus* growls in my ear. I let out a shout of terror and spin, slashing with my rocky dagger. My feet are torn anew as I twist them on the edge of the stony ground.

My swing finds only air. The wolf that was behind me is gone, vanished like the wind. Realizing my mistake, I turn back to face the first. My back aches in anticipation of a blow from its rending claws. But when I look back, it has not moved.

Once more, the *lupus* and I stare at each other. It tilts its head at me, as if surprised that I haven't run. I take a deep inhale and hold it for a second, trying to calm my nerves. I close my eyes and let out the breath I had been holding. I'm not as worried that it will attack me anymore.

I don't think it's that kind of test.

My eyes snap open, and I take a step toward the *mythus*. It doesn't move, only watches me with those too-intelligent eyes. Step after bloody step, I close the distance between us. My right hand opens, letting the sharp stone in its grasp fall to the ground. I won't need it.

I stop directly in front of the beast and take another centering breath. This is the most terrifying thing I have ever done. To encounter a wolf in the open plain is death. As a child, my parents would bring every servant inside if they even heard a normal howl in the fields. And these Ascended beasts are far more dangerous than their cousins.

Yet here I stand, readying myself to touch it. This close, I can see its teeth that are bigger than my fingers; they could tear me to shreds in an instant. I am stalling, letting my fear contain me. Every second I sit here paralyzed by fear is another cut in the slow death of my chances of earning a *Cor*.

Shamed by my cowardice, I reach forward with my right hand. My hand shakes, but it moves, and for that I am proud. The beast tenses, stiffening like a startled dog. I pause but hold its gaze, showing it that I have mastered my fear. After a few heartbeats, it relaxes, and I move closer.

My hand settles on the stiff, coarse fur of its head, and for a second, it relaxes, its pointed ears drooping. I exhale a long breath that I didn't realize I have been holding. Fear retreats, and I let out a small chuckle as I realize that I guessed the nature of the challenge correctly.

"Good boy," I murmur to it.

Faster than my eyes can track, the *mythus*'s head snaps around and its jaws open. I have just enough time to see that its mouth is filled with the gray haze of the test's boundary before it snaps shut on my right wrist.

Pain lances through me as its razor-sharp teeth slice through my soft human skin. I draw back my left to strike at the beast's head. If it doesn't release me, it could tear my whole arm off! The world turns bright for a second, and I'm forced to shut my eyes even as I cry in pain. The light retreats, and when I open my eyes, I'm standing on the other side of the gray field.

I scream again and fall to the floor. I'm no longer in pain, but the terror is still there. Gasping for breath, I hold my right arm up for inspection. My hand is still attached to my wrist, and my flesh is whole. But my heart skips a beat as I take in the sight of a row of scars in the shape of the *mythus lupus*'s bite.

Stunned, I sit up and inspect them. The dream was not real; it's not supposed to be able to leave a mark behind. My feet no longer hurt; they were never cut. Yet the scars from the wolf's bite are the dark purple of old skin trauma. The wound is completely healed, there isn't a hint of tenderness or blood. I rotate my wrist to see that they go around my wrist like a bracelet. I do not understand how dream relics work, but everything the magisters taught me says that should not have been possible.

I feel a comforting weight in my left hand, and I glance down to see that my fist is still wrapped around one of the sharp gray rocks from that world. I tuck the rock into my pocket, in case I need a weapon later.

Then, with a new sense of apprehension, I rise to my feet and eye the final field before me. It flickers with a hazy purple light, which chills me to the bone. It's hard to assign a color to a category of Symbols. There are only so many colors and far too many things to pair them with. Water is blue, but Air is also sort of blue, and so are all the ones contained within Ice. Plants and Crops tend to be green, but so do Poisons and Rots.

Purple tends to be things that are Intangible, like Ideas and Dreams. Having already been at the mercy of dream relics that were simulating physical things for the last three challenges, seeing something purple fills me with dread.

I have no idea how to prepare for this last terror. But I have no time to be afraid. Fear will rob me of my prize as sure as doubt. Steeling myself, I take a step toward the field.

"I should have fought Clintus," I grumble. Then I take another step and let the purple field consume me.

CHAPTER 10

"**C**astor, wake up! You're going to miss the *Sententia*!" My mother's voice pulls me out of my dreams like a horn of the legions, summoning the troops to muster. I gasp in shock and sit up in my bed, covered in a sheen of sweat.

My mind reels as I try to remember where I am. This is my room, where I have lived my whole life. My name is Castor Castus, and I am going to be late. I throw my sheets to the side and leap out of bed. Anxiety rages inside of me like a firestorm. I can't miss the *Sententia*! My whole life depends on it. If I fail, they will kill and devour me…

I pause in mid-stride as that last thought runs through my mind. Where did that come from? Who would devour me? *They* would, obviously. Frantically, I try to search my memory for who "they" are, but all I can come up with is a sense of unmistakable dread. I know without a shadow of a doubt that my life is on the line.

Shaking off my unease, I resume walking, and then I am in the kitchen, where my mother stands with her back to me, her hands on her hips. She is still, like a statue, but that doesn't bother me. Why would she be any other way?

"I'm awake!" I call to her, my voice ringing with the fear that I feel. "Don't worry, I won't miss the *Sententia*."

"You'd better not," she replies airily, without turning or moving her hands. "Your father would be *most* disappointed if you do not pass the Empress's tests."

"I know, I know," I assure her. "I won't disappoint him." She still doesn't turn, and I begin to feel like a plant that has not seen *Sol* for too long. Does she hate me so?

"Please, *Mater*," I beg. "Will you not look at me before I go on my quest? I crave your blessing."

"Be careful what you wish for," my mother's sing-song voice replies. There's a hint of playfulness to it, but it's deranged. It sounds evil. Slowly, the head of my statue-still mother turns. Her neck twists, and I stare in uncomprehending horror as her dead face turns to stare at me. Rot has claimed much of her flesh, and her eyes are milky-white with no pupils. Fire erupts behind her, sweeping through the kitchen as it devours even the stone. Her jaw hangs loose, but flaps as she speaks.

"Do you feel blessed now, my son?"

A scream of pure terror rips its way out of me, and I flee. I cannot be late to the *Sententia*. This is some sort of prophecy—a warning of what will happen if I fail. I cannot let that fate befall my mother. The world flickers by in scenes as I race through the house and down the road that leads to the arena.

As I run, my mother's dead laughter follows me.

I sprint through the open gates and burst into the arena, but it is empty. There are no crowds massed in the stands, no construction filling it for the challenge. It is as silent as a tomb, and I know I am too late. The *Sententia* is over.

Unwilling to give up, I march into the sands, hoping that I will find someone to test me. They expand to become a desert that stretches as far as the eye can see. The wind begins to whip up the grains and whip me with them, but still I persist. I will not let *them* get me too.

My heart leaps in relief as the form of Censor Atticus emerges from the swirling dust in front of me, dressed in his white *lorica*. I'm not too late; he's still here. I can still compete!

"Censor," I cry, waving for his attention.

The man whirls, and I recoil in horror. His face has been replaced with that of a demon. His eyes are black, and horns grow out of his forehead. He hisses in rage at the sight of me, and with a clawed hand, he draws his dueling blade.

"I'm here to be Sentenced!" I insist, ignoring his tormented appearance. "Please, you must let me compete."

"Sentenced you will be," the monstrous Censor promises, stalking toward me. "Grain must be beaten to separate it from its worthless parts. So, I will thresh you from that which makes you worthless."

He draws back his blade, and once more I flee. I make my way across the desert, but no matter how long I run, it never ends. The arena is infinite, and I have come here to die. To be devoured by them.

I run until *Sol* sets and plunges us into darkness. The monster that wears the Censor's face pursues me in the dark. For days and nights, I run, but whenever I look over my shoulder, the *daemon* in white is on my trail.

I do not hunger or thirst. At first, I assume this is because fear has driven these things out of me. But as my body continues to operate without the resources it needs to live, doubt begins to creep into me. How is it possible for me to survive without water?

On the second day of running, I begin to despair. This will never end. I have died and gone to a place of torment where I will be pursued by this creature for the rest of eternity. Never again shall I know peace.

On the third, I give up. I make the decision between the footfalls of my run. My left foot goes down, and my right foot comes up, and when it goes down, I do not lift my left again. For a moment, I stand as still as the dead statue of my mother did. Then I turn to face the monster that has dogged my heels for days.

The Censor is almost upon me. His black eyes gleam wickedly, and his white sword is drawn back to strike my head from my shoulders. Out of reflex, I raise my hands to ward off the blow. As my arms pass in front of my eyes, I feel a jolt in my stomach as I see the bite marks of the *mythus* on my right wrist.

Cracks appear on everything as it threatens to shatter. Slowly, I reach my left hand into my pocket, and my fingers close around the sharp stone like an anchor. The world shatters like ice as the illusion breaks.

This is a dream.

The *daemon* version of Atticus explodes into dust mid-step and vanishes. A mighty wind sweeps through and takes all the sand of the desert away. I cover my face to protect myself from the sudden windstorm, but I needn't have bothered. It vanishes as soon as it begins.

I lower my hands and open my eyes to find that I've left the world behind. I'm standing in a blank white space, a world without form or void. The floor and sky are indistinguishable from each other. Light comes from everywhere and nowhere. There is no up or down.

The only thing that breaks the monotony is a doorway with a purple tint. Still holding my rock, a piece of Reality that keeps the Dreams at bay, I head toward the door. Now that I am lucid, I remember what this is. I remember why I'm here. Vicious pride flows through me as I realize I've endured a nightmare created by the magisters.

I'm only a few paces away from the exit when the sound of a single pair of hands clapping stops me. I turn to find a man standing where I just was. He's tall and broad, bigger than almost any man I have ever seen. He would tower over Marcus.

He wears a white toga that is dirty and frayed, but otherwise the same shade as the void around us. Nestled in the crook of his arm while he applauds me is a bronze staff molded into the form of two snakes twisting together. A golden crown of olive leaves circles his head.

His flesh is not human; instead, it seems to be made of a golden, liquid metal that moves slowly as it swirls over his body. Dark black lines run through the armor, not mixing with its bright counterpart. Something about it sets waves of nausea roiling in my stomach. For a moment, I think I am about to be sick.

"Well done," he praises me in a sardonic tone. He leans back on his staff, hunching over it like an old man. A devilish light twinkles in his eyes as he surveys me. "It's been quite some time since anyone came through the Dream." Power radiates off him like a storm cloud. I have no idea who he is, but with one look, I can tell he is dangerous.

I lick my suddenly dry lips and take a step backward toward the door. I don't have time for this.

"Oh relax, boy." The giant rolls his eyes and takes a step to the side. A heavy clanking comes from the metal chains running from his ankle to an iron ball the size of a boulder. The clasp is closed over his golden flesh, and it seems to recoil from it. The sound echoes off the vast emptiness in ways I don't understand. "I couldn't catch you if you tried."

For some reason, his promise doesn't calm me. It only makes me more alert. His eyes glow a light blue and are too intense, like a predator. For some reason, it makes me think of something an *alligatoris* would say to its prey if it could only speak.

I take another step. The man lets out a hearty chuckle. It's warm and genuine and tells me that I was right not to trust his assurances. He seems pleased that I do not trust him, although I cannot imagine why.

"Why are you going so soon?" he asks, arching an eyebrow. The golden skin stretches as if it were made of flesh. "You summoned me, and I came. Despite my burdens, I still came. It is rude to turn aside a guest."

"I don't live here," I point out, taking another step toward the purple doorway.

"Well, I do."

"Then perhaps it is you who is being a bad host," I suggest.

He tilts his head as if surprised at my comment. Another genuine smile flickers across his face, replacing the arrogant smirk that seems to live there most of the time. It only serves to make him more unsettling. I do not like him. I suspect that he is another nightmare, sent to torment me. Something about him is inhuman, beyond the metal skin.

I take another step backward toward the purple door. I have a green flag to collect and a *Cor* Heart to earn. Whoever or whatever this creature is, all I have to do is leave the dream relic and never see him again.

My decision made, I trust that his iron ball will slow him down enough for me to make an escape. Fear spikes in my heart as I begin to turn away from the giant. His glowing eyes flicker with a knowing light. I don't hesitate, springing into action and dashing the final steps toward the door.

"Bah! Don't worry, boy, I shan't chase you," he calls after me. "We will meet again soon enough." The being's laughter chases me as I leap through the purple field and out of the Dream.

I emerge back into the dim room of the arena, still sprinting at full speed. I slide to a stop before I smash into the wall of the room. Feeling an almost frantic sense of hope, I turn and look at the base of the green flag. The maw of the box with a green ribbon sits open, waiting for me, and I snatch my prize out of its jaws, threading it through my armband with the blue one.

Confident that they're both secure, I make my way out of the challenge room. As I get to the front, there's a light hum as the fields turn back on. A shiver runs down my spine as I feel a pressure in the room that hadn't been there before. It is like a pair of heavy, unseen eyes stare at me without the need to blink. The scars on my wrist itch, and I rub them absently as I watch with bated breath to see if the gold-skinned man emerges from the Dream. Eventually, the pressure fades, and I don't look behind me as the door unlocks and slides into the air.

Eager to leave the strange presence behind me, I dash back into the *Labyrinthus* only to run into a different giant. I ricochet off the big boy and into the wall and shout as I feel a hand grasp for my wrist.

Clintus waited for me! What an idiot. I bounce off the wall, using it as a springboard to drive me forward, driving a fist at his stomach. There's a *woof* as my hand buries itself in his soft flesh. I jump back, settling into a fighting stance.

"Castor, it's me," Marcus wheezes, holding up a hand to stave off my next attack.

"Oh." Embarrassed, I lower my hands. "Sorry. Clintus chased me into that challenge room." I glance at my friend's wristband. He's already got a red one—of course. Strength is his greatest asset. The good news is that if my friend has only completed one challenge on his own, I haven't fallen behind while stuck in the Dream. He lets out a low whistle of admiration as he sees my second.

"What's in there?" He nods at the room I just left.

"Green. It's brutal," I reply, tapping my own ribbon. He makes a disgusted face; he probably wants to save it for last too, which means he needs a knowledge challenge. "Blue is back toward the beginning of the third floor." I gesture in the direction I came from. "Take a left, go around the circle, and first door on your left."

"Thanks." He holds out his fist, and I rap mine against it. "There's a red that way"—he jerks behind him—"but I wouldn't recommend it. It's all about carrying heavy stones. It's rough."

I nod in disappointment. After how intense the endurance test was, I suspect all of them will be like that.

"Seen any of the others?"

"Felix once—that madman was already at two ribbons too." I'm relieved that I'm keeping pace with the *Primus*. As much as I'd like to stick together for safety, I know time is running away without us. I give him a nod and set myself to go explore. Maybe I can find a red challenge more to my style. We part, and as we do, I remember that the knowledge challenge was no walk in the park either. I turn to call over my shoulder and call after my friend. "Marcus! The last question is a trick!"

My friend holds up his right fist in a salute and trots off. I take a steadying breath and stride deeper into the *Labyrinthus* to find my final flag.

CHAPTER 11

s I hurry through the next few turns, I pause to check every challenge door I encounter. I only find blue or green flags inside. It's not uncommon for the game masters to make one of the three challenges rarer than the others. It seems that this time Strength has drawn the short straw. I abort them and pop back into the *Labyrinthus*. All I need is a red, and I can escape.

My mind is focused on my hunt as I turn a corner and come face-to-face with a Nicodemian. The lean girl is at the far side of the hall, and when she sees me and the two ribbons on my wrist, her eyes light up. She throws back her head and lets out a trilling bird cry that makes my heart sink. Three more answer her from around the floor, echoing off the narrow walls.

It seems the interlopers have decided to have alliances of their own. Without a moment's hesitation, I spin and rabbit away from the hunters, shouting for reinforcements as I run.

"Marcus, Valentina, Felix!" The only answer is my own voice bouncing back to me. Mentally, I unravel the path I'd taken since leaving the green challenge as if I had trailed a spool of thread behind me. I burst into the hallway where Marcus and I parted and sprint along the strange, curved wall. It sounds like an entire war party is on my heels. Their footsteps pound like drums as they give chase.

"Dead gods!" I curse as I pass the door I directed my friend to. It's closed. Marcus will be no help to me now. My only hope is to lose them in the *Labyrinthus*. I shoot back into the third-floor landing and cut to the left, taking a ramp up to the fourth and final floor.

The sloped path doubles back on itself like a switchback, and I grab the corner to make my turn as tight as possible. I am moving at top speed as I catapult out of the exit and am forced to stumble to an abrupt halt so I don't fall into the abyss below.

I've arrived on the edge of a ledge. A giant circular pit stretches before me, filled with water. The waves, moved by a hidden relic, dance around, adding a current. In the center of the pool is a thick pillar that flies a red flag. At least I know what the curving wall is for.

A platform, powered by some sort of *aer* relic, hovers only a short leap in front of me. Looking further into the pit, I see more of the floating planks that eventually reach the middle, waiting for some idiot to leap between them.

To my surprise, Felix and Valentina are halfway through the challenge. The *Primus* already has three ribbons wrapped around his arm, but he's helping Valentina cross the leaps that would be too far for her shorter stature.

The two of them turn to look back at the sound of my approach. My friends both toss me a grin and wave from the middle platform, almost embarrassed to be caught working together. Valentina's expression turns to horror, and I know why. I can hear the footsteps behind me. The Nicodemians are coming.

With a curse, I take a few steps back and leap forward. My heart skips one of its furious beats as I soar through the open air and crash down on the floating platform. It wobbles slightly under my added weight, and I stagger to the side, waving my arms to catch my balance.

Immediately, I spin in time to see the girl who accosted me come flying out of the mouth of the ramp. She draws up shortly as three more of her interloper friends join her. They're all much bigger and meaner-looking than her. None of them have more than one ribbon. The would-be thieves gaze at me with angry glares. I give them a cheeky wave before turning back to the task at hand.

Grimly, I eye the next ledge. It's narrower than the first; I will have to be more precise with my landing. I eye the water below distrustfully, but there's nowhere to go but forward. Any second now, one of those brutes behind me is going to throw themselves at me and knock us both into the water below.

Taking two short steps, I leap to the second platform, which wobbles more aggressively under the weight of my landing. I windmill my arms and manage to catch myself before I fall into the drink. If it's protesting this much from my weight, I can't imagine how it would react if Marcus or Clintus landed on it.

I hear a dull thud behind me, and I turn to face the first brave thug who has chased me into the air. He's taller than me, but not that wide. He too flails his arms to catch his balance, then sets himself and leaps toward me.

My heart skips a beat as I twist to the side, extending my left palm in an open strike to his face. The force of his momentum makes me take a step back, but with his eyes covered, he loses sight of his target.

Our limbs flail against each other as he tries to grab my wrist, but he fails to get a grip as he plummets. I stumble back, managing to stop myself right before I run out of platform beneath my feet.

With an anguished scream, he falls into the raging waters below. I toss his friends a crude salute and then turn my attention to the next platform. Felix and Valentina are two ahead of me, almost to the center. I don't know how we're going to get out of this, but if we do, it's going to be together.

With a grunt, I throw myself to the next floater. It wobbles, but I find my balance more quickly than before, and it stays in the air. A victory by any measure. I wave to my friends, who are looking at me with a mixture of horror and delight.

"Hey." I pant. "I brought some company."

"You shouldn't have!" Felix shouts back over the roaring waters. I shrug back as if surprised by his lack of appreciation.

"Now you tell me!"

Felix laughs and leaps to the next platform easily. He turns and holds out an arm for Valentina, who catches his arm as she follows him. The tall *Primus* leans back, anchoring my friend as she lands on the edge of the platform, and they clasp arms to keep from falling.

Their platform wobbles even more than it did when I landed on it, but it stays in the air. Behind me, I hear a grunt as another Nicodemian throws himself into the chase. I look back at him and arch an eyebrow, making a point to look at their soaked comrade swimming below.

The ugly boy, with his shaved head and pimply face, merely snarls and leaps to the second platform. He's heavier than Felix and me put together, and the platform sags dramatically under his weight.

Suddenly, I begin to worry this task was designed to not let two people pass at once. If the magisters planned a way to prevent anyone from doing exactly what my friends are doing. I glance over my shoulder to eye the last jump the two of them have to make. It's smaller than any of the others.

"Felix!" I shout, trying to catch their attention, but they don't hear me. They're too focused, the roaring waters are too loud, and the red flag is too close. I can only watch in growing horror as *Primus* makes the jump easily and Valentina leaps on his heels.

But this time, when she lands on the platform, it shudders and tilts to the side, unhappy with the extra weight on it. As it collapses, my friends lose their grip on one another. Felix spins like a top and leaps from the rising edge of the platform to the pillar that holds the flag. Valentina plummets to the waters below.

"No!" I scream in despair at seeing Valentina, my Valentina, defeated by the challenge. Felix shares a look of horror with me, but then a look of cunning crosses his face. He turns to the red flag next to him and collects a second red ribbon from the box before it snaps shut.

We exchange bemused glances, and then the *Primus* lets out a bark of laughter. Valentina is going to be okay. There are no rules on how you get your ribbon. Relieved that we've averted the first disaster, I glance to check on my Nicodemian pursuer.

He's also been distracted by the show, but now that Felix holds another red ribbon, his focus turns back to me. Greedy eyes stare out of his puffy face, and I shudder at the thought of his ham-sized fists wrapping around my neck.

I turn and throw myself to the next platform, managing to catch my balance on the smaller space. Marcus was right: the strength tests in here are brutal. Without pausing for more than a moment, I leapt to the next, eager to stay ahead of my pursuit.

Felix waits for me at the flag, his eyes narrowed, as he watches the vultures that have come to loot our carcasses. I eye the final platform that spilled Valentina into the waters below distrustfully.

I'm fairly certain that the trigger for its collapse was due to the number of people or the total weight that the relic sensed on it. I weigh less than Felix, and there's only one of me, so it should remain inert when I land on it.

Should.

What a word to gamble my chance to earn the Empress's blessing on.. If Felix has already finished his third task, there is a good chance some of the other students were close to doing so as well. Every moment we delay is another second for them to get to the end before us.

With a scream of rage, I throw myself at the tiny platform. My heart almost leaps from my body as it begins to tilt underneath me, but I don't stop. Instead, I use my momentum to carry me up the angling floor before I leap for the flag. My foot slips at the last step, and I stumble off the edge.

I know as soon as I'm in the air that I'm going to fall short.

"Gotcha!" Felix cries, grabbing my wrist as I flail past. I let out a grunt of pain as I slam into the rocky pillar, and my friend drops to the ground, pulled by momentum. But his grip does not falter, and I wrap my hand around his arm, securing the hold. The raging water is far too close for my comfort. For a moment, I look down, stunned by the force of the impact.

"Please hurry," he grunts from above. "You are much heavier than Valentina."

Shaking my head to clear it, I plant my feet on the wall and pull on his wrist, walking myself up the side as if it were the floor. When I get to the top, I leap and throw my free hand over the edge. Together, we pull me up, and I slither over the edge like a snake. For a moment, we both lie on the ground panting. Then Felix taps my shoulder and struggles to his feet.

"No time to waste," he admonishes, eyeing the Nicodemian who is trying to make his way through the platforms behind me. He still has three jumps to go, but I have no desire to be here when he finishes them.

"Thanks," I gasp, reaching into the open box and taking the red ribbon that is waiting for me. Once more, it snaps shut, and I tie it around my wrist with the other two. Grim satisfaction runs through my veins. I have my ribbons. Now all I need to do is escape.

"Well?" Felix asks, eyeing the siege that we're under. The two Nicodemians who haven't braved the course are waiting at the edge of the water, watching us. "Any bright ideas?"

"Time for a swim?" I ask, pointing to where Valentina is treading water, waiting for us. There's no easy way out, as far as I can tell. That's how these open challenges tend to be. They're a trap, and we're in the middle of it.

"I was afraid you'd say that," the *Primus* grumbles, but leaps off the pillar in a clean dive, his four ribbons trailing in the wind. I jump after him, feet first into the frigid waves.

In the distance, the first Nicodemian I knocked into the water climbs up the ladder to rejoin his comrades on the landing. The three of them eye us evilly as we swim toward them. They know that we have at least three full sets of ribbons—there's no way they're going to let us escape. Valentina swims to join us, her face tight with strain.

"Tell me you have a better plan than to swim to the ladder!" she shouts over the crashing waves. I shake my head, saving my breath. There's no other way out, and we have no time to waste.

"I'll go first," Felix says grimly. "Follow me up."

The three of us swim across the miniature ocean to the ladder. The three interlopers hover around the top, waiting for us like buzzards. The fourth boy, the ugly one, hesitates on top of his platform. He's so close, he can taste the red ribbon waiting for him. No matter what happens, he and his friends will need more. Or maybe he isn't a strong swimmer and is afraid to join us in the water.

Felix grabs the first rung and lifts himself up out of the waves, looking back at me with a grim expression. After a moment of thought, he takes off his ribbons and passes them to me. "Hold these," he orders.

I nod in understanding, tying them around my relic with the others. It would be too easy for them to reach down and grab his wrist as he climbs up. Now that I'm loaded down with extra flags, I'm bait. Since I'm second on the ladder, they'll have to let him up or knock him off before they can get to me.

"Come on up, boys!" the girl jeers from above. "I am Decima Divitiae of Nicodemia, and you fools owe me your ribbons." Her black hair is drawn back in a ponytail, and she peers down at us with a triumphant glare. The other boys with her hover around her, waiting to pounce on us.

I do not know how we are going to get out of this. We have every disadvantage possible. We're outnumbered, out-positioned, and our wet clothes hamper our movement. If this was a castle and we were a besieging army trying to get on the wall, any imperator worth his salt would know that we're charging to die.

But time is running out, so charge we must.

Felix doesn't reply but grants her request, making his ascent up the ladder with a calm grace that I don't feel at all. I follow, shaking with cold and fear. The *Primus* hesitates a couple of rungs from the top, eyeing the gang waiting for him. They're a few steps back, as if promising him safe passage.

I can barely hear him sigh over the sound of the waves. "The things I do for bread," he mutters. Then his lean shoulders both flex, and he flies up the ladder like an arrow. Caught flat-footed, I scramble to follow in his footsteps.

Valentina climbs behind me, and the entire structure shakes under our combined weight as we race to the top. If Felix can hold them off for a few seconds for Val and me to get up, then the odds get a little better. But the Nicodemians, as much as I hate them, are not complete idiots. The two boys rush Felix and shove at him as he vaults up to the landing.

One of them wraps his arms around my friend, while the other slams into him from the side, spinning him toward the edge. I let out a shout of rage and reach for the top rung, racing to the *Primus*'s aid.

The dark-haired Nicodemian swoops in to cut me off. Her mouth is opened in a rictus snarl, and she stomps at my fingers with her boots. I shriek and jerk my hand back, narrowly avoiding having my digits crushed. There's a splash behind me as Felix falls into the waters below. Our charge has failed.

Immediately, the other two boys rush to grab me. I try to drop lower, but Valentina is right behind me and blocks my retreat. Strong hands claw at my wrists, and one of them manages to grab my left arm. I let my right dangle, keeping it and its precious cargo out of reach.

"Come on, idiot," Decima snaps. "Stop wasting time. It's over. Give us your ribbons, and maybe you'll have enough time to earn some more." A slow smile spreads across my face as I see something move behind them. The Nicodemians scowl at my expression.

"Are you sure?" I ask her, fighting against the laugh that's bubbling up in my chest. "I think you might have missed something."

"Like what?" one of her thugs sneers.

"Like Marcus the *Taurus!*" my friend roars, pounding out of the rampway where he has been lurking and smashing into the Nicodemians like a hammer. A blue ribbon has joined the red one he had earlier. One of the boys goes flying into the water, caught completely off balance. Marcus turns to the other, who lets go of my wrist to face this new threat.

Decima's eyes go wide as I explode up the ladder, pulling with all my weight. She might have the upper hand, but I outweigh her by at least two stones. She falls back in terror as I surge onto the landing. It's my turn to snatch at her wrist, trying to steal her ribbon.

Decima turns to flee, in time to see Marcus backhand her ally with a roar. The poor boy drops to the floor, and before he can get his bearings, my friend drags him to the edge and throws him into the pool. When I turn back, there's no sign of the girl.

"Time to go," Valentina pants, climbing up next to me. Her eyes find mine, and my heart skips a beat. Is this really happening? We survived the ambush and have our ribbons. We can escape the *Labyrinthus*. Wordlessly, I hand her the spare red that Felix collected for her.

She takes it from my hands with a shy smile and kisses me on the lips. We're both sopping, but her lips are wet in a different, much more pleasant way. My brain stutters, trying to comprehend this new sensation, and then it's gone. She moves past me, wrapping her third ribbon around her wrist. My smile is so big that I think my face might tear in half. Felix appears up the ladder after me, an amused look in his eye. I toss him his three ribbons back, and he nods in thanks.

"I still need one," Marcus says quietly, counting ours. There's a note of despair in his voice. How cruel would it be if our savior was left behind? If by rescuing us, he sealed his own failure? Felix and Valentina both bow their heads in guilt. But not me. A second massive smile splits my face, and I hold out my left fist, opening it slowly to reveal the green ribbon I swiped off Decima's wrist.

"I don't know about that." I laugh at the shocked expression on my friends' faces. "You can just use this one." Reverently, Marcus takes the ribbon out of my hand and wraps it around his other ones.

"Together or not at all," I remind him. For a moment, I look among my three friends and allies, marveling at the fact that we have completed the challenges of the *Labyrinthus*. We can earn our Hearts. All we have to do is escape before anyone else. "Does anyone know the path?" Valentina asks, her urgency shattering the moment.

"I do. Follow me," Felix announces confidently. In a moment, we're racing for the ramp and the exit. Our feet pound on the wooden floor as we go down to the third level and race along the curve of the pool.

A few students peer at us as we pass, but most flee when they see the size of our party. No one wants to get cornered by four people in these tight hallways. As we run, my excitement builds. We're so close! We find the long ramp down to the first floor that I took at the beginning of the challenge, and together we race down, turn left—and we're there. A glowing white door waits for us, preventing us from seeing anything on the other side.

Felix slides to a stop at the exit, turning to look at us with a somber expression. The entrance is empty; no other students are in sight. Silently, we all draw to a halt. Each of us is thinking the same thing.

Who crosses first?

We don't know how many students have finished the *Labyrinthus*. There are only so many Hearts. It is a drought year. Wordlessly, we look at each other, waiting for someone else to speak.

"Felix, go first," Valentina says after the silence stretches to an uncomfortable length. Surprised, all three of us turn to look at her. The girl's eyes are fixed firmly on the floor, and there's an embarrassed redness to her cheeks.

"You were done, but you stayed to help Castor and me," she continues, her blush deepening. "It's only right."

"I agree," I say after a moment's thought. It kills me to let anyone else go ahead, but it is the honorable thing to do. My parents would be proud of me, and for some reason that matters to me more than I thought.

Felix opens his mouth to protest, but Marcus cuts him off. "*Vade—go!*" he orders, pointing at the open doorway. "Get out of here. We're right behind you." The *Primus* lowers his head in shame, but when he looks up, there is gratitude in his eyes. He turns and heads for the door with a light step.

"I expect a discount on bread!" I shout at him as he walks. He pumps a fist in a salute.

"Well, that was easy," Marcus mutters, looking between the three of us. We have been friends and allies since birth, and now we are faced with a decision that would change the rest of our lives. Nervously, I glance over my shoulder, but no other students are coming. We still have time.

"You go," I insist, pointing at the door that Felix disappeared through. "You saved us. Without you, we would have lost all our ribbons."

"Yes," Valentina agrees after a moment. Her eyes are watering, as if she can't believe that she's doing this. But she knows it's the right thing too.

"I didn't even finish all my challenges!" Marcus protests, pointing at the green ribbon I gave him. "If anything, I should be after you."

"Will you just go?" I shout, stress turning my voice into anger. I appreciate that he didn't want to take it. He knows what this meant for all of us. But this is already hard enough without adding endless debate to it. Each of us would die for the other, or at least we thought we would. Making this decision is like abandoning your siblings to the wolves.

"*Vale*, my brother and sister," Marcus says softly after a moment, echoing my thoughts. The big boy turns to the door, and with one last look over his shoulder, he's through the door and gone.

"And then there were two," Valentina murmured, turning to look at me. Her brown eyes find mine, and there's a new note in the look we exchange. I feel like I can hear her heartbeat through her gaze. Maybe that's just mine, pounding in my ears. Maybe hers and mine beat in time now.

I want to go next. I want it more than anything. Letting each one of my friends go ahead of me had been like a stab wound in my soul.

Every time one of them disappeared through the door, I felt as if I died a little more. Will I be able to live with myself if my fairness is what costs me that which I want the most?

But as I stare at this wet, beautiful girl, I wonder if there are other things I want too. If other things are more important than getting a *Cor* Heart. *Maybe my father is right.*

"Go," I croak after a long moment of staring. I still want it, but this feels like a sacrifice that I can make. Valentina holds my gaze, silently. Her eyes feel bare, like windows to her soul that let hers look directly into mine. Eventually, she sees whatever she needs to because she tilts her head and nods.

I hear a frantic step behind us, and I turn in time to see a student I don't recognize emerge from the *Labyrinthus* with three ribbons in his hand. There's thundering of footsteps behind him as a horde of would-be thieves chases him.

"Now!" I shout, pushing her in front of me. With my heart in my throat, I follow Valentina out the white door and beat the *Labyrinthus*.

CHAPTER 12

The white flares and then fades as I race on Valentina's heels. We're back in the sandy entryway to the arena. Atticus and his Censors stand just ahead, eyeing a cluster of students against the wall. Felix and Marcus look back at us with blank expressions on their faces. The Censor moves to intercept us as we approach.

"Ribbons," he barks. Both of us hold up our wrists for his approval. He nods at hers and then mine and then gestures for us to get in the line. As we pass, he turns and points to Felix as if just completing the official count.

"*Tertius*," he announces.

He points at Marcus. "*Quartus*."

Valentina is *Quintus*.

I'm *Sextus*. My brain goes numb as I try to understand what he's telling me.

A student bursts through the doorway, clutching the three ribbons in his hands. It is not the student we saw holding them when we exited. It's Clintus—somehow the big boy managed to cut his way in.

"*Septimus*," Atticus grunts at him as he joins us in line. Slowly, I turn to face my friends. Marcus lets out a whoop of joy. Valentina tackles me in a hug. Felix turns away so we won't see his tears of joy.

In the last drought, the Censors brought six *Cor* Hearts.

As a *Sextus*, I would have received one.

I'm getting my Heart.

The world becomes a blur of bliss. I barely notice as the rest of the students trample in one by one. Dimly, I'm aware of the pained expressions on their faces as they see how long the line of people who beat them is. But their despair cannot dampen my fierce, unbridled joy.

I am whole. I am complete. I have achieved the dream of my youth. I will leave this town and explore the world. My father will be disappointed. Thinking of him and his distrust of the *Cor* Hearts is the only shadow that can be cast over my jubilee. I shake my head to clear it, snapping out of my introspection.

The line is silent. I'm not sure if that's because people are overwhelmed by their emotions or just intimidated by the Censors hovering over us like Imperial Eagles. I glance at my friends, enjoying seeing each of them process our victory. Felix's smile is like *Sol* breaking above the horizon. Tears still glisten in his eyes. I know what this means for the future of his family.

Marcus's gaze is unfocused, and he stares at the wall in front of him without really seeing it. I bet he's imagining himself in the purple livery of the Praetorians waiting outside the arena. By earning his own Heart instead of enlisting, it's an attainable goal. Valentina meets my eyes warmly. Her smile is small, but it's only for me. It gives me a different kind of thrill that even the ability to command the elements cannot compare to.

At last, the fiftieth contestant emerges from the arena into the hall. I feel a small surge of vicious satisfaction when I see that it's Decima. The raven-haired Nicodemian sees me and shoots me a killer glare as she takes her place at the tail of the line. Fiftieth or eleventh makes no difference, but seeing her embarrassed is a delicious little cherry on top of the dessert of today. If my soul gets any lighter, I might begin to float.

Atticus and his Censors sweep up the line, making sure that no one has swapped places. Satisfied that all is right in his world, the young man comes to the front of the line to stand next to today's *Primus*. He turns, running his cold eyes down the line before addressing us with his Air-powered voice.

"At my command, you will march in a single-file line to the top of the arena," he announces. Muted whispers run through the students as everyone realizes that the *Sententia* announcement is about to begin. "Once we reach the center, you will organize yourself in rows of five and await further instruction. Is that clear?"

"Aye, *Dominus*," we reply in unison. Satisfied, the man gives us a stiff nod and turns to march down the hall. His red cape billows behind him, caught in an unseen wind.

"Begin!" he calls.

We snake our way through the interior of the arena, trailing in the wake of the Censor. As we march, I wonder how Atticus and his escorts came to be Censors so young. All the others that I have ever seen were old. Not as old as Magister Vellum, but well into their fifth decade.

I have no interest in being a legionnaire, but the life of a Censor has some allure to it. They travel the empire speaking with the voice of the Empress. Plus, the white armor and red cape are a striking uniform. A small smile spreads across my face as I watch the man stride ahead of me. Perhaps one day Censor Castor would bring *Cor* Hearts to Segesta for their *Sententia*. The thought fills me with pride. Maybe one day, I would award my sister her own Heart.

I'm so lost in my daydreams that I don't realize we're about to enter the ring again. Atticus leads us out the door onto a platform that has been built over one side of the *Labyrinthus*. The crowd screams in delight as they see our crimson uniforms emerging in order. The purple-clad Praetorians stand at attention at the top of the arena, encircling the crowd.

I spot my mother and father in one of the lower rows, next to the mayor and his wife. My father's expression tightens as he sees how close to the front I am. I wave at them but look away quickly. Their disappointment threatens to overwhelm me.

The Censors stop at the center of the platform, and Atticus nods to the empty space to his right. As we were instructed, we line up in ten rows of five students. Anticipation soars in my chest as I settle into my place as leader of the second row. I'm practically giddy now.

Our new *Primus*, a dour-looking boy who was one of the Nicodemians released before me into the *Labyrinthus*, watches the crowd with an almost hostile expression. I suppose most of the faces looking at him aren't thrilled to see someone not from the hometown in first position.

One of the other Censors pulls out a scroll and passes it to Atticus, who unfurls it and gazes at the shouting crowd for a long moment. It is wrapped in the dull gray metal of a relic. They fall silent at the sight of the item in his hands. He holds the silence for another moment, until he is satisfied that the proper respect is being shown.

"My people!" Atticus says, but it is not him who speaks. The voice that emerges from his lips is feminine. It is rich and strong but carries a warmth to it like a late summer breeze. A thrill runs through me as I hear Empress Diana's voice for the first time in my life.

"I am most pleased by the prowess your *discipuli* have shown in the *Sententia*," she continues, using her Censor as a mouthpiece. "Our great empire is built on the foundation of its people, and today the young men and women of Segesta and Nicodemia have proven that they deserve to be counted among their ancestors—the Iron Lords."

There is a pleased murmur from the crowd, muted out of awe for being in the presence of the Empress but still noticeable. I feel a flush of pride myself. How special I feel to be among those who have attained her notice!

"My people, as my Censors have told you, this is a year of drought. The *Cor* showers have not fallen as we have grown used to. I know that for many of you, this has been hard news to bear. It is hard news for all of us. For each of you who attain my blessing are the future of us. It is not just a power for yourself, but for us."

"Here is what you do not know, dear friends in the South. Our enemies in the North and the East stir, testing the strength of our Iron Legions. The Senate has authorized an extra percentage of our harvest to go toward rebuilding our lost strength from battles waged far away."

Silence reigns supreme around the arena. The smile on my face begins to slip a little. Battles fought in the North and the East? We have heard nothing of it here; that was a world away. I don't know anything about politics or logistics. This is not the celebratory speech I was expecting. It sounded almost more like an apology.

"Our empire stands at the precipice," Diana's voice says after a pause. "We must do whatever it takes to protect our children, our mothers, and our way of life. To that end, my Censors have been sent with five *Cor* Hearts for you—" A shocked roar runs through the arena, interrupting the Empress. Gasps erupt from the students around me. Someone lets out a moan of despair. Maybe it's me.

I'm stunned, as if someone just hit me in the head with a poleaxe. Everything is blurry. I can't feel my fingers. I stagger backward a step, but hands grab me by my crimson tunic, stopping me from falling.

I snap back to myself to look into Felix's face. The tall boy is shaking me, a horrified expression on his face. It is the horror in his expression that makes my brain accept what the Empress just told me. There are only five Hearts. A hundred contestants for only five Hearts. I am *Sextus*, the sixth.

There is no Heart for me.

My knees feel weak, and it takes every ounce of my self-control for me to straighten myself. All three of my friends stare at me from the front row. The ones I let go before me. I don't look at them. I can't. Not because I am angry with them, but because I know if I see their pity, I will break.

I force my spine to be as straight as a spear as I focus on a spot above the crowd. I am a leaf adrift in the river of my own emotions. Despair and rage battle inside me as I try not to embarrass myself in front of my whole world. My vision is small, and the only thing I can see is the spot of the arena wall that I'm trying to stare a hole through.

"I know this is not what we are used to," Empress Diana's voice resumes. It is tinged with an imperial sadness that feels even richer than mine. Out of the corner of my eye, I see my friends turn back to face the front. "But we must do what we can to persist. Our empire survived the death of the gods; it will endure this. To the victors, you have my blessing. To those who fell short, do not despair—there is more than one way to be of service to the empire. *Imperium Aeternum!*"

Atticus closes the scroll-relic and gazes around at the crowd. Unruly shouting begins to emerge from the families whose hopes are devastated. No wonder the Praetorians are here again. The harsh-faced Censor gazes across the crowd before glancing at us. There is no apology in his cold eyes, only a grim determination.

"The Empress has spoken." His own voice booms off the walls with its magnified power. "In her generosity, she has granted five Hearts to these students. The Ritual of the Heart will be held tomorrow at dawn." He turns to us and speaks in his normal voice.

"Go." He nods toward the door.

Our *Primus* leads us back the way we came. I'm grateful to be able to follow Valentina. My mind doesn't feel capable of forming thoughts. All I can do is stumble along behind the person in front of me and hope they're taking me where I need to be.

We exit the same door, and someone leads us down a different windy path on the inside of the arena. Valentina keeps turning around to look at me, but I ignore her. I have nothing to say and nothing that I want said to me.

The entire purpose of my life had been to be bound to a Heart. What am I going to be now? What will I do? I feel as if I have died before I was ever been born. I am grieving myself without ever having gotten the chance to meet me.

We emerge from the arena into a small square on the side of the giant circle. I've never seen it before, but it's sequestered behind hedges. It's only when students break from the line to race to their families that I realize we're being released.

I look up from the ground and see mine waiting for me. Both of them wear pained expressions, but I can't help but notice the subtle signs of relief in my father's stance. His shoulders are straight, his brows unwrinkled. This is what he wanted. The copper veins in his arms glint in *Sol's* light.

For the first time, I hate him a little. Even though he had nothing to do with it, it feels like he personally took my dream away from me. Slowly, on leaden feet, I make my way toward them.

"Castor!" Valentina calls from behind me. I don't turn around. I can't bear to see her. Not now. My mother sweeps me into a hug, and I sink into her arms. I may be a man now, but all I want to be is a boy.

"Come, son," she whispers in my ear. "Let's go home."

CHAPTER 13

I'm sitting on the roof when they come. *Mons* Olympus glows a bright white as the *Luna* lends her light to the floating mountain. I've stared at the pair of them for the last two hours since I told my parents I was going to bed. As strong as *Luna's* light is, it seems weaker than usual. So do the stars. The world has grown a little darker for me.

I hear their whispers as they make their way up the path, but I don't react. There are two of them, and neither of them is good at being silent. Marcus and Felix pause under my window, and for a moment, I listen to them debate where they can find a pebble to throw at it.

I let them search for a while. Not because I am upset, but because I'm not ready to give up my solitude. The thought of them finding a wayward rock in the domain of someone bound to the Symbol of the Fertile Field is amusing to me. Even in my melancholy, I find a small smile tugging at the corner of my lips. My father could not rest if there were pebbles strewn across his ground.

At last, I take pity on them. I know why they're here. It's for me, but it's also for themselves. Each of them must be carrying a yoke of guilt, and only I can take it off them. With a sigh, I sit up and hiss at them from my perch up on the roof.

The two boys freeze like startled wildlife. They're still wearing their crimsons; I'm not. Marcus glances up and sees me before relaxing. I wave for them to join me and point at a nearby tree with low branches. It's a far easier challenge than the strength flag we earned today.

With a pair of thuds, the two boys drop next to me. At first, none of us speak. We just dangle our feet over the edge of the roof and stare at *Luna* and the mountain in the sky. What did it look like before the gods died? Did it have its own lights that shone in the night, or was it always an empty-looking stone house?

The silence stretches, and even though it is heavy, I feel no rush to break it. In some ways, it doesn't feel real yet. It won't until we talk about it. Deep down, I haven't admitted to myself that I am not getting a Heart tomorrow—not even to my parents. But after this conversation, I will have to.

Marcus and Felix clearly feel the weight of the awkwardness but try to bear it out of respect. I can see it combining with the guilt they already hold. Their shoulders hunch as if they carry heavy burdens. Eventually, I take pity on them; my despair doesn't excuse cruelty.

"Where's Valentina?" I ask. If Felix had not come, I wouldn't have been surprised. We were allies and newly minted friends, but he does not know me like Val and Marcus. As far as I am concerned, he held up his part of the agreement. I hold no malice for him in my heart—just a smidge of jealousy.

"She wouldn't come." Marcus's voice is hesitant—he's unsure how I will take the news. I'm unsure how I take it too. I'm too numb to feel any more pain, but there's still a dull ache in my chest somewhere where my flesh-and-blood heart is that feels new.

"I'm sure the mayor's daughter has a harder time skulking off in the night than we do," Felix offers, trying to sound reassuring.

"She never had a hard time before," I murmur. My peace offering of a conversation is backfiring. They both look even more wretched. Exhaustion rolls over me in a wave—not just physical, but an emotional one. If only I could turn them off like one of my grandfather's *lumos* relics.

I lie back on the roof and stare up into the night sky, gathering my thoughts. These two have both been good friends to me, albeit for different durations of time. I have been blessed to have them. Soon I will lose them. Marcus will depart for the legions. Felix might remain here to start his bakery, but there will be a social divide between us. He is an *electus*, and I am not. That is an even steeper incline than plebeian and patrician. It is only right that I release them from their burdens before it is too late.

"I am not upset with either of you," I say at last, staring into the inky void above us. It is far safer than looking at either of them. "Both of you were true to our *votum* and me. It's just bad fortune that we were destined for a drought year."

"Damned bad luck," Felix echoes in agreement. Marcus grunts too. After a moment, both of them lie back and stare at the empty heavens with me. I've never felt so small and insignificant.

"I will miss you both," I say honestly. "I suspect one of my great regrets will be that we did not become friends sooner, Felix."

The lean boy guffaws loud enough that some servants must have heard him. I'm not worried about being caught on the roof tonight. I'm an adult now. What can possibly be done to me that is worse than not getting a *Cor* Heart? "I'm not going anywhere," he protests. "We might be losing the big guy, but you're stuck with me." I smile in gratitude even though I know that he will move on. It is the way of the world. Already Valentina begins to drift.

"You could always come with me," Marcus offers softly. I open my mouth to mock his suggestion but pause. He's not wrong. I could enlist in the legions and be given a Heart in exchange for twenty years of service. There is still a way.

"No," I say after a moment of consideration. "My Heart was going to get me freedom, not a different cage." Marcus stiffens slightly, and I aim a gentle punch at his shoulder. "But thank you." He relaxes, nodding.

"You know, I've been wondering about that," Felix admits, sitting back up to look over at us. "Why are you so devoted to the idea of going to the legions? You're too bright to be in that meat grinder."

Marcus is silent for a long time. For a moment, I worry we've ruined his dream for him the same way mine has been damaged. But when he speaks, it is with firm conviction. "My grandfather was Seventh Legion." I arch an eyebrow at that. I never knew.

"The Seventh? Damn, man," Even Felix is impressed.

"He served his time in the North fighting the barbarians at Fortress Frigidus in the Winter Legions. Got wounded on the ice and awarded a bronze eagle for it. My *pater* wanted to sign up, but Grandfather got sick and died young, so Father ended up staying here and raising his sisters instead. He told me that Grandfather always said that protecting the empire from the things on the other side of the wall was the greatest honor that any citizen could ever have. Those of us in the warmth have no idea of the horrors that are on the other side: barbarians, *furiae*, *necromantae*." Felix and I laugh at how ridiculous that sounds, and even Marcus's lips twitch in a small smile.

"*Furiae* are real," Felix offers gravely, sounding like the smug *Primus* one last time. "*Necromantae*, on the other hand, I'm pretty sure are just a bedtime story."

"Even if they aren't, you heard what the Empress said," Marcus continues somberly. "The enemies of the empire are coming for us. Someone has to do something about that. Why not me?" I don't have a good answer for that question.

We're silent for a while. I'm stunned. Maybe I'm being selfish— maybe I should join the legions. I try to imagine myself bound to Iron and wearing the collar, but all I feel is trapped. I understand his desire a little better, but it's still not mine.

"Come work for me," Felix offers brightly. "You're much better at congruency. You can help me figure out how to use the Wheat Symbol in different ways to sell more bread." This time, all three of us chuckle at that idea.

"You still think you can force your Heart to attune to the Symbol you want?" Marcus asks.

"Of course." Felix laughs.

"But Magister Vellum told us—"

"If it is impossible, how is every legionnaire bound to Iron?" He reminds us of his earlier argument. "Tomorrow, our large friend here will declare for the legions, and they will fuse him with Iron. But for some reason, they can only do that for that one Symbol?" Marcus is still, deep in thought. Despite my bitterness about not getting a Heart, I too ponder Felix's words, trying to solve a mystery that I will never be a part of.

"Come now, do you think they tell us *everything*?" Felix chides the two of us.

I guess I always thought they had. But as I ponder his words, it seems so obvious. Everyone takes for granted that the legions require every soldier to be attuned to the Symbol of Iron. But we never discuss how they make that happen.

"Or," Felix continues, "how do they prevent someone from attuning to Iron who isn't in the legions?"

"If you become Ironbound, you are required to join on pain of death," I point out.

"Yes, yes." He waves my point away. "But it never happens. If it is truly random, don't you think some senator's son would draw the short straw and get dragged off to the legions? Why isn't that a story we ever hear?"

"There's a way to control it." The realization seems so obvious to me now that it is in front of me.

"There's a way to guide it," Felix corrects, still looking smug.

"How do you know?" I demand. In the moment, I've completely forgotten that I'm miserable. My friend has successfully sucked me into his theory.

"My family is plebeian, remember? I've got a cousin who works at the *collegium*. Last year, I convinced him to smuggle me in to watch the Ritual of the Heart."

Marcus and I both sit up in shock, staring at our friend. The Ritual is the only part of the *Sententia* process that is not held in front of the general populace. Only the students who partook in that year attend, deep in the basement of the *collegium*.

"You've seen it?" Marcus hisses in a low whisper.

"What is it?"

"I was able to witness part of one," Felix amends. "But from what I saw, the Censors and magisters bring out things that embody Symbols to evoke a response in the unbound *Cor*."

"Like a guide," I breathe in understanding. My mind is reeling with the implications of this. Our whole lives, the *collegium* has taught us that whatever your Heart bonds to is up to Fate. But Felix's shrewd insight has proven that to be a lie.

"So tomorrow, you'll demand to be shown a guide for the Symbol of Wheat?" Marcus asks, wrinkling his eyebrow.

"That's the plan." He shrugs. "If they show me other ones, I'll try to ignore them until I get one as close as possible."

Marcus is very still as he processes this revelation. I know him well enough to know that he is disturbed at the thought that we've not been told everything about how the Hearts work. I am too, but it's less relevant for me now.

"Still signing up, big guy?" Felix presses softly as Marcus's frustration becomes palpable.

"Yes," he replies after a while. "I'm not doing this for the Censors or even the Empress. I'm doing this because my grandfather said it is what good men need to do." It is Felix's and my turn to be silent, considering the weight of that statement. Once more, I feel a flare of guilt for my selfishness.

"What did he see in the North?" Felix asks, his voice betraying the same doubt that's in my mind. Maybe the world doesn't need more bread. Maybe it needs more swords.

"Barbarians and monsters." Marcus shrugs uncomfortably. "He didn't like to talk about them, but he said he saw *furiae* made of ice and snow that were taller than three men. That there are things there that have no name but seek to plunge the world into the eternal night." A shiver runs down my spine that has nothing to do with the cool wind swirling through the fields.

When I was a child, my mother would tell me stories of the monsters in the North and the heroes that defended us. As a student, my teachers would tell me that the legions protected us from enemies, but they made it sound more normal. It was far away and not important, they said. Maybe my mother had been the one telling me the truth all along.

We fall into a companionable silence. I am not healed or whole. The wound caused by my failure still aches deep in my chest, but it feels as if the first sutures have been sewn in.

Tonight is the first night we are men, but in some ways, it is the last night that we are boys. Together, the three of us sit on my roof watching the mountain and the moon.

CHAPTER 14

The Ritual of the Heart takes place deep in the bowels of the *collegium* in a room I've never seen before and will never see again. The magisters lead all fifty of us who braved the *Labyrinthus* down into the depths by a dark staircase, lit only by the torches they carry.

We arrive at a large square that is made of pure white marble. The center of the floor is sand of almost the same shade, with a border made of black marble. In the middle of the room, Atticus and the two other Censors wait for us, resplendent in their white *loricas* and red cloaks. Next to them is a heavy chest with an iron lock that sits on a solid rectangle of black marble like an altar. A giant bronze imperial eagle spreads its wings behind them, draped in purple and scarlet cloth, the signs of the Empress who bestows her blessing upon the best of us.

The severe young man watches us file in with flat, uninterested eyes. At the magister's direction, we file around the room, standing on the black marble, forming a human square around the sandy center, the red of our uniforms contrasting a burst of color against the monochromatic space.

We're assembled in order, so I stand as *Sextus* next to Valentina. She won't look at me. Her eyes are locked forward, and her body is tense. The wound in my heart feels less healed now, like I have just picked at the scab that was covering it. I swallow the bitterness in the back of my throat and settle into position. I will only get to see this once.

Atticus looks over the group with a cold expression, looking to make sure all is as it should be. Apparently satisfied, he steps forward and holds out both of his hands as if giving a benediction. "*Salvete, discipuli*," he intones. "Today, some of you will undergo the Ritual of the Heart. It is the sacred way that the Empress's blessing is given to the worthiest members of your generation. When it is fulfilled, the *Sententia* will be complete, and you will leave this place to never return."

"Those of you who did not earn this gift from your Empress are here to bear witness. Great things are expected of your peers. They took this from you. Today, they will swear to be worthy of the honor that has been denied to you." It takes all my strength to keep a grimace off my face as the Censor twists the knife in my raw wound. Of all the students here, I doubt any feel the pain as deeply as I do. Not that others didn't want it as badly as I did—I have no doubt that I am not special in that regard. But to be so close and still be denied stings in a different, cruel way. I'd rather have finished last with Decima than this.

"To those of you who will take the first step of Ascension, remember that you have proven yourself strong enough to carry these burdens. *Cor* is not meant for the weak-willed. You are the best of your generation, and to you is entrusted this most precious treasure."

I glance to my left at Valentina, but still she doesn't turn. Her gaze is locked on the square in front of us, her back and neck rigid as if her spine is steel instead of bone. I turn away, trying to make my own heart as hard, but the best I manage is broken glass.

"Let us begin," Atticus barks, and at his command, Vellum and three other white-robed magisters step into the sandy square with him. One of the Censors turns to the chest and inserts a key into its lock. She opens it and reaches inside with gloved hands.

A thrill runs through me as she pulls out a sphere of *Cor* that looks like a medium-sized ball. I've never seen it in its raw form before, just in the veins in the bodies of *electii*. It's pure white, the color of fresh milk. It seems that it is more liquid than metal, like some sort of quicksilver. The sphere ripples under the pressure of being held but stays together.

"Behold," Atticus announces to the room of stunned students. "An unbound Heart, chosen for your *Primus*. Silvester, attend me." Slowly, the Nicodemian boy who beat the *Labyrinthus* makes his way out into the sand.

The female magister who runs the foreign *collegium* gestures for him to kneel at Atticus's feet. The boy is shaking as he obeys, and I don't blame him. There is a solemn power that has gathered here, like opening the eye of a god.

Atticus fixes the kneeling *Primus* with his flat gaze and pins him there with it. Sweat begins to bead on Silvester's forehead, and I almost feel bad for him. But not really, for he is an interloper who stole my Heart.

"Do you swear on the bones of our gods to serve your Empress and empire from now 'til you are dust? To leave your relics in service to your people long after you are gone?" The Censor's voice is cold and harsh.

"I do." Silvester's voice is thin and reedy.

"Do you swear to be worthy of this blessing that you have taken from others?" There's a faint sneer on Atticus's face, as if he doubts that the boy is truly worthy. I do too.

"You shall be known as *rasa* until you earn your Symbol. Now rise and accept your Heart."

The *Primus* obeys, standing on shaking legs. His magister directs him to remove his crimson tunic, and he obeys. The Censor, carrying the *Cor* in her gloved hands, replaces Atticus standing before Silvester.

"Accept the blessing of your Empress!" Atticus cries, and without a moment's hesitation, the woman shoves the orb into Silvester's chest. The sphere breaks, and the metal runs like water across his chest.

"It's so cold!" the boy breathes, then gasps in shock as it begins to vanish inside his chest as his flesh absorbs the liquid metal. He arches his back and lets out a scream of discomfort before his legs give out, and he drops to the sand like a bag of rocks.

The forty-nine other students shift uncomfortably, but neither the Censors nor magisters seem concerned. All is silent as Silvester twitches in the sand and then, with a long sigh, grows still. Atticus watches him with hooded eyes, waiting for something.

With a gasp, the boy sits up like he just awoke from a nightmare. I stare enraptured as white metallic lines begin to grow from his chest, winding down his body like snakes. They wrap around his back and run down his legs, like creeping vines. His body has accepted the Heart, and now it fuses with him.

"Rise," Atticus commands, and the newest *electus* of the empire does, his eyes still wide. "You have been given a *Cor* Heart, but it has not yet been bound. Attend! We must find your Symbol."

More magisters step through our crimson lines, carrying different items that I can only describe as the essences of different elements. At his teacher's direction, Silvester kneels and bows his head in obeisance. The first magister steps forward and places a golden basin of water in the sand before him. She steps back, leaving it before Silvester.

"Focus on the water; search for its meaning. Listen for any of its Symbols to call out to you," Atticus instructs. The *rasa* obeys, staring at the water without blinking. A heavy silence descends as all of us lean forward, peering at him and the bowl, waiting to see what will happen.

Despite my jealousy, I am fascinated. A connection to a Symbol is deeply personal and profound. To witness this moment almost feels like I am intruding, but that is the design. This ceremony is meant to be uncomfortable, to burden those who were chosen with a sense of purpose.

After a few moments, Atticus waves at the magisters, and the woman collects the water. A second one steps in front of Silvester and places down a golden bowl of dirt—earth. The process is repeated. I glance over Valentina's head at Marcus, and we share a knowing look. Our tall plebeian friend is watching the process closely, his eyes burning with delight.

Felix was right.

They repeat the process until they have covered the rest of the base elements. Silvester's heart does not respond to offerings of fire or air. After that, they begin to get more specific.

Silvester's entire body is slicked with sweat from concentrating. Maybe he's doing what Felix will by holding out for something specific. From the sour look on Atticus's face, he might suspect the same thing. But the Censor says nothing, only gestures for the magisters to continue the offerings.

They bring out plants and rocks that also do nothing. Atticus openly scowls at the kneeling boy now, but he says nothing. It is when they place a bowl filled with branches from an ash tree that Silvester reacts.

He lets out a sigh as if he is releasing a death grip on the side of a cliff. Tension flows out of his body, and a gasp runs through the room as the white veins of his *rasa* begin to turn a shimmering orange. Before our eyes, he Ascends to Copper. His Heart has chosen a Symbol. Atticus claps, and the magisters collect the bowl. The woman takes one of the branches and places it at the feet of Silvester before she goes.

"What Symbol has your Heart taken?" he asks formally. Silvester reaches for the wood in front of him and clasps it tightly with his fist.

"The Whispering Ash Tree," he replies. His eyes almost pop out of his head as he realizes how many levels of specificity it has. His magister is practically beaming with pride. The teachers will see this as a good omen for the rest of us.

"Rise, Silvester Faber, and take your place among the Empress's chosen." The Censor watches dispassionately, like a mother bird keeping an eye on a hatchling as it breaks free of an egg. Silvester staggers to his feet, and a magister leads him to the corner of the black marble plinth that holds the chest of hearts.

Atticus repeats the process with Iris, the girl who achieved *Secundus*. She lets out a brilliant smile at the sight of the first element that they bring before her, a large river stone. Her *rasa* lines begin to change at once as her Symbol takes hold without the slightest bit of hesitation.

"The Smooth Stone," she whispers reverently when she is asked to name it. It's clear that she got exactly what she hoped for. My heart begins to race as I realize who is next.

"Felix Pistor," Atticus intones, and our lanky friend steps out onto the sand with a grim smile on his face. He winks at me as he passes by, reassured by what we've seen. For his sake, I hope he's able get his Wheat.

Atticus asks him to swear to the same oath to the dead gods that the first two *discipuli* did. My friend looks up from the sand for a moment and glances at me, a sorrowful expression on his face. I give him an encouraging nod, and he looks back down.

"I do," he affirms in a clear voice.

Then the world explodes.

Lightning strikes the center of the underground room in a pillar of blinding fire. The force of its thunder slams me against the wall of the room. Terror fills me as my vision clears. In its wake, a figure in gold armor towers over us. His metallic flesh flows like the strange being I encountered in the Dream. The same black lines run through it, not mixing with the gold. But despite these similarities, he is a different man. Instead of a face, his helmet is shaped in the visage of a snarling wolf. He does not carry a snakebound staff in his right hand, but a giant maul that glows with a fire that does not consume it.

The giant swings his weapon down to crush the kneeling Felix, but somehow it is blocked by the *tellus* sword of the Censor. Impossibly, Atticus managed to leap across the room with superhuman speed, quick enough to catch the thing's maul before it splattered my friend like a bug. When they separate, the white dueling blade has a black mark burnt into it, but it is still whole.

Felix dives to the side as the flaming maul sweeps toward him once more. The wolf is cackling. His mocking laughter echoes off the room as students and magisters scream in terror. With his empty hand, he catches a thrust from Atticus and wrenches the blade free from the Censor's grasp with casual strength. The razor edge of the dueling blade slices the palm of his golden armor, but there is no permanent damage. The liquid simply *flows*, refilling what the *tellus* cut.

The being steps toward Felix, raising its left fist in a grim mockery of the gladiator's judgment—holding the thumb out parallel to the ground. Then, with the ponderous weight of a metronome, it plummets, pointing down and calling for death. The golden monster lifts its maul for an overhead blow, which will splatter my prone friend like a bug under a bootheel.

"Hey!" I scream, leaping forward to get its attention, shouting at it as if it is a bear or feral dog. The wolf-man's helmet tilts in my direction as if studying me, then the maniacal laughter echoes from within one more. The weapon falls, but instead of on Felix, the fiery maul crashes down on the chest that holds the *Cor* Hearts.

The room explodes in a ball of fire and light.

I'm tossed like a doll. I think I scream as something spears into my chest. The world goes cold, and I constrict. I can't breathe. I can't move. I can't see. It is several long moments before I can force my eyes open. My body won't respond; it is overwhelmed by a thousand sensations. When my vision finally returns, I almost wish it did not. The room is devastated. Blood and gore stain the white sands and walls.

There are bodies everywhere, but there is no sign of the golden wolf. I'm sitting on the ground with my back against the wall. Ahead of me, I can see Felix's still form in front of the ruins of the chest. I try to get up to go to him, but I can't. Frustrated, I jerk myself forward but am stopped short by a dull pain that runs through me.

I look down at my chest and realize that I've been speared to the wall. A long, jagged piece of iron from the lockbox runs *through* me and into the marble behind me. I'm in shock. I reach for the shrapnel to pull it free, but freeze as my hands come into view.

The white veins of unbound *Cor* twist down my forearms, still growing right before my eyes. As I watch, a dark wave flows through some of the paths, changing from *rasa* to *cuprum*—from nothing to Copper. Awareness of the iron that skewers me explodes into me. I feel the piece of metal in my mind as if it is one of my limbs.

I have just enough time to marvel at the power of my *Cor* Heart before the world shrinks and fades to black.

CHAPTER 15

L ight returns to me with the roar of fire. My eyes snap open, and I try to sit up, but the muscles in my chest scream in protest. I let out a gasp of pain, and the figure next to me turns. It's Felix; he's still alive.

"You're awake," he whispers, giving my wound a once-over. Someone's bandaged it, but the cloth is stained red with my blood. "About damn time."

"What happened?" I manage to grunt. My friend motions for me to be quiet.

We're outside. It's night. *Mons* Olympus glows in the sky as it hovers above us, distant and out of reach. I shiver in the cold, even though a fire rages not far away. Confused at what is fueling the inferno, I turn my head to see that the *collegium* is burning. Not far from us, Atticus and his Censors confer with a Praetorian centurion and the city council. I see my father standing with them.

"The others?" I whisper.

"Alive," Felix whispers. "But there's trouble."

"Is that thing still…"

"Not from whatever that was, but them." He nods at the back of the red-cloaked Censors. "You may have damned us all."

"What do you mean?" But even as I ask, I remember the last thing that I saw. Shaking in anticipation, I raise my right arm into my vision and stare at the veins of my *Cor* Heart running through it. I sigh, unable to comprehend what my eyes are seeing. Hope's fire rekindles in my heart like stoked campfire coals.

"It's real," I breathe.

"It's *really bad*," Felix corrects. Something in his tone breaks through my shock, and the fire dims.

"Why?"

My friend grabs my wrist and holds my arm up in front of my eyes again. "Look at yourself! You took more than you should have." My vision swims, but as I focus, I realize that only some of the veins swirling through me have turned to Copper, the lowest rank. The rest are still the white of *rasa*.

Horror blooms inside of me as I realize that I have failed. Something went wrong when my body tried to bind to the *Cor*. I do not know if it was the wound that I suffered or because I lost consciousness, but my body has partially rejected the Heart. I am an *immundus*. I am impure. Exactly the sort of failure the *Sententia* is supposed to filter out.

Shaking, I reach inside for that feeling of awareness that I remember before passing out, but I only find a low, muted buzz. It's there but quiet, as if I can only hear it through several walls. Something burns coldly around my neck, and I raise my left hand to find that I've been fitted with a braided metal collar. Some of it is iron, but the rest of it is unknown to me.

"What's wrong with me?" I stammer, feeling like my dream is dying once more.

"Is he awake?" a cold voice demands from behind Felix. Atticus storms into view, his blue eyes dancing with fury as he stares down at me. "Get up." He prods me in the ribs with a booted toe. The men of the council follow in his wake like terrified ducklings.

It takes until this moment to occur to me that I wasn't supposed to get a Heart. I hadn't stolen one of my own volition, but I had not earned the Empress's blessing.

I groan and try to sit up. My chest screams in protest, but Felix reaches down and pulls on my other arm, helping me get to my feet. My father's face hovers over Atticus's shoulder, sick with worry. I try to give him a weak smile, but his frown only deepens.

"Let us see what you have stolen," the Censor demands, gripping my wrist roughly and pulling my arm forward. He sneers as he sees my incomplete transformation. He throws my arm away in disgust and glares at me. I retreat a step in the face of his rage.

"You bastard!" he screams. "Do you know what you've done?"

"I was struck by a flying Heart when that thing blew up the chest?" I ask, feeling light-headed. My earlier hope flees under the wrath of one who speaks with the voice of the Empress. "I know that my binding is incomplete, but I was wounded—"

"*A HEART?*" Atticus rages, spittle flecks the corner of his mouth. His arrogant composure has melted like the last of winter's snow in the spring. "You took *ALL* of them."

Dread floods through my veins, following the metal that is now a part of me. Felix's fear suddenly makes sense. My mouth is dry. I can't swallow—can't speak. I gaze down at the inert *rasa* lines and understand that my transformation wasn't incomplete—I'm just carrying extras that my body cannot bond with.

"What—what happens to the others?" I manage to ask finally.

"They're *wasted*! You can't have more than one *Cor*!" Atticus screams. I understand his rage now. It's not anger but panic. The Censors are entrusted with the Hearts to adjudicate who should earn her blessings. I may have taken them, but he has lost the Empress's most valuable treasure. I am not the only one in danger. When the time comes to account for today, it is he who will have to answer for what the empire has gained, not me.

"I didn't mean to—"

"I should cut you down where you stand and claim them as relics."

"Censor," my father objects from over his shoulder.

"Silence!" Atticus snaps. He seems even younger now. The shadows from the fires and the lines from his panic paint him in a new light. Only a few years older than me, he carries a great responsibility, and it is riding him to the ground. He has lost the Empress's property, a portion of her most prized possession. They execute men for that. "It wouldn't do any good," he murmurs to himself as if thinking out loud. "*Rasa* Hearts are practically worthless as relics, and you're Ironbound now. It's the legions for you."

"*Dominus*," my father implores, stepping around the Censor to catch his attention. "He is my only son."

"He is a thief. He has stolen from the Empress, the penalty for which should be death. I am being most merciful," Atticus retorts hotly. His hand strays to the hilt of his sword.

"He is a *victim*," my father insists, not backing down from the Silver Censor. His Bronze Heart glints in the light of the fires. "Surely the Empress would not—"

"He is bound to Iron. The law requires that he enlist in the legions." My world is collapsing in on itself. I gained my freedom only to lose it. The collar around my neck chafes like a dog's. I am destined to be a slave after all.

"I will appeal to the Senate!" my father snaps, his own cool slipping. "My son is a victim of a terrorist attack and will not be a prisoner for the rest of his life." I'm shocked. I've never seen him angry like this before. The veins in his neck twitch with his pounding pulse, and there's a light burning in his eyes that is a reflection of the fire raging behind us. Valentina's father, Brontus, places a gentle hand on mine's shoulder. The mayor's expression is grim, but he does not speak.

"It won't just be your boy," Atticus sneers. "The Empress will require an equal number of *electii* from these *discipuli* to restore what she has lost. She has only received one so far." He gestures at me with a sneer of disgust. "Marcus Drusu and Felix Pistor will be enlisted as well." He cocks his head and studies me with a malign gaze. Cool arrogance is resurfacing as he finds his path out of this mess. "I think the Twelfth will do nicely. We will conscript the other top students of the year to balance these scales." He nods to himself before glancing at the other two Censors. "We will mark them as *electii*, then let them get lost in the legion's rolls. No one will bother to check where they get their Hearts from as long as they die in the lines." One of the women nods after a moment of thought.

I close my eyes to block out the horror. Shame spreads through me like a cancer, eating me from the inside. Legion XII is the lowest of them all. Its roster is filled with murderers, traitors, and worse. My heart cracks as I think of Felix, who only wanted to bake bread, being forced into its ranks. It shatters when I think of Marcus and his Praetorian dream.

But Atticus isn't finished with his judgment. He's only claimed four souls so far. There's more debt to be paid. "Valentina Fluvius shall be taken into the Empress's service, where she shall be issued a Heart," he announces.

This time, my father's protests are joined by the other men of the council, by Marcus's father and Valentina's. Too timid to speak up when the Censor came for me, now they rage as their own children are claimed by the empire. I'm no hero, but I'm disgusted by their cowardice.

My eyes open, and I see my three friends standing behind the adults, staring at me. Marcus is heartbroken, his eyes full of hurt, as if I stabbed him in the back. A flash of anger surges in me upon seeing that look. I didn't betray him—I didn't ask for this.

Felix only looks grim, like a man stepping up to the gallows. I feel pity for him. The plebeian who dared to dream has been struck down through no fault of his own.

It is Valentina's eyes that break me. They're full of a thousand unspoken things but shame, guilt, anger, and fear stand at the forefront. We never spoke after I failed to earn my Heart, and somehow, I know we won't get the chance to ever again.

"Enough!" Atticus snaps, whirling on the group of protesting men like a wolf springing out of an ambush. His hand strays to the white grip of his dueling blade. "You've made it most clear that you will protest the Empress claiming what she is owed." A dark current enters his voice.

"We will need more than just five if we're going to hide what was taken," one of the other Censor's reminds him, her tone harsh. Atticus only nods, he's not done.

"Unfortunately, the attack that claimed the lives of some of the *discipuli* was not only centered on the *collegium.*" He waves a careless hand at the burning school behind them. The men grow still as his menace builds. My father's face pales. I am injured and overwhelmed, and I do not immediately understand their concern. Where else did they attack?

"Before our mighty Praetorians could drive off our enemies, these devilish villains attacked the farms of the city's leaders." The Censor's voice is cruel. He delights in the power he has, which he now wields like a sledgehammer. Still, I am too slow to understand the depths of his corruption.

"We put the attackers to the sword, but it was too late. The city council's farms were burned, their families murdered. It is out of a sense of duty and a desire for vengeance that so many *discipuli* volunteered for the Legions." I can only gape at the back of his red cloak. What is he talking about? Then he gestures at the centurion, and there's a hiss as a dozen legionnaires' swords slither from their sheaths, and I understand. The sound sends terror running through me.

The men of the council roar in protest and collapse with their backs toward each other, forming a shell. All of them are *electii*, and they call upon their Symbols. Weeds burst from the ground, twisting into ropes that reach for Praetorians as my father invokes the Fertile Field for something other than life.

But none of the Coppers are a match for the warrior that is Atticus. The Censor draws his blackened dueling blade in one swift motion and bursts forward, powered by his Wind Symbol. I scream before I even understand what I'm seeing. My father falls to the ground in two pieces, his face frozen in shock.

I sprint toward the Censor's exposed back. In my rage, the muted call of my Iron Heart grows stronger, as if it beats with more fury. I reach for its power, but I have no armor or weapons to make use of. The *lorica* and *gladii* of the legionnaires are out of my reach.

The Censor feels me coming. The Air itself probably betrays me to him. He whirls and slaps me in the head with the flat of his blade. He's so fast, I don't see him move. One moment I am sprinting, the next I am face down on the ground. My head rings like a bell. My vision shakes.

I press my hands against the ground and push, trying to rise. I have to stop them. I have to save my family. I can hear the cries of men as the council members battle with the Praetorians. There's a sickening wet sound as blades punch into torsos that I can hear even over the roaring flames.

The screams go silent.

Someone plants a boot in between my shoulder blades and shoves me down into the dirt. A sob of despair comes out of me as I crash down. The pressure stays on me, pinning me in place. "Centurion Brutus, send squads to each of the councilmen's homes. Kill everyone you find and burn them to the ground."

"*Dominus*, they have a stonehound," another voice calls. I manage to twist my head to stare at Aulus, who emerges from the shadow. My former classmate wears a patch over his eye and stares at me with naked hatred. I cannot speak; I am too stunned by his second betrayal.

"A *mythus?*" Atticus sounds almost impressed by our wealth. "Take some sledgehammers with you," he instructs the waiting officers.

"*Dominus*," Brutus growls, before turning and barking commands to his Praetorians. Footsteps drum against the cobblestone in unison as the men of the Iron Legion begin to move.

"You wait here," he says, looking at Aulus. "Your faithfulness to the empire will be rewarded." Atticus turns his attention back to me. I am still pinned to the ground, so he crouches low to hover just above my head.

"Please—"

"The name *Castor Castus* will be stripped from the Census. You are no longer a patrician of the empire, but a criminal. You are hereby sentenced to serve for your crimes." He pauses for a moment, studying me like a bug. "After tonight, you will be tempted to think that there is nothing else I can do to hurt you, boy, but you will be so wrong. You will not speak of this to anyone. Or I will come back here, with my Legion, and raze this backwater nothing-town to the ground. I will kill each man, woman, and child, and I will take my time. Do I make myself clear?" He waits for me to nod. "This is the will of the Empress. Back to sleep, thief," Atticus snarls, and the point of a boot crashes into my temple as the world fades to black once more.

I come to in the back of a rattling cart. I'm lying on the floor of its flat bed. A groan escapes me as I try to sit up. My head is pounding, my chest aches. But fear and adrenaline numb my wounds enough that I manage to get up.

We're in a prisoner wagon, made of bronze bars to prevent my Iron Symbol from being able to manipulate them. Alloys have no Symbol. Felix hovers over me, leaning against the bars and staring behind us as we rattle down the road. A dozen other boys from our class are jammed in with us like sardines. Some are from Segesta, like Clintus, Rufus, and Jasper, but some are strangers, Nicodemians claimed by Atticus's greed.

Marcus sits across from me, with his back against the far side of the cell. His expression is blank, but even from here, I can see the dancing flames reflecting in his eyes. I know what I will find before I even turn around.

Mons Olympus floats above us, a dark specter eclipsed by the full *Luna*. In its shadow is pandemonium. The last time I see the house my grandfather built is from the back of a prisoner's wagon, as the inferno consumes it.

PART 2

LEGION XII

CHAPTER 16

The journey from Segesta to the Iron City known as Agogia takes three weeks. There are ten of us from Segesta who have been force-recruited. Atticus took as many as he could. We spend the first in the copper prisoner wagon while those of us who were injured heal from our wounds. The cart is silent; no one feels like talking. The weight of the horrors I witnessed settle into my mind, where I know they will stay forever.

I spend most of my time leaning against the bars, staring at nothing as we roll through the wheat fields of the south. Rufus and Jasper glare at me when they think I'm not looking. I feel each glance like a knife thrust. Every time the cart bumps on a paved stone, the wound in my arm spikes in pain, and I welcome it. It's the only thing about me that doesn't feel numb.

And I deserve to suffer.

I hear my sister's screams in my nightmares on the rare moments I fall asleep. Of my father and mother, I see nothing, which is in some way even more devastating. Already, their absence creeps across my life like a shadow. I will never see them again, not even in my dreams.

On the third night, one of the Nicodemians tries to kill me.

My insomnia saves me. The boy, a tall, skinny one I recognize from the ceremony, slinks over to where I lie on the bed of the cart. Silently, he reaches for my neck to choke the life out of me. If I had been asleep, he would have succeeded. Instead, I twist away from his grasp, startled by his touch. I slam my fist down on his wrists, trying to knock him away. He grunts in pain, and then someone tackles him.

Marcus beats him bloody. He's unconscious by the time the Praetorians come to see what all the commotion is about. When they realize the boy tried to murder me, they take him away. One of them jokes that he's being "promoted to the Thirteenth Legion."

There is no Thirteenth Legion. We never see him again.

Only one of the boys will speak to me. In the quiet hours, Felix and I whisper about the doom that befell our city. How ironic that my childhood rival has become my only friend as an adult. I'm surrounded by boys I've known my whole life, but they treat me like a stranger, even Marcus—especially Marcus. I'm grateful for Felix's company. In truth, I think his patience keeps me from going insane.

"What even was that thing?" I hiss, frustrated by the dull pain in my wounds, by the cramped quarters, and by my own impotence. The scene from the Ritual of the Heart plays through my mind over and over again as I obsess about the doom that fell on our families and town.

"Some elite *electus*, probably," my friend grunts. He entertains my obsession, but he's already let it go. Maybe the dreams of plebeians are made with weaker foundations, but I don't believe that. I suspect that he's just more used to moving on when life does not go his way.

"Like a Gold?"

"Has to be." He rolls over on his back to stare up at the night sky above our wagon. "He was encased in a liquid metal like a suit of armor. No Silver could ever do that. That only leaves one tier."

He's probably right. The abilities of the upper echelon of ranks are a mystery to me. Coppers are able to interact with their Symbols through touch. Silvers can extend that will and sense beyond themselves. The magisters told us that Golds can reshape the world around them, although I've never seen it myself.

"But why would some Gold *electus* want to interrupt the Ritual of the Heart in our town?" I ask, feeling more confused now that I know something. "What makes us important?"

"You heard the Censor—"

"Atticus." I grate my teeth, letting the anger that burns in me leak into my tone. My friend turns to look at me in surprise. "Say his name," I insist.

"It is a drought year," Felix reminds me. "Perhaps some rival wishes to disrupt the supply of Hearts." I chew on that thought grimly.

"Who?"

"Everyone has enemies, even an Empress." Felix shrugs. He has a point. But the explanation is not satisfying to me. I feel as if there's another explanation, that this one only fits part of the puzzle. But despite my obsession, we do not solve the mystery from the back of a prisoner cart.

After seven days, the Praetorians bring us to the *Via Nordus*, the great northern road that runs all the way to the end of the empire. There they hand us off to a different group of legionnaires marching by that are escorting recruits. The banner they carry is stitched with a *VI*, which marks them as the Sixth Legion. The Empress's elite troops are too important to waste their time with the logistics of taking boys to be forged into soldiers. The column is impressive; hundreds flock to join the Iron Legions. Centurions and decurions ride up and down the line, screaming at the soon-to-be soldiers, trying to teach them the basics of marching. Almost none of the recruits wear a collar like the one that sits tightly around my own neck. These are not elite graduates who earned their Hearts in *Sententia*s, but boys who are willing to take the oath to be given one.

At the back of the line rumble several copper carts like the one that we are held in. Many are full of violent *captivi*—prisoners who have been given one of two options: death or service. Most of the men in those carts are mangy, hard-looking characters. They're destined for the dregs of the legions, the Twelfth—the same place we're going.

The column makes its way up to the northern end of the empire on the *Via Nordus*, heading toward Agogia. Almost daily, more boys are brought to the column and inserted into its ranks. Our force stretches for over a mile, snaking down the road. I'm blown away by the sheer number of us. I know the Iron Legions are vast, but the number of fresh recruits is beyond anything I ever imagined. I don't yet understand the scope of the world that I am being thrust into.

"What's that?" Matinius asks, from the front of cart. All our heads turn to stare at a massive hole in the ground. It could swallow my family's home easily and have room for more. The tunnel descends down into the earth and I can see no end. No one has an answer. We watch it go by in uneasy silence.

In my isolation, I spend time trying to learn about my *Cor* Heart. I can sense a sphere that has grown inside of me with my mind's eye. It is empty and dry. Despite being barren, I can feel its firm strength. It is cold and dispassionate, like a blade.

Part of me suspects that if I did not have the coldness of the Iron Symbol to lean on, I'd be even more of a wreck. At my current level, there isn't much that my Heart can really *do* without me being able to physically touch something that is made of its Symbol—and they are being very careful to keep me separated from iron.

The only bit I have on me is the collar that sits around my neck. I'm hyper-aware of it, to the point that I almost think it is a part of me. Sometimes I can't tell if I feel it on my skin, or my skin on it. But there is another element wrapped in it that eludes my understanding, blank spots in my knowledge.

The memory of being pierced by the shrapnel from the chest flashes in my mind. When the hunk of metal skewered me, it felt like a piece of my own body. I had total awareness of it until I blacked out. I haven't felt anything like that since. Despite my disappointment at being forced to bind the Iron Symbol, part of me is burning with curiosity to understand my new power.

They taught us the theory of it at the *collegium*, but now that I have a Heart, I realize the difference between being fed some vague concepts and putting them into action. The veins that run through my body are still mostly the *rasa* white of unbound *Cor*. Only a few branches have turned Copper to mark my Ascension. Atticus said that they would remain inert for my life, making me look like an *immundus* even when I am not.

Maybe Ascending to Silver would fix whatever went wrong, but it is a moot question. I will never advance beyond Copper. This is what the legionnaires' collars are for—to prevent a new crop of Iron Lords from rising up and conquering the world. Every soldier will wear them for the rest of our lives, even when our duty is done. I don't know exactly how they work. I never planned to join the legions, so why pay attention to them? All I know is that it's supposed to limit me, to keep me from rising.

"Wake up, you laggards," a harsh voice growls, and a baton rattles against the copper bars of our cart. A man in a white uniform, wearing the shoulder epaulettes of a decurion, eyes us with a distasteful look. His name is Flatunus, and he reserves a special glare for me. He's an officer of the Sixth Legion, and he's made it very clear that he does not appreciate babysitting men destined to die in the Twelfth. The fact that I seem to have earned a *Cor* Heart and still ended up at the bottom of the pecking order speaks poorly of me. By rights, I should at *least* be in his Legion, if not one of the higher ones.

The officer wears a white and gold uniform that marks him as a member of one of the Northern Legions. His *lorica* is strapped on, and he bears a straight *gladius* on his hip. He's no Praetorian in purple, but he cuts an intimidating figure nonetheless.

"It's supper time, lazy bones," he sneers and waves at a pair of legionnaires to bring over our food. "You'll never guess what the cooks whipped up for you today." A vicious grin slashes across his face. It's another giant pot of cornmeal gruel. The same thing it has been every day.

Silently, we gather around the copper pot and scoop some of the boiling hot mush into our tin plates before separating to our places on the side of the cart. It burns my mouth, but I've learned that once it cools, it hardens into something like cement, making it almost impossible to eat. A wave of grief crashes over me as I think of Gnaeus and his cooking. I doubt the monsters who came to my family's estate let him live. I will never enjoy one of his feats again.

I suspect—I hope that these are not standard rations but part of the process of turning boys into legionnaires. The lessons have already begun even though we're not in Agogia yet. I can only assume that they will get much worse.

After we eat, Flatunus and his men return to take the pot. "Get a good night's sleep tonight, Twelvies," he mocks, banging on the bars with his baton again. "It's your last night in the cage."

"What?" Felix breaks our silence to ask the question we all feel.

"Tomorrow, we hand you off to the Elevens, and everyone starts *marching*," the decurion replies cheerfully. He's happy enough to be rid of us that he doesn't scold my friend for his casual question.

"What about the other prisoners, *Dominus*? The violent ones?" Marcus asks carefully. The legionnaires haven't given him as hard a time as the rest of us. It's as if they can tell he *wanted* to be here. Perhaps they share some sort of unconscious bond that the rest of us do not.

"Everyone marches tomorrow, lad." Flatunus laughs, banging the bar one more time. "Better be on your guard, my pretties. Spoiled patricians like you don't last in the Twelfth."

We've been kept isolated from the rest of the recruits. But, as my gaze wanders over the hard men waiting outside, I realize it might be safer in here, like our own little tide pool. I hadn't considered that the other denizens of the Twelfth Legion might resent us, even though we all ended up in the same place. I glance around the cart and see the same look of concern on the other boys' faces.

But despite the danger, I find myself eager to be released. I haven't been able to stand up properly for weeks. I can't take the oppressive silence of this cage anymore. I can't wait to stretch my legs. If the men outside of here want to kill me, at least they might talk to me before they do it.

True to his words, the next morning, we are joined by another column. Wordlessly, I stand at the bars of our cage next to Felix, watching as a full century of legionnaires march in formation past us. The banner they carry at the front of their formation bears the marking *XI*, making them the Eleventh.

In their wake, *even more* boys march to take the Iron Oath. There must be more than a thousand of us. Ten times the number of students who competed for *Cor* Hearts in the *Sententia*. Segesta suddenly seems so very small.

"Dead gods," Marcus breathes in awe. "There are so many." I freeze, unsure how to respond. It's the first time he's spoken to me since we were put in this cage. Even though we've been together every day of the last two weeks, I have been alone. My heart pounds in my chest, and I have to swallow at least once before I can speak.

"I think this might be just a fraction of us." The big boy glances at me sharply, although whether he's shocked by my math or checking to see if I've accepted his olive branch, I'm not sure. He stares for a moment, and I take that as an invitation to explain.

"Agogia is in the North Central Province, right?" I ask rhetorically. It is. He knows this as much as I do. In order to make it to the top fifty *discipuli* and compete for a *Cor* Heart, we had to learn geography.

"We're coming up from the southeastern side of the empire," I continue, drawing a slanted line in the air to illustrate the angle. "It wouldn't make sense for recruits from other provinces that didn't border ours to meet us."

"Which means there's potentially three more columns this size heading toward Agogia right now," Felix finished, easily following my train of thought. "Four thousand new recruits."

"In a drought year."

His brown eyes flick to mine again, and we share a knowing look. We've both had the same thought. How is it that the empire cut the rations of Hearts to our town in *half* but still has enough to accept thousands of new legionnaires? Not only has the supply been reduced, but losing some was an issue worth slaughtering innocents over. The death of my family and my friends suddenly feels even more meaningless as I realize how small a speck we were in the eye of the empire.

"Out!" barks a harsh voice, and we turn to see Flatunus striding toward us, flanked by several legionnaires. The decurion carries a set of keys in his hand and is waving at us with irritation.

"Here we go," I murmur to Felix as the rest of the boys rise to their feet. "How bad do you think this will be?"

"What good are legionnaires that can't march?" the boy who dreamed of bread asks. "It can't be worse than what we've been through already." I don't find his words reassuring. I'm not sure he meant them to be.

"At least I'll look good in a necklace," Felix remarks to nobody in particular as we jump out of the open gate. There are a couple of dry chuckles from the other survivors. I take a moment to stretch my legs, trying to remember how to use them.

"Well, they're finally making the citizens walk with us dirty folk, I see," a voice jeers from the line. A frown passes over my face. Did they think we wanted to be in there? I look over the other prisoner recruits but can't see who shouted.

A big man steps into my path, shoving me with his shoulder. Caught off guard, I stumble backward, tripping over my own feet until I fall on the dusty ground. "Watch where you're going, *immundus*," he sneers, leaning down to loom over me. He's a big man, with a bushy beard and the scarred face of a fighter. A few of the other recruits laugh, watching our confrontation.

For a moment, I am surprised at being the target of his aggression. I forgot what I look like. Then I see his eyes on my *rasa Cor* markings, and I understand. I am scrap metal, the iron that smiths throw away because it is not worth forging into something better. This is not the last time that I will be judged for my apparent weakness.

I stare up at the man from my rump. I should feel something, I know. When other students bullied me in the *collegium,* I would be angry or afraid. But I am not. I'm just cold. Slowly, I rise to my feet, staring at the bigger man with an iron gaze.

Something uncertain flickers in his expression, as if he expected me to be different. My fingers curl into fists, driven by an impulse that feels like it's coming from outside of me. I take a step toward the brute, but before I can take another, Felix is between us. He places a hand on my chest and glances over my shoulder. I look and see what he sees. The officers are coming.

I have no interest in joining the Thirteenth Legion.

Under a new decurion's supervision, all the recruits destined for the Twelfth are shoved into formation. The column is five men wide, and our portion is ten rows deep. I'm not surprised, but up close, most of the men being forced into Legion XII are not impressive specimens. Many are smaller than me, skinny street urchins who have had to steal their whole lives to survive.

The rest are thugs. Big, hulking brutes who eye us like we're fresh meat. A shiver runs down my spine as I make eye contact with the one who shoved me. There's an anger burning behind his pupils that's just waiting for an excuse to boil over.

"Hup! Hup!" Flatunus shouts, calling the rhythm of the march as he strides alongside us. He and his fellow officers watch us with furious glares, looking for anyone not on their tempo. Any man caught out of step gets a hefty whack with their batons. I get three. The officers make sure I know they think I'm scum. Marcus and Felix get none.

When the decurion is satisfied that we can move as a block, they jam us into the back of the column under the watch of legionnaires from the Eleventh, and then they fade away. Flatunus and the Sixth depart later that day, taking the carts with them.

At first, it feels good to move again, but after a few hours, I find myself missing the wagon. The wound in my arm twinges as my body moves. I can feel blisters forming on my feet. The metal collar around my neck grows unforgettable as I begin to sweat. Men around me grumble, but I keep my mouth shut and focus on putting one foot in front of the other.

An officer, wearing the red-plumed helmet of a full-blown centurion, works his way down the line, watching all of us with tired, unimpressed eyes. Two decurions trail him like faithful hounds. He stops at the beginning of our section and falls in step with us.

"Right, my little recruits, I am Centurion Durus, First Spear of the Eighth Cohort of the Twelfth Legion. Listen up and listen up good." He's a hard man. His beard is more salt than pepper, and a pair of scars peel from his right eye. He has the air of a rock that's been pounded by the sea but still endures.

"From this moment on, I am your commanding officer. If I tell you to get up and march, you will be off the ground and in formation before I can count to twenty. Do I make myself clear?" There's a grumble of agreement from our column.

Centurion Durus stops mid-march, as if frozen in shock. His decurion shadows stop with him, in perfect formation. "Halt!" he screams, face turning bright red. We come to a ragged stop as people realize he's serious. Flatunus got us started but never gave us any more instructions. Durus stares at our disorganized pile with more disgust than if he had just walked in on it in bed with his wife. The rest of the recruits continue marching on, leaving our little tail-piece at the end.

"Fix this line!" he bellows, swinging his baton through the air with enough force for me to hear it even at a distance. Slowly, we shuffle around until we're back into a rough approximation of order.

The centurion glares at us for a few moments in angry silence. His chest is heaving. His eyes sweep up and down our formation, looking for something. I make the mistake of thinking that he is a teacher and hold his eye contact when his angry glare passes over me like a storm.

"You." He snaps his fingers at me and points in front of himself. "Front and center." My heart skips a beat, but I do as I'm told, slipping out of the ranks to stand before the centurion. Dimly, I'm aware that I should be more afraid, but I'm not. My new Iron spine keeps my fear at arm's length.

"What's your name, Copper?" He makes my rank something of a curse. Flatunus made it clear that I've got a target on my back. I do my best to copy the stance that I've seen the soldiers make the other recruits do, standing stiffly, staring straight ahead. I can feel the stares of all the other boys on the back of my neck like spider legs.

"Castor Castus, *Dominus!*" I shout, looking above Durus's head as I slam my fist into my chest in salute. For the first time, I remember that Atticus struck my name from the rolls. I do not care. That is what my father named me, who I am.

"Castus?" He chuckles, looking at me in amusement. "Do you know what *castus* meant in the ancient language, boy?" I swallow as a lump forms in my throat.

"It meant innocent, *Dominus.*"

"Well, if you're here, I think that time has passed," the centurion says with a wink. The men behind me chuckle in delight. I keep my lips pressed shut, not daring to respond to his taunts. Somewhere, the coldly logical presence in my mind helps me realize this is a right of passage, not cruel targeting. I am the only Ironbound marching with the Twelfth; how could he not single me out?

"We'll have to come up with a new one. How about *putris?*" It means rotten. Still, I say nothing, and after a moment, he lets it go, focusing on his true target.

"Ironbound already, are you boy?" Durus sneers, eyeing my collar with a sense of distrust. "What did you do to end up in my century, Castor?" I hesitate for a moment, caught flat-footed by his question. The other soldiers haven't bothered to ask. Being placed in the Twelfth is a lot like being sentenced to prison. Once you're there, no one cares what you have to say about how you got there.

My story has already gotten everyone I cared about killed or enslaved. Telling the truth now could only hurt those of us who were still alive. Atticus's threat to return and raze Segesta to the ground burns in my ears, convincing me to keep my secrets.

"I accidentally bound—" I started with a familiar lie, but the centurion's eyes narrow as he looks at the *rasa* veins on my wrist next to my iron ones.

"You some sort of freak, Castor?" he demands, cutting me off. "That why they didn't put you in the fancy legions, *Sententia* boy? What in the name of all gods, dead and dying, is wrong with your Heart?" If the rest of the recruits had been watching me get dressed down with mild interest before, now their attention is as sharp as a *gladius*.

"I do not know, *Dominus*," I tell him truthfully. "My ritual was… interrupted, and I ended up like this. When it was over, I was conscripted to the Twelfth."

Durus stares at me for a long moment, his gray eyes unimpressed. "Keep your secrets, boy," he grunts after the pause grows too long. "The Iron Pits of Agogia will sort you out as sure as the others." He turns his attention from me to the rest of the line, standing still.

"It's three days to the Iron City," he announces, sending a thrill running down my spine and a low murmur through the rest of the company. "By the time we arrive, I expect that each and every one of you will be able to march in formation. Any man who falls out of rhythm on the final day will be given five lashes. Do I make myself clear?"

This time, we all salute. Although from the grimace on his face, I'm sure we're all out of sync. The centurion nods to one of his decurions, who strides to the front of our line and sets the pace.

"Forward march!" I don't know what is waiting for us in Agogia, the legendary city of the legions. I have never wanted to be a soldier. But despite myself, I feel an eagerness to get answers. What is wrong with my Heart? Can they really fix me?

But those questions are only steps. Every direction that I turn, my vision is full of boys from my town who should not be here. Marcus, Felix, and Clintus are near me. Further down, I spot Jasper and red-haired Rufus. Haxus and Antony trudge along at the rear of the formation. No matter where I look, I am reminded that they pay the price for my punishment. Their lives have been stolen the same way that my family's was, the same mine was.

A punishment that is not fair. I did nothing wrong, and yet I am the scapegoat. There are others who deserve to pay for what they have taken. *Atticus.*

One day, I will kill him. The stray thought drifts through my mind for the first time like a shadow. It seems like madness to contemplate murdering an elite *electus* who bears the authority of the Empress. Only a fool who wishes to die would even contemplate such a thing.

But I am already dead. The only question is if I can avenge my father, mother, sister, and friends before my body stops breathing.

The only way to find out is to march.

So I do.

CHAPTER 17

"How do you bear it?" I mutter to Felix as we march. My body hurts, but that's not what I mean. Of all of us, the former plebeian seems the least troubled by our circumstances. I do not know how that is possible. In some ways, he lost more than all of us.

There's a resiliency to him that escapes the rest of the patricians stumbling along in the wake of the other recruits. Durus has pushed us hard to catch up with the rest of the column. I have not been made into a soldier yet, and already I hate marching.

"Bear what?" His voice is tired, but he's not winded.

"Everything," I don't bother explaining. He knows what I mean.

He's silent for a while, focusing on his paces. Eventually, I forget that I asked him a question. My world is nothing other than dust and counting, making sure that I don't get out of sync with the rest of the recruits.

"Pain is a kind of strength," he says, breaking the silence.

"Huh?" I ask, turning to look at him. "What does that mean?"

"You'll know when you find it." He shrugs, as if he doesn't know what else to say. We're interrupted by the recruits around us getting sight of our destination on the horizon.

The city of Agogia is the military capital of the empire. It is often referred to as the "Iron City" in honor of the legions that are forged here. But that is a younger, crass name for something that has survived since the ancients.

Before Prometheus stole the secret of *Cor* Hearts from the gods, before Titus and his Iron Lords went into the hallowed halls of Olympus and killed the entire pantheon, there was the *agoge*, the name of the way that they fought. Our legionnaires may have access to new power that their ancestors did not, but they are still steeped in ancient tradition.

I know this, and yet I do not. Because the understanding of a boy earned in a classroom is different from that of a man who has traveled the world and seen it with his own eyes. If the size of the recruitment column made me feel small, my first glance at Agogia makes me feel insignificant.

The Iron City is a massive fortress that sits at the end of the temperate plains of the empire. In the distance, a line of mountains rears up like a shieldwall, their tips covered with snow. The city itself is a giant ring, surrounded by a stone fortification that's at least fifty feet in height.

Scarlet-clad legionnaires man the walls in all directions, the tips of their spears glinting in the sunlight as they stand at attention. I am so shocked at the sight of it that I stumble, falling out of rhythm with the rest of the march.

Cursing under my breath, I manage to shuffle my steps and get back on pace before Durus or any of his decurions notice my misstep. True to his threat, men in line have already been whipped, and I have no desire to join their number.

"Mars's Bleached Bones," Felix breathes in awe from my right. I grunt in agreement. The recruits in our column are nothing compared to the population of the Iron City. Realistically, I know that not everyone there is a legionnaire. An army needs more than just soldiers to function.

There are quartermasters, cooks, *medici*, blacksmiths, and a dozen other professions that are needed to support the infrastructure of an Iron Legion. But all the same, for the first time, I think I truly understand the scope of the Empress's power.

We march for another hour, bringing up the rear of the column, choking on the dust that the boys in front of us kick up as we make our way through the arid plains. My feet are no longer blistered but cracked and bleeding. I am not used to this kind of hardship that we are only just beginning.

But even as I suffer, I notice that my body is different. I'm not in as much pain as I should be. My shoulder is still a little tender, but I barely notice it. Last night, I checked on it by the fire; the wound had completely sealed under a thin layer of fresh pink flesh. Likewise, my blisters are an irritant but not debilitating.

Once, when I was a boy, I impaled myself on a pitchfork, and the wounds left by its tines took months to heal. I'm certain that my body has begun to heal faster, which is what I was taught a Copper-level *Cor* Heart does for its bearer.

Relief floods through me as I realize whatever went wrong with my binding didn't ruin everything. I had begun to worry that my heart would be damaged and not work, but this was a good sign. Another sign is that my body itches with a new need—my *Cor* requires Iron essence to function, like a heart needs blood. But I have only a tiny amount in the binding around my neck, enough to keep me alive but not enough to slake my thirst.

Like a hovering eagle, Durus appeared at the side of the column, glaring at us as we marched. "When we enter the Iron City, don't stop marching, lads," he called, his voice easily carrying over the din of our marching. "Follow your decurions, and all will be well."

As we approach the massive walls, I risk a glance at Marcus. He's marching a few spaces ahead of me and has made every effort not to look in my direction since our brief conversation three days ago. He's still not looking at me, but the big boy's shoulders are slumped. I know that this moment must be like another hammer blow.

The legions were never my fantasy like they were his, but to be marched past the halls that he dreamed of entering, only to be forced into the lowest of them, has to be a special twist of the knife. As if he can feel me looking at him, he straightens his spine as we step into the shadow of Agogia.

We enter through the southernmost of the four main gates of the walled city, situated at the compass points on the wheel. Despite Durus's harsh warnings, all our heads swing around to stare at the spectacle of the Iron City. I grew up in a town with paved streets and a *collegium* by Jupiter's Grave! I knew that cities got bigger, but I didn't know *how* much bigger.

The entire place is bursting with industry. I hear a hundred blacksmith hammers ringing as they pound out iron for *gladii* and *scuta*, the iconic sword and shield of the legions. The whole place smells of smoke, horse dung, and sweat, as if its entire purpose is for war. This is where the engine that runs the empire is kept.

The main thoroughfare is wide enough for a legion to march in opposite directions at the same time. I know this because a cohort of blue-clad legionnaires from the Fifth, bearing a standard marked with a *V*, pass us, heading out of the gates we enter.

The inside of the ring is carved up like a pie, into four quadrants, containing three slices for a different Legion. Each Legion owns a sector, where they live and train. In the center is a smaller ring with a fortress, where the Imperators reside.

We come from the south, and my hands clench into fists as we pass the purple bedecked banners of the Praetorians on our left. None of the recruits are led into that camp, but I see a few boys being taken into the Second's sector. A larger portion breaks off toward the Third, and then the Fourth as we enter the second quadrant of Agogia. All those recruits are already Ironbound, like me.

It seems that all the higher Legions are billeted in the southern hemisphere of Agogia. They're closer to the Empress that way. Our column is only cut down by a third by the time we curve around the inner circle, which tells me a lot about how the legions are built.

After we leave the second quadrant, the Seventh and Eighth claim half of the remaining boys, but I don't see a single recruit that wears the iron collar among them. The rest of the column is sprinkled into the Ninth, Tenth, and Eleventh. All that's left as we march into the Twelfth's camp is our hundred-something reprobates and paupers.

Durus and his decurions lead us through our slice of the circle toward the wall. The inside of the Twelfth's sector is splintered into ten portions, one for each of the cohorts of the legion. We march into the one marked the Eighth. Stone barracks that can hold hundreds of men and supply depots run the length of the sector, and off-duty legionnaires eye us with an untrusting gaze as we make our way through.

Having just been at the mercy of Censors and Praetorians, I'm struck by how much less impressive these men are. Not just in size, although most of them are wiry instead of brawny, but in bearing too. The First Legion carries themselves with an innate pride, as if each of them were the centurion. These soldiers, by comparison, are dirty and downcast.

"Look out, boys. New fish just got caught," one calls from the doorway of a barracks.

"Welcome to the meat grinder," another hoots. The veterans around him laugh, as if he's said something brilliant. All of them wear the same metal collar that I do around my neck. One of them notices, and I see him pointing me out to the others. Murmurs spread along the way as more of the legionnaires see that I am already bound. They know even better than the recruits that I shouldn't be here.

Durus brings us to a halt and orders us to stand at attention in front of the thick stone building built against the wall of the city. For a moment, we stand in quiet tension, as all around us the city continues to bustle. I can still hear the blacksmith's hammers in the distance, ringing as they make more swords and shields.

But in our courtyard, everyone is silent, even the veterans who mocked us as we passed. They're all waiting for something with a hint of fear. Their concern breathes new life into mine, and I find my gaze drawn to the heavy door in front of us.

It bursts open with firm force, and a man who burns with a dark intensity steps through. He wears the iron *lorica* of the legions, with a red cape of command hanging from his shoulders. His hard gaze sweeps across us like a wave, and I almost shudder at the force of it.

Like every other member of the Iron Legions, the tribune wears a restrictive collar around his neck. My breath catches in my throat as I spy the Silver veins running through his forearms. He is a *Fidelis*! Only a handful of the most trusted of Ironbound are allowed to Ascend to the second level. He does not belong in the Twelfth any more than I do. The man steps out into the hush that gathers around him and joins Durus at the head of our formation.

"At ease," he commands after a long moment. Our group shifts uneasily, not really sure what that means—we've barely mastered marching. His contemptuous gaze sweeps across us for a moment before he sighs as if disappointed by us. Then he notices me, and his eyes narrow for a second before moving on.

"I am Tribune Gaius Marius," he informs us in a deep, resonant tone. "I command the Eighth Cohort of the Twelfth Legion. You are a group of miscreants and disappointments"—his voice hardens as he eyes us again—"but when we are finished with you, you will be legionnaires. Most of you know the way of the legions. Soldiers who prove their worth can earn a place higher on the wheel. Those who are unworthy will find themselves demoted. That is not how it works in the Twelfth. There is no Thirteenth Legion in the empire, only a noose."

A chill settles on my neck as I hear the legionnaires' jokes repeated by someone with authority. Any doubts I had about where the Nicodemian ended up fade to nothing. Atticus sent me and my friends here to die.

"Twenty years of service is the price you pay for your future," Gaius continues, unbothered by the shifting of the recruits in front of him. "Serve your Empress well, and all debts and crimes will be forgiven. You can retire and live as old men at peace. Whatever lives you led before you came here are over. You will be reborn as new iron men, purified in the forges of Agogia. Remember our Legion's motto, *redemptio in bello*." His lips quirk as he surveys the sea of blank faces before him. There are not many among us who are educated in the language of the ancients. "Redemption in war." I feel a grim sense of foreboding from the man. This will not be an easy transition, I think. I've never considered what metal must go through to become a sword.

Gaius eyes us for a moment, measuring the impact of his words. I can't help but notice that the tribune is different from the rest of us. His armor is meticulously maintained, and his posture is perfect. He carries himself with the same pride I saw in the other legions.

I'm not sure if he sees what he's looking for, but the moment has held long enough. "First Spear, assign the recruits to their barracks," he barks, turning from us and striding back into the command building.

"You heard the tribune, lads." Durus's strong voice picks up into the silence. "Off we go." The officers lead us to an empty stone structure on the edge of the Twelfth's slice of Agogian pie. It's the second closest one to the officers' building, probably so they can keep an eye on us.

Several dozen bunks run the length of the room, and slowly we claim them, organizing roughly by the cart we rode here in. I glance around the room, looking for my friends. Other recruits shove past me, bumping me with more force than necessary. More than one mutters "*immundus*" as a curse as they do.

I try to find a space in the back. I just want to be left alone. Anas, the big man who knocked me down a few days ago, intercepts me, blocking my path to the corner.

"Sorry, *Patrician*—this spot is taken." I let him have it because I can tell a lot of the men around him feel the same way. The last thing I need is to start a brawl, especially without anyone on my side. I just want a place to sleep.

"Taken," another man sneers as I work my way through the room.

I head toward the cluster of recruits from Segesta and Nicodemia that I rode with. They've congregated right in the center of the room, where everyone can see. The divide in the room couldn't be clearer if there were borders painted on the floor, with the exception of Felix, the other patricians and plebeians do not mix. I feel a moment of sympathy for my friend who is pulled between two worlds. Even among the lower class, there is a difference between the boy who was admitted to the *collegium* and prisoners sent here to earn their freedom.

Clintus eyes me darkly but says nothing. Antony watches me and nudges Petrus as I draw close. Approaching a bunk, I take the bottom bed, and Felix places his kit on the one above me. Marcus is lying on the next bed over, but he ignores me. A whipcord-thin boy named Lintus takes the one above him.

I look around the room and feel even more like a prisoner than I did behind copper bars. Maybe it's because the room has no windows, and the wagon did. Maybe it's because I know this may be the last place I live before I'm killed in the frontlines of some battle no one will ever hear about. Most of the men who have slept here before me are already dust. Soon we will join them.

"It's been a long day, boys," the centurion calls as we settle in. "You've earned some rest. Let's get you fed and in bed. The forging starts tomorrow."

CHAPTER 18

The centurion lied. There is no rest.

They come for us in the dark.

With my belly full from the first real meal I've eaten in days, I stumble back to my bed with the rest of the recruits. Spirits are high, despite our circumstances.

The beds are not comfortable. My mother would never have put one in her home. But after a couple of weeks on the road, sleeping in carts and on rocky ground, they feel heavenly. I rest deeply, entrenched in the empty halls of Somnus, long-dead God of Sleep, until I am violently wrenched from his domain.

There are hands on me, dragging me from my bed. Boys scream in anger and fear. I am one of them, although which of those two I feel, I am not sure. I fall to the floor as I writhe in the grasp of several men, twisting and struggling to break free like a calf about to be branded.

Heavy fists crash into my stomach, driving the air out of my lungs. I gasp in shock and go limp as my body tries to regain its breath. Blows rain down on me as I go still. Boots stomp on my back, forcing me to curl into a ball to protect my head. On instinct, I reach for the Symbol of Iron, and I'm stunned as a cold clarity descends upon me. I still feel the blows landing on me, but they're different—less.

At first, I think the other recruits have turned on me, or the students from my homeland have decided to exact revenge in blood. But as I focus on the screams all around me, I realize it's all of us. What is it that Gaius said? We will be *purified in the iron forges of Agogia.* Maybe that was more literal than I thought.

Satisfied that I won't struggle, rough hands grab my shoulders and drag me to my feet. At least a hundred legionnaires crowd our small barracks, in full battle dress. Two men hold me on my feet, and I find myself facing the tribune himself, who watches the proceedings with a solemn expression.

A few recruits still battle with the fully kitted soldiers, but slowly, the pandemonium begins to fade. The last holdout is silenced with a gurgle that fades into a pained groan. Then there is silence, broken only by heavy breaths and the shuffling of feet. Gaius surveys us for a moment before nodding sharply.

"To the pits," he orders, and immediately, we begin to move. Each recruit is dragged by a pair of legionnaires in the tribune's wake. Belatedly, I realize that mine aren't wearing their armor. They must not have wanted to risk me getting my hands on something made of iron.

Dressed only in a tunic and cotton leggings, I am pulled out of the Twelfth's district and back onto the main thoroughfare. Like ghosts, we head toward the center of the city toward the fortress that looms above the entire ring.

The main gate is open, guarded by legionnaires clothed in purple. They laugh at us as we are dragged through. A sneer curls at the corner of my lips as we pass the Praetorians. This place is the height of their power; they strut like songbirds.

The inside of the fortress is a grim place built for siege. Like the center of a stone fruit, this place was designed to be impossible for an opponent to digest. Even as a boy who knows nothing of war, I can see the cruelty in its design. Narrow hallways barely wide enough for three men circle through the walls before opening into a courtyard that has random walls constructed to create a permanent *Labyrinthus*.

Defenders on the wall gaze down on us with cruel eyes as we march exposed under their vantage points. Any army that wishes to conquer the Iron City would have to pay dead Hades a king's ransom in blood.

We do not proceed into the main castle, a dark, squat thing that hunches over us like a gargoyle. Instead, we are taken down a tunnel entrance that goes into the dark rock beneath the fortress. It is a gaping maw eager to swallow us all. Despite the cold iron that fills my mind and holds fear at bay, I am disturbed by the darkness.

The interior is a natural-looking cave, although I suspect that it was carved by someone with a Stone Symbol long ago. Torches flutter where they are set into the wall, lighting the narrow path wide enough for one recruit and his two legionnaire escorts. Gaius, Durus, and the other officers lead us as we are dragged down the spiral into the very bowels of the earth.

It feels like an hour has passed by the time we reach the bottom, and the room opens up to reveal a massive cave that has been claimed by the Iron Legions. The floor is cobbled around the stalagmites that have been here for centuries. Stalactites cling to the ceiling like teeth; some still drip with water like a serpent's venomous fang. The entire facility smells of mildew and rot.

In the far wall, a massive furnace has been built into the rock. Bellows roar as they pump air to feed the flames. The underground is filled with an oppressive, muggy heat like a sauna. A heavy, sleepy presence pervades this place. It reminds me of the one I felt in the endurance test in the arena. Giant iron doors are set in the walls every few paces, as far as I can see in the dim light. This is a place where weapons are made.

A secret place.

A fell place.

A magister and three priests wait for us at the bottom of the ramp. Both are old and wrinkled but seem a part of the cave itself, as if they have been here since it was made. The magister wears a white toga, but it is soiled from the soot that fills this place. Golden veins of an *aurum Cor* wrap around his arms as he watches us be dragged into his domain. I gape in awe at seeing *electus* who has reached the final Ascension.

The priests are dressed in black togas torn in mourning for their dead gods. All of them are blind, their empty eye sockets covered with strips of dark cloth. The man in front holds a black spear out over us like a scepter, chanting blessings in the tongue of the ancients. In his left hand, he holds a gilded *scutum*, the shield of the legions. The woman to his left raises a giant torch and wears a bronze helmet. The third man is covered in snakes, who stick out their tongues at us, tasting our fear. I feel nothing as I pass under his benediction. The gods are dead—what power do dead things have?

One by one, we are lined up on the large central floor of the cave, our legionnaire guards still holding us. I am pulled to the side, which I wonder at until I realize that this is the iron version of the Ritual of the Heart.

In civilization, when a citizen receives their *Cor*, it is a beautiful thing. It is a moment for a child to find their individuality and take the first steps of their adult life. But the legions do not want artistic individuals—they want weapons. We are not given instructions or a choice. We are here to serve at the Empress's will, and she desires that we be remade.

The legionnaires at my side force me to kneel, kicking out the back of my legs until I drop to the hard stone floor. When all of us are on our knees, silence falls across the cavern. It is large and imposing, deafening in its magnitude.

A dozen other priests appear around the corners of the room. Some are on balconies above us. The silence shatters as they begin to hum, a deep bass warble that echoes through the bowels of the earth like some forgotten call. The old, blind priest who carries the black spear steps forward and raises it.

"In the world above, they teach you that the gods are dead," he cries, his frail voice ringing with surprising power. "They lament the demise of the soft deities like Venus and Minerva. But here in the deep, we know the truth. Our elders may be dead, but they are not gone. The gods still speak through us."

Something catches in my throat. I've never heard a priest speak like this before. The theology of the *collegium* is as dead and dry as the masters of Olympus. But I've seen things I can't explain, and now I hear them too.

"Here in the Hall of Vulcan, the Master Forger, we invoke the art of Bellona and Pluto. The Iron Legions follow the path of Mars. These gods still live in each and every Ironbound that carries a sword in their name. The collars you will wear in service to this legacy are made from the relics of your fallen brothers. When you leave this place, you will bear a piece of our gods inside of you. War is not dead—he merely rests in you, his iron children."

Slowly, the magister makes his way down the line, followed by a handful of assistants, who push a large cart. Yet more priests appear, blind and carrying the Symbols of Mars. A jolt runs through me as I spot a wolf's head tattooed in the center of some of their foreheads. It is identical to the helmet of the golden-armored thing that attacked us in Segesta.

What connection does that creature have to the dead God of War? What does it mean that I was given my Heart by a being that bore the mark of the temple I now find myself in? Goosebumps prick my flesh as I eye the priests with a new wariness. Dead or not, there is still power here.

There is no individual ceremony as the recruits are Ironbound. Straight into the forge we are put, for these are the Iron Pits of Agogia. The old man pauses before the first recruit, dangling limply between the two legionnaires who have beaten him senseless. He reaches into the cart with a pair of tongs and pulls out a small globe of liquid *Cor*. Without hesitation, he lifts the dazed recruit's shirt and shoves the Heart against the man's chest.

Just like Silvester, the boy's body begins to writhe. He lets out a low moan as the metal fuses with his body and begins to spread. Satisfied, the magister steps back and nods at the two guards holding him. I watch as they drag him to one of the metal doors built into the rock and throw him in. It locks from the outside.

The magister moves on. Again and again, he thrusts a *Cor* Heart into the chest of a recruit, and they are taken through different doors. When he reaches Marcus, he pauses, grabbing my friend's chin and staring into his eyes for a moment. Then he grunts and jabs him with the liquid metal.

"Beat him again," he instructs as they take him away. This time, the guards go through the door with him and do not return for several minutes. When they do, one of them is chuckling as he rubs his wrist in his hand as if he sprained it. Anger surges in me, and for a moment, I forget that I'm being held.

I try to rise and confront the soldiers, but the firm hands on me yank me back, locking me in place. I snarl at one of the grim-faced legionnaires holding me, but he stares straight ahead, ignoring my vitriol.

It occurs to me as I turn back to the scene in front of me that I am the most aware recruit in the cavern. The rest have all been beaten into a dazed state of submission. Is that intentional, or another gift from my Iron Heart? Being an *electus* is supposed to increase my body's capability, but I suspect there's more at play.

Felix is next to be issued a Heart. My tall friend grimaces as the liquid begins to work its way through his body, although I think it is more sadness than pain. The boy wanted to be a baker, but that dream is dead, killed with an iron blade. Felix gets another beating too.

The magister keeps me for last. When all of the Twelfth Legion's new recruits have been made *rasa* and thrown into the cells, he comes for me. He's ancient. Even with the power of a Gold Heart, time has finally worn him down. Still, the eyes that he glares at me with are vibrant and full of life. He takes my wrist in his hands and turns it, tracing the white veins of unbound *Cor* next to my Copper ones. His lips purse as he thinks.

Tribune Gaius follows in his shadow, along with Durus and a handful of the other officers of the legion. There's an air of apprehension as they watch the old man inspect me.

"Well, Magister? Can he be saved?" Gaius demands after a few moments. For the first time, I realize that I might be in danger. I'm an *immundus*, a freak, not whole.

As I have just witnessed, the legions are not a place for individuality but efficiency. The Empress expects her Legions not to waste her weapons, but if I cannot be fixed, then I am a liability. In the *collegium*, they taught us that Legions are like living fortresses. Each man is a stone in the foundation, and together they can withstand any foe. But if my mangled binding is unable to channel enough power, I would be a weakness in the foundation. A broken sword is melted down to be made into something new. What good is an *electus* who cannot stand in the shieldwall?

Atticus is more devious than I gave him credit for. If I am killed by the legions, his problem goes away. He delivered his quota of *electii*, and someone else disposed of it. I am impressed by the coldness of it. He is a more efficient monster than I thought.

"Did something go wrong with your binding?" he demands, still inspecting my Heart.

"There was an… interruption. I passed out." The magister grunts as if he expected to hear something like that. He switches to my other wrist and glares at those lines too. The longer he is silent, the more my fear grows. At last, he releases my hand and looks me in the eyes for the first time. Squaring my jaw, I meet his gaze and call upon the coldness of Iron to make me brave. The old man arches an eyebrow before turning back to the tribune.

"There's only one way to find out," he pronounces. "If he can pass the test, he is worthy. The Iron Pits will either fix him or claim him." The priests' chanting cuts off abruptly as the magister begins to walk away. "Beat him thoroughly. He's already using Iron for endurance," he calls over his shoulder.

Even though I don't think I'm about to be killed, panic overtakes me. I struggle in the grip of the two soldiers who are dragging me toward the row of iron doors. No matter how hard I flail, they keep their grips on my arms.

"Go," Tribune Gaius's voice calls, and I hear footsteps as more men step into our wake.

Six legionnaires follow me into my cell. At first, I try to fight back, but there are too many. Whatever extra strength my Iron Heart has given me is more than equaled by their own. Slowly, they grind me down, and I stagger after a blow clips me in the right ear. Someone kicks out my leg, and I fall to the ground. Then they close in, using their boots.

I've been roughed up by classmates before. I survived a mock melee in the arena. None of these are like the beating that the professional soldiers rain down on me. I curl in on myself, trying to outlast their fury. I call upon my Heart, begging Iron for help. Awareness of the whole room floods into me as its strength fills my bones and its cold numbs my wounds. Iron essence pours into me, refilling a thirst I have not been able to quench, but the blows don't stop.

I can feel my hold on the power slipping as the legionnaires continue. I've taken too much abuse, and my tenuous connection to Iron snaps. The numbness fades, and the darkness takes me.

CHAPTER 19

I awake in the darkness. My eyes pop open, and for a moment, I worry that the legionnaires hit me so hard that I have gone blind. I panic, sitting up—or at least trying to—but my bruised body stops me short.

But what little movement I accomplish shifts my angle enough to let me see a faint stream of light coming from the cracks in the door of my cell. I'm not blind, just alone in the dark. Slowly, I manage to lever myself into a seated position, leaning on the wall for support.

I reach inside myself, looking for aid from my Iron Symbol. My pain retreats to a dull throb as the coldness fills me like a sword in its sheath. I close my eyes and let out a long sigh of relief as the noise of the injuries fades in my mind. I can think again.

My eyes snap back open in shock as awareness of the room floods into my brain once more. I can *feel* it, as if it is my own skin and bone. I take a deep breath to center myself as my mind explores this new sensation. Inside of my chest the gray sphere of power is no longer drained, my *Cor* has refilled a small portion of its reserve with the essence around me. It grows darker as it is nourished. As I expand my mind to study the entire room, I realize it is completely covered by sheets of iron. I'm surrounded by it on all sides.

A bitter laugh escapes my lips. This explains how the legions guarantee that their soldiers attune to the right Symbol. Felix was right—you can force your choice to some degree. They beat us to lower our ability to concentrate and then lock us in metal so that the only Symbol our *rasa* hearts can find is iron.

It's coldly genius and another example of the lengths that the empire is willing to go to make their weapons. I hold my hands up in front of my face, trying to see if any of my blank veins have changed, but it is too dark for me to tell. I understand now what the magister is trying to accomplish. If my binding was interrupted, then maybe I will be able to finish the process here.

Closing my eyes once more, I breathe in and hold it. I focus inward, trying to capture the feeling of the Symbol that I'm surrounded by. It is the most iron I've been allowed to touch since being bound. I feel its strength, its coldness, and its endurability.

This metal has been here for generations and will still be here long after I am but dust. My mind curls around the *thing* of it. It burns like a beacon to my closed eyes. Tentatively, I try to pull it into me, to draw on it with my soul the way a man drinks water.

The essence flows into me, and I feel my heart relax as the itch that has tormented me for days fades. A gasp erupts out of me as I feel my aches fade even more. It's as if I'm feeding my Heart, and in turn, it cares for me.

As my focus grows, I can feel the shape of the room. I see it in my mind's eye as clear as day. I'm sitting in a box, completely enclosed by iron. I can feel each rivet where they drove nails into the stone to hold it up. Every inch of this iron world reveals itself to me and becomes as familiar as my own fingers.

It's overwhelming; it's mesmerizing. My whole life, I have only had five senses: taste, sight, sound, touch, and smell. Now I have a sixth: iron. Already it feels as natural as breathing. In a day, I won't be able to imagine living without it. I know that when I step free from this cell, it will be like being blindfolded. This pure iron makes the mixed metal of the collar around my neck feel even stranger by comparison.

I exhale and take another breath, soaking up the Iron essence that surrounds me. That is the second purpose of this room, I realize. Magister Vellum once told us that after someone is bound, they are placed in a room full of physical manifestations of their Symbol to help the connection settle.

I did not have that opportunity after the creature knocked the Hearts into me. Maybe that is why my veins aren't all *cuprum*. A surge of excitement grows in me. This could fix me! I may not have chosen Iron as my Symbol, but if I am going to survive my term in the legions, I need to be strong.

With renewed vigor, I continue my controlled breaths, forcing my mind to pull on the essence of iron that surrounds me. It is like using two pairs of lungs at the same time. At first, my cultivation is slow and inefficient. Each collective inhale is awkward and halting. But an unusual patience fills me like the durability of Iron, helping me maintain my focus.

Eventually, I lose track of time until there is only the room and my breathing. With each cycle, I feel my skill improving. The veins in my arm burn like muscles being pushed to their limit. Their anguish fills me with hope that I am going down the right path. That cold sphere inside of my body fills, not unlike my stomach, as I grow close to the end of a meal. I'm almost sated, just a little more, and I—*urk.*

I gasp in shock as the iron collar around my neck tightens like a noose, cutting off my breath with a cold grip. My tranquility shatters as Iron abandons me. I jerk forward, hands scrabbling at the metal band.

I can't breathe.

The collar is like a serpent, choking the life out of me. My ragged gasps echo off the metal box, and I know that no one will ever avenge my family if I die here. Atticus's ploy will work, and he will never suffer for what he's done.

So, I must not die.

I rage at the iron in the collar that chokes me. I demand that it releases me, and to my surprise, I feel it go limp, like a dog letting go of its prey on command. But the other metal twisted inside it only tightens further, locking the band in place. I wheeze in pain, but no sound comes out. It will not obey me.

I reach inside myself and call on the Symbol of Iron. It is distant now. Faded and muted compared to the bright light that it was only a moment ago. But even so, we are bound, and so it must come.

I feel its icy calm settle over me, which banishes my panic and clears my head. If I am to survive this, I must use my brain. Fear and panic will kill me as sure as the absence of oxygen in my lungs. What good is knowledge if I can't use it unless I am comfortable? Wasn't that the reason Old Vellum made us answer congruency questions while riding waves?

The collar is trying to kill me.

It was made to stop us from becoming another *ferrum domini*—to prevent Ironbound from Ascending past *cuprum* to *argent*, from Copper to Silver. My lungs are burning, but the answer comes to me in an instant.

Of course.

How do you grow a *Cor* Heart? The same way you grow any other muscle. You feed it and exercise it. This is a room of pure Iron, designed to force legionnaires to only be able to bind to the Symbol that the legions wanted. But that also means it is rich in essence.

I gorged myself and have somehow grown too close to Ascending. Part of me doesn't believe that could be possible. Surely it is not that simple to advance to Silver. There are men and women in Segesta who never attained anything above *cuprum* in their whole lives. My own father is—was—one of them. How is it possible that I am ready to advance so soon? And yet, despite my doubts, I know this must be it.

If my Heart is too full, then logic would expect that the collar will release me if I dispose of some of the essence I have collected. I force my eyes to close, even as I feel my consciousness begin to fade. I do not panic. The rigid strength of Iron keeps me from being tossed around in the storm of my own fear.

I slap my right palm down on the metal floor and explore the box that I'm in. Like everything else, the door is made of iron connected to the walls by its iron hinges. I grit my teeth and try to command it to open. It rattles but doesn't move more than a few hairs.

Despite the door's refusal to obey me, I know I'm on the right course. It's not solid like the rest of my prison. I can feel the metallic pins sitting in the hinges. There are two of them: one at the top and one at the bottom. They're loose, only hanging on by a thread. This must be the next part of the test.

The room is still dark, but I'm sure the edges of my vision are going black. I'm almost out of time. With the last of my willpower, I command them to come free. I feel them wiggle in response to my order. They are like children, unsure if they're supposed to obey their older cousin. Gritting my teeth, I clench my hands into fists and *demand* that they do as they are told.

Like two missiles shot out of a ballista, the pins fire into the air, and when they break contact with the iron that I am touching, they vanish from my awareness, now out of my reach. As the hinges obey me, I feel a trickle of something flow out of me. It's minor, almost nothing, but my *Cor* Heart feels a little less full.

Instantly, the collar releases its grip on my neck, and I collapse to the floor, gasping for sweet, sweet air as my hold on my Symbol fades. Without Iron's sterile calm cloaking me, I feel the full pain of my burning lungs as I struggle to fill them.

I'm still panting as the door to my cell topples backward, falling like a tree. It slams into the ground with a heavy thud, and bright light pours in from the fires of the cave. I have just enough time to feel a sense of fear before legionnaires fill the door.

They're shouting, and my deprived brain struggles to understand what they're saying. Two of them grab me by the shoulders and drag me out of my cell. Numbly, I try to struggle, but I'm still weak.

They take me through the cave, suspending me between them like a sack of potatoes. My legs bounce on the paved floor of the cave as we go. In the distance, I see a knot of men waiting for us. Durus and the officers of the Twelfth Legion are among them. The soldiers dragging me don't stop shouting, and by the time they drop me off in front of Tribune Gaius and the magister, I realize they're cheering. I hope that's a good sign and not one that I'm about to be fed to the lions.

"First legionnaire ready for inspection, *Dominus*," the one on my right says, stepping back and saluting. I'm on my knees, still a little dazed, but I copy the salute as best I can.

The tribune eyes me with his intense stare, face impassive. He's surprised to see me, I think. Not displeased—he doesn't strike me as a man who feels pleasure or displeasure easily. He's merely surprised.

The old magister steps in front of Gaius without a word. Here in his domain, he seems to outrank even the tribune of an entire cohort. The white-haired man crouches down to peer at me. He too is unabashedly surprised to see me. He takes in my shortness of breath, and slowly, he reaches out and touches the collar running around my neck. There must be some bruise forming because his eyes widen and he steps back, eyeing me with a new interest.

He grabs my wrist and holds up my arm so he can inspect my *Cor* veins. My heart sinks as I see the white *rasa* lines among my Copper ones. Even soaking in the pure room of Iron essence wasn't enough to correct the flaw in my binding. Frowns grow on the officers standing behind him as they see what he is looking at. I'm still *immundus*, imperfect.

A forgotten fear curls in my chest as I realize that even though I escaped the cell, I may still fail. I'm not sure what happens to someone who fails to qualify for the legions after taking the Empress's Heart. Surely I would be assigned to some logistical division, put to work in a place where I wouldn't be a liability. *But the legions always need more relics.*

"Well?" Gaius demands after a few moments, his attention on the magister and not on me.

"He escaped on his own?" the old man asks the two soldiers who brought me to them.

"Begging your pardon, *Dominus*—he blew the door completely off." The man to my right chuckles. "Never seen anything like it." The stares from the officers are different this time, harder in some way.

"Is that not what you're supposed to do?" I ask, my voice still a little reedy.

"Most people find it easier to just tell the latch to open," the magister replies dryly, rising to his full height and dusting off his hands on his dirty toga as if I am somehow less clean. Oh. Now that he mentioned it, that does sound easier.

"Magister?" Gaius asks again. Part of me marvels at his restraint. There are few men in the empire that outrank Gaius, even if he is of the lowest legion. But once more, he shows deference to the man who makes us weapons.

"He passed the test." The magister shrugs, turning away from me as if bored. "I pronounce him worthy to bear Her mark." Something flows out of the rest of the men. Whatever decision needed to be made has been made. For some, it is already forgotten. But from the heavy gaze of a few, I know not all feel this way.

"You will take the Iron Oath," the tribune demands, standing above me. I swallow but nod in agreement. I know the words. They're taught to us when we're children. When I learned them, I thought it was so I could honor the sacrifice made by others. Not the one I was being forced to make.

A black-robed priest steps forward, extending the same black spear toward me. "Take the spear of the war god, lad," she whispers, staring past me with her empty eyes. I swallow, reaching out with my right hand to grasp it just behind the point. She nods encouragingly, face alight with rapture that I do not feel.

"I swear on the Bones of Mars to serve the People, the Senate, and the Empress," I say. "I will be the *scutum* and *gladius* of the empire so that her people may know peace. I will never desert my post, nor betray my fellow legionnaires."

Gaius nods, satisfied. "You are born into the Iron Legions. We do not bend. We do not break. On our strength is built the foundation of the empire. Rise, Legionnaire, and join the ranks of the unbroken." Relief floods through me as I stagger to my feet. I've survived this test. I'm one step closer to my revenge on Atticus. I inhale deeply, grateful to have my breath back.

"Mark him," he orders, his voice cold. Immediately, the soldier on my right buries his fist in my stomach.

"*Oof*," I gasp, sending all my air flying out once more.

They beat me again. I've learned some new tricks in the hours since my last one. I'm still full of essence, so Iron strength flows into me at my command, and I let its numbness fade the pain of their blows. I turn, catching the hook of the guy to my right, but his partner tackles me from behind.

We crash to the stony ground, and even in my metal shroud, I feel my entire body shudder from the impact. Quick as a pair of serpents, the two soldiers are on top of me. One grabs my arms, the other my legs. I struggle like a newborn calf, but it's no use—they hold me fast.

Another legionnaire appears above us and peers down at me. He's short for a soldier and missing an eye; it's covered by a black eyepatch. He wears an evil grin as he stares down at me like some puny god. For a moment, my Iron calm fades, and I worry that they're about to kill me anyway, but then he holds up a long metal pole.

I know what this is.

"Get his shirt off," he shouts to one of the men holding me down. Fear makes me stronger, but it's no matter. These are the Iron Legions, and there are always more soldiers. In the end, four men hold me down, one on each limb. There's a grim sense of completion in their motions.

After all, they've all had this done to them too.

My shirt is ripped off me, and as I lie on my back, the first soldier reappears. The brand in his hand is glowing red hot, and my calm shatters as he lowers it to my chest. On my left breast, above my heart, he places the mark of the legions, claiming my body for the service of the Empress.

I scream in pain as the brand sears my flesh. It's so hot that it burns cold. The nerves in my chest don't know how to process the feeling as my skin melts and scar tissue forms. My partnership with my Symbol is not strong enough to help me with this. My whole world is on fire.

They mark me in the ancient way, when they used numerals instead of numbers. After the first, they hold me down so Eyepatch can get the other brand to give me two more. The air stinks of burning meat and hot metal.

X.

I.

I.

Those bastards in the First, Fifth, and Tenth Legions have it easy. When it's done, they release me, like cowherds letting the calf get back to its feet. Every time I move my left arm, the skin gets pulled, and I want to scream. I manage to only let out a few whimpers as I rise. Dark chuckles echo around me as they watch me stare at the mark that's been branded into my chest.

Gaius and the other officers are watching, their faces stoic. On instinct, I snap to attention, standing stiffly, bare-chested and burnt under their heavy gazes. After a moment, the tribune salutes me, and I grit my teeth before returning it.

My left fist slams into the spot right above my heart, and it takes every ounce of self-control I possess not to scream. Over Gaius's shoulder, Durus gives me a slight nod of approval. I may have made a poor first impression, but my stubbornness is not going unnoticed.

"Welcome to the legions, lad." Eyepatch claps me on the shoulder with his right hand. The long pole of the "*I*" brand is thrown over his shoulder like a fishing rod. He grins at the confused expression on my face. "You're one of us now."

Still too stunned to speak, I merely nod and accept his welcome, twisted as it is. There's a commotion behind me as more soldiers approach, whooping and hollering as they drag another recruit for inspection. My heart skips a beat when they drop the boy in front of the magister for inspection.

I may have been first, but my friend is right behind me. The second legionnaire to be accepted to the Twelfth Legion is Marcus. The big boy looks a little disoriented, but not like he was almost choked to death. Thick *cuprum* veins run through his forearms as he kneels before the officers. Already, the iron collar circles his neck like a serpent.

His eyes are wild, and for the first time in a week, we make eye contact. He gives me a look that says, "*Can you believe this?*" and I realize that for a moment all is forgotten. He may not be a Praetorian, but for a boy who has always dreamed of being Ironbound, his experience is at least partially a dream come true.

I grin and give him a thumbs-up, and a ghost of a smile quirks at the corner of his mouth in response. Despite the pain in my chest, things suddenly feel a little better. Something between us has changed now that we have made it through the Iron Pits. Our friendship might be damaged, but now we are something more.

"How did he escape?" the magister asks the soldiers who brought him.

"Undid the latch with his Heart. Watched it meself," the soldier reports.

"Very well, mark him," the old man replies, turning away. He's far less interested in Marcus's process than mine. Marcus takes the oath, and Tribune Gaius nods his acceptance. The soldiers turn with gleeful delight to brand their new fellow.

Marcus knows what's coming. The big boy holds out a hand to stall them. To my surprise, they pause. Whether that's because they're so caught off guard by his actions or because he's bigger than most of them, I'm not sure. He calmly strips off his tunic as he rises to his feet. The orange veins of his Copper Heart shine brightly against his dark skin. There's a beatific expression on his face. He looks like a groom preparing for his wedding day.

Shirtless, he steps toward an open spot of the floor and lowers himself to the ground, lying on his back as mild as a lamb. The legionnaires all exchange disbelieving glances. None of them have ever seen anything like this. In the background, the officers watch with a similar level of surprise. Maybe in the First the young Praetorians come with as much eagerness, but in the Twelfth? Men only come here to die.

Eyepatch returns with his glowing brand, but this time, his face is solemn. Even with his one eye, he can sense that this is a transcendent experience. Our gods might be dead, but this feels like something bigger than us.

The short man looks up and gestures for me to join him. "Come, lad," he calls, his tone serious. "You were the first of your brothers to be Ironbound, so it is your duty to baptize them in the fire, *Primus*."

Startled, I move to stand next to Eyepatch before it even occurs to me to protest. The iron rod is already in my hand, and I feel it with my Symbol as I hold it. The "*X*" at the end glows a cherry red.

Primus.

It feels like another life where I wanted to be *Primus*. It was certainly a different place, deep in the halls of a sterile *collegium*, not buried in some forgotten temple to the war gods. But still, it feels good. I am the first, the best. All others who emerge from the Pits do so in my footsteps.

A dormant coal catches fire in the cold void of my chest as ambition flares. It doesn't banish the cold that's lived inside me since my family died, but it warms my living corpse. I reach for it, like a sailor at the beacon of a lighthouse in a storm. It stabilizes me—guides me.

I look up from the brand to my friend. Marcus meets my eyes. I see the same fire burning behind his pupils that I feel in me. He nods once, telling me to get on with it.

I brand him with the mark of the legions. He doesn't even grunt as it sears his flesh.

CHAPTER 20

In the end, I sear a hundred and fifteen new recruits in the fire of the Twelfth Legion. Felix was third. All the boys from our *collegium* were in the top twenty. Fourteen doors of the Iron Pits do not open. I ask Unus, the one-eyed soldier who branded me, how long the magister and priests will keep them closed.

"As long as they have to," he replies grimly. I understand. I see the world with new eyes. Now that I have seen death, I see it everywhere. It's been here the whole time; I was just blind to it. Before a blacksmith makes a blade, he must purify the metal. Not all iron makes it to the forge. It is the same in the legions.

By being the first out of the pits, I've become something I never thought I would be. *Primus*. In the elite legions, it is not uncommon for someone to go through the ritual already bound to Iron. In the Twelfth, it is an anomaly. My advantage practically guaranteed that I would be the first one out.

When no more legionnaires emerge for a long time, we march back out of the cave and to our district of Agogia. *Sol* is just beginning to crest the horizon, and the sky blazes with its fire as we emerge from the bowels of the earth.

"A good omen!" Unus shouts, clapping me on the shoulder with wild abandon. I don't share his excitement. To me, it seems more like a warning. Everywhere I go, it seems, fire follows. Segesta burned, my family burned, and now the sky burns. Some of the others cheer, but I am silent.

As we enter the Twelfth's Srea, I am surprised that we are dismissed to our barracks. "One last break," Durus treats us with a small smile. "I know the process of being Ironbound is not gentle, lads. Let it settle today. Tomorrow, we start forging." Despite his soft expression, that sounds like a threat.

Presented with the first free day that I have had since my parents died, I wander through the Twelfth's Sector, unsure what to do with myself. Some go back to sleep, but rest evades me. The grief that hovers just over my shoulder threatens to break free of its dam and flood everywhere. I ignore it, electing to keep myself busy so I don't think too much.

Felix follows me, a loyal shadow. I cannot tell if he enjoys my company or if he worries about me. Either way, I am grateful for the tall boy's presence. I am less likely to cry in front of him. We are instructed not to leave our slice of the Agogian circle, but there are no rules against watching at the exit. I've never been in a city this size; the sheer volume of people threatens to overwhelm me.

But at the same time, I find solace in seeing the men march by. I am part of this organism now. The brand on my chest burns every time I move my arm, reminding me of my new place. I never wanted to be a soldier, but the Iron Legions have been the sword and shield of the empire for hundreds of years. Now that I am here, I can't help but feel the tug of belonging to such a mighty and noble tradition. Even as a member of the lowest legion.

"Look at their uniforms." Felix chuckles as a century from the Fifth marches by. Their tunics are the same cut as the ones our quadrant wears, but they are a deep blue instead of red like our legion.

"Fourth, Fifth, and Sixth are the naval Legions," I reply quietly, remembering a lesson from Marcus what feels like a lifetime ago. "Praetorians are purple; Second and Third Legions wear black."

"Then the blue boys make up the Second Quadrant."

"Seventh, Eighth, and Ninth are white."

"That's right. Flatunus was dressed in white. I thought that was just because he was on recruit duty. Why is the Third Quadrant white?"

"To blend in with the snow, I think."

"Ah, of course, the *Northern* Legions. How fancy. Didn't Marcus say that was what his grandfather was in?"

"Seventh, I think."

"Where is the big guy anyway?" Felix glances over his shoulder as if Marcus will suddenly appear.

"Not sure," I reply glumly. Since we left the forge, Marcus has gone back to ignoring me. The absence of my friend feels like a fresh wound next to everything else. I had hoped after I branded him with the *XII* of the Twelfth that things between us would be fixed. Now my crushed hope threatens to destroy me.

"Ah, well, it's up to you to explain to me why we're stuck wearing red uniforms, then," Felix replies, his voice full of forced cheer.

"Marcus told me is because it's the bottom legions that bleed."

"Lovely." Felix's voice is as sour as I feel. Atticus's intent could not be clearer than if it was written on our foreheads.

For a while, we watch as the crowds make their way past our sector in silence. There are so many people! Not just legionnaires, but teamsters, heartsmiths, *medici*, and magisters stream by in a never-ending parade. The reach of the Iron Legions is massive and stretches across the entire Empire. Agogia is a training city—many of the legions' cohorts are in the field, but still, I am in awe of the Empress's might. What enemy could ever withstand the Iron Legions? After getting a taste of what my *Cor* Heart can do this morning, I cannot imagine that such a power exists.

"Hungry?" my faithful friend asks after hours have gone by. *Sol* has begun its evening descent, kissing the tip of the mountains in the distance of the desert. Felix's voice pulls me out of my daze, and I turn to look at him.

I haven't eaten since before we went down into the cave. My stomach rumbles, and I realize that I'm starving. I nod, and together we rise from where we sit to head to the mess hall. Long shadows begin to dance through the sector as the light falls behind the massive walls of the Iron City.

Veteran legionnaires move throughout the cohort's area, ignoring us recruits with a practiced air. We are lumpy iron that has not yet been forged into a sword. We are not worth their notice.

"If it isn't our fancy new *Primus*," a voice sneers from one of the pools of shadow. I turn, surprised at being addressed. A pair of recruits I recognize as friends of Anas glare at Felix and me from the wall they lean on, passing a bottle between the two of them. I can smell the strong scent of lunashine from where I stand. How they already managed to find a supply is a mystery to me.

"I'm sorry?" I ask, confused by their hostility.

"Lextus, did the patrician just address me?" the shorter one with black teeth asks.

"It sure seems like he did, Ramus," the bigger one agrees slowly. A bad feeling creeps down my spine as I glance around the mostly empty alley that we are in. There are no officers within my line of sight. I glance at Ramus's hands and grimace as I spy the *M* branded there, for *Murderus*.

"We don't want any trouble," Felix cuts in, stepping up to tower over the two former *captivi*.

"Well, that's too bad," Lextus remarks grimly, smashing the bottle against the wall, shattering it into a jagged edge. "This is the Twelfth Legion. There's only trouble here." The two men stalk toward us, shoulders hunched for violence.

I freeze, unable to look away from the murderer brand that is burned into the back of Ramus's hand. Lextus's shows an *R* for a different horrific crime. I'm terrified, but also disgusted. I hate being here with these thugs and being associated with them. Tentatively, I reach for the Iron Symbol, letting it sweep over me, filling me with its calm. I have no metal, but my reserve still teems with essence I took from the forge. It won't help me fight, but it keeps me from running in fear.

Lextus lunges at me, wielding the jagged bottle like a knife. He stabs at my throat, but he's drunk and hilariously slow. I duck to the side and jab at his wrist, punching it as hard as I can. The taller *captivus* hisses in pain, dropping the weapon, which shatters on the ground.

"Now you did it," Ramus remarks, shoving past his friend. "That was our last bottle."

"But he already broke it—" I protest, but the murderer leaps at me, fists swinging wildly. He's not as inebriated as his taller friend, or at least he's able to hold his drink better. Lextus tries to join in, but Felix jumps on him, holding him back.

"Here we go." Felix sighs mournfully as if this is my fault.

The four of us bounce around the narrow alley, grunting as we kick and punch. I've never been in a fight like this before. I threw a few punches as a child, but this is something far more vicious. There's a difference between the blows that *discipuli* fighting over hurt feelings throw and hardened criminals who have been sentenced to the legions.

The sound of our fight echoes through the quarter. I punch Ramus in the chest, forgetting about our fresh brands. He screams in pain and tries to grab my arm to bite it. I wrench my wrist free of his grip, not eager to add another set of teeth scars next to the wolf marks.

"What's going on here?" a voice demands, and I turn, letting out a groan of annoyance when I see two more former *captivi* whose names I don't know. They're staring at our fight with confused expressions, unsure if they should join in. Their expressions narrow when they see that it is Felix and me.

"Dacchus, jump 'em!" Lextus slurs, and that's the only encouragement they need. They wade in, splitting up to reinforce both of their comrades.

"Surely you don't need help to kick two patricians' asses," I protest weakly as they join in.

"Technically, I'm a plebeian," Felix points out, ducking under a blow from drunk Lextus.

"But you went to *collegium*."

"Oh, *now* I belong," he replies sarcastically.

"I never—" My protest is cut off as I take a blow to the stomach, forcing out my air. I slam into the side of one of the command buildings, holding my stomach and wincing as my own brand twinges in pain. One of the new brutes jumps on me, pinning me against the wall, while the other two do the same to Felix.

"Come on, patricians, why aren't you smiling?" Lextus pauses to pick up a jagged piece of glass off the ground. "Let's see if we can make sure you feel properly welcome." Fear spikes in me, too strong for my Iron Symbol to drown out.

The *captivus* leers at me as he takes a stumbling step toward me, brandishing the weapon toward my face. "I'm gonna give you a new smile," he promises, licking his lips. Madness burns in his eyes, but his hands do not shake. I struggle, trying to break free of the man who holds me against the wall, but I can't get my arms free.

"I'll give you something to smile about!" screams a familiar voice as someone slams into Lextus from the side. A thrill runs through me as Marcus sends the drunk flying. Before anyone can react, he turns to the man holding me in place and drills two punches into the *captivus's* exposed stomach. My captor crumples, and I break free, gladly kneeing the man in the face as he collapses.

I turn to thank my friend, but he's already moving, tackling one of the men who challenges Felix. They go down in a pile of limbs, but before I can blink, Marcus is back on his feet.

"Don't worry, reinforcements are here!" a cheerful voice calls out, and I turn in time to see Petrus and red-headed Rufus charge into the alley in Marcus's wake. The five of us pummel the thugs as they flee. When they are gone, I lean against the wall, inhaling deeply, trying to get my breath back.

"Titus protect us, we're really in the Twelfth now, aren't we?" Petrus remarks. Nothing ever seems to truly faze him. He blows on a skinned knuckle, eyeing it skeptically in the fading light.

"So it would seem," Marcus grunts. He walks away, not sparing me a second glance. My heart breaks at his cold demeanor. The other three boys turn to look at me, their expressions full of exasperation.

"What?" I hiss at them, gesturing at the retreating boy.

"Just go." Felix sighs. "You have to talk to him." I eye Marcus's broad back with a glare, hurt and unwilling to compromise, but the pressure from the other survivors builds up, and finally I can't resist any longer.

"Fine," I snap, chasing after my oldest friend, "but this is not going to work."

Marcus has made it to the main quad of the cohort's section. He doesn't turn as I chase after him, even though I make enough noise that he has to know I'm behind him. "Hey, idiot," I yell at him, which finally stops him in his tracks. He freezes but doesn't turn, just looms large and brooding.

"I'm sorry!" I scream at his back, unable to think of what else to say. "I'm sorry that you're here. I'm sorry that your family is dead. But mine is too. I didn't want to be here. I didn't want to take your Heart. But we are here. This is our life now. You're either going to have to get over it and forgive me or wait 'til we die, because it won't be long! If we don't get killed by our fellow soldiers, I'm sure wherever they're sending us will do the trick."

Marcus is quiet for so long that I think he is going to ignore me and walk away. My anger spikes, fueled by the battle rage that's still fading from our skirmish in the alley. For a white-hot moment, I consider hitting him. Maybe that would at least get him to make eye contact with me for more than a second.

At last, he turns, looking at me over his shoulder. His dark features hide his expression in the low light, but his voice is soft and contrite. "I know," he admits. "I'm working on it." Then he walks away, and I let him go, not sure if we're still friends.

CHAPTER 21

Part of me hopes the next morning that Lextus and the other drunkards will be so hungover, they'll get punished by the officers. But my hopes are dashed as Durus grabs us before breakfast.

"Line up!" he roars. His decurions echo his call, running up and down the line, screaming at us until we stretch down the length of the field two deep. I spy my attackers in line. Two of them sport black eyes, but they are all upright, which is good enough for the Twelfth.

The Iron Pits were not the forge, merely the furnace. It is not enough to heat us to the proper temperature. Now we must be beaten into shape. Durus strides up and down the line, eyeing us with a baleful eye.

"You lot are reinforcements," he growls, striding up and down the field, making sure that we are all paying attention. "You are now legionnaires under the command of Tribune Gaius Marius, in the Eighth Cohort of the Twelfth Legion. That makes me your centurion and First Spear, understood?

"Yes, *Dominus!*" we answer raggedly.

The officer frowns but lets it pass. I risk a glance over my shoulder at the mass of men standing around me. A legion is made up of ten cohorts. Each cohort is made up of roughly five centuries, amounting to just over five hundred men. I know from firsthand experience that we had more than one hundred of us as recruits, which means we would either eventually be broken up or they expect more of us to die.

"The officers and I will build your formation. Do not forget your place." Durus's voice hardens as he scans us, the threat more than implied by his tone. At once, they begin dragging newly minted legionnaires out onto the field. Bit by bit, they arrange us into five columns.

Clintus is the front of the leftmost column. Marcus and Felix are placed on either side of the center to him. Anas, my favorite person, is on the right. They don't fill the center spot as they pull more soldiers out of the line-up and place them in the formation.

A thrill runs through my gut as the officers pass over me time and time again. It can be no coincidence that they have not filled the center and are ignoring me. I was the first one out of the Pits. I branded each and every one of my new brothers. They are saving that place for the *Primus*.

My suspicion is confirmed when I am the last soldier standing along the field. The center spot at the front of the column is still empty. My heart races as Durus and the decurions approach me. None of them are smiling. I swallow and raise my chin to meet the officer's gaze calmly.

I am a soldier now. I cannot show fear.

"Come on, *Primus*," Durus growls as he draws abreast of me. "Let's see if you're worthy of your shield." The officers surround me as I stride to the front. I can feel the eyes of a hundred and fifteen of my century mates on the back of my neck as I walk.

I channel the lessons I learned in the *collegium*, in the *Labyrinthus*. I ignore them and take my place. I earned this. I did not ask for it, but I paid for it. The price was not worth it. I would trade it all in to have my family live again. But this is all I have, so I'm going to take what is mine.

At the centurion's direction, I step between Marcus and Felix and stand at attention. The officers walk up and down the line, shouting at soldiers who are not in the right places or are not standing as sharply as they ought.

"Right!" Durus shouts after they're satisfied. His voice carries through the entire district as if he is channeling it somehow, but it is just his own power. I know of no way Iron could increase his volume. Even my congruency skills see no way to make that happen.

"Memorize your position, boys. For the next week, when your officers command you to fall in, you will form this line. Each of you will be in the exact same spot, standing next to the exact same men. When I decide it has been too long, if you are out of place, you will be whipped. The last man in place will be whipped. Am I understood?"

"Yes, *Dominus*," we reply, more in unison this time.

"Good." He nods sharply. "Congratulations. You're all legionnaires now. In the cities, when the fancy patricians and palatines get gifted their *Cor* Hearts, their parents throw them a party. We don't do that here." The century chuckles. Somehow, we already feel different from civilians.

"The best I can offer you is a double portion of rations before a full day of training." We chuckle again. Even though it's not a joke, it feels like one. "Fall out." He dismisses us with a wave. "Let's get you some grub." The line dissolves, and we begin to make our way toward the mess hall.

"Well, that's a relief," Marcus mutters to Felix and me as we walk. I glance at him in surprise but keep my mouth shut. He feels like a nervous dog. I worry that if I react too strongly to his overture, he will flee. But after the fight last night, I will gladly accept his olive branch.

"What is?"

"I thought that was going to turn into something more intense," the big boy replies. His dark eyes are narrowed as we walk, like he's waiting for something.

"It does seem like they're letting us off easy," Felix muses, glancing over his shoulder at where we left the officers. I follow his gaze and see them all watching us with an air of anticipation.

"Dead gods." I sigh tiredly. I know where this is going. We may be in the legions now, but Vellum and the magisters love their surprise quizzes just the same.

"Fall in!" Durus screams in his best parade voice.

"Fall in! Fall in!" the decurions echo like parrots, storming toward us. Even prepared for the test, I find myself flustered. Like a school of fish, our century had mixed and mingled as we headed toward the mess. There is no order; the officers scream, and we panic, which is exactly what they want.

A legionnaire bounces off me as he shoves his way toward the middle of the pack. I stagger to the side as another passes me, heading to the rear. Gritting my teeth, I follow in Marcus's wake as the big man carves us a path to the front.

I'm *Primus*—I can't be last. I have to set an example for the men. Durus told me to show that I am worthy, and I have no intention of letting him or the rest of my century down on our first challenge. The column begins to form, crooked and awkward, as the rest of the hundred and fifteen soldiers find their spots.

Men call each other's names and organize themselves while the officers rage. I'm caught in a maelstrom of flesh as we wriggle into our places. It's overwhelming, and I feel like I'm drowning. At last, Marcus punches out the top of the column, and he and Felix take their places on either side of my spot with haste.

Straightening, I step into formation and stand at attention, staring straight forward. I feel the eyes of every officer on me, judging me for being toward the end of my list. I resist the urge to grimace as I resolve to be faster next time. I must set a good example.

A flash of dry amusement runs through me. I never wanted to be a soldier, but all my life, I dreamt of being a *Primus*. It seems that I am easy to bribe. Who would have thought that I would be so quick to fall in line? If only Vellum could see me now.

"That's enough!" Durus bellows, and the line is still. Men stop shifting and fall into a tense stiffness. The officers prowl up and down the column, inspecting each soldier to make sure they are in the right spot. How they know who should be where is beyond me.

The centurion stomps up to the front of the line and eyes me with a displeased look. I return his glare, unsure what he's upset about. It seems like everyone is in their place, which is impressive for the first time we've done this. I guess everyone took his threats seriously.

"Centurion Murex, who was the last man in line?" the First Spear calls, not looking away from me. A pit opens up in my stomach as I remember that no matter what, someone is being punished.

"A moment, *Dominus*," Murex exclaims from the back of the line, where he confers with two of the other officers. Durus's glare deepens, and I realize he's waiting to see if I'm going to do something. My mind races as I try to understand. I have barely been *Primus* for a day, but already it has become the cornerstone of my sanity. I cannot give it up.

The answer comes to me in a flash.

When I was younger, one of our servants ran over a boy with a wagon. It wasn't his fault—the child darted out into the street without looking. He wasn't seriously injured, just a broken arm, but he was a patrician, and our driver was a plebeian. The punishment for such a crime against his betters was an astronomical fine, some fifty *denarii*. My father paid the fine and rescued our servant from debtor's jail. When I asked him why, he only smiled softly and told me, "That is the price of leadership." When I was a child, I did not understand. Today, I think I finally do.

Proving my worth as *Primus* isn't about being first. It's about leading. This century is made up of oil and water, patricians and plebeians. We have been forced together, but we do not mix. Someone has to bridge the gap, and that lucky bastard is me.

For a moment, I hesitate, dreading weathering the displeasure of Durus and the officers. I did not mean to put myself in this position. I didn't want to be responsible for the men behind me. I was just doing my best, and now I must suffer for it. But my father would if he were in my place, and that knowledge takes the step for me. I see something glimmer in the centurion's face as he sees me move.

I stride out of line and stand at attention two paces in front of the rest of the column. I hear a dozen gasps of surprise behind me as the soldiers in the front row realize that I've volunteered.

"What are you *doing?*" Marcus hisses behind me. I ignore him and keep my gaze trained on the empty air straight ahead of me as I salute Durus.

"Why are you out of line, *Primus?*" the centurion demands, striding toward me. His baton whirls in his grip as he stares at me. My heart is racing. I can hear the pounding of its drum in my ears as the blood sings in my veins.

"I was the last to find my place, *Dominus*," I reply in a crisp, emotionless tone. Without looking, I take two steps backward and resume my place at the front of the column. "I will do better next time, *Dominus.*"

"Murex, what did we say would happen to the last man to find his place in line?" Durus calls over the line to where his decurions wait. There are murmurs behind me as the soldiers understand where this is going. I'm not surprised. I knew the game already.

"Whipping, *Dominus*," comes the immediate reply.

"A whipping," Durus agrees calmly. "Let's get to it, then. Forward march!" Awkwardly, we begin to troop forward as we learned to on the way to Agogia. The column is silent, and I can feel their nerves as they stare at my back.

I know some of them don't understand. Many of the men pulled into the Twelfth are *captivi*, straight from prisons around the empire. Many of them probably grew up starving in the streets, doing whatever it took to survive. What killer or thief would ever do this?

Minerva's Bones, I barely understand it myself. I feel the shade of my father riding on my shoulder, watching over me. I'm merely following in the footsteps of what I was shown. The others, who attended a *collegium* and competed for a *Cor* Heart, have spent their lives dreaming of being *Primus* too, but the one in school was not a leader, just a winner. There's a difference between the two, I think.

In the center of the Twelfth Sector is a wide, cobbled square where men can be assembled. At the front is a raised dais for the officers to address the troops or the soldiers to watch punishment be doled out. A pair of poles stand in the center, each with a dangling cuff for a man's wrist.

My smug satisfaction at understanding my role deflates as I eye the well-worn whipping posts. Maybe being *Secundus* would be better. Durus marches the column through the square, perpendicular to the stage, before halting us and ordering us to turn to our right so that the century stands five men deep the length of the platform.

"*Primus!*" he barks, striding toward the platform with the other officers. I hesitate for only a second before stepping out of line and following after him. It is too late to let fear slow me down. If I was going to let it do that, I should never have gotten out of line.

The cobbles click under my boots, but the boards echo hollowly under each footstep. None of them are loud enough to drown out the pounding of my heart. I'm terrified, but I keep my head held high. I have to play the part in front of my peers. We may be newly made men, but one day, we will fight together. Cowardice will be remembered more than foolishness.

This is nothing, I tell myself. I have been stabbed. I have seen my family and friends murdered in cold blood. What can be done to me by a whip that comes close to what I have already endured? Something hardens in my heart, and I feel the corner of my mouth tug in a smile. There is nothing for me to fear here.

I see a glimmer of the strength that lurks underneath my pain. Felix was right.

I strip off my tunic at Durus's command and step between the whipping posts. The day-old brand on my chest stings as I lift my arms too high. I kneel with my back to the century, and two decurions fasten my wrists into the shackles. They're made of leather, not iron.

I should be panicking, but I'm already deep in the tranquil presence of my Iron Symbol. It fills me with strength, and I cling to it. The hurt of my burn fades and gives me a clear mind. Durus steps next to me and leans down to murmur in my ear.

"You're one of a few that's learned to hold Iron to dull the pain, boy. Use it." I glance at him, and he must see it in my eyes. The stone face of an angry executioner cracks slightly as his smile quirks at the corner. I'm already ahead of him.

He holds a whip in his hands, a thick, knotted thing. It's not designed to rip or tear flesh. It's a blunt object instead of a cutting razor. I suppose that makes sense. They're going to expect me to be able to keep training. I can't do that if my back is a ruin.

"For being the last man to get into formation, the punishment is five lashes," I hear him announce to the assembled men behind me. This show is for them, not me. Of all the soldiers, I am the one who will be hurt the least by this, thanks to my head-start with Iron.

"Centurion Murex, five lashes as you please," Durus calls to his right hand.

"Aye, *Dominus*," the officer replies smoothly. Even deep in the cold logic of Iron, I feel my heart skip a beat in anticipation. I force myself to relax. This isn't a real punishment, purely theater. I'm sure the decurion will take it easy on me—

My world shatters, and my hold on the Symbol slips out of my mental fingers as the stroke lands on my back. Fire, as hot as the one that burned my chest, runs down the length of my spine. A ragged scream comes out of my lips as the shock fades.

"One," Murex calls calmly. I only barely manage to summon my Symbol again before the second blow lands. This time, I'm ready. My control slips, but I don't lose it completely. It still hurts, but more distantly, as if my skin is numb.

"Two." I'm already hysterical with pain. Whatever strength I thought I had found isn't a physical one. Being a leader is not worth it! Why would anyone ever choose to do this? My back arches as another blow slams into it.

"Three." Another scream is ripped from me as my tenuous grasp on Iron flickers. Raw, hot agony surges through me as the stripes on my back all radiate pain. Again, the whip slaps into me.

"Four." My vision fades around the edges as my torture builds. I'd rather be branded again than suffer this.

The final blow is the heaviest of them all. I might have been expected to take this on behalf of the men, but the officers wanted everyone to know that they were serious. "Five."

I list forward, letting the manacles hold me up. I still have my grip on Iron, but it's not strong enough to keep all the pain at bay. Rough hands seize my wrists and pull me to my feet. I let out another moan of pain as the flesh over my back stretches. I stagger, but the decurions on either side of me hold me up.

"Stand up, boy. If you want them to respect you, stand." Durus's voice is low, just for me. Somehow it penetrates through the iron and pain. I grit my teeth and raise my head, making eye contact with the hundred and fifteen brand-new legionnaires looking at me.

Their faces range from disgusted to awed. The harder cases can't believe I was stupid enough to get myself whipped. Others are shocked that I'm standing on my own two feet. The cluster of boys from Segesta are staring at me like I am a stranger. They haven't learned about the strength their Hearts give them yet.

The only thing I've learned is that I never want to be whipped again.

CHAPTER 22

None of Centurion Murex's blows broke the skin, for which I am more than grateful. But still, my back is raw. I stumble my way through a day of marching, lost in a fugue of pain. Every step jostles the wounds on my front and back, keeping me suspended in a state of misery. Tonight, I will sleep on my side. My back and chest are both far too tender for me to put any weight on them.

But even as I am kicking myself for getting whipped for no reason, my actions begin to show the first sprouts from seeds I planted. A skinny—too skinny—soldier approaches my bunk as I'm getting ready for bed. He's fidgety and keeps looking at the floor. A *T* is burnt into the back of both of his hands, marking him as a thief.

"You're Castor, right?" he asks softly, standing a few feet to the side as I try to remove my sweat-encrusted tunic without screaming. It's not going well, but I don't want to ruin my new reputation for being tough by asking someone to help me take my shirt off.

"I am." I turn to face him, ready for whatever new abuse one of my fellow legionnaires has come to bring to me. I glance at Felix watching from the other side of our bunk, but I shake my head slightly, stopping him from inserting himself. "Who are you?"

"Most people call me Macer."

"What can I do for you, Macer?" The boy hesitates, flustered. "I just wanted to say thanks," he mumbles after a moment.

"You were the last one to get in place?" I ask, understanding the source of his hesitation.

"I think so," he mumbles, still not looking at me. He's waiting for me to blow up on him, I realize. A lot of the men in this room would. An eye for an eye is the way of life that he's used to.

I don't get angry. I'm not entirely sure what's happening. I feel like I'm sliding down a path that's been chosen for me. I should be angry with this beanpole. Because of him, I am in an agony like I have never known. Instead, I smile thinly and clap him on the shoulder.

"Do me a favor and try to be a little quicker next time?" I ask. The expression of wonder on his face is like the rising dawn. I hate it because it feels like something I did not choose.

"Yes, *Dominus!*" He salutes.

"I don't think you're supposed to do that," I mumble as he scampers away, but on the inside, I'm equally blown away. It can't be that easy, can it? I glance around the room, but no one seems to be watching. Yet I feel their eyes when I turn away.

Anas is the only one who glares openly at me. The others' acceptance seems to only fuel his hate. I can feel it from across the room like a fire, raging at being contained. I hold his gaze before deliberately looking away—not afraid, just bored.

I'm not some savior to these men. I have not magically healed the rift between plebeian and patrician—*captivus* and conscripted. To a lot of them, I'm an idiot who took a beating that was meant for another. But as I scan the faces of the century, I see a few people who look at me differently. Before, I was a spoiled member of the middle class who managed to get himself thrown in with the regular people. Now, I'm something they don't understand. I feel like a man hanging from a cliff who has just pulled himself up to the next rock. That will have to be enough for now, I decide as I crawl into bed.

It's a testament to how exhausted I am that I am able to get any rest at all. Even the tiniest movement sends agony running down my front or back. I'm in too much pain to even try to hold Iron. I am tired enough to fall asleep standing; otherwise, I'm sure it would have been a sleepless night. My dreams are dark and tormented, but I remember nothing of them.

Despite our injuries, the next day is even more intense than the first. We march until our feet break out in blisters. The tender flesh surrounding my wounds burns as sweat runs down it in waves. We learn more than a dozen formations. At first, it is only simple ones like the marching column and the basic battle line, which is three men deep. Then Durus begins to make it more difficult; we learn the turtle, square, and pyramid. Each has its uses, we are assured. But that's for officers to worry about. Grunts like us are here to be the bricks in the formation. We go where we are placed and hold our weight until we break.

The decurions scream at us to call upon our Symbol, to let it dull the pain and strengthen our limbs. "You are Iron. You do not bend. You do not break!" I hear over and over as they march us beyond exhaustion. Already I can feel that my *Cor* Heart carries me further than I could ever have gone before.

Men collapse and are taken to the *medici*, but we keep marching until Durus is satisfied. It's brutal and breaking. I am numb, deep in the embrace of my Iron Symbol. The world is muted. I feel nothing. I only obey.

At the end of the day, my feet hurt more than my wounds.

There are no more whippings, but the threat hovers above all of us like an executioner's axe. Every time I make eye contact with skinny Macer, he gives me a look of intense focus, showing me that he's paying attention.

Remarkable.

After three days of marching, we're ready to learn how to fight.

We marshal on the training field in the Twelfth District as the fiery orb of *Sol* rises over the horizon. Murmurs run through our tired collective as Durus and the officers carry out a pair of weapon racks holding a dozen *gladii* and *scuta*. Even I feel a thrill at the sight of them. I've been a legionnaire for days and still have never held a sword.

"You boys are getting a break today," Durus calls, rubbing his hands together as he steps in front of the racks. "No marching, just fighting." We chuckle darkly. It doesn't sound like much of a breather, but I am willing to do *anything* not to take any more steps. My feet are a ruin.

"Most of you have figured out how to use the Symbol of Iron to ease your suffering," he says, "but that's only a fraction of what your Heart can do. Today, you're going to learn how to use it like a legionnaire." The whispers that run through the century aren't muted this time. For once, Durus gives us a grin instead of a scowl for our lack of discipline. Even the old soldier isn't immune to the excitement.

"Now, I know we have some *discipuli* among us." He makes it sound like a curse. Most of the recruits chuckle evilly with him, happy to join in on the mockery. "But for any of you not gifted with an education in the *collegia*, listen up. I'll only explain this once." There's absolute stillness as every man in the line leans forward, drinking in his words.

"Your *Cor* Heart needs two things to function: the essence to power it and the will to guide it. The will part comes from you. You must train your ability to use it, just like every other muscle in your body. Essence, on the other hand, is like your Heart's blood. It comes from being in contact with the physical form of your Symbol. For us in the legions, that's easy to do." He kicks at the pile of *scuta* at his feet.

My eyes widen as I realize the symbiotic nature of the shield for the first time. We carry our iron with us. Not only are they our weapons, but the source of our power.

"First things first: if you're going to stand in a shieldwall, you have to learn to take a hit." The centurion draws his own *gladius*, the long, straight blade of the legions, and gestures to the decurions. "Bring me the first sheep, lads. Let's see what these *collegium* boys can do."

The decurions grabs the ten of us from Segesta and instruct us to pick up a *scutum*. It's a rectangular shield with sharp edges that is bigger than my torso. There's a strap on the inside that ties around my forearm and a handle for me to hold.

The moment that I grab it, a wave of knowledge crashes down on me. The iron shield whispers its secrets to me the same way my own body tells me its needs. It feels like an extension of me, a natural addition to my hand. The shield is me, and I am it. I feel Iron essence flowing into me, refilling my Heart like the rooms of the Iron Pits did, but on a much smaller scale. Compared to that feast, this is merely a snack.

My eyes go wide as the implications fill my mind. Iron is the most dangerous of all the Symbols because of its natural affinity to war. This is why we wear collars—why it is forbidden to all except those in the legions. I have been taught this since I was a boy.

But now that I hold it in my hand, I begin to understand *why*. I glance over at Marcus, whose face has gone white with shock. My old friend glances at me, and a slow grin spreads over his face. He seems the most alive he has been since we were taken.

"Form a line!" Durus bellows, and the ten of us condense into a tight formation, just as we have drilled for the last three days. We form on Marcus, standing shoulder to shoulder. The *scuta* snap together like a wall, perfectly designed to fill the space in front of us. I gain the same sense of knowledge from the other shields as mine rubs against them, bridging our connection. For a moment, I can feel the entire wall like a single organism before some of us separate, breaking the link.

"You will begin to see." Durus laughs at the expression on our faces. "The Iron Legions can take hits and dish them out in a way nothing else can. When we call upon our Symbols in the shieldwall, we become one."

"*Dominus.*" I raise my left hand to get the centurion's attention, waiting for him to nod before I continue. "Are there any congruencies we can use to strengthen the line?" I realize the question is a mistake the moment the words come out of my mouth.

"Congruencies!" he shouts, making sure that every recruit on the field hears it. "Our fancy *collegium*-educated *Primus* wants to know if the legion uses congruencies." Several of the decurions behind him chuckle evilly, like I have just fallen into a trap.

"Let me ask you something, *Primus*." He uses my title like a whip to scourge at me. Once again, I forgot that this was the legion and not a classroom. "What is like Iron?"

"Other metals, some rocks if they come from the earth," I start, listing off every category I have ever studied. If he is going to put me on display, I will at least show him that I know what I am talking about. "Things that have been refined in fire…"

"Very impressive." He holds up a hand to cut me off. "And which of those things makes a better *gladius* than Iron? Which would be a stronger *scutum*?" I have no answer for him.

"You are a soldier of the Iron Legion. You do not bend. You do not break." He is talking to me, but his voice is loud enough to carry to all the assembled recruits. I see now the direction that this lesson goes. "Congruencies are for fancy patricians and palatines in their soft lives. Other things bend. Other things break. Cast them from your mind, *Primus*. You are *only* Iron. Understood?" The centurion holds me in his glare until I nod.

"Then back to the forging," Durus says, striding up to our line, twirling his sword like a bat. He stops in front of the man on the edge, Petrus, and looks back at the rest of the century. They're watching with open jealousy, but they don't even know what they're missing. "A wall is only as strong as its weakest brick."

Quick as a snake, Durus's blade whips back and surges forward in an angled slash that lands square on the shield of the legionnaire. Petrus grunts as he takes the blow, then his eyes widen as his shield warps, parting like butter for the blade.

Gasps echo from every recruit as we watch Durus cut through the *scutum* like it is nothing. A hole opens, and the centurion mimes stabbing his sword through it. "Dead," he says grimly.

The field is absolutely silent.

If this is what a Copper Ironbound can do… no wonder they keep us in chains. My mind conjures visions of men tearing through armies with the ease of a child peeling an apple. I try to swallow, but my throat is dry.

"Fix it," he commands Petrus, stepping to the next man in the line. Without warning, he strikes again, his blade tearing into the shield. As I overcome my shock, I begin to understand what's happening.

When Durus's blade makes contact with the shield, it gives him a link to the iron in the *scutum*, the same way that I can feel them when they touch mine. Once he's able to reach it, he's channeling his own Iron Symbol and using it to warp the shield. It's not enough to feel my shield with my Heart, but I have to protect it too.

Marcus is up next. He grits his teeth and takes the centurion's attack. He might be the strongest man in the whole century, but this is not a strength that comes from muscles. His shield holds for a couple heartbeats before it bulges and warps under the pressure of the veteran's *Cor* Heart.

On instinct, I step forward, placing the edge of my shield against his. They touch, and my awareness spreads to cover his shield as well, then continues to Durus's *gladius*. I almost stagger in awe at the force of the assault radiating from the centurion through his blade.

It's a direct command, an undeniable order that tells Marcus's shield that it should be different. It speaks with authority, demanding that the iron obey. For a moment, I am overwhelmed by the drowning chorus that fills my mind with its volume. But as my shield locks with my friend's, the voice splits, divided between the two of us. I grit my teeth and pour my will into Marcus's shield through its connection to mine. I call on my Symbol and remind the *scuta* that they are made of iron. It does not bend; it does not yield.

Durus's *gladius* jerks to a stop like it ran into a pillar of bedrock. A scowl flickers across his face, and he glances up at Marcus in surprise. His eyes narrow as he sees my shield touching my friend's, locked in place next to his. The centurion's gaze flicks from Marcus to me, and my gut does a flip as I see him evaluating me once more.

"Well done, *Primus*." He chuckles, but the laughter doesn't reach his eyes.

"This is the true power of a shieldwall," he announces, turning back to the century watching. "We do not fight alone. Two *Corda* are stronger than one, and eighty are stronger than two." He turns back to me, watching me with that same cool expression. It's my only warning to set myself as he strikes.

"First. You. Need. To. Defend. Yourself." With each clipped word, his blade flashes, slicing my shield to ribbons with a speed and violence that he had not used on the other legionnaires. I stagger under the force of his blows. Before, he had been holding back; now, he does not. Every time his *gladius* hits my shield, it's only for a moment, but I feel his will cutting into me with hard, unrelenting precision. *Part.* It commands, and my *scutum* obeys, peeling like an orange. I call on my *Cor*, invoking the Iron Symbol to repair my shield, but it's too slow. His speed is overwhelming. Each attack carves out a different space, bending and twisting it, then is gone before I can focus my attention on defending it.

This is what they were trying to prepare us for in the *collegium*. I can command Iron; force it to operate within my definition of reality. But compared to Durus, I am a chirping cricket caught in a hurricane.

Six blows fall like lightning, and the centurion pauses, taking a step back so everyone can see my shredded *scutum*. He doesn't need to say that I would be dead; anyone with eyes can tell. My cheeks burn red with embarrassment. I hadn't meant to show up the officer; it had been instinct that led me to lock shields with Marcus.

"Fix it," he commands, turning his eyes on Felix to warn him that he is next. This time when he attacks, it's a single blow that he holds, like he used on the others. I am being made an example of. Again.

Disheartened, I turn to the ruin of my *scutum*. A shiver passes through me as I examine the ruin that the centurion made with such ease. If I were on the front line of a shieldwall, I would be bleeding my life out on the ground.

Anger sparks deep in me. The same flame that began burning when they named me *Primus* welcomes it eagerly. There's always room for more fire in the hearth. I place my empty right hand on the shield and invoke my Symbol. I feel its cold strength running through my veins.

The world fades as I embrace Iron. I can *feel* the wrongness in my shield. Deep down, the metal knows that this is not its shape, that it has lost its form and failed in its duty. There's something twisted and broken at its core, lurking like a sickness.

I reach in with my mind and find that wrongness. I remind the *scutum* what it is supposed to be: a wall, a shield, a thing that protects. Slowly, in front of my wide eyes, the edges of the gaping wounds begin to stretch toward each other, healing like a wound.

The edges of the rents touch, and I feel as one lip folds over the other, covering the hole but leaving a scar. I frown, trying to force them to fold back together, but the gaps refuse to merge. I cannot force it to meld back together in this state; it was hot when the blacksmith first beat it into this shape. Perhaps if I were more than just a Copper, I could force it to flow together, but for now, it seems impossible to do better than this.

I open my eyes to judge my handiwork. It's ugly but serviceable. I cannot add new mass to the shield; the places where Durus cut through it are weaker now than they were in the first place. If I need to, I can fix my shield in the middle of a battle, but it would be better if I never let it get cut in the first place.

"Lesson Two," Durus calls, striding back down the line toward me. "Your Heart can repair the damage done to your *scutum* in the field of battle, but—" He breaks off midsentence as he sees my shield in my hands. I glance up in fear, but this time, he isn't angry. There's a different light burning in his eyes now. "As the *Primus* here has demonstrated, you're an *electus*, not a blacksmith." He holds up my shield, still attached to my arm, so that the rest of the century can see the scars.

None of the other legionnaires' shields are close. A few of the other *collegium* students have managed to reduce some of the damage, but none have managed to completely close their holes like I did.

"How in the name of Dead Vulcan did you manage that?" Marcus hisses at me while Durus is occupied.

"Does it feel wrong?" I turn to look at him.

"Does what feel wrong?"

"The *scutum*. When I used my Symbol to look at it, I could feel that it was *twisted*—something left over from whatever the centurion did that was convincing the iron to be soft and give way." Marcus closes his eyes and focuses on his shield. After a moment, he opens his eyes and sighs in frustration.

"I don't feel it at all."

"Here." I reach out and place my hand on his shield, questing inside for the same corruption that I sensed before. It's there, lurking in the center of the *scutum*'s being. It's as if when the blacksmith made it, he pounded an identity into it. He made it a shield, and it knew what that meant. But when Durus attacked it, the centurion's Heart twisted it and told it something new. I banish those lies and remind it of what it is supposed to be.

Marcus twitches as his shield begins to knit itself back together. I feel his own will leaning into it, almost reassuring it that it is doing the right thing. It may have lost its way for a moment, but it is time for it to be a shield again.

When it's done, his is almost as neatly repaired as mine. My friend looks at me with wide eyes, and I grin. "See? Nothing to it," I tell him, giving him a pat on the shoulder. Felix has been listening and begins to repair his own *scutum*. It's better by far than anything any of the other recruits manage, although not quite as good as mine.

"I don't really sense what you're talking about," he complains, eyeing his shield with frustration.

"Me neither," Marcus admits.

I shrug. I'm sure it will come to them.

Durus spends a few minutes demonstrating the technique to the rest of the century. He does not look at me, but I feel his scrutiny in the stiffness of his shoulders. I'm not sure why I'm able to command the iron better than my peers. Maybe because I've been bound longer. But the centurion's discomfort puts me on edge.

The next lesson is how to make an actual shieldwall. Durus lines us up against the officers in formation. Murex and the rest of the decurions draw their swords and charge our formation.

"Shields!" Marcus bellows as they close in on us. Together, we raise our *scuta* as we have been shown, locking them together to form a single unbroken line of metal. The six veterans barrel down on us and begin cutting at us with their blades and the power in their *Corda*. Our shields ring like bells as the legionnaires hack at them. The sound is deafening.

I shake with each blow that rains down on the line, my wounds protesting under the strain. I feel like an elephant besieged by wolves, being nipped at from all sides. Sensing a weakness in the line, I send my will down the right side of the flank. I can feel more *wrongness* as the officers' Hearts warp the metal of our shields to their will.

Endure! I command, and I feel the wall strengthen as more of my comrades reinforce it. Shields stitch their wounds at our urging, and the line remains whole. A laugh escapes my lips. It's working! There's something beautiful and satisfying about being part of a unit like this. I've never felt such shared purpose.

But my laughter turns to horror as I feel the left side of our wall collapse. The shields tear under the pressure of the officers carving into our line. In our panic, too many of us protected the weak spot and created a new one.

"Hold!" Durus calls, stepping back. The rest of the decurions follow, sheathing their blades. "In a wall, your ability to work together increases," the centurion lectures, striding along the field. "But in order to hold the line, you have to trust the men next to you to do their job, or you leave your defenses open. Let me tell you, when a shieldwall falls, men die by the fistful."

Something about this education strikes me as odd. Why were we learning how to defend against other Ironbound? The only soldiers in the world who use *Cor* Hearts are the Iron Legions. Why would we be taught how to fight against our own kind?

Unbidden, my mind raises my hand, trying to catch the centurion's attention. Durus turns right as I start to lower it, suddenly thinking better of interrupting. "You have another question, *Primus?*" The centurion's voice is mild, but I know that I'm skirting into dangerous territory. But it's too late now.

"How often can we expect to face an enemy that can control Symbols like that, *Dominus?*" I blurt. Durus's eyes narrow, and he gives me another perceptive stare. I don't know what he's looking for, but he doesn't seem to find it.

"Worry about what's in front of you, Legionnaire," he snaps, and my hand reflexively snaps into a salute. He glares but lets it pass. "Murex, get me another ten men on the line!" the centurion orders, turning away. Over his shoulder, I see Tribune Gaius watching our line with hooded eyes. His expression is unreadable as he turns and walks away, leaving Durus and his men to their work.

But something in his bearing tells me that he is watching us with more intention than he wants me to know. For a second, fear grips me. Did Atticus send some sort of message to him? Before I can worry further, our instructors pull me back into the shieldwall. I grip my *scutum* with relish as I rejoin the line. No matter what happens, I will need to know how to use it.

CHAPTER 23

The days turn to weeks as time begins to pass in a blur. My life is made up of three things: marching, drilling, and sleeping. Our brands heal, so do the stripes on my back. My shoulders broaden, and I lose the layer of baby fat that still clung to my frame. Slowly, the scraggly boys who were sentenced to service in the Twelfth Legion begin to harden and grow into soldiers.

Even in the lowest legion, the *mythos* of the Iron Legions is infectious. The more I am shaped into a soldier, the more I want to be one. I find joy in being a part of the shieldwall of the empire that protects the people, that serves the Empress, who is fair and just. The void in my heart is not filled, but it does not feel as deep now that I have found my purpose.

We learn to form sixteen different formations in under a minute, even if we're asleep. I know this because the decurions love to burst into the barracks in the dead of night and order us to fall in. Men are beaten, but rarely. We learn how to defend a shieldwall with our *Corda*, and bit by bit, I begin to feel ready—for what, I do not know.

I spend so much time holding on to Iron that my life is numb. I don't mourn my family, or fantasize about killing Atticus, or worry about Valentina. My *Cor* Heart takes the pain away and buries me in the cold of my Symbol.

But the day they put a sword in my hand is the first day I truly feel alive.

"This is the *gladius* of the Iron Legions," Durus lectures, holding up his blade for us all to see. Every one of us is more than familiar with them. The officers have been using them to batter our shields for weeks. The sword is a simple affair, with minimal decoration. It's made to serve a purpose, not impress. Its blade is about two feet of straight metal, which flares in the middle before tapering down to a slimmer edge. It has no wide crossguard to prevent it from catching on to the soldier standing in line next to its wielder. It is designed for short, brutal stabs and heavy cuts.

It's beautiful.

The *scutum* radiates an aura of strength that my *Cor* Heart reads like a book. It is strong and durable. It protects. It does not give in. These are the tenets that have been imbued into the iron by the smith who forged it. When I invoke the Symbol of Iron, I remind it of this to help it stay whole.

The *gladius*, on the other hand, was made to cut. It burns with hunger and power like a starving animal, like the wolves of long-dead Ares. It was made for battle—to fight and conquer.

When I hold my shield, I feel safe.

When I hold my sword, I feel dangerous.

Like the *scutum*, the *gladius* immediately feels like an extension of myself. The tang, the part of the sword that is contained within the wooden pommel, is cleverly connected to the surface by a series of nails to give me unbroken access to the iron.

Our first day is spent stabbing tree trunks with our sword.

"Forward thrust!" bellows Durus as he paces around the training square, watching us with intense eyes. The other decurions circle us like sharks, screaming corrections. All hundred and fifteen of us stand in front of a thick chunk of a tree that still has the bark on it.

"Huah," we roar in unison. I stab my blade forward, low at waist height, leaning into it with my hips as I have been shown. Legions don't fight in the way that heroes in stories do. Being in a shieldwall is more like being in a butcher shop than a duel. All the thrusts they teach us are made to fit in the gaps of our defense, allowing us to strike without exposing ourselves to danger or disrupting the line.

Normally, hacking at a tree would be a great way to ruin a sword. But thanks to my connection to the iron, I insist that it remain sharp, and the weapon obeys me. I can feel the edge knitting itself back together as I wrench it free of the wood. We will do this for hours. At the end of our exercise, every blade will be tested. Any man's *gladius* that cannot slice through a piece of string will be whipped. I'm pretty sure they're more serious about that threat than they have been in a while.

"Shields low, blades high!" the centurion calls, not giving us more than a moment between strikes.

"Huah!" we reply, and I follow the order. I drop my left arm and raise my right, pretending to stab at an enemy's eyes over the top of the shield. My weapon bites into the wood but only goes in an inch.

"*Primus*, don't be scared!" Livius, another of our decurions, screeches at me. His voice is shrill, and reputation cruel. "Are you some sort of tree lover, boy?"

"No, *Dominus!*" I reply, pulling my sword out of the wood.

"Then stab it like you want to hurt it!" he shrieks, leaning down to scream right into my ear. "Do it again, Legionnaire!"

"Huah!" I acknowledge, repeating the stab with more force. My weapon sinks into the tree deeper this time, and I give myself a satisfied nod before pulling my blade free.

"Dead gods, how did you survive being born?" Livius berates me. "I said to kill the tree, maggot!"

"Yes, *Dominus!*" I reply, drawing myself up to my full height. I've learned by this point that sometimes the officers pick on me to encourage the rest of the men. My role is to be an example, a leader to the recruits. But that can mean eating crow to keep those falling behind from despair. At least that's the only thing that makes sense to me. Maybe they just like being mean.

Gritting my teeth, I draw on the Iron essence coming off my sword and shield deeply, trying to cultivate enough to refill the dark sphere-shaped reserve inside my chest to give myself more fuel for the task at hand. It is remarkably simple to do. This is the most iron I have touched at once since being locked in the Pits, and I delight in the abundance. As I feed my *Cor*, I bury myself in Iron, going deeper than I've ever gone before. I become one with my Symbol, commanding the *gladius* to be sharper than it has ever been. I can feel the metal shift in response to my command. My veins feel like they are stretching as I push them to channel more essence than I ever have before.

I draw the blade back and leap a step forward to give myself momentum as I stab my sword into the trunk with all my might. Its new razor-sharp edge cuts through the wood with terrifying ease. This time, I bury half my blade before it stops. I have to reshape it to pull it free. Essence pours out of me as I rework the blade to return to its killer shape.

No wonder the Iron Legions are devastating. What can you do against soldiers whose shields won't break and whose weapons cut through yours as if they were made of butter?

"It's a good thing your mother isn't here, *Primus*," Livius sneers, cuffing me on the back of the head. "She'd never get over what a disappointment you are." I'm so deep in the clutches of Iron that I don't feel the impact of his blow or the pain that his words cause.

The Symbol of Iron protects me from feeling, but the rational part of my brain that is free knows that the officer has crossed a line. I'm not angry when I decide to kill him; I just know that he deserves it.

I turn on the ball of my right foot, and my *gladius* slithers forward in the low stab at waist height. In the depths of my cold maelstrom, I have time to take in everything. The decurion has already backed up several paces, almost as if he expected me to attack, but he seems caught off guard by the speed of my turn.

His own blade leaps free of its scabbard as he draws it in a horizontal slash. I feel the impact in the palm of my hand as his *gladius* deflects my stab, twisting it to the side. I feel the calm presence of his own will in his sword as our blades touch. I twist my wrist, freeing my weapon from his and bringing it back toward his exposed stomach. Already, I know that I have him.

It's almost too easy, but the decurion shouldn't have said that.

I falter mid-step as the iron band around my neck tightens, cutting off my air. Stunned, I stagger, dropping my sword to clutch at my neck. My grasp on the Iron Symbol fails, and the world crashes back into me. Horror grows in me as I stare at the decurion I just tried to murder. I'm gasping for air, but all I feel is ashamed. Livius steps back a few paces and lowers his sword. Surprisingly, his face is wary but not angry.

Panicking, I fall to my knees, trying to remember how I saved myself the last time. My Heart is full, overfed on the Iron essence that I drew to satisfy the officer's demands. I must be close to the threshold, which is what triggered the limiter once more. I need to burn off the excess before I pass out and die.

I reach for my sword's hilt and command my Symbol to dull its sharp edge. A trickle of power flows out of me, and I sag, but the ring doesn't relax. Gasping like a fish on dry land, I use my will to sharpen the blade once again. More essence flows out, but I am still too full. Again, I coax it to dull. My lungs are burning, but I don't know what else to do.

I can feel the eyes of all the other legionnaires on me. I don't want to die with all of them staring. I sharpen the blade again, and this time, it is enough. The essence in my heart is low enough that the collar relaxes its death grip on my neck. I sag in relief, taking huge breaths.

"Sorry, *Dominus*," I gasp, waving at Livius. The practice field is completely silent around us as all the recruits stare in horror. Fear begins to build in me as I realize that I have just tried to kill my superior officer. I don't know what punishment will befall me, but a court martial wouldn't be unreasonable. What a stupid, stupid way to die.

"*Primus*, what in the name of Dead Mars has gotten into you?" Durus bellows, stepping between us in fury.

"I don't—I don't know," I stammer, trying to understand. How could I just decide to kill someone? What was wrong with me? "It was so cold…"

"What are you babbling about?"

"The Iron it… I couldn't…" Words fail me as I struggle to explain the numbness that had just enveloped my world. It had all seemed so reasonable, so logical for me to kill the decurion. He had insulted my dead mother, and thanks to the sword I held in my hands, I had the power to do something about it. Why wouldn't I punish him for it?

My hand strays to the metal collar. I've only been wearing this thing for a few weeks, and it has already almost killed me twice. How am I supposed to survive the rest of my life with it coiled around my neck?

To my surprise, something in the centurion's harsh face changes as he watches my confusion. He crouches down to look into my eyes and places a hand on my shoulder. He peers into my eyes for a long moment before stepping back.

"You got lost in the Iron, boy." His voice is sympathetic. "Most men don't ever get that in tune with their Symbol—not at Copper and not without being in full battle kit." His eyes narrow as he looks at me more intently.

"This isn't the first time your collar has restricted you." It's not a question.

"In the Pits," I croak. He nods, as if not surprised.

"Come with me, Castor," he orders. "Leave your *scutum* here." His voice is gentle, but there's no debate. He extends his arm to me and yanks me to my feet. I pull my sword out of the ground and slide it into the sheath that rides at my hip. Marcus and Felix shoot me concerned looks, but I wave them away as I undo the strap that binds my shield to my forearm. If this goes poorly, there's no sense in dragging them down with me.

"The rest of you, back to work!" he bellows, turning to glare at the silent training field. "Murex, you will lead the exercise." The centurion immediately calls out a strike, and the men rush to follow his order. Despite the activity, I can still feel the eyes of my peers on me as I'm led away.

Durus doesn't speak to me as he marches us to the command building. I've never been inside it, but the centurion opens the door and gestures for me to enter.

I'm not sure what I thought it would be like, but it's softer than I expected. A full *tigris's* pelt sits on the floor in front of an empty hearth. Several hallways branch off the entrance, full of doors to what are either officer quarters or offices. It's quiet in here, almost serene compared to the nonstop thrum of activity in the Twelfth Sector.

We set off down the path to the right. By all rights, I should be hanging from the whipping posts, being flogged with the whips designed to actually cut skin. But for some reason, I don't think that's where Durus is taking me. Part of the way down the hall, the centurion stops in front of an unmarked door and raps it with his knuckles.

"Come," a voice calls from within.

Durus opens the door, and I follow him into a subtly ornate office. Even in the Twelfth Legion, the bottom of the barrel, the title of Tribune merits some luxuries. Gaius sits behind a large mahogany desk, sorting through a stack of papers. A pair of old *gladii* hang from the wall behind him, next to a bloody and burnt legion standard marked with *II* in golden thread. In the bottom right corner is a smaller *X*, denoting the Tenth Cohort.

My eyes widen as I realize that our tribune was once a member of the Second Legion. It's always been obvious that he's different from most of the men who end up here. Not only is he a *Fidelis*, a Silver Ironbound, but he carries himself with an innate pride that belies the legion he's an officer in. What did he do to fall to our level?

Gaius's eyes flick up from his work to Durus and then to me. They stay on me for a long moment, measuring and judging. The centurion salutes as the tribune drops the piece of paper with a small sigh and folds his hands. The silver lines of his *Cor* Heart wrap around his forearms, disappearing beneath the scarlet of his uniform.

"What can I do for you, Centurion?" His voice is crisp but irritated.

"Sorry to bother you, *Dominus*, but we have an issue with one of our recruits that needs your attention." The tribune's heavy gaze flickers to me, knocking me out of my stupor enough to beat a hasty salute. I hold it, standing at attention.

Just because Durus isn't screaming at me doesn't mean that I'm not in trouble. If there's one thing I've learned about the legions so far, it's that it runs cold. My death sentence could be given in this very room with only a few words from Gaius. The tribune flips his hand toward the centurion, giving him leave to speak.

"This legionnaire just triggered his collar during a practice with only a *gladius* and *scutum*," Durus informs him grimly. "This is not the first time that he's done so, and he figured out on his own how to expel enough essence to make it release him." Gaius's heavy eyes turn from the officer to me once more. Before this moment, they were bored, but now they are sharp as ice picks, and they dig into me with relish. I swallow and hold my salute.

"Before his collar restricted him, he attacked a decurion who was berating him. He was too deep in the Iron to stop himself." Durus sounds tense, as if he's not sure what the tribune will make of it.

"You're certain?" Gaius's voice is deep and heavy. I feel a thrill of fear to hear the anger lurking in his words. I don't fully understand what I've done. Well, I know what I did, but from the way they're talking about it, I'm beginning to suspect he doesn't actually care that I attacked Livius. He's angry about something else.

"Saw it myself, *Dominus*. Boy was blank-faced and cold. Then his collar choked him, and he collapsed. Said this happened in the Iron Pits as well." The silence in the room is heavy. The tribune frowns as he looks between his officer and me. The panic inside of me rises, but I do not call on the Symbol of Iron to ease it. I don't trust it right now.

"*Gladius* and *scutum* only? No *lorica*?"

"No, *Dominus*. Been keeping them away from full iron until they are more acclimated." Gaius grunts in tacit agreement to whatever that means. Given how my Heart reacted to having more than one source of iron to pull essence from, I can guess.

"Have you ever lost yourself to Iron, Centurion?" Gaius murmurs, still studying me with an intense stare.

"Once, *Dominus*, at Octodorus."

Gaius grunts as if that is to be expected.

"Arausio for me," he replies, his voice growing distant.

"I heard it was bad, *Dominus*."

"It was." Gaius taps his desk with his fingers, as if weighing some heavy decision.

I've never heard of these places, but I can fill in the blanks.

"You were right to bring this to me," Gaius tells Durus after a moment. "Give me a moment with Legionnaire Castor, would you, please?"

"*Dominus?*" The officer's relief is tempered by his surprise at the request. I flinch. Something in Gaius's tone reminds me of being in trouble with my father, when he would take me into his study and kick everyone else out. There's a severity to it that makes my palms sweat.

"Guard the door if you please, Centurion." Understanding glints in Durus's eye, and he salutes before stepping past me. He gives me a flat look that I don't know how to interpret and steps through the door, closing it behind him.

Then I am alone with the tribune. My heart rate spikes, and for a moment, I debate reaching for Iron to help center me. But after a moment of consideration, I don't. Part of it is because I'm afraid of losing control, but I also suspect that a Silver-level *electus* would be able to tell if I did use it.

"Sit." He gestures at one of the chairs across from him. I obey, feeling a little relieved. I don't think they let condemned men sit in the tribune's office. The older man leans forward and stares at me for a long while. Unsure what to do, I return his heavy stare openly. I want him to know that I feel guilty for attacking Livius, but I am not a coward.

"I think it is time that you and I finally stop lying to each other," he says after the moment has passed. He leans back in his chair and steeples his fingers in front of him, peering over them.

"*Dominus?*" I ask, confused by this.

"It is clear that you are not what you pretend to be," the tribune snaps, a hint of anger appearing at the corner of his eyes. "You are clearly a *collegium* graduate—that alone would make you an extreme rarity in the Twelfth. But not only are you educated—you were already Ironbound before you arrived, yet you were still assigned to the lowest legion. It's been more than a decade since that happened. On top of all of that, you arrive surrounded by a group of boys who are equally as trained that watch over you day and night."

"What—that's not…" I stammer, trying to catch up.

"Then you continue to demonstrate a faculty for your *Cor* that overshadows most of the elite recruits that the Praetorians bring in. Even the weakest of the other boys you arrived with show enough to promise to be the Sixth at least."

"How?" I'm floundering, unsure what he's accusing me of and unsure how to answer. I knew that my affinity with Iron is more advanced than the rest of my century, but I assumed that is because I was paired with my Heart longer than any of them. Like any muscle, it must take time for one's body to get used to working it.

"You reached your Copper limit while only holding a *gladius* and *scutum?*" Gaius is yelling now. He's frustrated by my confusion. He thinks I'm playing dumb, but I'm not playing at all. "You got swallowed by Iron on a practice field without being in full battle kit?" The tribune leaps to his feet and hammers his desk with a fist. "Do you think I am blind, boy?"

"No, *Dominus*," I say softly in the crisp, angry silence. "But I don't understand."

"You're not the first by-blow of the Imperium to find their way to the Twelfth Legion." Gaius snorts. "Which of the imperials fathered you on some poor servant and arranged for you to be sent away?"

I'm too stunned to speak. The tribune thinks I'm a palatine bastard, some illegitimate relative of the Empress, sent to bury any embarrassment that I might cause to the family. I want to laugh at how wrong he is. I was sent here by Diana's White Hand, but I do not share her blood. I can't tell him that. The specter of Atticus and his threats lurk in my mind like an *alligatoris*, lying in wait.

"I'm no imperial, *Dominus*. I was sentenced to be here because of this." I hold out my arms to show him the white *rasa* lines that still run through my skin. The tribune's eyes trace my disfigured *Cor* veins as if trying to solve them like a *Labyrinthus*.

"And your bodyguards?"

"Childhood friends, nothing more. We were in the *collegium* together."

"As your commanding officer, I order you to tell me the truth," Gaius snaps, frustrated by this dance. For a moment, I hesitate, and his eyes narrow. He knows there's more to the story. I grimace, trying to figure out how to earn his trust without endangering the home I left behind.

"Begging your pardon, *Dominus*, but if I was sent here in secret, then it would stand to reason that I would be under command to keep that secret." To my surprise, some of the tension fades out of his shoulders as he processes my words. He takes it as an admission, which means that his world makes sense. He doesn't know how much worse it could be.

"Commands that supersede my orders?" There's no challenge in his words, only a pressing curiosity. There aren't that many people whose authority trumps that of a legion tribune. Nervous, I lick my lips. To let him think that I am sort of an imperial bastard has its own set of dangers. For all I know, that would get my throat cut in the dark just on rumor alone. I need to give him enough of a clue to dispel that notion but to leave it alone.

"Depends, *Dominus*. Do you think the Censors part with their secrets easily?" Gaius's face darkens at the mention of the Empress's enforcers. Too late, I realize that might only confirm his suspicion rather than discourage it. Mercury's Ashes I am bad at this!

"We will discuss this further," he warns, dropping back into his chair. "In the meantime, I am ordering that you and the rest of your 'friends'"—his tone makes it clear that he is still skeptical that we were all boys from the same small town—"start an advanced training regimen to adequately prepare you for the use of your Hearts."

"*Dominus?*" Once again, I'm caught off guard by Gaius. I expected him to dig deeper into my secret, not give us a reward.

"You may have noticed that I didn't start my career in the Twelfth," Gaius remarked dryly, nodding at the banner of the Second Legion hanging on his wall. "I know the difference that men who can really use their Symbols make in a shieldwall. I don't know why you've been assigned to my cohort, but I intend to make the most of it. You and your men will be examined as potential *Fidelis*." He pauses to see if the word has meaning.

Of course it does.

A shiver runs down my spine as I realize what he intends. It is my turn for my eyes to track along his *Cor* veins. There is one path for an Ironbound to rise above the level of Copper. Only the *Fidelis*, the Faithful, are trusted to attain such heights. They are the elite soldiers used to hold the center of formations and smash through enemy lines.

Gaius sees that I understand. "I expect each of you to excel at the trial and training, or you will be whipped until you can't stand. Do I make myself clear?"

"Perfectly, *Dominus*." I stand up and salute. It's a threat but also a dismissal. The tribune returns it, and I turn to go.

Gaius calls after me, stopping me in my tracks. "Men only get sent to the Twelfth for one of two reasons: to hide or to die. Which one are you here for?"

"Make no mistake, *Dominus*," I told him. "I'm here to die."

CHAPTER 24

aius brings the old magister from Vulcan's Cave to inspect us. The twelve of us from Segesta marshal on the training field while the rest of the cohort run laps around the outer wall of the city. Endurance is a huge part of our training, but I suspect that the officers have purposely sent the rest of the trainees away so they don't witness our testing. I'm glad to be missing that miserable experience, but I'm sweating all the same with the tension of what is about to happen. It feels like I'm waiting to go into the *Sententia* arena all over again.

The graying man barely spares a glance at us as he strides up. His white toga is still dusty from the work he does below the earth. He fixes our commander with an irritated stare and does not salute. I'm not sure how the old magister figures into the ranks of the legions, but it's clear that he does not consider Gaius to be his superior.

"Tribune, surely you jest," he grumbles, finally giving us a second look. "Just because you are the Twelfth Legion does not mean you are entitled to twelve *Fidelia*." A shiver runs down my spine once more at the ancient word. I do not feel like some hero or worthy of being in the tradition of Titus and his *Ferrum Domini*. From the wry look on his face, the magister agrees.

"There are only ten," the tribune replies easily, as if making a joke. His dark eyes glitter as they watch the magister.

"Not even the Praetorians make me test this many soldiers. I am a busy man, Gaius."

"It is my duty to the empire, Magister Lucas, to present anyone possibly being worthy of inspection," our commander reminds him mildly, unperturbed by the old man's tone.

"Yes, yes," Lucas snaps, irritated at being lectured. "Very well, let us review this crop of worthies." His tone makes it clear how little value he thinks we have.

Lucas stomps forward toward our line and starts with the legionnaire on the left end of our line, Jasper. Lucas pulls a perfectly round sphere of polished iron from his pocket and holds it out to the confused soldier.

"Flatten it!" he barks as the dark-skinned boy nervously catches the sphere. Jasper gives him a shocked glance, looking between the magister and the iron like a panicked child.

"Uh," he stammers, cupping the ball and staring at it with a desperate intensity. The iron wiggles, but its shape does not change dramatically.

"Next," Lucas snaps, swiping it out of his hands and advancing to the next soldier.

Antony is more prepared, but still, he fails to manipulate the iron sphere to the magister's satisfaction. The old man spares a glare for our tribune, who watches the process with a grim expression. His eyes flick to me, and there's a glint of latent anger burning in his eyes. He thinks these are my men and that they are failing on purpose.

I'm under no illusions that if I do not pass this test, Gaius is prepared to make life miserable for all of us. While he's wrong about who I am, I understand his reasoning. If I'm some bastard sent to the Twelfth to hide, then he intends to make use of me. Having some *Fidelia* among the men would save lives. If I fail the test by sandbagging, then I'm a selfish brat who will get men killed.

I give him a serious nod, trying to allay his fears. I am hiding, but I am not some imperial's bastard. I don't think I deserve to be *Fidelis*, but he has nothing to worry about. I have every intention of trying to become one. Atticus had already Ascended to Silver before he murdered my family and burned my town. If I am going to have my revenge, I am going to need every ounce of power I can get.

"Worthless," Lucas proclaims of Matinius, the fourth candidate, and I glance down the line to see Clintus's sour expression. He glances at me, and I give him a commiserating shake of my head.

So it continues. Rufus manages to turn the sphere into something that resembles a cylinder. Lucas's right eyebrow arches as the shape constricts, but it flattens out when the iron does not.

"It has to be some sort of relic," Felix murmurs from my left. I glance at the tall boy and nod once. I'm thinking the same thing. Even as Coppers, any legionnaire should be able to manipulate the iron better than this. Something is preventing them from doing so. Is that part of the test or a deliberate tactic to keep us from passing?

Marcus is silent further down the line, a tense pillar of human flesh wound far too tight. This is a chance for him to reclaim something that was lost. He may have been denied the chance to serve in a prime legion, but becoming *Fidelis* would be a step toward his former dream. A new kind of stress blooms in my chest, an anxious hope for my friend.

Seven boys are tested, and seven fail. With each one, Lucas becomes a little more smug, and Gaius's stare deepens. Marcus is next in line. The boy's eyes narrow as he accepts the sphere from the magister, the shiny silver a bright contrast from his dark flesh. His right hand clenches into a fist at his side as he commands the sphere to constrict.

For a moment, nothing happens. The sphere remains perfectly whole, gleaming with its polished shine. Then it convulses wildly, as if struck by a hammer. For a brief second, it seems almost liquid as it collapses into a flat puddle of iron. Then, with a vicious spring, it rebounds back to its original shape.

A heavy silence descends on the training field as everyone's gaze moves from the sphere to Lucas to see his reaction. The old magister ignores us, pursing his lips as if torn. After a moment of thought, he shrugs and nods, taking the sphere back from Marcus.

"Well, what a surprise! It seems the Twelfth has found a candidate for the *Fidelia*," he proclaims to Gaius, turning his back on the line and striding away. I feel a flash of joy for my friend and see a smile creeping onto his face as he realizes what he's done. "Have him report to the *castellum* for special training."

My mouth opens slightly in shock as I realize Lucas has no intention of testing Felix or me. But before I can say something stupid, the tribune cuts in. His irritation is a deep current in his voice. "Apologies, Magister, but I think you missed two of my soldiers."

Lucas draws up short at the tone and fixes our commander with a sharp glare. Gaius matches it with a heavy stonewalling gaze. "Surely you are satisfied at having one of your recruits accepted, Tribune? If I didn't know better, I would almost suspect you're trying to be greedy. There haven't been three *Fidelia* in a single Twelfth Cohort in the history of the empire."

"Yet it is my duty to bring any eligible recruits before the magisters. I would not be serving my Empress if I were negligent in doing so."

"Yes, Tribune Gaius, your reputation for precision of duty precedes you," Lucas hisses, and for the first time, he seems truly angry to be here.

"It has always been my understanding that the shortage of *Fidelia* in the Twelfth had to do with the nature of our recruits. Perhaps there is another reason that I am unaware of?" Gaius's tone is mild, but there's a threat lurking there—an accusation of favoritism. I cannot begin to fathom the levels of politics at play here, but it's clear that this is not the first time this tune has been danced.

Lucas sneers but doesn't deign to respond. Instead, he spins and thrusts the sphere into Felix's hands. "Get on with it," he snaps, and the tall boy nods, bowing his head to stare at the iron ball with blazing intensity.

This time when it crumples, it does so in an entirely different way than it did for Marcus. Under Felix's command, it slowly begins to constrict, as if wrapped up by some sort of python. Bit by bit, the sphere collapses in on itself. It doesn't become completely flat, but when it is very small and dense, it explodes back outward to its original size.

Lucas is still for a deadly moment, glaring at the sphere in Felix's hand before snatching it and turning toward me, his face purple with rage. "Tribune, this legionnaire will also report to the *castellum*."

"Of course," Gaius replies mildly, his mockery evident by the pure blandness of his tone.

I hold out my hand expectantly, waiting for my turn. My heart hammers in my chest as I make eye contact with Gaius over the old man's shoulder. The tribune's arms are crossed, and he looks relaxed for a martial man, but his eyes burn like coals as he waits to see what I will do. The magister pauses before giving me the sphere, his eyes tracking down to the white veins of my heart still winding through my arms.

"You're *immundus*, *Primus*?" he turns to ask in scandalized rage. He shoves the sphere into his toga pocket to show that he wants nothing to do with me. "Being attentive to your duty is one thing, Gaius, but this is beyond the pale. The *Fidelia* would never accept someone so disfigured—"

"I think that I have some idea of what the *Fidelia* will or will not accept," Gaius interrupts dryly, crossing his Silver-veined arms in front of his chest.

"Be that as it may, there are *rules*—"

"Then it should be an easy thing to test him and dismiss him."

My heart skips a beat as Lucas turns to look at me, fury radiating off him. I know my *Cor* Heart appears to be crippled, but I've not felt impaired by it. Among my fellow legionnaires, I was the first to open the iron doors of Vulcan's Forge. I was the first to learn to repair my *scutum* in the field. Iron calls to me despite my apparent deficiency, and even though it was never the Symbol I wanted, I find myself answering it gladly. Confidence grows in me like the dawning sun. If Felix and Marcus were able to pass the test, then I should be able to as well.

Lucas sighs in frustration but reaches into his pocket for the sphere and tosses it to me with a look of disgust. He takes great pains not to touch me, as if my impurities are an infection he might catch. I give him a smile full of teeth as the iron lands in my palm and understanding floods into me.

I know it the same way I understand my own flesh. I feel it like a living extension of me, and manipulating it is as easy as closing my fist. I look into the old magister's eyes and command the sphere to flatten. The iron constricts at my will, and my smile expands.

Then it halts, stopped cold by something indomitable. My smile falters, and a new one begins to sprout on Lucas's face. My mouth drops open, and I look down at my hand in stunned disbelief. The sphere is smaller than it was, but it is not small enough to be impressive—and I know that to be accepted into the *Fidelia*, I must be impressive.

Something is wrong, but I can't tell what. I can feel the exterior of the sphere, but then my understanding stops, and there is only darkness. I frown, concentrating on the sphere, trying to discern its secrets.

"As I suspected, the *immundus* is not a worthy candidate," Lucas announces, holding out his hand for me to toss him the sphere. He still doesn't want to touch me. Gaius's anger builds like a volcanic eruption. I can already feel the whip scoring my back as he promised.

"This isn't iron." The truth slips out of my mouth before I can consider the implications of it.

"Preposterous," Lucas scoffs, gesturing imperiously. "Your worthy peers had no problem—"

I ignore him and wrap my other hand around the sphere. Instead of commanding it to shrink, now I twist, telling the metal to part for me. The iron exterior comes apart like an orange peel in my grip, revealing the fruit inside. The core is shiny and metallic, but it's bronze, not iron. This is why I could not crush the sphere. The alloy will not listen to me. Lucas's protests die on his lips, and his eyes bug out of his face as I dissect his sphere.

"Magister, perhaps it is the other ball in your pocket," Gaius's tone is so mild, it burns. His Silver veins flash in the sunlight. "Perhaps you accidentally gave my *Primus* the wrong one when you put the orb back in your robe?" His words give Lucas a way out, but his voice makes it clear it is not a question. He can feel the other sphere from where he stands. My throat goes dry as I realize the difference between his Heart and mine. I want that power. I need it.

"That must be," Lucas stammers. His face is a bright red, but his eyes are locked on me with a murderous rage. I copy my commander and give him a bland look as if I don't understand the underhanded trick he just used. He switched them to make me fail on purpose.

"Shall we resume the test with the correct relic, then?"

"That won't be necessary," the magister admits, staring at the remains of his second sphere in my hands. Acting surprised, I press my hands back together, commanding the iron to knit itself back into a ball. With a stupid smile, I hold up my hand, presenting it as good as new.

Lucas snatches it out of my hands with barely-constrained contempt. "The *castellum*. Tomorrow," he snarls before storming out of the practice yard, leaving the twelve of us with our commander. Pride soars in my chest as I realize that we have found a path to vengeance. I will be one of the *Fidelis*.

I will be Silver.

For a moment, the realization brings a sharp pang of grief. My father never wanted me to become an *electus*. He never Ascended above Copper himself and would caution me against this. But my father is in the dirt now, among his plants. I must follow a different path.

I feel a separation between me and my family grow, the same way that my veins stretch as I push them. My loved ones are dead—they cannot go with me. Each step I take on this journey takes me further from the Castor they knew. Soon the boy who was their son and brother will be dead. The man I am becoming will be someone they would not recognize.

"The rest of you are dismissed." Gaius's voice is smooth and calm as he nods at the nine who failed. "There is no shame in not being selected to be a part of the *Fidelia*. Thank you for your efforts." The men salute and trail off in the wake of the angry magister. I catch Clintus's eye as he looks back over his shoulder, his expression unreadable.

I nod at him, and after a moment, he returns it. Once he might have hated me for Ascending above him when we competed in the *collegium*, but things have begun to change. I am *Primus* now, and we aren't boys anymore. We're survivors bound by the same tragedy.

Marcus, Felix, and I remain in formation as Gaius approaches. The corner of his lip is turned down as he surveys the three of us. For a long moment, he holds his silence, judging our worthiness. I stiffen, worried he is angry that so few of us were chosen, despite his words. I know that we are not special. But I can tell that my performance has only convinced him that I am exactly what he thinks I am.

"This will not be the last time that happens," he murmurs.

"What happens, *Dominus*?" Marcus inquires, his voice as surprised as I feel.

"You will not be allowed to succeed," the tribune replies. "But you *must*."

"Who will not let us?" It is Felix this time, but I feel the shape of our commander's answer already. It feels like the stink of Atticus and men like him. The rust that grows on the Iron Empire, hidden out of sight from the Empress and those who work for the good of the people.

"Think, boys," he hisses, an iota of frustration creeping into his voice. "Think where you are. The Prime Legions will not welcome you into their halls. We are the Twelfth. We are made to die in the desert, not to be able to challenge their power."

The three of us exchange a glance that he sees. His expression darkens as he realizes that we like the sound of that. He takes another step forward, clenching his fist, and his stern anger makes him loom like a mountain. I do not fall back from him, but it takes more will than I'd like to admit.

"Politics and power are appealing things to legionnaires, but they are even more deadly than the front of a shieldwall. I did not send you to become *Fidelia* as a favor. I did it so that when our enemies come screaming out of the sand, our line holds and our cohort endures. Each of you will save lives that have been thrown away. There is no greater good than that."

A chill sweeps down my spine. I knew the Twelfth is often sent to the desert wastes, but I'd never thought about going there myself. I glance at Marcus once more, but my oldest friend is no longer looking at me. He stares back at Gaius, enraptured in this new version of following his grandfather's legacy.

I snap to attention, and after a moment, my friends follow me. "What are your orders, Tribune?"

"The magisters will be watching you, looking for an excuse to cast you out from the *Fidelia*. You must be clever. You must be strong. You must pass their tests so completely that they would not dare deny your Ascension to Silver."

"We will not fail," Marcus promises fervently. I nod my head, but already the doubt is beginning to grow in the back of my mind. I was not good enough to earn a heart in the *Sententia*—how am I supposed to compete with the elite to become *Fidelis*?

CHAPTER 25

I can't sleep.

Dead Somnus's domain is closed to me as I lie on my lumpy Legion mattress. More than a hundred men snore around me, a symphony of noise that keeps the silence of night at bay. But it is not the sound that keeps me awake. My own thoughts rush through my head with the fury of a river, and their torrent is deafening.

Tomorrow, I will begin my training to become one of the *Fidelia*, but that is not what I think about. I cannot forget the look on Clintus's face as he walked away from the training field. It is not the same glare of hatred that he used to give me when I would show him up in the *collegium*. That one was easy to identify, equal parts frustration and jealousy. No, this expression had been full of shame.

But why? Clintus has nothing to be ashamed of. He did his best during the *Sententia*, and it is certainly not his fault that he is here. That blame lies at the feet of Atticus, Brutus, and the Golden Wolf. If any of us are at fault, it is me, not him. But his family is as dead as mine and that guilt is not something you can shrug off with logic.

Since we began our legionnaire training, the other boys have begun to treat me differently. Not in a bad way, quite the opposite. I am no longer ostracized as I was in the cart. They are not my friends like Marcus and Felix, but they look up to me.

I think it is because my dream is their dream. Even if I haven't shared it with each of them, somehow they know that I have found a direction. All of us are adrift, thrown into deep water far beyond our ability to navigate. Every one of them is floundering, trying to find the way back to a place that makes sense. I am on a path; it is one of revenge. The others can see that I am moving forward, and they want that too.

Clintus's shame isn't that he failed to be chosen as an elite soldier; it's that he missed an opportunity to follow the course I have been setting. He worries that he has missed his chance and will be lost forever. No wonder Gaius thinks that they are my men. I've been their *Primus* the whole time—I just didn't notice.

I sit bolt upright on my lower bunk as inspiration hits, almost hitting my head. I know what I need to do. Valentina already showed me the way. We are in the *Sententia* again, and this time, we must win.

Valentina.

I haven't thought about her in weeks. What has become of her in service to the Empress? What did that even mean? Does she think of Marcus and me and wonder if we still live? Is she now bound to a *Cor* Heart? Pain, a different sort of heartbreak, flares as I relive her icy silence after we came out of the arena.

Without meaning to, I summon my Iron Symbol, and its calming presence settles over me, numbing the hurt with its cool strength. *It does not matter*, I tell myself. I will never see Valentina again. But she showed me the way, and now I will use that light to guide the others. If I am going to win, I am going to need allies.

I rise out of my bed silently, not even bothering to strap on my sandals. I place a hand on Felix's shoulder on the bunk above me. The plebeian raises his head without twitching—I'm not the only one banished from the world of dreams tonight.

I motion for him to meet me out front and turn to Marcus. My old friend's eyes are open, watching. I glance around the barracks to confirm what my instincts have already guessed. The rest of our cohort are sleeping, but all my former townsmen are awake. Goosebumps prick my flesh as I feel the faint stirring of something beyond my understanding. What grand luck that Somnus and his children had not claimed the men I needed.

Or maybe it is something else.

Our eyes strike sparks as I meet them one by one. Each of them gets up without complaint. Clintus doesn't even wait to be summoned but pads to stand beside me, looming like a faithful hound. Gone is the rivalry of our youth, as recent as that was. The forges of Agogia have beaten it out of us both. Rufus and Jasper creep along the outer edge of the room. Matinius follows in their wake. There are too few of us left from Segesta to let old wounds fester. Petrus, Haxus, and Lintus sneak out the door ahead of me.

Silently, we troop out of our barracks. None of them question me, even though we are breaking curfew. If we are caught outside of our quarters, we will all be whipped. Do they also feel the heavy hand that lies over this place like a fog or do they just trust me?

I shake my head to clear it. My heart is not racing—it beats at the steady pace of someone lost in the sea of Iron's peace. It is not the soulless calm that I was sucked into on the training field but a pale shadow. I know where I am going and how to get there. The Twelfth's Sector is dark and silent; there is not a single guard in sight. Only the command building glows with the light of *lumos* relics. I lead them across the empty training field in our bare feet, the sand still warm from Sol's rays. *Mons* Olympus floats far above, the dead mountain dark except for the light from *Luna* reflecting off it.

At the far side is a small armory where they keep the *gladii* and *scuta* that we train with. It is not locked—they're not real weapons. But tonight, they will work well enough. I pull open the door and motion for the boys from Segesta to enter. Jasper shoots me a long glance but doesn't hesitate longer than that.

I move to follow the last of them in, but a sudden pressure on my back stops me. I glance over my shoulder to see Tribune Gaius standing in the courtyard on the far side of the training field. He stands alone, his red cape fluttering behind him, backed by the light of the command building.

We stare at each other for a long moment. My connection to Iron makes my spine straight and holds me firm. The commander does not move, only watches—and wants me to know that he watches. I have confirmed his suspicions even though they are not true.

Well, they *were* not true. After tonight, they just might be. But if I am becoming what he suspected, then he is to blame. It was he who planted the seed that I nurture now. I continue into the armory, closing the door with me. I know he will not interfere. Tonight, we are safe from him.

The other boys wait in a circle, looking at me with hungry expressions. They all know something changed today on that field. They feel a part of the path that I have found and are eager to take the first step of their journey. They are tired of being lost. I have found the strength in the pain and now it guides me. Tonight, I will show them the way.

I pause for a moment, taking in the sight of these nine boys from my town. They should not be here. Marcus should be training to be a hero. Felix should be baking bread. Clintus—I don't know what he would be doing, but something other than this. All of them are here, sucked in by the vortex that surrounds me. I cannot change that, but maybe I can lead them out of it.

A single *lumos* relic hangs from the ceiling, casting a harsh light, casting shadows on all their faces and making their Copper veins shine. For a moment, I think of my grandfather—of the light he left behind that has now been burnt and destroyed. This path is for him too.

I say nothing, striding past them to the wall where a training *gladius* hangs. I take it in my hand and draw deeply, inhaling its Iron essence to feed my Heart. As my awareness plunges into the blade, I focus on its edges, commanding them to sharpen. A proper *gladius* has an edge hammered into it by a legion blacksmith to make sure that it knows its true form; it helps a soldier keep it sharp in the heat of battle.

Training blades are created blunt on purpose. They can cut into a log, but it would take a lot of effort to take a limb off.

"We are lost men," I say softly, breaking the anxious silence that fills the room. I turn to make eye contact with all my comrades as I speak, making sure that each of them knows that I want him here.

"We are a long way from our homes and can never return. They burned them down behind us." There is a grim murmur of anger from the other boys. "They killed our mothers and fathers. Our sisters and brothers. Our dogs." I pause for a moment, letting the cold logic of the Iron Symbol keep my own emotion at bay.

"But they made a mistake. They left us alive. They sent us to be forged into weapons and then forgot about us. But Iron has a long memory." I hold up the blade and twist it against the light, letting my friends see its edge glint. A couple of them look more nervous, but none of them move. Whatever current is nudging me along has caught all of them in its grasp.

"But what can we do?" the red-haired Rufus challenges me. He does not look angry or belligerent, only despondent. The burdens we carry have worn him down and bowed his back. I understand—they almost did the same to me.

"We endure." Slowly, I slide the newly sharpened weapon against my left palm. Bright red blood wells up from the slice, but I feel only a faint tug thanks to the numbing from the Iron Symbol pulsing in my *Cor* Heart. Still holding the *gladius*, I drop into a crouch and pry a small stone loose from the floor with my left hand. Rising, I hold it out for everyone to see. Felix and Marcus both have dark looks on their faces. They have done this before. I squeeze my left hand closed around the rock and roll it around, staining it with my blood.

"This is a *votum*," I say for the benefit of the boys who still look confused. "Tonight, I make an oath before the bones of the gods. The magisters told us that they are dead, but the legion priests claim that war still lives even if Mars is dead." The laughing thing wearing the wolf's head flickers in my mind before it is gone. "Our families were killed, our town burned for a wrong that none of us committed."

Dark murmurs echo through the room. My *rasa* veins glint in the light, but none of the boys look at me with anger. I am their *Primus* now. My portion of the blame has been forgotten, drowned by the crimes of others.

"If war is not dead, then neither is vengeance." I squeeze the rock again; my blood has begun to drip down to the floor. None of them are even breathing; they are caught up in the rush. "I swear by Nemesis's bones that we shall avenge our families. Let their blood water the earth and descend into Hades as our offering." I'm looking into Clintus's eyes as he realizes what I am doing. He burns with the same hunger that I do. I have him. The pressure in the room grows heavy, trying to hold me down. Something is listening.

Dimly, I wonder if I should feel guilty. This oath will likely get us all killed. But we've been sentenced to the Twelfth Legion. We are already dead—it is up to us what we do until then.

"Censor Atticus," I chant the first name. Their hungry eyes grow sharper like the sword in my hand.

"Centurion Brutus."

"The Sixth Cohort of the Praetorians."

I hesitate for a moment, glancing up at the ceiling, toward where *Mons* Olympus floats far away. This has been the easy part. But I am not done. These are the men who killed our fathers and burned our mothers. But there is another name on my list. Marcus stares at me like he hasn't since our city burned. I give him a smile full of teeth.

"The Golden Wolf," I whisper in the heavy silence. The pressure from above heightens. Even holding on to Iron, I almost stagger to my knees, but I don't fall. I am tall. Unyielding like the Symbol in my Heart. I do not bend. I do not break. Then it fades and withdraws, returning to wherever it came from.

I hold my breath as I measure the gazes of the boys looking back at me. The Praetorians might be elite, but our training has made them feel within reach. Atticus is a Censor, but he's still just flesh and blood.

But the wolf, the howling, laughing wolf that wore the living armor before he smashed the chest, seemed to be something more. I do not know what he was, but I suspect he walks a different path, tied to a different dead god. These are things I shouldn't say out loud, much less think.

My friends are still, but none of them leave. I take their silence as an agreement.

"Any others whose hands are stained with our parents' blood."

I hand the *gladius* and stone to Rufus on my left, who is only too eager to add his blood to mine. The oath makes its way around the circle. Marcus. Clintus. Petrus. Antony. Rufus. Jasper. Matinius. Haxus. Lintus. None of them refuse. Felix pauses for a second, giving me a long look before cutting his own hand. I frown but let it go. I'm surprised that he of all people is hesitant. He's sworn a *votum* before, so he should know that they are meaningless words. It is the idea that will bind us together.

Then it is done. We are oathbound. Before, we were held together by tragedy; now, we are bound by purpose. I bury the blood-marked stone in the floor of the armory; it feels appropriate. When I finish, I rise and look around the room. The boys who took the oath are gone for good now. They stare back at me with the eyes of men. I raise my red right hand.

"Tomorrow, Felix, Marcus, and I will train to become *Fidelis*. What we are shown, we will teach you. But the rest of you must keep pushing yourselves. Excel. Make it impossible for them to ignore you. We will learn their secrets, and one day, we will kill them with it."

I dull the blade and hang it on the wall before reluctantly letting go of Iron. I can feel my *Cor* reserves getting close to full, and triggering the collar's judgment would ruin the moment. As we leave to make our way back to our barracks, there's no sign of Gaius, but I'm certain he is watching. Felix drops back from the rest of the group to grab my arm.

"Are you sure about this?" he hisses, keeping his voice too low for the other men to hear.

"They needed a purpose, and we are going to need allies." I shrug my arm free from his grip and keep walking. I'm still not entirely sure why I did it. The certainty that was coursing through me has begun to fade.

"You've taken quite a risk just to give them a purpose."

"You're worried about risk?" I turn to look at him. "We're destined for the front lines of the Twelfth Legion. We were dead the moment we marched into Agogia. Why are you scared of an oath? It's just empty words."

"The four of us—you, me, Marcus, and Valentina—swore that none of us would get their Heart without the others," he reminds me with a troubled expression.

"And that worked out so well, didn't it?" I reply, feeling a flush creep up the base of my neck. "I don't know if you remember, but I—"

"—got a Heart anyway," Felix interrupts me smoothly.

My protests die on my tongue. I freeze in shock, and my friend pauses with me. For a moment, we stare at each other, thinking the same thought but not daring to voice it. Too many ears might hear it.

We made a *votum,* and it was going to be broken. Then *something* interfered, and all of us ended up getting a Heart. I glance down at the white *rasa* veins running through my forearms. I would never have chosen this path, but technically, our oath is whole. Our families died, and our city burned, but we did not break the pact.

Chills run down my spine as we both turn in the empty training field to look up at *Mons* Olympus floating above. What have I done?

CHAPTER 26

awn.

Sol breaks over the towering wall of Agogia, sending long lines shooting down her long streets, chasing the shadows into their corners. Marcus, Felix, and I approach the closed main gate to the fortress in the center of the city. Each of us bears a pass signed by our tribune, allowing us to travel throughout the city without an officer.

The palm of my right hand stings each time I move it, but not as much as it should. I marvel at how much my body has changed since I became Copper. There is no sign of infection, and already the wound is mostly closed. It burns a little, but I feel like I have taken an important step forward. I have been lost since the night the *Sententia* ended, and my life was taken from me. But now I have a direction, and nothing will stop me from walking the path of the Faithful.

But despite my joy, Felix's words from outside the armory shed still ring in my ears. We swore a *votum,* and it came true. It was going to fail, *because of me*, and then it did not. All four of us got our *Corda*. It is my greed that has brought us here. I cannot bear the blame for *how* the oath was fulfilled, but I did swear it. I promised to do anything to get my *Cor*. Now that I have it, the price does not feel worth it.

As we draw near to the gate, I chuckle at how different I feel this time. I have not been back within these walls since the rest of the company was made Ironbound. They seem smaller now, less imposing than they were when I first came to this place. We are the only legionnaires waiting.

"It's a little empty," Felix remarks dryly, looking around with narrowed eyes.

"The *Fidelia* are elite. Perhaps we are the only—"

"That's definitely not it," I cut in over Marcus's monologue. This means everything to him, but he's on his way to becoming unbearable since being chosen. We know that there are others who have been selected. But where are they? Gaius's fears hover over my shoulder like the commander himself, tall and imposing.

"You suspect tampering?" Felix is paying attention.

I nod and stride forward to the smaller guard gate, rapping it with heavy blows until someone finally answers. A legionnaire in full battle kit opens the door, his eyes narrowing in displeasure as he takes in our appearance. We're dressed in our cotton training tunics that are stitched with the *XII* of the Twelfth Legion.

"Get lost, recruit," he snarls, taking in our white training uniforms. He starts to pull the door closed, but my words stop him.

"We were ordered to report to the magisters by our tribune, *Dominus*," I snap, raising the pass in my hand so he can see the wax seal by the signature.

He pauses, looking at the paper with an uncertain expression. It doesn't matter what legion he is in, disobeying someone like Gaius could get him whipped.

I continue, taking advantage of his hesitation. "If you would give me your name and legion so that I might report to him the soldier that countermanded his orders…"

"Give it here," he demands, pulling the door open to step through. I hand him the pass, and his eyes narrow further as he slowly reads the short description. "*Fidelis?* Why would they send you here? There's no *Fidelia* here." My heart sinks as he hands the pass back. The sun's rays taunt me, telling me that I am late. We've not even made it to muster, and already the games have begun.

"Where?" Marcus demands, shouldering me aside in his eagerness. "Where are they gathered?"

"Training fields out the south gate." The legionnaire points down the main road toward the gate in the distance. "Better hop to it, recruit. You've got a long way to go." The small door slams shut in our faces, and we exchange dark glances.

"Come on!" Marcus shouts, turning and breaking into a sprint. Felix and I follow him as he makes a mad dash into the main thoroughfare of Agogia. A century of Fifth Legion regulars, fully trained, professional soldiers, marches in front us. They take up the entire right side of the road but are in no rush—their journey is just beginning.

Marcus cuts to the left and dodges a blacksmith's wagon. I let out a curse as I follow my friend, spinning to avoid being crushed by the heavy wheels. Felix trails in my wake, and together we carve a path against the current.

Officers and civilians scream at us as we race, but none of us stop. Finally, we're in front of the century, and we switch to the right side of the road. A couple of the veterans let out mocking whoops, but we don't stop running.

My world becomes narrow. Even after weeks of intense physical training, the sprint is draining. Sweat pours down my brow, but I barely pause to wipe it off. We still have a quarter of the city to cross.

By the time we make it to the gate, I am gasping for breath. "Halt!" A grizzled decurion stops as we descend on the South Gate at top speed. Marcus screeches to a stop, his sandals scrabbling for purchase on the cobblestone as Felix and I slide into him, bouncing off him like a wall.

"Where do you think you're going?" he demands with a smirk of mild amusement. "No recruits outside the gate without an officer."

"Special permission," I manage to gasp out, waving my pass in his face like a flag. He frowns and studies it for a moment before giving us another skeptical look. "*Fidelia?*" he asks in mild disbelief, looking at the legion number stitched into our training clothes.

"Not yet."

"Clearly. Good luck, lads." He steps out of the way and waves us through.

We pound across the path toward a training field with a score or so of white-robed recruits going through exercises. A dozen white-robed magisters look up as we approach.

"What are you doing outside of the walls, recruit?" a decurion in Praetorian purple bellows, stepping forward to intercept us on the path. We stumble to an abrupt halt, and I salute, panting from my run. It takes everything in me to keep myself from sneering in disgust at the sight of his uniform.

"We've been ordered to report for *Fidelis* training, *Dominus*," I gasp out as politely as I can.

"From the Twelfth?" he barks a laugh. "Get back to your—"

"Here's my pass, *Dominus*," Marcus interrupts politely, stepping forward to show the paper. The officer's eyes almost pop out of his head when he sees Gaius's seal at the bottom.

"There must be—"

"What is going on here, Decurion?" a rich voice demands, cutting the officer off midsentence. A woman dressed in the toga of a magister steps into our view. Her black hair has begun to turn gray, but she moves with a vitality that belongs to a much younger person. Golden veins of a *Cor* Heart glint as she crosses her arms.

"Begging your pardon, Magister, but these recruits are claiming to be *Fidelis*, but they're from the Twelfth."

"Ah yes, Lucas mentioned he got bullied into accepting some farm boys by Gaius." She snorts dismissively. She has aristocratic features that are as palatine as they come. Bright eyes tear us to shreds. I feel naked under her piercing gaze. Something about her is familiar, but I cannot quite place it. She sees my *rasa* veins, and her lips thin into a frown.

"And like farm boys, you are late and not dressed appropriately." She clicks her tongue in disappointment. It's only then that I realize that the rest of the recruits are in full battle kit, *lorica* and all. I open my mouth to protest, *I'm not even allowed to wear a* lorica! but I am cut short.

"Decurion, ten lashes each." She turns away with a wave. "Once that's done, send them back to Gaius and tell him not to waste our time in the future." The recruits practicing in the field have stopped their training and are watching us with cold, speculative eyes.

"Yes, *Domina*." The officer gestures to some more Praetorians who rush over to grab us in a sea of purple. I hiss as the first legionnaire grabs my arm, and he's only too happy to slam his fist into my stomach, knocking the air out of me.

There's no whipping post here, so instead, they force us to kneel in a line, and a soldier holds each of our arms. They don't bother to strip our shirts. One of them jokes about how I shouldn't have worn my dress uniform. The rest laugh, delighting in their cruelty.

I see the world through a haze of red. I want to kill them. Their uniforms mark them as the Third Cohort, which means they had nothing to do with Atticus's work, but the purple of their uniforms is enough to make me start trembling.

They whip Felix first. I hear him grunt as the first blow lands. I can't see him, but the crack of leather striking against flesh paints a vivid picture. I'm next. I'm so angry, I can't even focus on the Symbol of Iron, and so it slips out of my grasp like a snake as I try to seize it.

I feel the first blow, but my rage dampens the pain. The unfairness of it all stings more than the whip. Gaius was right—they are trying to keep us out. Lucas told us to report to the wrong location so they would have an excuse to deny us. We were never going to be given a chance to become *Fidelia*. Even the Iron Legions suffer from the rust of corruption.

My body is jerked forward by the force of the second strike. Unlike Durus, who first whipped me, these legionnaires don't care if I am able to walk after. The two soldiers holding my arms stumble with me, laughing at my plight. As they shift, their *lorica* rub against me, the iron touching my bare arms.

My pain fades as my consciousness sweeps into the iron that makes up their armor. My Symbol's essence pours into me, and distantly, I know that I have been swallowed by Iron's calm once more. I remember that it is dangerous, but I don't care.

These men are hurting me. They are taking something from me, and I have lost more than enough already. An idea forms in my mind, an echo of the words that I said to the boys in the armory shed last night. *Make it impossible for them to ignore you.*

I draw deeply from the iron that I can touch. The Praetorians are still whipping me, but I'm glad. Now, when all eyes are on me, is when I must show them what I am. I must become unforgettable. As the essence within me grows, I resist the urge to grab the *lorica* of the men holding me and squeeze them like rotten fruit. I could do it. I feel their distracted will. They're not on guard, and by the time they tried to stop me, it would be too late.

But as much as I want to kill them, that would only be remarkable. I want to be more than that. Brimming with Iron power, I smile as I feel the collar begin to constrict around my neck, cutting me off from drawing any more essence or air. Durus and Gaius were shocked by how easily I triggered my collar's safeguard. Now, I use that against this magister.

My body seizes, and the two men drop me in surprise as I begin to twitch violently. I land on my side, staring straight at the harsh-faced woman and the other magisters. My smile is sharp and toothy as I stare at them. Slowly, her mouth opens in shock as she realizes my collar is preventing me from Ascending. Her eyes flick from my iron-less body to the two men who were holding me.

She gestures toward me, but I can't hear her over my own choking. Someone grabs my hand and forces a metal bar into my rictus grip. "Bend it, boy! Bend it!" a girl is shouting in my ears. I glance at her for a moment—a different woman, much younger than the one who is having me whipped. Struggling to control my body against the ravages of the collar, I raise my fist holding the rod and make eye contact with the old palatine.

Her eyes are hard now. I am not panicked enough. She can tell this is not the first time I have been limited by my collar. Still holding her gaze, I release the raging inferno of essence inside me, channeling it into the iron with one single command.

Break.

The rod shatters into a thousand pieces. The collar releases its control over my body instantly as the essence stored in my *Cor* pours out of me. I cling to my Symbol like a drowning man to keep my pain in check as I struggle to my feet. This is my moment. This is how I make sure I am unforgettable.

The old woman purses her lips as she looks at me; everyone around us totally still. The other magisters, Praetorians, and recruits are all watching. She's trapped, and we both know it. The Iron Legions are made to serve the Empress, and despite the politics at play here, I'm betting that she doesn't dare deny me if I show enough promise. Her eyes burn with a cold fire as she studies me, but there is no way out for her.

"Decurion, whip the third boy, then find them training kits." She turns away to the recruits who have ceased their exercises on the field. "Did anyone tell you to stop?" she screeches, driving them back to work.

Activity resumes at a frantic pace as everyone scrambles away from the old magister's ire like cockroaches from the light. Felix struggles to his feet beside me with a grimace of pain.

"Well, that was illuminating," he murmurs, standing close to me.

"Very," I agree softly. "We will need to be on our guard."

"It's not that different than growing up a plebeian in the *collegium*," my friend says with a casual shrug. I wince in shame; although I was never the cruelest to Felix, I know that I was a part of that cycle. I clap a hand on his shoulder, taking care to land far from his fresh lashes. We both laugh in shared pain. Behind us, Marcus grunts as the first blows fall on him.

I wince in sympathy but don't worry for my friend. No one wants to be a *Fidelis* more than him. He will gladly suffer this punishment for a chance to achieve it.

"That is not your first time being restricted by the *inhibitus*, is it?" a feminine voice interrupts. I turn to see the younger woman, the one who handed me the iron rod, standing before me. She's older than me, but not by much. Dark black hair spills to her shoulder in waves, making her blue eyes stand out. Her features are sharp but elegant, hinting at her palatine heritage. But it is the attentiveness she studies me with that I find unsettling.

I squint at the unfamiliar word. Guessing at its meaning, I point a finger at my collar, arching an eyebrow. She nods impatiently. "No, Magister," I admit easily. "It has happened before."

"Not a magister yet; just an apprentice." Her lips quirk wryly. "How soon after you were Ironbound did it first occur?"

"A couple weeks, *Domina*," I reply. Something in her interest fades. I don't like that. I need to stand out if I'm going to stay on this path.

"Although I didn't have the opportunity to be around much iron until I got here," I add casually. "Once they got me down into that cave, it started happening pretty often."

"You were bound before you arrived at Agogia?" Her eyes flicker to the *XII* stitched into my tattered training uniform. Another strike cracks against Marcus's back, underscoring our conversation.

"I was." My smile is broad and smug. She thinks the same thing that Gaius does. At this point, it might as well be true. I was sent to the

Twelfth to spare someone important embarrassment and die. I have no intention of doing either of those things.

"My first time being choked by the… *inhibitus*, was it?" She nods. "My first time was in the iron chambers in Vulcan's cave beneath the *castellum*." She studies me for a moment before nodding. I continue, "My second was when I held a *gladius* and *scutum* for the first time."

"What about the *lorica*?"

"I have never worn one." I shrug as her heavy gaze intensifies. It reminds me of the pressure that I felt bearing down on us while we made our *votum* the night before. I give her a fey smile. "Who knows what will happen then?"

We're interrupted by the soldiers hauling Marcus to his feet. My loyal friend groans in pain, but he's grinning widely. His eyes dance with gratitude as they meet mine. I shake my head with a bemused smile at his joy. Only a madman can be so thrilled after being whipped. Even the Praetorians seem rattled by his mood.

"Put these on," the decurion grumbles, appearing at my side. He throws three cotton tunics on the ground. They're purple, marked with the single *I* of the Praetorians. My stomach roils in disgust as I look at them. I can't make myself wear their colors, even if I should.

"I wo—" I begin hotly, but Felix is too quick. The tall boy tosses his shredded white tunic to the ground and picks up one of the purple ones. He shoots me a glare as he pulls it over his head, shaming me. I put mine on in silence. My back screams in pain as I stretch it, but I don't let it stop me.

Three more legionnaires approach, each one carrying a *lorica*. I resist the urge to look back at the young woman. It seems we will find out what happens when I wear one sooner than I thought.

"Help them," the decurion barks, just holding back a sneer.

The first soldier stops at my feet and orders me to hold out my arms. With my heart in my throat, I obey. I don't know what's about to happen, but it feels momentous. The same instinct that woke me last night thrums through my body with anticipation.

He lifts the *lorica* up and holds it out like a coat. At his urging, I slip my arms through it, and he steps forward, shoving it over me to swallow me whole. I let out a gasp of shock as knowledge of the armor envelops me. My *Cor* drinks greedily from its supply of essence, and I stand up straighter as the pain in my back fades to a whisper. I force myself to stop cultivating any more. I've proven my point. Now I need to show that I can control myself—that I am worth the investment.

The *lorica* is made up of a series of iron strips that overlap but are not attached, granting me a high degree of flexibility. Perpendicular strips run over my shoulder, growing smaller as they tighten over my biceps.

The suit is open at the back, but I sense a series of iron latches that are just waiting to connect. I shift my body, coaxing the edges to meet in the middle of my back. With a nudge from my Symbol, I click them into place, tightening them until they are snug but not restrictive. It fits like a second skin.

"You'll need to use your Heart to feel the latches on the back…" The soldier begins to lecture me as he walks around me to check the other side. He trails off as he sees that I have already intuited his instructions. Over his shoulder, I see the magisters and their apprentices watching me.

Another legionnaire hands me a training *gladius* and *scutum*. I loop the blade's belt around my waist before strapping the shield to my left forearm. For the first time, I feel like a true legionnaire. A broad smile crosses my face as I stand there, thrumming with Iron essence. I dare not even take in another iota, but dancing on the brink of inhibition is intoxicating.

I turn in time to see Marcus finish securing his shield. His smile dwarfs mine, and I laugh out loud to see it. Even Felix is smirking now, encased in iron.

"Get in line!" the decurion bellows after all three of us are in battle kit. "Did you not learn your lesson, little Twelvies? Do you want to be whipped for being late again?"

The three of us trot out onto the sandy field to join the score of other recruits who are waiting for us. The weight of the iron on me slows me down, but after a moment of thought, I command it to be less. I feel essence flow out of me as the metal changes, obeying my command. The armor wrapping around my body feeds my *Cor* a steady flow, making it possible for me to maintain the effect. My kit does not become weightless, but I feel lighter. Each step becomes easier, and I start to outdistance my companions with each stride.

"What are you doing?" Marcus hisses at me as I begin to pull ahead.

"Tell the iron to weigh less!" I laugh, and after a moment, the two of them stop losing ground as they figure out what I mean.

Now that I wear the full gear, I'm floored by the brilliance of the Iron Legions. A soldier's *Cor* Heart needs essence to fuel its control over a Symbol. But every legionnaire carries a supply of it with them. When they are connected in a shieldwall, the effect must be overwhelming. I shudder with dark delight. I can't wait to feel it—to ride that wave.

"You must be the recruits from the Twelfth." A centurion steps up to intercept us as we approach. He is tall and lean like a spear. His brown hair is cropped close, and his beard is short. But it is not his face that draws my attention. Silver *Cor* veins run through his flesh, telling the story that he has attained the highest rank an Ironbound can achieve. His *lorica* is marked with the *II* of the Second Legion, and a dark *F* has been branded over his heart.

This centurion is one of the *Fidelia*. Tiberius and his god-killers were the first of the Faithful. They Ascended beyond Silver in the days before the empire, but the soldiers who earn that title now carry on in the tradition of heroes. Even I, a boy who never wanted to be a soldier, feel a sense of disbelief that I have been given a chance to be an heir to their legacy.

"Yes, *Dominus*," Felix answers for us. I tap my chest with my fist in a reluctant salute, fully expecting to be treated with the same scorn that the rest of the legions heap on us.

"Fascinating," is his only reply. His eyes do the now-familiar dance down my mismatched *rasa* veins, but he does not comment on them. "In the line, if you please." He gestures toward the assembled recruits and turns away from us.

We stride toward the rear of formation under the heavy gazes of our peers. Some of the recruits from elite legions openly sneer. Felix ignores them, staring straight ahead. Marcus and I follow his lead. Our tall friend has more experience surviving this kind of attention.

"We will resume, and our new arrivals will observe," the lean *Fidelis* declares. "You, from the Third." He gestures to a boy in the second row of soldiers. The boy grunts and steps forward, giving his *scutum* a shake as he marches to meet the centurion. The officer points to a training dummy in the ring and the legionnaire from the third faces across from it.

My eyes narrow as I study it. It is clearly different from the logs that we have been stabbing so far. The dummy is shaped like a soldier—if their flesh was made of wood. It's even wearing a *lorica* and holding a shield and sword. The centurion steps up next to it and places his hand on its back for a moment. I let out a small gasp as the entire thing twitches, coming alive with a false humanity.

"Hades's Grave! That's a relic," I whisper to my companions. It feels like another life where I survived the trial of the *Sententia*'s Arena.

"Never seen one that could impersonate a man," Marcus says with awe.

"But what is it for?" Felix asks.

"I don't know," I tell him, "but it's another test."

"Will we ever leave them behind?" my tall friend laments with an amused grin.

"I think the true tests are yet to come."

"Legionnaire, are you ready?" the centurion bellows, his voice no longer mild.

"Aye, *Dominus!*"

"Draw your sword!"

The recruit obeys, pulling the *gladius* from its sheath and gripping it firmly in his right hand.

"First, you will receive. Good fortune, soldier. Advance!" The centurion pulls his hand from the back of the automaton and crosses his arms.

The legionnaire from the Third steps into range of the relic, *scutum* forward like a single brick of the legendary shieldwall. Immediately, the machine raises its own *gladius* and brings it down on his shield with incredible force. The man grunts and falls back a pace before stepping forward, raising his now-dented *scutum* to block the next blow. He staggers further under this one, and his shield warps more, but it holds.

A third time, the dummy's arm comes crashing down like a sledgehammer, and a loud peal rings out as a fissure appears in the soldier's shield. The fourth strike comes even faster than the others, before he can get his feet under him. With a thunderous *crack*, his *scutum* splinters into two large pieces as he's sent flying. The automaton leans forward, its *gladius* rising to finish him while he's down. My heart skips a beat, and instinctively, I take a step forward even though I could never reach the downed soldier in time.

Quick as a thought, the centurion steps up to the back of the machine, placing his hand on the dummy's back. It pauses mid-stroke before leaning back into its original stance and raising its shield.

"On your feet, soldier," he calls to the legionnaire. "You will have three strokes to return the favor."

"Ahh," I breathe, beginning to understand what the test measures.

"It's not a particularly impressive relic, is it?" Felix asks under his breath.

"Seems to hit pretty hard," Marcus grunts.

"No, it's nothing compared to the *collegium*'s tools," I agree, thinking of the challenges we faced in the arena. "But it's an Iron relic, so that makes sense."

"Ah, of course." Felix understands my meaning immediately.

"It's so annoying when you two do this," Marcus complains. "It's not like I am an idiot. I was *Quartus.*" Despite the intensity around us, I chuckle at my friend's frustration.

"Think about it—the relics that were used in the arena were not Iron. They were from other Symbols, which means that they were able to be harvested from powerful *electii*."

"No Ironbound has Ascended beyond Silver in over four hundred years, and the majority of Iron relics that are available are only Copper," Felix points out. "Only a Gold *electus* can manipulate elements at range with their Symbol, which is why the centurion has to keep touching it to give it instructions."

"Okay, okay, I get it," Marcus huffs, but his eyes are narrowed as he studies the automaton with new eyes.

The soldier from the third finishes unbuckling his ruined *scutum*, tossing it down into the dust. He twirls his *gladius* once in his hands, which I must admit looks impressive even if it is needlessly flashy, then nods to the centurion.

"Advance!" the officer commands, stepping back from the dummy once again.

The legionnaire steps into range, and the automaton raises its shield to meet him. With a shout, the man lunges forward, driving his point straight into the other shield in the standard stab of a shieldwall. The blade scrapes a slice across the surface of the relic's *scutum* with a vicious squeal. Despite the horrible sound, the automaton's shield does not bend or break.

"One," calls the centurion from behind the relic.

Panting from the exertion, the legionnaire brings his weapon in an overhead smash, aping the style the automaton had used on him only a few moments ago. Iron clangs on iron, but again, no dent appears.

"Two."

With a cry, the man abandons all form and steps close to the relic. His strike is full of fury, a wild, diagonal slash like the one that Durus used to slice my own shield to ribbons the first time I held a *scutum*. But his *Cor* Heart is not able to keep up with the demands of his will. With a metallic *ping*, his sword bounces off the shield, and his test is at an end.

"Three." The centurion places a hand on the back of the automaton, and it slumps forward, shoulders sagging as the false life inside of it fades. A shiver runs down my spine at the thought of having a part of me turned into something like that after I die. The magisters say that our souls do not remain with our *Cor* Hearts, and I certainly hope they are right.

"Failure," the officer announces after withdrawing his hand from the training dummy. I wonder if it gives him some sort of report of information about the actual Symbol use done by the soldier. "You will report back to your commander at once."

The soldier, who is little more than a boy, frowns with disappointment, but he bows his head and salutes before stumbling off the field. I watch him go with a twist of sympathy and fear. If I'm not careful, I might find myself following him shortly.

"You, next," the *Fidelis* commands, and another recruit steps into the ring with the automaton. I narrow my eyes and lean forward—there's always a trick to these tests. I just need to find it.

This soldier, also from the Third Legion, survives four blows before his *scutum* is shattered. In exchange, he is given four to damage the shield of the automaton. On his fourth, he manages to crack it, earning him a "pass" from the centurion.

I watch the ruined shield, curious how they will replace it before the next recruit takes their turn. Then, before my eyes, the metal begins to flow as it reforms itself until its *scutum* is as smooth and pristine as it was before it was broken.

"Jupiter's Rotting Beard," Marcus breathes in awe. I think of how proud I was to stitch my shield back into something usable and shake my head. We have only begun to scratch the surface of the power of our Symbol.

The next three boys fail quickly. None survive more than two blows from the automaton's *gladius*, and when they fail, they have no more strength left to shatter its shield in return.

"It's an endurance test," I murmur to my friends, keeping my voice low so the single recruit from the Ninth, the next lowest legionnaire present, can't hear me.

"The longer you survive, the more chances you have to wear down its shield," Marcus agrees.

"I'm not sure it's so simple. I think it's about balance." My eyes narrow as I follow the thread of an idea that is forming in my mind.

"What do you mean?" Marcus shoots me a confused look.

"You have to have enough essence left to be able to crack the thing's shield. It's a relic, a machine. They reset it between rounds, but they don't give the soldier more than a moment." The more I think about it, the more certain I am that I am on the right path.

"Are you proposing that we fail on purpose?" Felix asks. Marcus makes a horrified sound of disgust.

"Not fail, but don't let them tire you all the way out," I reply, my eyes fixated on a boy from the Fifth whose last blow fails to break the shield. "The magisters and officers want to see that you understand how to use your Heart. It's the rank and file's job to hold until they break. *Fidelis* are supposed to be something more."

"No wonder no one from the Bottom Quadrant ever makes it this far." Felix snorts in disgust. "We've barely even been taught how to reinforce our swords. Most of these elites came from the *collegium*." Which is exactly why our fellowship sticks out like a sore thumb. I understand Gaius's skepticism of us a little better.

The dozen recruits ahead of us take their turns one by one. Only four of them pass the test. The last is from the Seventh Legion—all the challengers from the Eighth and Ninth fail. While the rest of the pack struggles, we watch and plan.

"You, next." The centurion gestures at Marcus to step into the field. Our big friend hefts his *scutum* and draws his blade. A couple of soldiers jeer from the sidelines as he passes them. As he steps into range, it slams an overhead blow into his shield. The force drives him back a couple of paces. His feet dig deep furrows in the sand.

Gritting his teeth, he keeps his shield high and steps back into range. The second blow drives him almost to his knees and leaves a massive dent in its wake.

"Come on, one more," Felix whispers at my side.

The relic's *gladius* slams home a third time, deepening the dent, and a crack appears in the center, but it holds. Marcus lets out a roar of joy, but the automaton does not let him get set before striking again. His shield shatters under the force of the blow, ending the first half of the test.

"It goes faster after every strike." Felix confirms our theory. "I counted."

"Three blows," the centurion calls, stepping up to place his hand on the back of the relic. It shifts its posture from attack to defense, raising its shield and squaring its shoulders. He eyes Marcus, who is standing tall for a moment before withdrawing and nodding once.

"Begin."

Marcus lets out a shout of understanding and charges the thing. Unlike many of the other recruits, he is not completely worn out. By not resisting the fourth blow, he preserved some of his strength for the second part of this challenge.

His sword slashes in a flurry of strikes. *One. Two. Three.* Each carves a sharp rent through the iron of the *scutum* like a claw. Marcus steps back, panting now, and sheathes his sword before the centurion can react.

The officer glances at the shield for a moment before looking at Marcus again. For a moment, I think he is going to fail my friend anyway. Perhaps he too thinks that the Twelfth should not have any *Fidelis* among its ranks. Then he places his hand on the back of the relic, and its shield repairs itself before the machine goes still.

"Pass," is all he says before turning to look at us. The recruits from the other legions are still, stunned by what they have just witnessed. I smile slightly at their backs. Marcus takes his place among their ranks and gives us both a nod. Our plan worked.

"You." He points at Felix, leaving me for last.

"Luck," I whisper after my friend as he strides to the front. The other soldiers don't make any snide remarks as he passes. Their confidence is shaken seeing someone from the lowest rung pass the test with ease.

Felix draws his *gladius* and nods at the *Fidelis*, who watches him with hooded eyes. The officer activates the automaton with a touch, and it swings at the plebeian without hesitation. The field rings as Felix survives one, two blows. I see a small dent in his *scutum*, but it seems otherwise unharmed.

He only needs to survive one more hit. We noticed from watching the others that most of the successful attempts took at least three hits to crack the relic's shield. By stopping to resist after the third blow, he would save his energy but still have plenty of chances to—

With a horrendous *crack*, his *scutum* shatters as the automaton's blade comes crashing down. Felix glances at me, his face tight with concern. His chest heaves as he tries to recover from the assault. I give him a slow nod. He can do this. I know he can.

"Two blows." The relic's shield comes up.

Felix does not attack like Marcus—he's more winded. Taking a deep breath, he steps into range and drives his blade forward with a shout. Despite not surviving as many blows as Marcus, he must have released his will on the third strike because he still has enough power left for his stab to dent the automaton's *scutum* easily.

I clench my fist, trying to contain my excitement. He can do this.

"One."

Felix rolls his shoulders and lunges forward, bringing his *gladius* down from an overhanded blow onto the dent his first attack made. The relic's *scutum* crumples and cracks as it fails. The centurion places his hand on the back of the dummy and withdraws it, a frown forming on his face as it reforms its shield once more.

"Pass," he says at last before his brown eyes turn to me and fix me with a heavy stare. Even as full of Iron as I am, my heart begins to race because I know what comes next.

"You."

CHAPTER 27

I make my way along the line of recruits who passed their tests with my head held high. On the other side of the field, I can feel the weight of the magisters who have been observing these trials with attention. I am surrounded by enemies, but I refuse to show them fear.

On the inside, my guts roil with panic. I am more anxious than when I went into the arena. I spent my whole childhood wanting to earn my Heart. I've only had the dream of becoming a *Fidelis* for a day, but already it means everything to me.

As my nerves tense, I cling to the Iron Symbol's cool presence within me. It takes every ounce of self-control not to pull any more essence into my body from the ocean that surrounds me. I'm at the brink of triggering my *inhibitus*. My body moves with a new power as if it is completely rested. The lashes on my back do not hurt anymore. I cannot feel them—it is almost as if I were never whipped.

As the calm of Iron settles around me like a second *lorica*, my focus narrows until my world only consists of two things: the *Fidelis* centurion from the Second Legion with the familiar face and the relic.

"Draw your sword," he commands. I do, grateful to have another source of iron touching me. It is comforting. The officer looks at me for a long moment, his eyes flickering from my *immundus* veins to my eyes with that same burning question. I don't know what the answer is yet. We're about to find out together. I helped Marcus and Felix come up with a plan to beat the test, but I have a different one for mine. Today, I am going to find out if I am worthy.

"Advance."

I nod and raise my left arm that's bound to my *scutum* and step into range of the relic. The dummy's arm rises and crashes down on my shield with enough force to rattle my bones. I *feel* the blow physically as well as on the symbolic level. Essence pours out of my Heart as I reinforce the shield against the automaton's automatic attack.

Bend, it seems to whisper to my shield. It does not truly speak in words, but I get a sense of its intent as its will seeks to infiltrate and corrupt my defenses.

207

Straighten, I command as I pour my will into the *scutum.* The attack lasts an instant but feels like an eternity. I gasp as the connection between us is broken when the automation raises its arm for another blow.

My shield is whole.

I inhale, drawing in air and essence from the iron I carry at the same time. I spent my reserves freely defending from the last attack, which means I am in no danger of triggering the *inhibitus.* My Heart surges as it feeds, and I feel a thrill as the collar begins to tighten in warning. By the time the second blow slams into my shield, I'm as full of essence as when I started.

Crack. The relic's intent is heavier now, and the force of the strike drives me back a pace.

Withstand. Once more, I feel the essence flow out of my *Cor* veins as my Iron Symbol exerts my will to protect the integrity of my *scutum.* My veins burn as I push them to new heights, using them more than I ever have before. Then it is over—we part, and the machine resets itself. I take the opportunity to pull in more essence, filling myself to the brim once more.

My shield is whole—I am whole.

REND. The sense is overwhelming, like the roar of a waterfall, drowning out everything else around it. Its will is a foreign thing jamming its way into my mind.

MEND, I command, forcing my *scutum* to stitch itself back together.

We are still whole.

Breathe.

I have survived three strikes. If I was going to follow the plan that my friends and I made, I would hoard the essence in my Heart on the next blow and let the automaton destroy my shield. But I am not going to take that path. I need to know if I can do it another way.

I have been paying attention. There's something different about my *Cor* Heart. That much is obvious just by looking at me—my white *rasa* veins are plain to the naked eye. But there's another clue, written on the faces of the commanders and magisters who have evaluated my process. A trickle of something that I can't quite place. Fear or awe, maybe.

No other member of the Twelfth has had their *inhibitus* restrain them. From the expression on Gaius's face, no recruit has ever done it without wearing a *lorica.* For some reason, I am different, and today, I want to find out how different.

My heart is still brimming with Iron essence. I'm in no danger of running out. So instead of letting the relic destroy my shield, I pour my will into the *scutum* and resist.

PART.

I refuse.

FRACTURE.

I do not bend.

DIVIDE.

I do not break.

SHATTER.

My shield rings like a gong as the automaton's *gladius* smashes down with more force than it ever has before. My heart skips a beat as I feel my essence reserves dip dramatically as I burn them to contest its will. The strength of its attacks increases with the pace. I don't have enough time to refill before—

DISINTEGRATE.

My *scutum* explodes under the force of the assault from the relic's Symbol. I'm knocked out of the peace of Iron as my reserve is emptied in a single blow. The power that hits me outclasses me by an order of magnitude.

My world spins. I gain control of my body only after it has come to a rest. I'm lying on my back, staring up at the morning sun. The lash marks on my back burn once more, the pain igniting like a dormant fire after my hold on the Iron Symbol failed.

I cannot stay here. I gasp and reach for any source of Iron—the *lorica* that surrounds me, the *gladius* that is somehow still in my hand. My pain eases as essence flows into me as easily as air into my lungs.

I lever myself into a sitting position, marveling at how flexible my armor is. Thanks to my Symbol, I'm able to bend it with me, making it easy for me to get to my feet. The training field is deathly silent as I rise. The magisters to my right are staring at me like I'm some sort of monster. The palatine woman who had me whipped is white as a sheet.

I try to not let my smile look like I am gloating.

My gaze settles on the centurion, whose hand is on the back of the relic. He opens his eyes and meets mine without fear. "You will have seven blows," he announces with a flat tone. No recruit that we watched survived more than four.

I nod, doing my best to look unfazed. I'm still running low on essence. Like losing your breath, it takes a few moments to regain composure. Mentally, I curse myself for being so arrogant. I have fallen into the same trap that I warned my friends of. It took longer, but now I will pay the same price unless I can fix it.

"Begin," the centurion commands, stepping back from the relic one last time.

I stride forward and stab forward with my *gladius*. The tip of the blade slices across the surface of the automaton's *scutum*, leaving a scratch in its wake. As our weapons touch, the awareness of its shield floods into my mind, and I feel its will push mine back like a wall.

Resist. Resist. Resist. Resist. Resist. Resist. Resist. Resist. Resist. Resist. Resist. Resist, it seems to chant.

My own instructions are weak, charged with a minuscule amount of essence, and bounce right off its defenses. My sword slides off the edge, and the connection is broken. The relic's *scutum* shimmers as it repairs the tiny scratch.

"One," calls the centurion, his expression disappointed. I take a deep breath and pull in more essence. My stress is gone as I become like Iron, grounding myself in its cold stability. I ignore his look and set myself for the second strike, an idea forming in the back of my mind. If I need more essence, why not borrow some from the relic?

I repeat my attack, stepping into a driving strike aimed right at the middle of its *scutum*. But this time, instead of trying to destroy, my will has a different demand.

Feed.

Resist. Resist. Resist. Resist. Resist. Resist. Resist. Resist. Resist. Resist. Resist. Resist, the relic hums again, but I am not attacking it in the way that it expects. As the iron of its shield joins my awareness, I cultivate essence from all of it, gorging myself on an expanded supply. My reserves surge as I feast. I suspect that this would never work against another legionnaire, but this automaton is not a living, thinking man. It is the remnant of someone long dead, given very specific instructions by the Heartsmiths who forged it. It was never designed to protect itself from something like this.

Once again, my blade skitters off the side of the shield. This time, its passage didn't even leave a scratch.

"Two," the centurion announces after glancing at the untouched shield. His frown is growing. I hear murmurs from the recruits behind me, but I am deep in the grips of Iron, and I do not feel the weight of their whispers.

I'm ready.

The *inihibitus* tugs at my neck as it warns me that my reserves are too full. I smile as I step forward to strike at the relic. I repeat the same stroke that I used the first two times, but this time as I step into the lunge, I bundle my will, fueled by all the Iron essence inside of me, into the tip of my *gladius* as it stabs into the automaton's *scutum*.

PART, I command.

The tip of my sword cuts through the surface of the shield like a hot knife carving into butter. I use my Copper strength to drive the blade all the way in, burying in its chest up to the hilt. If this machine was a man, he'd be dead.

As the iron of my *gladius* sinks into the dummy, knowledge of its inner workings flares in my body and mind. Underneath the wooden shell is an intricate network of iron and something that tastes similar. It is not actually a flavor, but I can think of no other way to describe it.

It must be the relic itself. An idea flares in my head, and I'm so deeply nestled in the confidence gifted to me by my Symbol that I don't hesitate. I will be unforgettable. I raise my head to make eye contact with the Silver centurion as my will seizes every scrap of essence I have left in my *Cor* veins and channels them into a single command.

BREAK.

My body shakes with the force that channels out of me, but it is a pale comparison to the dummy's reaction. The automaton shudders for a heartbeat as its chant of *Resist* tries to fend off my assault. But its focus is on its *scutum*; it doesn't know that I have broken through its defenses.

A horrendous crack echoes through the training field as the inner workings of iron and relic are hit by an attack they were never designed to handle, like a fishing town struck by a tidal wave. The machine's upper torso explodes, sending wooden shrapnel flying. My *lorica* rings as a piece bounces off the armor of my chestplate. The automaton's shield slides off my blade like a dead weight as it collapses. There's nothing left to tell it to resist.

I lose my grip on the Symbol of Iron as I glance at the wreckage at my feet. Panic flares up in me as my doubts come rushing back in. I hoped that my attack would damage it more than my peers had. I thought any recruit who could actually wound the dummy behind the shield would be impressive. I did not expect the destruction to be this absolute.

Relics can only be made from the Hearts of dead *electii*; I have no idea how I was going to ever be able to replace what I had demolished. Screams of outrage from the magisters to my right only increase my concern. I don't look at them; I already know that the old palatine wants to murder me. Instead, I train my gaze back on the centurion. So far, he has been fair to all the recruits. I can only hope that I have impressed him enough to earn his protection. His face is impassive as he glances down at the ruined relic and then back up to me. What does his Silver Heart tell him about what just occurred?

"Pass," he says after an eon of silence.

Pandemonium erupts. The magisters swarm the field, led by the woman who had me whipped. She steps up to the centurion, glaring at him right in his eye. His face does not even so much as twitch as a Gold *electus* screams in his face.

"This *immundus* destroyed a relic that has belonged to the Censors since the *Ferrum Domini* fell," she rages. "Who will tell the Empress that it has been lost?" My blood turns cold as I imagine Atticus coming to investigate the loss of this priceless artifact.

"I suspect that is your job, Magister," the centurion replies smoothly.

"Seize this soldier and beat him bloody!" The crone extends a single finger in my direction. A couple of Praetorians from earlier take a few steps in my direction.

"Halt." The Silver officer does not raise his voice, but the purple-clad legionnaires freeze. Even the First Legion respects a *Fidelis*.

"You dare counter my orders, Centurion Marius?" The barely restrained fury in her voice is like a storm hovering on the horizon. I can tell that it will break at any moment.

"You have no authority to order this man to be punished." The welts on my back disagree, but hope begins to burn in my chest.

"The Empress has given us the right to oversee—"

"To oversee the testing of recruits chosen to become *Fidelia*. The testing has concluded. This legionnaire has passed, and as such, is no longer under your purview. You are not Legion; you may not have this man whipped."

"He has not passed!" she screams. The ground beneath my feet shakes slightly with her rage, and I feel a thrill. Centurion Marius is right; she isn't Legion. Her Golden veins make it impossible for her to be bound to the Iron Symbol. But still, the earth is vibrating because she's growing angry.

Such power.

I marvel at his bravery as he stares down the palatine woman without blinking. His Silver Heart makes him an order of magnitude stronger than me, but hers is yet another step above his. Is he using his connection to Iron to keep himself calm, or if he is just that brave?

"By what metric would you judge that he has failed his test?" The officer glances away from her to look at the scattered relic pieces at their feet. He doesn't say anything further but turns back to her with a hint of challenge in his stare.

The magister gapes for a moment, trapped by her own rage. I marvel at the deftness with which the centurion handled her objections. If she says that the destruction of the automaton was not enough to merit my acceptance into the *Fidelis*, then she must claim that I did not do this. On the other hand, if she admits that I did pass, I am out of her clutches. A weight lifts from my shoulders as I realize that I'm probably not about to be whipped for a second time today.

"Your father will hear of this," she hisses after a moment, drawing herself up to her full height. It's not as impressive as it might be in civilian circles, now that she's squaring up against a professional soldier.

"Please tell him that I say *salve*." The centurion nods as if he had been expecting her to say that. The older magister hisses in irritation and storms off the field. The rest of the toga-wearing palatines follow in her wake, except for the younger woman who spoke to me before my test.

"Well done." Her gaze travels up and down my body as if searching for an answer to some mystery. I feel myself flush in embarrassment.

"Be careful. She may not seem like it in this moment, but she is a very dangerous enemy to have."

"Why does she hate me?" I blurt, too surprised to stop myself.

"It has nothing to do with you." She tells me grimly. That only makes me more confused. I glance at her, hoping she will expand, but we are out of time.

"Come, Alessandra!" her mentor's voice snaps from the distance.

"I hope you survive."

CHAPTER 28

enturion Marius dismisses us after the magisters storm off. "Each of you will report to your commanding officer and inform him that you have been selected for training as a *Fidelis*. You are expected to muster at this field every second day."

He glances at Marcus, Felix, and me with a knowing eye. "I will make sure that your tribune is aware of the expectations for this new experience." I'm surprised by the dismissive remark, but I don't rise to the bait. Gaius was a *Fidelis* himself. I'm sure that he is more than familiar. A small smile quirks at the corner of my lips as I imagine an arrogant soldier coming to lecture our commander. It seems everyone was in for surprises today.

We strip off our battle kits, leaving them with the Praetorians who loaned them to us. Our white training linens are ruined, so we keep the purple ones we are wearing. The decurion who whipped us gives us a stern look but doesn't press it. The veins in his arms are Copper; I wonder if he regrets the beatings he gave out after what he just witnessed.

The pain in my welts grows as I lose the sources of iron around me. I refilled my reserves with essence before taking it off, but it's not the same as carrying iron with me. I seize my Symbol and leave it simmering in the back of my mind to help numb the pain. It's worth the drain on my Heart.

The three of us make our way back to the main gate at a much more leisurely pace than we did this morning. The legionnaires from the Fifth at the checkpoint don't even question us. They take one glance at our purple tunics and wave us through. A sneer grows on my face, but I rein it in, calling on Iron to help me keep my temper.

The journey back could not be more different. As we walk through the Prime Quad, where the First, Second, and Third have their districts, soldiers get out of our way without a word. Civilians greet us warmly. Companions working at the taverns and brothels call as we pass, asking us to join them.

"I didn't even know there were places like that in the city," Marcus grumbles, eyeing a beautiful woman who waves at us. Felix snorts but says nothing. This is not a new experience for the plebeian. He seems to be enjoying watching us learn more about how the world works.

"None in our quad," I tell him. I'm even pretty sure that's true. The difference between the quality of life for the elite legions and ours is stark.

We make it only a few blocks through the central corridor of Agogia before Felix shoves us into an alleyway and corners me with a furious expression on his face. "What in the name of all gods, dead and dying, was that?"

"What do you mean?" I sputter, surprised by the anger on his face.

"We had a plan!"

"And it worked!"

"You didn't follow it. Why didn't you show us how to do what you did?" Suddenly, I understand why he's angry. He feels abandoned, like I've been keeping secrets from him, like he's still a plebeian and not my equal. I'm so relieved, I let out a laugh. His face darkens. Marcus looks between us, still confused.

"No, Felix, I didn't keep anything from you. I just had to try something."

"Why?" The single word holds so much weight. An entire friendship hovers in the balance of the answer to that simple question.

"Something is different about my Heart."

"Well, obviously," Marcus cuts in with a chuckle, trying to defuse the situation.

"Not that," I snap, rubbing a self-conscious hand on my wrist over some of my white veins. "Well, maybe. I don't really know what it is."

"What are you talking about?" Felix's patience is still thin, but he's listening.

"Have either of you triggered your *inhibitus*?" I ask. They both give me blank looks. I point at the collar that circles my neck. "This. Have either of you pulled in so much essence that it chokes you and cuts off your ability to draw any more?" Both of them shake their heads silently.

"I've done it three times. Durus tells me that's not normal; so does Gaius."

"Is there something wrong with your collar? Maybe because your whole Heart didn't integrate with your Symbol, you can hold less, like having a smaller stomach?" Felix suggests.

I pause, caught off guard by his question. That might make sense if the *inhibitus* measures how full a Heart is rather than how much essence it holds. That hadn't occurred to me. A chill settles over me as I realize how reckless I was during the test. I could have discovered that I lacked the power to stop a blow from the relic the hard way.

"I think I'm actually exceptional at drawing in essence from iron." I shrug, a little embarrassed. "I have to be really careful not to overdraw all the time or I'd be choking out on the floor."

My friends exchange surprised glances. "So you were refilling your reserves between each hit?" Felix's voice is incredulous.

"Well, only after it got stronger," I admit. "In the beginning, it wasn't really using up that much."

Marcus's jaw drops open, and he stares at me in shock.

"What?" I ask, looking between them.

"It was all I could do to refill enough to hold off those first two hits," Felix admits grimly. "If I had taken the third one, I'd have been as dry as a whistle. I can't imagine surviving *seven*."

"I almost blacked out on that last strike," Marcus says quietly.

My heart races as I process what they are telling me.

"You boys lost?" a cruel voice calls from behind us. I look up from my friends' faces to see a group of recruits at the mouth of the alley. My mouth dries as I take in their purple training tunics.

Marcus and Felix see the expression on my face and turn to face the interlopers. They each take a step back, hovering over my shoulder like a pair of gargoyles. There are five recruits—I recognize two from the training field. Their eyes are cold and unfriendly. I feel a flash of anger at the sight of them—that same rage that burns every time I see anyone from the First Legion. I lean into the Iron Symbol, letting its coldness flood through me.

"Nope, exactly where we're meant to be." I give their leader, a burly blond recruit, a small smile. "I appreciate you asking."

"Well, that's funny," the boy drawls, taking a step forward, "because Spurius here says that three legionnaires that look like you are walking around wearing Praetorian training tunics despite being dogs from the Twelfth." My eyes flick over to the rat who had been on the field with us. He flinches as our eyes make contact but doesn't back down.

"Well, that would be a problem." I shrug, still hoping I can talk my way out of it. "If we see any Twelvies running around in purple, you will be the first person I tell."

"Don't suppose you'd mind showing us your brand?" He smiles, revealing a set of perfect white teeth, like a miniature shieldwall. "Can't be too careful when our reputation is on the line. Our words are *excellentia ex excellentia* after all." His lips quirk condescendingly, assuming that we do not speak the ancients' language.

"That means excellence from the excellent," he explains with a cruel smile, as if he was our magister. "I do not think an *immundus* is any sort of excellent." He already knows the truth of who we are. This is a formality—an excuse for the bullies to get their licks in without getting in trouble. Mentally, I curse the old crone for ruining our tunics.

"Surely Spurius told you what we are," I offer, changing tactics. "Are you so sure you want to make enemies of us?"

"Oooh, you might become *Fidelia*." Scorn fills his tone. "I'm so scared. You're the next Iron Lords. Whatever shall we do?" He pulls a white *tellus* knife from his belt and twirls it in his hand. It bears a *krakenus*, the many armed monster as a seal. My eyes almost pop out of my head at the sight of the ceramic weapon. It is the same thing that Censors' blades are made of—strong enough to scratch iron and immune to all Symbols.

"Let's teach them a lesson, Brennus," one of the recruits begs their leader.

"Maybe we should just gut them like pigs now to spare us all from their Ascent?" He takes a couple of paces toward us, and the pack follows him like eager hounds, nipping at his heels. I crouch down to scoop a loose stone from the cobbles. Marcus and Felix step next to me, their fists raised.

"Enough." A quiet voice cuts through the impending violence like a blade. The Praetorian recruits spin to reveal a single officer standing behind them. My eyebrow arches as I realize it is Centurion Marius. Is he here to save us, or did he send them?

"Give me that," he snaps, holding a hand out to Brennus, who carries the *tellus* knife.

"It was given to me by my mother." The legionnaire sniffs and raises his head in challenge.

"It is against regulations for a recruit to carry one," the officer replies calmly, unimpressed. "Give it to me now, and I will not have you whipped." A cruel sneer passes over the boy's face, but he hands the blade to the centurion, who tucks it behind his belt.

His attention turns to us with the same cool intensity. "As for you three, I ordered you to report to your tribune."

"Yes, *Dominus*." I salute, bowing my head. "We got lost on our way back. We are not used to the routes of the Prime Quad."

"Idiots, come with me." He snaps his fingers, and the Praetorian recruits part for us like a gate. We march past their baleful stares to join Marius. He glances back at our would-be killers and waves dismissively. "As you were."

He leads us away from the alley and down the long, main road toward the Fourth Quad at a brisk pace. I trot, trying to catch up to him. "Thank you, *Dominus*—" I begin, but he raises up a hand, cutting me off.

We march the rest of the way back to the Twelfth in silence. As we enter our legion's sector, I feel the eyes of all the men settle on us with the intensity of jackals. I glance down at the purple training clothes I wear and know that this color has become dangerous for a different reason. We left this morning for the *Fidelis test* and return wearing the uniform of the First Legion. Mars damn that palatine magister!

Without breaking stride, I pull the tunic over my head and throw it over my shoulders, leaving it in the dust. I feel Marcus and Felix copy my movements just behind me. Marius doesn't turn, but a sense of wry amusement radiates from the dry officer.

I am no Praetorian. Let the men see the red welts on our backs and know what they did to us. The anger continues to simmer in our wake, but I feel its direction change. It is no longer aimed at me but walks at my side.

Marius leads us to the stone headquarters building at the back of the sector. Durus meets us at the front. The First Spear's eyes take in our bare torsos before moving to the *Fidelis* centurion, who escorts us.

"This way," he says without asking any questions. What will our commander say when he sees our whipped backs? When he finds out what I did to the relic? I am not afraid—perhaps I should be, but Iron succors me, keeping my spine straight and my heart cold.

The four of us follow him down the hall and pause outside Gaius's closed door. The Twelfth's centurion knocks once before placing his hand on the handle.

"Come," a serious voice calls from inside.

"Tribune, they're back, and they brought Centurion Marius with them," Durus announces. He opens the door and gestures for us to enter. The *Fidelis* leads us in. Gaius is sitting behind his desk underneath the banner of the Second Legion. He looks up from a stack of papers, and his eyes sharpen when he sees who escorts us.

Durus closes the door in our wake, and the room is silent for a long time—too long. It's obvious that our commander and the *Fidelis* know each other. The tension grows so thick that I feel it even with Iron dulling my nerves. There's a similarity in the expression on their faces. A suspicion begins to form in my mind when the centurion breaks the peace.

"What have you dragged me into this time, brother?"

Of course.

The familial similarity is obvious now that I look for it. The clue was in the centurion's name—I just didn't notice. The Marius brothers do not look completely alike; they are more like two rocks that have weathered in the same place. They're both tall and lean, but that's not what tells me that they're related. There's an aura of solemn competency that exudes from both.

Gaius's eyes flick from his brother to me before going back. "He passed, then?" He does not sound surprised.

"Passed…" my instructor scoffs in disgust. "They all *passed*, Gaius. That one hit the *custos* relic with his will so hard that it shattered."

"I see." Gaius lowers the papers in his hands to the desk and folds them, staring at me with an unblinking gaze. I can feel the wheels of his mind spinning as his suspicions are confirmed. I'm not sure why he looks upset; he told me to be unforgettable. I just followed his orders.

"Three *Fidelia* from the Twelfth?" the centurion pushes, finally showing a measure of his frustration. "Not a single recruit was chosen from below the Ninth, and then you find *three*?"

"It should have been more, but that bastard Lucas was tricky," Gaius mutters, leaning back in his chair.

"*More*?" The younger Marius makes a strangled sound somewhere between delight and horror.

"Yes, Percy, I found more." Gaius sounds tired.

"Is this why you—" He bites off the sentence before he finishes it. The two brothers glance at us as if they briefly forgot we were here.

"Father is right about some things," Gaius replies. The silence in the room grows heavier. I can feel Percy's disagreement even if he does not say so.

"Thank you for testing them fairly. Can I count on you to train them?"

"You know I have no interest in these games."

"I do know, which is why the responsibility to play them falls to me." Gaius looks over us again, a frown forming on his face as he fully notices our missing shirts and some of the welts that wrap around Marcus's ribs.

"Why were my soldiers flogged?" His voice is soft, but there's a sharp note of steel that runs through it. A shiver runs down me as the two Silver *electii* eye each other.

"That was a gift from our mother." Percy raises his chin in defiance. Surprise flares in Gaius's eyes for the first time, and he leans forward, staring intently at his brother. Felix lets out a little choking sound next to me.

"Plautia was here?"

"Here? She was the senior magister on the committee. She whipped your men."

Gaius's eyes darken.

"She knew they were yours," Percy says, answering his unspoken question. "Whipped them for being late and not in *lorica*. Tried to keep me from passing them too."

"You were late?" Our tribune turns to look at us with a light of suspicion in his eyes. He knows when we left; there is no reason we should not have been on time unless we did something else while his eyes were not on us.

"The training was not at the *castellum*." I snort. "Had to run across the entire damn circle to get to the southern training fields."

Gaius gives his brother a look.

"More games." Percy sighs. "This will not end well, brother."

"It was never going to." Gaius shrugs. "Thank you for protecting them." The full scope of what Percy did by standing up to his mother is clear to me now. My head spins as I try to comprehend the politics at play.

"Thank you, *Dominus*," I repeat sharply, standing to shirtless attention. Marcus and Felix copy my action, and we stand stiffly as the centurion turns in surprise. He studies us for a moment, his face unreadable, before he turns back to our tribune.

"Every other day, Gaius. South training fields, full battle kit."

"They will be there." The brothers toss each other lazy salutes, and Percy departs, closing the door behind him, leaving us alone with our commander. For the first time, I notice he's not that much older than me. When I first arrived, he seemed so different. But he's barely thirty and already the tribune of a cohort. A cohort in the Twelfth Legion, but there are only one hundred in the entirety of the Iron Legions.

It's obvious that the Marius family is connected. To have two sons that were in the Second Legion and the *Fidelia* as well as a mother who is a senior magister is… uncommon, to say the least. But for one of those sons to fall to the Twelfth speaks of another layer that I don't even begin to understand.

"I told you these games would continue," Gaius comments softly, turning to look at the three of us. His face is thoughtful, and he gestures for us to sit in the three chairs in front of his desk. I perch at the front, keeping my tender back from hitting the back.

"You will not be caught off guard again." It is an order, not a question.

"Yes, *Dominus*," we echo each other.

"But why, *Dominus*?" Felix broaches the question we are all thinking. "Why are the magisters trying to stop us from—"

Gaius holds up a hand, interrupting him. "Think, boy. Who gets sent to the lowest legions?"

"Criminals, cowards, and failures," I offer.

"Not exactly the kind of people that those at the top would want to wield more power, eh?" Gaius chuckles. "The elite feel a lot more comfortable when their loyal dogs are bigger than the ones with a little bit of wolf in them."

I wince at his words. Wolves and I do not have the best history. But as I trace the logic of his point. It makes a cold sort of sense. If you have a legion dedicated to reprobates, why would you want to make them stronger? Everyone knows the Twelfth is essentially a death sentence.

"If this is a legion where they send problems to be disposed of, then what are you doing here, *Dominus*?" I keep my voice neutral, but his head snaps up as he stares at me. Instead of anger, a small smile flashes across his stoic face, then it is gone.

"I chose to be here, recruit. Now, it is up to you all to choose to survive." The three of us exchange glances and nod. I can tell there's more he isn't telling us, but he knows that we haven't told him the truth either.

"*Dominus*," I begin my next question slowly, delicately. "If that was your brother and mother, does that mean Alessandra is your sister?" I *feel* the weight of Felix and Marcus's gazes on me, and a flush begins to grow at the base of my neck. I throw myself deeper into Iron's clutches to keep my embarrassment at bay.

Gaius stares at me with a knowing eye that threatens to shatter the calm that my Symbol gives me. I studiously keep my face blank. Cupid's Bones! I didn't mean it like that. I was just making sure I understood the players in the game I found myself dancing to.

"A distant cousin," he grunts after a moment of inspection. "She was there too, I take it?"

"Yes, *Dominus*. She didn't seem to share your mother's opinion of us."

Gaius grunts in acknowledgment but doesn't comment on his family drama. After a moment of silence, he leans forward, his brown eyes boring into mine.

"You've done well so far. But my brother won't always be there to save you. I expect the three of you to become *Fidelia*."

"*Dominus*, why is this so important?" Marcus asks, a frown on his square face. "I have always dreamed of being worthy..." His voice trails off, his question only partially formed.

"I will worry about why it is important. It is enough for you to do as your commanding officer tells you. I am ordering you to Ascend to Silver. Do I make myself clear?" The snap of command is back in his voice—our quiet conversation is at an end.

"Yes, *Dominus*," we reply.

"*Vade*. Go. Do my will."

CHAPTER 29

Time loses all meaning.

One day we are marching in line with the rest of the Twelfth, learning over a score of different maneuvers that our commanders might demand we perform in the thick of battle. When we are not drilling, we are running, carrying battle gear, and sweating as they push us beyond our physical limits.

Then we are suffering under the scrutiny of Percy Marius as he teaches us how to use our *Corda* to the maximum potential of what the *inhibitus* around our necks will let us achieve. Even if we do not become *Fidelis*, every recruit who follows his teachings will be more capable with their Heart than when they began.

My *Cor* veins burn constantly from the strain I am putting them through. The cold Iron sphere in my chest seems to grow, expanding my already impressive capacity to hold essence. I am even faster at drawing it from my *gladius* and *scutum* than I was before. My will grows like a muscle, getting better at protecting my weapons and twisting my enemies'. I know that these are all signs that I am advancing through the stages of Copper and toward Silver, but my *inhibitus* stymies any true breakthroughs. I think I have reached the peak of what Copper can be. My collar thrums with warning at all times, a nagging presence that irritates me to no end.

The routine sucks us all in. Every day is similar enough that they blend together. I could not guess how many weeks we are hammered in the forges of Agogia. The boys of Segesta all push themselves, doing their best to keep pace with Marcus, Felix, and me.

We meet behind the shed every night to show them what Percy has taught us. They may not be able to Ascend, but all of them are hungry to reach the maximum potential of what their *Corda* can do. I do not know if it is forbidden for us to do this, but we do it anyway. I am certain Gaius knows and equally certain that he will say nothing for now. Why should he complain if his soldiers become stronger?

"I think I missed my nameday," Marcus comments to no one in particular one night as we carry the *gladii* and *scuta* back inside the shed. I freeze in shock, trying to figure out what day it is.

The *Sententia* happened during *Octobris*, the eighth month. Here in the desert, it got cold at night, but there were not seasons here the same way that there were back home.

"Saturn's Bones! Is it *Maius* already?" I ask in horror. Has it truly been four months since our parents were killed? It does not seem possible, and yet it must be true. The changes that have been wrought in my body and mind cannot happen overnight.

"I heard some of the decurions talking about the date," Marcus answers with a shrug, walking ahead of me. His expression is hard to read, his skin blending in with the dark night. But his voice is full of a bravado that I'm not sure is real. I think I understand. What kind of man complains about their nameday being forgotten after what we have lived through? My heart breaks for the boys we once were.

Self-hatred runs through me, bringing a flush to my face that I can feel burning. Yet another thing that my greed has taken away from my friends. Even if Marcus had joined the legions like he planned, something tells me they celebrate birthdays in the Praetorians.

"Happy nameday, Marcus," I murmur, my voice full of self-pity. It feels like I will never escape this guilt. Every day, I see something that has been twisted or taken away from my friends. I will carry this burden with me wherever I go.

"Will you stop doing that?" he snaps, whirling around to glare at me. I have no problem making out that expression even in the dark.

"Stop doing what?" Unconsciously, I take a step back, startled by his sudden aggression. We have been on better terms lately, not quite what it was before the *Sententia*, but part of me had dared to think that I was forgiven. But now that seems to be a false hope.

"Making everything *your* fault."

"But… but it is."

Marcus crosses his arms and glares down at me. "And how do you figure that?"

"The *votum*—everything. I was the one who failed to get a *Cor*. I am the reason that whatever that thing in the wolf armor was attacked. I am the reason that our families…" My voice trails off, unable to finish the sentence.

"You think that they were killed because of the *votum*?" Marcus's voice is dangerously quiet. We tease him about being the stupidest of us, but that is unfair. He is beyond clever; he just rarely needs to use it. I feel the sharp edge of his mind cutting against me as he angles his argument.

"Well... yeah. Felix said—"

"A *votum* that you swore all by yourself, with no input from anyone else," he interrupts, not letting me explain any further.

"Obviously, all four of us swore—"

"Oh, all *four* of us swore it. But it was your idea, then?" I know what he wants me to say. That Valentina pushed us to do this. That if anyone is to blame for putting us on this path, it is her. But that is not the only thing that went wrong.

"I am the only one who didn't get their *Cor*. I am the one who broke it."

"Not true," he snarls, pointing an angry finger at me. "'We earn our Hearts together, or not at all.' That was the exact oath. And if you would stop feeling sorry for yourself for even a single moment— you would remember that although you did not get a *Cor* from the *Sententia*, the rest of us were ready to take ours."

"Uh," I try to interject, my mind reeling.

"The wolf did not appear until Felix was kneeling before the Censor, about to get his. That was the moment the *votum* was broken. If all three of us had refused to accept ours, it would have stayed whole."

I am silent for a long moment, reeling from shock at being spoken to like this.

"You do not get to have a monopoly on our pain. You do not get to take all the responsibility. The four of us—Valentina, Felix, you, and I. We did this. We played with things we should not have, and now we pay the price." Marcus's chest is heaving, full of barely contained rage.

"I didn't realize..." I manage to choke after a moment. "I thought that was why you were angry with me."

"I wasn't angry with you," he says, deflating with a long sigh. "Well, not about that. I was sad. I was broken. I needed my friend, but you were too busy making yourself into a martyr for something that you didn't need to bear alone." A new feeling of guilt spreads through me, although unlike the old one, this one doesn't feel like it will break me.

"I'm sorry," I say when the silence between us has grown uncomfortable. "I should have been there. I was... lost too."

"Yeah, I figured." He chuckles dryly. "Not a great admission from the guy who is telling us where to go." I can't help it; I throw back my head and laugh. I can't stop. It keeps bubbling out of me like a hot spring bursting out of the ground. After a moment, Marcus joins in, adding his own voice to mine.

Tears run down my face. I am the one who is supposed to be showing them the way. I promised them that I knew the path, but I am just as lost, just as broken. It would be even more hilarious if it were not the only choice that we had.

Still, even though my merriment is tinged with a hint of madness, it feels good. I have not laughed like this since I came to Agogia. A piece of the cold, hard crust that has begun to form around my soul seems to crack and slough off, lightening my load. My shoulders straighten, and my spine unbends. I needed this. I needed my best friend to help me carry through. I have been trying to do it alone, but that was foolish. We are a unit, and together we will go forward.

"I'm sorry that I wasn't there when you needed me," I tell him when we finally finish laughing. Marcus wipes at the corner of his eyes as I apologize. "I let my guilt strangle me, and I forgot the most important rule. We're stronger together than we are apart."

"I won't lie to you," he says softly. "I was sad. I didn't want to look at any of you. Everything I ever had, everything I ever wanted, was taken away in a single night."

"Me too."

"I'm still sad," he admits with a sigh. "No matter how hard I train, no matter how far I push, all I see is what could have been." It must be almost impossible to heal from that pain—to be so close to his dream but prevented from reaching for it. Every step is like a cut, reopening a wound. In some ways, I'm lucky. I never wanted to be here. I'm spared from being haunted by the specter of lost dreams.

"What can I do to help?" I ask, not sure what else to say.

"Share the load, my friend." His teeth flash in a tight smile. "We're stronger together."

"I will," I tell him, stepping forward to clasp hands with him and pulling him into a hug. "I promise."

CHAPTER 30

urus and the other officers don't relent on our training. If anything, it feels like they increase the amount of work that they expect from us. The First Spear is in front of me, walking backward as he watches us march. His expression is grim, but that might just be the disappointment of a strict father.

"You are soldiers of the Iron Legions of the empire!" he chants in the familiar cadence.

"We do not bend! We do not break!" we call back.

"Faster, you dogs, or I'll have every man of you whipped!" one of the decurions shouts at the back half of our formation, which must be lagging. My hand tightens on the grip of my shield. I really hope they don't whip us. Our Copper bodies can take more punishment than a normal man's, but I am getting tired of being beaten.

"Halt!" Durus screams from the front. I take one more step to let the command trickle down the line and then stop, perfectly in line with Felix, Marcus, and the two other line leaders.

"Form battle lines!" the centurion calls, and there is a flurry of movement behind me as our long, trailing formation shrinks in length and expands in width. Men from the back run up at an angle until the entire unit stands three lines deep.

A heavy shoulder jams into me as someone passes behind me. I let out a grunt of surprise and stagger a half-step before catching myself and getting back in place.

"Sorry about that, *Primus*," a voice sneers. I can't turn to look at him, but I know it is Anas. The big man has become something of a leader for the more traditional members of the Twelfth. The rift between patrician and plebeian is still strong.

"Didn't you hear?" another snide voice joins in. "Our dear *Primus* has been tested to be a *Fidelis*."

"Mars's Bones!" Anas replies as if he had no idea. "Is that true, *Primus*? You really can't stand slumming with us poor people, can you? I bet your mother would get along with us just fine—" Marcus begins

229

to turn, a dark look brewing on his face, like a thunderstorm gathering around *Mons* Olympus on a hot summer's day.

"Try it, big boy," Anas calls lustily. "I've been wanting to knock you down a peg since the day you walked in here." I kick my friend's shin and shake my head when he glances at me. Gaius's warning that the magisters will look for any reason to exclude us from *Fidelis* training rings in my mind.

"That's what I thought," the thug taunts as my friend turns back to the front.

"Shields!" comes the call.

"Shields," we thunder back, raising our *scuta* to form the shieldwall that the legions are famous for. Awareness floods into me as the iron rectangles touch, forming an unbroken connection. Today, we are only using our *gladii* and *scuta*. I feel the other men's wills flickering through as they join, like fireflies in the night.

Essence floods into me from the incredible amount of iron that I am now able to reach. This must be why we are not wearing our *loricae*: the combined mass would be more than any of us are ready to handle. Even this much is intoxicating. I would stay in this ocean forever if I could. Its peaceful cold is like a siren song to my tired body and mind.

"Swords!" A hundred blades slither from their sheaths. The metallic sound is deafening. I grip my *gladius* in my right hand, holding the blade low between me and Marcus. My shoulder blades itch; I can feel the eyes of men who hate me holding naked swords at my back. I am exposed, but force myself to breathe, leaning on the calm that comes with holding my Symbol to keep me steady.

"Fighting advance!" Durus calls.

"Huah!" we reply, and I rap my *scutum* with my will. The wave ripples through the connected iron like a stone thrown into a pond. Again, I strike the wall, beating it like a drum, setting the pace for our progression. As one, we advance, shields forward. I slide into my step like a miniature lunge and stab my *gladius* forward, shifting my shield slightly to allow it to pass between mine and Marcus's. After a full extension, I pull it back and snap my *scutum* back to where it belongs.

All around me, I feel with every part of my being the individual pieces of our wall as they click back into place. Durus does not call for us to halt, so I strike my shield with my will again, and we advance, blades shooting out after each step.

"Ordered retreat!" Durus cries after we repeat the process a dozen times.

"Huah!" we cry. This time, I strike the shieldwall with a double beat. Every legionnaire rotates his shield at an angle, connecting his own to the top of the *scutum* to his right and the bottom of the one to his left. The gaps leave space for our swords to strike out at anyone pushing our line as we give ground. In time to my drum, we step backward, holding the line as we go. Officers walk along the front, pointing at men who "die." They fall out of line, and the next person steps forward to fill the gap, keeping our front seamless and whole.

"Halt!" the centurion calls as we reach the end of the field. We pause and wait for our next orders. Durus puts his hands on his hips and frowns, looking up and down the line. "Well, you can kind of march," he admits after a long moment. "It's time to see if you can fight."

They divide us into twelve decades and have us face off. I'm left with a lot of men I don't know, from the rear of the formation. They're real *captivi*, sent here to be punished for their crimes. Many of them look at me with evil eyes that tell me they'd rather follow Anas than me.

"Don't worry, *Dominus*, we'll make you proud," a light voice says at my elbow. I turn to find Macer, the skinny kid who I got whipped for, standing at my right. He's put on a few pounds since we first got here, but he's still thin for a soldier. He looks at me like an adoring pup, and I feel a little sick to my stomach.

"Yeah, '*Dominus*,'" one of the harder recruits, a man named Bror, sneers.

"Don't call me that," I snap at Macer, who wilts a little at the anger in my tone. I didn't mean to lash out at him that hard. But the needling from the rest of the cohort has begun to get under my skin. I sigh in frustration and sink deeper into the Iron Symbol, letting my stress fade away.

"Tribune on the field!" one of the decurions shouts from the far end.

"Attention!" As one, we snap into a stiff stance, shields raised.

"Carry on," Gaius calls calmly after a moment. His brown eyes sweep the field with his usual disinterested stare. They pause on me for only a moment before continuing their inspection. He doesn't show it, but I know he's here to watch his *Fidelis* hopefuls in action.

"Form lines!" Durus shouts, needing no further encouragement.

I know that there is more to this than he has told me, but a thrill runs through me as I settle into a line with my other nine. I feel important—a new sensation for me. When I came to the Twelfth, I expected to die in obscurity, forgotten because all my family is dead. Thanks to Gaius, I have a chance to escape that future. My heart, the blood and flesh one in my chest, beats with excitement for the chance to show my commander that I am worth the investment he is making.

The officers organize us into two lines of six companies. Colored armbands are distributed to mark us as allies. I tie a black band around my forearm and take stock of the rest of the field. Each team has another decade across from them. My group is placed toward the center, across from Marcus's. My big friend is wearing a red band and gives me a cheerful grin as we settle into our shieldwalls. He lives for this. Felix and his squad are also opposite mine further down to the left, wearing purple.

"The last decade standing will be excused from running a lap around Agogia tonight!" Durus announces, striding down the open center between the two battle lines. We all groan at the punishment. "And their dinner will probably be warm when they get to it. Just in case you needed some extra motivation." A wicked grin flashes across the officer's bearded face.

My heart, which is already beating quickly, picks up the pace as I realize that we're going to fight each other. We've practiced taking and giving hits, but never something like this. This will be my first taste of what it's like to be a legionnaire.

For a moment, I'm transported back to the melee in the arena, where I convinced a group of boys and girls to form a shieldwall. I thought I was very clever stealing the tactics of the legion to use against the interlopers from Nicodemia. While we survived, my plan cost a lot of my peers the chance to earn their *Cor*. But this time, it's different—I am a legionnaire in the Iron Legions. I carry the *gladius* and *scutum* and bear a Copper Heart.

"Blunt your swords and present them for inspection!" he barks. I reach into my *gladius* with the Iron Symbol, tracing the sharp edges with my mind and commanding them to soften. The blade ripples as it obeys my command without too much effort. It was made to train, not to kill. After a dozen heartbeats, it is done. I raise my head and extend my sword out from our shieldwall for an officer to approve.

I'm the first recruit for what feels like a long time. Durus narrows his eyes at me but doesn't comment, opting instead to wait for the rest of the century to catch up. Felix and Marcus also finish before the rest of the recruits complete the task. All of the other boys from Segesta are not far behind us.

The centurion boldly walks down the line, his hands extended out like wings, striking the edges with the palms of his blades. A shudder runs down my spine as I imagine the penalty any legionnaire will suffer if their blade cuts him.

"Pass, pass, pass," the veteran calls as he touches each sword. I *feel* when his hand settles on my *gladius* the same way that I would if he shook my hand, for the sword is a part of me. His presence runs down the length of the blade, then withdraws as he moves on, breaking physical contact.

"More!" he snaps at one or two recruits, pausing until he is satisfied at the level of dullness. It only takes him a few moments to work his way through the entire field. When he reaches the far end, he turns and spits at us with the glare of a longtime officer.

"Shields!"

"Shields!" we echo. My decade lifts their *scutum* together, and my awareness expands as our small shieldwall forms. The fear is gone as I sink into my Symbol, replaced by the hard cold that is central to Iron. I lean on that stability to keep myself from overdrawing essence and triggering my *inhibitus*. With this much iron connected to my body, I am walking a razor's edge—the slightest slip could send me over.

"Begin!" Durus commands, and the melee begins. For a moment, we all hesitate, afraid to advance.

"Watch our sides!" I shout from the center, aware that it would be easy for one of our neighbors to turn on us and catch our unprotected flank. I feel the shieldwall constrict into a curve as the men on our wings step back, twisting so they can watch all directions.

Then there's a crash of metal on metal as one of the squads on the edge of the field barrels into their opponent, confident because they are not surrounded like the rest of us. Their surge forward sets off a wave of action as the new edges throw caution to the wind and rush their opposite, chanting battle cries.

The decade to our right charges, and I feel the men in line gathering themselves, their shields wiggling in the wall as they prepare for our turn. But as I watch the melee develop, I can't shake the sense that following them is a death sentence. The squads on either side are fully entangled with their opposite, shieldwall against shieldwall. There is no room for tactics; only a brutal, bloody fight until only one decade stands. I might be the strongest Copper in the century, but I don't like those odds.

"Hold!" I shout, hesitant to be dragged into the quagmire before us. I see Felix's frustrated expression as his squad rushes to meet their opposing group, which reinforces my thought. Marcus's decade does not charge but keeps their line tight and sharp, mirroring us.

I meet my friend's eye and toss my head to the side, offering him a way out of our stalemate. He looks at me for a second, then laughs, nodding once. I raise my blunted *gladius* and point at the exposed back of the shieldwall to our right, locked in a brutal battle with the squad they charged.

"Advance forward-right!" I order.

"Who made you—"

"Oh, shut up and just do what he says, Bror," one of the other men grunts. "He's the Mars-damned *Primus* anyway."

Bror mumbles another curse but doesn't resist. I strike our shieldwall with my will, beating out a tempo as we advance on the exposed backs of the squad to our diagonal.

Across from us, Marcus's squadron copies our move, attacking the rear of the battling squad to our left. Satisfied that we're safe for a moment, I pick up our pace so that we're jogging by the time we close with the unsuspecting decade wearing yellow armbands locked in combat with another group wearing brown.

A smirk runs across my face as I see Anas turn at the sound of our charge. His sour face turns white at the sight of us crashing down on him. I hadn't realized he was in this decade when I chose to attack it, but I'm certainly not sad about eliminating my biggest enemy.

The yellow squad in the middle of our sandwich doesn't last more than a matter of seconds. Some turn to face us as we slam into them, only to take blunted blades to their backs from their original opponents.

"Strike!" I order as we step into range, ceasing my drumbeats on the shieldwall.

"Huah!" my squad echoes as we grind to a halt. In unison, we swing our *scuta* to the side and stab out with our blades. I'm not the one who takes down Anas, but I see him fall as the opposite line takes advantage of the chaos that we have sown. The yellow squad shatters, and all of them drop to the ground, playing dead as we have been taught.

"Strike!" I command again without missing a beat, striking a blow against the shieldwall with my will as I do.

"Huah!" the men echo, and we take a step forward, not giving the group with brown armbands a moment to recover. A couple of their fellows are down, their line scattered and disorganized. My *gladius* slams into the shield of one of the other recruits, and for a second, I feel the entirety of their will pushing back at me, rejecting my blow. A flurry of haunting commands tickles at my mind.

Hold. Stay. Please. No! Resist, they seem to say, but even though there are more of them, they pale in authority compared to the *custos* relic that I destroyed. The voices cut off as I step back, raising my shield to catch the return blow. I make sure to keep my *scutum* in contact with the rest of my squad, letting their will reinforce mine.

A frown creases my face as I feel one of the shields on my line warp, twisted by the will of an attacking legionnaire. I'm brimming with essence, and I burn it as I shove my will down the line to encompass the entire wall for a moment.

Resist, I command. The *scutum* springs back to its rectangular shape, fitting back into our formation like a perfect puzzle piece. I stagger slightly as my reserves almost run dry at the strain of reinforcing something so far away. All the extra strength flows out of my body as my grasp on the Iron Symbol flickers and threatens to fade. I grasp like a drowning man, pulling from all the sources that I can touch.

Essence pours into me, reinforcing my connection to my Symbol. My exhaustion fades, my strength returns, and with a grunt, I step forward, getting back into line with the rest of my squad. I catch a second strike on my *scutum*, dismissing the weak command—*Shatter*—with a mere thought.

I keep pulling essence as I follow up the soldier's reset. The *inhibitus* constricts around my throat like a serpent as I dance at the limits of Copper. The point of my blade stabs at the center of the other man's shield, and as the chorus of their tiny wills protest, I trigger a command of my own.

Break.

The brown-banded recruit's shield cracks down the middle, parting for my blade like an eggshell. The dull tip of my *gladius* slams into his chest, knocking him back a pace as I deal a blow that would be fatal if this were truly battle.

The rest of my strike's power ripples through the enemy's shieldwall. My jaw drops in shock as I see the *scuta* on either side of the recruit crack in obedience to my will. Durus's incessant training takes over, and I step back, pulling my sword free of the other man's shield and lifting my own to protect my comrades. The legionnaire I "killed" glances at his ruined *scutum* for a moment before looking back at me in terrified awe.

"Plaius, you're dead!" an officer booms from the sidelines.

"Oh, right," he mumbles, collapsing to his knees before falling over.

The brown squad crumbles quickly after him. The two recruits whose shields I broke try to mend them, but they're too slow—the distraction makes it even easier to tear them apart.

"Watch the right!" someone shouts on the side of our formation as we step over our fallen century mates.

"We gotta shift!" another man cries in panic.

There's a flurry of voices as the men react to a threat I can't see. Another squad has decided to challenge us. Our formation is uneven, broken up by victory. We've got to get back into a fighting stance, or we'll die faster than the two squads we just eliminated.

"Box! Form a box!" I order, turning to face the way we came. More of the decade takes up the call, and we form up into a square with our backs facing inward, our shields making a wall on every side. It's claustrophobic inside the formation, and I can't see anything beyond my own *scutum*. Something smashes into our now left flank, and I get a flash of insight as our shieldwall touches theirs.

"Reinforce!" the men around me call, and they turn to join the portion of the line that is under assault. Our box dissolves as we flow into the new formation, adding our shields to the wall. For a moment, we're deadlocked. The new challenger, wearing blue armbands, spent their charge's momentum, but we did not break. Now we fight with the slow grind of the Iron Legions, as our people have done for hundreds of years.

My *scutum* bangs against another's as I try to force my will through some crack in their defenses, as a tree root sunders a mountain. But even as I fight with my Heart, my *gladius* is moving. I draw my shield back and stab forward with the blade in the gap it leaves, searching for my enemies.

There is only the dull thud of metal on metal and the grunts of men as we shove and are shoved, each line trying to break the other but holding strong. I draw in Iron essence as fast as I can, desperate to hold on. There's no danger of triggering my *inhibitus* now—I spend essence as quickly as it comes in, and even my increased efficiency in cultivating is not enough to keep my reserves full. We're losing. I can feel the battle beginning to get away from us. The edges of my *scutum* are crumpling—every blow against our shieldwall feels like it rattles my brain inside my skull. A Copper Heart might make me stronger and faster than a normal man, but even it can't keep exhaustion at bay forever.

My grasp on the Symbol begins to weaken. I pant with exertion. I have to do something, or we will lose. The other decade is fresher, or their Hearts are stronger. Whatever the reason, it doesn't matter. In a war of attrition, they will win. A gap appears as the contact of our *scuta* breaks further down the line. I can no longer feel the other side of our wall in my mind. My *Cor* cannot reach what it cannot touch. We are reunited a moment later as my men condense the formation, but we're down from ten shields to nine.

I take a risk as I raise my *scutum* to block another legionnaire's blow and glance over my shoulder, surveying the rest of the field behind us. There are only two decades left, locked in the same struggle a dozen paces away. I spot purple and red armbands among the fray and can't stop the amused smirk that comes out of my mouth. Marcus and Felix have been drawn into battle against each other. Of course those two are still in the fray.

I eye the backs of the men behind us, and an idea begins to take hold. "Ordered retreat! Ordered retreat!" I bellow twice to make sure no one is caught off guard by the command. Then, as I did just a little while earlier, I ring our shieldwall with the beat of our march.

As one, we fall back a step, creating space between us and our opponents. Sensing our weakness, they eat it up greedily, hungry for the kill. Our line holds as we pull back, beat by beat. Our attackers throw themselves at us trying to bring us down.

Step. Block. Counterstroke.

Step. Block. Counterstroke.

Pace by pace, we drag our stronger opponents into the melee that rages behind us. With every step, I look over my shoulder, waiting for the other decades to notice our approach.

We're only a couple of feet away from the backs of the other squad when one of them begins to shout the alarm to the rest of his comrades. Panic sweeps through the different groups as everyone tries to react at once.

Half of the decade behind us begins to turn to face the new threat, leaving themselves exposed to the one they've been holding off. Their leader tries to collapse them into some dense formation like a square, but it's too late. Their enemy swarms through the cracks like a horde of locusts. Any organization left on the battlefield vanishes as both lines collapse into a blood frenzy.

Our instructors will be furious.

"Box! Form a box!" I shout, trying to pull off the move that the other line failed to do. If we can just hunker down before the storm hits us, we might have a chance—

A maelstrom of iron and men envelops us like the hurricanes that plague the coasts. Our line evaporates as we are hit from both sides.

"Break!" I shout, releasing the men to fight on their own, and then I am thrust into the midst. My awareness shrinks down to the iron *gladius* and *scutum* in my hands as I lose contact with all the rest of my line. My Heart feels a pang of loss for the easy access to so much essence, but now that I'm not being hammered by a dozen attacks at once, I feel my reserves begin to swell. The Iron Symbol settles back over me like a mantle as I catch my breath.

A recruit wearing a blue band spins into view, his face twisted in frustration. They've chased us across the field only to be drawn into a nightmare. I raise my shield to ward off his blow, readying my own thrust at the same time.

I feel his sword tip scrape across the surface of my shield numbly, as if it's part of me. His will is weak compared to mine, and it barely even takes a thought to keep his *gladius* from getting any purchase. But... what if I wanted it to? A stray thought flickers through my mind, and I feel the corner of my lip quirk as I intuit another use of my *Cor* Heart.

Grab, I whisper to my shield, and the iron begins to soften at my command. The blue recruit's blade jerks to a halt as my shield clutches at it. I see his eyes widen in shock as I wrench my shield to the side, dragging him into an awkward position. He tries to cover himself with his *scutum*, but it's too late. My blunted tip stabs into his chest, and he drops with an *oomph* of pain.

I release his sword from my shield and order the iron to return to its natural state. A laugh rips out of me as I step over the fallen recruit and into the fray. I am learning. Another blue boy has one of my own black bands cornered. I slam into him from the side, my blade stabbing as he falls. He does not get up.

"Mars's Beard, I'm glad to see you, *Dominus!*" Macer pants as he lowers his shield. A red-banded recruit looms behind him with his blade raised.

"Don't call me that!" I snap, darting forward and shoving him to the side. My *scutum* rings like a bell under the force of the attack and the will backing it up. It feels like a creeping vine, growing over me inch by inch, constricting my ability to breathe—to think.

Break. Break. Break, the recruit's Heart demands of my iron. I gasp in shock at how strong his assault is. Caught off guard, I almost lose hold of my Symbol, but before it can slip through my fingers, I grab it with my mind and pour all the essence I have left into my defense.

No.

The vines recoil in surprise, as if burnt. I stagger, now losing my connection to the Symbol. In my panic, I used too much. My reserves are almost out; I can feel my Heart burning like an empty lung. But I'm still on my feet, still able to fight. I grit my teeth and pull as much essence as I can from my *gladius* and *scutum.* Compared to the torrent that I can glut on when wearing a *lorica,* it is but a trickle.

The red recruit's blade flashes in another attack. I catch it on my shield, but I'm not able to put any of my will into keeping my *scutum* whole. The blunted sword cuts through it like it's paper, leaving a diagonal rent that I can see through. Desperate for essence, I try to use the same trick I used against the *custos* relic and use his sword as another source, but he rebuffs me easily.

My attacker smiles as he draws his blade back for a stab, aiming for the hole he's already torn in my shield. I grit my teeth and suck in as much essence as I can from my tools. The Copper veins in my body burn as they stretch, obeying the demand placed on them by my will. The Iron Symbol begins to glow in my mind, banishing my tiredness. His arm shoots forward, and even though my Heart is fueled again, I know I don't have enough essence to stop this attack.

"Watch out, *Dominus!*" A scrawny figure pushes past me, throwing themselves at the blue recruit in a full-body tackle. My attacker grunts in surprise, staggering under the force of the dive, but manages to keep his feet under himself. He probably weighs at least two stone more than Macer, who makes up for what he lacks in mass with spirit.

The two of them grapple, their sandals kicking up the dust at our feet. I seize the moment that my squadmate has gifted me and inhale, drawing in as much essence as my Heart can manage. *I'm not out of the fight yet.*

I lower my head and charge forward, rushing to join the squabble. The blue recruit sees me coming and tries to disengage from my skinny little ally, but Macer stays on him doggedly, not giving him an inch. Then I barrel into our enemy's left side, leading with my *scutum,* and send him flying.

To my surprise, he stays on his feet and turns to me with rage burning in his eyes, Macer already forgotten. A dark *M* is branded onto the top of his hands, marking him as a murderer. He must be another of Anas's friends. I may not have been the one to personally bring my rival down, but I can certainly put one of his cronies in his place.

"Help the others! I got this," I shout to Macer, moving to meet the former *captivus*'s advance.

"Yes, *Dominus!*" the skinny boy replies before turning to sprint away.

"Don't call me that!"

My Copper veins buzz with essence, and the Iron Symbol burns brightly in my mind as I lunge forward, *gladius* extended like a duelist. The soldier catches it on his shield, but it's his turn to be on the backfoot. My will slams into his shield, crushing his resistance like a bug, and my sword punches through his shield with ease and its dull point slams into his chest. I pull my blade out with a flourish and turn my back on the stunned boy before he even finishes falling to the ground.

Essence continues to flood into me, and my reserve is almost filled to its Copper brink. Our little duel brought us to the edge of the skirmish. The rest of the field is a madhouse. All four decades have lost any sort of unit cohesion. I see a red fighting with one of my black-banded recruits. Two blues chase a fleeing purple like wolves. From the outside, it's impossible to judge who's winning, which means my only path is to start cutting and see what happens.

Across the field, I spy Gaius and the rest of the officers spectating the battle with dark expressions. The tribune's arms are crossed, and he is watching the living recruits with something like contempt. As if he feels my gaze, his eyes flick up and narrow into a glare when he sees I'm on the outside.

Taking the hint, I square my shoulders and circle the edge of the melee, looking for an opportune moment to strike. A red recruit with his back to the edge is locked in a duel with a blue band. Their swords crash into each other's shields as they give and take blows. The red legionnaire is so focused that he doesn't notice me coming up behind him until my *gladius* slams into his back. He drops to his knees and looks over his shoulder in disbelief.

I ignore him, flowing to face the blue band that he had been battling. The legionnaire turns to face me, but he's panting from the exertion, and I am coming off a slight rest. First, I slam into him with my shield, making its surface stick to his like glue. I twist my left arm to the side, forcing him to rotate with it. He lets out a gasp of surprise as he realizes what I've done, but by then, it's too late. My *gladius* slams into his stomach, doubling him over. I release his shield from mine as he topples to the ground.

I march through the field, keeping my essence reserves full, striking at any exposed legionnaire I can reach. Bodies slam down into the dust, and a bad feeling begins to grow in my chest as I realize that I've not seen another black band for minutes. I fear that my squad has fared poorly in this melee.

A purple legionnaire challenges me, and I catch his lunge, using my shield to knock his blade low while striking with mine. The steps of this battle dance has begun to feel familiar to me. It is different than the organized lines of the Iron Legions, but a part of me loves it.

The purple-banded man falls to the ground with a dull thud, and suddenly, the field is silent. I look up from my fallen enemy to see that there are only two other recruits on the field. One wears a purple band, the other a red one.

It's Marcus and Felix, my two closest friends.

CHAPTER 31

Of course the three of us who have been chosen as potential *Fidelia* are the last standing. Marcus barks an amused laugh as he looks from Felix to me. The big boy looks completely unruffled from the skirmish. I have no doubt that he could do this all day. Felix is quiet as he studies the two of us. There's a big dent in his shield, but as I watch, the iron begins to flow as it shifts back into something resembling its original state.

"Well, get on with it!" Durus barks from the outside. A chorus of laughter follows his order, drawing my attention. At least a score of full legionnaires has gathered behind the officers, waiting to see the outcome.

"Come on, *Primus*, I've got a dozen *denarii* on ya," shouts a voice I recognize. It's Unus, the soldier with the eyepatch, who branded me into the Twelfth Legion. More catcalls echo from the rest of the regulars, and even some of the recruits playing dead chime in. They're not betting; they just don't want to run around Agogia after this.

I glance between my two friends, trying to plan. I can tell that both of them are thinking the same thing. If one of us starts to fight another, the third wins by default. The legionnaires begin to call us names, shouting for us to fight. With a shrug, I start to make my way to the center, and after a moment, both of them copy me.

We make the three corners of a triangle so that we can watch each other. Felix is to my left and Marcus to my right. I raise my shield in salute, which they copy, and then we're off. Roars of excitement break out as I raise my *scutum* to catch Felix's blow. His will is like a python, twisting and crawling around me.

Relent. Relent. Relent, it insists as his Heart battles for control of my iron.

Hold, I command, and I feel my shield shudder as it wants to constrict under the pressure from Felix. It trembles but does not give, as my will keeps it firm. I step forward, spinning past Marcus in a risky move, but it forces Felix to reposition lest I get behind him. His sword's contact with my shield breaks, and I gasp in relief as his mental assault vanishes.

My *gladius* flashes out at Marcus as we reset our triangle, and his will is like a wall of sound shouting over mine in one long roar. Not to be left behind, Felix swipes at me again as his blade meets my shield, and I stagger under the assault of juggling the force of both of their minds. The noise from Marcus drowns out my own voice, and I stare in horror as Felix slices through the iron of my *scutum* easily.

I retreat a few steps, breaking the contact. It is blissfully silent in my head as I shake my body, trying to clear my mind. I feel both of their eyes settle on my damaged shield with the hunger of a predator spying a weak member of the herd. We may be friends, but we grew up in the *collegium*—competition is in our bones. A chance to take down the *Primus* is as delicious as any meal.

I lift my head in defiance, calling upon my *Cor* Heart to mend that which is broken. The iron on my shield ripples as it flows slowly like molasses, melting to cover the hole that Felix tore. It is better by leagues than the first time I showed them how to do it on this very field. Both of my friends blink in surprise before looking at each other.

"Shall we?" Felix drawls to Marcus with an amused grin.

"About time someone reminds our dear *Primus* that he's still human." As one, they drop into fighting crouches and begin stalking toward me, shields high, blades low.

I'm not angry that they are working together. If anything, I take it as a compliment. Something warm ignites in my chest, burning so bright that it overcomes the cold logic of the Iron Symbol. I am the greatest threat. No one else survived seven blows from the *custos* relic. We may all be Copper still, but I am straining the limits of what a Heart can do at this level.

Even with my unusual ability to draw in essence, I don't think that will save me from them. Both have the same education that I do. Their wills are too trained, too focused. Essence is the blood that pumps in the veins of a *Cor* Heart, but that is only one piece of the puzzle.

They close in on me like the *mythii* wolves that hunted me in the dream relic back in the arena. I glance at the purple bite marks that still circle my wrist. I survived that; I can survive this. Marcus angles himself toward my right, while Felix circles to my left, threatening my shield. I give ground, trying to keep them from being able to hit me at the same time. The hands of recruits playing dead surreptitiously grab at our ankles as we step over them—no one wants to run around the city.

I block an attack with my *scutum*, disengaging to catch Marcus's sword with my own. Their wills bore into mine. Felix's slices like a knife; Marcus's smashes like a hammer. My shield begins to dent; my sword bows in the middle. I could hold off against one of their assaults, but under their combined barrage, my essence reserves begin to wither. I'm running out of time.

Sensing my weakness, their blows grow even more reckless. I have no space to counterattack, so they stop defending themselves, throwing everything they have into breaking down my barriers. The regular legionnaires are shouting encouragement and insults as I try to weather the storm. I don't have time to look, but from the sound, I think even more have come to watch.

Crumble. Collapse. Submit, Felix's will whispers as he smashes yet another dent into my ruined *scutum*.

AHHHHHHHHHHHHH! Marcus's follows, coursing through my sword and into me like a thunderbolt. An idea flares in my mind with the same intensity. I can't continue to retreat; they will wear me out and tear me to pieces. I think I know what to do. I just need to find my moment.

It comes with sudden violence; I wrench my shield to the side, breaking contact with one of Felix's blows. Doing so leaves me open to another strike, but I don't plan on blocking anymore. If this doesn't work, I'll be joining my squad in the dust. I feel the gaze of everyone that's watching, from Gaius to Macer, wherever he vanished to. They're all counting on me to succeed in different ways. I can't fail them. The pressure mounts like a physical weight, demanding that I bow. I draw more deeply on my Symbol, reinforcing my spine with the strength of iron.

I step forward, turning my shield sideways and shoving it toward Felix like a plow. He slams his sword into it to stop my assault. His voice whispers in my head, demanding that my iron obey him. At the same time, I catch Marcus's incoming *gladius* with my own and pin it against the edge of my horizontal shield.

His rage pours into me, and instead of resisting either of their wills, I welcome them, letting my iron become a bridge, passing their reckless offense onto each other. I add my will to theirs in one strong command:

Shatter.

I have just enough time to see Felix's eyes go wide in surprise before the iron obeys our combined will. The connected metal explodes into a thousand pieces. My *scutum* and *gladius* disintegrate into shards of iron that rain down on the training ground at our feet. So do both of their blades, caught in the same maelstrom of will.

The shouts from the watching legionnaires go silent. I don't look to see what the officers think about the destruction we just caused. I can't spare even a moment. My world has shrunk down to hold only two other men, and I'm trying to beat them.

I stagger forward between them. My shield's leather strap dangles uselessly from my left arm, the only piece still intact. I bend low as I race, scooping up a dropped *gladius* from the ground and turning to face my two friends. Their shields were isolated and remain whole, but for the moment, they are disarmed. Quick Felix is the first to realize that I have found a new blade. Both of their heads turn, desperately scanning for a spare sword. I don't give them the time to look.

With a roar, I throw myself at Felix, blade flashing. He still has his shield, which can be a weapon in its own right, but it is most effective in the line, not in a duel. I dance around him, not even bothering to use the Iron Symbol as I hack at him. I feint high, forcing him to raise his *scutum* to block his vision. With a quick flick of my wrist, I slice downward, striking at his exposed thigh.

The tall boy lets out a grunt of pain as my blunted blade bounces off his leg. My second blow slams into his ribs, and he collapses with an irritated grimace. A thrill surges in my chest as I turn, searching for Marcus. I can do this.

All my life, I wished to be worthy of a Heart and to earn my place among the *electii*. I failed, and that has sent me down a hard road. But today, I finally feel worthy of being *Primus* of the cohort. The elation in my chest chills as I see Marcus taking a sword from one of his fallen blue squadmates. The "dead" boy is only too happy to let go of it. I let out a groan of frustration. I took too long finishing off Felix.

My massive friend looks up to see me watching him. He tosses me a grin, saluting with his intact *scutum* and *gladius*. No matter how much more essence I have than him, I know I won't last more than a few heartbeats with only a single blade. I glance at the still forms of the cohort, debating trying to steal another shield, but I know it will take too long to undo the leather strap.

I spy another *gladius* lying next to a fallen recruit's hand, and with a shrug, I snatch it up in my left hand. I've never used a sword in this hand before, but it's better than nothing. Awareness of the second blade flows into me as it becomes an extension of me.

"How rebellious of you," Marcus calls, striding over the prone forms of a dozen of our peers to come toward me. He's confident, and he should be. His shield gives him an incredible advantage in this fight, and we both know it. The big boy strikes a pose, shooting me a broad grin. For a moment, he looks every inch the hero he has always wanted to be.

"You know me," I call back, striding to meet him. "I like to think outside the box."

"Ever since we were children."

I sprint toward him, relying on the fact that I'm carrying less weight to give me an advantage. I have no massive shield to hide behind, so I try to use aggression to my advantage. I slash at my friend's *scutum* with both blades one after the other, keeping up a fierce flurry of blows, trying to overcome his defenses.

Break.

Part.

Succumb.

Give in.

Every strike carries more of my commands as I try to tear his shield to shreds. If I can destroy it, finishing him off with two swords should be easy. Marcus's own will repulses me with a constant incoherent roar of defiance. I don't know how he does that; I've never experienced anything like it. Even the relic felt like it had a sense of coherent thought behind its attacks.

The dark-skinned recruit gives ground, holding his shield up to block my attacks, and I follow him through his retreat, not letting him get any space to strike back at me. The training field is silent except for the peal of iron ringing on iron as I beat his *scutum* like a drum. I can feel my essence beginning to wane as I keep up my assault. I'm carrying less total metal to draw more from now. I won't be able to keep this up forever.

But at the same time, I can feel the mighty wall of his will beginning to fade too. The roar is quieter in my mind every time our iron connects. If I can just keep it up a little longer, I think I can wear him down. Suddenly, Marcus changes direction, charging me with his shield like a boar. I'm caught off guard by his move, and his *scutum* slams into me hard enough to send me staggering back a half dozen paces. More hands grab at my ankles as I stumble by, but I kick them off and keep my feet.

He keeps up the chase, shield forward, blade shooting out in little stabs, trying to catch my undefended chest. I block his sword with my right one, parrying it wide. He shoves his *scutum* at me again, forcing me to retreat.

I gnash my teeth in frustration as I fall back. He's laughing at me from over the top of his shield. He has the upper hand, and he's loving it in a way only one sibling can appreciate beating another. I'm dimly aware that this is the happiest I've seen him since the night our parents were killed. It delights me to see him smile once more. It doesn't make me willing to lose, but I am glad to see my friend look like himself again.

I can't beat him, not like this. He's bigger, stronger, and better equipped. But none of those things have ever been my gift. Old Vellum often accused me of being too clever for my own good. That was how I became *Sextus* in the *collegium*. That is how I can stay *Primus* in the training field.

I stop retreating, meeting Marcus in the middle and going blow for blow with him. He uses his shield like a weapon, swinging it at me with almost inhuman strength. I hammer at it with the *gladius* in my right hand. With the one in my left, I turn the thrusts of his sword. Already the second blade is already beginning to feel natural in my hand.

We circle each other, blades flashing as we attack, searching for a crack in each other's defense. The bigger boy uses his shield menacingly, forcing me to dodge. It's not something that our instructors ever taught us—it's not how the Iron Legions fight—but as we dance, I begin to find the steps.

My mind races as I duck another shield strike, trying to solve the puzzle in front of me. Marcus is not afraid of me; he's known me his whole life. He's not going to panic and make some easy mistake that I can capitalize on. As long as he has that shield and enough essence to hold it together, getting a killing blow will be almost impossible. Which means that if I'm going to win, I'll have to cheat.

An idea begins to take root in the back of my mind as I consider the two swords in my hands. There's a freedom to no longer being weighed down by a large shield. I just need to take advantage of it. Cautiously, I reach out with my will into the *gladius* in my right hand, commanding it to change.

It does so begrudgingly, resisting my commands with every fiber of its being. When it was forged, the smiths who made it poured a purpose—an instruction—into it with every peal of their hammers. It is straight. It is strong. Now, I ask it to betray one of those tenets. I grit my teeth as I split my focus between matching Marcus's tempo and forcing the sword to change.

Clang. Clang. Clang. The field is silent except for the sound of our weapons ringing against each other. It takes several moments, but eventually, it shifts. The tip of my right *gladius* begins to curl, forming a rudimentary hook. Sweat drips down the back of my neck, and I feel my Heart drawing on the last scraps of essence in my Copper veins. This had better work, or it was all for nothing.

Satisfied that my modification is as good as it's going to get, I change my pattern, lunging forward with my right blade angled toward Marcus's eyes. My friend raises his shield, and I lean into my momentum, driving the sword upward over the lip of his *scutum*.

I feel the *gladius* crest the top and twist my wrist before bringing it down, catching the hook on the edge of his shield. I pull with all my might, forcing his arm to come down, leaving his chest exposed. Using that leverage, I lunge forward, stabbing with my left blade through the gap that I created.

The tip of my blunted sword slams into his chest, and Marcus stumbles backward, dropping to his knees with a shocked expression on his face. The field is silent as he crumples, leaving me the last one standing.

I have won.

CHAPTER 32

A roar begins to build as the watching legionnaires recover from their shock and shout their approval or disappointment. All around the field, the "dead" recruits begin to return to life, sitting up out of the dust and shaking themselves off. Marcus laughs from where he lies at my feet, and numbly, I hold out an arm to pull him to his feet. Together, we begin to walk off the field.

"I swear you're a descendant of Mercury," he says with a chuckle. There's no trace of anger in his eyes as he claps me on the shoulder. "How else could you be so tricky? How did you do that?"

"I just made it bend." I shrug, suddenly uncomfortable with the attention. In the middle of our sparring, it had seemed like the only logical thing to do, but the long glances from other recruits tell a different story.

"Just made it bend," Marcus repeats half-reverently, half-mockingly. "That's all. Why didn't I think of that? Felix! He just made the sword bend!"

"I saw." Our tall friend joins the triangle, a slight frown on his face as he studies me. "Can I look at that?" He motions at the *gladius* in my right hand, still curved into a hook. Wordlessly, I pass it to him, and I watch his eyes narrow as he probes it with his will.

"There he is!" I shout, recognizing the slight form of Macer, who is climbing to his feet, wincing from some bruise hidden under his tunic. "Thank you for the rescue, my friend." I place my hand on his shoulder and give it a squeeze.

"You're welcome, *Dom*—"

"No!" I snap, cutting him off and giving him another pat. "I said '*friend*.'" The smile that begins to grow at the corners of his mouth is brilliant and somehow feels better than winning did.

"It's the least I could do after you… you know."

"The way I see it, we're even now." His eyes widen in shock. This is not a concept he is used to. The boy with the thief brands on his hands has grown up in a world that does not watch out for each other or forgive debts. But today, he is free. We leave him standing on the sands, looking stunned as we keep walking.

"Remarkable," Felix murmurs after a moment. I'm not sure if he's talking about the bent sword or Macer.

"What?" I ask hotly, feeling a flush of embarrassment creep up the base of my neck. I miss the cooling presence of the Iron Symbol but don't reach for it, as tempting as it is. A silence descends upon the field, making its way to us like an arrow.

"Later," Felix promises, passing the sword back to me as Tribune Gaius marches into view. The red cape of his office trails behind him as he approaches. His face is grim, but it always is. Yet something in his eyes tells me that he is not pleased. I have plenty to answer for, from tactics to shattering several pieces of Legion equipment.

Durus appears at his right hand and begins bellowing out orders to the milling recruits. "If your band isn't black, form up for running! Stack your swords and shields at the armory. You all got a nice little nap. Now back to work!"

Groans echo from the other squads, but they move toward the front of the field, following the centurion's command. Felix and Marcus shoot me sympathetic glances as they leave, but not too sympathetic. I might be in trouble, but at least I don't have to run around Agogia. They depart, leaving me alone with the Silver *electus*. He stares at me for a moment, brow furrowing into a frown as he studies the two blades in my hands.

"You need to be careful," he says at last.

"Careful of what, *Dominus*?"

"Of the eyes that you are drawing."

"*You* told me to become unforgettable." I can't keep the accusation out of my tone.

"And now I am telling you to be careful," he hisses, taking a step closer to me. "I need you to excel, not shatter their expectations. My mother already seeks to block your Ascension. When she hears about what you did here, it will not be hard for her to find allies in her mission."

"What did I do here that will cause such a problem?"

"You shattered two shields and a sword into a thousand pieces." The tribune kicks a chunk of iron at our feet. "That's not something a Copper recruit should be able to do. That's something that those veterans watching can't do."

"I didn't really do it myself," I protest. "I used their own—"

"I know what you did." Gaius cuts me off effortlessly, gesturing at the *argentum* veins in his own arms. "I am the only one here who could feel it." A shiver of jealousy runs down my spine at the thought of being able to sense iron that I could not touch. "It doesn't matter how you did it, only that you did it. After today, your reputation will grow."

"Why is that a problem? I know you said that the magisters do not like to make soldiers from the Bottom Quadrant into the *Fidelia*, but—"

"Think, boy!" Gaius snaps, finally seeming frustrated. "I've already told you that they don't want the dregs of society to have power. What you did today will make them *fear* you now."

I pause, truly listening to his words. There's danger lurking here. It feels the same as what followed in Atticus's wake. Goosebumps prick my flesh as a chill deeper than Iron's runs down my spine. I'm caught in another game; I will never escape them.

"I understand," I manage weakly. Gaius must see some of my emotions warp across my face, but he doesn't push. He holds me in his commander's glare for few heartbeats, then nods once before turning away, leaving me in the dust of the training field.

As the tribune departs, I feel a new presence settle the back of my head like a pair of weights. It's lighter than Gaius's glare, but equally impossible to ignore. I turn to find Durus staring at me pointedly from the other side of the field.

The other black bands are lounging around, chuckling to one another at the fate of the rest of the recruits streaming out of the Twelfth's sector to run their laps. My gaze flicks back to the centurion, who raises a single finger and mouths one word: *Primus*. I feel my shoulders sag under the yoke of responsibility.

I know what the officer wants me to do.

I know what my father would do.

Leaders don't sit in the dirt while their comrades work, even if they've earned it. They run with their people every step of the way. A cohort is made up of a series of decades, but to truly function, it must be one cohesive unit. I can't help but chuckle as I take my first step, springing into a light jog. I spent my whole life wanting to be a *Primus*, but it is turning out to be a lot more work than I ever thought. I should have let Marcus have it.

The low buzz of conversation among my squadmates cuts out as I trot through them. I don't turn to look at them, although part of me thinks I should. It's only fair that they be shamed the way that Durus is shaming me. But despite the temptation, I resist. It doesn't feel like my place to do that to them. Even if I am *Primus*, I am not an officer. We are equals.

The First Spear gives me a slight nod of respect as I jog past him. I roll my eyes but lean into my pace, stretching my legs longer to eat up the distance between me and the rest of the recruits. I hear crunching in the sand as some of my fellow black bands begrudgingly get to their feet. A wry grin twists my face as I run faster. I'm not sure if I'm running from the recruits behind me or chasing the ones in front of me.

I feel lighter than I have in months, and despite my exhaustion from the skirmish, I let out a laugh of joy as I burst from the Twelfth Sector and into the main thoroughfare of Agogia. I spy the dusty white training uniforms of the rest of the century ahead, and I lower my head as I break into a sprint, trying to catch them.

I'm flying as I close in on the back of the pack, weaving my way around a marching column from the Seventh and dodging a wagon train heading to the blacksmiths. Shouts of outrage follow me as I blaze past the other recruits, and the entire formation lunges like a hound as they catch sight of me shooting past them.

"Oh, come on!" Marcus bellows in indignation as he spots me. "I didn't mean that you should start running like Mercury too!" Some of the recruits from Segesta laugh. They welcome my rise. Others do not. Felix says nothing, only runs faster. I let out a *whoop* and add as much speed as I can, trying to catch my longer-legged friend.

We're still racing when we enter the space between the First and Second Quadrants, the home of the elite legions. Angry shouts follow the horde of Twelvies as we cut around marching units, but we do not stop. I spy a group of Praetorian recruits, clad in purple, who sneer as we rush past. Brennus, the blond boy who threatened us with a *tellus* knife, is among them. He glares at me, but I am moving too fast for his irritation to reach me.

The guards at the front don't even bother to try stopping us; instead, the centurion steps aside and waves us through, confident that we are on assignment. I hook to the right as I exit, following the leaders of the group as we begin the long marathon around Agogia.

The wheeled city is massive—it will take us at least two hours to return to our original gate. There is no road circling the massive walls, but a path has been beaten into the dry ground by a hundred thousand legionnaires before us. We run on the tracks of our ancestors, following the course they charted. Yet another thing that makes me feel like a part of a mighty and noble tradition.

Now that we are out of the city, we settle into a more sustainable pace. The journey is long. Only those with patience make it to the end without collapsing. Felix falls in step with me, and we jog in companionable silence as I try to catch my breath from the sprint.

"There's something wrong with your Heart," my friend remarks after some time. Surprised, I shoot him a glare, but none of the other recruits around us seem to be paying attention. "Well, maybe not wrong," he amends after a moment, "but not normal."

"It doesn't seem that weird to me." I keep my voice low enough to be covered by the crunching of our sandals.

"You mean aside from the sheer volume of essence you seem to be able to absorb?"

"Maybe a little unusual, but I wouldn't say it's a cause for alarm," I protest. "I'm still only a Copper. I'm bound to the same restrictions as anyone else here."

"You survived seven blows from the *custos* relic," Felix points out flatly, not even looking at me. "No one else lasted more than four. Not even any of the Praetorian recruits."

"Well... yeah—"

"Then you beat Marcus and me, even though we both are also being tested to become *Fidelia*." Now he turns toward me, not breaking stride. "That is not normal. But then again, neither was how you got your Heart."

I'm silent for a few moments, focusing on putting one foot in front of the other instead of the questions that Felix is asking. They're not too different from the ones that I've been asking myself already. The white *rasa* veins in my arm glint in the setting sunlight as I run. Most people think they are a deformity, but in reality, they're a clue to whatever happened to me when the golden wolf attacked.

"Could it have something to do with the other Hearts that I absorbed?" I ask even more softly, not wanting to risk another recruit overhearing it. Felix gives me a knowing look that tells me he is thinking the same thing.

"Maybe they somehow increase my ability to pull in essence even if they aren't attuned to the same Symbol?" I shrug uncomfortably, focusing my attention back on my feet. I don't like thinking about the night that I got my Heart—or Hearts. The price that I paid for becoming Ironbound is still too dear.

Without meaning to, I embrace the Iron Symbol, letting its cold logic wash through me and drive back the painful feelings. I can't afford to let my hurt keep me away from this. Not if I want revenge on Atticus and Brutus.

"It could be," Felix grunts after a moment of thought. "Maybe they are also able to store extra essence for you? It feels like you have more reserves than I do too." Mentally, I sweep my senses inward, studying the cold ball of Iron essence that sits in my chest like an organ. I cannot feel the blank *Corda*. It's as if they do not exist.

"I don't know how that's even possible. Vellum always said that it wasn't possible to carry more than one Heart. Atticus also thought that the extra ones were wasted."

"Maybe since they all went into you at the same time, they…" Felix trails off with a frustrated shrug. Neither of us has the words to describe this phenomenon.

"Maybe," I allow, still feeling unsettled. "Gaius says I need to be careful."

"I agree."

"It just doesn't make sense," I hiss, the frustration that has been building in me finally beginning to boil over. "Why wouldn't the legions want soldiers to be the best they can be? I know this is the Twelfth, but even the lowest legion still must serve the Empress's will."

"You really were a patrician."

"What's that supposed to mean?" I snap, glancing at my friend sharply.

"You still think the world is fair."

I don't know how to respond to that, so I look away, seething. Felix is silent for a few moments as we run. Part of me suspects that he's waiting to let me cool off before he tries to reason with me. I know I'm being dramatic, but his logical acceptance of the rust of corruption irritates me further. Did my upbringing really shield me from so much?

All my life, I've wanted to be the best at something, to excel. I failed to become *Primus* in the *collegium*, but now that I've finally done it, all of a sudden, everyone around me wants me to be worse? I gnash my teeth in frustration and run faster, taking out my anger on the ground with the soles of my feet.

"I don't think it's just about being in the Twelfth," Felix says when he feels like my tantrum has faded enough that I will listen. "Well, maybe that's part of it. I think they're afraid of anyone who seems like they could become another Titus."

"That's what these are for." I tap the *inihibitus* around my neck with a free hand. "Not much danger in that with these around." I probe it with the Iron Symbol, tracing the twists of Iron relic mixed with the thing I cannot identify. The metal collar throbs, in warning, as if irritated by my scrutiny.

"So we're told, and yet they still seem afraid." My friend's eyes are dark and heavy. For once, I don't have anything smart to say. Troubled by his thoughts, we run in silence, pushing toward the front of the pack.

It's well into dusk by the time we round the final bend of Agogia, and the South Gate springs into view once more. The recruits of our cohort are strung out in little groups of two and three as their endurance fades and they plod through the final stretch. Felix and I chase the leaders, our breath ragged. My leg muscles are on fire, and my ability to call upon Iron has long since faded without any essence to draw on. I'll never forgive Durus for pushing me to do this when I didn't have to.

Dimly, I'm aware of the sound of shouting off to my right as the path goes through several low dunes. I'm so tired, I don't even turn, assuming it's some other member of the Twelfth making a final dash for first. Let them win—I already won the battle today. I may be *Primus*, but I don't need to be first at everything.

A flicker of shadow out of the corner of my eye and a gasp from Felix is the only warning I get before someone slams into me from the side. We go down in a tangle of limbs, and what little breath I still have explodes out of me as we tumble.

Instinct takes over, and I slam an elbow into something soft, causing whoever has grabbed me to let go. We roll apart, and I manage to get my feet under me, panting with rage and exhaustion. I kick up sand as I charge my assailant, a shadowy figure I don't recognize.

He's slower getting to his feet, and it's my turn to slam him to the ground. I only wish we were on cobblestones instead of soft desert. I drive a fist at his stomach like my instructors have taught me, and he barely manages to catch it on his forearm.

Before I can follow up with a blow to his throat, I'm tackled by another assailant, pushing me off him. I stagger to the side, turning to face this new threat with my fists raised. In the faint light, I can just make out the purple of his training tunic.

Praetorians. The arrogant fools don't even try to hide who they are. Over the rush of blood in my ears, I can make out the sounds of Felix fighting and voices shouting. I recognize Brennus by a flash of pale blond hair in the moonlight. A chill settles on me as I realize this isn't some sort of mad drill by our instructors.

This is an ambush.

There's at least a half-dozen of them, and they circle Felix and me like a group of coyotes, trying to bring down their prey. Spurius, one of the Praetorians who is trying to become a *Fidelis,* steps into range, his right hand balled into a fist, hatred shining on his face so brightly, I can see it in the dark.

I dodge his first blow only to get clipped in the side of my head by someone else's strike. My vision swims as I stagger backward, and several of them follow me, shoulders hunched, ready to get to work. The Iron Symbol slips through my fingers as my empty reserves lack the essence I need to make my *Cor* function.

There are too many of them for me to even try to fight back. I hold up my arms to ward off the flurry of blows that descend upon me. It helps, but they surround me, raining their fury down on me from all sides. In the distance, I hear shouts as some of the other Twelfth recruits realize something is wrong. Despite my exhaustion, a small smile crooks at the corner of my mouth. Soon the Praetorians will be outnumbered and will pay the price for their challenge.

Brennus, the ringleader, appears in front of me, moonlight glinting off the iron blade in his fist. I eye the weapon with a sinking heart. If I were already a Silver *electus*, it would be easy for me to avoid it, but my Copper veins will offer me no protection from his weapon until it is too late.

"This is for making a mockery of your betters," he hisses. I feel myself lock up as he stabs forward with the weapon. I've been taught to fight for the last few months, but no one has ever actually tried to *kill* me before. Despite all my training, I'm caught flatfooted, exhausted, and unarmed as the Praetorian tries to murder me.

"No!" a voice screams as someone slams into me from the side. I hear him grunt in pain as we both fall in a tangle of arms and legs. Roars of rage echo off the dunes as more of my fellow Twelves arrive, furious that these elites would dare attack us. The Praetorians scatter as my reinforcements arrive.

I scramble out from under my rescuer, but they're not moving. As I drop to my knees, I stare in horror at the sight of Macer bleeding in the sand with a knife that was meant for me buried in his guts.

"No, no, no!" I scream, placing my hands around the wound, trying to stem the tide of darkness that's seeping through the white of his training tunic. The skinny recruit gasps like a fish out of water, but his eyes are locked on my face with fanatical desperation. This is the second time today he has tried to save me. This time, it carries a much heavier price.

"Sorry I was late, Castor," he wheezes.

"Shh," I interrupt, choking back a sob of fear. My hands are wet and sticky with his blood. "Don't you dare waste a single breath talking, Macer. You're going to be fine; you hear me?" The boy lets out another gasp of pain, twisting in pain.

"Dammit, man, use the Iron in the knife!" I scream in desperation, trying to help him find his Symbol. "You've got essence—use it!" I don't know if he can hear me above the pain or if his mind is too clouded to even begin to use his *Cor*. I feel a trickle of it flow into me as my own starved body soaks up some from my contact with the weapon.

"What in Jupiter's Rotten Corpse is going on here?" a harsh voice thunders over my shoulder. My head snaps around to find Anas lurking behind me, his face red enough to glow in the low light. The hard man's eyes glide from me to the knife in Macer's gut with animal-like quickness. Fury like I have never seen before flickers across his face as he sees the Praetorian recruits fleeing in the face of our reinforcements.

"Bastards! I'll kill you!" he screams, rushing after our assailants as if he hadn't just run around the entirety of Agogia's walls. Macer lets out another gurgle, and I press harder, trying to stop the blood flow.

Sand sprays as Felix slides to his knees next to me. "We can't move him. Marcus is going for help." He places his hands on Macer's bloody stomach without hesitation. "Just hang on. The *medici* will be here soon."

"I never thanked you…" Macer wheezes weakly to me, his voice a weak croak.

"Yes, you did," I hiss, cutting him off. "You did that first night. I told you today that we're even. You gotta stop trying to save me. Someone is going to get hurt." He doesn't laugh at my weak attempt at a joke. His eyes are unfocused but stare at me in rapt attention.

"Not for the whipping… For treating me like I belonged."

"You do belong. You belong here. Pluto cannot have you. You are a recruit of the Eighth Cohort of the Twelfth Legion, and as your *Primus*, I am telling you—" I'm not kneeling on the desert outside of Agogia anymore. In my mind, I'm at my father's side, watching his blood leak out onto the cobblestones. I'm in my family's kitchen, staring at the empty eyes of my mother and sister before the fire consumes them.

"Castor... He's gone." Felix's voice pulls me back, his bloody hand resting gently on my shoulder. I glance into his brown eyes and know that he's reliving the same horrors that I am. Slowly, against my will, I look down at the still form of Macer.

He seems smaller now. His arms are frail and thin, his face gaunt and pale. The knife that was meant for me sticks out of his stomach like a flagpole. I sit with him, unsure what else to do. It doesn't feel right to leave him alone. Felix stays with me, and the two of us stand guard over him, watching as his Copper veins slowly fade to the dull gray of a relic. We are still kneeling at his side half an hour later when Gaius arrives.

CHAPTER 33

The tribune gets to us before the rest of the relief column, dressed in full battle kit. His Silver-powered body races ahead of the rest of them, red cloak trailing behind him in the wind. White-robed *medici*, legion doctors, race in his wake, carrying a stretcher, racing to save a man who is already gone. It's fully night now. Our commander's face is lit by a *lumos* relic that he carries on the end of a wooden baton. The light only serves to sharpen the shadows clinging to the rage etched on his face.

He takes everything in at a glance: the other recruits milling around behind us like lost sheep, Felix and me kneeling in the sand by the still form of Macer. An inferno lights in his eyes that burns brighter than the light of *Luna* reflecting off *Mons* Olympus floating above us.

The *medici* shoo us from our friend, going through the motions to see if there is anything worth saving. I don't watch; I already know that he's gone. If I allow myself even a glimmer of hope, I may shatter.

After a few moments, the leader rises from Macer's body and shakes his head at Gaius. "He's dead," the *medico* confirms. "He needs to be taken to the Heartsmiths to reclaim his relics." I shiver at the cold efficiency of the Iron Legions. His body is barely cold and already they harvest him for his *Cor*. I know that this is the burden of being an *electus*, but it feels inhuman.

"What happened?" Gaius asks me, turning from the *medico*, face dark with rage.

"We were attacked." I stumble over the words as I learn to use my mouth again. It feels like a lifetime since the last time I spoke.

"By Mars's Chosen, Praetorians!" a voice shaking with the rage I feel shouts from behind me. I don't need to turn to see that it's Anas, returning empty-handed from his chase of Macer's killers. Gaius's eyes flick to the former *captivus* for a heartbeat before coming back to me for confirmation. I nod, not trusting myself to speak.

"Would you recognize the ones who did this?"

I nod again. Brennus's face is seared into my mind like a painting. I will never forget him as long as I live. Already he has joined the shrine of hatred in my heart that holds the visage of Atticus and Brutus.

"Come." Gaius spins on his heel without waiting to see if I obey.

I'm on my feet before I even process the command. Felix and the rest surge forward, and our commander freezes as he hears all the recruits begin to move. He turns slowly, a rebuke forming on his lips. I see it in his eyes, a cold order, sharp as an executioner's blade. I feel the rest of the men behind me halt, but no one turns away. A dozen angry faces stare at our tribune, daring him to tell some of us to stay behind.

A flicker of another expression ripples across his face, fighting to break through the mask of anger on his face. It fails, but he doesn't reprimand us. Without a word, he turns and begins striding toward Agogia. Struck by some foreign instinct, I raise my hand and wave the rest of my fellow recruits forward.

We rush into the wake of Gaius, like a pack of wolf pups following their father. His powerful strides eat up the distance back to the city, and I find myself trotting to keep up the pace. Not a single man with me complains at the pace. The anger we carry looms over us like a storm cloud, driving us forward.

The gates of the city are open, and the centurion from the Ninth doesn't say a word to our tribune as he leads us back into the city. The soldiers on guard duty wear grim expressions, like men at a funeral. This late in the evening, the wide cobbled streets are mostly empty, but our anger fills them up as if we were a full legion.

Gaius storms into the First's Sector, glancing over his shoulder for the first time, his dark eyes looking to me for guidance. Remembering the stitching on their tunics, I make the hand symbol for five . First Legion, Fifth Cohort. The tribune's pace picks up, and I feel like I'm in the middle of a charge as I follow. My heart hammers in my chest, a horrible tempo of rage and fear.

We pass banners for the first four cohorts. Purple-clad soldiers on guard eye us warily, but none of the rank-and-file dare to question a Silver Tribune who looks like the second coming of Mars's rage, even if he is from the Twelfth. We turn into the section for the Fifth, and despite everything, I can't help but notice how much nicer their sector is.

Their paths are immaculately cobbled like the main highways, rather than the dusty, hard-packed dirt that fills our home. Grass, which is clearly tended to by a gardener, grows along the paths. Their buildings are taller, the space between them wider. The sons of the noble and elite might be made into legionnaires in the same place as the rest of us, but their forge is much less austere than ours.

"What is the meaning of this?" a voice demands as a decurion steps out of one of the barracks and into the light of one of the *lumos* relics, placing himself in Gaius's path. He's not armored or armed, but the haughtiness on his face looks sharp enough to cut. "Twelfth Legion are not—"

"Who is your commanding officer?" Gaius demands, his voice cold and imperious enough to belong. For a moment, I had forgotten that once he was an officer of the Second. The decurion blinks in surprise at the interruption.

"Tribune Dorcas, but—"

"Where is he?"

"In his headquarters, where he belongs. I must insist—"

Gaius steps forward, coming into the light enough for the junior officer to see the pale *F* burned into his *lorica* and the Silver veins in his arms. He falls silent, less confident than he was a moment ago.

"Take me to him." The Praetorian opens his mouth to protest but thinks better of it, turning to lead us deeper into the Fifth Cohort's quarters. Gaius follows, dogging his heels like a dark specter, forcing the man to march at a double pace.

Just like everything else in the First Sector, the headquarters are larger and nicer than ours. The stones used to make it are white and clean, as if they have been washed regularly.

The tribune of the Fifth Cohort of the Praetorians meets us at the patio of his command building. Someone must have warned him that Gaius was coming, because there's an edge to his stare as he watches us approach. The veins of his *Cor* Heart flash copper in the light of the *lumos* relics, but he crosses them contemptuously, armored by his superiority. Two centurions flank him, wearing their full *lorica*.

"Tribune Gaius, I understand there's something troubling you?" Dorcas calls as we cross the stone assembly square. "I can think of no other reason for a commander of the Twelfth to darken my doorstep at this hour with a gaggle of recruits in tow like a mother duck with her ducklings." The centurions with him chuckle darkly, their eyes sweeping over us with disgust.

"I'm here to oversee punishment," Gaius calls as he steps up to the base of the patio. There's a pair of steps leading up into the building, letting Dorcas tower over his counterpart. But despite the difference in their height, our commander looms larger than the Praetorian does by an order of magnitude.

"Punishment?" Dorcas makes an amused face, like a man humoring a child, and looks at his two centurions to bring them in on the joke. "Well, that's fine of you, but I'm sure whatever your rodents did can wait until tomorrow. Whip them until you're satisfied, and I will be as well."

The silence that follows his words is deafening. It echoes off the paving stones and the manicured lawns, and with each heartbeat, it grows in size. The armored centurions shift next to their tribune, sensing the approach of violence.

"I fear you misunderstand me, Dorcas," Gaius replies through gritted teeth. "I am here to oversee the punishment of one of your recruits."

"My recruits?" Elite outrage enters his voice as the Praetorian stares down at us in surprise. "Mars's Bones, man, in what world would *you* ever punish one of *my* recruits?"

"The *Lex Legionis* grants the right of any commander to discipline a legionnaire who abuses someone under their command in order to maintain brotherhood between the legions."

"The *Lex*—" Dorcas scoffs, cutting himself off in disbelief. "What is this about?"

"Several of your recruits attacked mine with vicious intent while they trained. One of them *died*. I am here to see that they are appropriately punished, as is my right."

"You're serious?" He leans forward in shock. "What year do you think it is, man? Are you Titus himself? Or perhaps Scipio, come again to lead our Iron Legions?" The centurions laugh dutifully at their leader's jokes, but their hands are on the hilts of their *gladii*, and their eyes are hard. For all their faults, the Praetorians are real soldiers who know their business.

"One of your men killed one of mine, Dorcas. Give him to me." The hairs on the back of my arms rise at the violent chill that lurks in his voice. I may not be Silver yet, but I don't need to be to sense the Symbol of Iron thrumming around him.

"Your man?" Dorcas chuckles dryly, his flat, humorless eyes passing over me and the other recruits like we are cattle. "Wasn't aware you had those in the Twelfth." There's a hum of vicious anger from my fellows. A sea of red washes over me, and I'm grateful to be low enough on essence that I can't smother my emotions in the cold embrace of Iron. I want to feel this, to add this to the fire of anger that burns in the forge of my heart.

"There's a difference between the upper legions and the bottom ones. I would have thought you learned your lesson the first time, Marius," Dorcas taunts, striding down the stairs, flanked by his two officers. "The last time you tried to treat the chattel like humans, you got sent to live with them. You must like it down there in the mud with the piggies."

"Give him to me," Gaius repeats, his voice flat.

"I will not." Dorcas shrugs, as if it is decided. "The imperators will never side with you, and we both know it. Now leave me. It's long past time I had my supper. What's on the menu tonight, Riter?"

"Roast chicken, Tribune," the centurion to his left supplies instantly.

"Roast chicken," he emphasizes with a tight smile. He cares not for the death of our comrade. I doubt he even remembers what the actual complaint is. We are rodents, and he is important. Felix was right—the world is not fair. A long shadow passes across my soul as I realize that kind Macer may go unavenged, just like my parents. Silently, I add his name to the list of deaths to atone for before I die.

"I knew it." Anas's voice shakes with rage as he speaks from somewhere behind me. "He's gonna let them get away with it. So much for being one of us."

I say nothing, but in the deepest part of my heart, I agree with the former *captivus*. The Praetorians who murdered my parents saw no reprisal for their actions—why should it be any different here?

A chorus of laughter interrupts the two tribunes' staring contest. My head snaps over my shoulder at the sound of a group of boys' cruel snickering. A dozen purple-clad Praetorian recruits stumble into the courtyard, dusty and in high spirits. Brennus is in the center, surrounded by his cronies.

They stop short at the sight of us, their eyes widening. I find the blond boy's gaze and hold it with my own, channeling every ounce of hate I can muster. Brennus returns it, although his is a cold, academic thing. He hates me because of what I am—a lesser being that dares to outshine him. Mine is hot—I hate him for who he is.

I feel Gaius's attention settle on me with a physical weight. I turn to meet his questioning look. For a moment, we stare at one another, having a conversation that no one else can hear. Something will happen if I tell him the truth. I can feel the rage that quivers in him, like an arrow on a taut bowstring. It is not that different from mine; we're brothers in a way. The world shrinks. I nod once. My heart is pounding so hard that it almost drowns out every other sound. I can taste the violence on the wind.

"Give him to me," Gaius demands once more, jabbing a finger at Brennus.

"No."

"Then I will take him."

The two centurions step forward at our commander's threat, *gladii* hissing like snakes as they pull them from their sheaths. I clench my fists and take a step forward, hoping to tackle one of them to buy Gaius enough time to deal with the other.

I shouldn't have bothered. He doesn't need me. The tribune's own blade leaps free in a blinding flash as it reflects the *lumos* relics around us. He explodes toward the right guard, striking in a series of slashes that our officers never taught us.

The Praetorian catches the first on his blade, but Gaius's *gladius* simply slices through it as if it were a piece of cloth. It rings against the cobbles as it lands on the ground. Again, he strikes, shearing off another piece of the man's sword. The second centurion, Riter, lunges forward, blade extended for a stab into our commander's unprotected side.

I open my mouth to warn him, but his Silver senses need no help. Without looking, Gaius twists perfectly, letting the sword slide past him into thin air. He slashes at the first man's broken sword a third time and hews it down to the crossguard.

Spinning, his blade flicks out, striking Riter in the temple with the flat side. The snotty centurion collapses to the ground like a sack of potatoes. Wheeling on the swordless soldier, Gaius headbutts him in the face, sending him reeling. The man staggers backward, holding his face with his hands before tripping over the unconscious form of his fellow centurion.

The entire fight takes fewer than ten seconds. Dorcas's mouth is open and working in stunned disbelief. Gaius rounds on him before he can speak, blade flashing. The Praetorian tribune's tunic explodes with each slice as the *Fidelis* carves our Legion's name into his chest.

X

I

I

His strikes are precise to an inhuman level—not a single drop of blood wells up on the other tribune's chest, but the threat is there all the same. Gaius's *gladius* flicks out to the side in a sharp salute before crashing into Dorcas's temple, sending the man crumbling to the ground with his men.

Gaius's eyes are wide and furious as he turns to stalk toward the group of Praetorian recruits, who cower before the *Fidelis*. Brennus has only a moment to let out a whimper before our tribune grabs him by his hair and begins to drag him from the courtyard. He screams in pain, pleading with his friends to help him.

Not a single one of them moves.

Silently, like ghosts of judgment, we follow our commander as he drags the weeping boy from the First Sector and down the main thoroughfare of Agogia. Soldiers and civilians watch our progression with wide eyes, but anyone who sees the furious Silver Tribune with a naked sword and screaming Praetorian in his grip decides it is best not to get involved.

"Assemble the men, full battle kit," Gaius snarls at me over his shoulder as we enter the Twelfth's sector, beelining for the Eighth Cohort's section. Brennus lets out another whimper of pain, hands wrapped around the tribune's wrist, trying to alleviate some of the pressure on him. "At the double," he murmurs after a moment of thought. A shiver runs through me as I realize that there's only one reason he would order us to be fully armed and armored.

Anas and the rest don't need to be told twice. Recruits fly past me, sprinting toward our barracks like they didn't just run around the entire city after fighting in skirmish. Our sandals beat out a stampeding tempo on the dusty path as we race to spread the news.

None of us can catch Anas, and we follow on his heels as he bursts into our bunkroom. Heads snap up from where recruits are moping. The room stinks of despair and melancholy, but our arrival is like the breaking of dawn. Marcus sits up in his bunk, his gaze sharpening as he takes in our breathless excitement.

"Up!" I shout, doing my best to channel Durus's best parade voice. "Tribune wants us assembled in the courtyard, double time. Full battle kit: *gladius, scutum, lorica*." A groan of reluctance echoes across the room. I see some of their faces fall as if I had just crushed their hope. They took our urgency as good news about Macer, not as an opportunity for more work. I hesitate, looking for the words to reassure them. I have no hope to offer, no warmth. I come bearing the words of revenge, and its chill can only numb the pain, not cure it.

Anas sees no need for delicacy. "Hurry up, boys," he growls with dark delight. "Gaius got his hands on the boy who stuck Macer, and he's going to make him pay." The room empties faster than it ever has for screaming officers. I stand by the door watching every recruit who rushes past me with a growing sense of belief—this is really happening.

Many of them give me a new look as they go. It's not one of hatred or disgust, a reminder that I am different from them and not welcome. Maybe those will come back tomorrow. Tonight, they are aflame with the fire of a shared rage, passed from one another like candles at a vigil.

I follow the last man out the back, racing toward the armory where the weapons and armor are kept. Someone wrenches open the shed where we buried our *votum* and starts yanking things off the walls. Recruits grab weapons and pass them down the line. We still only have our training blades, but they can still be made sharp enough to harm. I throw a *lorica* over my head and let out a sigh of relief as essence pours into me, refilling my almost empty reserves. Calling on Iron, I adjust the size to fit me. Whoever had worn this last was far skinnier than me. I wonder if it was Macer.

Someone passes me a *gladius*, and I grab a *scutum* from a stack before rushing to meet Gaius in the square. We sprint, flying toward what we are owed. In the back of my mind, I know our commander told us to hurry because there will be a response. The Praetorians will not tolerate what Gaius did to them. The tribune of the Fifth Cohort might not have been one of the *Fidelia*, but there are plenty of their number among the First Legion. They will come, they will take their recruit back, and we will not be able to stop them.

Unless they are too late.

I burst into the same quad where I was whipped in Macer's place what feels like an age ago, in time to see Gaius drag Brennus up onto the wood dais. We summoned the recruits, but someone told the regulars. The soldiers stream in, filling the square to the brim, armed like us. Durus steps up next to our tribune, his eyes hooded and uneasy.

"Do you know who my mother is?" the Praetorian screams and sobs at the same time. "Do you know what she will do to you?" Gaius ignores his rants, forcing him to his knees and binding his wrists into the leather cuffs one by one.

"You're dead, I swear on Jupiter's Ashes. You stupid, damn Twelvie." The tribune turns away, striding to the back of the dais where the whips are kept. He shifts through them for a moment, pulling out one, then frowning and replacing it before selecting another.

Murmurs run through the real soldiers among us as he stalks back toward the kneeling boy. The whip ends in a series of thin cords like Medusa's hair, and they scratch at the wood as they drag against it.

"That's a ninetails," Felix whispers in horror. I blanch in horror as I recognize it. Unlike the whip that Durus used on me that was designed to punish but not injure, a ninetails was made to maim. Thick thorns jut out the length of its many cords, sharp and eager to devour flesh.

The cohort's murmurs rise as more and more of the men understand what they're about to see. The blond boy's face grows tight with fear, and he twists frantically, trying to look over his shoulder to see what we do. When he does, he screams again, a choked, animalistic sound. His feet scrabble for purchase on the dais, but the leather straps hold him in place. The square is silent as Gaius steps behind him. The only sounds are the boy's pathetic whimpers as his pleas and threats fall on deaf, iron ears.

"Tonight, this legionnaire committed a cardinal sin of the legions." Gaius's voice carries out across the assembled men with a cold strength. He is not shouting, but every soldier can hear him clearly.

"He took up arms against his Ironbound brother and slew him in cold blood." A dark murmur sweeps through the regulars. Many of them hadn't heard the news, and now they understand what they've come to see. "The *Lex Legionis* declares that the punishment of any legionnaire who spills the blood of another belongs to the fallen soldier's legion. As such, in the name of Macer, I sentence you to bleed."

In the distance, I hear a faint rolling thunder.

Gaius raises the ninetails with a *snap*, letting its cruel tendrils uncoil above his head like a dozen scorpion stingers. With a furious snarl, he jerks his arm down, lashing his weapon into the back of the flailing boy. Brennus's scream is loud and primal. Blood splatters on the wooden dais around his feet.

The tribune's face is hard as stone as he raises the whip again, its tails wet and red. Again, he strikes, driving a scream of pain from the boy who killed Macer. The men around me lean forward, hungry to see something they never have before—a Praetorian elite suffer for wronging a Twelfth.

Gaius picks up the pace, raining a half-dozen strikes down on his back. Brennus hangs limply from the leather restraints, his blood pooling around his knees like a dark lake. I swallow, feeling suddenly hollow at the sight of the unconscious boy.

He deserves this, I tell myself angrily, and I'm right—he does. But something about it feels emptier than I thought it would. Maybe it's because he's still alive. Maybe it's because Macer is still dead. Will killing Atticus and Brutus feel as empty? I shake my head, clearing these treasonous thoughts.

I will kill Atticus. I will kill Brutus.

It is justice. It is what my parents and friends deserve. It's not about me or how it makes it feel. It's about doing what's right, about making them pay for their crimes. Even if it doesn't bring them back, at least they will be avenged.

The distant thunder grows. I hear its continuous rumbling over the cracks of the whip and the murmur of my fellow soldiers. It's not thunder, I realize, cocking my head to listen. It's more like the relentless crashing of the sea—

"Praetorians!" someone shouts from the entrance of the Twelfth's sector. Gaius's head snaps up, but he doesn't stop what he is doing. That is no natural sound, but the noise of several hundred feet marching in perfect sync. The First Legion has come to claim their recruit.

Horns blare throughout the entire sector, and I hear shouts of alarm in the other cohorts' districts. The rest of the tribunes may not know what Gaius has done, but the purple-clad elites are not welcome here. I glance over my shoulder in time to see the fully kitted soldiers rush into view. They're in a battle march, the top speed a legion can travel while holding formation. Despite my hatred, I marvel at how clean their lines are. I've trained enough to know that these soldiers know their work.

A furious Tribune Dorcas stomps at the head of his entire cohort, a red welt marking the right side of his face where Gaius struck him. Without being told to, the rear line of men turns, getting close enough together to form a shieldwall. The second line steps forward to reinforce them, and so does the third. I'm several layers away from the Praetorians, but my hand caresses the hilt of my *gladius*, drawing comfort from the Iron essence that flows into me.

Gaius watches them walk into view with the same hard expression. His gaze holds his rival commander's for a moment before he strikes Brennus, drawing a deep groan from him.

"Halt!" Dorcas bellows, and the Praetorians behind him stop at once, in perfect unison. "Tribune Marius, you are under arrest for assault of another officer, abduction, and violating another legion's sacred autonomy." The sound of a score of *scuta* rattling against each other as the men of my cohort raise theirs to form a shieldwall is deafening.

"Praetorians, draw swords!" Dorcas snaps in response, and the sound of several hundred *gladii* slithering from their scabbards fills the plaza with their hisses. The front lines of the Twelfth respond in kind, drawing their blades. My heart hammers in my chest as I pull my own free.

I'm under no illusion about our chances against one of the elite units of the Iron Legions. I may have been chosen to train to become *Fidelis*, but that doesn't mean that I'm the equal of a veteran legionnaire. We're just recruits, and they are some of the most professional warriors in the empire.

The ninetails cracks again as Gaius whips the boy once more.

"That's enough!" a strong baritone voice barks as a new contingent of men storms into our sector. In the lead is an older man in a golden *lorica* that I don't recognize.

"Bloody Jupiter, that's Imperator Tyrus himself," a regular whispers loud enough to be heard.

"Who?" one of the recruits demands.

"The man with *imperium* over all of Agogia." Shocked murmurs run through us, and I turn to study him again. He's older than most soldiers but still carries himself with strength and vitality. There's an *inhibitus* around his neck, and his arms are worked with Silver veins, making him a match for Gaius. The imperator's expression is neutral compared to the furious tribune next to him, and I shudder as his dark eyes sweep across the sea of assembled Twelves.

"Imperator Tyrus, this man has stolen one of my—"

"Yes, Dorcas, I heard your speech." The man cuts him off effortlessly, turning his full attention on Gaius still standing over the kneeling form of Macer's murderer. Our commander doesn't strike him again but holds the ninetails raised as if he might at any moment. Even he doesn't dare defy the imperator to his face.

The rival cohorts stare at each other with drawn swords, quivering with the proximity to violence. I reset the grip on my own *gladius* and imagine shoving forward to fill the gaps in the shieldwall as my fellow soldiers die for real.

"This man murdered one of my recruits in an ambush, Imperator," Gaius calls after the silence begins to feel heavy. "I am merely exercising my rights."

"His rights? That is a *Praetorian* recruit."

"Enough." Tyrus doesn't shout, but his voice cuts through all the protests with the ease of a sword. "Do you have proof, Tribune Marius?"

"Who here witnessed the death of Macer?" Gaius barks, not backing down. I raise my blade straight into the air. Around me, almost a dozen other recruits lift theirs. The imperator's iron gaze falls on me for a moment. His scrutiny is a physical thing that almost drives me back a step, but I hold my ground.

After inspecting us all, he seems satisfied. "The scales between Legions must be balanced," he grunts. "That is the law."

"Balanced?" Dorcas screeches, his face turning the same shade as the welt that Gaius gave him. Tyrus silences him with a raised hand.

"They must be balanced, and now they have been. Release this recruit back into his tribune's keeping, Gaius." Dark murmurs sweep through the Twelfth's ranks as we realize that he's being spared. Once again, the Praetorians are above the law. Cold fury lights a new fire in my chest where the first went out. I no longer care if revenge feels hollow. I'm certain it's better than this. I risk a glance over my shoulder at our commander, wondering what he plans.

Brennus is unconscious, dangling by his wrists from the restraints. He's pale from the loss of blood, and if I didn't know he had been laughing about murdering my friend less than an hour ago, I'd say he looked pathetic. But to me, he just looks far too alive.

Gaius's face is a stone. Something cold and cruel flashes across his face, and for a wild moment, it looks like he's been lost to the coldness of Iron. I half-expect him to cut the murderer's throat on the dais right in front of Tyrus and the rest of us.

"Let it be enough, Tribune," the imperator calls, his own voice full of the strength of iron. With a snarl of disgust, Gaius tosses his ninetails to the ground and motions for Durus to release Brennus.

The centurion and another legionnaire pull his unconscious form through our ranks, letting his feet drag behind him. I catch sight of his back as he passes by. It is a ruined mess that almost makes me sick, but the calming presence of the Iron Symbol settles my stomach.

Reluctantly, the front ranks part to allow our prize to be taken back to his masters. Durus and the other soldier drop him at Dorcas's feet like a bag of waste, turning without saluting and returning to our lines at a trot.

The shieldwall closes behind them like the gate of a keep. Neither the Praetorians nor we have put our swords away. Dorcas signals frantically to two of his men, who drop out of their formation and pick the boy up. One of them shoves his *gladius* into the unconscious recruit's hands, trying to give him access to more Iron essence.

For a long moment, the purple-clad tribune glares daggers at our lines, his hands clenched into fists. His rage is still boiling, and his pride is burnt. He glances over his shoulder at the imperator and his coterie, and I'm certain that if they were not here, we would be shedding each other's blood even now.

"It will be dealt with, Dorcas," Tyrus promises.

"I want his head," the Praetorian hisses.

"It will be dealt with." The imperator's voice is cold and hard. It sends a chill sweeping down my spine. Tonight will not be the end of this. What will Gaius suffer in retaliation for embarrassing the Praetorians? They've already demoted him to the Twelfth. What more can be done to him?

"You'd better hope he lives!" Dorcas hisses, spinning his fist over his head, ordering his cohort to do an about-face.

"Did you see how pale he was? There's no way he escapes being pulled down into Pluto's Grave," Anas murmurs to me as we watch them leave. I can only hope he's right.

CHAPTER 34

The next week passes at a crawl. It feels like we are men waiting for judgment, but it never seems to come. As we promised, every other day, Marcus, Felix, and I train with the other *Fidelis* hopefuls. Spurius and the other Praetorians glare at us from across the field, with the boys from the Second and Third hovering around them like loyal dogs.

The rest of the recruits keep their distance, not wanting to be caught in the clash between the First and Twelfth. Percy has us practice against him or against other relics, never against each other. I wonder if that is normal or if he is taking steps to avoid more bloodshed.

Under his watchful eye, we are tested in all manners of using our Hearts. One relic forces us to deplete our essence and then times how long it takes us to refill our reserves. Every second that we are unable to stop it, it constricts around us like a python. Of all the recruits, I am the best at this by far.

Another simple device holds an iron bar that we are instructed to shatter. Its only thought is telling the rod to resist our attempts to reshape it. I am able to overcome it, but only by cheating. Instead of competing against it with brute force, I tell the bar that it is too soft, forcing it to collapse in on itself until it becomes so brittle it shatters. With a whisper, Marcus and Felix also succeed at besting it.

Percy gives me a frown but is silent. The other recruits glare but can do nothing. Gaius has given us an order, and after what he did for Macer... None of us are willing to fail. We have enemies in powerful places and fallen friends to avenge. Ascending to Silver is the first step on the path to being able to put things right.

"This was your last training session," our instructor informs us when *Sol* begins to set. "The *Argentum Consilio* will meet in three days. Those of you who are chosen will be allowed to Ascend to Silver and join the ranks of the *Fidelia*. Those of you who are not will return to your units to continue your service." I share a glance with my friends as excitement begins to uncoil in my belly. I am the best *electus* on the field—well, the best Copper anyway. Soon I will take the next step on my path to power.

Back with the cohort, we mourn the loss of Macer in the tradition of the Iron Legions. We may only be recruits, untested and unblooded, but it was the regulars who insisted, who taught us the way. As far as anyone in the cohort is concerned, the skinny boy died a warrior's death.

The day after Gaius's showdown with the Praetorians, three veterans led by Unus, the one-eyed man who branded me months ago, march into the mess hall, carrying a *gladius* and helmet. The room falls silent as they stride through the ranks of eating soldiers, stopping at Macer's empty seat.

With casual strength, Unus stabs the point of the sword into the bench deep enough so that it can support itself. Another soldier places the helmet on top of the pommel so that it rests at head height with the rest of us.

The third carries a small brazier that burns with a splinter of the everflame, smuggled from some Mars temple in Agogia. For a moment, I am a boy, standing before the mausoleum that held my grandfather's remains, watching that same fire burn, trying to guide his soul home.

Unus raises his flagon, glaring around the room with his single eye as if daring anyone to question this memorial. From the officer's table, Gaius and Durus watch but say nothing—a tacit approval.

"To a fallen soldier!" he barks, pouring out an ample sip onto the helmet. The water sings as it bounces off the metal of the helmet and bathes the seat below. The recruits on either side shift uncomfortably as they are splashed but do not complain. "He fell protecting his brothers from their enemies." A pang of guilt tugs at my guts like the knife that killed Macer. He died saving me. "For his sacrifice, his name will be remembered in the halls of the Twelfth forever."

The regulars slam their fists against the tables once in sharp punctuation. Quick on our feet, most of the recruits copy our elders, eager to belong to something that binds us to those who have come before. Unus turns to scan the crowd, still holding his glass high.

"Is there anyone who will speak for our fallen brother?" He only has one eye, but its gaze feels like it weighs as much as Durus's two when he wants me to do something. This is the price of being *Primus*, of being a leader. My father knew this and tried to show me the way—but he was just a farmer, not a soldier. Some of this I will have to figure out on my own.

"His name was Macer!" The words spring from my lips as I rise. I hold up my flagon as I step around the edge of my table and make my way to the effigy that sits in his place. "He was the worst soldier in the whole legion." Surprised chuckles ripple through the room from the recruits. The veterans are silent, but I see a few grins throughout the room. Iron men tell hard jokes.

"But he was worth more than any of those Mars-forgotten *Praetorians*." I spit their name as a curse. A roar of approval echoes out of the room that shakes the foundations of the buildings. "He died saving me from an ambush, but he lives still with me. With you." I point at another recruit who was there around the room. "With you." I point directly at Anas, who surprises me by not looking away. For once, there is something other than hatred in his eyes.

"My mother once told me that we burn the everflame by the graves of our lost to keep them with us, because Thanatos and Charon are dead and cannot carry them to Hades. But Macer is not lost! As long as we live, we carry him with us. Every victory will be his victory; every enemy vanquished will lose to him too. He is not dead until we all are." The men pound their fists against the table in rigorous approval as I pour a sip of my water onto the helmet. Unus gives me a wink—well, I think it's a wink. It's hard to tell with a guy who has only one eye.

Suddenly embarrassed, I return to my seat. Marcus claps me on the back in approval, and slowly, the men return to their food. When the meal is done, no one touches the effigy of Macer. He stays there, waiting for us at our meals, as we hope to one day find him waiting for us when we cross over the River Styx into the land of the dead.

I'm still thinking of Macer and his sacrifice when I make my way to the training fields three days later. The *Argentum Consilio* is waiting to pass judgment on our desire to become *Fidelis*. Marcus and I both brim with nervous excitement that Felix doesn't share. His expression is grim, as if we are walking to an execution. I pat him on the shoulder, giving him a reassuring smile, but he only shakes his head.

He's wrong—the world is fair. The Iron Empire has its failings, its spots of rust. Men like Atticus, Brutus, and Brennus exist, and some even have power. But there are good men like Gaius who balance them out. We have worked for this day. We are worthy. We will be *Fidelia*.

All the recruits of our cohort are waiting for us at the entrance of the Eighth's region of the sector. My hands clench into fists as I see Anas standing in the center of the road, blocking our path. Most of them are former plebeians, although I spot Clintus and the remaining Segestans off on the side, watching with blank faces.

"What's this?" Marcus calls, his hand resting on the hilt of his *gladius* with familiar ease.

Anas glares at my friend for a moment before glancing past him to me. He licks his lips once before growling with irritation and extending his hand. "We've come to wish you luck," he grumbles.

The three of us stare at his hand like it's a snake that suddenly appeared in our path. This cannot be the same man who's had it out for us since the march into Agogia. "Luck?" Marcus repeats incredulously to himself as if he's never heard the word before.

"The three of you are going to become *Fidelia*, yeah?" Some of his familiar hostility makes its way back into his tone. "Gonna show those *Praetorians* what a real soldier looks like?"

"You're damned right we are." Marcus steps forward and clasps the man's wrist with his own.

"Do it for Macer."

"For Macer," I agree, following Marcus's example and shaking hands with the man who had been my biggest enemy. Felix still hesitates, before finally following suit.

"You may have been patricians once, but we've decided to forgive you for that particular crime," Anas announces, looking between me and Marcus. "'Sides, didn't seem to do your lot many favors, did it? You're here too."

"I suppose it didn't." I snort after a moment of thought. "I suppose it did not." The rest of the men reach out to us as we pass, patting our shoulders or shaking a hand if they can reach it. I find the smile on my face is no longer forced as I accept their well wishes.

"Well, that was something I thought I'd never see," Marcus mutters to both of us as we enter the main thoroughfare of Agogia, making our way toward the fields where the council awaits.

"Guess they really do forge us anew here," Felix agrees absently, eyes fixed on the distant South Gate. The tension that grows between us feels familiar, like I have been here before. I laugh out loud when I realize that this is just like when we sat in the stone room outside the arena, waiting for the *Sententia* to begin. We three are still together, bound by our *votum*. Only, this time, there are three of us instead of four.

I wonder what has become of Valentina—what the Censors have made her into. I have no doubt that the Empress's enforcers rebuild their recruits the same way that Agogia reforges her Iron Legions. I can only hope that she's found some sort of peace in her new life.

I never wanted to be a soldier; this is Marcus's dream. But becoming Ironbound has given me a new purpose, a path to vengeance, and a new home. Every time I walk through the ancient city, I feel as though I can sense the men who have come before me, forming the backbone of the empire that has kept our people safe for centuries, since the death of the gods. Before the *Sententia*, all I wanted was to explore the world and be free of my home. Now, I feel as though I am a part of something that is bigger than I will ever be.

"Who do you think is on the council?" Marcus pesters Felix as we walk.

"Iron Legion officers certainly," the former plebeian replies without a thought. His expression is still dour, but Anas and the cohort's gesture seems to have lightened his mood.

"I'm still not stupid," Marcus grumbles. "I know there will be legionnaires—I mean, who else?"

"Magisters." The word is harsh in my voice. I have not forgotten our last meeting with the erudite order—how they whipped some of us and tried to eliminate us from the ranks of *Fidelis* hopefuls.

"Most likely," Felix agrees. "Probably Censors too. The Ascension of any Ironbound is highly regulated by the Empress. There's no way that it would be left up to only the legions. Otherwise, I think more of us would pass."

"Makes sense," I agree after a moment of thought. There are political struggles at play at all levels of the legions. It is only logical that those would extend between the military and the other branches.

"Can you imagine the power?" Marcus half-whispers as we approach the open South Gate. "To be able to feel Iron at a distance? No wonder everyone is so afraid of the return of the Iron Lords." Visions of Gaius dancing around sword strikes he didn't even see flash before my eyes. Yes, I can imagine it, and I want it.

The training field has been redone to welcome the members of the *Argentum Consilio*. My heart sinks at the sight of it because I know at a glance that some of Felix's fears are true. The barebones military field has been redressed as a venue for the social elite. Dozens of figures mill inside a gazebo constructed out of pristine white wood. Servants clad in crimson uniforms meander through the crowd of toga-wearing nobles who shelter in the awning away from the sun.

Next to the shaded structure, a small amphitheater has been constructed, a dais surrounded by raised seating as if prepared for a play. My heart chills as I realize my fate will be decided in that tiny arena and not on the field.

"Fortuna's Bones," Felix swears as we see the crowd waiting for us. A Praetorian decurion spies our approach and waves us toward the center of the field, where the remaining trainees assemble in formation around Percy.

The centurion of the Second Legion nods at us in greeting as we step into the rear rank of the hopeful. Like the rest of us, he is dressed in full *lorica*, and his *gladius* rides on his right hip. His brown hair is cropped short, and his eyes are tight with stress.

The group of candidates has fewer than twenty of us left in it. There are four purple-clad boys standing in the first row but only two in the second. The Third Legion has three representatives still in the running, but no other rank after theirs has more than two members awaiting the trials. There are no representatives from the Ninth, Tenth, or Eleventh Legions. But in the last row, lurking like ill shadows are the three of us from the Twelfth.

The other boys ignore us today, too distracted by their own fear.. No one dares step out of line in front of this august company that has gathered to judge us, not even the Praetorians.

"In a few moments, the Silver Council will convene," Percy announces in a low voice. I lean forward with the rest of my peers, drinking in his words. "One by one, you will be called forward to stand before them. They will question you and test you however they desire to see if you are worthy. Answer truthfully, and you may earn your place among the *Fidelia*." He pauses, his dark eyes sweeping over our assembled ranks once more.

"Each of you has earned your right to stand before this council," he reminds us. "I have pushed you to see if you are worthy of the title of Faithful, and I have found you acceptable. Go before these judges with confidence that you are the best of your year." I feel my spine stiffen as if his words added Iron to it. Calm flows into me as I embrace my Symbol, and I feel my shoulders roll back as old fears bleed out of me. I know that I am one of the best *electii* in this formation. Unlike when I went into the arena during the *Sententia*, I am *Primus*. Today, I will not falter.

I will become *Fidelis*.

Over our instructor's shoulder, I see the toga-wearing officials begin to make their way from the gazebo to the amphitheater, settling themselves into the tiered seats as they gossip among themselves. My eyes sweep through them, trying to guess who they are. All of them have Golden *Cors*. Their veins are on bold display, glinting in the sun. Scarlet-clad servants stride among them, passing out goblets of wine and food like this is a festival rather than a solemn event.

I spot Imperator Tyrus in his golden *lorica* as he makes his way to the low center of the seats. The gray-haired commander of Agogia is stoic, and I look away before he can notice me staring. Despite his promise to balance the scales, nothing has happened. It would do no good to remind him that I was involved in Gaius's challenge. Sitting a few rows behind him, I spy my tribune's mother, Magister Plautia, scowling at our formation with open hostility. A few of the other palatines wear the golden bangle of a senator around their right arms, a thing I've only read about, never seen.

Gaius sits at the back of the little stadium. A handful of other serious-looking tribunes sit next to him. All are dressed in their iron *loricae* and red cloaks, making them a stark contrast to the rest of the luxuriously dressed elite sitting below them. The soldiers are the only members of the audience who do not have Golden *Cor* veins. My commander catches my gaze and nods slowly in my direction. I swallow my fear and return it. This next part is up to me.

My heart chills as a familiar figure steps out onto the dais, taking stock of the seated nobles. The tall woman is armored, although her *lorica* is different. It is not made of iron like we wear of the legions; instead, it is pale *tellus*, the Symbol-less ceramic worn by the White Hand of the Empress, the Censors.

Felix was right. Diana would not let this council occur without her eyes present, watching.

My world slows to a crawl as I study the Censor. Cropped raven black hair hangs to the length of her chin, hiding her face from view. As I watch, she turns to study our ranks. She is older than me, maybe early into her fourth decade. Crow's feet claw at the corner of her eyes. Her features are harsh and imperial, with a strong forehead and sharp nose. Golden veins work their way through her arms as she crosses them over her chest.

For all my belief that Atticus does not represent the empire, rage blossoms in me as I take in her haughty glare. I grasp at the Iron Symbol like a man adrift at sea, desperately holding it against the waves of fury that crash down on me. She is not Atticus, but she might as well be. She is a Symbol of the evil that came to my home and killed my family, that destroyed my friends' dreams, and dragged us to this place to die.

"Easy," Felix murmurs just above his breath at my side, snapping my attention from the Censor and onto him. "Ascend first. Revenge after." His voice is pitched so low that not even Marcus, standing on the other side of me, can hear it.

"Right," I reply just as softly. "Revenge after." Gooseflesh prickles across my skin as an unseen wind sweeps over me, its touch playful and faint.

"Honored Counselors," the Censor calls, her voice sharp and cutting. "As the voice of the Empress, I convoke this meeting of the *Argentum Consilio*, whose solemn purpose is to judge the merit of our Ironbound, choosing only those who are worthy to Ascend to the level of *argentum*."

"It has been four hundred and thirteen years since we first began to inhibit those attuned to Iron to prevent the rise of another generation of *Ferrum Domini*. But our enemies are many. Our Iron Legions require strength to protect us from those who would tear us asunder. Since the death of the gods, only a select few have been allowed to advance beyond the rank of *cuprum*, selected by the advisors of the Agrippa line. Today, you carry on that legacy on behalf of the Empress; I bid you to judge their faithfulness in her name.

"Before us, the legions assemble their most promising recruits for your inspection. Choose wisely, for the fate of our empire rests on it." With a gesture, the Censor cedes the floor to Percy, who strides up to stand before the assembled nobles.

"Crastos Fabii, Praetorian," the centurion intones, and as instructed, the first boy steps up next to our instructor. "Recruit Crastos excels in control of his Iron essence and the strength of his will. He will make an excellent addition to the *Fidelia*."

"An excellent family, the Fabii. Descended from one of the Iron Lords," remarks one of the senators from his seat. My eyes go wide as I realize why that surname sounded familiar. "You are the second son?"

Crastos glances at Percy for permission before replying, "Third, Honored Senator." His voice is tight and nervous.

"Primed for a fine career in the legions." A magister nods approvingly.

"Any disciplinary infractions?" one of the tribunes calls from the back row.

"No, *Dominus*," replies the recruit, saluting as he replies.

"Oh enough. The boy is clearly a worthy choice, and he comes from excellent stock. Saturn himself would be daunted by the amount of time this is going to take," a slim senator calls, her voice bored. She raises her right hand in a fist, holding her thumb upward in approval.

"Too right you are, Senator Claudia," another magister chuckles, copying her gesture. One by one, the rest of the toga-wearing counselors raise their hands. The vote is unanimous. The tribunes do not get a vote.

"Recruit Crastos is formally accepted into the rolls of the *Fidelis*," the Censor announces. A scribe at her right hand makes a note on a large scroll. The Praetorian beams at the council before stepping to the side of the dais, standing at attention.

"Spurius Demoris, Praetorian," Percy calls. I glare at the back of the boy as he walks up to stand before the elites. He might not have been the one who killed Macer, but he was the first inciter of problems between our groups. We still owe him for that.

As the process continues, my stress begins to fade again. The *Argentum Consilio*'s questions seem largely perfunctory. I had been afraid that this would be a difficult test, but they barely seem to be paying attention. No one from the First or Second Legion is denied. None even get a vote against them.

"Where did you attend *collegium*?" one magister asks Arctor, a dark, hulking boy from the Third.

"Antioch, *Dominus*," he replies in a heavy baritone.

"At Magister Sirena's school?"

"Yes, *Dominus*."

"I know Sirena. She never fails to deliver excellent results from her *Sententia* winners," the magister tells the rest of his peers. His thumb goes up, and the rest follow his lead.

A recruit from the Fourth is the first not to get unanimous approval from the council. Two senators protest the elevation of a boy named Victorio, but as far as I can tell, it's purely because his father is a rival *politico*. There's some good-natured chuckling among the rest of the counselors, but still, the boy is elevated.

My shoulders feel like they have been released from a great weight, and I stand at full attention next to Marcus and Felix in the back of line. I can already taste my vengeance against Atticus and Brutus on my tongue. This is just a formality for something that has already been given to me. Felix's expression, by contrast, has only grown more sour. I am not sure why.

Despite my increasing confidence, I can't help but notice that some of the councilors can count. As the ranks in front of us are called forward and there are fewer of us still waiting to be approved, I sense an increasing amount of scrutiny on the three of us in the back. There are only seven hopefuls left—two recruits from the Sixth, then one from Seventh, and Eighth, respectively. The three of us standing behind them begin to stick out like a sore thumb as the thicker ranks from the Upper Quadrant no longer obscure us.

But that makes us merely a curiosity. Let them be curious—none of them seem to care who becomes Silver. Maybe a pack of Golden elites isn't worried about a handful of soldiers who scrabble to attain a rank that is below theirs. A few of the counselors are showing signs of being drunk, their faces flushing, their words slurring. Servants continue to scramble through the stadium seating, refilling goblets with haste.

The next four recruits are all accepted into the *Fidelis*, although the boys from the Eighth and Ninth are asked more questions than the rest. A few senators and magisters abstain from voting, it seems like they are growing bored of this farce.

At last, Marcus, Felix, and I are the only three boys left to be evaluated. The scrutiny on us builds as even the counselors who have not been paying attention realize that the three of us are from one of the bottom legions. Even the drunk ones seem to notice something is out of the ordinary.

Gaius's mother stares at me from her seat at the front, her vision of me no longer blocked. She's not drunk—I've not seen her touch the goblet sitting at her right hand once. The new *Fidelis* recruits are glaring at us with unabashed hatred. Suddenly, the mood of the day seems to grow dour, as if a cloud passed over the sun. A chill that has nothing to do with my connection to Iron runs through me.

"Well, this should be interesting," one senator remarks loudly to another one of his peers, sipping from a golden goblet.

"Castor, Twelfth Legion," Percy announces. My world distorts as I step forward to meet him on the dais. Unlike when the others were announced, there is no polite silence. An outburst erupts from the counselors as they protest.

"The Twelfth Legion," one red-faced senator screams, leaping to his feet. "You cannot be serious, Centurion. A *Fidelis* from the Bottom Quadrant is practically unheard of, but three from the Twelfth?"

"Castor is *Primus* of his cohort—"

"That's like being *Primus* of a group of monkeys!" an outraged magister erupts.

"He is the strongest Copper user in this group of recruits—"

"He probably can't even read!"

"He is a graduate of the Segestan *collegium*—" Percy continues, not flustered by the constant interruptions.

"Segesta? A backwater town full of idiots! Vellum couldn't reason his way out of a paper bag!" From the center of the crowd, Plautia's eyes find mine, and her cruel palatine face stretches as she smiles at me. Did she do this? My eyes scan the protesting council, suddenly wondering how many of them are truly outraged and how many are just playing a role.

There is no warmth in her grin, only the sharpness of an eagle's beak as it tears into its prey. What kind of mother plots against her own sons like this? Behind her on the top row, I see Gaius's face grow darker, a direct inverse of his matron. He's not looking at me but rather staring down at her, face boiling with barely-contained fury.

"What's wrong with his *Cor*?" a magister pipes up from the rear. "Surely the Iron Legions are not suggesting that an *immundus* be elevated to the ranks of the *Fidelis*?"

Wholehearted murmurs echo through the crowd as more of them point at my deformity. I resist the urge to bow my head and cover the white *rasa* veins with my hands. No matter the appearance of my Heart, I know what it is capable of.

"You are being foolish!" Percy snaps, stepping forward as if to shield me from the assembled aureate elite. The base of his neck is flushed with a creeping red that slithers through him like a poison. In that moment, it could not be more obvious that he and Gaius are hewn from the same stone. "Castor is the most capable Ironbound I have ever seen—"

"Have a care, Centurion," the Censor interjects mildly. "You address this august company as a placeholder for the Empress herself. These are not common soldiers for you to rebuke so."

"Says something about the quality of our legions, I fear, if a cripple is the greatest among them," says a drunk senator between sniffs. The row of tribunes behind him shifts in anger. I may be of the lowest legion, but I am Legion. The division between civilian and soldier is not that different between plebeian and patrician.

"Capable or not, he *is* Twelfth Legion." Plautia speaks for the first time. "I myself was present when these three recruits faced the *custos* relic. They were late and had no respect for authority. We all know the quality of men who are sent to the lowest legions. There is no wisdom in granting them the responsibility of *Fidelis*. What's next, murderers and thieves becoming *argentini*?"

"Hear, hear," another magister calls loudly. Several more thump their fists on their chairs in hearty support. My heart is in shambles, its pieces broken and scattered around the floor of my chest. The votes have not been cast, but already I know their results. The *inhibitus* will remain around my neck—I will not be allowed to Ascend.

Felix was right.

"No to them all!" calls a drunk senator, holding up his fist with the thumb pointed down at the ground. A dozen other counselors follow suit, casting their votes against us. Without meaning to, my eyes flick over to the other recruits, the ones who have all been accepted. They're laughing, mocking us as we are cast away. I'm frozen, too shocked to know what to say, like a climber sliding off the side of mountain. There are no handholds. I feel myself about to hurtle toward the edge, about to shoot off into the abyss.

"Are you truly so petty?" Percy roars at the elites, his face red. Not even the Iron Symbol can help him hold his calm—it has melted in the forge of his fury. "You would deny a legion the strength of Silver just because of its number? They may not be *Praetorian*, but they are men! They bleed and die for you, and for the crime of being lower, you will let them die freely? May Dead Mars judge you all."

"That's enough, Centurion!" the Censor warns again, stepping forward with her hand on the hilt of her *tellus* sword. The counselors fall silent in the face of Percy's rage, but their votes do not change. Slowly, more rise to join them, thumbs pointing down. Imperator Tyrus's face is cold and hard as he casts his own vote against me. Even the legions do not want me to Ascend.

My world has gone flat, and I cannot process what has just been taken from me. I feel as if my arm was cut off, but I have not yet realized that it is missing. I no longer take joy from being part of the Iron Legions. They are not what they told us as boys. There is no honor here, only corruption and favoritism. A black despair creeps up my chest as I learn once again the way of the world. Is there nothing safe from corruption's insidious growth?

Felix was right—the world is not fair. Tyrus has his revenge for Gaius daring to treat us like equals.

"There's that famous Marius rage," a senator scoffs after a moment, breaking the silence.

"Just like his father," Plautia crows.

"You would know, my dear magister." Laughter flows through the counselors like warmth, dismissing the rage of Percy like waving away a fly.

"Enough," Tyrus barks, leaping to his feet. His glare settles on the centurion and me with the weight of a millstone. "The *Argentum Consilio* has spoken with the Empress's wisdom, and the Iron Legions will obey. The recruits from the Twelfth will not be permitted to Ascend to the ranks of *Fidelis*. I apologize for the outburst of my centurion. He will be duly reprimanded."

"Well said," a senator calls, rapping his knuckles against the arm of his seat in dry applause. Imperator Tyrus does not return to his seat. Instead, he strides down to stand on the dais, standing in front of Percy to address the assembled counselors. I'm still reeling, but somehow, I sense a new danger, poised at my ribs like a knife in the dark.

"However, my worthies, I fear this does leave us with a smaller crop than expected," Tyrus begins, waving toward someone standing off to the side that I cannot see. "To that end, I have taken the liberty of selecting three special recruits for consideration. All of them are Praetorians, with names I'm sure you will find familiar…"

"Oh, you fiend!" A magister laughs from the back row. "You baited us all with those grunts, didn't you?"

"I merely thought that we deserved a little bit of sport. This process is always so dry and boring." Tyrus shrugs, but I can hear the cruel expression on his face. It doesn't take any imagination; it's the same one that's plastered on the sea of vultures looking at me like I'm carrion.

"Bring out the real candidates, then!" Plautia calls. I turn to see three boys in the purple tunic of Praetorian recruits file onto the dais, heads tall and proud. The first two ignore me, but I recognize them. Their faces are burned into my memory. The third one shoots me a cruel glare as he goes by. I can't believe that Brennus is able to walk after what Gaius did to him. He's stiff, and I feel a savage pleasure at his weakness, but it's not enough to overcome the despair of what I know is about to happen.

"Counselors, I present Tyrus Manis, Domitius Languens, and Brennus Valerus—"

"Come now, Tyrus. I think we all recognize our Empress's greatnephew," a senator cuts in with a dry chuckle. My head snaps from glaring holes in the back of Brennus's head to stare at Gaius in shock. The tribune doesn't look at me. Instead, he glares hatefully at Macer's killer, his right hand blatantly caressing the hilt of his *gladius*.

The Empress's great-nephew? This thing is a descendant of Agrippan blood? The puny, cruel creature that murdered my friend simply because he could? She must not know. Diana would never tolerate such behavior if she were aware. The Empress was just! She was… just not here.

"Do we really need to vote, or can we just sort of make a sweeping gesture?" Another magister laughs from where she leans in her chair. "Surely no one is opposed to this?" The silence has an edge to it that's almost strong enough to be congruent with the Iron Symbol.

"I thought it would be expedient to do it all at once," Tyrus chuckles, gesturing toward the Censor, who lurks in the corner like an executioner. "The Iron Legions appreciate the counsel's tolerance of our little show and the approval to bolster our ranks so that we may better serve the empire."

"Thank you, Imperator," the Censor replies smoothly from where she lurks over my shoulder. "Honored Counselors, you have acquitted your duty well. Empress Diana thanks you for your peerless judgment."

"Now, where's that wine girl?" one senator calls to the crowd. They laugh as they begin to rise and exit the theater, leaving our dreams dead in the dust. I look back over my shoulder once as we too depart, to take one last look at another life that was taken from me. My eyes find Brennus's, and his flash with a hateful promise. We will meet again, he and I.

Marcus, Felix, and I do not speak as we walk back to the Twelfth's district inside the city. My feet feel as if they are full of lead; every step takes too much effort. My shoulders hunch from the weight of failure that hangs on them. I see the faces of my father and mother, of my sister, and of the parents of my friends killed by Atticus and the Praetorians. They are tortured and unsettled, unable to rest because they are not avenged. They cry out to me for failing them.

The Eighth Cohort's sector is frantic with activity as we enter. A row of wagons lines the assembly area; teamsters rush back and forth, filling them with supplies. Soldiers dressed in full battle kits scurry around on urgent missions while officers scream at them.

"There you bloody three are!" Durus barks as his attention falls on us. The Prime Spear seems more tense than usual, the lines on his weathered face deeper and more pronounced. "Good thing you're already in your gear. Grab your packs and get ready to march."

"March, *Dominus*? Where are we going?" Marcus asks.

"You lot have been graduated, recruit. Welcome to the legions."

"Graduated? *Dominus*, I thought we were months from finishing our training."

Durus shrugs like a man who has given up. "Make sure you bring a warm cloak. They're sending us to the ice."

PART 3

WINTER'S HEART

CHAPTER 35

We have been sent to die.

Even the least educated members of the Twelfth know this truth. The bitter cold wastes of the North are traditionally the domain of legions from the middle, not the Twelfth. The mighty Fortress Frigidus, the last bastion of the Iron Empire, is held by the Seventh, Eighth, and Ninth.

We are the only cohort of the Twelfth in living memory that has been sent to serve there, months before we recruits were slated to have finished their training. There are not even winter kits made for our Legion. We carry coats and cloaks that have hastily been stitched with a *V* underneath the Seventh's *VII* insignia to add up to twelve. Imperator Tyrus was not subtle with his punishment.

"I hear the ice *furiae* can be as tall as any two men," a man named Poros whispers to another as we march. Agogia is on the northern edge of the empire, but to get to the true cold, where Winter never sleeps, we must travel further north still.

"My grandfather told me they could be as big as three," Marcus grunts, joining their conversation. A wry smile twists my lips as I remember him telling us about his ancestor fighting in the cold. It feels like a lifetime ago now that we were just three boys sitting in the dark on my parents' roof.

"I guess your dream will come true after all," I murmur to my friend.

"I have a different one now." His voice is heady with something I recognize—a latent anger that burns in me, the same fire. My pack feels heavier as I remember what I carry there, nestled among my winter clothing. Before we left, I dug the bloody *votum* rock up from the floor of the training armory and brought it with us. I don't think you're supposed to do that with an ancient oath to the gods, but they're dead, and I do not want to forget the task that is before me. I may not have been allowed to become *Fidelis*, but my oath for vengeance will not release me.

"Do you remember when we were in that little sandy room below the arena and Castor wished for a Fire Symbol?" Felix asks, rubbing his hands together, trying to warm them.

"That was a long time ago." I smile at the memory.

"I'm sorry for laughing. If you were Firebound, you could keep my fingers from falling off in this Aquilo-damned cold." All three of us chuckle at the lost dreams of youth—and because it is very, very cold.

But despite understanding the punishment we are under, I do not know the depths of judgment against us until a week into our journey when I am summoned to Gaius's command tent with Marcus and Felix. The tribune's pavilion is a large red structure put up by a team of hostlers every night as we make camp. We're wearing our borrowed fur-lined coats over our *lorica*. Already, the nights have a chill to them like a knife's edge.

I dread seeing our commander. We have not spoken since the *Argentum Consilio* denied us from Ascending. We failed at the task that he gave us, and I fear how he will respond. A legionnaire standing guard waves us through the slit as we approach—we are expected. I lead my friends through the entrance, drawing up short in surprise at what I find waiting for us.

The room is expansive but undecorated. A thick rug provides a makeshift floor, and a small *ignis* relic burns with a smokeless fire, heating the room. Felix elbows me before nodding at it as if to remind me of how cold he is. Gaius sits at a long folding table that has been set up for his officers to dine at, but only two others are waiting for us.

Durus looks up from the tribune's left as we enter and gives us a tired smile. The good centurion seems as if he has aged a decade in the couple of days, but I imagine the logistics of an unplanned march fall heaviest on his shoulders.

Seated at our commander's right hand is the last person I expected to find on our campaign. He should be back in Agogia, with his own Legion. Percy raises his hand in greeting, a wry twist of his lips showing me that he is here for the same reason we are. He wears the same white coat marked with a *VII* and *V* to make twelve. He is one of us now.

"Sit," Gaius calls, gesturing at the far end of the table. "We have much to discuss."

"Yes, *Dominus*," I reply, leading our trio to face theirs. The tribune is silent for a moment, staring at us with a dark, understanding gaze. Even here in the cold, he burns with that same intensity.

"I don't blame you," he tells us eventually. "You were never going to be allowed to Ascend, no matter what you did. That is clear to me now."

Percy snorts derisively but does not comment. He simmers with his own anger, a mirror to his brother. The three of us are silent. It feels as if the barrier between officer and legionnaire is thinner here, like the Veil during *Feralia*. But none of us dare press the familiarity, not yet.

"It is no secret that we are being punished," he continues after a moment, his eyes flicking to the stitching on our coats. "Ostensibly, we are being deployed as reinforcements to Fortress Frigidus, due to increased pressure from the Normans and the ice. The garrison is being stretched thin, trying to maintain order for the mining towns across the expanse."

"But that's not happening?" I hazard a guess.

"Oh no, it certainly is. Even Tyrus would not dare send us off on a falsehood." Gaius shrugs. "But just because it is true does not mean that it is not useful to their ends. Half of the Ninth is still in Agogia training their new recruits, so instead, they send us."

"How can they do that, *Dominus*? Were you formally reprimanded for whipping Macer's killer?"

"Of course not." The tribune laughs darkly. "I was completely within my rights, and every one of them knows it. Legally, I could have executed the boy for what he did, but I did not think that wise."

"So our orders are a facade. We are being punished."

"It is how the empire works."

I frown at his words, my world growing a shade darker at what he has shown us. Yet another rust spot on the legacy of the Iron Legions. It seems like a laughable fiction to me, but on the battlefield of politics, shields do not need to be as thick.

Gaius continues, "Just because we are being thrown into the kingdom of ice doesn't mean we have to freeze."

"What do you mean, *Dominus*?" Felix asks eagerly. He truly hates the cold.

"Percy is going to continue your training," he announces bluntly. "You may not be able to Ascend, but he will push you to get every inch of use out of your Copper veins." I blink in surprise, looking at the recently demoted centurion.

"Tyrus told me that if I was so worried about the Twelfth having *Fidelis* in its ranks, I should supplement them myself," the tribune's younger brother tells us with a grin. "I took that as permission to spend more time with my brother."

"It is time for us to be fully honest with one another," Gaius orders, giving his brother a glance that is concerned. "I did not press you when we were in Agogia because that is a place of games and politics. But in the North, there are no games, only ice and death."

My heart skips a beat, and it feels like my entire body goes still, locked up in rigid defense. I do not know what to tell him—the price of sharing our secret is one I am not willing to pay. After a moment, I glance at my two companions, searching for wisdom. All three of the officers are leaning forward, eyes burning with interest, even Percy.

"*Dominus*," Felix says slowly, drawing the attention off me. "I know how your brother came to join the Twelfth, but I have not heard the tale of how you descended down to our depths." The pressure in the room mounts for a moment as Gaius stares at my tall friend, face unreadable. For a moment, I think he is about to explode on us, but then he snorts and leans back in his chair. The barrier *is* thinner tonight.

"I was the tribune of the Third Cohort of the Second Legion," he says after composing his thoughts. "At the battle of Arausio, I ordered my men to reinforce a line that was crumbling and needed to be relieved. I was punished for that because the formation that was in jeopardy was part of the Twelfth. According to my legate at the time, Seconds should never die for Twelves."

Horror blooms in me as I hear his story. Not at the tale, but at how little I am surprised by it. I have seen firsthand the classism at work between the different legions. In my mind's eye, I see the drunk, laughing senators finding out their sons died for criminals and chaff. Gaius is lucky to still be alive. No wonder he made sure that the Praetorian who killed our friend was punished.

"I ordered *men* to die saving other *men*." Heat enters Gaius's voice, the familial rage that bubbles so close to the surface. "But according to those I answer to, they died for animals. And for that crime, I was sent to live among them." He spreads his arms with a small smile. The crackle of the *ignis* relic is the only sound inside the tent as we process his words.

"Tell him." Marcus breaks the silence, turning to look at me. "I trust him."

"As do I," Felix agrees softly.

The tribune's eyes sharpen as he realizes that I truly am not their secret master but one of equals. I smile slightly, nodding at the understanding in his eyes.

"I told you that we were all in the same *collegium*—that is true." I begin our story, almost unsure where to start. I've never spoken it aloud before. "As the *Sententia* approached, we were told that it was a drought year, and we were made to compete against a second *collegium* for the same number of hearts."

I tell them the whole story. The melee in the arena, our battle in the *Labyrinthus*, and about being *Sextus* when there were only five *Corda*. Their eyes all slip to my discolored veins as I admit I failed to earn a Heart. I tell them about the thing that appeared during the Ritual of the Heart and how its attack sent all them into my body.

"By Dead Jupiter," Durus breathes as he understands what all the *rasa* veins truly are—empty, wasted Hearts. I am not impure; just greedy.

I tell them of Atticus's butchery; of the plot he and the Praetorians hatch to cover up their failures. Gaius's eyes go flat and hard as he learns of the legionnaires slaughtering women and children to cover up the loss of a few Hearts.

"So you see," I tell the officers as I finish. "We too were sent here to die." The tent's silence is oppressive as the three of them process the secret that they now hold.

"Castor, you are hereby promoted to the rank of decurion," Gaius announces after what feels like an eternity. He tosses a pair of copper epaulettes on the table and gestures for me to take them. My mouth drops open in surprise, but no sound comes out.

"*Dominus?*" I manage after a moment.

"You are *Primus* no longer," he chides me. It's true. Our column has been merged with the real legionnaires. I march in the middle now, far from the front. "That is a title for *discipuli* and recruits. You will report to Percy, along with the rest of your fellow *collegium* graduates. We may not have a *Fidelis* detachment, but you and your boys will do well enough."

"Yes, *Dominus*," I croak, reaching out to scoop up the rank insignia without thinking about it. My hands shake as I snap them onto the shoulders of my *lorica*, using my connection to Iron to coax the little grooves to open and hold them.

"We'll march in a separate formation tomorrow, Castor," Percy informs me when I'm done. "Marshal the decade off to the side and meet me at muster."

"Yes, Centurion." I salute fist to heart, as I have done a thousand times before. It strikes me that this is the first time I've done it since I became a legionnaire instead of a recruit. In the whirlwind of the last week, I've had little time to understand that I've graduated once again, and like the last time, it only brings despair with it.

CHAPTER 36

The march to Frigidus will take over a month. As our column winds deeper into the North, a bitter chill begins to seep into everything. Tautus, who once was in the Eighth Legion before being demoted down to the Twelfth for "taking liberties with an officer's belongings," teaches us how to cut our long-sleeved tunics and wear them beneath our armor, making holes so that some of the iron keeps in contact with our skin. It's still miserable, but better than being completely encased in icy metal. Sometimes our blades freeze in their sheaths, and we learn to keep them away from any source of moisture.

Our sandals have been replaced with a pair of thick leather boots that have a row of nails poking through their soles, leading back to an iron plate in the heel. With our Symbols, it's easy work for a legionnaire to sharpen them, allowing us to climb treacherous footing, then flatten so we don't tear the floors to shreds.

The cobbled road fades into one of packed ice mixed with dirt. We've made it to the land of permafrost, where it never melts, even in the peak of summer. The trees are dull, dark, and full of pines, but they thrive despite the harsh conditions.

"Never thought I'd miss the desert," Marcus grunts to me as we march behind Percy, ranging ahead of the main column. We're off to the side of the road, scouting for any surprises along the way. It's hard work, but we get to leave our packs with the wagons, and I'll take the extra walking over being a beast of burden any day.

"What?" I'm too absorbed in my study of the climate to hear my friend's comment.

"Sorry. I never thought I'd miss the desert, *Dominus*," he growls, irritated that I wasn't listening.

"Stop that." I sigh, shifting my shoulders uncomfortably. Since being promoted, the rest of the Segestans have been relentless with their teasing. No one seems to take it seriously, which I appreciate, but their mockery still rankles a little.

"Can't help it." Marcus shrugs, but I hear the grin in his voice. "Instructors taught me to respect my officers."

"Respect? Is that what we're calling it now?"

"Yes, *Dominus*."

I let out a long sigh, which only prompts another chuckle from my childhood friend. Ahead of us, Percy draws up, raising his fist for us to follow his lead. We halt, dropping into crouches to copy our leader.

Since the *Fidelis* has taken us under his wing, I've learned that Silver legionnaires are often used as scouting parties. Their enhanced abilities make them more dangerous in small groups. Percy may be the only true *Fidelis* among us, but the rest of us do our best to follow in his footsteps. The other soldiers call us *argentulae*, which means "little silvers" in the language of the ancients.

Silently, the centurion waves for us to join him, holding up five fingers pointing to his left and then five to his right. The first few days of serving under the *Fidelis* were spent learning fieldcraft, which included hand and trail signs to let us communicate silently. Obeying his commands now, the ten of us split into two groups and crouch-walk to the top of the hill on either side of him. My feet crunch a thin layer of ice with every step, and I wince at the sound.

We crest the small ridge that Percy waits for us on, and my hand leaps to the hilt of my *gladius*, but the centurion grabs my wrist, stopping me before I can draw the blade. I glance at him, and he shakes his head once before releasing me and pointing ahead.

Watch, his gesture says.

A small clearing is nestled among the trees below, where a dozen Normans are camped. They are dressed in leather and gathered around a small, smokeless fire. I've never seen a tall, pale Northerner before, but they seem much more *human* than the stories I heard as a child made the barbarians seem.

But that is not why Percy wants to wait. Something moves in the back of the camp, emerging from the trees, and I stare in horror at my first sight of a *furia*. It's tall—Marcus was right about that. It stalks about on two legs like a man, although its mass is easily two to three times that of a fully kitted legionnaire.

It is not a *mythos*, a living animal that somehow bound itself to *Cor*. Instead, it's as if the elements themselves have come to life. It has no flesh; its entire body is made of dark blue ice. Although it has two arms and two legs, the *furia* is more triangular than organic, as if pieced together by a master mason. Its limbs end in giant, pyramid-shaped fists that are larger than my helmeted head. I glance down at the *scutum* strapped to my left arm, giving it a skeptical look. How in dead Mars's name am I supposed to hold back a blow from something like that with just a shield?

I let out the breath I'm holding, only to see it mist in front of me thicker than it ever has on the coldest night in the North. There's an extra sharp chill in the air around this frigid *furia*. Beside me, Marcus has gone stock-still, staring at the thing that his grandfather spent his entire Legion tour fighting against. He is no longer smiling.

"What do we do, *Dominus*?" I whisper to Percy.

"Hope it doesn't see us," the centurion muses softly. "It's not often that one makes it beyond the wall, but it's colder than Aquilo's Bones today. I doubt it will last long once things warm up."

"But the column will march by soon!" I protest softly. "Shouldn't we—

"Protect five hundred men from a single *furia*?" His sarcasm is loud even though his tone is hushed. "I'd rather face one with the entire might of the cohort than with the eleven of us. I think they will be just fine, Decurion." I don't reply, too embarrassed to speak. Of course, the main cohort is in no danger. If anyone is, it is us, the ones spying on the monster. I eye the massive thing with distrust, but it shows no sign of being aware of our presence. It wanders idly through the glade as if bored.

"Come," Percy commands after we observe it for a few moments. "We have more ground to cover." The centurion turns away from the idle *furia* and motions for us to move back toward the main road.

I obey, following my commander, but as I turn, I catch a flicker of motion in the corner of my eye. I pause, my head snapping toward the flash of color before my brain even processes what I saw. A man snaps into view, dressed in white furs. A bow is in his hands, arrow nocked and drawn back.

"Percy!" I shout in warning, drawing my own sword. The man releases his bolt, and it shoots across the glade, thrumming with death. I needn't have worried—the Silver centurion is more than equipped for the task.

Spinning as the arrow enters his range, Percy reaches out with his right hand and snatches the quarrel out of the air with his palm as if it were a ball being thrown to him. Its iron tip gleams in the cold sunlight as he tosses it aside, drawing his own *gladius*.

"On me!" he roars, banging his sword against his *scutum* like a drum. We press around him, forming a loose circle as he taught us. Clintus slides in next to me, touching his shield to my own. Awareness of our ring blooms within me as our iron connects, forming an unbroken wall.

An undulating battle cry echoes from the wood, and a dozen Normans burst from the trees, clad in furs. They are tall and pale. Men and women alike have long, flowing hair that is braided into tight tails. They lack all the uniformity that defines the Iron Legions—some carry long, straight swords while others sport axes. Many bear round wooden shields. Scalps dangle from their belts. Most are fresh and dark-haired, different from barbarians' universal blond.

As I watch, one of the women pauses, raising a small horn to her lips. She blows it, sending out a shrill call that is echoed a moment later, as the *furia* emits a deep bass rumble in reply. My head whips to the side in time to see the giant begin to lumber toward us like a giant hound.

"Stay together!" Percy calls, snapping my attention back to the pressing fight. Iron *pings* as a handful of arrows slam into us a heartbeat later. My arm tingles from the force, but none of them penetrate our defenses. There's no will behind their attempt to punch through our shields, and after training against other *electii*, it's a simple matter to refuse their damage.

I lower my *scutum* enough to glance over its rim, watching as the raiders close with us. My heart races, and not even Iron's cold calm is enough to soothe it. The first Norman steps into range, wielding an axe in one hand and a sword in the other. He strikes with the axe, a wild, overhand attack teeming with strength. My shield rings with the blow, but it is easy to reinforce it with my *Cor* Heart. My body moves instinctively, the motions burned into me by months in the forges of Agogia. I step into his blow, shoving him backward. My mind is somewhere else, caught off guard by the burst of violence. This kind of fighting is almost second nature to me now.

But I trained against *gladii*, not axes, and there I get my first surprise. The edge of his weapon slides up the top of my shield before catching on the upper rim like a hook in a move I recognize. I feel a burst of panic as the raider pulls with his weapon, forcing the upper edge of my *scutum* down, exposing my upper body.

My eyes widen as he draws back his sword to stab me in the neck. I reach out through my Symbol, flowing from my shield and into their axe. The Norman's weapon feels wrong, muted compared to my legion gear. Maybe their smiths are not able to refine their ore as well as ours, but there is iron enough for me to work with. I attack the nails that hold the head on the shaft, rending them with my will.

As I weaken them, I redouble my effort in raising my shield. I feel a *crunch* as the axe head shifts, then flies off, freeing my *scutum* to pop up between me and my enemy's blade. The longsword's tip slams into my shield with enough force to dent it, and I repay his trick with one of my own.

I encourage the iron around his sword to give way to his thrust, trapping his weapon in the folds of my *scutum*. With a vicious wrench, I rip his weapon free of his grip, sending it spinning to land on the icy ground.

The Norman's eyes are wide as I lunge forward, *gladius* extended in a low, vicious stab. His mouth goes wide as my sword bites into him, and the wooden haft of his headless axe drops from his senseless fingers to join the sword on the tundra.

It is so easy.

I slam into him with my *scutum*, driving him off the edge of my blade. He staggers back a few paces before falling to his knees. I stare at him, engrossed despite the fighting raging around me. I've never killed anyone before. His mouth works soundlessly, like a fish out of water, until a red bubble grows out of it and pops. After another moment, his eyes roll back in his head, and he collapses to the ground, empty.

Slowly, I tear my gaze from the still form of the man I killed, the *gladius* in my right hand. The blade drips with his bright red blood, and it feels *sticky* to me through my connection with it. A horrified shudder runs through me as I realize that I can sense some of what the blade does.

"Castor!" Felix screams from across the field, snapping me out of the horrified trance that I am trapped in. My head whips around to see another raider charging me from the side. A pair of scalps bounce on his belt as he runs. Rage blooms in me at his approach. These people are interlopers, come to murder my people. I may not have chosen to join Iron Legion, but I am a part of it now. I am the shield of the people. The sword of their justice.

This time, I am prepared for his tricks. The Norman strikes at me with one of his axes, trying to hook my shield so he can kill me. I let him grab the edge of my *scutum*, but before he can take advantage of his leverage, I slam my *gladius* into the head of his weapon, shattering it like pottery.

Fools. What chance did they think they would stand against an *electus*? I'm furious now as I strike at his second axe, seeking to disarm him. I will kill him. I have to for the lives he has taken. He should never have come here.

The raider keeps his grip on his ruined weapon, using its haft to block my sword as he continues to hammer at my shield with his second axe. I accept his blows easily, keeping my *scutum*'s integrity with a fraction of my will. Essence thrums in my veins, and I force myself to stop drawing more of it in. I'm close to triggering my *inhibitus*. I've been pulling it in like I would in a skirmish back in Agogia. Without other Iron Symbols to oppose me, there's barely anything for me to spend it on here.

Gritting my teeth, I step into brawling range with the Norman, making it harder for him to swing his axe. I batter him with the flat of my shield, like a ram against a castle. He gives ground, unable to block my assault.

I follow him, pressing the attack, not giving him a moment to breathe, just as Durus taught me. The raider has never fought a legionnaire before—I can read it in his panicked movements. He backpedals further until the icy ground betrays him.

He trips over a rock behind him and stumbles backward, falling to his rump on the ground. He looks up at me with horrified blue eyes as I strike, my will-enforced blade sinking through the leathers of his coat and into his chest with ease.

We both freeze for a moment, staring at the *gladius* running him through in disbelief. My hands begin to shake as I realize how quickly I killed him. I didn't even mean to, but the instructors of Agogia forged me well. I kill without thought, just like they want me to.

I pull my blade free from the Norman's chest, tearing my eyes away from his pleading gaze. There's nothing to be done for him, and while part of me is horrified, I do not feel sorry for him. I feel sorry for me and for my parents, who watch from whatever life waits beyond this.

A dull roar rattles the entire glade as the *furia* bursts into the midst of the skirmish. It towers above us all as it charges at the first legionnaire it sees, the black holes it has for eyes burning coldly.

Marcus raises his shield to accept the monster's sledgehammer of a blow as it draws near to him. The giant ice creature slams into his *scutum* with enough force to pick him up off his feet and toss him backward a dozen paces, where he slides to a rest at my feet.

"That went well," I comment down to my childhood friend, who lets out a groan of pain but seems otherwise unhurt.

"Form a line!" Percy bellows from the other side of the creature. He gestures at Felix, Clintus, and the rest with a bloody *gladius*. "Draw its attention while we strike its flanks. Castor, Marcus, you're with me. Go for its legs!"

"Aye, *Dominus*!" we roar, setting to work. I scan the glade, searching for other threats. There are no living Normans in sight; the raiders are either dead or fled. My heart skips a beat as I make out the form of a legionnaire who lies still on the tundra. From the shock of red hair, I know it must be Rufus.

"Come on, old boy," I call down to Marcus, stabbing my bloody sword into the ground before offering him my wrist. "We've got a *furia* to kill." I pull him to his feet as the other eight men of our decade form a shieldwall and begin to advance on the icy beast. The thing lets out another roar, despite having no visible mouth, and begins to lope toward them, eager for the challenge.

"It hits like a horse, but it's not very bright, is it?" Marcus pants as he regains his feet. I clap him on the shoulder before retrieving my blade from the ground.

"Well, just brace yourself harder next time," I chide with a chuckle, starting to trot at the thing from an angle.

"Why don't you let it take a whack at you once or twice before you give me advice?"

"I'd rather not," I admit as the *furia* slams into our line like a berserk *elephanti* that our ancestors once faced in battle. The line scatters under the force of its charge, letting it barrel through before regrouping to challenge it again.

The beast ignores them, continuing its rush toward Rufus's still form, raising one of its giant fists to crush him where he lies.

"Protect him!" I bellow. Out of panic, I use the Iron Symbol to release the clasps that bind my *scutum* to my wrist, tossing it to the side. I pour everything I have into charging after the *furia*, but I know I will be too late. There's just too much distance to cover, even without my shield slowing me down.

Percy flies past the monster in a burst of Silver speed that I could never match. His *gladius* flashes in an arc, and sparks fly as he strikes at the back of one of the ice creature's legs. The *furia* lets out a roar of pain, like a wounded animal, and spins to track our centurion, but he's gone, already out of range of the monster's rage.

Instead of chasing its new attacker, it refuses to be distracted from its quarry. With lightning speed, it whirls, crashing its boulder-like fist down onto the still form of Rufus, squashing him into a bloody pulp like a rotten watermelon. I can only hope that he was already dead.

"No!" I scream, my voice raw. My feet fly as I race at the *furia*'s exposed back. It ignores me, raising its red-stained appendage to strike a second time. I leap as I come into range, my *gladius* held in both hands above my head like a scorpion's barbed tail.

As I slam into the thing's rear, I drive my weapon down with all my rage, channeling all my will into my blade, commanding it to cut. Ice explodes from the *furia*'s back as my *gladius* bites hungrily into it, carving right through where its spine should be.

I let out a gasp of shock as I slam into the icy beast. Instead of slicing easily, my will runs into something equally impenetrable. A wall of resistance pushes back against my Iron Symbol as I try to cut into the monster, halting my blade's progress.

I cannot sense its desires as clearly as I could against the *custos* relic that Percy trained me on, but I feel its defiance in a similar but muted manner. For a moment, I think I know it—the language that it speaks. It's harsh and cold—far colder than the chill of Iron. I cock my head, trying to listen to its whispers, but before I can hear it more, I slip from the beast's back, unable to find enough purchase with my *gladius* to hold myself up.

I lie on the ground, frozen with shock as the *furia* turns slowly to stare down at me with its evil black eyes. That one blow is enough to tell me a truth they never told me in the *collegium*. This isn't a creature at all, but something like a relic, crafted from *Cor* and ice. We are not the only ones who have mastered the use of the metal that falls from the sky.

The *furia*'s bloody fist begins to rise as it prepares to smash me like it did poor Rufus. Fear frees me of the truth that has frozen me, and I throw myself to the side as its hammer-like blow comes crashing down where I had lain.

"Look at me, you great icy bastard!" Marcus roars, dashing in from the side to strike at its legs like Percy did before. He too no longer carries his shield, opting for speed. It lets out another roar of rage as it turns to swat at him like a pest.

I scurry to my feet and sprint away from the thing, using my connection to Iron to make the nails in the soles of my boot bite into the slippery ground, giving me traction. Marcus's distraction gives me enough time to get out of its immediate range safely, and I turn to watch as the main group of our decade begins to advance on the *furia*, shields at the ready. They hammer their swords against their shields, shouting curses at our opponent, creating a wall of sound that pulls the monster's attention.

Percy flashes behind the distracted *furia*, his *gladius* biting deeply into the same leg, deepening the crack that he made before. What level of Heart does this thing have? Our centurion's blade seems to be able to cut it much easier than Marcus's or mine can. But that could mean that it is at the peak of Copper and Percy's Silver *Cor* is overwhelming the construct with its strength. Or that it too is an *argentum*. I shudder at the thought.

So much for not needing my essence. I pull at my *lorica*, refilling my reserves to the brim, the world seems to sing before I choke on the Iron that fills my Heart. If I could defeat the *custos* relic, surely I can cut this thing.

Following Percy's lead, I circle around behind the distracted creature, looking for my moment to strike. The *furia* ignores me, focused on the tight group of eight legionnaires who are making all the noise.

They give ground at a steady pace as it lumbers after them, leading it in a circle around the glade. Felix stands at the center of the line, the tall man's gaze flicking between his group and the three of us roaming, timing their turns to give us an opening to strike.

Marcus makes another pass, aiming for the crack made by our centurion. His expression is wild as the *furia*'s *Cor* pushes back against his will, but the fissure widens. I salute him for the attempt and cut across the clearing from the opposite direction. Unable to get an angle on the weak spot, I try to make a new one.

A few pieces of ice bounce off its right leg as I slash at it. Its will is still as impenetrable as any fortress's wall, rebuffing my attempts to do anything other than surface damage. Again, I feel the harsh cold of its Symbol and its brush is familiar…

—esist, I think I feel. It isn't communicated in words, but a primal, base impression that I can think of no other way to explain. It is the sentiment of resisting, on a fundamental level. I can't be certain before I am past the thing, no longer able to touch it to maintain our connection.

Despite its raw strength, it has nothing to guide it, and bit by bit, we chip away at its reserves. The crack on its left leg grows deeper until it begins to limp. Felix and the rest of the decade continue to distract the *furia*, luring it into a never-ending dance. Every time it charges, they scatter like the wind before reforming behind it, taunting it mercilessly. It roars in increasing frustration but seems helpless to come up with a solution.

"Castor, together!" Percy barks from across the glade, pointing with his blade at the left leg. "Give it everything you have." I swallow in fear but nod in understanding. The thought of emptying my reserves while staying in range of the *furia* fills me with dread, but we can't do this forever. The Normans who fled could return with reinforcements at any moment.

"Now!" the *Fidelis* orders, rushing toward the right leg at a slower pace that I can match. Understanding what he wants me to do, I dash across the clearing, aiming for the left, my *gladius* angled for a strike.

The thing vents its frustration by turning on our centurion as he sprints behind it. It twists with shocking speed, sweeping its giant mallet of a hand across the ground at Percy's legs. The *Fidelis's* Silver reflexes save him. Quick as a thought, he springs into the air, easily clearing the icy limb that reaches for him.

He's safe but cut off from making his run with me. I tighten my grip on my *gladius*, deciding not to waste this opportunity to get another hit on the growing fissure in its leg. I sprint at top speed, letting my sword trail to the side, using my momentum to fuel the attack. I pivot on my left foot as I step behind the distracted *furia*, swinging my weapon in a lateral strike powered by my hips.

I pump as much of my will as I dare into the blow, commanding the Iron in my *gladius* to shatter everything in its path, to hew this leg from its frozen bone, or whatever it has going on in its anatomy under the ice.

My weapon slams into the *furia's* leg with enough force to make my hands go numb, and I watch in delight as a massive chunk of ice flies from the crack, widening it into something I would comfortably call a wound.

The thing's own will slams into me with frigid authority, stopping my weapon's progress cold, trapping it in its frozen flesh. I gasp as I feel my sword grow frosty under the assault of its *Cor*. Once more, I feel like I can almost understand the impetus behind the will, like half-forgotten words.

Dimly, I'm aware that the *furia* is turning, its attention pulled from Percy and the rest of the decade, so that it can strike at me. Furiously,

I pull at my sword, trying to free it from the glacial trap that it is stuck in, but it will not budge. With a shout of rage, I try to let go of my *gladius*. I cannot stay here; I'm only a few heartbeats away from ending up like poor Rufus. But my hands won't release the hilt of my blade—they're frozen fast to the metal in the grip.

"Aquilo's Frozen Bones!" I scream, flailing at the icy wall with my mind, burning more essence than I can spare, trying to free myself. I might as well have been hammering my fists against the wall of a fortress for all the good it does.

A shadow passes over me as *Sol* is blocked by a massive, icy hand. Terrified, I look up to see the thing drawing back its arm for a mighty overhead smash. Fear makes me grow still and quiets the raging of my mind against the will that holds me in place. *This is it*, I realize, watching in horrified silence. This is where I die, and my oath of vengeance with me. At least Rufus will not lie alone in this cold place.

For a moment, the world seems to freeze.

A frigid knowledge sweeps into my mind, filling the now-tranquil space that had been full of my wrestling with the Iron Symbol. The barrier between me and the will of the *furia* shatters like a piece of fragile ice, and suddenly I can understand its impetus effortlessly.

Frozen power floods through me, a deeper chill than Iron could ever manifest. I can feel every inch of the *furia*, as if it is a part of me, an extension of my body. My body shakes uncontrollably, not from the cold but from the alien presence invading me—joining with me. My world begins to fade as the fist begins its descent. My body is already losing consciousness, unable to process the overwhelming cold that fills this thing.

HOLD. DEFEND. DESTROY. I feel the impetus that the thing is under. With my fading mind, I rip at its ice, pulling it into me. Whatever the *furia* is, it is not a relic, but like the *custos* training device—it does not know how to fight against this type of attack. I speak its frozen language and am therefore a master, not an enemy.

SHATTER, I command, pouring every ounce of cold essence that teems within me into enforcing my will over the thing. It resists me, but not as resolutely as it had once before. After a moment, its defense falters, then collapses.

The last thing I hear before the world goes dark is a resounding *crack* that I hope is not my skull.

CHAPTER 37

"Pastor, wake up! *Wake up!*" a voice demands from the darkness. Something slaps me across my face, driving a groan of pain from me.

"Thank the dead gods," another voice breathes. "He's alive!"

I mutter in discomfort again, debating if that is true. My body aches in a way that makes me wish I wasn't. For a moment, I consider never opening my eyes and letting the dark carry me off to join Pluto in his grave. I feel wispy and ephemeral, as if my soul might slip out of me at any second.

But then I remember my oath, and something warm and heavy begins to build in my gut, trapping my spirit inside of me like an anchor. It feels about the same size and weight as the stone that we all bled on for our *votum*. The same one that rests in my pack back at the camp.

Against my own wishes, I open my eyes and return to the land of the living. Percy kneels above me, his face tight and stressed. Marcus and Felix hover over each of his shoulders, their expressions comedic shadows of his.

"I take it we won?" I manage to croak after we stare at each other for a few heartbeats. A flash of disgusted amusement crosses each of their faces like a lightning strike before their stress returns.

Something is wrong; I can feel it. I can feel *everything*. A frown grows on my face as the ground around me complains of the footsteps made by three of my fellow legionnaires as they approach. I turn my head to spot them a half-dozen feet away. Clintus raises his own bloody sword to me in an exhausted greeting.

"Glad you're still with us, *Dominus*." Abruptly, I feel less concerned. I must be fine if they're still mocking me. With a grunt, I place my elbow against the ground to lever myself up into a sitting position. Percy offers me his arm to pull me to my feet while the other two back up to give me space.

"Why are all of you looking at me like I'm about to fall apart?" I complain when I'm off the ground. "You made me think the icy bastard got me—" My banter dies on my lips as I turn to survey the scene around me. We're standing in the epicenter of what used to be a *furia*. Shards of ice as big as my head are scattered around us in every direction as if the thing had exploded. Dumbfounded, I spin in a circle, taking in the scene. I know that I had told it to shatter, but this far exceeded my expectations.

"Oh," I manage after a few moments. "I see."

"Mars's Rotting Beard, how did you do that, Castor?" Marcus demands, his voice full of breathless awe.

"I… am not entirely sure," I reply, still reeling. My mind is overwhelmed by the knowledge that is pouring into it unfiltered. I've felt like this once before, in the iron cage in Vulcan's Forge. How is this possible? Surreptitiously, I glance at my feet, checking to see if we are somehow standing on a giant slab of forgotten iron. But all I see is frozen ground. Clintus marches over to inspect a dead Norman, and I feel each of his steps crunching on the tundra as if he walked down my spine.

Oh.

There's only one explanation for how I tore the *furia* to shreds, but it's impossible. My breath comes out in rabid gasps as I wrestle with something world-shattering. *It's happening again*, I tell myself. In the distance, I think I hear a wolf's howl.

"Breathe, Castor, breathe," Percy commands, clapping me on the shoulder. "You did a great thing. If I hadn't seen it myself, I never would have believed it. Mars's Bones, man, I don't think I could have hit it that hard, and you're only Copper! I hope Minerva's ghost haunts all of the *Argentum Consilio*, for they were fools to deny you. What a *Fidelis* you would have made."

Despite my panic, I beam with pride at the centurion's praise. But the longer I think about his words, the more uncomfortable I grow. He's right, I am *only Copper*… but am I? Was it possible for someone of my level to do what I had just done? I glance down to check the veins on my arms, but they are covered by my thick winter coat. Perhaps that is a mercy, just now. I fear what they would show would create questions I cannot answer.

"Thank you," I tell him after a moment. "I'm still collecting myself after—"

"You used up all your essence at once." The *Fidelis* nods knowingly. "When your *Cor* Heart has nothing left to feed on, it stops. I've seen it knock even the toughest veteran off their feet. Some of the men call it the *crassamentum*—the dregs."

"Yeah… That was not fun," I agree, wincing. Struck by a sudden panic, I extend my senses inward, feeling for my Iron Symbol. It comes to me readily. The *lorica* around my body still feels like a second skin, and the essence pours into me when I call for it. A colder source lurks around me, but I do not dare touch it, fearing some sort of corruption from the *furia*.

Slowly, the world returns to normal, and I begin to convince myself that I am being paranoid. There is nothing wrong with me; I am just panicking after almost getting smashed by a monster my mother used to tell me scary stories about. I do my best to ignore the awareness that creeps through the frozen ground at my feet as I walk around the glade. There is a totally reasonable explanation for this! It must be some sort of congruency between Iron's chill and the coldness of the *furia*. I tell myself it will fade as I begin to warm up and the memory of the thing's deep chill is banished from my mind.

Relieved that I am going to be fine, I follow the rest of my fellow legionnaires to the body of our comrade, who is not going to be. My stomach roils as I stare down at the mess that was one of my childhood companions. Rufus and I were never close, but we were in the *collegium* together since a young age. We were bound to the same *votum*, but now he is free.

"Rest easy, brother," I whisper softly, my promise meant only for most of the men around me. "We will carry your oath for you." A pressure settles on the glade, like some distant eye watching us. It sends shivers running down my spine that have nothing to do with the extremely cold temperature.

"I swear it," Clintus growls from beside me, his eyes distant. Rufus's parents owned the farm down the road from his.

"Poor lad," Percy laments, appearing next to us. He makes no mention of what we said, but he must have heard it. "We will bring him back with us, so he can keep watch over the road, yeah?"

"Will he be lost forever without a flame to guide him?" Antony asks from across the circle. His face is drawn and pale as the dusty snow all around us. We have no piece of the everflame with us and have no nearby temple to borrow it from.

"I always try to leave my brothers in places that they won't mind spending eternity in," Percy continues softly, answering without answering. "And I hope that one day someone does the same for me, when my time comes." No one responds to his words. None of us know how. We may be men, blooded legionnaires now, but this is still beyond us. Percy has sailed an ocean of blood, and our voyage is just beginning.

"Who will carry him?" the centurion asks, unfurling a cloak that he took from one of the dead Normans. "Who will walk with our brother one last time?"

"Me. Give him to me." Clintus's voice is choked and weak, but his face is hard as iron. He kneels next to Percy, and together they move the ruin that was our friend onto the makeshift stretcher to take him on one last march.

It is dusk by the time we make it back to the cohort's encampment. Watch fires blaze around the perimeter, and the tribune's blood-red tent dominates the center. Its color makes me sick to my stomach; it reminds me too much of today. With every step away from the *furia's* body, I expect the cold awareness that fills my mind to fade, but it hasn't. I feel every step my comrades take as we make our way through the tundra.

"Welcome back, *argentulae!*" the veteran on watch booms as he spots us filing in out of the dark. "We were beginning to get worried you had gotten lost out there in the dark, hadn't we, Tryndamus?" A flash of rage burns through me, like white-hot lightning at the sentries' jeers. There's a rattle of iron along our line as all of us shift, settling ourselves. My hand settles on the hilt of my *gladius*, and I welcome Iron's clarity, although it no longer seems as cold as it once did.

"Like a pack of lost lambs, bleat for me, little Silvers, just so I know you're all there—" The legionnaire's voice cuts off abruptly to the sound of something ringing off his *lorica*.

"Shut your gob," Unus growls, his baritone low and threatening. I can just make out the three figures around the fire as we step into view. The one-eyed soldier stands in front of the other two, his face solemn.

Tryndamus and his companion's faces go pale as they see the body we carry on a stretcher. Percy and Clintus hold either end, keeping it steady as if poor Rufus could feel every bump.

The centurion gives the two loudmouths a long glance but doesn't say anything as he leads us past. Before I can do something stupid, Marcus is more than happy to demonstrate our decade's frustration for me. He steps up to the trio of sentries, face dark and threatening. The two veterans lean backward from his challenge, their faces contrite. Felix and Petrus follow, hands balled into fists.

"Easy, lad," Unus says softly, not stepping out of the way. "They didn't know. It was just legion banter. Go and see to your brother. They'll bother you no more." Marcus glares at the two offenders for a moment before snarling a curse under his breath and stalking back toward us.

Shouts of dismay begin to echo through the camp as off-duty soldiers spy our procession. We're out of the dark now, and it's easy for the rest of the cohort to see what has happened. The red tent's flap is thrown aside, and Gaius Marius storms out, looking furious.

His gaze softens as he sees his brother and the rest of us, relief visible on his features even at this distance. It crumples when he sees the body we carry. Without hesitating, he rushes toward us, parting the sea of legionnaires effortlessly.

"What happened?" he asks in a calm voice, already in control of the situation.

"Ran into a Norman raiding party," Percy says, still carrying Rufus forward. The tribune's eyes flick from his brother to the ruined figure before returning to his brother. "They had a *furia* with them." A low murmur of shock breaks out among the regulars. Some of them look at us with new respect. We have fought something even the other veterans have not seen before.

"Where are they now?"

"Most are dead. A couple fled."

"And the *furia*?" The men around us tense in eager anticipation, like a wolfhound right before it is taken off the leash to hunt. I have no doubt that the entire cohort is ready to march into the forest to avenge Rufus.

Fortunately, they don't have to.

Percy doesn't answer for a moment. For the first time, he pauses, turning to look at his brother. Slowly, he drops his left hand into a satchel he carries over his shoulder. He pulls out a chunk of dark blue ice, the size of a large egg, holding it up to the light before tossing it at the feet of the rest of the cohort. I feel it land on the cold ground as if it is my own skin.

"We smashed it into a thousand pieces." Gaius looks at the shard at his feet before looking back at his brother, a knowing look on his face. He does not look at the rest of our decade, but I feel his scrutiny nonetheless. He knows there's more to the story. I scratch at my covered arms, which feel suddenly itchy.

"Well done," is all he says before turning his gaze to the body we carry. "We should see him to rest."

The entire cohort gathers at a small clearing that borders the road to Fortress Frigidus. Our decade does the digging—we will not let any of the others help. In angry silence, we hack at the frozen ground with our shovels, watched by the eyes of five hundred men.

The spade is made for use by the Iron Legions, so a long network of metal runs through the length of the pole, connecting me to the metal of the head. This allows me to use my will to sharpen its edges as it tears at the stubborn northern earth.

I feel every blow from my fellow legionnaires as they dig. It tears at my frigid awareness like a pack of rats, burrowing through me. I am certain that I could command the frost to retreat, to make the ground more pliable, but I refuse. There is no reason to hurry. I want this to hurt.

I'm sweating from the exertion by the time the hole is deep enough to reach my shoulders. Some of the decade pull off their coats and roll up their tunic sleeves. I do not dare.

"It's good enough," Percy tells us after a while. None of us stop digging. We're not ready to say goodbye to another one of us. Macer was a good kid, but I didn't *know* him. Rufus's death feels too much like my parents' own demise. The centurion lays a gentle hand on my shoulder, halting my effort. Slowly, the rest of the men around me pause.

"You've done enough," Percy says softly. "It's time to say farewell." Numbly, I nod and follow the officer out of the hole. I'm cold, far too cold for the sweat that beads on my forehead. It's not the chill of Iron that fills my soul, but something deeper and darker.

The hole is no different from any other grave. We dug it deep to keep the predators at bay, but all I see when I look at it is Hades's open mouth—a maw waiting to devour us all. Today, it is Rufus's turn to be swallowed.

"There is one more thing," Gaius says quietly, his voice gentle but firm. I shudder in disgust because I know what the tribune is going to say. This is the Iron Legions; it is cold and efficient. "We are bound by our oath to the Empress. We must reclaim his relics." The elder Marius looks at us with true sympathy. "You need not see this."

"I'll do it." Clintus steps forward, his eyes hard. His lower lip trembles, but his spine is straight. He boldly stares the tribune in the eyes, daring Gaius to deny his right. The commander is silent for a moment, judging the young recruit. At last, he accepts, pulling a long knife from his belt and offering it to Clintus hilt first.

"I'll help, lad," Unus growls, joining at the front. "It is not easy."

Clintus nods stiffly, sniffing dryly. Not a single man of the cohort judges him for his sorrow, not even these hard men. The one-eyed veteran steps up to the stretcher and kneels next to Rufus's broken body. Clintus joins him, and together they set to their grim task, removing the now-dark metal veins of his *Cor* from his corpse. I try to watch but cannot stomach it, turning away from the sight after a few moments. What horrors we endure for our empire!

When at last it is finished, the two men rise, wrapping the bloodstained metal in a spare cloak. Clintus solemnly hands it to Gaius, who accepts the relics with a comforting smile. He moves to the head of the grave, waiting patiently for us to collect our friend's body and lower him into his resting place. Despite the frost that fills me, I'm touched by the care that he and the veterans are showing.

Most of them have been deployed before. They've lost friends so many times that they should be as numb as I am. And yet, something about the fact that they all know we have been condemned to die has made each life count in a way it might not have before.

"Rufus was a soldier of the Iron Legions," Gaius says after we step back from placing him in the ground. The tribune reaches behind his shoulder, unhooking his red cloak of office from his *lorica*. There are gasps among the men as he crouches down to spread it over Rufus, covering his body.

"Our legion's motto is *redemptio in bella*—redemption in war. Rufus died in service to his Empress, defending his people from a monster from the North. There are few deaths that can be considered better." The cohort murmurs an uneasy agreement, our own future looming in our minds.

"But he was more than that," Gaius continues after a pause. He looks up from the cloaked body to sweep his gaze over us all. "He was one of *us*. The palatines of the empire like to pretend that the soldiers of the Twelfth Legion are not men but some sort of automaton or *furia* to carry out their will.

"Many of you have taken dark paths to get here, but this is not a place of condemnation—it's one of redemption." Fire builds in his dark eyes, and I feel some of winter's chill fade from my own heart. "You may have lost your humanity once, but today, you have taken a step toward taking it back. Your brother died for you. He shed his blood so that the rest of this cohort might live. The forges of Agogia may have reforged you into a soldier, but it is Rufus's blood that quenches you.

"*Never* forget that," he demands. "We are bound by his blood, and the blood of every soldier who has died for another. *That* is what makes us a legion. No matter what is waiting for us at Frigidus, that is a binding that cannot be broken. It is deeper than one of Iron." The men around me seem to be standing straighter, their spines stiffened by our commander's words. Glancing to my right, I make eye contact with Anas. The former thug gives me a slow nod of respect, which I return after a moment.

Maybe we are bound by blood now.

"Remember those words. *Redemptio in bello*. For some of you, that journey has begun today."

The tribune gestures at us, and we begin to bury our friend. Slowly, the dirt obscures the red cloak until it rises into a mound, displaced by the body below. When we finish, we place stones on top to stop any wolves from digging for him. Every man of the cohort finds at least one, placing it above Rufus to form one final shieldwall.

It is totally dark when we file back into the encampment. The handful of men left behind as sentries welcome us, and the cohort disperses to get what rest we can before we resume our marching in the morning.

I wave off Marcus and the rest as we approach. "Hand me a torch. Gotta relieve myself," I mumble, walking along the perimeter toward a large copse of trees. I'm shaking by the time I get under cover. I can run from the truth no longer. I'm safe here from prying eyes—the cold earth would tell me if anyone was close.

Gasping in fear, I rip my coat off, throwing it to the ground, heedless of getting it dirty. With numb hands, I roll up the sleeve of my tunic, holding my wrist close to the light. For a moment, I'm disappointed at what I find.

The *Cor* veins running through my skin look much the same as they ever have. The copper-colored metal flashes dully in the reflection of the torch, intertwined with the purple marks from the scar the *mythus* wolf left me. Confused, I lower my arm. I was so certain that...

Inspiration hits me like lightning, and I let out a gasp of shock as I inspect my wrist once again. There are no Silver veins, like I had hoped. I am still a Copper *electus* like I was when I left the camp this morning.

But as I trace my fingers along them, I am certain that something is different. There are fewer *rasa* lines than before. Some of them have changed from white to Copper. A cold fear grips me, somehow even colder than the burden that I carry. Somehow, I have done the impossible. I know what the new presence in my mind is now. I can feel the second reserve of essence that forms within me a darker, colder sphere next to the first.

I have bound a second Symbol.

I am tied to the cold of Ancient Frost, that which lies at the center of Winter's Heart.

CHAPTER 38

Frigidus's squat form rears on the horizon like some underworldly gargoyle, hunched over the path. The fortress is made of a dark stone, almost black, that seems to drink the light around it. It's much smaller than Agogia, but still large enough to comfortably hold the bulk of the three Legions that are stationed there.

A mountain range runs in line with it, acting like a natural wall to hold back the Normans and their frozen allies. Frigidus fills the only pass I can see like a wine cork, making it impossible for an army of any size to march through without first breaking its dark fortifications. I always wanted to come see the mountains that make up the Northern Wall, but now that I'm here, I thought they'd be taller.

For some reason, the sight of this famous range makes me think of Valentina. She always wanted to see a mountain—there were none to be found among the wheat fields of Segesta. Maybe the Censors will bring her here to see them one day. My heart pangs with a coldness that even my new Symbol cannot protect me from, and I turn my thoughts from her.

"There it is, lads," Durus calls from the side of the formation, his voice full of a brightness that none of us feel. "We'll be sleeping under a roof tonight, nice and toasty!" A couple of men let out a halfhearted cheer. The First Spear eyes the line askance but does not press it.

"Maybe for a day," Percy murmurs to himself from where he leads our decade to the side of the main column.

"What was that, *Dominus*?"

"Nothing." The *Fidelis* centurion eyes me with surprise, as if he had not been expecting me to be paying attention.

"Understood," I reply just as dryly, causing him to chuckle under his breath. We return to our collective brooding silence as Frigidus slowly begins to grow in the distance. At this pace, I estimate that we'll arrive shortly after *Sol* sets.

The rest of the decade marches in two rows of three and one row of two behind Percy and me. There are only nine of us assigned to Percy's special squad now. Gaius has chosen not to replace Rufus, for which

I am grateful. Adding someone new would only make me feel like we were replacing him. Keeping his spot empty feels like we're saving his seat, just like we did for Macer back in Agogia.

My new awareness, the one granted by being bound to Ancient Frost, is overwhelming. I feel the step of every legionnaire around me for twenty paces, beating an incessant, rhythmic beat against my mind. I'm grateful that we march on the edge of the main line—being in the thick of the column would have driven me mad by now.

I still cannot believe what has happened. In the history of the empire, no one has ever borne two hearts attuned to two different Symbols. Even Atticus thought it was impossible; it is that very reason that made him condemn me to the Twelfth after I had absorbed more than one. And yet, I can feel the frost layer all around me, ancient and permanent here in the far north. I carry a second reserve of essence within me that is *not* Iron.

Could it be because the *Corda* were inserted at the same time? Surely the magisters have tried that before. I doubt it could be that simple. I have learned enough about how the world works now that I know if it were that easy to bind a second Symbol, the palatines would all have multiple.

It must have something to do with the wolf-man, but what part did he play? Did he do something to the Hearts before he jammed them into me that changed them? And if he did, why did it take so long for me to bind my second Symbol? It's been months since the attack at the Ritual of the Heart. I've never heard of anything taking that long to bind to anything.

At first, I foolishly suspected that I had somehow Ascended to Silver. How else could I be sensing things so far away? That I was like Percy, who caught an iron arrow out of the air with his bare hands because he could feel it.

But I am not Silver; my veins are only Copper. I wasn't sensing anything at the distance; rather, I am walking on an unbroken layer of frost that has existed for generations. The iron nails in my boots act as a bridge connecting me to the ground below me. Thanks to my Ironbound Heart, I *am* Iron—why shouldn't it count as a part of my body?

My senses seem able to extend only so far before they fail, but as long as the ground is iced, I am connected to it all. The same way that I was able to feel the entire room of iron in Vulcan's Forge or the entirety of a shieldwall when we join our *scuta* together.

If before I was an *immundus*, now I am something else. Something that isn't supposed to exist. I'm under no illusion of what will happen to me if anyone discovers what I have done. The Censors will come for me, to torture me until they discover the source of my new power. Then they will kill me to keep it secret. Already I have learned that it is the nature of those with power to hoard their secrets like *hydrae*. What more will they do to learn how to do something like this?

That is only one aspect of the danger that my new Symbol offers me. I'm surrounded by an ocean of essence compared to the limited amount of iron that I carry on me. It was already a struggle not to trigger my *inhibitus's* punishment for hovering too close to the Ascension to Silver. Now it is almost impossible for me not to. Every second is an agonizing dance of precision.

Twice this morning, I have gotten careless and gone over the limit. I blame the choking on a cough that I don't have. No, I am fine, I tell my comrades. There is nothing to worry about, I am just unused to this Northern chill.

I am not fine. I am like a man holding his breath on a tightrope. With every step, I force my *gladius's* edge to dull then sharpen again as I take the next, just to bleed as much out of my heart as I can.

"You all right, Castor?" Percy asks me after a time.

"*Dominus?*" The centurion turns to glance at my right hand, which is wrapped around the pommel of my *gladius* in a tight fist, before turning back.

"I can feel that, you know," he reminds me. My heart skips a beat, and I snatch my hand from the hilt. Of course he could. I might as well have told him that I wasn't struggling to hold myself together.

"Sorry, *Dominus,*" I reply abashedly. "Having some trouble with… essence overload." The centurion turns to look at me in surprise, one dark eyebrow cocked. It's plausible enough. I'm dressed in my full iron *lorica*, carrying my *gladius* and *scutum* with me. My ability to gather essence is what earned me Gaius's attention in the first place.

"Jupiter's Bones! I forget how restrictive being Copper was," Percy muses sympathetically after a moment. "I felt my collar around my neck every waking moment."

"Do you not anymore, *Dominus?*" I ask eagerly, forgetting that I will never be one like him. The need to Ascend crawls under my skin like a living thing, begging to be released.

"Oh, I do," he chuckles, looking off into the horizon. "But in a different way. The path to Gold is much more complex than it is to

Silver. You cannot trigger it just by cultivating too much essence like you can as a peak Copper. The *inhibitus* makes it impossible to move beyond the beginning of that journey. What you need is a way to control your intake."

"You can control your intake? Do you think that could help me?"

"It's worth a shot," he muses after a moment of thought. "Never tried to teach it to a Copper before, but if anyone might be able to use it, it's you. I think the principle will work similarly for you. You'll have to figure out how to adapt it for your own use. I wasn't shown it until after I Ascended."

"Please."

"As a Silver, I can feel the Iron around me. I can also draw essence from anything within the range of my *animus*. A physical connection is still more efficient, but it isn't required."

"*Animus?*"

"The ancients used it to mean something like spirit, I think. For *electii*, it's what the magisters define as the range that our *Cor* can reach. The strength of my *animus* determines the range that I can sense or draw from Iron." I nod slowly, realizing that is probably what limits how far I could feel across the frosty ground. Percy didn't think that it was relevant to Coppers, and why would it be? How often did an Ironbound get to stand on a surface made entirely of Iron?

"The trick is," the centurion continued, eyes distant, "to withdraw your *animus*, to suppress it while still holding the Iron Symbol. For me, it shrinks the radius of my awareness, but sometimes it can be overwhelming." He tosses another glance at me. "I'm not sure if it's possible to not draw from things you're touching, though."

"It's worth a shot," I reply, trying not to sound too excited. It may not help me reduce the amount of Iron essence around me, but perhaps I could limit how far my own sphere of knowledge extends across the ice. I am only physically touching the frost at my feet through the nails in my boots. If I could somehow ignore the rest of it, then I might be able to breathe easily again.

"The idea is simple in theory but hard to maintain. Your *Cor* Heart becomes as much a part of your body as the rest of your senses. But when you first start to bear it, it is easy to not realize you can regulate it, just like anything else. Most Coppers are like babies, their eyes either open or closed. You need to figure out how to do something in between."

I tilt my head in surprise. He was right; I had never thought of my Heart like that before. I turned my attention inward, reaching for the two Symbols that burned brightly in my mind. "That's the trick?" I ask, uncertain. "Just squint?"

"Just squint," Percy affirms with a shrug.

Instead of releasing Iron and Ancient Frost, I merely... loosen my grip, letting them slip slightly but not fall away completely. I let out a gasp as I feel the sphere of knowledge around me constrict, matching the slack in my mind.

Bit by bit, I continue to release my hold on the Symbols, and I let out a sigh of relief as the overwhelming surge of essence around me continues to dim, like a setting sun. The incessant drumming of the cohort's marching blessedly fades from my skull. I'm still just as aware of the iron on my body, but that makes sense—it's closer.

On a whim, I try to change my grip, holding my Symbols differently. It feels like trying to close one eye while leaving another open. It's awkward and unwieldy, but after a moment, I manage it. My awareness of Frost winks out of my mind, leaving only Iron. I'm so startled that I pause mid-stride, causing a pile-up in our ranks.

"Keep moving, *Dominus*," Marcus growls good-naturedly from behind me. "Officers gotta march too."

"Sorry," I manage, not even bothering to respond to his banter. I'm too focused on the task at hand. The ever-present chill creeps back into my bones, invading the space that my Symbol has vacated. I hadn't realized that I wasn't cold anymore.

Well, *I* am cold, but the cold that dwells inside me like a sleeping behemoth kept the outside chill at bay. Now that I banished it, the air around me seems content to wreak its vengeance.

I reach for the Ancient Frost Symbol, brushing it lightly as if it is a sleeping kitten that I am trying to get to love me. Gently, I grip it, trying to hold it with only the faintest touch while keeping Iron firmly in my mind. I stagger as I fail to be gentle, and the awareness of the icy ground around me comes crashing into me like a rockslide. Frantic, I release both before I can trigger my *inhibitus's* restrictions. *That was a close one.*

Taking a deep breath, I try to find a calm center before restarting the process once more. I want to hold Iron as firmly as I can while only barely calling upon Ancient Frost for its relief from the cold.

It takes hours for me to become competent, but I can practically march in my sleep at this point. As Frigidus grows larger before us, I practice switching between the two Symbols, carrying one then the other, then holding both at different strengths.

It's awkward. If I was really learning to wink, my mouth would be open and my entire face contorting to pull it off, but by the time *Sol* has set and we approach the fortress's drawbridge, I think I'm no longer in danger of overflowing my essence reserves just by existing.

At the front of the column, a horn plays, blowing three long notes announcing our arrival at the gate. In response, the wall returns the notes, followed by the creaking of chains as they begin to lower the door.

Torches decorate the dark stone of the fortress, hanging on the outside so they do not illuminate much on the other side of the defenses. I can barely make out the glint of armor as legionnaires move around in the murky dark. Any archers looking to take out the sentries at night would have their work cut out for them.

"Easy, lads! We're almost home!" Durus calls out brightly as the giant iron and wood bridge thuds down in front of us. "One last bit and we can sleep!" The Twelfth lets out a ragged cheer as we enter Frigidus. Percy guides us to join the rear of the column, and I glance over the edge as we make our way over the chasm.

It's far too cold for there ever to be water in the moat, and I can't see the bottom of the drop in the dark, which tells me all I need to know. Any invaders attacking the imperial fortress from the south would be risking a free fall into the abyss.

Although, I realize as I march through the giant stone gates like I'm being devoured, why do they need such defenses on this side? The only thing that lies to the south is the empire. The only army that has come this way in generations is the Iron Legions.

"Jupiter's Rotting Beard, those really are Twelvies," a guard says overhead as we pass beneath their watchful gaze. I shift my shoulders, trying to ignore the gossip I know is spreading like wildfire above us.

"Cohort, assemble!" Durus barks as we emerge into an open courtyard. Our booted feet ring as the iron nails beat against the solid stone of the fortress. There's no permafrost here. I let out a sigh of relief at not having to focus on splitting my Symbols power any longer.

As instructed, we form twenty ranks of twenty-five men, standing at parade attention. Gaius is at the front, with Percy and Durus hovering behind his shoulders like a pair of Muses. We wait in tense silence for a few moments. Our officers don't look at us but at the far entrance to the courtyard. Legionnaires on the wall shuffle behind us, muttering among themselves. They know we're not supposed to be here too.

"I did not believe it!" a man's voice booms as he strides into the light. He's tall and powerful with a dark mane of hair that is far too long for regulation. But he wears the golden *lorica* of a imperator, so maybe the rules don't apply to him. "I read the orders three times, and still, I did not believe them."

"Jupiter's Brittle Bones," Marcus whispers in reverent awe. "That's Imperator Brodigan, the Lion of the North." I eye the man with even more interest. Brodigan's fame extends far beyond his military record. According to legend, he once sought the Empress's hand, but he was not a palatine, and the priests rejected him. Brokenhearted, he took an oath of celibacy until he was worthy of her. That promise brought him here, where he waged war on the Normans in Diana's name. A pair of centurions follow in his wake, wearing the white uniforms of the Northern Legions instead of crimson like ours.

Brodigan draws up short in front of Gaius, studying him for a moment before turning to look at Percy with a piercing, knowing gaze. "Yet here stand the two sons of *Domus* Marius, bearing the mark of the Twelfth, standing in my fortress."

"*Dominus*." Our tribune's voice is colder still than the air around us. His fist thumps against the metal of his chestplate, and five hundred men follow suit like thunder following lightning. The imperator glances at us, an eyebrow arched in surprise as if he wouldn't have expected that we were capable of such a thing.

"Tribune," he replies easily, returning the gesture. "Welcome to Frigidus. Sorry it's so bloody warm. We've been having an unusually hot summer." For a moment, the square is still in stunned silence before the imperator gives us another skeptical look. A pair of blue sapphires glint from above his shoulder, marking him as the Commander of the North.

"That's a joke, lads," he calls, chuckling warmly. "We tell those here. It's colder than Aquilo's Areolae out there! Welcome to Hades; I hope you brought an extra coat." An amused burst of laughter sweeps along our ranks. A imperator has never addressed most of us before. Already I like the man far more than Tyrus. I exchange glances with Felix, who shrugs, as confused as I am by the familiarity.

"My centurions will show you where your men can bunk for the night, Gaius," he tells our commander. "Get your lads settled, then bring your officers to my quarters for a late dinner and wine. Lots of wine," he adds under his breath.

CHAPTER 39

As a decurion, I'm not expected to join the imperator for dinner. That's for the centurions and other senior officers. I make sure our decade is settled into the barracks that we've been given. It's like the one we lived in at Agogia, only made of stone and full of fireplaces that burn brightly, casting light and warmth throughout.

It feels a little like coming home.

"That's the nice thing about the legion," Marcus grunts as he tosses his pack onto an upper bunk by one of the hearths. "They make everything the same."

"It's also the bad thing about the legion," Felix grumbles as he flops onto his bed, his feet sticking off the edge slightly, just as they had in our last one.

"The legion expects you to be the appropriate height," Marcus shoots back with a grin. "If you are too big for the bed, you will need to adjust accordingly."

"Castor, Gaius wants you at dinner," Percy calls, sticking his head in from the door.

"*Dominus?*" I stutter in response, caught off guard. "The tribune wants me to have dinner with... the imperator?" The men around the room *whoop*, mocking my favoritism.

"I'm just the messenger, Decurion." He is amused by my discomfort. His eyes narrow as he takes me in, still dressed in my full battle kit. "What are you wearing?"

"Um," I reply, glancing down at my *lorica*, not sure how to answer what feels like an obvious question. "My... uniform?"

"Lose the armor," the *Fidelis* orders with a hurried gesture. "You can wear your *gladius* if you want to, but it makes you look nervous." I glance at his belt to see that he's still carrying his, so I decide to follow his lead. Besides, I am nervous.

"Give me a hand," I say to Marcus as I use my connection to the Iron Symbol to undo the clasps down the back of the armor, letting it relax so that it's easy to slip off. I toss my helmet on my bed—I'll take care of them later.

"Yes, *Dominus*," my friend calls cheerfully, catching it as it falls off me. I feel a pang of regret as I lose contact with my major source of Iron essence. My reserve is full, but its presence is still comforting, like a warm loaf of bread even when you're not hungry.

"Make sure your boots' *clavi* are flat," Percy warns as I follow him out of the barracks. "If you tear up a imperator's carpet, they'll whip you until you join the Thirteenth."

"That's the nails, right?" The quartermasters didn't bother teaching us the proper term for them; just made sure they fit and sent us off to die. The centurion grunts in affirmation, and I check to make sure that they are. Percy leads me toward a tight cluster of officers waiting in the courtyard. Gaius stands in the middle; it is strange to see him without his red cloak.

"Good. Come." The tribune turns as we approach, leading our pack deeper into Frigidus. His spine is rigid and tense, like a taut bowstring ready to release its arrow.

"I expect you all to behave tonight." He does not pause or turn to look as he lectures us.

"Yes, *Dominus*," we reply in a disjointed chorus. We're much worse at it than the enlisted men. I half expected Durus to scold us for our terrible showing, but he says nothing.

"Murex, I swear on Dead Jupiter's Right Hand, if I see you eat anything without a fork, I'll whip you myself." Murex's gulp is audible before he replies.

"Yes, *Dominus*," he repeats.

"Make no mistake. This is not a dinner; it is a battlefield. Do not speak unless spoken to. Do not drink unless offered a drink. Do not get too drunk, but drink enough to appear grateful that a imperator is sharing his personal collection with you." He pauses, turning to look at all of us. "On second thought, drink as much as he gives you. The Seventh deserves to have their stores plundered." We chuckle in dark appreciation.

"But under no circumstances are you to comment on the details of our assignment to the North. Am I clear?"

"Yes, *Dominus*." This time, our reply is crisp and uniform. Gaius nods once in satisfaction, looking at each of us, measuring our mettle. His dark gaze pauses on me, and for a moment, I think he's about to send me back to the men. Part of me hopes he does. But then it passes, and he nods once at me before moving on. A warm feeling begins to grow in the center of my chest. It feels good to be accepted—to belong.

"Let's go to battle."

The imperator's quarters are high up in the main fortifications of Frigidus. If it were daylight, I have no doubt that we would have an unparalleled view of the wild, snowy expanse to the north. Instead, at night, all we can see is an endless dark void through the thick, double-paned glass windows. *Mons* Olympus floats in the sky, blazing like a beacon under the power of a waxing *Luna*.

A dozen other men join us, the legates of the Seventh and Eighth, as well as several tribunes from their legions. It is a room full of powerful people, maybe even more powerful than the *Argentum Consilio*, although in a different way. These men don't wield the same political strength; instead, they command the Iron might of the legions. I feel like a fish out of water, caught in a place I do not belong. I am the only decurion present.

The room is dominated by a long mahogany table sitting on top of a thick, red carpet, loaded with a feast. A fire roars in the wall, casting the entire stone room with a warm, cheery light. The dishes and cups are made of gold, and many are set with precious stones that dance with the flames. I eye them with distaste as I sit in a comfortable chair. It seems so needlessly opulent compared to Gaius's austere traveling tent.

"I know what you're thinking," Brodigan chuckles from across the table, marking the sour look on my face. "This is a bit gaudy for the Iron Legions, isn't it?"

Gaius's head turns slowly so he can glare at me.

"*D-Dominus?*" I stutter, surprised by the imperator's sudden, intense focus.

"You're fresh from Agogia, still suffering from a little shock about what the Iron Legions *really* are. Do I hit the mark?" I gape at the Lion, feeling as helpless as a gazelle. Now that we're out of the cold, I can see he too is a *Fidelis*. Silver veins glint around his wrist as he rubs his hands together in amusement. Gaius's eyes bore into me—a dark fury that I can barely withstand.

"Relax!" Brodigan laughs, a genuinely warm sound that echoes around the room. "You're with the real legions now, Decurion. Not the pretenders you left behind."

"You're scaring the lad," Boris, the legate of the Seventh, scolds his commander with a chuckle. He's tall and severe, with a wicked scar that runs down the right side of his face. But despite his cold appearance, his voice is warm and welcoming. "Have no fear, Decurion. He does this speech every time there are new guests." Out of the corner of my eye, I see Gaius relax. I do not dare to follow suit.

"Each of these pieces was claimed in battle," Brodigan announces, raising his own goblet to inspect it in the firelight. They're spoils of war, taken from Normans who dared to invade our empire. They've been paid for not with coin but in blood from our soldiers. This collection has been maintained since the time of the Iron Lord Frigidus, who built this fortress after he slew the winter god Aquilo. These are not luxury, but a reminder of the victories that those who defended the North before us have won. It is our duty to add to it so that the next generation may have an even greater collection."

"Hear, hear," the two legates chorus, drumming their hands on the table. The rest of the room follows their lead, and even Gaius looks properly assuaged.

I can't help but like the Lion of the North more. He has a charisma about him that is both genuine and powerful. The attention of the room naturally flows to him, but he welcomes it like an old friend. This feels like the legions that Marcus told me stories about, the iron shield of the realm.

"To victory in the North, gentlemen, *Frigus Victoria!*" Brodigan raises his cup, and the rest of the officers follow.

"*Frigus Victoria!*" we bellow in response before sipping our cups. They're full of wine, warmed and spiced. It spreads through me, banishing the chill that settled in my bones and has been there so long I have grown used to it.

The imperator claps his hands, and a pair of servants sweep through the room, delivering food that makes my jaw hang open. There's a soup full of leeks and meat. Steaming roast pork with mashed potatoes and asparagus that's been grilled over an open flame. There's bread—fresh bread! So warm that it falls apart in my hands. After a month on the road, eating dried legion preserves, it feels like I've found my way to Olympus. I slip a roll into my pocket for Felix, the tragic baker. Percy sees me but only winks when we make eye contact.

I glance to my right to see Murex staring at food on his plate with a tortured expression as he tries to cut the pork with a knife held in his fist. Trying to hold back a laugh, I inhale my bite and have to drink most of my wine to stop from choking to death on that heavenly food.

"How was the journey from Agogia, Gaius?" Pordus, the legate of the Seventh, inquires pleasantly when I've finished choking. "As the good imperator says, it's been colder than Aquilo's Grave this season."

"It was certainly cold, *Dominus*—"

"Nonsense," Brodigan interrupts, glaring over his bowl at my tribune. "At my table, there are no ranks, Gaius. Not while there's eating to be done." The rest of the Northern Legions laugh warmly, used to this level of familiarity.

"Understood," Gaius says slowly, looking as confused as I feel. "It was cold, but we had more trouble with the Norman raiders we encountered."

"You found a raiding party on this side of Frigidus?" Brodigan demands, pausing mid-bite to stare intently. "Where?"

"My brother was leading a detachment of scouts when they encountered it—Percy?"

"It was a small group, maybe less than a score in total. We encountered them about a week south." The *Fidelis* hesitates, glancing at his older brother for a moment before continuing. "They did, however, have a *furia* with them."

"A *furia* is loose on the other side of the wall, and you're just now mentioning it?" Brodigan throws his half-eaten roll to his plate in a burst of anger. His dark brows furrow as he turns his rage on Gaius. For the first time, I see that he earned his nickname for more than his long hair. He seems every inch a lion learning that his territory has been invaded.

"Not anymore," Percy says softly, cutting off the imperator's tirade before it can begin. The table all twitches in surprise, turning to look at my centurion in surprise.

"You killed it?" Boris asks, impressed. "I know you are *Fidelis*, but that's impressive work for any legion, especially one not trained in the North. We have relics for those frozen bastards."

"Not me." Percy shakes his head, raising his fork to gesture at me with something like a cruel smirk on his face. "He did."

An imperator, two legates, four tribunes, and a handful of centurions turn to stare at me with the same unbelieving expression. I swallow hard, barely managing to not choke on my food again while under their scrutiny.

"You killed a *furia*?" Boris's voice is skeptical.

"This is your protégé?" Brodigan asks Gaius. My tribune nods once, sending a thrill through me even though I do not feel as though I have earned this praise.

"I didn't do it alone," I protest, looking at Percy for some help, but the centurion shoots me a big grin and waves away my protests with a dismissive gesture.

"I barely cracked its thick skin. Young Castor here hit it hard enough to make it shatter. He was nearly made a *Fidelis* himself, actually."

"A *Fidelis* from the Bottom Quadrant?" Pordus asks, voicing the doubt that I know all will feel. "Surely you jest—"

"Pordus." Brodigan's voice is hard and cold like an avalanche, cutting off the legate mid-sentence.

The legate stiffens for a moment before lowering his head in a demure nod to his superior officer and then, to my surprise, to the rest of us. "Forgive me," he murmurs. "I've been in the cold too long, and my manners have clearly frozen."

"Think nothing of it." Gaius snorts, raising his golden goblet in the direction of Pordus. "You're not wrong, obviously." I feel the rest of the room trying to look at my arms, trying to verify that my veins are Copper and not Silver. I'm grateful for the long-sleeved tunic that I wear for hiding the white *rasa* lines, saving me from questions I do not want to face from an imperator of the empire.

"Is that what brings you to my Northern Domain?" Brodigan asks as he takes another large bite. His voice is mild, but there's a sharpness to his eyes that sends shivers down my spine. He may be kinder and less formal than the palatines, but that doesn't mean he's not deadly.

"We've been sent to supplement your garrison," Gaius replies in an equally uninterested tone. "Something about the cold and increased raid from the Normans." The northern officers all exchange glances. They know what that really means.

"It's true that the barbarians grow bolder this year than any in memory," Boris allows, absently tapping at his long scar with a pointer finger. "Something drives them out of the cold with a whip."

"Yet much of the Ninth is still in Agogia, refilling their ranks with recruits. The Seventh and Eighth also have not been fully recalled to Frigidus," Pordus remarks. "It seems strange that we would be sent a single cohort of the Twelfth to replace more than five thousand men."

"I think we had best be careful speculating too hard on the mind of Agogia," Gaius warns softly, his voice tense. The room falls silent, heavy with a shared knowledge that even I understand. These men know that we have not been sent to reinforce them but to be punished.

"What my men are saying so delicately, Gaius, is that sending you and your soldiers here seems like a much more effective way to lose a cohort than to save a fortress." Brodigan sets his utensils down with an aggressive clink. The eating around the room halts as we are all drawn in by his power. There is an energy to him that borders on furious, like a thunderhead on the horizon.

"I would not presume to know such a thing, Imperator," Gaius replies delicately. His face is a stone mask, revealing nothing.

"Bah! Spare me the answer of a *politico*," Brodigan snaps, slamming a palm against the table. "This is the North, not that den of vipers in Agogia. Even here in the ice, we have heard the tale of the youngest tribune in the history of the Second, who ordered his men to bleed for the Twelfth." The legates peer at Gaius over steepled hands, their gazes intense, their respect obvious. These are truly different men—ones worthy of the legacy of the Iron Legion.

The Second would never sacrifice for them either, I realize. But Gaius is something other than a former Tribune of one of the elite legions. He's proven his mettle in fire and blood, and that is the only language that matters here in the North.

"And now here you are on my doorstep with your brother similarly demoted. This is doubly surprising to me since I know who your father is." He turns to give Percy a hard stare. "What did you do?"

The centurion glances at Gaius for confirmation before responding, "I scolded the *Argentum Consilio* for their corruption. To their faces. During the assembly."

"Did you really?" A deep chuckle rips from the Lion of the North as he leans back in his chair. "Now that, I would have loved to see. What did they do this time?"

"They refused to raise the three strongest Coppers I've ever seen to the *Fidelia* because they were in the Twelfth."

"Ah." The imperator's heavy scrutiny turns back on me. I know how a jewel must feel under the eye of a master smith. "It seems that we are on similar paths, young Gaius." It occurs to me that Brodigan's own fate is congruent to our story. After being denied the right to marry the Empress by political schemers, he was sent here to freeze and die—alone and out of the way.

"You might be right," my commander allows, nodding his head.

"I have received orders for your deployment. They arrived by *mandatum* relic a week ago," the imperator says, eyes still dark and watching. Gaius stiffens but nods once.

"I will accept them."

"Unfortunately, I left them in my quarters." Brodigan waves airily, leaning back in his chair. "I'll get them to you in the morning. You were tired after a long march and you and your men retired early, so I was unable to give them to you immediately upon your arrival."

"We are quite exhausted," Gaius agrees, some of the tension leaking out of his shoulders. I understand now. Once he has his orders in hand, he must follow them, but since he has not been given them, there is a moment of peace—a moment for this meeting to take place. It is a fiction that he could not be given them tonight, but it is enough of one to shield us all. This far north, even Agogia's reach begins to grow short.

"Tonight, we are merely talking about the future." Brodigan produces a pipe from his pocket and puts it in his mouth. A servant steps forward with a burning brand and lights it before refilling all our cups with more wine. The imperator puffs on the stem for a moment before continuing.

"It is true that the Normans are coming out of the ice in numbers like we've never seen," he says after a moment. "There's something going on, deep in their territory, but we have no idea what it is. All we know is that we've almost drowned under the waves that are pouring out of the frost. Twice, Frigidus has almost fallen."

I let out a cough of surprise, choking on my wine. Brodigan arches an eyebrow in my direction while Gaius glares at me. "Sorry," I manage to wheeze out. "I just don't understand how that's possible."

"You've witnessed the power of a *furia* and you're confused how they are a threat to a fortress?" Boris asks me incredulously.

"Not that part, I guess. But the raiders were… Well, they didn't put up much of a fight," I explain embarrassedly. I'm not sure how to politely say it, but my Ironbound companions and I tore through them like a wind through a washing line. It feels cavalier to dismiss the death of men like this.

"Ah." Brodigan understands my meaning in an instant. "You got your first taste of combat and found it disappointing, did you, lad?"

"No—th-that's not what I mean," I stutter.

"Well, have no fear, young Castor, because there are far worse things waiting for you in the cold." The rest of the northern officers laugh in grim appreciation.

"Raiding parties tend to be made of their youngest and weakest," Pordus tells me, taking pity on my lack of understanding. "They'd rather sneak past our patrols than face down a cohort of the Iron Legion."

"Their true warriors, on the other hand, live for the chance to break through a shieldwall," Brodigan promises me. "No doubt you noticed the *Cor* that powers a *furia*?" I nod, still uncomfortable about that revelation. "Their elite warriors are called *berserkirs*. Trust me, you'll know if you ever see one. They are covered in tattoos from head to toe with ink mixed with ground-up *Cor*." My eyes widen at the blasphemy. Before we killed the gods, Prometheus stole the knowledge of how to use the metal from them, but to hear of another people using our knowledge and defiling it so makes me feel sick to my stomach.

"Their tattoos give them fearsome strength, enough to tear through any Copper's shield. But more than that, it gives them dark powers to attack our Hearts." I gape at the imperator in shock before looking at the other northern officers, hoping one of them will tell me that this is joke. When none of them laugh, I slowly begin to realize that it is true.

"So, you see, Castor, holding the line in the North is harder than it looks."

"I had no idea, *Dominus*," I manage, still overwhelmed by what feels like my world collapsing. The magisters told us stories of the Norman barbarians; of their primitive existence out in the snow. None of them ever told us that they harness the same power that we do—that they've found new ways to use it. Brodigan smiles slightly, letting me know that he isn't offended by my ignorance.

"I don't blame you, you're fresh from the forge. They've been screaming '*You are the Iron Legions. You do not bend. You do not break*' in your ears until you believe it. The real world is far messier than you can ever be taught."

"Isn't that the truth?" Boris chuckles from further down the table.

"I do need men, Gaius." The imperator grows serious as he turns back to my commander. "Yours are healthy and"—he glances at me once again—"capable. I would welcome such reinforcements among my troops."

"But?"

"But I cannot simply take you under my command... Not yet."

"What is the nature of our orders?"

"Scouting. Apparently, you're some sort of tactical experiment. A Bottom Quadrant cohort, equipped with a *Fidelis*, designed to range out into enemy lines without support." The familiar chill, which had been banished by the fire and food, begins to fill my guts again at his words. We are to be fed to the wolves.

"I take it we're supposed to discover the source of unrest for the Normans?"

"If you survive, that would be lovely. But we both know you're just expected to die."

"What do you need?"

"An excuse. I don't have the *imperium* to claim you as a part of my legions without the approval of Agogia. But if Frigidus was under siege, which it certainly will be soon…"

"Then you will," Gaius breathes out in understanding.

"It would be well within my rights to issue a battlefield promotion to any men who fought on my lines protecting the fortress." Brodigan shrugs as if that is no big thing. "It could be the Seventh, Eighth, or Ninth, whichever needs reinforcement the most. But once you are a part of my legions, then you fall under my command and become untouchable."

I exchange a wide-eyed glance with Murex, too stunned to speak. A promotion out of the Twelfth? For an entire cohort? It's unthinkable. But as I stare at the Lion of the North, my doubts begin to fade. Who would dare stand against him?

"What do you need from me?"

"Follow your orders. Slowly. You're the Twelfth—they don't expect you to be efficient or capable. The invasion is coming. Stay alive, or better yet, find its source for me, and then I can protect you." Gaius glances down the table at his officers. A thrill runs through me as I see his cold eyes have begun to burn like an old coal catching fire once more.

"Consider it done."

CHAPTER 40

F ollowing the imperator's orders, we spend the next four days preparing to embark beyond the wall into Norman territory. Gaius stalks through the courtyard, screaming at us to move faster, his face turning red with rage. But at night, we decurions move through the barracks, carrying his dark whispers to move even slower. The men do not know why we stall, but the rumors fly like ravens, zipping this way and that. Anyone with eyes can tell that something has changed. They need only look at our commander to see it written on his face.

We're deserting.

No, we're being chosen to be a part of a new Legion.

That's not it. We're heading back to Agogia.

Idiots, anyone with eyes can see that we're going to be sacrifices to the gods.

I'm surprised at how many of the rumors contain a morsel of the truth, although none of them are quite right. Every day, the slowest century is rewarded with an extra ration of whiskey at dinner. The men love it. Even if they do not know why their commander wishes to drag his feet, they have no desire to go back out into the cold. Besides, this is a legion made up of liars and thieves. Agogia may have tried to burn the laziness out of them, but some of it still lurks in their bones.

Brodigan warned us that there were those in the fortress who were not a part of his command—logisticians and quartermasters who report directly to the Iron City. The farce we put on is for them so they cannot report we are disobeying orders.

The Lion also sees to it that we are properly equipped for the Arctic waste that awaits us on the other side of Frigidus's walls. Our supply wagons are replaced by sleds. We're issued five hundred pairs of something called snowshoes—flat, circular platforms that attach to our boots, allowing us to march across the powder without breaking through the surface.

More precious than any of these are the *venator* relics Boris spoke of, special spearheads on the ends of long pikes forged by the Heartsmiths of the North to kill *furia*. They're made from a pairing of two different sets of relics—one bound to Iron and one to Ice, and the sight of their dark, faded metal sends shivers down my spine. I've known my whole life where relics come from, but now, after Rufus, I've witnessed the price with my eyes.

Gaius is everywhere, overseeing the cohort's training with the new gear, poring over scouting reports with Brodigan and the legates. He seems like a new man, reborn from the walking corpse that he had become after we were sentenced to the North. Hope burns like a fire in him, and its flame is infectious, spreading to even the cruelest member of the Twelfth.

Every morning, I scale the sweeping walls of Frigidus, looking for a spot of darkness on the horizon, growing like a cancer. But despite my vigilance, the days pass, and no barbarian horde appears to besiege the castle. Our collective bonfire begins to fade, burning through its supply of hope like kindling. Eventually, even our cohort's legendary ability to fake work is exhausted, and we are out of excuses.

"We march at dawn," Durus tells my barracks. It is strange to receive this news standing behind him instead of with the rest of the men. This is the fourth room I have accompanied the First Spear to as he makes the announcement. There are still two more to go after this. The expected chorus of groans echoes as the legionnaires voice their displeasure.

"Relax, lads!" Durus calls, shouting them down. "We'll be taking a leisurely stroll in the ice, but have no fear—Tribune thinks we'll be back in no time to eat more of the imperator's hot suppers and drink his beer!" I suppress a grin as the soldiers exchange glances. The First Spear deliberately fans the flames of the rumors, keeping hope alive. I'm more impressed at the effect his words have on them all. The tension that began to creep into their expressions at the centurion's announcement begins to bleed out of their faces.

"But for tonight, curfew is in effect—no drink but water. Tribune wants us sharp and ready for muster before the rooster crows tomorrow. Full battle kit, understood?"

"Aye, *Dominus*," the room thunders.

"That was amazing," I mutter to the First Spear as we make our way to the next room. "They were afraid, and you made them all relax with a joke. I saw it."

Durus pauses in the hall, turning to look at me with an earnest glance. It occurs to me that I do not know how he came to be in the Twelfth Legion. He does not seem to belong here anymore than the Marius brothers. "It's easy to think that because we have this." He glances down at his wrist, where his Copper veins lie underneath his coat. "That the only kind of shield is made of metal. That the only kind of attacks are made with iron swords. But that's not the case, lad. There are knives that cut in from the inside, that slice at a man's confidence, at his belief. A line will crumble from doubt before it does from a loss of blood. It's our job to give the boys another set of armor to protect against that."

I don't have the words to reply to the First Spear as he turns away to tell the next set of men. All I know is that I am forever changed by the wisdom of the durable man. My father would have been friends with him, I think.

Dawn breaks cold and hard, the only way it can in this place. There is nothing soft in the North. It is a place of rock and ice, compacted over eons into a land that man should not enter. The five hundred men of the Eighth Cohort of the Twelfth Legion stand assembled at the far end of the fortress, waiting for the gates to be opened so that we may advance into the Norman Wastes. Nervous energy thrums through the column like lightning. This is the first time that many of us have ever marched into hostile territory. We may have encountered raiders on the road to Frigidus, but that was still in the empire. When we leave this fortress, I will be beyond the Empress's reach for the first time in my life.

"Aquilo's Frozen Balls, it's cold," Marcus grumbles to me from our position in the line. We're not separated for scouting. Gaius wants the line together in case we have to—get to—beat a hasty retreat.

"Thought this was where you always wanted to end up?" I ask him cheerfully.

"Shut your gob," a veteran hisses, rounding on us both with a fury. His face pales as he realizes that he's just shouted at an officer, but I give him a wink. No harm done. My unbothered response doesn't soothe the legionnaire, only emboldens him. "Begging your pardon, *Dominus*, but he should be keeping his mouth shut. No good can come from cursing a god in his own house."

"Come off it, old-timer." Marcus laughs, amused by the superstition. "He doesn't live here anymore; he's dead." The younger soldiers around us laugh at the exchange, bleeding off their nerves. "The North Wind hasn't blown in over four hundred years."

"I don't know," another older legionnaire spits. "Seems plenty cold to me." The line falls silent as another blade of frozen air sweeps across us, cutting as sharply as any *gladius*.

"Easy, legionnaire," I call. Durus's words still ring in my ears, guiding me like a North Star. "That's not Aquilo, just some centurion's fart after eating at the high table last night." I sniff the air deliberately, calling on the Symbol of Ancient Frost to dull the searing pain from the cold that rakes at my nostrils. "Some sort of fish, unless I miss my guess." A few dry chuckles echo from the enlisted men.

"Maybe some peas?" a voice growls from further down the line. I glance over to see Anas looking in my direction. The former *captivus* gives me a slow nod; he knows what I'm up to. I return it slowly, marveling at the change that a little bit of blood can make.

"There's a hint of rosemary," someone else calls, and the dam of tension breaks.

"You fools, it's porkchops!"

A dozen other suggestions echo down the line, growing more ridiculous with each moment. A tight grin spreads across my face. I did it—gave the men something to laugh about instead of stewing in their own fear. It's silly, but it matters.

The jokes fall silent as a loud *crunch* comes from the gate as it begins to move. The chains begin to clink rhythmically as the forward drawbridge lowers over the front moat. Despite the levity a moment ago, I feel a surge of panic in my own chest, almost as cold as Ancient Frost.

I rise to my tiptoes, trying to peer over the sea of helmets at the frozen expanse that waits for us. I've seen it from the top of the walls, but never at this level. It's disappointingly familiar. Snow stretches as far as the eye can see as a path winds down the other side of the mountains' swell. The trees have all been cleared for several hundred paces so that no army could approach under cover.

The bridge slams into the cold earth, and for a heartbeat, all is silent as our column gazes out into the wintry abyss that waits for us. Then the horns begin to sound, and the moment is over.

"Eighth Cohort, forward march!" Durus roars, and we acknowledge his command with a shout that echoes off the fortress with a thunderous roar. On the parapet above, Brodigan appears, bedecked in his golden *lorica*, his face impassive. Two black toga–wearing priests stand on either side, their garments torn in mourning. As one, they extend black spears above us, chanting in deep, warbling tones. One last blessing from the dead God of War before his children depart. As the first line passes under the arch and out into the cold, Brodigan salutes, holding it as we pass beneath him.

"I'm going to miss the bread," Felix bemoans to no one in particular.

The world that waits beyond the empire's last fortress is barren and empty. It immediately feels more remote. It's the first time I've been somewhere that has no road in the direction I'm traveling. Why would the legions build something to make it easier for things to come from a place they do not go? It's too bright; *Sol* reflects off the white around us, magnifying into something crueler than the desert one I'm used to. There are no houses, no signs of life. Only rocks and snow, as far as I can see. A crushing weight builds on my shoulders—a dread that tells me that this is not a place for me. Here I will die.

Marching in the snow is treacherous and slow. There is a path for us to follow, but it is rarely used and covered by a layer of fresh powder. The first ranks have it the worst. They must battle through the unstable ground, packing it down for the rest of us to follow. Even the snowshoes can only help so much. The wind on this side of Frigidus cuts at us with a fury that almost makes me think the veteran was right—maybe it is alive. Our red uniforms stand out against the white expanse, reinforcing that we do not belong here. As the day goes on, we make depressingly little progress away from the fortress, compared to what we are used to.

Our camp is bitterly cold. We use fires, having no fear of ambush this close to the border. But the flames do little to chase away the cold; instead, they tease us, reminding us what warmth feels like. It seems like a form of torture rather than a luxury.

"Look," Felix shouts, staring up at the sky. Men all around us lift their heads from the cookfires, watching as a pair of bright lights streak through the sky, burning like little *Sole*s as they fall. Excited murmurs sweep through the camp as we watch its descent.

"Is that?" Marcus breathes, voice tinged with awe.

"*Corda*," Felix confirms. I watch it with a hint of bitterness. No one knows where *Cor* comes from or what causes more or less of it to fall. I wonder if this year is will be another drought, or if the *discipuli* who follow in our footsteps will not face the same hardships that we did. All I needed was one more Heart to be brought to Segesta.

I know the magisters at Frigidus will report the rain, and Censors will be dispatched to claim it wherever it falls for the Empress. The cycle will continue. Eventually, the new *electii* who gain those Hearts will become relics, just as I will. The Iron Empire will grow stronger, but some of us will be ground to dust in the wheels of its industry. My dreams are full of falling light and resentment.

It takes four days before we are finally out of sight of Frigidus and its mountain wall. "Dead gods, this is slow," Marcus complains as we come to a halt for what feels like the hundredth time while the men in front feel their way through the treacherous footing.

"Look on the bright side," Felix points out. "When we have to retreat, the path behind us will be ready for us." I shoot him a glare and motion for him to keep his mouth shut. They are the only two that I have entrusted with the truth of the game at foot and how we might escape the noose that Tyrus has put around our necks.

"Castor, marshal the decade! Have the men stow their packs and let's get out there," Percy shouts, cutting off our conversation.

"Aye, *Dominus*," I call, turning to wave over my head at the other Segestans still lurking in the column. "You heard the centurion. Move!" Marcus grumbles along with the rest as we break formation and scurry to the rear, where the sleds wait. On a whim, I slip the *votum* stone from my pack and into my pocket. No matter where I go, I will carry my oath of vengeance with me.

Anas is waiting for us by the teamsters, a strange look on his face. Percy spies him and nods approvingly. "I've chosen a new member of the decade," he announces, turning to look at us with a serious expression. I freeze in shock, eyeing the former *captivus* with a distrusting gaze. Anas meets my scrutiny calmly, missing most of his usual scorn. He looks nervous, instead of angry.

"Any problems?" Percy asks mildly. We're silent as we judge this interloper. It feels like burying Rufus all over again. Filling his spot is the final confirmation that we will never see him again. And of all people with *Anas*! But as I study him, I remember the change that has been growing in him—growing in us.

"I said, 'any problems'?" The *Fidelis*'s voice gains an edge that cuts at me sharply.

"No, *Dominus*," I reply, and the rest of the Segestans echo me softly. Percy nods once, then moves on, checking every man to make sure they are equipped as he wants.

"Tribune wants us to range ahead. See if we can find anything *interesting*," Percy announces, He gives me a knowing look, which I return, trying to be as mysterious as the other officers. Felix rolls his eyes but keeps his mouth shut.

"So, let's go find my brother something interesting, eh?" Percy claps Clintus and Matinius on the shoulders before setting off into the snow along the edge of the column, not waiting for us to follow.

"Maybe I'm glad I didn't get made into a *Fidelis*," Felix remarks to me, hefting one of the *venator* spears over his shoulders as we follow our centurion. "They all seem a little mad."

"What does that make us for following him?"

He pauses for a moment, considering my question. "Stupid, I think."

"You both have thought I was stupid for years." Marcus laughs, turning to look at us. "Yet we all ended up here, so how bright could you two really be?"

"He has a point," Felix mutters to me.

"Don't tell him. I hate when he gets smug."

Even with the snowshoes, it's treacherous going once we break away from the main line to carve our own path. Percy orders us into a single-file line to try to save as much of our energy as possible. We are expected to range far to find what our tribune needs.

Using an extreme force of will, I loosen my grip on the Iron Symbol until it is barely hanging on by a thread. My *lorica* is more like a tunic than a part of my own flesh. I feel naked for the first time that I can remember, being so absent from my armor like that. But by limiting it, I am able to seize more of my second Symbol, Ancient Frost, without drowning in essence and triggering my *inhibitus*. Awareness blossoms in my mind like an unfolding lily as the snow at my feet whispers its secrets to my second *Cor* Heart. I feel nothing in this barren wasteland other than the presence of my companions, marching across the powder's surface with the grace of a pack of drowning swimmers.

The sheer amount of essence that is at my beck and call is staggering. It is a torrent here in the snow compared to what is on the other side of the wall. But it is not just the quantity, but the *quality* of it. The drifts here are older, undisturbed. They are a more accurate match to Ancient Frost than anything I have tasted before. As this new supply crashes into me, I gasp in delight, sucking it down greedily like a lush with his wine. But the collar around my neck tightens in warning, and I master myself. I'm glad that I have access to so much because I intend to use it.

The awareness is not why I chose to embrace my secret Symbol. Instead, I direct my will at the powder beneath our feet, calling upon the loose snow to bind together, hardening into something that can hold my weight. I am technically bound to Frost, not Snow, but the congruency between them is about as simple as it gets—they are equal parts water and cold, just worked into different shapes.

A series of *cracks* sounds all around me like miniature explosions, and I let out a grunt of surprise as essence *pours* out of me as if I am being drained by a *striga* sucking on my blood. I've never felt a demand like this before. The *custos* relic hit harder with its individual blows, but this is a continuous pull that eats at me. Gritting my teeth, I unleash my *Cor*, allowing it to pull in as much Ancient Frost as it can.

I shiver from the energy running through me, trying to hide the work that I am doing, willing the snow to make easier footing. Slowly, I feel the resistance at my feet begin to increase. With each step, I sink a little less and my pace increases.

"How are you doing that?" Marcus grunts irritably as I pass him, making my way to the front of the line. I do not have the strength to harden the powder underneath everyone's feet, but if I move to the front, the rest can follow in my wake.

"Think I'm getting the hang of these snowshoes." I shrug, pressing past Antony and Petrus to join Percy at the front. "Let me spell you a bit, *Dominus*," I call. "I'm feeling good." The *Fidelis* eyes me warily. As our lone Silver, he has more strength and energy than the rest of us, but he knows even he has limits. I give him a confident grin, and after a moment, he relents, letting me pass by him to take point.

"Over the ridge, *Decurion*," he orders. "Let's see what we're dealing with."

There's nothing but a valley full of more snow and rocks on the other side. In the distance, a series of mountains claw into the sky, towering to heights that make the ones we just passed through seem like little more than children pretending to be gods.

The only other change to the world is the beginning of a pine forest. It stretches as far as the eye can see, growing so thick that I can't imagine how a legion is supposed to navigate through it, let alone form a shieldwall.

"That's going to get us killed," Felix drawls from behind me as we pause to take stock of the valley before us. "Good thing we're well-versed in alpine battle tactics, isn't it, *Dominus*?" the former plebeian calls to Percy. The centurion shoots him a dour look but doesn't reprimand him. What would be the point? He's not wrong. The legionnaires assigned to Fortress Frigidus are trained for the climates they will be fighting in. That's part of the reason that legions are traditionally assigned to different regions of the empire, so their soldiers can be prepared.

We barely know how to wear our snowshoes.

"I don't see an invading horde," I grumble dispiritedly. The warmth of the hope given to me by Imperator Brodigan is fading in this cold hell. "All I see is a bunch of Silvanus-damned trees."

"Our job, Castor, is to find out what's in the trees," Percy says with grim determination. "In we go."

It's dark inside the forest. The sun's cruel light no longer reflects off every surface. The snowfall is not as deep and piles up on the pine branches instead. The whole woods feel alive, and my skin prickles as if a hundred unseen eyes stare at me from every shadow. There's a grim edge to this place that tells me I am not welcome. I know that. I don't want to be here either. But I am a legionnaire—I can only go where they send me.

I no longer need to use my connection to Ancient Frost to harden the ground beneath me. Instead, I stretch my awareness to its maximum, trying to sense enemies before they draw close. But there is nothing, only a vast emptiness that feels aware, hungry.

We string along in a loose line, covering as much ground through the forest as we can. Percy is certain we must find *some* sign of the Normans. We're still on the only route to approach Frigidus. The horde that Brodigan is looking for has to be here—we just have to look hard enough.

The afternoon begins to fade into the evening. Darkness falls heavier on us under the long arms of the trees. We're tired and wet with nothing to show for our labors other than blisters. The cold grows, but mercifully, I am spared that burden thanks to my second Symbol.

"Can't believe my grandfather spoke fondly of this," Marcus complains as he passes around another tree. "I'll never be warm again."

"Shh," Felix hisses, silencing him. I don't know why he bothers. Our feet crunch on the snow, announcing our presence with every step. If any enemy sentries are lying in wait, we do not need to be speaking for them to hear us. I turn to tell my friend to relax, but he is frozen, staring at something in the waning light.

"Oh, come off it," Marcus snaps, turning on the taller boy. "I'm so sick of you—»

"Marcus, shut up," I order, dropping a hand to the hilt of my *gladius*. "Look."

Ahead of us, only now visible in the dark shadows of the evening, burns a fire.

CHAPTER 41

We approach the fire in a pack, like wolves stalking their prey. Percy orders us to take off our snowshoes before we get close; we leave them stacked under a pine that was burnt and blackened by a lightning strike. As we do, I find myself praying to Dead Mars that all of us return to put them back on. He cannot hear me, but it makes me feel a little better.

We move slower without our shoes, but now we do not sound like a horde of elephants making our way through the forest. We move from tree to tree, lurking in their growing shadows. As we draw close, I begin to smell the scent of burning meat. My stomach rumbles in jealousy. It's only been a few days since we left Frigidus, but I have grown used to eating well.

Cautiously, moving as Percy taught us, we encircle the light that comes from the center of a small glade. There are no sentries waiting for us—no one raises a shout of alarm as we creep closer. I follow Felix as he creeps forward, unable to see over his tall frame, trusting him to guide me. The Symbol of Ancient Frost tells me there are people in the glade ahead, but the reports from my senses are confusing. The world feels muted, covered in something sticky that my Symbol doesn't recognize. Nothing moves, but I feel the heat of the fire, feel it burning painfully against my own skin. Apart from that, everything is still.

It's not until my friend freezes that I realize why. A chill that has nothing to do with the cold settles on me as I step around him to see the camp with my own eyes. I walk forward numbly, no longer afraid of being discovered. Slowly, the rest of the decade emerges from the forest, stepping into the small glade to join me. *Gladii* hang limply from their hands as they stare at the tableau before us. We've fought and killed before, but none of us except Percy have ever seen anything like this.

Everyone is dead.

The sticky substance that covered the frost and snow is their blood, painted across the plain white canvas in sheets. There are corpses everywhere. My stomach roils as I realize that they're not warriors but civilians. I see mothers and children among the victims. The fires that dance are not contained to the pits but race along their sleds and tents, devouring everything in sight.

Whoever did this is not long gone.

"Shields!" Percy hisses, apparently realizing the same thing I do. Instinctively, I raise my *scutum* and turn so I stand back-to-back with Felix, forming our own little shieldwall. "Together," the *Fidelis* snaps, motioning at us with his sword to bring us into a cluster. We're all breathing raggedly as the battle song begins to sing in our veins.

No one questions his order. We group together in the center, our eyes watching every tree that had so recently been our ally and now harbors our foes. I reach out with Ancient Frost, releasing my connection with the Iron Symbol completely, straining to extend my sense as far as I can.

But no matter how far I push, I sense nothing; only trees, rocks, and… corpses.

I glance at Percy, trying to follow his lead. I am the only one other than the *Fidelis* who can try to use a Symbol to hunt at a distance, but from his expression, I don't think he feels anything either. My heartbeat begins to slow; whoever did this must have left in a hurry.

"Centurion?" I ask, unsure what we should do. We cannot stay here forever, standing in the middle of a slaughter. The song of battle no longer rings in my ears. "Maybe they're—" My voice cuts off as something rains on the ground. I feel its weight through the Ancient Frost Symbol in the distance, like the faint thump of something falling on my head.

Snow. It's snow falling from above. My eyes track upwards, and I feel my stomach clench in dread as I realize there are piles of snow on the limbs of the pines. I can't feel them because they're not on the ground.

They're in the trees.

"Shields up!" Percy screams in command, and my body responds with the obedience beaten into it in the forges of Agogia. My arm rocks as a trio of quarrels slam into the iron of my shield with enough force to punch their heads through. I let out a squeak of fear, dropping the Ancient Frost Symbol and grasping at Iron with all my strength.

The awareness of my shield flows back into me as my knowledge of the snow around me fades. I snarl in rage, closing my shield back over the wooden shafts of the bolts that almost killed me, snapping them in half like kindling. *Idiot*, I berate myself for almost getting myself shot.

Ancient Frost gives me a unique advantage in this place, but Iron is what makes me a killer.

I risk lowering my shield enough to peer over it, cursing as a shaft bounces off the top of my helm, unable to penetrate my defense now that my will infuses it. I see them now, clothed in drab colors that let them blend in among the pines.

"Hold the line," Percy commands grimly, risking a peek out of his own shield. "They won't have the power to break through our *scuta* with arrows alone. When they attack, they'll break on our shields."

"Aye, *Dominus*," we all reply lustily. The battle song is back, filling our ears with its rousing call. We are the Iron Legions. We do not break; we do not bend.

True to the *Fidelis*'s prediction, we weather a few more storms of bolts, but none of them manage to do any serious damage. Jasper's ear is clipped by a stray bolt, but that only raises our bloodlust. I slam the flat of my *gladius* against my shield, banging it like a drum, taunting the ghosts that haunt us from the trees.

"Come and face us, cowards!" I cry. I do not know if these Normans speak our language or only know their own barbaric tongue. It does not matter; my tone requires no translation. The rest of the decade joins in with me, rattling their weapons against their shields, screaming at our attackers. Even Percy follows along, laughing as he shouts at the trees.

"We are not mothers and children for you to murder," Felix calls, adding to the insults. "Come and see what real warriors can do." Another barrage of arrows slams into our shields, but none of us fall. I can feel the frustration of our enemies rising as their bolts fail to even penetrate our shields.

"Here we go," Percy shouts, suddenly ceasing to beat on his shield. We follow suit and watch as the Normans, men and women, begin to leap from the trees, casting aside their bows to unlimber their axes and swords. They're tall, towering like the pines in the forest around us, blond hair tied behind their heads in thick tails. Their armor is made of leather and chainmail, which I know will part for my *gladius* like smoke. Despite looking similar to the raiders we faced before, there is an economy to their movement that tells me these are more dangerous than their kin. There are more than a dozen of them, but not enough that I feel truly outnumbered.

"Hold the line, boys, and we will get through this just fine," the *Fidelis* promises. "If we get separated, work together in battle pairs."

"Vrok!" calls one of the men in the front, a tall bastard with a long blond ponytail.

"Vrok!" the rest of them echo in response.

"Vrok! Vrok!" the leader calls again, raising his axe to pump it in the sky.

"Vrok! Vrok!" they scream in response, their faces contorting in ecstatic rage.

"Odd sort of battle cry," Felix muses to me, not taking his eyes off the Normans.

"Maybe it means 'welcome, traveling stranger' in their language?" I offer, trying to laugh, but my mouth is dry. Now that the moment is here, I can feel panic and fear circling me like rabid wolves trying to break into my house and eat me in my bed. Only the calm strength of Iron holds them at bay.

"Vrok! Vrok! Vrok!" the leader screams, bringing the edge of his axe down to slice at his own arm until it draws blood. He waves his arm wildly, splattering blood on the white snow on the edge of the glade. As his people echo the cry, a thirteenth figure appears in the trees. He's massive—taller than Felix and broader than Marcus. He's shirtless, clad only in a pair of furry breeches, which makes it impossible to miss the dark, swirling tattoos that scrawl across his chest like an unbroken serpent. They move as if they're alive, trapped on his skin. I swallow as fear slams against the iron wall protecting my calm with enough force to shake it to its foundations. I know what he must be.

The *berserkir* pumps his double-bladed axe above his head with both hands while howling like a wolf. When his warriors have finished chanting his name, Vrok leaps from the tree, slamming into the ground at the front of their formation like a god descending from Olympus.

"Or maybe not," I admit with a sigh.

The man points his axe at our formation and spits a furious word that needs no translation. Howling with mad fury, the Normans charge us, following their champion like faithful hounds.

"Together!" Percy cries, but I can hear the stress in his voice. He was at the imperator's table too. He knows what we face, perhaps even better than I do. The *berserkir* bounds across the ground between us, flying like a deer. His ponytail trails behind him, dancing in the wind. He aims straight for the center of our formation, hurtling like a battering ram.

Our shields ring as we condense into a single organism, curling like an *armadillo*, the strange, armored rodents of the South. The Iron

Symbol fills my mind with knowledge as my *animus* fills our shieldwall, adding my will to the rest of my squad as we prepare to hold the line.

Vrok barrels into range, sweeping backward with his axe for a reckless two-handed attack. Everything slows down as two worlds meet—the iron might of the legions and the wild, untamable fury of the Normans. Petrus squares his shoulders at the center of our line, *scutum* held high and firm. The *berserkir* leaps, swinging his weapon at our line.

I tense, waiting to reach out with my will to grab and twist the warrior's weapon, shredding it with my mind. Instead, I feel its cold corruption as it slams into Petrus's shield with the force of a charging boar.

My mind screams as a presence scrapes along it, pouring through our shieldwall. Something tears into me, ripping and eating with a hunger that can never be filled. The Iron Symbol twists in my grip like a fish trying to return to the river. It slips from my grasp, and the last thing I sense before I lose connection to the shieldwall is Petrus's *scutum* shattering like glass.

The legionnaire is blasted back by the force of the blow, landing in a heap a dozen paces away. He's far too still. One of his legs is twisted at an unnatural angle, broken in a handful of places. I have only a heartbeat to feel sick with worry before I am swept away.

Our line fractures as Vrok slams into it. He's on us before any of us can blink, moving so fast that I can barely follow him. Panic fills me, greedily filling the void left by Iron's calming presence. Desperately, I reach for my Symbol, begging for it to come to my aid.

But there is only an echoing silence, a gaping wound where the steady power usually is.

Numb, I turn to face the Normans that descend upon us, following in Vrok's wake. My *gladius* is foreign in my hand, like I've never held one before. My *scutum* is bulky and unwieldy. My *lorica* feels like it was made for another man.

The world is muted, as if I have lost my hearing. I barely manage to bring my shield up in time to block the first barbarian's axe. It bounces off my *scutum*, and I'm startled by how my body shakes from the impact. I don't feel the edge of their weapon scraping against my mind. I am blind behind my defenses.

Again, my world rocks as the Norman slams his axe against my shield, and I retreat, alone and off-kilter. The barbarian presses his advantage, battering me like I am a fortress, and he is a ram. I can't focus. I am lost. I chase the Iron Symbol, but it evades me.

My *scutum* begins to dent, no longer protected by my will. I am going to die. Without Iron, I am nothing. I do not know how to fight like these savages; how to kill with my rage. I am a boy who was sent to contend with monsters.

Something cold and wet sprays me from the side, splashing my face. Its arctic touch shakes me free from my shock. A deeper cold invades me, filling the empty, grasping hand in my mind with its frigid power. The Symbol of Ancient Frost coalesces in my mind, and the world resumes normal speed. The sound of battle crashes down on me, jarringly loud, but I am no longer overwhelmed by terror.

I am awake.

My *animus* floods into the snow around us, filling my mind with knowledge. A score of warriors dance around me, fighting their individual battles. Between them, I feel the still forms of the fallen, their lifeblood leaking out onto me. I am still blind to my iron, but I have gained a new pair of eyes, giving me a different perspective. My attacker presses his advantage, lunging forward brazenly. I feel his reckless footsteps on the frozen ground.

My *scutum* rings as his axe hammers into it, but this time, I am prepared. I twist my shield, angling it so that his attack doesn't land on a flat surface. Instead, his wild force bounces off me, leaving him overextended. I see his wide, shocked eyes as I step forward, driving my *gladius* into his gut with cold force.

We pass each other, driven by momentum, and I wrench my blade free as he continues by. I do not need to turn to see if he remains on his feet. I feel the frosty ground welcome him in its cold arms as he falls.

The battlefield before me is something out of a nightmare. Our shieldwall is shattered, torn asunder by the *berserkir's* blasphemous power. I can identify Vrok from the speed of his movements as he terrorizes the far side of the glade. There are too many still forms wearing the red of the legions.

Felix is a dozen paces from my side, hemmed in by three Normans who herd him like a lamb. The tall legionnaire bleeds from a cut on his face, and his shield is dented and battered, but his eyes are alight with the battle fury.

I rush to my friend's aid, slamming into the side of an attacker, a woman wielding two swords who is the only enemy here shorter than me. She staggers under the force of my charge, giving ground. I slash at her retreating form, stepping into the ring to stand back-to-back with Felix.

"Took you long enough!"

"Sorry I'm late. I had to deal with a problem."

"I saw, but you only had one; I have three."

"Do you want to be rescued or not?" The snow whispers a warning to me as the woman I knocked to the side recovers her balance and lunges at my left flank. I lift my *scutum*, blocking her attack, while striking with my *gladius* at one of the other barbarians, driving him back from my exposed side.

Felix follows up on my distraction, hammering at the woman with his blade, forcing her to drop to her knees to avoid being bisected by the tall legionnaire's strike. Over her shoulder, I see Antony swept away in a tide of Normans, dragged to the ground by another trio, who pummel him even after he is down.

We're losing. Without our Iron Symbols, we're no match for these vicious killers, who excel at this kind of fight. Anger begins to build in me, stoked by the betrayal that sent us here in the first place. The Northern Legions are trained to battle in these conditions. We were served up to the wolves like lambs, all because we dared to reach for something more than we were given.

I feel my *Cor* Heart react to my rage, twisting and pulsing like the flesh and blood one in my chest. If it worked like the other organ, I would say that it was racing. Awareness flickers within me. For a beat, the Iron Symbol flares cold and bright. I feel all the metal that touches me: *gladius*, *scutum*, and *lorica*. I even understand the *inhibitus* relic coiled around my neck. But then it is gone, falling through my grip like grains of sand.

Only the Symbol of Ancient Frost remains.

I pour my will into the unfamiliar power, driving my *animus* at the Norman's boots, calling on the snow to grab at them as I press my attack. The woman's eyes widen as she tries to step out of the way, only to find her foot stuck. I batter her with my *scutum*, forcing her to wield one of her swords defensively.

I use the shield's bulk to hide my true intent, keeping my *gladius* behind it, like Durus taught me. I twist my arm, angling the shield to the side, and stab forward with all my strength. She sees the attack too late and lets out a grunt as the tip of my blade stabs into her.

One of her companions tries to come to save her, but the frosty ground betrays him. My will pulls at his feet, slowing his mad dash, while I track his progress. When he is in range, I spin, sword extended to slash at his throat. My weapon slices easily, passing under his axe, which is raised above his head for an overhanded strike. I stare into his wide blue eyes as blood bursts from the wound. The Norman shakes like a leaf before falling to his knees, the light fading from him.

My Symbol whispers another warning, and I spin to catch the third barbarian's blow on my *scutum*. The man lets out a scream of rage that is cut short into a gurgle as Felix tears into him from behind. I feel the cold welcome another body as I lower my shield, nodding in thanks to my friend.

Together, we advance on the field, trying to reform something like a shieldwall. The Normans are excellent one-on-one fighters, warriors to their core. Legionnaires are not trained to be individuals. We are a machine designed to devour all that stands before us. By shattering our line, the barbarians have the advantage. Our only hope to withstand their fury is to rebuild our cohesion.

"On me, on me!" I scream, remembering that I am an officer. I do not know where Percy is, which means the responsibility falls on my shoulders. We liberate Jasper from a duel, and Marcus fights his way to my side, raising our squad to four.

"Where's the centurion?" I demand as each man joins us.

"Further in, fighting that Mars-damned maniac!" Marcus pants. There are tears in his *lorica* that leak blood, but he's not yet turned pale—they must be shallow.

"Does anyone have their Iron?" I ask, glancing between the three. I can almost feel it, like the glow of *Sol* before it rises above the horizon. They all shake their heads. I can read the despair on their faces plainly. All of them think we are going to die here. So do I, but I cannot show it.

"Yes, you do!" I shout at them, thinking of the First Spear again. I slam the flat of my *gladius* against my shield. "It's right here. Together." Hope lights in their eyes, kindling like a dormant flame.

"Together!" Marcus bellows, hunching his shoulders.

"Let's finish this." I lead them toward the center, where the rest of the fighting is still going.

A pair of Normans see our cluster advancing and retreat toward their other fellows—they know to fear our iron wall. I spy the still forms of Lintus and Haxus on the ground, the snow around them red. Two more souls whose *votum* we will have to carry, unless we join them in this cold grave.

In the center, Percy stands alone, battling against Vrok. The *Fidelis* has discarded his shield, replacing it with a second *gladius* taken from one of our fallen brothers. They flash as he dances around the *berserkir*, slashing at the shirtless warrior. I can tell at a glance that the Silver's connection to the Iron Symbol is intact. He is far too fluid to be moving like this without its insight.

Vrok twists at inhuman speed, dodging Percy's first strike, before swinging his axe at Percy in a vicious sideswipe. The centurion dances backward, letting the blow pass between them while dropping his left hand so that his blade doesn't connect with the weapon.

"Anas!" I shout, spotting the former convict tearing himself free of a duel with a vicious Norman woman wielding a two-handed sword. He ducks a monstrous attack from her great weapon before sprinting to us, leaving her standing in the snow.

Now we are five. I cannot see Antony, Matinius, or Clintus, but I can hear the sound of iron-on-iron ringing on the other side of the Norman cluster. I can only pray to dead Mars that they will not join him in the afterlife. I must first save those that I can.

"Form up!" I scream, banging my sword against my shield in mimicry of the pulses we would create with our Symbol to time marches.

"Huah!" the men grunt, raising their *scuta* to form our wall with me at the center. Together, we begin to advance on the cluster of barbarians who watch us, suddenly wary. A tall man with a hooked nose points at two of their number with his bloody sword, and they break to the side, circling us like sheepdogs trying to herd us toward our pen.

"Marcus, Anas, watch the wings," I order, keeping us advancing.

"We know our business," the former *captivus* growls, but I feel his feet shift in the snow, turning to track the flankers. The Norman leader barks a command to the rest of his group, and the four of them begin to stride toward us, willing to meet us head-on. Despite myself, I feel a grin growing on my face as I watch the confident fools saunter toward us, unconcerned. They may have caught us unawares, but we have recovered. We are the Iron Legion; we do not break.

As we get close, Hooknose lets out a roar and charges toward me, his companions trailing along behind him like faithful hounds. "Steady!" I shout to Felix and Jasper as we meet their charge head-on. I raise my battered *scutum* to catch the blow of his longsword, gritting my teeth as the impact rattles the bones in my body.

Before he can react, I angle my shield, stabbing forward with my *gladius*, aiming for his guts. Hook lets out a grunt of surprise, dropping his round, wooden shield low to catch my thrust. I pull my blade back and block his second strike, twisting my *scutum* to let it slide past me. Again, I stab, forcing him to dance away to prevent himself from being skewered.

I can feel my grim smile as I press my attack, advancing the line to push on their stalled charge. I feel blind in this combat without the knowledge the Iron Symbol could give me, but my hands have done this dance a thousand times. The barbarians are caught off guard by our resistance. They thought we would still be easy pickings, but they don't understand where our true strength comes from. Anas was right—we know our business.

Marcus and Anas fold behind us, holding off the flankers with their shields. Ancient Frost whispers to me as Hooknose shifts his weight, watching us with uncertainty. He's leaning away from me, and I can tell that part of him—the wise part—wants to flee.

An idea occurs to me as we push forward. I crouch down as I walk, letting the bottom of my shield trail in the snow for a moment. Using my Symbol, I call the ice of the ground, commanding it to crawl onto my shield like a child picking up a pet.

"What are you doing?" Marcus hisses from my shoulder. He cannot see the front of my *scutum*. All he knows is that I have broken the shieldwall, endangering us all.

"Trust me," I murmur, rising to my full height, smirking at my opponents.

Hooknose's eyes widen in something like fear as the ice spreads across the surface of my shield. I feel a familiar sense of knowledge fill my mind as the frost covers the iron. I may not be able to call upon my other Symbol, but I am not helpless.

I push us forward, constantly advancing, not giving Hooknose and his companions time to think. The sound of combat rings behind me as Anas blocks a strike from one of the flankers, but we do not stop. This momentum is our power. We roll like a boulder down a mountain about to cause a rockslide. I feel the ridiculous confidence of the empire's legacy boil in me. They had their chance to break us, but now they will be broken.

I leap forward, thrusting my shield at Hooknose. He scowls at the frost-covered *scutum*, striking at it with his longsword to bat it to the side. I welcome his blow, commanding my ice to bind him to me. His eyes widen in shock as his sword sticks to the frozen surface. I smile at him as I wrench my shield to the side, ripping his blade free of his stunned grip. With a thought, I instruct the frost to release it, and the sword thumps against the ground.

The Norman's feet betray him to the snow as he turns to flee. Ancient Frost tells me of his fear and shows me that he will run. But there is no escaping the Iron Legions. As he turns, I step forward, battering him with my shield. I catch him off balance, and he staggers. The snow hardens around his right foot, and he falls flat on his face on the cold ground. He flails, trying to escape, but I bind him with my will. Essence pours from me as the snow freezes, holding down his feet, hands, and face.

I ignore my victim, saving him for later like a spider with a fly in its web, turning to strike at the startled barbarian who stands next to him. Together, Jasper and I overwhelm his defenses. The blond barbarian gurgles as we both stab him until he falls, staining the ground with his blood.

The enemy line crumbles and collapses under the weight of its own fear as two of their number fall. We do not let them escape, turning their retreat into a rout. The sight of Lintus's and Haxus's torn bodies burns bright in my mind as I cut down any who would flee. The hate is warm enough to keep the North's bitter chill at bay without the help of Ancient Frost.

When the slaughter is done, I turn to where Hooknose lies, still frozen to the ground, twisting in fear. His sword lies nearby, still red with the blood of my fallen brothers. I stand above him for a heartbeat, watching him struggle, trying to feel something other than satisfaction. A dim, distant voice wonders what my father would think.

I'm not sure I care. He was a gentle soul, and they killed him. I am cold, and they are welcome to try. My *gladius* bites deeply into his back, driving into the Norman's heart. I am not cruel; I do not seek to make him suffer. I pull my blade free with a wrench and rise to find Felix watching me, a strange expression on his face.

"What happened to him?" he asks, glancing at the frost that binds the Norman.

"No idea," I lie. "Maybe Aquilo's ghost is watching over us today."

"Maybe," he agrees, turning away with me as we rejoin the fray. He doesn't believe me. My secret creates a void between us—a space where before there was none. I'll tell him the truth later. We still have a fight to win.

The remaining Normans flee before us as we descend upon them. We outnumber them, and they have no confidence facing us without their champion to shatter our line. Clintus hobbles over to join our line. Blood flows from a wound in one of his legs, but his eyes dance with the same burning rage.

It is our turn to circle the battle like prowling wolves. Vrok is the only barbarian who does not flee. He roars in frustration as he chases Percy around the glade, unable to pin the *Fidelis* down. The centurion's Silver strength allows him to match the *berserkir*'s inhuman speed, and the two dance, striking at each other but never landing a blow.

I raise my hand to grab the attention of my fellows before spinning it in a shrinking circle, the instruction obvious. This barbarian has had enough free rein. It is time to tighten the noose. Slowly, the six of us begin to advance, hemming in their battlefield with our shields.

As we draw closer, I reach out with my will, commanding the frozen ground to claw at the Vrok's feet. The *berserkir* stumbles slightly, but he's too strong for me to hold in place. He turns in a circle, noticing our pack as we step out of the dark, framed by the fires of the massacre that happened before we arrived.

"*Kom og dø små hunder.*" He smiles broadly, welcoming us. I don't know what his harsh words mean, but the teeth he shows us need no translation.

With lightning speed, he leaps toward Clintus, whose wounds make him the weakest. The legionnaire raises his shield, but without his Iron Symbol, he does not have the strength to withstand Vrok's assault. His *scutum* crumples, and he is knocked off his feet. I watch, helpless from the far side of the ring, as *berserkir* raises his axe above his head to deliver a decapitating blow.

Anas tackles Vrok from the side, slamming into him with his shield held tight and low. The inhumanly strong Norman staggers under the assault but doesn't fall. He swings his right hand in a dismissive slap against Anas's *scutum*, knocking the soldier back three paces from the force.

Truly, this is a monster in human form. But Anas has given us the distraction we needed to hunt. I break into a sprint, racing across the ring as my squamates descend upon Vrok. Felix is the next to slam into the man, hammering him from the left. The *berserkir* turns in rage, but he is like a bear beset by hunting dogs on all sides.

A sword bursts through his chest from behind as Clintus regains his feet. Vrok looks down at it in surprise but does not fall. Whatever power he gains from his heretical *Cor* tattoos holds him upright.

Vrok roars in anger and slams into Felix, knocking the man onto his back as the *berserkir* breaks free of the knot that he has been trapped in. Clintus's sword still runs through his back, but he doesn't seem to notice. He goes on the attack, charging at the person directly in front of him.

Me.

The Norman lifts his heavy axe over his shoulder as he runs, angling for a diagonal slash across my chest. Instinctively, I start to raise my shield to catch the strike, only to realize that's exactly what he wants me to do. With his strength, he will shear right through my shield and the arm behind it.

Instead, I pour my will into the icy ground at his feet, calling upon Ancient Frost to obey my will. The *berserkir* is too powerful for me to bind with my Copper Heart, but with the right application of cunning, strength can be turned on its owner.

Instead of making the ground beneath the charging Norman grab at him, I coax it to become slick, like the ice cap of a river—smooth and flat. Black ice forms on his path, but still, he barrels toward me, blue eyes glinting with murderous intent.

At the last moment, I dash to the side, daring the *berserkir* to follow. He does, cutting sharply to keep me in front of him, but his feet find no purchase and slip out from under him. I have just enough time to see his eyes widen in shock before he shoots past me, collapsing into an uncontrollable tumble across the snowy ground. He slams into the corpse of a fallen barbarian with enough force to rip his axe from his grip, giving Percy his opportunity to strike.

Vrok tries to rise, but his feet slip on the black ice that forms beneath him at my command. Our centurion is at his side in a heartbeat, the blade in his right hand drawing back for a final blow. The *berserkir* senses him, turning to look right before the *Fidelis* strikes.

"*Sic semper paganus*," Percy growls in a voice of Iron judgment. His *gladius* sings, and Vrok's head drops to the icy ground, and it is done. A heavy stillness settles on the glade as only we men of the legion are left among the living.

Despair, darkness, and twisting fill my guts as I turn to look at the three forms of my fallen friends. Their red uniforms were striking against the snow, but now there is so much blood that they almost blend in.

We were eleven, but now we are seven. Something on the back of my neck crawls as the *votum* in my pocket calls to me, whispering its demands that I fulfill my promise. I snarl, turning away from the dark voices, staying in the present. I need to be here.

"Check the bod—" Percy begins, before he is cut off.

Bwooooooo! A hunting horn sounds from within the dark forest.

Bwooooooo! Answers a second and then a third in the distance.

The Normans who fled the battle have found reinforcements. We may have found Brodigan's horde after all. Percy turns to look at us with a grim expression. His gaze tracks from Marcus's bleeding chest to Clintus's limp, and his frown grows.

"Run," is all he says.

CHAPTER 42

We move through the dark forest at a miserably slow pace. Clintus's leg isn't working properly. Marcus and Anas walk at his side with their arms around him to help him keep up. During the day, it did not seem like we ventured that far into the pines, but now it feels like the trees extend beyond the horizon.

We carry a pair of torches made from the burning wreckage of the camp. Why did the Normans butcher them all? From the ruins, it looked like they had been traders, no threat to anyone. Are they just rabid like dogs, or do they have their own plans?

"Mars damn you all, just leave me!" Clintus shouts for the fifth time, grunting in pain between every step. Our Iron Symbols have still not returned, although Percy says they will. We could all use that strength right now.

"Shut up," I snap, turning to look at him with fury. "No more. Do you hear me? We're not losing another one." I glance up at Percy, who ranges ahead of us, trying to find a path in the dark. He looks at me with a sad expression but does not reprimand me. I know what he is thinking. At some point, we will have no choice.

The horns still echo through the forest as the reinforcements pursue us, and my skin crawls with the sensation of being watched. I imagine a dozen *berserkir* stalking us even now, waiting for the perfect moment to strike. I reach out with my senses through the Symbol of Ancient Frost, but I feel nothing around us. That doesn't mean they're not in the trees.

"Keep moving," is all the centurion says, picking up the pace.

We are not subtle as we tramp through the dark. We might be scouts, but we are still legion. Our armor rattles, and we swear as we stumble on roots and stub our toes on rocks we cannot see. It will not be hard for the Norman hunters to find us. Speed is our only hope.

"Castor," the centurion calls from the front, and I struggle to join him. Even though my legs work fine, I still cannot match his Silver strength.

"Yes, *Dominus?*"

"I want you to take this torch and go ahead." The *Fidelis* does not look at me but holds out the burning brand in his hand.

"What? Why?" I'm so startled, I forget to call him by his rank. He doesn't notice, or maybe he's too tired to care.

"Our first duty is to report what we have seen and found to Gaius." Now he looks at me, his face in shadow from the harsh light. "We are scouts—that is more important than any of us. The message has to get to the main column."

"So we tell him together," I hiss, pushing the torch away. "I'm not leaving."

"No, we won't." His voice is soft as he glances back at Clintus. "We can't outrun them. But the rest of us can buy you some time." I am silent for a few heartbeats, trying to choke back tears. This cannot be how it ends. I will not leave my friends—my people—to die. There has to be another way.

"You go," I say after a moment. Percy's head snaps toward me in shock.

"I'm not—"

"You're the only one of us that is actually *Silver*!" I snap, cutting him off. "We're only *argentulae*, remember? You have the best chance of staying ahead of the Normans and getting back to the cohort. We can buy you time."

It is Percy's turn to fall silent. He knows I am right, yet he does not want to leave us. He is our commander; we are his responsibility. But we have a mission, and he is the one who has the best chance to complete it. My logic is cold and heavy, and even one as strong as him cannot hold against it. His shoulders sag as he accepts the burden that I offer.

I sigh in relief to be spared this load. I would rather stay here and die than abandon my friends, my brothers. Death feels light compared to the heavy yoke of duty. "Honos damn you," he growls after he surrenders to the path before him.

"He'll have to get in line." I snort. "I think a few others of the dead want a piece first." The centurion looks back at the rest of the decade like a father leaving his children for the last time. Marcus, Felix, Anas, Jasper, and Clintus return his look with silence. We are all that's left.

"Well, hurry up?" calls Anas after the moment stretches. "We don't have all night."

"The sooner you're gone, the sooner you can bring the reinforcements, *Dominus*," Marcus offers Percy as an olive branch.

"I'll be right back in a moment," Percy agrees, his voice dry. "Don't worry, boys. Tribune Gaius and the Twelfth will—" Whatever they will be is interrupted by the long call of a hunting horn, far too close.

"*Vade*," I command. "Go."

Percy nods once, then grabs me by the shoulder, his grip far too strong. "They're your men now, Decurion." He tells me. "Bring them home." Before I can reply, he springs forward, bounding away on his Silver strength. We watch as his light bobs through the darkness, growing smaller until it is swallowed by the pines, leaving us alone with the barbarians that hunt us.

My men. I think to myself as I watch him go. I thought I would feel lighter once he left, buoyed by the knowledge that one of us might escape and warn Gaius. Now I only feel heavier. I'm in charge again.

"Never liked having a *Fidelis* around anyway," Anas grumbles to the gloom. "They're damned bad luck."

"Aye," Marcus agrees. "That's all officers for you, isn't it, *Dominus?*"

"Shut up," I snap. "Our orders are to rendezvous with the main column and get this wounded soldier to a *medico*. Let's get to it."

"Aye, *Dominus*," they chorus. This is the first time it sounds like they mean it. Together, we set to work.

The hunters grow close. As the hours pass, we can hear them calling to each other in the dark. Sometimes we see their lights bouncing as they race through the murk. We extinguished our torch hours ago to prevent being seen the same way, but now our progress has slowed to a crawl that even Clintus can easily keep pace with.

A howl sounds in the night. They have dogs. The noose begins to tighten. They are on all sides; it is only a matter of time before we are discovered. We move in a single-file line, with me in the front, picking our footing through the inky blackness. I rely on the Symbol of Ancient Frost to guide me across the ground, but my men don't know that. Jasper follows in my wake, left hand on my shoulder, *gladius* in his right. We discarded our shields for the sake of speed. I find myself regretting that decision as the hunters get closer.

The snow whispers to me as a foot breaks its crust at the edge of my *animus*'s range. I freeze, hissing a warning to the rest of my squad. There are muted curses as we jerk to a stop, but the men follow my lead, crouching low by the base of a broad pine.

The hunter's steps are slow and measured, like a stalking predator not wanting to startle its prey. A second pair of feet joins the first, then a third. I tighten my grip on the hilt of my sword, confident that I am about to put it to work.

The trio breaks apart, circling the center of my awareness. They know we are here. The barbarians must have been tracking the sound of our shuffling in the dark. Strangely, I feel no fear, only an eagerness for the violence to come.

Ancient Frost pervades through me, filling me with its cold power. It is not as strong as Iron—just as ice is not as strong as metal—but it's deeper than my original Symbol. I breathe in, filling my reserves from the frosty essence that surrounds me.

I feel the crunch of a boot on the ice on the other side of the trunk of the tree that we hide next to. I close my eyes, which are practically worthless in the dark, and wait, tracking the hunter's progress.

As the footsteps round the corner, I explode forward, *gladius* extended in a lunge. I feel a hint of resistance from their leather armor, but it gives way against the sharp edge of my blade. A scream shatters the quiet of the dark.

"There are more!" I roar, ripping my blade free of the Norman's chest. I can only see the other two warriors as patches of dark on darkness. One of their blades glints against a hint of moonlight, but I do not need my eyes to know where they are.

I sidestep a reckless charge from one, swinging my blade behind me as they pass. The Norman lets out a high-pitched cry, staggering as they continue toward my brothers. I hear the telltale sound of iron cutting into flesh as my squad mates finish off the wounded barbarian.

The next warrior approaches more cautiously, shuffling his feet to keep himself grounded as he searches for me in the dark. I slash wildly at where he stands, but my *gladius* bounces off the haft of his axe. The barbarian leaps forward, trying to cut me in two. I dodge his lunge and burrow my empty left fist into his stomach with as much force as I can muster.

The Norman lets out an *oomph* of pain as the air rushes out of his lungs. I shove him backward and feel as he trips over some unseen root and falls onto the cold, hard ground. I reach for him with my icy power, grabbing him and keeping him from getting back on his feet.

I cut through his neck with one clean stroke, guided by the outline of his body in my mind. The Norman gurgles out the rest of his life as I turn toward my brothers. "Keep moving," I pant.

They are silent as they obey my orders. They can tell that something about me is different, but they don't know what. If we manage to escape, I will have to come up with an answer that will satisfy them, or the Censors will kill me. It would be a shame to survive all of this, just to be executed by my own people.

The dogs howl, and the damned hunting horns echo their cries. They will find the bodies of their scouts soon; we are out of time. I reach inward, searching for the sturdy presence of the Iron Symbol, but it is still distant and muted, like *Sol* behind a thick cloud. I know it is there, but I cannot see it.

Ancient Frost is a powerful ally. Already, I grow more comfortable with its applications, but it is no substitute for the greatest of the War Symbols. We stand no chance of fighting our way free without our Iron *Corda*. Our only chance is to flee and hope that Gaius comes to meet us.

I lead the men forward as quickly as we can go in the dark with a crippled companion. It is agonizingly slow, but I dive deeper into the cold embrace of my Symbol and let the anxiety freeze to death. I cannot succumb to panic; I must lead. I draw deeply from the essence around me, filling my reserves until the *inhibitus* around my neck twitches in warning. My fatigue fades, and my limbs feel strong, but I know my brothers are spent.

"We can't keep running," Felix pants in my ear as he makes his way to the front of the column. He's traded off with Jasper to help carry our wounded member. "Clintus is still bleeding, and *most* of us are starting to fade." His voice carries a subtle accusation that I ignore. There's no time.

"They have dogs," I snap back, deep in cold logic's embrace. "If we stop, they will find us."

"We could fight." The tall man's voice is skeptical. He knows we would die.

"Running is our only chance. If we can break free of the forest…"

"Percy can't have reached the column yet. Even if Gaius mobilizes the sentries, they won't be on the move for hours."

"I know. But what else can we do?" My friend is silent for a moment, frustrated by this puzzle with no solution. We have no advantages. We are outnumbered, Symbol-less, and wounded.

"Then we keep running," he agrees eventually.

"Maybe they won't follow us out of the trees," I suggest, not really believing it. "In the open, a cohort could fight them in full formation. Surely that's something they would want to avoid."

"That's only if they know there's a cohort waiting for them. But legions don't really get sent to this side of the wall, do they?" I can feel the knowing glance he shoots at the back of my head. This is exactly what Imperator Tyrus expected to happen to us.

"I'm beginning to see why."

"I wouldn't recommend it to anyone looking for a vacation," Felix chuckles. I turn to stare at him for a moment, the ice in my brain cracking a little from the warmth of his humor. A wry laugh forces its way free from my lips.

"Me neither," I agree.

"Look! Look ahead! Lights!" Anas bays from the back. "It is the cohort! We are saved!"

I whip my head back to look ahead of us. My heart skips a beat as I see he is right. In the distance, a sea of flames dances between the gaps of the trees. Gaius has come. Somehow, against all odds, Percy has rescued us.

Behind us, the hunting dogs howl. I hear their claws scrabbling across the rocks as they come for us. The barbarians are here.

"Come on!" I bark, leading the charge.

We're close enough to the edge of the forest that the lights illuminate our path. Even Clintus finds some last vestige of strength to outrace the hounds that chase us. Hope is even more powerful than fear. We only need to make it a hundred paces and we will be safe.

I burst from the dark woods at top speed, hardening the snow beneath my feet to make it easier for my brothers to follow. As we emerge into the open snowy plains, I slide to a halt, taking in the sight of several hundred warriors waiting for us with torches in their hands.

They are Normans, not the Iron Legions.

My companions slam into my back as I come to an abrupt stop, spreading out around me as they take in the horrifying sight that waits for us. I see no sign of Percy, for which I am grateful. There's still hope that he will get the message to Gaius.

A dozen *berserkirs* pace toward us like snow leopards. They carry their massive weapons with casual grace. One woman holds a warbow that I could never hope to draw, nocked with an arrow that could kill an elephant.

A different woman steps in front of her peers, a giant two-handed sword held loosely in her right hand. A golden circlet worked with precious stones wraps around her upper arm like a snake. Her *Cor* tattoos are thick and dark; they swirl slowly as they dance across her flesh. Her heavy gaze flicks from me to the men who follow me, and the corner of her lip twitches in a snarl.

I tense, readying the Symbol of Ancient Frost for one last defense. But on the inside, I have already begun to bury us all in my heart. None of us could contend with Vrok on his own. What chance do we have against a dozen of his kind?

But the woman does not attack. Instead, she snarls a single word in their language. "*Afleggja.*" We stare at her with confused looks, and her frown deepens.

"Surrender," she demands in a thick Northern accent. I feel the eyes of my men on my back as I consider her words. If I ordered them to fight, they would, but that would be condemning them to death. Part of me wants to do it—to die on the field of battle with my brothers in the tradition of the Iron Legions. But something otherworldly tickles my spine, and I feel the weight of the *votum* stone in my pocket that binds us together. I glance up at the sky at the glowing sight of *Mons* Olympus floating above us. I do not think the Normans are known for their mercy, but it is the only chance we have.

I toss my *gladius* into the snow at my feet, and after a moment, the rest of the decade's weapons join mine. The *berserkir* nods in acceptance and gestures to the rest of her kind, who grab us, dragging us roughly to our knees and binding our arms behind our backs.

We are captured.

CHAPTER 43

The *berserkir* we surrendered to appears to be named Astrid. She speaks a little of the imperial tongue, but it is enough to convey her meaning. Each of us is assigned a pair of warriors to watch over us. The Normans march us through the night, skirting the forest. The host we travel with is far too large to be able to move through it quickly, and these barbarians seem to be in a hurry. They grow frustrated with Clintus's slow pace, and after a beating does not magically enable him to walk faster, they throw him over a giant horse and tie him down like a saddlebag.

They are not overly cruel, but we are not allowed to speak. If any of us makes too much noise, the guards cuff us on the head to remind us of the rules. Most of them do not seem to speak our language, so they won't tolerate any sound, just in case.

They take our *loricae* and helmets, which is a pity because by the time *Sol* begins to rise, my Iron Symbol has recovered from whatever Vrok did to it, but now I have no iron to work with. The only metal I have within my reach is the little *clavi* nails in the soles of my boots and the collar around my neck. Greedily, I drink up what essence I can gain from them. I did not have time to use much before it was taken from me, but even refilling the missing amount in the gray sphere of my reserve will take hours.

I don't want to risk missing an opportunity to use a sword if I get my hands on one. We cannot talk, but through glances, I can tell that the rest of my squad's Symbols have begun to return too. We are dangerous again, if only we had teeth.

Dawn's first light banishes the shadows, and I'm surprised by how far we've made it into the valley. The thick forest still looms to our left, but we continue deeper into the embrace of the mountain ridges that frame it. In the distance, hundreds of columns of smoke ascend in thick columns. My stomach grumbles, and I do my best to ignore it. I doubt the Normans plan on feeding us soon.

We march for hours, well into the morning. The barbarians move in a cluster. They could not be more different than the organized columns of the Iron Legions. And yet, despite their lack of formation, we make good time through the snow. The pine forest eventually tapers off, allowing the rest of the valley to open up before us. It acts like a natural shield, making it difficult for an army to maneuver into this place unless they know the path. A frozen river runs through the center, gurgling in a few places that have not been completely covered by ice.

It is a beautiful and strange place, but my eyes are focused on the camp itself. It is nestled in the far end of the valley, backed up against the mountains, where it is sheltered from the winds. Thick fur tents that are more like huts stretch as far as the eye can see. The smoke from their campfires billows thick enough to form its own cloud above. Men and women warriors loiter about the camp, watching us with bright eyes.

There are *berserkirs* everywhere. My heart sinks as I realize that even if we got our weapons back, we would have no chance of fighting our way free of this place. An entire Legion might not be enough to stand against this army. We have found the den where Brodigan's horde lurks. More terrifying still is the sight of the host of *furia* that wander about like beasts of burden. They carry massive logs to feed the fires of the blacksmiths; others pull wagons full of supplies. There are hundreds of them. My mind's eye flashes with visions of them smashing through the walls of the Frigidus with casual ease.

I feel foolish for once having asked the Imperator how the Normans could hope to challenge the Iron Legions. Now I marvel that he has managed to hold them back at all. Marcus's grandfather truly was a hero to have survived his tour here.

At the back of the encampment is the open maw of a giant cave, like the mouth of some dreadbeast about to devour the army whole. Thick ice stalactites and stalagmites jut out like fangs, and a heavy presence settles over me that seeks to hold me in place. It is a familiar burden—it reminds me of the iron vaults beneath Agogia, where they forged us into Ironbound.

Scaffolding surrounds the cave entrance as if they are trying to hold it open. Here Norman men and women scurry about with purpose. I see piles of rock and ice they have excavated from within. Crews of workmen move around the outside, sawing logs and preparing tools.

Our captors force us into a dark tent with no torch or windows. The *berserkir* holding my arm shoves me with enough force that I trip and fall onto the thick rug, turning on my side to land on my shoulder instead of my face. The rest of us are crammed in, and then they seal it, plunging us into darkness.

"Well, it's not exactly the most secure cell I've ever been in," Anas chuckles grimly. Surprised laughter sparks around the room, and even I chuckle. Although his newfound sense of humor worries me, I've never heard him talk about his past life before. It seems an ill omen, like something that happens right before we die.

"Sound off," I command, finally managing to wrest myself upright, despite my arms still being bound behind my back. "Everyone here?"

"Yes," Felix replies.

"Present," says Marcus.

"I'm alive," Jasper echoes.

"—m doin' my best," Clintus wheezes. It is not convincing. Someone shuffles closer to check on him. I'm sure it's Felix, but I can't see. I just know my friend. A heavy silence settles on our group as no one else calls out.

"Anas," Marcus growls after a moment.

"Oh, sorry. Obviously, I am here also, *Dominus*." The brute's voice sounds amused rather than challenging. I let it go. It might be the last joke he ever gets to crack.

"Anyone have any iron?" I ask, knowing the answer is no. The Normans were thorough in their search. We are not the first legionnaires they have taken prisoner. They know better than to let us keep anything we could harness with our Symbols.

"Just my boots," Marcus confirms as a chorus of negatives echoes through the darkness.

"That could work," I muse after a moment of thought.

"What could?" Jasper challenges.

"Someone come here," I order. "Let me see if I can weaken the cords around your arms with my *clavi*."

"That's impossible, even if you could see. If you cut too deep and break it, they're going to kill us for trying to escape," Jasper protests, sounding more like a boy than a soldier. His fear is infectious in the dark. I feel it spreading among us all like a cloud.

"They're probably going to anyway," I point out.

"You don't know that!"

"Boy, we were sent here to die!" Anas's voice cracks like a whip, full of his usual anger. The tent falls silent, what little fire of rebellion we still carry extinguished by fear.

"What can we do?" Jasper's voice is soft and broken. "What hope do we have against an army like that?"

"We endure," I say firmly, turning to look in his direction in the dark. I cannot see him, but I hope that he can hear me speaking directly to him. "We are the Iron Legions of the empire. We do not bend; we do not break." I can't help but smile as I remember Durus shouting that at us in the training yards of Agogia. A few of the men chuckle dryly, no doubt thinking the same thing. Their laughter is like a wind, banishing the cloud of fear that hung heavy in the room.

"He can do it." Felix's confidence is firm. A grin flashes across my face that he cannot see, but it's not for him. It's for two boys waiting to enter an arena what feels like a lifetime ago.

"Try it on me," Anas grunts, and I hear him shuffling toward me in the dark. "I'm not afraid."

"This way." I thump my feet on the ground, helping guide him. The burly man positions himself facing away from me at my feet, and slowly, I move the soles of my boots over him, trying to get a sense of where he is in the dark.

"Stop hesitating and do it, *Dominus*," Anas growls after a few moments, the challenge back in his voice. I close my eyes, trying to focus. Seizing the Iron Symbol, I command the *clavi* in my right boot to rise. I mold their tips to be rounded instead of sharp while I hunt for my target. Through my connection to iron, I can feel Anas's arms as if I touched them with my own fingers, letting me find my way even though I cannot see. I move my foot down, locating the bundle of knots that bind his wrists together. Confident that my nails will not connect with his skin, I sharpen them into points and drive them into the fibers of the rope. It parts easily, but I stop myself from tearing it too much. I seek only to loosen his bonds, not free him. We need to wait for the right moment.

I withdraw the *clavi*, shifting my foot slightly to the side before stabbing them out again, creating another series of tiny holes in the cord. Sweat begins to bead on the back of my neck as I focus, trying to overcome my blindness. I pull the nails back again, but before I can drive them in a third time, the flap of the tent is yanked open. I jerk my foot back and open my eyes against the blinding light, trying to look as if I am merely startled and not terrified.

"Come," grunts Astrid, grabbing me by the arm and leading me out of tent. I look over my shoulder to see my men being pulled by regular warriors in our wake. Even Clintus is being dragged with us. He's pale and looks weak, but he is alive. I relax a little, glad that we are not being separated. If we are to be killed, I would have it be together.

The powerful woman leads us to a large tent made of furs that sits by the entrance to the cave. A guard at the front throws the flap open, and we are shoved inside. The floor is covered in more skins, forming a thick carpet. Incense burns from several braziers, filling the room with cloying, sweet smoke. Ancient Frost is faint here, driven away by the warmth.

In the back sits a large golden throne, its base so wide that it stretches almost the entire width of the space. A terrible man perches on it like a monster. His entire body is covered with the living tattoos of a *berserkir*. He is more shadow than flesh, and I gaze in horror at the dark, writhing mass that covers his entire body. At his feet sits a demented helm mounted with a pair of antlers. He turns from the woman who sits at his right hand to stare at our approach.

Despite his terrifying appearance, I forget about him as I stare at her with shock. She is draped in fur, covering all but her face, but even that is striking. Hers is a cold beauty, different than the land beyond the wall, but that is not why I stare. It is obvious from a glance that she is not Norman. Her hair is dark, not blond, her features sharp and palatine. She must be a prisoner, like us.

I feel the heavy stare of Anas burrowing into the back of my neck, and I make eye contact with him for a moment, just long enough to give him a tiny shake of my head. The idea of taking the leader of this army hostage is tempting, but we are surrounded by warriors. We would be cut to shreds before our rebellion even began. It is not yet the moment. He snarls in frustration but nods in agreement.

My *berserkir* minder forces me to my knees, and I hear the *thumps* of my men following me to the ground. The man and woman both stare at us like predators. She is not a prisoner, I realize with a chill. She is something else.

The monstrous man asks a question in his language, and the woman shifts, settling the thick wrap around her. "High King Knut wishes to know your name," she translates. I barely manage to hold back a gasp of surprise. The Normans have no kings.

"Decurion Castor, Twelfth Legion, Eighth Cohort," I reply as I have been trained. She twitches with a faint chuckle, turning back to the man to tell him.

"Where is the rest of your cohort?" she asks on his behalf. Despite being on my knees, I feel a fey mood settle on me. I may be a prisoner, but I do not have to be an obedient one. I jerk my head back at the four men kneeling behind me.

"I think you found them all," I reply dryly.

"*ljóst!*" the woman snaps at the *berserkir* standing behind me, her face darkening with a scowl that feels all too familiar. My face and chest slam into the carpet after the inhumanly powerful warrior cuffs me in the back of the head. I let out a groan as strong hands pull me back to my knees. It hurts, but not as much as it could. The forges of Agogia made me strong, but I don't need them to know that. They'll only hit me harder.

"The High King asked you a question," she hisses, drawing herself up to her full height. She could have been a senator on the *Argentum Consilio*, so intense is her condescension. It makes it easy for me to hate her.

"At Frigidus," I lie after taking a moment to orient myself. "We were sent ahead to scout—" The woman nods, and the *berserkir* hits me again. I gasp, leaning into the theatrics even harder. I am pathetic. She knows what the Twelfth Legion is; let her think me exactly what she expects.

"They're at Frigidus," I repeat, panting. "Please don't hit me again. I swear it on Jupiter's Bones."

"Shut your mouth," Felix snarls at me from behind, trying to sell my story. I wince in sympathy, letting my eyes go wide as I hear the warriors strike him. My shoulders quake as if I am terrified. In truth, I should be, but the deep chill of Ancient Frost keeps my fear at bay.

"Please, I'll tell you whatever you want to know," I beg. I lower myself into a bow before this High King. "Our officers will ransom us back…"

High King Knut cuts me off, his Northern tone thick with disgust. His teeth are white against the shadow of his writhing tattoos that feed him power. As far as he is concerned, I am no warrior. The woman responds in his tongue, and for a moment, they debate. The ruler makes a dismissive gesture at us, like a man shooing a fly. Clearly, he does not think we are of any use. The woman turns to look at us with obvious satisfaction. She has won something here, but I do not know what. As she raises a hand to signal the *berserkir* to take us away, her furs fall, revealing the *Cor* markings that run through her forearms.

The world freezes as I stare at them, unable to process what I see. Her veins are not Copper, or Silver, and they are definitely not Gold. Instead, they are black and viscous, tinged with spots of acidic green. They remind me of something. The woman watches me noticing, and her mouth sharpens into a hideous smile, like the grave-made flesh. There are only three levels an *electus* can attain, but hers is none of those. She wants me to see what she is, to fear her. And as much as I do not want to give her the satisfaction, not even Ancient Frost can stop me from falling into her trap.

Astrid, my *berserkir* shadow, grabs me, and we are dragged from the High King's tent, not even given time to get off our knees. I kick my feet, trying to wrench myself off the ground, but she is too strong. The dark-veined woman rises, following us with that sinister smile.

Tired of my twisting, my guard pauses long enough for me to stand. Then she sends me stumbling with a snarl and a shove, straight toward the yawning maw of the ice cavern. My fear rises, haunted by the evil look of the woman and the cave. The heavy presence that I noticed before rises from the ice again, bearing down on me like an avalanche.

I struggle to find my breath for real this time as Astrid drags me toward the entrance. Even the powerful woman seems to be slowing down, as if she is equally not eager to enter its icy jaws. The woman in furs strolls past us, stepping easily into the opening as if it were her home.

We wind down the sloped entrance, our journey like being swallowed in the throat of some massive beast. It twists and turns as we descend until we lose sight of the entrance and daylight. Only smoky torches mounted on the wall provide illumination.

Further down, the tunnel expands into a room, wide enough for a dozen men to stand side by side. It feels as if we have made it to the stomach, ready to be digested. The Normans throw us down to the cold, hard ground and leave us there with our bonds tied. Astrid pauses for a moment, eyeing the room with distaste, but as the last of her warriors trudges past, she follows.

This space has been set up as some sort of staging area. *Lumos* relics hang from the walls instead of torches, casting bright light throughout the room. Thick, red wooden tables run the length of both walls, and my eyes run over a series of hammers, picks, saws, and knives with growing alarm. Some of those do not seem like the kind that are used for digging in the snow. More scaffolding has been erected here, reinforcing the ceiling.

"Do you like it?" the twisted *electus* asks as she removes her outer furs, dropping them casually on the frozen floor before turning to pace toward a series of tables that are built along the wall. Her arms are exposed, and I trace the black veins running through her with growing horror. They cover her left arm, but her right has far fewer lines, and none make it past her elbow. A vicious white scar runs down the entire back of her left arm, and its twin does the same on her right, but only halfway. It looks like someone tried to skin her.

She is an *immundus* of some kind, although her symptoms are different than mine. I wonder what she will think if she sees the *rasa* veins that fill my arms. Could she too have bound more than one Symbol? Despite my terror, my curiosity is piqued. If I wasn't certain that I was going to die here, I might be able to learn more about what I am.

She pauses halfway and turns to study us with a mocking pout on her face. "You have no idea what this place is, do you? Poor legionnaires, sent to die in the cold without even knowing why." She tilts her head, her gaze flicking among us like a cunning fish wife at a sea market. "You little lost sheep have no idea what I am either." Her smile turns cruel as she looks over our shoulders at someone approaching. "But you will soon," she promises.

Warned by the eerie tone in her voice, I turn my head to see what she watches. My stomach roils as I recognize the red uniform of the Twelfth Legion. A group of Normans carry the corpses of our brothers who died in the fighting in the trees. I weep to see Petrus's broken body, shattered from the force of Vrok's *berserkir* rage.

"Just here." The terrible woman gestures at the tables lining the side of the cavern. Too late, I realize they are red with the blood of bodies who have lain there before. The Normans set our friend down before beating a hasty retreat. Even these hardened warriors want no part of what is to come. Next, Lintus, Matinius, Haxus, and Antony are laid down in a row. I look over my shoulder, terrified that I will see them carrying Percy's body, but he does not appear. The centurion may still be alive—and with him, our small, fragile hope.

More warriors drop off our stripped gear in piles. My eyes stare hungrily at the *loricae* and *gladii* that are just out of reach. But as much as I long to take hold of my iron weapons and show them the wrath of the legions, I know it would be futile. It is a testament to how unconcerned these Normans are by our presence that they do not care to keep our gear more secure. What can five Coppers hope to do against a horde of *berserkirs* and *furia*?

The last barbarian leaves, and I feel the dread of this place grow in me as they depart. I wish they would stay; I would much rather be tortured by Astrid and her kind than left alone in this woman's clutches.

The black-veined woman wanders down the line of tables, dragging her fingers lightly over the edges of them, peering down at the bodies of our brothers. I'm going to be sick. There's something about the way that she sizes them up that makes me feel like she is a butcher, and we are all cows.

"I think I'll start with you," she murmurs, tapping the still form of Lintus on the chest. "But have no fear." She laughs, looking down the line at Antony. "You'll get your turn too, my dear." She turns to face us again, leaning back against the table and crossing her arms. The blackness in her veins *moves* like sludge.

"I am called Vixa," she announces. None of us offer our names, and she chuckles to herself, amused by our silence. "Have you realized what I am yet?" The tip of her tongue plays along her lip, tasting the air like a snake. She's enjoying our fear, delighting in its scent. We stare at her in silence, helpless and afraid to move.

"You seem like bright boys." She chuckles, turning back to the corpses behind her. "I'm sure you'll figure it out." She reaches for the handle of a long knife, its blade stained and rusty. I shudder to think what it has seen and done here in the cold.

A groan sounds from the tables, and her head whips around to stare at Antony. The blood drains out of my face as I realize what that means. I can just see the corner of her mouth as it curves in evil delight. "Oh my," she gushes. "You're still alive? I thought we had lost you, my dear. How delightful." She moves from Lintus to Antony, raising the tip of her knife as she moves.

"*Necromanta*." Felix gasps in horrific realization. Part of me wants to deny his answer as ridiculous—they are just a story. But I feel something inside my mind shatter, an innocence of some sort, as I realize that is exactly what she is. A myth made flesh, like the icy *furia* that serve the Normans.

As *discipuli*, we used to tell stories of dark magisters who stole relics from the bodies of *electii*, using them to give themselves powers that they had not earned, but none of us had believed them. Once, Clintus had asked Old Vellum if such a thing were possible, and our teacher mocked him, asking if he also believed in the *fenix* or the *hydrus*? We stopped telling those stories after that day.

But now, as I look at the black, rotten veins running through Vixa's body and the scars that trace her flesh, I know that is what she is. A nightmare vulture. A Heart thief. Relics are the property of the empire, the last gift of an *electus* after they die. For her to steal them is a profane act.

Anas lets out a screech of rage, struggling to his feet. I turn my head over my shoulder in time to see his shoulders bunch, straining against his weakened bonds. For a moment, the cords hold him tight, despite the damage I did to them. But before I can despair, there is a *pop*, and his arms separate as the rope falls to the ground. He's free! The brutish man bounds forward, hurtling toward the woman, with his shoulder low to ram her with his weight.

As one, the rest of us leap to our feet. The nails in our boots *crunch* as they catch the ice as we try to follow his example. We've been trained like wolfhounds to stay in a pack. I grab the Symbol of Ancient Frost, calling upon it to harden the surface beneath my brothers to make our footing sure. Awareness of the tunnel fills me, but so does something else. The heavy presence that permeates the air bores into my mind as if it is noticing me for the first time, and it does not appreciate me manipulating its home.

The cavern rumbles in response to my command, like a hibernating bear. The room shakes, and chunks of snow and ice rain from the ceiling in a deadly storm. Panicking, I release the Symbol, praying to Fortuna's Ashes that I did not start an avalanche. I do not understand what Ancient Frost showed me; it's like nothing I have ever seen before. Already my mind seeks to forget, to drive the memory of the presence from my skull.

The cavern's shaking groans to a halt, appeased by my retreat.

The woman spins at the sound of Anas's charge. Never in my life have I seen someone move like that, not even Atticus when he called on the speed of the wind. Her pleasant smile is gone, replaced with an enraged snarl as she leaps at the soldier. She flashes past him in a blur, ripping him off his feet with a casual grace.

He lets out a scream as she spins, throwing him at the wall as if he weighs nothing. Anas's back slams into the ice, and he slides down the side to the cold ground. His head lolls to the side, and his mouth hangs open. He does not stir.

"Sit. Down," Vixa snarls, looking at the rest of us with icy imperium. The rest of us are frozen mid-charge, stunned by her terrifying strength. Slowly, I obey, dropping to my knees in obeisance. The rest of the squad follows my lead. She studies us for a moment, as if trying to decide if we will charge her again the moment she turns her back.

Silently, she glides forward, extending the tip of her knife to rest on the bottom of Felix's chin. My skin crawls as she forces his head up so she can stare into his eyes. I reach for the Symbol of Ancient Frost but stop myself just short of fully grabbing it. It hovers just out of my grip, beckoning me to embrace it, promising to shield me from the danger before me. I do not know what will happen if I do, and for some reason, I am more afraid of the other presence than Vixa.

"You're the smart one," she murmurs, staring into his eyes. Felix meets her gaze boldly, back straight, face hard. No legionnaire of the Iron Legions could fault his courage in the face of terror. After a moment, she chuckles again, patting his cheek with her empty hand before turning away.

"Your friend is right," she tells us as she walks back toward the tables. "*Necromantia* was what the ancients called my art. It has many names, but I've always liked that one the best. It has a certain *severity* to it that *evocator* never did. Wouldn't you agree?" She reaches out to place a hand on Antony's still form. He does not move, and I find myself hoping that he faded while Vixa was throwing Anas around. I would not want to be alive in her clutches.

"Still hanging on," she murmurs after a moment, sending a rush of relief and fear through me. I am terrified for him. "It's so much easier when they're fresh."

Vixa begins to root around her tools, searching for something specific. "This is a sacred site to the barbarians," she tells us as she hunts. "Surely you feel it? The *animus* that hangs around this place like a cloud of smoke." She gives me a wry glance that makes my skin crawl. "Your decurion surely does." I'm glad once again for the coat that covers my *rasa* veins. I dread to think what having her full attention would be like.

"This is where they bind their *furia*," she continues, unperturbed by our silence. "For generations, the various clans would come here on holy days to raise their monsters with the *Corda* they stole. But now it all belongs to the High King." She selects a long saw from her tools and lays it next to Antony.

My pulse quickens as I stare at my fading friend. I know I have no chance against the *necromanta*, but I cannot bear to watch one of our brothers be butchered like a pig. Antony stood with us and did not falter when he was called upon. He deserves better than this. The ghosts of Macer and Rufus hover over my shoulders, watching me with heavy eyes. I could not save them, but maybe I can save him.

"The barbarians believe that this is the home of Winter itself, the place that all ice and cold come from. They think that is why they are able to create their *furia* and imbue them with their will. They're right—well, after a fashion. Winter did live here once, but that is not all this place is. Our ancestors called it Hyperborea."

She pauses, laughing to herself in surprise. "Listen to me prattle on. Can you tell I haven't had the chance to speak *lingua imperia* in months? Living Gods, it feels good not to have their thick tongue clogging up my mouth. It's like having my cheeks full of pebbles."

Shaking her head in amusement, Vixa raises the rusty knife, and I give in to Ancient Frost's call. Knowledge floods into me as my *animus* spreads out through the floor, flowing over the walls and diving into the floor. It is a vast structure that my Copper Heart cannot fully plumb, but even the fraction of it that I perceive is overwhelming. It is infused with a presence that seems to glow like the sun.

It is blinding.

It reacts instantly, turning its focus on me with violent speed. The entire cavern rumbles in warning like a growling dog. I ignore its complaints, placing my hand on the ground and pouring my will into a simple instruction—*bind*. I feel the snow crunch as it begins to condense into hard ice, like coal becoming a diamond. Essence flows out of me in a flood, but I hardly notice. This cavern is like an ocean; I have access to more than I could ever need.

Vixa pauses, her knife hovering just above Antony's chest. She turns to study us, a curious expression on her face, and her gaze spears me with an intensity that almost matches the presence's scrutiny.

The cavern shudders again, more fiercely this time. I can feel a palpable anger growing in the air like the scent of smoke from a forest fire. I grit my teeth and pour more of my will into the task. A bar settles into my grip, and with a thought, I trim the edge, sharpening it into a razor. I twist my wrist, letting the edge catch against the cords that bind my arms behind my back. They part with a snap, and I laugh as I rise to my feet in front of the staring *necromanta*.

Vixa's eyes go wide in shock as she sees the ice weapon that I've formed. It's about as long as a knife, but it is only a simple bar with a sharp edge. I grip the base and command the weapon to come to a point. It cracks in response as it obeys, shifting before my eyes.

"You fool!" Vixa screams, her shock turning to terror as she realizes what I have done. The cavern shakes a third time. Across the room, a scaffold collapses under the strain. "Release it. You cannot hold a Winter Symbol here—"

Then the world goes white.

CHAPTER 44

I am standing in a void made of snow.

The ground crunches under my feet as I turn, taking in my new surroundings. A chill wind moans through the emptiness, cutting through my coat like a blade. Everything around me is white, even the sky. I do not think I am in a cave; it is too bright even though I see no sign of *Sol*. It reminds me of the dreams that I was pulled into during the *Sententia*.

I look for my friends, for Vixa, but there is no sign of any of them. Even my Symbols are nowhere to be found. There is only a dark emptiness in my mind where they were once kept. I am alone in every sense of the word. The only things I carry with me are my ice sword and the wolf scars on my right arm, which glow with a purple light. The coldness of the blade eats into my palm now that I do not have the power of Ancient Frost to keep it at bay. I welcome the pain, unwilling to drop my only weapon.

The swirling wind grows, circling me with sinister intent. The presence that has watched me since the moment I came to this place grows with it, as if carried by the same current. A flurry of snow begins to spin around me, a flicker of white-on-white as it fills my vision. It crescendos like a mighty storm before vanishing in an instant.

When I can see again, I am no longer alone.

A massive throne sits before me, carved of deep blue ice. It is made for a man far too tall. If I stood on Felix's shoulders, its back would still reach above my head. A being sits on it. He also dwarfs me. I am not as surprised by his size as I should be. He is not the first unnaturally tall man that I have seen.

He looks like a corpse, withered and dry, but is clearly alive. I can see his bones where the flesh has rotted away, but he does not seem to be bothered by his state of disrepair. A pair of wings sweeps out of his back, featherless and decrepit. The only part of him that shows any vitality are the golden orbs in his eye sockets, which burn with a feverish light. In his right hand, he holds a large conch shell that must have come from the king of all its kind. An iron shackle is wrapped around his right leg, with thick chains that run around the back of the throne.

Frigidus, he rumbles in a voice like thunder. The giant does not speak, but his voice booms in my head as if it were my own thought. *Why have you returned to my domain?* Terror clutches at me as I realize that this creature thinks I am one of Titus's Iron Lords. My mouth works silently as a dozen denials die unspoken. I do not utter them, but he seems to sense them all the same.

You are not one of the iron apostates, the voice muses after a moment of thought. It rattles my skull with its force. *You are but a shadow. A pretender. Why have you come to my house?*

"Um," I reply, licking my dry lips. I'm not sure that I need to speak out loud, but it feels rude not to. "I'm sorry, *Dominus*, but I do not know where I am. I was brought here against my will."

You are in my house, he repeats. I resist the urge to look around at the vast emptiness that surrounds us.

"And who are you… *Dominus*? I mean no disrespect, but I am lost and without knowledge of this place or its people." The giant is silent for a long moment. I am not sure that time flows here—this feels like a place that Saturn never entered—but even after an eon passes, the corpse does not reply.

When it finally does, it is with an amused chuckle that is so dry, it could create a desert. *You have wandered far from home indeed, Ovicula.* He calls me "Little Sheep" in the language of the ancients. *Has my name truly faded from your minds? Or are you simply too foolish to see what is right before you?*

It is my turn to fall silent, staring at the dead thing with trepidation. I know who he is. Or perhaps who he was. But my mind does not want to accept it. I cannot. Because he cannot be what he is. The priests, the magisters, and the Empress have told me my whole life that the gods were dead.

But I suspect that Frigidus didn't finish the job with Aquilo.

I see, he says at last with a dry chuckle. *What a curse you carry.* The skeleton cocks its head, studying me with those glowing orbs. *Did you pick it up yourself? I see the blood of your oath—your oaths. Did you not learn your lesson the first time you tempted my siblings, Ovicula?* Panic threatens to overwhelm me as my world comes crashing down, and I desperately reach for my Symbols, but they are still absent, blocked by the god's power.

"You're dead!" I protest. It sounds weak and pathetic to my ears. It can only sound worse to the god. "Frigidus killed you. Titus and the rest of the Iron Lords…"

This is not what the priests and magisters told us. The gods are dead. We killed them, and they are gone. The Iron Law was made to protect us from those who would become tyrants, but what use is being safe from men when the gods still waited in the shadows?

Killed me? His voice is thunderous but amused. *How do you kill a god, little lamb?* Mocking laughter echoes off the inside of my skull. *Long have I slept since those iron apostates betrayed me and my kin, but you are bound to me, and your voice pulled me from my slumber.* His voice trails off, and his presence fades slightly, as if he had turned away from me to study the world before him.

What is this? he demands, a bitter cold entering his voice that freezes me to my core. *Who dares to profane my home?* The void shakes again, this time with rage. *What have you brought here, mortal?*

Something wraps around me like a serpent, coiling to hold me tight. I am ripped off my feet by a force I cannot see. Fear, total and absolute, fills me as I am hauled up to the god to stare in his eyes with my own. I am as dangerous as a mouse to him—I feel it in the strength of his power and the frailty of my own.

"I wasn't a part of this!" I protest weakly, unable to get a full breath. "I am a *captivus* here, much like you." I don't know if he's truly a prisoner. He doesn't seem to be in the best health, and the chain around his ankle does not seem like a fashion choice.

BARBARIANS, he thunders, not listening to me. His gaze rises to the heavens as he rants. *APOSTATES.* There is a pause, like the building of a storm before it surges. *NECROMANTIA IN DOMUM MEAM?* His voice slips into the ancient tongue in his rage. I realize that we have been speaking it the entire time; something about his presence was translating his intent to me.

"They are my enemies also, *Dominus*," I assure him weakly. "I am a legionnaire of the empire, not a follower of these—"

YOU ARE A BROKEN TOY, Aquilo, the God of Winter, screams over me. His rage is unhinged and blinding. *YOU DO NOT KNOW WHAT YOU ARE OR WHAT YOU HAVE BEEN MADE TO DO.*

"Well, either way, I'm still not with the barbarians," I wheeze. Aquilo looks down from his rage-fueled diatribe to study me. I feel his *animus* sweep through me like he is washing me from the inside out. Something inside of me clicks, like a bone being set into its rightful place, and for a moment, I feel *connected*, whole. Iron and Ancient Frost flare in my mind, bright as stars. Power fills me like rushing water. I stare back at the dead god, whole and complete. A spark of something flickers between us. Like this, I could kill him. The *inhibitus* around my neck throbs in anger but does not constrict. It does not dare to rebuke me. Then the spirit withdraws, and it is gone.

Aquilo is silent, as if he too felt that spark. After a heartbeat, he releases me from his will, and I plummet a half-dozen paces to land in a crouch on the cold ground. We stare at each other for a moment, man and god. My heart is racing, but I am no longer terrified. I am afraid, the same way I would fear finding a lion in front of me, but something has changed, and we both feel it.

My siblings, he sneers. *Always they think they know what is best. They will reap what they sow again. I want no part of their misery.*

I do not reply, only hold my stare. To look away feels like it would invite him to destroy me. I am being tested, but I do not know for what.

I will make you my storm, son, Aquilo declares after the silence stretches. *You will carry my wrath and restore my home.*

"How will I do that?" I ask, caught off guard by the god's capriciousness. "There's an *army* out there. I am but one man with a couple of friends."

I will give you the authority to summon ice, the god offers. I twitch in shock, unable to comprehend the offer that he is making to me. Some *electii* are able to manifest specialized uses of their Symbols instead of purely manipulating the world around them, but it is something that even most elite Golds cannot do. I've never heard of a Copper possessing an ability like that.

"You can do that?" I whisper.

Can? Aquilo thunders in rage. *Can? I am COLD. I do not need permission to do anything with my imperium. I command, and ice obeys. You merely echo me with your stolen power.* I do not think now is the moment to point out that Mars or one of his avatars gave me my Hearts. Unless he means that they were taken from the Empress?

The god raises a bony arm and gestures at the snow in front of me with a single finger. The ground at my feet rumbles, parting as something is drawn out of the depths. My mouth drops in shock as I realize it is the hilt of a sword made completely of ice. It grows until only the tip is still buried in the cold ground. It is etched with every detail, every facet that a sword that a soldier of the Iron Legions would bear. The pommel even has the grooves for the cloth wraps that most legionnaires use to make gripping it more comfortable.

Since you like oaths, make a votum *with me, Ovicula,* the God of Winter and the North Wind taunts me from his throne. I shudder to hear his tone; it fills me with ice and damnation. I bear too many burdens already. I do not know if I can carry another.

Take my sword and use it to clean my house. Rid it of the necromanta who dwells in my frozen halls. Do this in my name and I will grant you power like you have never seen.

"What about the army that waits outside the cave?" I ask, not feeling confident about where this is going. Vixa is fast and strong. She is some sort of *electus*, and I do not know what Symbol she is bound to. Even with a sword, I am not sure that I would be able to fight her.

Aquilo gestures at the *gladius* again, and the circle on the end of the hilt begins to glow with a deep sapphire light. Even without my Symbol, my eyes know that it is filled with frozen rage. Inwardly, I shiver with terror at what has been laid before my feet. Almost a seven hundred years ago, Prometheus took something from the gods—the knowledge of *Cor* Hearts—which he brought back to his brothers and began the rise of men.

Who am I that I should stand before a god, dead and dying, to be offered the same kind of power? I feel unworthy, like a lame donkey burdened by treasure. I should not be here. I am a soldier of the Iron Legion, not a hero. This is a place for men mightier than me. If only Percy or Gaius were here, they would know what to do.

I cannot leave this place, but you will carry a piece of me with you, the god promises. *Set me free and see what doom visits these barbarians.*

I shiver at the dreadful glee in his voice. "And if I do these things, you will let me go?"

Let you go? Ovicula, I am not the spider whose web you are caught in. The wind around us shifts, and I think I hear the mocking howl of a wolf in the distance. *I merely offer you a knife to cut yourself free.* The giant head turns to look pointedly at the icy sword that rests between us.

The wind continues to swirl around us as we fall silent. There is no need to rush. I am trapped in this place with him, and he has nothing to fear from me. I ransack my brain, trying to find a solution to this problem that does not involve me swearing another oath to a god.

Felix was right. Only fools do that more than once. I should have learned my lesson the first time. But no matter how I look at it, I'm trapped. Aquilo hasn't really given me a choice, just a way out. I have no power here; I cannot threaten him. He can keep me here for an eternity, until I am bones and dust just like him.

The only way out is to take his deal.

"What is your *votum*?" I ask, dreading the answer.

Kill the necromanta and feed her bones to the deep dark of my caves, Aquilo replies at once. *You will be my cold wind and bear my storm to sweep the barbarians that infest my home. Do this, and you shall be free of my aegis.*

"And if I fail?"

You return here and take my place. The god leans back in his icy throne and kicks out his shackled leg, making the heavy iron chain rattle. His skull smile seems to grow as he sees the expression on my face. *Long has it been since one of the Ironbound came to these halls,* he chortles. *But even one such as you could undo* Frigidus's *cursed handiwork.*

I am silent for another eon as I consider his offer. It is not often that one is given the chance to undo your entire world. My whole life, I have been taught that Titus and the *Ferrum Domini* killed our gods, that they were *dead*. Not only is Aquilo somewhat alive, but he seeks to be released from this prison my ancestors trapped him in.

What sort of terror would a half-dead god unleash on the world when he emerged? The priests tell us that before the legendary warriors threw them down, the gods ruled over us with a heavy yoke. Does he harbor anger for being trapped in this empty expanse for hundreds of years? He may be immortal, but how could he not? I would.

But as I look at Aquilo, I remember how we have changed since then. Titus and Iron Lords were powerful *electii*, most of them bound to the Symbol of Iron. None of them wore collars like the one around my neck. If this god were to get free, who could stand before him? Where have all our heroes gone?

And yet, here I am, trapped with no way out. It feels wrong to take such a risk on behalf of the empire, my people. Resolving to not give in to temptation, I draw myself to my full height, squaring my shoulders, and clasp my hands behind my back, preparing to out-stubborn a god.

Aquilo watches me for a moment, cadaverous head tilted as he studies me anew. He seems amused by my resistance, like a parent watching a toddler try to escape. After a moment, he leans forward, resting his arm bones on his rotting knees.

By the way, he asks almost casually, *you wouldn't be a member of the little legion that's being hunted by barbarians, would you?*

I twitch in surprise, and his laughter booms in my ears. My vision blurs as Aquilo's presence jams something into my mind. It is not sight—it is knowledge. He knows this frozen wasteland the way I know my *gladius* when I hold it and the Iron Symbol. Now he shares that understanding with me. It is overwhelming, like drinking from a waterfall, and I fear I might drown.

I feel the pounding of hundreds of feet as the Twelfth maneuvers through the ice, cutting through the snow, like they are tearing lines in Aquilo's—our flesh. The legion marches north, toward Aquilo's cave and the High King. Panic flares in my chest as I realize they are racing into an ambush. Did Percy not make it to Gaius? Did he not warn them?

Then I see that they are not hunting, but being hunted. A second force of barbarians has gotten behind them, cutting off their retreat to the fortress. Now that formation drives them forward like dogs, bringing their prey right to their masters. The Twelfth is outnumbered and outmaneuvered, just like Imperator Tyrus wanted.

The knowledge fades, and my vision returns. "Is that happening now?" I demand, trying to understand how it could be when I thought we were trapped in some dream world beyond its grasp.

It is what is and what will be, the god promises unhelpfully. I glare at him, and he shrugs, unwilling or unable to explain it to me beyond that. *I swear to you on my throne.* That sets my mind more at ease. The priests say that the gods never broke their oaths. Granted, they also said that the gods were dead, so maybe I should take their advice with a grain of salt.

Aquilo glances down at the icy gladius before me with a pointed stare. He grows tired of my performative resistance. We both know how this ends. With a defeated sigh, I reach for its hilt, but the sword does not budge. Confused, I look at the decaying god, who leans back in his chair with a relaxed air.

Come now, Ovicula. He chuckles. *You have sworn a* votum *before.* The stone that I carry in my pocket grows heavy, I can feel its weight growing under his scrutiny. *Blood oaths require blood.*

I grit my teeth in frustration. Now that I know the fate that awaits my cohort, I feel Time's heavy hands on my shoulders, forcing me to kneel. The loyalty I share with my brothers compels me to take up this weapon and come to their aid. I crouch by the blade, running the back of my left hand along the icy *gladius*'s razor-sharp edge. I don't feel any pain as the cold blade cuts me open. My bright red blood flows down the length of the blade, and the sword quivers as if suddenly released from incredible pressure. Confident that this time it will come to me, I grab its hilt with my right hand and pull it free from the snow in one swift move.

I raise the icy *gladius* high in a mocking salute to the dead god. I have drawn his blade and sworn his oath. Now he must deliver to me the power he promised. The golden orbs of his eyes narrow as he watches, waiting for something. Frozen knowledge hits me like an avalanche. I cannot do anything other than shudder as the icy tide envelops me, filling my mind.

The barrier that banished my Symbols parts, allowing Ancient Frost to slip in like a courtesan. It burns brightly in my mind, shining brighter than it ever has before. Cold flares in my right hand as the *gladius* begins to absorb into me, lured by the song of my *Cor* Heart. It sinks into my palm hilt first, inch by agonizing inch, as it answers the call.

I gaze in horror as my weapon vanishes into my skin, until even the tip is gone. The blade's frozen presence breaks up inside of me, swirling around my body as if being carried by my Copper veins. The *inhibitus* around my neck tightens threateningly, but that coldness flows up to my neck and rebukes it, freezing it in place. I lower my now-empty hand and clench it as the power courses through me, bowing my head and closing my eyes.

As it spreads, I feel an instinct swell inside of me. It is as if I just grew a third arm, but I understand this new ability as if it has been a part of my body since I was born. It is *Glacialis Falx*, the Frozen Blade, and it is mine.

My eyes open, and slowly, I raise my head to stare at Aquilo. He seems like so much more a frail thing now than he did at first. Maybe he is dead. I hold his golden gaze and extend my right hand, calling upon the Symbol of Ancient Frost to activate command of the Frozen Blade.

Essence pours out of me into the palm of my hand, just like it would into my *gladius* or *scutum*. But now it forms a weapon of its own. I breathe deeply, cultivating the frozen essence that surrounds me in this frozen void and manifesting it into a physical form. After a dozen heartbeats, it is done. I do not need to look to see it is a perfect replica of my own sword carved out of dark blue ice.

The sapphire storm that Aquilo gave me roils below my grip in the hilt. I can feel its fury rattling within the blade like a caged *tigris*, desperate to get out and hunt. The magnitude of its force awes me—it is a greater working than I could ever hope to manage as a Copper.

Well? thunders Aquilo, shifting back in his throne at the sight of me wielding some of his power. *Have I not kept my word, Ovicula? Is it not time for you to do the same? Or would you prefer to take my place now and spare yourself from the dangers to come?*

"No," I reply, brimming with my new cold power. "I'll take my chances."

Then go, Ovicula, and bear my wrath with you. Aquilo's golden eyes flash with something like a fire, despite being the God of Cold and Winter. The winds around us pick up, and a wall of snow flurries between us, obscuring my vision of his rotting corpse.

The world flashes white, and then I am back in the cave, facing down Vixa's rage. But now I'm armed.

CHAPTER 45

The *Glacialis Falx* is still in my hand when I return to my body. The bar of ice that I pulled from the floor has been replaced with a weapon worthy of a legionnaire. Otherwise, the room is just as I left it. I feel my brothers preparing to follow me, even though they are still bound. I glance over my shoulder to make sure that they are unhurt. Marcus and Felix stare at me with wide eyes, while Clintus struggles with his lame leg. Relief pours through me like a wave. I am not too late.

"Fool!" Vixa screams again, her face contorting in terror. "Release it before you wake the Sleeper." Does she know the truth of who slumbers here? Or does she think it some legend? It does not matter; she will meet him soon.

"He's already awake," I tell her with a small, sad smile. "He asked me to give you his greetings." Aquilo's presence deepens as if he is leaning closer to study us like bugs. Her face pales, the white of her fear standing in stark relief against the black of her rotting, stolen *Cor* veins.

"You are no threat to me," the *necromanta* hisses, regaining some of her poise. She doesn't understand what I am, but her mind has already made assumptions. I wear the uniform of a legionnaire and the *inhibitus* of an Ironbound, but I have shown that I bear a Winter Symbol.

She thinks I am a spy, perhaps even a Censor in sheep's clothing. Even if I am not truly a soldier of the Iron Legions, I must look the part to blend in, which means that I am only a Copper, and whatever she is, it is an order of magnitude in power above me.

That would be true if I hadn't been given an ability of a god, the same way that Prometheus was so long ago.

I glance at the sapphire set into the hilt of my icy *gladius*, and it boils with Aquilo's rage. Lightning flares within it, hammering at the sides of its prison. It begs to be unleashed; to be allowed to wreak havoc. *Not yet*, I rebuke it with my will, and it relents, resentment burning bright.

But the *Glacialis Falx* is not only a sword—it is a focus. I feel my connection to Ancient Frost sharpen. My *animus* can carve through the ground with ease, reaching farther than ever before. I am stronger and faster than I ever have been. Again, the *inhibitus* around my neck seeks to punish me for brushing the limits of Copper, but the cold power within me lashes back, holding it at bay.

When I look at the black-veined woman, I do not need to hide my satisfaction at the fear my ability brings to her. "What are you?" she whispers in horror. The corner of my lip quirks in savage delight at seeing such the profane woman afraid.

"I am the cold wind," I reply, although the words do not feel like my own, as Aquilo's presence builds to a crescendo. I am merely a conduit for a power that speaks with my lips. Did Atticus feel like this when the Empress used him as her mouthpiece during the *Sententia*?

"You are an abomination to the *Pax Deorum*, *necromanta*," I snarl, burning with a hatred even colder than the one in my chest. "And for that, you must die."

"Then come and kill me, slave, if you can," she spits at me, flashing forward at inhuman speed.

I react with a soldier's instinct, doing what my instructors beat into me. I twist to the side, out of the way of her headlong rush, slashing my frozen blade in a horizontal strike meant to cut her in half. It feels too easy—fighting against someone who is strong but not trained to be a warrior.

Then I find out what her Symbol is, and it turns out that it is not an easy fight at all.

The *necromanta* lifts her right hand and flares her fingers as she dashes toward me. I only have a flash of insight from my knowledge of the frozen ground to warn me before I am skewered. I leap to the side, just in time to see a spike of rock burst from the ground where I stood, like the fang of some cave monster. If I had not moved, it would have speared me through my guts as easily as a *berserkir*'s blade.

Vixa lets out a roar of rage and sweeps her hand again, summoning a half dozen more lances from the ground that stab at me as I dance across the cave floor, narrowly avoiding their razor-sharp edges.

She must be some sort of earthbound. *What incredible power*, I think, jealous of my own comparative weakness. Her black veins must be the equivalent of at least a Silver, if not Gold, *electus*.

"Castor!" Marcus bellows, taking a few steps toward me, trying to help. I shake my head and wave him back. She would gut him like a pig. The only reason I'm not dead is the layer of ice and snow over the ground betraying her moves to my Ancient Frost–powered senses.

Screaming in frustration, Vixa presses her attack. My mind flares with panic as I sense a spike tunneling out of the wall next to me. I leap in front of it, sidestepping her second shard that stabs up from the ground below.

"How are you doing this?" she demands, running up one of the spears, using it to leap toward the tables on the far side. I do not reply and instead push forward, trying to catch her in the air while she is not touching the ground. She is too fast. She lands on the other side of the room, just out of my reach.

The ground beneath the ice rumbles, and this time, I am ready for it. I reach out with my will, hardening the ice above her spear. I feel the sharp point of her rocky lance shatter as it slams into the crust beneath my feet but fails to penetrate. Three more stalagmites surge toward me, and again I block their path. The essence cost is staggering, but I am drowning in it here in the *Domus* of Aquilo.

Vixa is panting with exertion, sweat running down her face despite the bitter cold. She clenches both of her fists, and a dozen spears launch at me. I block most of them and dodge the last two. She's so strong! I cannot keep this up forever, even with my unusual aptitude for drawing in essence.

Fortunately, the *necromanta* seems equally spent. Her connection to the ground is diluted by the ice, which must affect her own ability to cultivate. She stares at me with naked fear, aware that I am something that she doesn't understand, afraid that despite all the power she has stolen, she is about to die. With a wave, she conjures a wall of spikes from the ground between us, forming a wall. Momentarily out of my reach, she turns toward the tables, confident that she is safe from me.

Snarling with frustration, I hammer at the wall of stone blocking my path with the Frozen Blade. My will reinforces the weapon to be as hard as iron, and I shatter through them with the extra strength from my Copper *Cor*.

Vixa's head whips around in shock as she feels her constructs break. I'm stronger than she expected me to be, and I know she feels an echo of my power through her connection to the stone. She stands over her tools, scrambling to find something. For a horrible moment, I think she means to kill some of our comrades who still live, but she is only looking for a weapon. She grabs a pair of long, cruel knives and turns to face me.

"Come and die," she hisses.

"You first." I step forward to meet her, leaping off the ground in time to dodge two grasping hands of flowing earth that grab at my feet, seeking to hold me still. My prescience only makes her angrier. Her eyes are red, bloodshot with fury, and more of her veins are turning sickly green. Whatever she is, she isn't a true *electus*. The essence strain seems to be eating at her like a cancer.

I feint at her left side before twisting and driving my frozen *gladius* forward in a lunge at her gut. She whips one of her daggers around, catching the edge of my sword and forcing it wide while slashing at me with her other. I dance backward, leaning away from the attack as I bring my sword back to force her out of my range.

A low laugh echoes out of my throat as she retreats, and she tilts her head, confused by my amusement. I understand why she is puzzled. She doesn't know what I am. She doesn't know what her attack revealed.

"You mock me?" she rages, spittle beginning to form at the corner of her mouth. Maybe the practice of *necromantia* drives someone mad, or maybe they must be mad to begin it in the first place. "You are nothing. I have Ascended to heights you could never dream of. I have walked the ancient halls of long-dead gods, feasted on the greatest relics of this world, and lived for over three centuries." Her breath is ragged. Despite her accolades, I can tell she is almost spent.

"And yet, today is your last." The voice is my own now, cold and harsh. I feel something like a flash of amusement from the *animus* of Aquilo that hangs over our battle, watching like an Augur. I guess he is content with my offerings.

"Die a slave!" she screams, charging forward with her lightning-quick speed. But she is not faster than the knowledge of the Symbol of Ancient Frost. It shows me how she gathers her weight on her back foot before she springs forward. It traces her footsteps on my skin like kisses. I do not need to be as fast as her because she is already dead.

She leaps into a dive, one dagger extended to match my frozen *gladius* while she holds the other in reserve, waiting for its moment. I let her grapple with my sword, feeling the smile on my face grow as my ice meets her blade. If we were both normal *electii*, then that would be the end of it. But I am far from normal. Her weapon greets me eagerly, letting my *animus* flow into it unblocked, unprotected.

I am Ice. I am Iron. Together in me, the two things are bridged.

Shatter, I whisper with my will. Her Earth Symbol, while powerful, has little overlap in congruence with her weapon to shield it from me. She is not Legion. She is not Iron.

Vixa's dagger explodes into a thousand pieces, torn asunder by my command. I stagger slightly as I feel the essence pour out of me at an unsustainable rate. I have never used this much at once. The veins in my body burn as I push them to new heights. It does not matter—this fight is over.

The *necromanta*'s eyes go wide in shock as her weapon disintegrates. My *gladius* stabs forward, letting her impale herself on it as she shoots toward me. We stare at each other for a few beats, like a bride and groom at the altar. In a way, this moment is just as sacred, but it is an end, not a beginning. Vixa gurgles once, but no words come out of her mouth. I know what she wants to ask, but I shake my head. She will die without knowing my secrets. A dark red bubble bursts out of her mouth, and I pull the *Glacialis Falx* from her with a vicious wrench, spraying bright blood across the floor of the cave.

Vixa falls to the ground in a pile of limbs. She twitches violently several times but does not rise. I leave her there on the floor of the cave. For a moment, I stand over her body, watching as the life fades from her eyes. I feel no remorse but a morbid sense of curiosity to see such an ancient, wicked life end. What knowledge did she have that we will never recover? A shiver runs through me as I glance at her rotten veins. Maybe none of it was worth having in the first place.

Slowly, I become aware of the eyes on my back. I bow my head, taking another long breath, feeling the rush of energy that comes from restoring some of my essence before I turn to face my men. Marcus, Jasper, and Clintus stare at me with demanding eyes. Even Anas, who has regained some level of consciousness, is wide-eyed from where he slumps on the floor. Only Felix seems unsurprised—he nods slightly as if he has just had a guess confirmed.

"Later," I snap, hunching my shoulders against the accusation in their gazes. "First we survive, then story time." Yet another calculated risk I must take. If any of them decide to report me to the Censors, I'll be executed as soon as we return to the empire. At least then I could join my family.

"Armor up," I command, pointing at the pile of *loricae* and *gladii* waiting for us. "We don't know how soon the barbarians will come to check on her. Get Clintus into his first. The Iron should help." The men move to follow my orders while I turn to Anas, who is still reeling from Vixa's strength.

"You alive?" I demand, holding my hand out to the brute. He stares at it for a moment, and I cannot tell if it is because he is deciding whether to slap it away or if his brains are addled and he isn't sure what it is.

"I will be; just get me in my kit," he promises after a moment and grabs my wrist with a strong grip. I pull the former *captivus* to his feet. He staggers slightly but finds his footing and makes his way toward the rest of the men.

A series of pins prick up and down my spine like spider steps, building in intensity until I cannot ignore them. I do not need to be a priest to know that this is the gentle whisper of an impatient god. I turn to look at Vixa's cooling body, reminded of the exact terms of my *votum* to Aquilo.

Feed her bones to the deep dark of my caves.

I barely manage to hold back a sigh. To do that requires that we go in the opposite direction that we want to travel. I do not know how I will explain this to the men, but I hope that they will obey me. I will not allow Aquilo to break free of the prison that Frigidus made for him, even if it costs my own life.

Shaking myself, I rush to join them in pulling on a set of armor. Once again, I'm struck by the efficiency of the Iron Legions. The *lorica* that I shrug over my shoulders is not my original one—judging by the width of its shoulders, it belonged to Marcus. But thanks to my Symbol, it is a simple matter to adjust it to fit my frame. In moments, we are battle ready.

My original *Cor* surges with joy as I am reunited with iron. I feel whole again. Having access to only one of my Symbols' essences felt like I was full but dying of thirst. At last, I am properly sated.

"Check on them," I order, pointing at our brothers still on the tables. Some of them are dead—poor Petrus is lying in too many angles to be anything but—but Antony was alive, so maybe some of the others' souls still clung to their bodies.

As my men rush to aid their brethren, I make my way toward Vixa, gritting my teeth as I reach out grab one of her wrists. Her skin is cold and slimy, like something I would expect to find under a rotting log. Her presence assaults me as if it could infect me from a simple touch. I shudder, but do not release the *necromanta*. I made an oath and am bound to see it through.

"Castor." I glance up from my grisly task to see Felix looking at me with somber eyes.

"Anything?" I release Vixa and trot over to my tall friend's side. Haxus and Lintus are gone; they're stiff and pale. The *Cor* veins on Matinius's dark arms have begun to fade to gray as they fill with the cold of death—I recognize its presence at once. It is a cousin of Ancient Frost, one of the few things older and colder.

"Antony has a pulse," Felix tells me grimly, "but he's unconscious. He's lost a lot of blood." I gaze down at our friend, feeling a profound sense of loss. There is nothing we can do for him. I wish he was already dead, if only to assuage my guilt. There is no way we can bring him with us, and I have a responsibility to the living.

"Dress him in his *lorica* as best you can, and put a *gladius* in his hand," I say after a long moment. "We can give him a chance at least. If his Symbol helps him heal, maybe we can rescue him on our way out."

"What do you mean 'on our way out'?" Jasper asks, eyes narrowing in suspicion. "The way out is right in front of us."

"And we cannot take it yet," I tell him, shaking my head somberly.

"Are you insane?" Anas hisses, taking an aggressive step toward me. "We have iron and are free, and you don't want to flee?"

"And go where?" I challenge, looking the dangerous man in the eyes. "The cave exit literally empties into the middle of the High King's camp. There's no way for us to walk out of here without barging right into the entire barbarian horde. Several of us won't ever pass for Normans." I cast a significant glance at Marcus and Jasper, whose complexions are both far darker than any of the fair-skinned barbarians.

"True." Marcus chuckles grimly.

"Especially now, in broad *daylight*." The men shift uncomfortably as they recognize the wisdom in my words.

"But why go that way?" Felix points deeper into the cavern.

"We don't know when someone might come to check on the *necromanta*'s work. If we take her body and go deeper, we might avoid alerting any suspicion until night falls. Then we can try to escape under the cover of darkness." The men are silent and exchange reluctant glances. Even Marcus looks worried about venturing away from the exit. For a moment, I worry they will mutiny and refuse to follow my command. I may be a decurion, but I am not an officer whose opinion they truly respect. Most of these men have known me since I was a child.

It is Anas who breaks first. He grunts in irritation, shifting his shoulders before he nods once. "Let's get moving, then. No point in waiting around here to get caught." The three other men agree, reluctance clear on their faces.

"Good," I say as if I never had any doubts in their obedience. Bending down, I grab Vixa's corpse by the leg, avoiding her flesh, and begin to drag her behind me. "Let's go see what the Normans are looking for."

CHAPTER 46

The cavern twists as we make our way deeper into Aquilo's home. It must be cold, but the Symbol of Ancient Frost shelters me from its bitter chill. My men huddle in their coats, rubbing their arms against their chests to generate warmth. Clintus is able to keep up now that he can lean on Iron again. His face is still drawn and tight, but he can kill the pain enough to be mobile.

Since I have sworn his *votum*, the God of Winter no longer objects to me using my *Cor* Heart in his domain. I sweep my *animus* ahead of us, searching for any Normans lying in ambush. I find none, but there are signs of their presence everywhere we go.

Scaffolding reinforces much of the roof and walls, and we pass piles of lumber and rope that have been stacked in an orderly fashion. *Lumos* relics shine in the walls, a remnant from when priests of the empire must have come to this place to pay obeisance to Aquilo. I've never seen so many in one place. I shudder to think how many lives were given to illuminate this temple.

"Well, at least we won't get lost," Anas grumbles from the back of the group. "It's just a bloody straight line."

"Yeah," pants Clintus. "It could be worse." Dry chuckles run through the group at his humor.

"Silver linings, I guess," Felix murmurs in agreement, but his voice is thoughtful, skeptical. I remember hearing the same tone when we were *discipuli* and he was trying to solve a complex question from the magisters.

Thanks to my knowledge, I can sense that the winding tunnel begins to expand before we can see it. As we draw closer and my awareness grows, I begin to divine the breadth of a massive antechamber. This is where the barbarians have clearly spent most of their time. The icy ground is scarred where it has been broken by picks. My skin itches as I feel the bite of the iron tools digging into it. Even now they carve into this frozen place, searching for something.

I feel as though I am walking on a grave. Well, in one sense, that is true—a god *was* killed here, or rather, mostly killed. But that is not the death that I feel as I follow the path of my ancestors. It is a bigger death. This is where peace is buried. The Normans are digging it up, and once they find it, we will only know war. I am alone as I walk with the other legionnaires. We are together, but I am the only one who knows what this place is. Even so, the rest of my men are somber, cowed by the presence that lurks here.

We turn the bend, and my jaw drops at the sight of the room that waits for us. It is so massive that my *animus* cannot stretch across it. I knew that the expanse we were about to enter was big, but this is something beyond my wildest dreams. A vaulted ceiling rises several stories above us, and thick support beams made of deep blue ice jut down to the surface. Murals depicting Aquilo in many different ways are etched into the entire span of the roof. I see him old and young, as snow and as the wind. The whole thing makes Vulcan's Forge look like a wild animal's den by comparison.

"Dead gods, what is this place?" Felix breathes in horror from my side, gazing around in wild shock.

"You're closer than you know," I can't resist replying. I lead the men into the temple, still dragging Vixa's body behind me. I can feel Aquilo's presence beaming with delight at our approach. His *animus* is still heavy, but there is a gentleness to it that was not present before. We are welcome guests, not interlopers.

The rest of the cavern has fallen into disrepair since Aquilo's death. Many of the great columns of ice that run up to the ceiling are shattered. Perhaps some of them were broken by Frigidus and the rest of the *Ferrum Domini* when they came to strike down a god. Over the centuries, ice and snow have built up in drifts taller than a man.

Lights shine from all over, but many have gone out, leaving pools of darkness in between their warmth. At the far end of the temple, a massive work site looms. Bonfires burn all around it, illuminating the giant pile of scaffolding that a dozen Normans scramble over, digging at the ice with their picks.

"What in Jupiter's name are the barbarians doing?" Marcus asks, peering at them in the distance.

"Looking for a weapon," I say with certainty. The other men look at me sharply, startled by my confidence. "Why else would their High King be here, sending his people to dig in the cold dark unless he could find something to make him stronger?" I challenge. "You heard Vixa— this is where *furia* are made. What are they but weapons?"

"Frigidus protect us," intones Clintus in a horrified whisper. "Do you think that's what they're doing right now?" Aquilo's presence pulls on me like an eager hound on its lead, desperate for me to finish my journey.

"Well," I murmur, glancing down at the *gladius* in my right hand, relishing the feel of being back with my iron. It was my first Symbol, and I felt its absence like a gaping wound. "Why don't we find out?"

"Castor..." Felix begins, sounding wary.

"There are only a few of them," I cut him off urgently, turning to look at my tall friend. "They're probably not armed if they're working."

"So? Why would we risk exposing ourselves? Isn't the whole point of being down here to *hide*?" Marcus asks the question everyone else is thinking. "We should go hide behind some of those pillars in the dark and wait for them to leave."

"Or we kill them, take their clothing, and walk right out of here dressed as Normans," I counter, tilting my head and giving him a savage smile. "The *lorica* is kind of hard to miss."

"Anas, where are you going?" Jasper demands in a hushed whisper as the burly man begins walking toward the construction site.

"That's the best plan I've heard yet," he calls over his shoulder. Felix only shakes his head in silent disagreement, but he follows the rest as we catch up to the former *captivus*.

"What are your orders, *Dominus*?"

"Anas, take Clintus and set up an ambush for any who try to escape." I gesture ahead of us. "We can't let any of them get out of the cavern to sound the alarm."

"I'll take the lame horse," the burly man agrees. "No survivors."

"Jasper, Marcus, Felix, and I will split up and attack from two directions at once. We hit them fast before they have a chance to organize."

"All right," Felix agrees with a deep sigh. He doesn't like this move, but he knows that everyone else has accepted my leadership. "I hope you know what you're doing."

"We'll find out," I snap at him. The stress is eating at me, even if he thinks it isn't. This is different than fighting in a skirmish on the training fields of Agogia. Some of us might die based on my orders. Some of us already have. But I know that if I do nothing, all of us will, and that alone gives me the confidence to act. Well, that and the demanding presence of Aquilo, which hovers over us hungrily, focused on Vixa's corpse.

I drag her with me as we cross the massive floor of the cavern. A couple of the men eye me with concern, wondering why I haven't ditched her body in a pool of shadow. I ignore their glances. They wouldn't believe me if I tried to tell them the truth. The temple is so grand, it takes more than five minutes to cross it. As we draw close, I finally drop Vixa's body, promising the presence around us that I will come back for her.

We move from cover to cover, hiding behind shattered pillars and snow dunes to spy on the Normans. They are completely ignorant of our presence. There are no sentries posted to watch over them while they work. Why would there be? We are deep at the bottom of a cavern whose entrance is protected by an entire army. There should be no safer place for these barbarians.

Ancient Frost essence comes to me easily. The snow and frost have been here a long time, undisturbed. The permafrost that pervades the North is old, but this is even older still, making it a closer match for my Symbol.

I motion for Jasper and Marcus to circle to the left while keeping Felix with me. He may not like my plan, but I trust him to watch my back once the fighting actually starts. Together, we work our way to the right, staying in the shadows.

This close, we can see what the workers are doing, and a chill floods through me that not even the Symbol of Ancient Frost can keep at bay. The scaffolding centers around a giant lump of ice where the room ends. Beyond it is a sheer drop filled with an encompassing darkness. I know at a glance that this is where Aquilo wants me to throw Vixa's body.

Three stone altars carved with glowing runes are laid out before the massive frozen mound. On each one lies a figure made of ice, pieced together by chunks that the workers have harvested from this very room. A man and woman dressed in furs that cover them from hood to toe march around the forms, swirling censers full of smoke while chanting in a language I do not know.

A third shaman, a grizzled old man, naked save for a loincloth, raises a lump of white metal in two hands to the ceiling. I would know it anywhere. It is the same thing that twists through my body. Felix and I exchange an understanding glance. This is how *furia* are made.

He lowers the *Cor* and gestures to a much younger blonde woman who watches from the side. She approaches the first stone altar and kneels at its head, lowering her head and bowing her eyes. I watch with bated breath, transfixed by the scene unfolding before me. Suddenly, the woman looks up and produces a long knife from under her furs. With a scream of defiance, she slashes it across her left hand and holds it upward, letting the blood pool in the palm.

The shaman walks forward toward her and bows to stare at her blood with intense scrutiny. After a moment, he inhales deeply as if smelling it. Apparently satisfied, he stands up straight before dipping the shimmering metal in her blood and turning back toward the not-yet-finished *furia*.

Again, he raises the *Cor* into the air before smashing it down onto the chest of the lifeless ice golem. The liquid metal passes through it without resistance, just as it did when it sank into my own skin.

Horror blooms in me as the ice construct shudders to life, or some approximation of it. Its limbs twitch, and the *Cor* inundates it, filling it with its power. When the metamorphosis is complete, it rises to its feet. The massive thing towers above the kneeling woman in absolute stillness, waiting for something.

A long, tense moment passes as the shaman and his companions watch the interaction closely, like magisters judging *discipuli* during the Ritual of the Heart. Eventually, they are satisfied. The man in the loincloth barks a command, and the woman's head comes up to look at the *furia* for the first time.

She stands and, with a bright smile, snaps a command at the thing. Without hesitation, it lumbers forward to stand beside her, like a faithful hound. The blonde woman claps her hands in delight, and even the grizzled shaman smiles in satisfaction.

I tear my gaze away from the ritual to look again at the massive frozen structure behind them. Workers swarm over it, digging at it with their picks. They did not pause even when the *furia* was being created. If anything, they seem to have increased their pace. I reach for the Symbol of Ancient Frost, sending my *animus* sweeping toward it, wondering what about it commands their attention.

A resonance slams into me hard enough to make me stagger as I gain knowledge of the miniature glacier. It is like an echo that begins within my own mind, shaking me violently. I grunt, dropping to my knees and releasing the Symbol, desperate to get the vibrations out of my head. In a moment, they fade. I do not know what is causing this resistance, but I dare not use my power this far into the depths of the cave, lest it tear me apart from the inside out.

It must have something to do with what the barbarians are mining. Studying the block of ice more closely, I glimpse the rounded edge of something white and massive just beneath the surface, and panic fills me. That can only be the real skull of Aquilo, the mostly dead God of Winter. No wonder he is so upset that his home has been infested. They are literally robbing his grave for power.

You begin to see, Ovicula, the dead god's voice seems to whisper in my skull from where he watches.

"Castor, if we're going to do this, we should not wait until they make more of them," Felix whispers urgently. I look from the god's bones to where my friend points. The priests have moved to the second unborn *furia* to begin the ceremony again.

"Mars's Ashes! You're right. Come on." I slide out of the shadows with my gladius in my right hand, staying low as I stalk forward. The last time we faced a *furia*, I was able to break it thanks to the Symbol of Ancient Frost, but Percy had been the only one who was otherwise able to crack its icy armor. If I can't use my cold power, I'm not sure how we can possibly stand up to the creature without our *Fidelis*.

I hear Felix's footsteps as he follows. Together, we move quickly, relying on the barbarians' comfort to let us get close. There should be no wolves this deep, the sheep thought, but they were wrong. Without my connection to the cold, my footing is not as sure. I stumble into a chunk of ice, knocking it free. It clatters from the top of one of the frozen dunes, echoing throughout the massive chamber. With a curse, I spring forward, not willing to lose the element of surprise.

The shaman turns, curious at the source of the noise. In his hands, he holds another lump of *Cor*. It slides from his fingers to crash on the frozen ground as he stiffens in shock at the sight of us. He gapes silently for a moment, stunned beyond words at the sight of two Iron Legionnaires running at him with their swords drawn.

We're too far away to kill him before he can raise the alarm. I surge forward, pumping my legs as fast as they can go, shrinking the distance between me and my prey. The shaman recovers from his fear enough to shout a warning to the rest of his party. The others turn to follow his finger, screaming in terror at the sight of us.

Cries of alarm spread through the cavern, echoing like the calls of ravens. I know the workers will come to investigate swiftly, which leaves me only one course of action. I close the final few paces to the frozen shaman and leap into the air, extending my *gladius* like a spear.

He screams as my blade takes him through the chest—then goes flying as I slam into him at full speed. The difference in our mass is already significant before factoring in my *lorica*, and he careens backward into one of the stone altars. I ignore him, turning toward the priestess on the right, trusting Felix to cover my left.

The woman does not suffer from the same hesitation. She charges at me, swinging her smoking censer like a flail. I lean to the side as the sphere shoots past my head like a missile before she yanks it back on its iron chain.

I cluck my tongue in disappointment at the sight of my favorite metal. Her priestly tool can double as a makeshift mace, but it will not help her against an Ironbound like me. She gathers the slack of her censer up, spinning it loosely in her right hand, watching me with crazed eyes. I feint forward, and she shoots it at my head again, throwing it with incredible strength.

I sidestep the attack, slashing my *gladius* at her chain. The Symbol of Iron blazes as I channel my will into the edge of my blade. Knowledge floods me of her weapon as my blade touches it. *Shatter*, I whisper. The links explode without a hint of resistance, and her smoking sphere sails off into the room behind us.

The priestess's eyes widen in shock and stay that way as I whip my *gladius* around, cutting through her neck with one blow. Her body falls one way and her head another as she crumples to the ground. Shouts of anger sound from the work site. Marcus and Jasper must have struck in the wake of our confusion.

I glance to my left in time to see Felix dispatch the other shaman. My friend's head snaps toward me, checking to make sure I'm alive. I wave at him to join me, but then my vision of him is obscured by a moving wall of ice.

The newly made *furia* charges me at the behest of its minder. I drop to a roll, ducking under its massive fist as it hurtles through the space I just occupied. Cursing myself for being careless, I release some of the Iron Symbol to make room for Ancient Frost.

This close to Aquilo's bones, the resonance immediately begins to shake through me, and I push it away, loosening my grip until I barely hold any of it. I'll need as much of it as I can bear if I am going to defeat the *furia*.

It presses its attack, goaded on by screams of rage from the woman bound to it. I retreat, keeping its attention focused on me. Like the one in the glade, it is big and powerful, but not particularly agile. I have just enough of Ancient Frost humming in me to guide my feet as I walk backward, confident in my footsteps.

As I flee, my mind scrambles for a solution to our problems. I don't bother trying to hammer it with attacks—I know that I lack the strength to break through its shell. If I must, I can distract this thing for a long time, but we are outnumbered. Even if the *furia* only takes me out of the fight instead of smashing me into little bits, it still prevents me from helping Felix as he battles with a worker who swings a pick at him like a war hammer. If my men don't win the larger skirmish, eventually, I will have to deal with more enemies.

Over the thing's icy shoulder, I spot two more workers sprinting off into the giant cavern, rushing to get help. I resist the urge to shout a warning to my waiting men as they flee. I must trust Anas and Clintus to be ready to do their job. If they escape, we are dead.

But their flight gives me an idea. I was able to hold more of Ancient Frost's power when I was further away from Aquilo's frozen mausoleum. If I can lure the *furia* far enough away from the god's bones, I might be able to deal with it.

I twist my course, pulling the thing in the direction that the other barbarians fled. It lumbers after me, lowering its head and charging like a *rhinoceros*. I leap to the side, letting it career past me. It smashes into one of the ruined pillars but turns quickly, unbothered by the ice. The woman screams a command in the northern tongue, trying to get it to circle me and force me back toward the work site.

She sees me looking at her and backs up a dozen paces, keeping me well out of striking range. I give her a smile full of teeth, acknowledging that she guessed what I was thinking. A horse with no rider is much less of a threat.

Again, the *furia* stumbles after me, and I fall back, watching it closely. We fade back into the darker parts of Aquilo's ruined home, but I don't need light to know where I am going in the cold. The sounds of battle have faded a little as we progress further away.

Tentatively, I tighten my grip on Ancient Frost, letting its cold fury fill me. The resonance hums threateningly, but I can hold more than I could at the base of the work site. I can feel the god's gift roiling under my skin, desperate to get out. I try to summon the *Glacialis Falx*, but the vibrations build, and I release it, unable to hold enough of my power yet.

Gritting my teeth, I continue falling back, knowing that every step I take adds more distance that I will have to transverse to get back to my men. I pass another column and keep my face expressionless as I feel a hint of movement whispered to me by Ancient Frost. I lock my gaze on the *furia*, putting all my concentration on dodging its attacks.

The construct lumbers past the pillar, and I leap backward as one of its fists smashes down on the ground in front of me. I lick my lips but do not look away, drawing it deeper into the dark. We continue to dance, and step by step, I lead it further into the ambush.

Slowly, its minder follows, staying close enough to watch but far enough to be well out of my reach. She passes the column, hooked like a fish on the line. As she crosses its shadow, my glance flicks from the *furia* to her. She pauses in wary paranoia, ready to run if I charge at her. But it is not me that she needs to fear.

Anas rises from the darkness behind her and steps forward, stabbing his *gladius* through her back in three savage thrusts like a back-alley cutthroat. He cups a hand over her mouth to muffle her screams as he lowers her body to the ground. He moves to follow us, to try to hound at the thing's heels, but I wave him off. There's nothing he can do against it. We cannot risk any Normans escaping while we're both distracted. He nods and slinks back into the cavern, hunting.

Her death's effect on the *furia* is immediate. It staggers as if dealt a heavy blow to the back of its skull. Slowly, it rights itself, keeping its gaze locked on me. It may not have a master to give it orders any longer, but it still intends to fulfill her final command.

I pull it further into the open area of the vault. Dodging its strikes is easier now that it's lost some of its earlier speed and aggression. As I distract it, I probe the Symbol of Ancient Frost, testing how much interference it experiences as I get further from Aquilo's frozen corpse.

Halfway back to the tunnel we entered from, I feel the god's overbearing physical presence fade and the resonance vanishes. I'm out of range of its disruption. I take a few more steps to give me some room to work with and wait. A dark smile grows on my face as I settle into a ready stance.

The *furia* takes my bait, thundering at me with heavy steps that shake the icy ground beneath my feet. I pass my *gladius* to my left hand and grab the Symbol of Ancient Frost firmly, calling on the *Glacialis Falx* to summon its icy twin in my right. The essence cost is heavy, but I draw deeply from the frozen room around us. It takes a score of heartbeats before the ice manifests in my hand, forming the cold sword.

I stalk forward, breaking into a sprint as I rush to meet its head-on charge. The construct doesn't react. It has no curiosity about why I have suddenly changed tactics, only a single directive—*smash the legionnaire*. As I enter its range, it draws back a massive fist to obey its orders, and I cut to the left, striking with my Frozen Blade as we shoot past each other.

Knowledge of the icy construct blooms in me as my blade touches it, and its frozen skin resists the edge of my sword, but I insist, pouring my will into the sharp edge, commanding it to cut. After a heartbeat, the *furia's* resistance crumbles, and my weapon slices through it with ease.

I plant my left foot and spin, turning to watch as its arm falls to the ground, shattering under the impact. The *furia* pauses, processing its missing limb before coming around to face me. For a moment, we stare at each other, and a chill runs through me. I know it is only a construct, but I feel its gaze as it studies me. What are these abominations the barbarians have made?

As one, we spring forward, triggered by the same imperceptible clue. I angle myself toward its armless side, staying out of its reach, but it has learned. As we draw close, it screeches to a halt and spins, extending its single arm like a mace. I drop into a slide, calling on Ancient Frost to make the ground beneath me slick. I can feel the veins in my body surge, fed by the rich essence here. My new Symbol grows within me, working toward Ascension.

The *furia's* massive limb *whooshes* overhead, and I feel the wind of its passage on my hair as it goes by. Still gliding across the ground, I extend my Frozen Blade and cut at its thigh as I careen past. Again, it resists my attack, but its will fades before my authority. My sword eagerly slices through, and I hear the construct collapse as I slide past.

I stop coasting, rising to my feet and jogging a few steps to bleed off my momentum before turning to survey my handiwork. The *furia* is on the ground, missing an arm and a leg. It glares at me with its black eyes, trying to crawl in my direction to finish its final directive.

Slowly, I pace around it, careful to stay out of range of its remaining limbs. Blazing with victory, I dash forward, stabbing down with my blade into its head. The point of my icy blade sticks for a moment, caught by its final act of defiance, but I grit my teeth and channel my will into the tip, making it sharper than a thought.

Slowly, it cuts through the construct's thick forehead. I feel the ice shudder under my assault as it gives way. Then, with a loud *crack*, the *furia's* last bit of strength fails, and my sword punches through its skull, burying itself to the hilt.

At once, the construct goes limp, and as I watch, it begins to crumble like a rotting corpse. Chunks fall off it in a rain, littering the ground around us. In a matter of heartbeats, the *furia* is no more—just a mound of ice that did not live up to its potential.

Gasping for breath, I turn to the sound of fighting that still wages from the work site. The battle is not yet done. With a sigh, I release the Symbol of Ancient Frost, tossing the Frozen Blade to the ground next to the ice, where it decays in a similar fashion.

I pass my iron *gladius* to my right hand and break into a run. My men need me. There are more barbarians to kill.

CHAPTER 47

With the *furia* destroyed, we finish off the rest of the workers quickly. They fight to the death—whether that is because they are fearless or because they know we cannot risk letting them live, I do not know. They are brave but not equipped for battle. There are no *berserkirs* here to protect them from Ironbound like us. The last man dies on the point of Marcus's blade, cursing us as his sledgehammer falls from limp fingers.

An awful silence falls upon the cold expanse of Aquilo's home. It is harsh, but this place is the origin of winter—it has no warmth to give.

I take stock of my men. Jasper and Clintus both bleed from new wounds, but they seem minor. Marcus has a limp, but he shrugs when I give him a questioning look.

"Thanks for the help," I tell Anas as the burly man approaches. I hold out my forearm to him in an offering. He stares at a moment before clasping it with his own. We are not enemies anymore. We haven't been for a while. But this is a formal acceptance of that truth.

"Just doing my job, *Dominus.*" I nod and release him from my grip. I don't need to push it. Not now.

"What in Hades's name is this thing?" Felix asks, staring at the frozen obelisk that the workers had been chipping at. "Some sort of icon for a frost Symbol?" He steps close, peering into the distorted depths. "There's something in there."

"It's the corpse of Aquilo." I don't know why I tell them the truth. I should lie. They won't believe me, and I don't want to explain how I know.

"Truly?" Felix turns to look at me with a pair of raised eyebrows. I blink at his acceptance but nod once.

"Dead gods," he whispers, raising a hand toward the ice but stopping himself from touching it. "I guess Frigidus really did kill him."

"I think he tried." I narrow my eyes at the edge of the skull I can see, imagining those glowing yellow orbs that filled it when the god spoke to me. "I'm not sure it's so simple."

The men look at me in surprise for my blasphemy. I can feel their eyes from all around. I shrug, gesturing at the stone tables where the *furia* are made. "There's still some power here. Even the barbarians can feel it." Their attention is diverted, and I shake myself to get rid of the existential thoughts that haunt me. We have survived the battle, but we have much more work to do if we are going to escape.

"Marcus, take two men and smash those tables." He looks at me in surprise. "We are still soldiers of the Iron Legions," I remind them. "We have a chance to ruin our enemy's ability to make one of their greatest weapons. We should take it." My friend nods and motions to Jasper and Anas to follow him.

"Felix, Clintus, find us disguises." I gesture at the fur-clad bodies all around us. "There should be enough for us all. Once you've stripped them of their supplies, toss the bodies in the hole."

"What are you going to be doing?" Felix asks, his eyes narrowed.

"The same thing," I lie.

It's not really a lie. I will help them find clothing for all of us. But first, I will appease a dead god. I return to Vixa's corpse, dragging her the rest of the way to the edge of the cliff. This close to Aquilo's body, I don't need to touch the Symbol of Ancient Frost to feel his presence. My skin buzzes with his similar power, and I clamp my jaw shut to keep my teeth from chattering together.

I pause, gazing into the abyss that stretches before me. I can barely make out the faint edges of the far side of the cave in the darkness. This chasm could swallow my entire family's estate in a single bite. I cannot see the bottom; it seems to go on for eternity.

I study the *necromanta* briefly, disturbed by how the black of her metal veins matches the same color of the void that stretches before me. My spine tickles as Aquilo's presence urges me to complete my oath. Grunting in exertion, I tug at her corpse, using my Copper strength to throw her off the edge. She spins as she falls and is swallowed by the blackness.

Immediately, Aquilo's impatience fades, sated by my obedience, but it does not vanish. There is still one more task that I must complete. Instead, it curls up in the corner of my mind like a cat. Watching. Waiting.

I shiver and turn away from the deep, joining the rest of my men in cleaning up the aftermath. Marcus, Anas, and Jasper grunt as they hammer at the altars with the very tools the Normans provided. The incomplete *furia* shatter easily, and the stone only lasts a little while under the sustained assault from three Ironbound. The first one breaks with a sharp *crack* that echoes through the cavern like a curse. Jasper and Anas pulverize theirs a few moments later, and the deed is done. I suspect the barbarians will be able to replace them. It would be too easy if this were the end of their *furiae*, but I hope that it takes a long time and is expensive.

We dress in the thick, brown furs that we collected from our opponents, pulling them over our *loricae* to hide them. I study my men with a dour chuckle. None of us are pale and blond enough to pass for a true Norman, but at night and with our hoods up, it might work.

"Okay, *Dominus*," Anas asks when the work is done. "What next?" It's weird to hear him show me respect without sounding sarcastic. I turn away so he doesn't see the surprise in my eyes.

"We hide." I gesture at the ruins around us. "Wait for it to be dark and then walk right out the front of the cave."

"And when the people we killed don't come back up to the surface when their shift is over?" Felix challenges. "That will cause some sort of alarm, surely."

"It was morning when we were brought here," I point out. "Right now, it should be full daylight, and there's no way we make it a hundred paces before someone realizes we aren't Norman."

"I don't think we'd make it fifty," Marcus chuckles dryly, gesturing at himself and Jasper. I toss them both a spare hood from the pile of clothes to cover their heads. Every little bit will help us make it further out of the cave before we're discovered.

"So, we either rush out and die or wait and maybe don't die." I shrug. "I'm open to a better plan if you have one."

Felix frowns, turning to look around the vault. After a moment, he shrugs in defeat. "If I come up with one, I will let you know," he promises.

We make a little makeshift camp nestled between several massive chunks that fell from the ceiling eons ago. The six of us huddle together, short on space and warmth. The moment we settle, I feel exhaustion begin to sweep over me in waves. The barbarians marched us overnight after chasing us through the woods. I am spent, and a glance at the rest of my men tells me they are the same. My stomach rumbles as I realize how long it's been since I last ate.

"Here," Clintus murmurs, passing me a leather sack that he took from one of the dead workers. I reach inside and pull out some sort of cured meat. Delighted, I jam it in my mouth before passing it to

Marcus. It's dry and gamey—venison perhaps—but my body rejoices as I swallow.

"We'll set a watch," I announce when I finish chewing. The men nod in agreement as they partake in our meager stores. "Who is the most awake?"

"I am," Marcus offers at once. He looks exhausted, but I trust him to be responsible.

"There's no *Sol* or *Luna* down here," I remind him. "Count to five hundred four times, then wake the next man."

"Why don't I just count to two thousand?"

"If you can do that without losing count, you're welcome to." The big man grins, his bright smile erasing the exhaustion on his face for a moment. "Five hundred four times it is."

"That's what I thought." I lie back against one of the stones, closing my eyes and letting the welcoming darkness sweep over me. The last thing I murmur before it takes me is, "If you will excuse me, your officer needs to get some sleep."

"*Dominus.*" A soft voice rips me from my slumber as a hand shakes my shoulder. I jerk awake, sitting upright as everything comes crashing back into me. It feels like I have only been asleep for a second. Exhaustion still pulls at me, trying to hold me down, but fear helps me pull free of its grasp.

"Shhh," Felix commands, crouching next to me. The rest of the men are awake, watching us with grim expressions. "They're here." The tall man motions for me to follow him, and together we peek over the ridge of one of the boulders sheltering us.

A group of about a dozen Normans has emerged from the tunnel that leads to the entrance and is making their way through the vault, torches held high. They are moving at a casual pace, their laughter echoing to us as they head toward the work site. It's the next shift, and they have not yet realized that something is wrong.

"Fortuna's Ashes," I snarl as they head further in. My mind is scrambling to form a plan. We have only a few moments to act before the choices will be taken from us. "How long were we asleep?" I glance at the rest of them.

"It's been hours," Clintus offers after they look at one another.

"Hours?" I scowl. "Why did no one wake me?"

"Need you fresh, *Dominus*," Marcus drawls, gesturing at the group of Normans. "We all agreed. Now what do we do?"

"Could it be dark?" Everyone shrugs, uncomfortable with judging the amount of time that has passed. I grimace as I try to make a decision. Responsibility grinds me like a gristmill, tearing at me and trying to rend me asunder. I exhale slowly, trying to let the tension bleed out of me as I plan.

We only have two real choices: fight or run. We could ambush this group of workers like we did the last time and kill them, perhaps buying us enough time to slip out once it is dark. But when the first shift didn't return to the surface, someone was bound to notice and come to investigate.

Or we could run now and slip out before the Normans figure out something is wrong and return to the surface to report it. If we time it right, we might slip out into the camp perfectly and get lost in the crowds. Anyone who sees us emerge might think we were the relieved workers, coming back up for air.

I eye my men with a commander's gaze. They're tired, hungry, and on edge. The workers are not armed for battle, but every time we fight, we use up more of our energy. It's too much risk for too little of a reward. No, it's time for us to roll the dice and see if we can escape.

"Come on," I whisper, rising to my feet. My body aches in protest, but I grab both of my Symbols, feeding the pain to Iron and letting Ancient Frost guide my feet as I begin to make my way through the dark. "We're getting out of here."

It's easy enough to slip past the workers. They are relaxed as they head to work, confident in their safety down here in the center of their High King's power. I lead the men from ice pile to pillar, staying out of their line of sight until we are behind them.

As they draw near to the work site, I abandon all pretense of hiding and motion for my men to follow. The six of us slip into the entrance of the tunnel as alarmed shouts begin to echo behind us. I understand their confusion. The bodies are missing, but there is still plenty of blood. It's clear that violence was done there, but I can only hope the mystery will slow them down.

We race through the tunnel. Clintus is still slower than the rest of us, but being reunited with Iron has sped up his healing so that he's no longer hobbling. We circle back upward, past the *lumos* relics, and with every turn, my stress builds. This needs to be perfect for us to pull it off, and so many of the pieces are out of our control. I do not even know what time it is.

I say a prayer to dead Mars, asking him to watch over his legionnaires. I don't think it will help, but it makes me feel a little better.

We burst into the chamber where Vixa did her cursed work, and I draw up short. Attendants have been here, cleaning up after her. The tables that held the bodies of our friends are empty. There is no sign of Antony. I feel sick at the thought of their corpses in the hands of another *necromanta*. Percy ordered me to get my men home. I can't help the dead ones, but I can still save the rest.

Marcus shares a grim look with me but doesn't comment. Together, we lead the group forward, heading for the surface. As we round the bend, I pull my hood up over my head, trying to hide my dark hair. I hear the rustle of metal as they follow my lead.

We're close now.

We round the final bend, and I gasp in relief. *Sol* has begun to set, casting long shadows across the camp in the valley. It's not true nightfall yet, but it has begun to grow dark. I motion for the men to follow, and together we emerge from the ground back in the realm of the High King.

My heart pounds as I take my first steps. It takes every ounce of self-control not to reach for the hilt of my *gladius* tucked under the bottom of my furs. I feel naked without my *scutum*. A few Normans glance in our direction, but no one accosts us as we march purposefully into the tents. And why should they? A new shift of workers has just gone down into Aquilo's grave. It only makes sense that some would come up to take a rest.

We move with purpose, threading our way past clusters of tents laid out without the precision of a legion encampment. With every passing moment, my confidence begins to build. Our disguises are good enough. In a moment, the other workers will come running up and pandemonium will break loose, giving us an opportunity to escape.

"Where is everyone?" Felix murmurs loud enough for me to hear. I glare over my shoulder, reminding him to keep quiet. The last thing we need is for a Norman to overhear us speaking the Imperial tongue. He shakes his head, gesturing at the tents around us.

I follow his hand, feeling a new sense of dread. He's right—the camp does feel like a ghost town. When the *berserkir* dragged us to meet the High King, there were warriors everywhere. Now there were only a few lonely individuals making their way about the camp. My concern spikes as I realize that I have not seen a single *furia*. I turn back to exchange glances with the men, whose faces share my concern. Where have they all gone?

Memory of Aquilo's vision flares in my mind. I see the Twelfth fleeing before the Normans who hound them, being driven right into an even larger host. The winter god told me the truth. I close my eyes for a moment, trying to remember everything I can about what he showed me.

There's a branch of the valley toward the southeast that the hunters were pushing Gaius and the rest of the cohort toward. Once there, our brothers will be unable to flee when the High King and the rest of his army march to pin them in the narrow pass from the front. There is only one way they might escape, but I doubt they will find it without the knowledge Aquilo gave me. My skin pricks as the god's *votum* pulls at me, reminding me of my second task. It's clear where I must head.

"We need to go that way." I gesture where the fight will happen.

"But, Castor, Frigidus is south," Felix protests with an exasperated tone, pointing over my shoulder. "Why would we go any other direction?"

"Because that is where Tribune Gaius and the rest of the cohort are," I announce. Silence greets my words as the men exchange glances. I'm pushing their faith too far. They know I am different; I have done things I should not have been able to. But that could be a trick. Perhaps I have discovered that Iron and Ice are congruent because both can be cold. That would be believable. But knowing the Twelfth's location from miles away beggars their belief.

"Castor..." Marcus begins after a long moment. "I think it's time you tell us the truth." The rest of them bunch behind him, demonstrating their agreement. I am alone, staring at the five soldiers still alive under my command.

"We are supposed to be brothers, but you hide things from us." I wince to hear the suspicion in Felix's voice. He is right, I have not been faithful to them. Fear has kept my mouth shut, cutting me off from my brothers.

Slowly, I shake my head, glancing around to make sure that no Normans are within earshot. But the camp is practically deserted; we are safe. I need them to trust me—for their own good, if nothing else. So, in order to preserve their faith, I lie, "I told you those were the bones of Aquilo."

Felix nods, and the rest slowly agree.

"That is the truth. But he's not dead."

Clintus lets out a gasp of horror.

I press forward before he can object. "When I fought the *necromanta*, he woke up and gave me a vision and a gift. He showed me how to create that frozen blade with my Symbol." I avoid mentioning *which* Symbol to protect myself. "In exchange for this weapon, he made me swear a *votum*."

Felix's face falls in horror.

"The first promise was to throw the *necromanta*'s body into the abyss behind his grave." I gave them an easy smile to let them know they don't need to worry. Fulfilling the undead god's request is not going to be a challenge. Their expressions tell me that they don't buy my optimism.

"The second is to bring his judgment to the High King of the Normans."

"What kind of judgment?" Felix asks suspiciously, his eyes narrowed. Behind us, shouts of alarm begin to echo from the mouth of the cave as the workers we slipped past come running to the surface.

"The only kind winter knows—a cold wind."

CHAPTER 48

Now that the men know I carry the boon of the winter god, I use Ancient Frost freely, letting it harden the ground beneath our feet. We make even better time than a troop of scouts equipped with snowshoes. Poor Clintus is able to keep the pace, now that he doesn't have to battle his way through the drifts with every step. I let the ground relax in our wake, obscuring any tracks, making it impossible for anyone to follow us. I can feel my veins stretching under the load, but that only makes me push them harder. Is the *inhibitus* only designed to prevent me from Ascending to Silver as an Iron, or will it stop my new Symbol as well? If I keep using Ancient Frost like this, I will arrive at the peak of Copper soon, and then I will find out.

We pass around more cured meats that we liberated from a larder tent on our way out of the camp. A lone guard tried to stop us, but Anas cut him down before he could raise the alarm, and we hid his body behind some sacks of grain.

Sol finally sets behind the horizon, but I press us forward, knowing that night is our only chance to catch up before it's too late. The larger groups will not keep marching in the darkness, and we don't need a light for me to be able to guide us. We're exhausted, but fear gives us wings.

Aquilo's presence urges me forward like a hostler, driving me with his whips. I follow in the direction he leads, as eager to find the High King as the dead god is. I can only hope that we will not be too late to save them. Above us, a full *Luna* rises, shining her cold light on the snow. *Mons* Olympus glows under her baleful eye. Is it as dead as the stories say? Or is that just another myth?

"Castor, look," Felix calls from my elbow, pointing at the distant ridgeline.

I glance down from the floating home of the gods to see where my friend points. A glow hovers on the horizon, like a second *Sol* just before it rises. I do not need to feel the excited flare on my spine to know what awaits us just over the hill.

I extend my *animus* to its furthest range, leading the men forward at a slow pace. I sense no sentries but do not trust the Normans. Their *berserkir* blasphemy is powerful, and I do not know the extent of what it can do.

Crawling on top of the snow, we peer over the crest to the war camp below. A hundred bonfires blaze, illuminating the horde that the High King has brought with him. They travel without supplies, eager for the hunt. I see still forms of warriors sleeping in their bedrolls, while others group around the flames. Lurking on the edge of the light, an entire army of *furiae* waits silently for their minders. There are no sentries, for they are not afraid. The only imperial legion within twenty miles is their prey.

Aquilo's presence spikes, demanding to unleash the storm that I carry within me. I grit my teeth and shake my head, refusing to obey. First, I must find Gaius and the rest of the cohort. *Soon*, I promise. Reluctantly, the pressure within me abates, watching me with untrusting eyes. I resist the urge to chuckle at his lack of faith. I have no desire to take his place frozen to that throne. I will do as I swore.

Just not yet.

"Come on," I whisper, pulling back from the ridge and starting a path parallel with the Normans. "Gaius and the men can't be far." Silently, we continue further into the darkness, looking for our brothers.

Luna continues her ascent as we continue our search for the next two hours. Aquilo's presence is silent now, waiting to see what I do. Sharp-eyed Felix is the first to spot the next fire, burning brightly in the distance. Our group pauses, watching the glow warily.

"What do you think?" I ask. "Normans?"

"Tribune wouldn't light fires if they were running from an enemy," Marcus grunts.

"Or he'd light the fires, then make everyone march," Anas suggests. A chorus of dry chuckles echoes from all of us. That does sound like something Gaius would do.

"Either way, that means it isn't the Twelfth," I point out. I reach out with Ancient Frost, but my Copper Heart does not have the range to find our quarry. "If the hammer is in front of us and the anvil is behind us…" I turn to our left and investigate the yawning darkness that we have traveled alongside for hours. "Then the iron must be this way."

No one disagrees, so I lead us forward, cutting back across our path at an angle, heading back toward the High King and his larger army.

Gaius wouldn't let the men sleep in the eyesight of the Norman camp, which means that we had to have passed them.

We cross the valley until we draw near the far wall before we turn again, sweeping for our friends. Nervously, I glance at *Luna's* position in the sky, checking the time. It's approaching midnight. We only have a few hours to find our cohort.

"*Dominus*, I'm not sure how much further I can go," Clintus pants after a while. I study the man, feeling concerned. He's marched without complaint, but it's obvious that even Iron can only carry him so far. His face is drawn and pale, and the rings around his eyes are dark enough to look like bruises.

"Understood. Let's find somewhere safe to take a breather," I tell him, looking around for a place we can rest. This close to the wall of the valley, clumps of pines grow together, safe from the sweeping winds that course through this northern wasteland. It is not as thick as the great forest in the main valley, but dense enough. On a hunch, I lead the group toward them. It is foolish for a legion to hide among the trees—the trunks break up their ability to form shieldwalls and outmaneuver their opponents. Which means it is exactly the kind of place that Gaius would use to throw his enemies off. If he's not here, it will at least be a safe place to rest or leave Clintus, if it comes to that. I feel guilty for even considering it, but Aquilo's burden rests heavily on me. I have to find the Eighth before it's too late.

We make it a dozen paces into the woods before Ancient Frost warns me of feet breaking through the snow all around us. "Ware!" I cry, drawing my *gladius* from underneath my furs. My men respond instantly, collapsing into a ring and drawing their own blades.

Legionnaires burst from the trees, shields high. I laugh in joy before I remember that we're disguised as Normans. The first soldier charges me, and I slam my *gladius* against his shield, calling upon the Iron Symbol to shake it. I don't want to damage the thing but to rattle him enough that he knows that I too am legion.

The soldier stumbles in surprise as my will clashes with his. "*Redemptio in bello!*" I shout. "*Redemptio in bello!*" The skirmish freezes as the men hear our words. A light flares in the darkness, and none other than Durus, First Spear of the Eighth Cohort, steps out from behind a tree with a torch in one hand and *gladius* in the other. I whip back the hood of my fur cloak and give the surprised centurion a bright grin and a salute.

"Decurion Castor and the *argentulae* reporting for duty, *Dominus*. Sorry we're a little late." There's no time for me to say anything else before the tough man sweeps me into a warm embrace.

The First Spear takes us to see Gaius immediately. As we move deeper into the wood, we encounter the rest of the cohort desperately trying to get some sleep in the snow. Whispers follow our passage as word of our return spreads like wildfire.

The tribune's tent must have been abandoned long ago, but the officers are nestled in a makeshift shelter pieced together from cloaks and pieces of leather strung between the trees to block the light of a small fire. Gaius pores over a map in the low light, his sharp features tight with stress.

"Durus, what in Bellona's—" His angry question dies on his lips as he spies us following in the First Spear's wake. "Percy!" he snaps, and a figure just outside the circle of light stirs from a cocoon of cloaks.

Delight pours through me as the centurion's tousled dark hair emerges from beneath his covers. "What is it?" he mumbles before his eyes focus and snap to me. Shock flashes across his face, followed immediately by a massive grin that I feel echoed on my own face.

He made it. I knew he could.

"Mars's Bones! You did it!" the centurion shouts, leaping to his feet to charge at us. I'm caught off guard as the Silver slams into me, lifting me off the ground with his superior strength to give me a back-cracking hug. "All of you?" His voice is desperate, hopeful. He drops me to make his way through our group. No one is spared an embrace, even Anas.

I laugh and turn back to the tribune, who is on his feet, staring at me with the same questioning intensity that he once had on the training field back in Agogia.

"Reporting for duty, Tribune." I salute, stepping past Percy to join the commander in the light.

"Welcome back, *Decurion*," he murmurs, sitting back down. "Sorry we don't have a warm bed waiting for you."

"I'm just glad you're all still in one piece, *Dominus*."

"Yes, the group that followed Percy back has been an annoyance, but so far, we have stayed ahead of them." Gaius gestures at the map he had been studying. "They got ahead of us, but tomorrow, we should reach a gap in the valley branch that will allow us to circle back around and make our escape back toward Frigidus. I'm not of a mind to engage them in a straight-up fight if we can avoid it. Percy says they have *berserkirs* in their number."

My stomach drops as I realize he does not know. I glance around the sparse encampment and see just how undersupplied we were for this kind of expedition. Gaius has no more *Fidelia* to range forward and scout for him. He had been relying on us to be his eyes, but we've been gone for days. Without us, he's been blind, reacting to the enemy he can see, not understanding the trap that has been laid.

"*Dominus,*" I begin slowly, my heart breaking. "I'm afraid that won't be possible."

"Why not?" Gaius's expression is sharp, and despite myself, I lean back from his focused stare.

"Because there is a second force of Normans approaching from the North. They've already sealed the gap and are waiting for you." Despair digs at the corner of the tribune's eyes for a moment before he looks down at the map with feverish need.

"How is that possible? The barbarians never come together in these numbers…"

"They have joined under the banner of a High King; one they call Knut." Gaius's head snaps up to fix me with a glare.

"The Normans have no kings."

"They do now. We snuck past his fires this very evening, not two hours from here."

"Tell me everything," Gaius demands as Percy sits next to him, still smiling. Our survival has lifted a weight of guilt from his shoulders that even my bad tidings cannot replace.

"We were captured after we sent the centurion ahead. The *berserkirs* marched us all night to their encampment. There is a great host that shelters there at the back of the valley." I harden my lips into a thin line, trying to decide how much to tell him—how much truth should I trust him with? I feel the eyes of my men on my back. If I do not do this story justice, I know they will.

"We were taken before this Knut and questioned. He wanted to know where the rest of our legion was and why we had been sent." The tribune's dark eyes flick between us, measuring our mettle.

"Did you tell him?"

"No, *Dominus*. I think they must have already known. They barely questioned us before they gave us over to his advisor, a woman named Vixa." Gaius twitches in surprise at the imperial name.

"She was indeed a woman of the empire, *Dominus*." I nod at his guess. "But she was also something else." I lick my cold, dry lips before continuing, "I do not wish to sound like a superstitious child, but we believe she was a *necromanta*."

Gaius says nothing, only stares at me, waiting for me to continue. I cannot tell if he believes me or is waiting to see if he should strip me of my rank.

"She had black *Cor* veins on her arms," I explain, trying to communicate the horror of what Vixa had been. "She planned on harvesting the relics of our fallen brothers for her own use."

"Pluto's Rotting Bones," Percy breathes, staring at me in horror.

"So it is true," Gaius says at last, leaning back in his seat. His gaze is dull and unfocused, as if he is looking somewhere else. It is my turn to be surprised.

"You believe me?"

"A pity neither of us will be able to tell Father," Percy muses to his brother, looking away from me at last. I do not know what the Marius patriarch has to do with *necromanta*, but I do understand the meaning of his regret. He thinks we are going to die here. He might be right, but we still have one trick left.

"He'll find out soon enough, I suspect," Gaius grunts, returning to the present. "How did you escape this *necromanta*'s clutches?"

"Well," I say, glancing at Felix, who hovers just behind my shoulder. "That's where the story gets really unbelievable. But if you're willing to trust me, I might have a way for us to survive this."

CHAPTER 49

The sunrise is brutal in the snowy wasteland. Every surface reflects its light into my eyes, cutting at them like blades. The Eighth Cohort of the Twelfth Legion of the Iron Empire stands at attention in battle formation with our backs to the rocky wall of the valley.

I'm in the front line, just behind Gaius, who stands alone. The tribune did not believe me when I told him how we escaped from the cave. He refused to accept that Aquilo was still alive and had given me the ability to summon ice. But after I performed the feat three times, he was forced to admit that there was *some* sort of power at work here.

In the distance, two Norman armies approach at a leisurely pace from either side of us. They know we are trapped with nowhere to go. My heart quivers at the sight of them. The horde is big enough to fill the width of the valley on both sides, although Knut's contingent is much thicker than the hunters that drove Gaius and the cohort to him.

"You're certain?" he murmurs to me for the tenth time, turning from the front of the line to study me.

"As sure as I can be, *Dominus*." I shrug unhelpfully. "I only know what it feels like, not what it will do." The god's fury rages wildly as we watch the barbarians.

Release me, it hisses eagerly. *Release me!*

Soon, I promise the god. *Soon.* The storm inside me goes still, calmed by my oath. It can feel the truth in the air.

At last, the two armies meet, curving to form a crescent around us, trapping us against the rocks that protect our rear. Despite my faith in Aquilo's rage, dread builds in me as I stare at the sea of barbarians that has come to drown us. They laugh, pointing at us with axes and swords. My breath is ragged as fear swallows me. I am not the only one in the formation who is terrified. Heavy breaths echo from all around me.

Even if all three of Brodigan's full legions were here, I do not think that we would have a chance. Tattooed *berserkirs* dot their lines in droves. A complement of *furiae* march to reinforce the smaller army, drawing murmurs from the line.

"Easy, lads," Durus murmurs from the front, his voice somehow carrying even though he doesn't shout. "There'll be plenty of work to do soon." Cruel chuckles echo from the line as men desperately cling to the First Spear's hope.

"Find your targets," Percy calls to the soldiers who carry the *venator* relics, spears designed to kill the *furiae*. I glance at Felix and Marcus, who stand on either side of me in line. Both of them carry one of the precious weapons, and their eyes are hard with concentration.

Gaius stands in the front of our formation, red cloak flapping in the wind like some martial god. He carries no *scutum*, but a *gladius* hangs from his right hip and a longer dueling blade from his left. As the horde settles in around us, he stares at them, unbothered by the teeming masses who have come to kill him.

He is everything I always thought the men of the Iron Legions would be, worthy of the legacy in a way few others have been. Alone, he stands to face the enemies of the empire, fearless and unbothered. I'm certain that he draws some calm from his Iron Symbol, but his own mettle is strong on its own.

I settle myself, drawing strength from his example, grounding myself in the ice and iron that surrounds me, feeding it my fear until I am only cold logic. My reserves teem with the twin essences, gray and blue. I hold both just under the limit that will trigger my *inhibitus*. With my right hand, I finger the *votum* stone in my jacket pocket, still with me even after all we have endured. Mentally, I try to find some level of calm, preparing to call upon the weapon of a god.

"I seek your High King!" Gaius roars, his voice sharp and cutting. "I am Gaius Marius, Tribune of the Iron Legions and I challenge this Knut to single combat." He wants to do this his way before resorting to relying on Aquilo's aid. The Normans shift, and I wonder how many speak our tongue or if they just ready themselves to charge.

Silence greets our commander's challenge.

I scan their troops, looking for Knut's fearsome features, but there's no sign of the High King. My gaze lands on a familiar *berserkir* in the front ranks. It's Astrid, the woman with the golden band who I surrendered to at the edge of the forest, who left me in Vixa's clutches. She turns toward me, as if sensing my stare. I'm easy to find. We *argentulae* stand out amongst our brethren; other than Gaius, we're the only ones without shields. Our eyes meet, and she arches her blonde brows in surprise. I do not react, afraid that any expression I make will warn her of our plan.

"Coward!" Gaius bellows, taking a step toward the horde that encircles us. He is fearless, unbreakable. I feel his courage ignite in the men around me like a fire as they shift, eager to face these barbarians, to follow their commander into the fray.

The *berserkir* woman looks away from me, casting a surprised glance over her shoulder, as if waiting for something. But whatever she is looking for doesn't come.

The silence grows.

"Come and face me, barbarian dog!" Gaius bellows again, trying to prey on the king's vanity. The Normans are a militant people. They do not respect leaders who cannot kill in their own name. More warriors begin to look around, surprised their king has not responded to this challenge. Confusion is written on their faces.

At last, there is a motion in the sea, and it parts for High King Knut, who strides out from his army at a brisk pace, rigid with anger. He wears his horned helm, which frames his tattooed face, making him seem more beast than man. He's even bigger than I remember. A longsword dangles from his right hip, its scabbard marked with the same glowing runes that decorated the stone altars in the deep. The horde roars their approval as their leader steps into the space between our forces.

Two figures race after him, calling to him, but the barbarian ignores them. Immediately, I understand why he did not appear when Gaius first challenged him. The High King is not alone. A murmur of shock runs through the soldiers as they see the two Imperials who follow in his wake. The figures wear veils obscuring their faces, but it is obvious from their hair and clothing that they are not Normans.

Gaius tightens at the sight of them, turning to glance at me as the trio approaches. *Be ready*, he commands with his eyes. I nod, flexing my hand again.

"What do you want, *Legionnaire*?" Knut demands as he approaches. I resist the urge to gasp in surprise. His voice is deeper than it was in the tent, so rich that it vibrates in my chest. He speaks perfect *lingua imperia*, without accent or need for a translator.

"Single combat, to the death," Gaius offers without hesitation. "The victor allows the loser's forces to disperse in peace."

"Do you think I am afraid of you, little man?" Knut seems amused by the offering. Gaius does not bother to respond. "Do you think you will kill me?"

"Easily."

"High King, please, you must listen!" a woman's voice cuts in smoothly as the Imperials reach Knut's side. She's tall and lean, like a dancer. A pudgy man follows right behind her, breathing heavily. I try to check their arms for signs of a *Cor* Heart, but they are covered. "You cannot duel this man. He is Gaius Marius, son of—"

"He is a great warrior?" the king interrupts, turning to look at his advisor with interest.

"Well, yes, but—"

"I accept." Knut turns back to Gaius with less disdain than before.

"My liege, you are being foolish. Our agreement—"

"I am High King." Something dark and dangerous enters the giant's voice, matching the tattoos that swirl across his entire skin. "You do not command me."

"No, of course not, Your Majesty," the woman huffs, giving a small bow at the waist that seems entirely ceremonial. "But I have been sent to advise you, and your benefactors will not appreciate—" The High King interrupts her for a third time, backhanding her in the face with a massive hand. She staggers to the side but does not fall, telling me she must have a Symbol feeding her strength.

Her eyes glitter with hatred above her veil as she straightens up to her full height. "When the crows feast on your eyeballs, barbarian, just remember I warned you."

"I shall not remember anything. I shall be dead and feasting in the halls with my fathers." The giant laughs scornfully.

"Thank you for that lovely introduction, Tullia," Gaius remarks dryly, glancing at the woman. She stiffens but does not respond to his barb. "I haven't seen you since the *collegium*."

"Enough talk. Fight me if you wish to save your people," Knut chimes in.

The Imperial woman shakes her head, turning to storm away, once again drawing the pudgy man on her heels. Knut gestures with a massive hand, and a half-dozen *berserkirs* in the front line lope forward, forming half of a ring in the center of the field.

"Choose your six," he commands, turning his back on our army and striding away without fear.

"Percy, Castor, Felix, Marcus, Unus, and Anas." Gaius rattles our names off without looking. Felix and I exchange surprised glances at the inclusion of the former *captivus*, but after a moment, I shrug. He's earned his place.

"Durus, you have the cohort."

"Aye, *Dominus*," the First Spear responds grimly from the center of the line.

"Let's move," Gaius orders as Percy springs to his older brother's side, leaning in to confer with him as we move forward. I fall in step with the rest of my decade, trying to keep myself from shaking as we draw closer to the horde. Not even Ancient Frost can keep all of my fear at bay.

"He's a *berserkir*," the centurion reminds Gaius urgently. "He's going to be faster than you, stronger too. He probably can swing that sword with one hand."

"I know."

"You can't let him hit you, or he'll damage your Heart—cut you off from Iron."

"Brother, I'm going to kill him." Gaius pauses midstride and turns an exasperated expression on his younger sibling. "I am going to cut him into tiny little pieces and get us out of here."

"Just making sure you've thought this through," Percy grumbles, chastised.

"*Dominus!*" Durus shouts from behind us. Surprised, Gaius turns to look at the First Spear. I follow his gaze to look at the solid iron block that watches us leave.

"*Tribunus!*" roars the First Spear.

"*Victorius!*" the legion thunders in unison. The hairs on the back of my neck stand at attention as goosebumps sweep through my body from the fury channeled into the single cry of my comrades. I look back at our commander in time to see him nod once in acceptance before turning back to his task.

"Castor," he calls as we approach the centerfield where Knut and his seconds wait. The two Imperials stand off to the side, watching our progression with an air of irritation. I feel the burden of their stares through the veils that hide their faces.

"Yes, *Dominus?*"

"I believe the Normans will honor their king's agreement, but the palatines… complicate things."

"They can't let us live." He gives me a shrewd look and nods. I do not know why so many of our countrymen flock to the court of the High King. I can better understand a Censor murdering my family for his own gain more than these traitors. What could they possibly hope to gain that is worth unleashing these monsters upon the empire?

"Be ready. If they try to break the agreement, then invoke your god's power and see what wrath he brings."

"What about you, *Dominus*?" What if you—"

"Only if they break the *pax*, *Legionnaire*." His voice is hard as he fixes me with another penetrating stare. "I want your word." I hesitate, torn between lying to my commander and telling the truth. My *votum* to Aquilo demands that I unleash his storm on Knut and his horde, but I cannot deny Gaius. Not here. Not now.

"Aye, *Dominus*," I promise, bowing my head in his direction. The oath's pressure on my spine builds, like the *inhibitus* just before it strikes, but I ignore its warning.

"Come and die," Knut calls from the center of the field, impatient for glory. Gaius turns to look at the massive high king for a moment. Knut has removed his furs and stands bare-chested in the snow like Vrok before him. His entire chest is covered in more of the thick, black tattoos that cover his face. Only a few white lines mar their surface, though whether they are scars or negative space I cannot tell. They move like living things. The antlers of his helmet spread wide above him, making him look like a monster.

The tribune smiles slightly, clapping his brother on the shoulder before striding forward. He draws his dueling sword as he approaches Knut. It's longer than a *gladius*, with a slightly curved half blade at the tip. Atticus's was the same shape, although his was made of *tellus*, not iron.

"I am Gaius Marius, Tribune of the Eighth Cohort of the Twelfth of the Iron Legions," he declares in a bold voice. "I am Ironbound in the name of Diana Agrippa, Empress of the Iron Empire. I come before you today in challenge: a duel to the death. The winner shall be victorious and claim the other's life. The loser's people shall be allowed to depart in disgrace."

"I accept," the Norman agrees eagerly. He draws his longsword from the sheath at his hip. Glowing runes are carved into the blade itself, a match for the ones on the scabbard. "I am Knut, son of Knut, High King of the North. If the gods bless me, I shall use your skull as a drinking cup in the mead hall tonight." The horde roars their approval, although I cannot tell how many understood the exchange.

"Yeesh, at least give it a little bit to settle," Marcus complains under his breath.

The time for talking is done. Gaius raises his blade in salute to his opponent. Knut mirrors him, but as his blade lifts, it bursts into flame, wreathed from the crossguard to tip in a black flame. Dread rolls from it like a distant heat, and I feel it crawling on my skin as I gaze at that fell weapon.

"What is that?" Felix demands, looking at the glowing weapon in horror. I shake my head, unable to speak. The only soldier who isn't cowed by the weapon's aura of fear is Gaius. The tribune walks forward calmly, sword held low.

Before he even seems to be in range, Knut leaps forward with a roar, swinging his massive sword in a horizontal slash to cut Gaius in half. Our commander explodes in a burst of Silver speed that stuns me. I've seen Percy fight, but it's clear in the first moment of this duel that his older brother is a warrior of a different caliber.

Gaius leans close to the ground, letting the black blade pass over him like a stormfront. He dashes past the king, slashing at the big man's chest as he streaks by. Knut is caught off guard but did not become High King because of his looks. He staggers into his momentum, letting the swing carry him out of the range of Gaius's strike. He spins, following the tribune's dash, and raises his blade overhead for a devastating downward blow.

Our commander does not turn, but he does not need to. His Silver Heart warns him of the danger, tracking the iron as it moves through the air. He leaps to the side the black flame crashes into the ground where he had just been standing.

Spinning, Gaius's sword licks out at lightning speed, trying to catch Knut before he can reset his stance. The tip of the dueling blade bites deeply into the tattooed flesh of Knut's ribs, exploding in a blast of red blood as it cuts through.

The *berserkir* king doesn't even grunt in pain; only raises his blade and slashes at Gaius in a series of strokes that I can barely follow with my naked eye. His power is incredible! That sword must weigh as much as my entire kit, but he wields it comfortably with one hand or two.

"Dead gods, he's strong," Marcus whispers in awe.

"I told him," Percy mutters darkly, voice tight with tension.

Gaius retreats, dodging the strikes like a dancer, refusing to block or parry with his weapon. He cannot risk having his access to the Iron Symbol disrupted. Without its speed or strength, he would likely already be dead. I shudder, trying to imagine holding a shieldwall against a monster like Knut. He would shred through us with ease.

I can't help my curiosity. Tightening my grip on the Symbol of Ancient Frost, I let my *animus* sink into the icy ground beneath their feet, feeling their tempo as the two fighters work their way around the arena.

I'm in awe as I sense our tribune floating across the ground, never getting trapped, always forcing the king to turn. I've never seen anything like it. It is the opposite of how they teach legionnaires to fight. We are a wall, an impenetrable fortress that cannot be broken. He is the wind.

It is only because of my connection to the cold that I feel another worm of *animus* work its way underneath the fighters, hunting them like a shark. I stiffen as it creeps past me, not sure what it could be. On instinct, I glance at the two Imperials who watch from the Norman side. They are still, watching the fight with intense scrutiny.

Heart pounding, I track the other Winter Symbol, watching as it circles the fighters, looking for an opportunity. I am certain that it is one of the other traitors. Who else could it be? I am the only member of the legion who can touch anything other than Iron. Which means that it is my responsibility to be ready.

Gaius lands another blow on Knut, a slash across one of his forearms that leaves a flap of ink-blackened skin dangling. The Legion roars with thunderous approval as Knut's blood anoints the snow once more. The High King doesn't retreat but presses his attack, snarling with focused anger.

The tribune turns to dodge, and the enemy *electus* chooses that moment to strike. I feel the snow surge like a wave, sweeping over his boot and hardening into a frozen grip before I can stop it. Gaius stumbles, caught off guard by the ambush. Knut takes advantage of his hesitation with another one of his brutal attacks, twisting his hips as he swings his blade horizontally with the ground to take our commander's head.

Gaius recovers quickly, dropping to his knees to duck under the sword's black fire. As he falls, he draws his *gladius* in a reverse grip with his left hand. With uncanny precision, he raises it and stabs downward at his own foot, using the iron to shatter the icy bonds that hold him.

"What is he doing?" Percy moans in despair, unaware of the trap that has been sprung.

I feel the other Imperial's *animus* reach for his boot, trying to snare him again, and know it is my time to act. With a snarl, I clench my teeth and slam my mind against theirs, battling them for control of the frost beneath the fighters. My veins burn as I push them to their limits, burning essence like a wildfire.

The other spirit wriggles in my grasp like a furious snake, trying to break free of my grip. I've caught the other *electus* off guard, but as they struggle, I feel the power of their will grow, swelling in power. I may have ambushed them, but it is obvious they have Ascended to heights above me.

I glance at the two Imperials, trying to see their reaction. The pudgy man is twitching, looking at our line with an intense stare that I can feel through his veil. I school my face into a concerned expression, trying to shield my identity.

Now that I am its focus, the foreign will breaks free of my grip easily before turning on mine and slamming it to the side. I'm stunned—it feels as if I have just been thrown into a wall. I shake my head to clear it, but the other *electus* has already left me behind, chasing after Gaius once more.

I grit my teeth and send my *animus* racing after them, harassing them like a puppy chases its parent. They ignore me, sending another wave of snow to grab at the tribune's feet. As they order it to harden, I throw my entire will into rejecting it. The intent of their command echoes in my skull as my Symbol reacts to the strength.

FREEZE.

No, I demand weakly. I am no match for their raw power. This *electus* is far beyond my Copper capabilities. But despite my weakness, I feel a hesitation in the snow, like a child torn between toddling to two parents.

In a flash, I realize that their Symbol is not as direct as mine. Using the laws of congruency, an *electus* can command snow with any Winter Symbol, but there is a loss of power in the transfer the more removed it is. I have no such inefficiencies with my will. I am bound to Ancient Frost, and this snow has been here for a very long time. My authority is direct.

No, I command again, and the snow shudders before collapsing back into powder, refusing to grip Gaius. The tribune dances to the side, narrowly avoiding another powerful swing from Knut. He's free and able to move. I grin in relief at the sight of his unfrozen boots. The other *animus* retreats a distance, watching for another opportunity to attack.

My smile begins to slip as I realize the damage has been done. Gaius is free, but his tempo is thrown off by the Imperial's attack. He backpedals, trying to create enough space to dodge, but the *berserkir* follows him, matching his pace easily.

"Come on, reset," Percy groans, steepling his fingers over his nose in stress.

Gaius dances, but he is trapped in the bigger man's orbit, unable to escape. Knut's speed is inhuman, despite the blood flowing from several wounds. Finally, the tribune makes a mistake. Despite the *argentum Cor* in his body, he is still human. Knut brings his fiery blade in an angled slash before halting the strike mid-swing, turning it into a feint, and lashing forward with the hilt.

Gaius sees the trap too late and raises his left elbow to take the hit, shielding his face. The force of the blow drives him back several steps, and before he can recover, Knut explodes forward, blade extended for a killing thrust.

The tribune twists, using his *gladius* to catch the king's cursed blade and force it to go wide.

"No, no, no," Percy screams, watching as his brother is finally forced to block.

Gaius leaps backward a few steps, finally regaining the space that he had lost, but the damage is done. He raises his *gladius* to inspect it, and even from the sidelines, I can see that Knut's sword carved a slice of iron from it like butter. The *berserkir*'s dark power has done its work.

The cohort behind me sits in stunned silence at the sight of their commander's ruined weapon.

The tribune is panting as he looks from his damaged sword to the massive man who grins at him evilly. Despair runs through me as I realize what is going to happen next. Without his Iron Symbol, the tribune will not be able to keep up with the High King's power. Gaius might be able to hold him off for a while, but eventually, he will tire, and then he will die. Distantly, I feel the other *animus* retreat from the snow, its work done.

"Now you see, little man," mocks Knut. "You see the blessings that our gods have given us to destroy you. We will tear down your walls. We will burn your cities. We will take your wives and kill your children. We will plunder the graves of your gods. You cannot stop us. Your time is at an end." His horde hoots and hollers, shaking their weapons in the air.

"I'm not dead yet," Gaius replies between gasps, rising to his full height. He stabs the damaged *gladius* into the snow, choosing to rely only on his still intact dueling blade. "Might as well finish the job before you start gloating."

Knut chuckles but does not disagree. The High King explodes forward on the attack. He swarms Gaius, who does not have the speed to evade him any longer. Our tribune dances around the attacks, but he is slower, less prescient than he was before. He cannot rely on his supernatural senses to guide his blade. Yet despite his weakness, he is fearless. His face is set like stone, and he holds his form, not surrendering to fear or panic. I grit my teeth in frustration, tempted to ignore his orders and summon Aquilo's storm now. I do not want to watch my commander die.

But I obey.

The end comes quickly. Gaius's speed flags as his human heart struggles to keep up with the *berserkir* who hounds him. At last, the king traps him, forcing him to block with his sword again. The black fire cuts off the top third of Gaius's dueling blade, sending it spinning into the snow.

The tribune grimaces but charges forward into the space behind Knut's attack, swinging his broken weapon at the giant's neck. Knut laughs, slapping Gaius with his free palm. The force of the blow sends the tribune reeling. Desperate to help, I try to copy the other Winter *electus*'s trick, grabbing at Knut's boots with the snow at his feet. But the distance is too great, and he is too strong. I barely even manage to slow him before he breaks free of my grasp.

"No..." Percy begs to the dead gods as his brother's weapon spins from his grip. The centurion falls to his knees, tears streaming down his face. His pain almost makes me manifest the *Glacialis Falx*, but still, I obey. Though it may damn me, I obey.

An exhausted Gaius collapses facedown into the snow next to the ruined *gladius* that he stuck into the ground. As I watch, he reaches for it, resolute until the end.

"It is time for you to become my cup, little man," Knut announces, crouching over our fallen commander. He reaches for the back of the tribune's head with his massive hand. As his fingers brush Gaius's neck, the tribune bursts into motion, all signs of fatigue gone in an instant.

Gaius twists on the ground, pulling his ruined *gladius* from the ground and jamming it straight into the eye of Knut. I have the perfect view from behind to see the point explode through the back of the High King's skull and into the daylight. As I watch, the iron of his blade begins to shift, reforging its edge at the tribune's will.

He still has access to his Symbol.

Calmly, Gaius rises to his feet to a silent field. With a wrench, he pulls his blade free of the barbarian, turning as the massive *berserkir*'s body collapses to the ground like a tree. The legionnaires recover from their shock and clang their *gladii* on their *scuta*, roaring their love and approval for their commander. Percy is on his feet, sprinting to his brother's side, screaming in delight. The centurion slams into Gaius, wrapping his arms around his older brother. For the first time I can remember, the tribune smiles—a broad, warm thing like a perfect sunrise. I feel an echo growing on my own face. *We might actually survive this.*

"He did it!" Marcus thunders as he bangs on the back of my *lorica* in delight. "Mars's Ashes, he did it!"

"How?" Felix asks the question that lurks in my own mind. When I used my Symbol to defend from Vrok's attacks in the glade, he had cut off my ability to access the Iron Symbol for half a day. Was that just another difference between Copper and Silver, or was there something else at play here? An idea tickles at the back of my mind, but now is not the time to get distracted.

I tear my gaze from the brothers to look for the Imperials who had been with Knut. I spy the two veiled figures at the front of the line, speaking urgently to another *berserkir*, gesturing in our direction with frantic motions. The man's gaze snaps from the Imperials to us, burning with wild hatred. He screams something at the warriors around him, gesturing with his axe for them to follow as he begins to run in our direction.

The cheers of the cohort die at the sight of the horde's line beginning to tear as more and more Normans join in the charge. Like the grains of an hourglass, they pull the rest of their companions into a headlong rush toward us. The six *berserkirs* that Knut brought with him watch the rush with confusion, unsure what to do. Astrid looks at me with narrowed, suspicious eyes.

Gaius and Percy react instantly, sprinting back toward us. The centurion waves for the honor guard to follow him as we race to the cohort. We obey, running with our officers toward the line while the barbarians roar behind us. Durus screams a command, and several men turn their shields, opening an entrance for us to get into the formation.

"Castor!" I turn as Gaius calls my name. He stands at the front of the formation and motions for me to join him. Heart racing, I jog to his side.

"Well fought, *Dominus!*" I shout over the frenzy. He shoots me an amused look before it is swallowed by a serious expression. For a moment, we gaze at the horde of thousands crashing down on us. The *furiae* charge toward us, their long legs devouring the distance even faster than the *berserkirs*. I feel my chest tighten in fear. I call upon Iron's calming presence, but it can only do so much. I know what is about to come.

"We tried my plan. Now it's time for yours. Do it!" he commands.

Yes. Yes, yes, yes, yesyesyesyes, Aquilo's voice begs in my mind, ravenous for its revenge.

Aquilo's presence spikes, peering down on me with heavy intensity. I stagger as I take a step forward to face the charging barbarians alone. I stare at my empty right palm for a second, grateful that I will not have to serve as the dead god's replacement in his frozen prison, terrified about what I am about to unleash.

"The sooner, the better, I think," Gaius murmurs from behind me, startling me out of my reverie. I nod and get to work.

It is not hard to summon the *Glacialis Falx*. The Frozen Blade comes eagerly, leaping into my hand as if Aquilo himself had placed it there. Essence surges from me, but I replace it easily, drawing from the frozen wasteland we stand in. The sapphire light that burns in the hilt seethes, glowing with a dark light.

I glance up to see that the Normans have already covered half the distance between us. Steeling myself, I draw back my left palm and slam it into the bottom of the hilt, commanding the ice to shatter. My strike cracks its seal, which begins to grow at its own pace as something within begins to claw its way out, like a bird hatching from an egg.

With a roar like thunder, it shatters, and in the grasp of a cold wind, I unleash the fury of a god.

CHAPTER 50

For the first time in more than four hundred years, the North Wind roars again. Lightning strikes all around the field, targeting the *furiae* with delight. The ice constructs shatter as I shut my eyes that burn with the afterimage of its furious light. Thick, black clouds appear out of nowhere, spreading like a rot across the sky, blotting out *Sol*. Thick snow whips at me as it hurtles toward the charging horde.

"Dead gods," Gaius murmurs in awe from behind me. I can barely hear him over the cacophony of the storm. As if summoned by the tribune, a figure forms in the wind, taller and broader even than Knut. For a moment, I see Aquilo as he must have looked before Frigidus and the rest of the Iron Lords killed him. He is a man, graying at the temples, but still in his prime. He carries a long wooden staff, and his eyes twinkle. Then he smiles, and the veneer is shattered as his madness is laid bare. His eyes stretch too wide; his teeth are too sharp.

"You are released from your oath, mortal. Now flee while you still can!" he cackles and then begins to spin, whipping the vicious wind into an even deadlier frenzy. The weight of my *votum* lifts from my shoulders, but I take no joy in being released.

"We've got to get out of here, *Dominus*," I scream, turning to Gaius. The tribune is staring over my shoulder, eyes narrowed as he tries to peer through the snowstorm. I do not think he saw what I just did.

"Not yet." He gestures for me to follow him. "Get back in line. We're going to take a few hits first." I glance in the direction he is looking to see the front wave of barbarians emerge from the murk, still rushing toward us.

"We are the Iron Legion of the Iron Empire!" Durus calls from the front.

"We do not bend! We do not break!" five hundred men roar back. Goosebumps prick my flesh as pride burns inside of me. This is never the road I meant to walk, but Jupiter's Rotting Beard, I wouldn't leave these men to face this alone.

"Brace!" screams Gaius as we rejoin the line.

"Brace!" the men echo, repeating the command down the line so that all hear it. I'm shoved to the back of the formation with the rest of the *argentulae*. Without our *scuta*, we are no good at the front of the formation. I grit my teeth in frustration, hating not being able to do anything.

A roar goes up as the front edge of the Normans slams into our line. The formation crunches as the men absorb the force of the charge and then spring forward, pushing our attackers back.

"Shields up! Blades low!" Durus chants.

"Shields up! Blades low!" the men reply. I watch with pride as the line holds. We may be the lowest of the Iron Legions, but we were trained by Gaius Marius. We know our business. Iron rings as blows glance off the shieldwall, and men scream as the *gladii* of the legionnaires slip out, stabbing and cutting. Against any normal warriors, our defenses would be impenetrable.

But these are not normal opponents.

"My Iron! Where's my Iron?" a man screams as a *berserkir* tears into his shield.

"I can't feel it!" shouts another, voice full of panic. Terror grows like an out-of-control fire in the line as the officers try to restore order. The blasphemous power of the Normans eats into our formation like a cancer.

"Hold, lads, hold!" Durus cries, trying to rally the men, but the panic tears the formation apart as men lose the reassuring calm of Iron to help suppress their fears.

"Gaius needs us," Percy announces, appearing next to us out of the snow. He doesn't wait for us to respond but dashes off into the storm.

"Here we go again," Jasper mutters to no one in particular. We race off after our centurion, following him as he leads us out the side of the formation and circles around.

"Those *berserkirs* are eating us alive!" he screams over the raging North Wind as we run. "Gaius wants us to hit them from the side hard enough to back them up, then we rabbit for your path. Follow me! We go in fast, then get out, clear?"

"Aye, *Dominus*," we chorus. Percy pauses for a moment, watching us with sad eyes. I suspect he blames himself that we are still only Copper. This is not an easy task that he and his brother ask of us. Even if we had Ascended, some of us would likely die.

"Stick together. Don't let them hit you," he instructs, and then he moves, eager to join the fight.

As we come around the side of the formation, I understand why Gaius is risking us in this move. The storm is fracturing the Normans' assault. The frontrunners managed to get to us, but the rest of the horde is still trapped inside Aquilo's fury. If we can break free now, it will give us a head-start to slip away.

Legionnaires and barbarians litter the ground where the two armies meet. The snow is now thick, red slush. The cohort holds, but the *berserkirs* carve huge swaths into the shieldwall with each push. Percy falls on them from the side with a righteous wrath that would make even Nemesis pale. The *Fidelis* carries two *gladii*, and I copy him, holding the *Glacialis Falx* in my right and my iron in my left.

He pounces on the unsuspecting barbarians, slicing off limbs with every stroke. Their assault buckles under the attack, and as they crumble, the rest of the *argentulae* decade slams into them, blades flashing.

The *Glacialis Falx* cuts as easily as my legion-issued *gladius*. I reinforce its edge with my will the same way that I do with Iron. With my right hand, I stab a Norman in the stomach, ripping the icy sword free of her as I slide past. Percy blazes a path through their lines, and I follow in his wake, preventing the barbarians from collapsing on his heels.

Anas leaps into my shadow, covering my back as I do for the centurion. A glance over my shoulder shows the rest of us following in the gap, hammering into the weakness that the *Fidelis* has created. I call upon Ancient Frost to harden the ground under us, protecting our footing as we shove our way through.

It is fast and brutal. I've never fought like this before. My knowledge of the ground is an overwhelming roar. A hundred feet pound on my senses, making me unable to isolate anything. I stab wildly, striking at anything wearing furs, until abruptly, we punch through the other side of their line.

I whirl in time to see the barbarian formation crumble, torn to shreds by our assault. The survivors flee into the thick snowstorm, choosing to risk their lives against the elements instead of the Iron Legions. I pump my Frozen Blade above my head in glee as I watch them run.

But that joy dies in my throat as I see the sea of red-clad bodies among the snow. A third of the cohort lies dead, a bloody tax for this chance to escape. My heart breaks. Which of my brothers will never rise from the cold ground?

"Form up!" a decurion roars, running down the line. "We're on the move in one minute. Form up!"

"Come on," Percy calls, waving to me. "Gaius is going to need to know where to go."

We race to the tribune's side, easy to find thanks to the red cloak that flutters behind him in the wild storm. "It's time!" he shouts when he sees me. "Lead us to this miracle."

We chose this battlefield on purpose. When Aquilo showed me the vision of the Twelfth being hounded by Knut's armies, he gave me knowledge of this place. The Normans were happy to use this valley as a funnel because there is no other reasonable exit for an army. The only other way out is a narrow mountain path that is suitable for no more than one or two people at a time.

A legion might as well give up and die instead of marching in a single file. Our superiority comes from our formations. If Gaius had tried to escape through it, the barbarians would have been only too happy to pounce on the spread-out cohort and kill us one at a time. I shudder at the thought of fighting a hundred *berserkirs* in such conditions. But under the cover of the worst storm in centuries? We have just the distraction to let us get through the pass safely. All we have to do is get there before it runs out of steam.

"Aye, *Dominus*," I shout, moving to the front of the line and setting forward. I call on Ancient Frost to pack down as much of the snow in my wake as I can. My *animus* cannot reach the outer edges of our formation, but every little bit helps. Essence pours out of me as my will shudders under the weight of the effort. I grit my teeth and bear the strain, pulling every ounce I can from the winter around me. We don't have that far to go.

The storm rages so heavily that I cannot see a dozen paces in front of me. The men walk with their arms on the shoulders of the ones in front of them. I rely on the knowledge given to me by Aquilo to navigate.

"Don't wear yourself out; we will still need you," Gaius shouts into my ear as the gale screams above us.

"I'm sorry, *Dominus*?" I gasp, pulled out of my focus.

"Whatever you're doing to the ground, it isn't worth it."

"I'm not doing anything to the ground." The lie pops out of my mouth before I even consider the dangers of lying to my tribune. Gaius doesn't respond; merely looks down at the Frozen Blade that I still carry in my right hand.

"That's different," I protest weakly.

"I felt your interference during the duel," he scolds me. "You should have trusted me. I had it in hand."

"But they cheated first!" I protest. He shakes his head, tired of arguing with me.

"Save your energy. There will be more fighting," the commander promises, clapping me on the shoulder. I search his eyes, looking for some condemnation of what I am, but I find none. At last, I nod, releasing my will and sighing in relief as the essence stops pouring out of me. I breathe deeply, trying to replenish my stores.

The entrance to the mountain pass is hidden in the long rock wall of the valley. A large boulder juts out, blocking it from view. I lead the column around it, revealing the narrow gap in the rock that leads to freedom. A hushed cheer breaks out down the line, muted by the storm that rages above.

"Well done. You may have saved us all," Gaius shouts in my ear. "I want you to take your men and scout ahead. Make sure it's clear."

"Where will you be?"

"Right here, making sure every man gets through."

"*Dominus*, surely—"

"*Vade*," he commands, like I once did to his brother. "Go."

So we go.

I range ahead with the rest of the *argentulae* except for Clintus, who is too slow to keep up. Gaius does not wait to make sure the pass is completely safe but sends men right on our heels. We do not have time to waste. The barbarians will regroup and follow us soon. Aquilo's fury is centered on the horde behind us, and the pass is nestled between two mountains, offering some shelter from the storm.

The North Wind still shakes the valley, but we can see further and hear ourselves think now. As we progress, the path winds upward, running along the edge of a sharp cliff.

"Is now a bad time to say I hate heights?" Marcus complains from the middle of the pack.

"How far does this go?" Felix asks suspiciously, ignoring the banter. Now that the path is so narrow, it is easy for me to pack down the snow with Ancient Frost. I can just barely make out the red uniforms of the first legionnaires behind us.

"A few miles, then it comes out near the mouth of the valley. From there, we can head straight to Frigidus."

"Lucky you found it."

"Sure is."

"When exactly did you find it?" Felix's voice is bitter with something I can't place.

"I told you, Aquilo—"

"Ah yes, of course. The God of Winter showed you this secret path that we can use to escape."

"Will you two shut up?" Anas rounds on us from the side. "We're here to scout, not listen to a lover's quarrel." I open my mouth to object but think better of it after seeing the expression on the former *captivus*'s face. He's right anyway—now is not the time.

"Well, thank Aquilo we're not trying to cross this while fighting barbarians," Marcus murmurs as we round a tight bend that requires us to go single file. "I would hate to find one of those lunatics waiting for me on the other side of one of these corners."

No one disagrees with him. The path widens, and we bunch up, making sure to stay away from the edge. I cannot spot the bottom through the snowstorm, but it is a drop that no one can survive. We keep our eyes forward as we move, rushing to clear the path for the men who follow behind us. Any delay could be deadly.

But we are not the only ones who know of this secret pass.

A light thud sounds behind me, causing me to turn. "Ware!" I scream as a bald *berserkir* lands neatly on the balls of his feet behind Jasper. My friend spins, extending his *gladius* in a wicked slash at the barbarian, but the cursed warrior is too quick. He dances to the side, swinging his large double-bladed axe with inhuman strength. I hear more thumps in front of us as more of them spring their ambush. The weapon cuts through Jasper cleanly, rending him in two. His body tumbles off the side of the mountain, vanishing into the swirling snowstorm.

"*Furiae!*" Marcus bellows, pointing toward the front of our formation. I risk a glance over my shoulder to see three of the ice constructs peering down at us from the mountainside. Five *berserkirs* stand next to them, and three more block our path. I catch sight of their leader and feel a shock of surprise. It's Astrid, the gold-banded woman who captured us once before. How did she know?

"Barbarians ahead!" I scream, hoping the legionnaires are getting close enough to hear my warning. Then I throw myself at Jasper's killer. The bald *berserkir* grins, tattoos swirling on his head with living ink. He rushes to meet me, unafraid of a single legionnaire. I call upon both my Symbols, letting them make me cold.

The barbarian feints a low blow with his axe before twisting his grip and whipping the weapon up vertically, trying to split me from groin to breastbone. I remember Percy's advice, dodging the strike, but that maneuver forces me closer to the edge. The Norman cackles as he charges after me, trying to force me over the precipice.

I trust Ancient Frost to guide my footsteps as I circle away from the cliff, trying to keep the *berserkir* at bay with my weapons. He laughs, offering to parry any of my strikes with his axe, forcing me to pull my attacks before they can land.

Licking my lips, I glance at the two weapons in my hand, trying to figure out how to kill him. Against a normal opponent, it would be easy to tie up his axe with one sword while I finish with him with the other. But even if I did kill him, I would die without my Symbols in a matter of moments.

Unless…

Unless I can do what Gaius did.

Seized by a sudden, insane idea, I step forward, pressing the attack. The *berserkir* laughs, thinking that I am a fool. I stab with my *gladius*, aiming for his exposed neck. He sweeps his axe up to catch my blade and push it wide.

But before his weapon can touch mine, I release my Symbols, dropping them like a pair of marbles. When the *berserkir's* axe slams into my *gladius*, it carves a chunk from the blade because it is no longer protected by my will.

I twist my wrist, locking our weapons together, and step forward, stabbing with the now-brittle Frozen Blade. The ice takes him in the neck, and I laugh cruelly at his shocked expression as I pull my sword free. The barbarian collapses to his knees, and I strike his head from his shoulders, sending it falling into the snowy void after my friend. It does not fill the gaping hole in my chest, but I take some solace in the fact that he, at least, has been avenged.

As I turn to help my brothers, I reach for my Symbols, praying to the mostly-dead gods that I am right. Ancient Frost and Iron leap to my call eagerly, filling me with their cold presences. I understand. *Cor* is the bridge that makes the connection between man and the Symbols. The *berserkir* are tattooed with ink made from it—I carry it in my flesh. If I am holding Iron when we come in contact, they can reach through me to sever my connection to the Symbol. But if I am not, there is nothing for them to touch. I just have to be vigilant, and they will not be able to take my power from me. That is why Vrok only took my Iron and left me with Ancient Frost.

The Normans have chosen their ambush spot well. The path is wide enough that they can comfortably swing their large weapons, but not spacious enough for us to form a cohesive defense. The ground rumbles as a *furia* drops into the middle of the fray, raising its fists to smash down on Felix's back.

"No!" I scream uselessly, sprinting toward my friend. I'm too far to strike at the construct. I'll never make it in time. But fortunately, our other friend is faster than me.

"Felix!" Marcus bellows, leaping past me, hurling the *venator* spear that he carries with all his fury. The javelin whistles as it cuts through the air, its relic tip glistening darkly in the low light. It slams into the *furia*'s back, burrowing into the ice just like it was made to.

The construct freezes, hands high. Felix disengages from the *berserkir* he's dueling with and dodges to the side, warned of the danger behind him. But he needn't have worried—the *furia* is already dead. A horrific *crack* echoes throughout the pass dangerously as fissures shoot out of the wound caused by the *venator*. They grow wider with every heartbeat until the *furia* shatters like a teacup, collapsing into a pile of frozen chunks in the snow.

"Kill them all!" Marcus screams, surging forward to retrieve his thrown relic. The rest of us roar in agreement as our hearts soar.

I spy Astrid at the front, shouting orders to the barbarians on the ledge above, and decide to take the head from the snake. I snarl as I cut past the *berserkir* Felix duels, aiming a cut at his leg with my *gladius* as I pass. The barbarian whips his blade around to parry my strike, and I release Iron, letting him carve a weal out of the blade in exchange for his life. Felix drives his sword through the man's chest while he's distracted, and the Norman is dead before I extricate my weapon from his. Around us, the storm grows as it begins to sweep toward the pass. The horde must be on our tail. We have to clear the pass before they catch up.

"Have you lost your mind?" my friend bellows over the suddenly rising wind.

"What?" I scream, not sure I heard him properly. He follows me as I push toward the front to challenge their leader.

"Why would you let him touch your *gladius*? Now you're..."

"Don't hold your Symbols when you make contact with them. They can't cut you off if you're not touching it!"

"Are you sure?" I seize Iron once more and smooth out the notch that the *berserkir* carved in my blade in front of him so he can see I am still whole. I glance back to see his eyes widen as he understands that I still have my Symbols.

"Trust me!"

"More secrets," he grumbles bitterly. I ignore him, promising myself that I will explain everything when we survive. I summon a new *Glacialis Falx* in my right hand. Its hilt no longer glows with the light of a storm, but I am relieved by that. I have no desire to carry a piece of a mad god with me wherever I go.

The barbarians on the ridge above us are gesturing frantically at something behind them that I cannot see. Astrid screams orders, but they do not seem to hear her. I cannot imagine what fresh horror awaits revelation, but I ignore them. I cannot afford to be distracted by my next opponent.

The *berserkir* sees Felix and me approach and turns her attention from her disobedient warriors. She draws her massive longsword and swings it once to limber up her arms. It does not bear any glowing runes or burn with black fire, but I am dismayed to see that she seems as fast as the High King was. In this narrow space, there will be no way to avoid her longer reach. The only way to get to her is to go through it and she knows it.

"Follow me," I command my friend. "I'll hold the blade away; you get close."

"This is a bad idea," he cautions from my right shoulder.

"That's all we have here, I'm afraid." Behind us, Anas and Marcus roar as another *furia* drops into the fray. I trust the two men with *venators* to keep us safe from the construct while we deal with their leader. "The storm is moving, which means we're running out of time."

"May Mars's Bones protect you, then," Felix agrees after a moment. I shake my head in amusement. I'm no longer sure that Mars is any more dead than Aquilo, and if he is alive, I'm more afraid of his plans than this Norman's.

The maelstrom's fury grows, shaking the pass around us.

I lunge forward, charging at the blonde woman where she waits. She responds as I expect, swinging her longsword in a horizontal slash that covers the entire path. I catch it with the Frozen Blade. My icy weapon cracks warningly, straining under the force of her inhuman strength without my will to reinforce it.

I rush forward, sliding my blade against the edge of her sword, preventing it from passing any further. Her eyes widen as Felix dashes to my left, racing at her with *gladius* drawn back for the kill.

With a snarl, she drops her long weapon, hands flashing for a dirk that rides on her belt. I stumble, caught off guard by the sudden absence of pressure. Regaining my balance, I follow my friend in his charge.

Felix closes in on her, driving his sword forward in a vicious stab. The *berserkir* catches the edge of his blade with her knife, twisting it to the side as she steps inside his guard. Before he can adapt, she headbutts him viciously, sending him reeling.

I hurl my damaged Frozen Blade at her head. It's not balanced for throwing, but it distracts her before she can finish off Felix. She bats it to the side, sneering at my poor aim. I return her disdain with a quiet smile, summoning another icy sword in my empty hand. Here in the depths of Winter, it is a trifle for me to replace the lost Ancient Frost essence. Astrid's expression goes still, and she looks at me with wide eyes. She knows that should not be possible.

"Castor, I'm coming!" Marcus shouts from behind me, racing toward me as his opponent falls lifelessly to the ground. I nod in understanding, deliberately angling toward the edge to give my friend as much space to pinch Astrid as possible in these cramped quarters.

Lightning strikes close by, blindingly bright. Its thunder is a roar that does not cease. It builds and builds like an echo feeding itself. The path shakes as the storm rages, and I take my first step toward Astrid, eager to finish this fight so I can help my friends.

But the ground does not settle. Instead, the vibrations grow, rattling me down to my bones. The *berserkir* looks over my shoulder, her eyes going wide. The Symbol of Ancient Frost flares in horrified warning as a wall of motion enters the range of my *animus*. Slowly, I tear my gaze from my enemy and look up the mountainside where the Norman stares.

I have just enough time to see a mass of snow crest like a wave before the avalanche is upon us. A giant creature, like a frozen worm, leaps from the rush, maw gaping with a thousand teeth. My jaw drops at the sight of the *mythus* before the powder slams into me with the fury of the ocean, sweeping me off my feet. My breath is torn from my lungs, and I hurtle over the side of the cliff, carried out into the open air like a riptide.

I'm falling, encased in an immeasurable amount of snow and ice. I call on the Symbol of Ancient Frost with every ounce of will that my Copper *Cor* can leverage. Reaching out with my *animus*, I pull the free-falling snow around me, packing it around me like pillows. I feel the powder stick to itself, forming layer upon layer around me, like a snowman. It swells, burying me at the center of a sphere that I could never escape from.

Dimly, I can sense three blank, human-shaped spots among the snow, others who were caught in the avalanche and swept with me. I cannot tell friend from foe, so I bundle them all in my cocoon, choosing to save all instead of none.

So much time has passed that I am beginning to fear that we have fallen off a cliff that has no bottom, that we might fall forever. Still, I take advantage of the length reinforcing the soft snow with layer upon layer. My veins burn as I push my *Cor* beyond anything I have ever done. My will shakes as I extend my *animus* to its limits. The wintery-blue reserve inside of me is running dangerously low. I burn more essence, trying to hold on just a little longer.

The end comes quickly, like all ends do. My giant snowball slams into something implacable, but as I connect with it, I coax the waiting slush to catch my passengers and me. It is by no means gentle; I scream as I feel one of my legs twist too far to the side. Something snaps, and pain burns through me, overwhelming Ancient Frost's calm. Then the momentum stops, and I sag inside my soft cocoon of snow, bruised and broken.

I am alive.

The avalanche continues to pour down for a few minutes. I don't need a Winter Symbol to know that it still rages; everything around me shudders under its assault. I can't breathe, crushed by the forces that can carve mountains. Gritting my teeth against the pain, I use Ancient Frost to expand a bubble around me and the other human spots to give us places to shelter and breathe. I huddle in the dark, praying for it to end.

Escape while you still can, Aquilo had said.

At last, the rumbling stops, and I let out a tortured sigh of release. My ribs are probably broken too. Each breath feels like a knife blade stabbing into my side. I can only hope my friends are in better condition than me. I force myself to wait, making sure no more is coming.

When I can bear the dark no longer, I gather my legs under me in my tight little sphere, gasping in agony as I put weight on my right leg.

Gingerly, I add pressure to it, holding back a scream as the pain flares. I trade some of Ancient Frost for Iron, letting its metallic embrace dull the pain. In a moment of clarity, I realize I should have used it to reinforce my bones before I landed.

Idiot.

At last, I manage to stand, leaning to my left a little. Now, I just have to get out of here. Calling upon Ancient Frost once more, I push forward at a slight angle, carving a path for myself through the compressed snow. It shifts ponderously, reluctantly accepting my command after being packed down so firmly. I do the same for the others around me. If there are Normans among us, then we will just have to deal with it.

I grit my teeth and reduce my hold on Iron, allowing myself to channel more of the cold Symbol. It opens me to more pain, but I have to get out of here before we run out of air. The snowbank parts more freely, recognizing my authority, and I climb, racing toward the surface. It's hot and stale in the dark, but I make my way forward, guided by the knowledge that Ancient Frost gives to me. Sometimes I feel other things in the pile, like rocks and trees. But others are fleshier things, squished into oblivion. I do not pause to investigate them; they are dead and buried. If I am not efficient, I will join them in this tomb. I must save who I can.

At last, I burst free from the snow and emerge into the storm. I inhale deeply, gasping as I take my first proper breath in minutes. The North Wind whirls around me, cutting at me with its hard, icy flakes. I glance upward, but I cannot spot the pass above—it is shielded by the clouds. As I survey the mass of snow that I rode to the bottom, I am grateful I cannot see more. It would force me to accept a truth that I already know.

Whether or not the avalanche swept away all my friends, the pass is closed. Gaius and the rest of the Twelfth are trapped in a rat hole by the barbarian horde. Most of them will likely die wishing that they had been crushed by the snowy tide. Those legionnaires are the lucky ones.

I shake myself, forcing the maudlin thoughts from my head. The other paths that I carve in my wake are beginning to reach the surface. I pray to every dead god and every Iron Lord that I was able to save my friends and not my enemies.

I claw myself to my feet as the first hole opens, leaning on my right leg to keep my weight off my broken left. I have no *gladius*; I lost it in the fall. I hold out my right hand, trying to use my ability and manifest the *Glacialis Falx*, but the pain makes me slow. If the person inside is a *berserkir*, then I am no better than the little sheep that Aquilo named me.

My heart stops as Felix's head emerges from the thin crust, eyes wide like a diver coming up from the deep. He collapses against the snowy surface, halfway out of the hole, gasping for air.

"Brother!" I shout, hobbling to my friend to help pull him from the ground. "You're okay. You're okay." I'm hysterical, babbling with joy that one of my brothers lives. I am not alone. Not yet.

"*Okay* might be a bit of stretch," the lanky plebeian groans as he slithers free of the snow. He's cradling his left arm against his chest, unwilling to use it. I suspect it suffered a similar fate as my leg. Our *lorica* and Symbols are the only things keeping us functioning.

"More coming." I turn to another spot as a figure bursts free, following the path I created for them. I recognize Marcus's dark skin against the white snow immediately. His eyes are flared, ready for a fight. Somehow, he has kept his grip on his *gladius*, further proof that he was always destined to be a hero and soldier.

"That's it!" he says as he climbs to his feet. He does not seem to be injured like the rest of us. "No more gods. No more oaths. No more! I'm sick of this. I will not be riding *any* more avalanches over the sides of cliffs and into chasms. Is that clear?"

"Crystal," I manage through a delighted laugh at seeing my oldest friend alive and well. "No more avalanches."

"You left out the part about *vota* and gods." His eyes narrow.

"Those ones are a little harder to promise," I admit.

His mouth opens to protest, but before he can admonish me, the fourth survivor emerges. A blonde head erupts from the snow, and my heart stills as Astrid claws her way free from the avalanche's detritus. She glares at us with wild, wide-eyed rage. She still grips her dirk in her right hand, and the dark tattoos inked in her flesh dance like flames.

"I'll handle this," Marcus intones, stepping between us and the *berserkir, gladius* held low. I grit my teeth, finishing the manifestation of the *Glacialis Falx*. I have managed to *cultivate* some Ancient Frost to refill my reserve, but I burn much of it to remake my weapon. Now is no time to not be armed.

A *crunch* interrupts me, and I turn in time to see a massive icy hand punch free of the ground. My heart hammers in my chest as a second fist emerges from the mound. I only shielded three others as we fell. How could anything else survive that drop?

A *furia* levers itself out of the detritus, and I gape in horror. It is twice as large as it was before. Somehow being mixed in the avalanche seems to have allowed it to increase its mass. *It was me*, I realize, studying it with a rueful gaze. When I bound more ice and snow, it was hidden among the rest and got caught up in the command.

Now fully free, it turns to look at us with its black gaze, sending chills down my spine. For a moment, I wonder if it doesn't know I am an enemy. Maybe its minder is dead in the rubble and did not leave it with a command to attack.

"*Hyökkäät*," Astrid snarls in command from over my shoulder. The construct takes a slow, ponderous step toward me, raising its fists into an aggressive position, responding to her command. So much for that.

"That one is all you," Marcus says into the stunned silence.

"Right." I sigh, shifting to face the *furia* and calling on Iron to dull as much of the pain as I can. I have dealt with these before. Ancient Frost is a powerful weapon against them. All I need to do is get one good blow in.

At least there's only one of them.

The snow shudders again as a second *furia* bursts free of its snowy cocoon, as if summoned by my thoughts. A third emerges on its heels like a loyal dog. Both have also swollen to immense proportions, and the three of them tower over me like titans.

Drip. Drip. Blood leaks from my a cut on my left leg to splat at my feet. I eye the wound wistfully before looking at the three constructs that stride toward me. At least my essence reserves aren't empty any longer.

"Felix, I am going to need some help."

CHAPTER 51

In my wounded state, I'm far too slow to dance with three *furiae*. There's a difference between being able to stand and springing about like a madman. The first construct charges me, leaning low to punch me directly in my face. In its evolved form, the thing's fist is about two-thirds the size of my body.

Unable to dodge, I lean forward, striking out with my Frozen Blade, sending my will coursing through it to attack the *furia*. SHATTER, I command, demanding that the fist break instead of crashing into me.

I let out a scream of pain as the construct's hand slams into me, sending me flying. My will bounces off the massive thing. It burns with a new level of defiance fueled by its increased mass. I slam into the packed snow on my back a dozen paces away. This time, I remembered to reinforce my bones with Iron, so I am only bruised as I claw back to my feet.

"What do you want me to do?" Felix demands. Behind us, the sound of metal rings against metal as Astrid and Marcus begin their deadly duel.

"Distract some of them," I pant as I pull myself to my feet. "I can't move fast enough to dodge."

The three titans pace toward me leisurely, their giant legs eating up the distance at a terrifying pace. I pant as I watch them approach, feeling helpless. I'm too tired and wounded to run, too weak to fight them. Each of their heavy steps shakes the ground at my feet, rattling the foundation of my confidence. We are going to die here.

Felix races to my right, bending to scoop up a chunk of ice from the ground. "Here, you devil!" he roars, voice echoing off the mountain wall behind us. "Come and get me."

One of the *furia* takes the bait, turning ponderously to study my comrade with its beady black eyes. It takes a few steps in Felix's direction, leaving me with only two giants to deal with, which is better, but still too many for me to handle in my current state.

The lead *furia* continues stalking me, unwavering in its hatred. I sigh but set myself, wishing I still had my *scutum*. The behemoth closes in on me, fist pulled back to crush me like a bug. At the last moment, I dodge to the side, screaming at the pain that erupts from my left leg as I do.

I lash out with the *Glacialis Falx* as I pass it, aiming for its upper left thigh. My sword bites deeply, but the appendage is too thick for me to cut it off with a single blow. My will flails at it impotently, unable to find any purchase. The increased mass seems to give it more power, making it feel like it has Ascended. If the others I have faced were the equivalent of a Copper, this one is a Silver.

I scramble to my feet, cursing over the pain as I force myself to keep moving. Dread fills me as I study the two *furiae* that hound me. I am not enough. Even if I were whole and healthy, I would not have the power I need to force these creatures into submission. I cannot fight; I cannot run. We are out of options.

Iron grates against iron as Marcus and Astrid continue their battle. Marcus lets out a shout of surprise, and my head whips around to see the tip of my friend's blade fall to the ground, shorn off by the *berserkir*'s inhuman strength.

Slowly, Marcus raises his head to stare at the Norman. His shoulders are tense, and his fear makes him brittle. He knows what I know. That we are too weak—too small—to stand against these opponents. Felix and I are both cut off from him by the *furiae*, unable to reach our friend. His fear only serves to highlight his bravery.

He does not retreat; he does not back down. In this moment, he is the hero that he grew up wanting to be. The wolves have come to the sheepfold. He stands bravely in the entryway, standing against the predators.

But bravery is not armor. It cannot protect soft flesh or turn away blades.

Astrid closes the distance between her and Marcus, knife flashing. His shortened blade can no longer keep her at a safe distance. Iron rings as they exchange a quick series of blows. With each strike, the *berserkir* takes a step forward, getting inside his range.

I see it too late to warn him. She twists, catching his right hand with her left, spinning backward to stand against him like a lover as she stabs her knife behind her and into his stomach. For a moment, the whole scene freezes, even the *furiae* watch the two of them trapped in this deadly embrace.

Then Astrid steps forward, wrenching her knife free, spraying red blood across the sand. Before I can blink, she spins, plunging her knife into his chest again and again, turning his flesh into a ruin. Slowly, Marcus falls to his knees. It takes an eon for him to collapse.

The *berserkir* stands above him, chest heaving as she watches him die. I cannot move. I cannot breathe. Distantly, I am aware that I am screaming. To me, it sounds like the howl of a wolf crying out its rage into the night.

The North Wind's ire increases, and the hairs on the back of my neck stand on edge as I feel the scrutiny of the god descend upon me once again. Mocking laughter dances in my ears, rejoicing at my misfortune. I stare at Marcus lying still on the ground, his dark skin stark against the white snow. I cannot look away. Aquilo always meant to destroy us all, barbarian and legion alike. What love does he have for the iron people who killed him?

Rage, cold and furious, sprouts in me, like a blacksmith's forge in the center of Winter's Heart. With every breath, it grows as if my lungs are the bellows, feeding it until it is something wild and out of control. This is the strength that Felix once told me of—the power of pain. My brothers are dead, but I am not, so I must endure. I must survive for them. Their names swirl in my mind as I glare at the gray sky swirling above me. *Gaius, Percy, Clintus, Anas, Durus, Unus,* Marcus. The list goes on as the divine pressure on me spikes, growing as if I am drawing the eyes of all the dead gods like moths to a flame. I channel that rage inward, demanding that my body fix itself—that I be made *whole*. But something blocks my path, a dark thing that denies my progress. The collar I wear about my neck flares in warning as both of my *Corda* seek to become more.

Something broken finds its home—a jagged edge clicks into place. I feel whole, like I did in that brief moment when Aquilo spoke to me in the void. Perhaps it was he who showed me the way. My *inhibitus* activates, choking me with its cold, unrelenting grip. But its secrets are laid bare to me now. I understand both of the twisting metals that circle my neck as if they were a part of me. There is no *Cor* in existence that would dare defy me in this moment. They answer my call as I speak my will to them now.

Shatter.

My slave collar explodes into a thousand pieces, littering the ground at my feet like falling stars. I inhale, pulling in as much essence from around me as I can. It feels like I am taking the first full breath in my life. Ancient Frost pours into me like a torrent, filling its reserve beyond what I can hold, overflowing like a cup at a feast. My *lorica* too feeds the Iron Symbol, which drinks from its supply greedily. I throw back my head and scream in defiance as the *furiae* draw close. I will not die here. I will avenge my family, my friends, and my legion brothers. The constructs pause as I roar, unable to process my strange behavior. I ignore them. They cannot stop what is coming.

Ascendo. I Ascend.

Fire plays along my limbs, like the veins of my *Corda* are becoming molten metal. Strength fills me, banishing my exhaustion and pain. My essence reserves expand, each growing from a thimble to a jug. My awareness grows, and I feel every snowflake dancing on Aquilo's wind, every *gladius* beneath my feet. Iron and Ancient Frost pour into me, drawn from all around me, filling me with more than I have ever held in my life.

It is done in a flash, like the head of a match catching fire. Shaking with excitement, I drop the Frozen Blade in my right hand to peel back my left sleeve. I hiss as my broken leg complains at the weight I put on it. It is not healed, but my Ascension has touched it. My body is far stronger than it was just heartbeats ago. But even that miracle cannot distract me from the change to my Cor. I stare in stupefied wonder at the new veins that cover my forearm, replacing the Copper ones that I am used to.

I am *Argent*.

I am Silver.

There are still plenty of white *rasa* lines, I notice with a hint of exasperation. It seems I am still plagued by the wolf-man's meddling. I had hoped that when I Ascended—it does not matter. Now is not the time to dwell on my own desires.

"Dead gods," I hear Felix whisper in shock.

The first *furia* shifts, taking a tentative step forward, and even at this distance, I sense it. I no longer need to be physically touching something from my Symbol to give me knowledge of it. I cannot affect it without touch—I am no Gold—but I can feel it. I let my sleeve drop and smile up at the gods staring down at me. Even though I cannot see it, I'm sure *Mons* Olympus drifts up above the storm.

A cold unlike any I have ever experienced swallows me, devouring my emotions. My anger and rage no longer burn. I am lost, not just to Iron, but to Ancient Frost as well. Deep in their frigid embrace I am only sharp edges and killer focus.

"Stay back," I call to Felix, striding to meet the titans as they come to kill me. I debate summoning another *Glacialis Falx*. I'm pretty sure

I could make two swords with the essence that rages in me. But I don't bother. I don't need a blade to destroy these constructs.

Thanks to the wound in my leg, I'm still slower than I should be, but the new strength filling my body lets me move comfortably as I move to meet the first *furia*. It raises back its boulder-sized hand for another blow, and I leap at it using my good leg as a spring. I'm delighted at how fast I move. As I close with it, I cock my fist back and punch the thing in the chest. My will parts the ice of the giant *furia* with ease, and my hand grabs the *Cor* Heart that rests in its center. I rip it out with a savage twist, throwing it behind me as I move onto the next one.

I leap upward, rising above the hands of the second construct as it tries to grab me. Its black eyes stare at me as I draw level with its head. My fist smashes through its face with the ease of a sledgehammer punching through a rotten log.

The third *furia* charges me as the first one is still collapsing to its knees, and I sidestep, backhanding it in the leg as it thunders past. Its limb shatters above the knee, and the lopsided construct tumbles onto its face. I'm on it before it can try to get up, laughing as I crush its other leg. For a moment, I debate leaving it there, helpless, unable to die. But then I remember it is just a thing, and I break its head into tiny pieces.

I feel Astrid's iron as she charges me from behind.

The *berserkir* closes in on me at inhuman speed. Even my new Silver strength would struggle to match her power. But the snow shows me her footsteps, and her knife betrays her to me. I know where she is even without looking.

At the last moment, I step to the side, ducking under her blade and stabbing behind me with the *Glacialis Falx*. My icy blade cuts into her side, but her own power allows her to react quickly, pulling away from my blade, preventing it from carving more than a scratch into her.

Her momentum carries her past me, and I lash at her feet with my will, commanding the snow to harden into ice, and grab her. She snarls, ripping her left foot free, but I attack the right while it is undefended.

Layers of ice sweep over her boot, hardening into stone. She leans down to hack at it with her dirk, and I withdraw, protecting my Symbol from her attack. If she still had her giant sword, it would have been easy to break free, but now her weapon is short and light, and it buys me the time to get close to her.

Ice sprays as she digs at it with furious strength, heedless of her own foot's safety, like a rat caught in a trap. Astrid's head snaps up at my approach, and her expression turns cruel as she whips her long knife at me.

Iron traces her movement, showing me the angle of her wrist, and I sidestep it easily, getting inside her guard like she just did to my friend. Slowly, I extend my frozen blade to hover a hairsbreadth from her neck. My hand does not shake; the blade is still.

The *berserkir* does not beg for her life or surrender. The blonde Norman lifts her chin proudly, exposing her neck further. Both of my cold Symbols, Iron and Ancient Frost, delight in this. They do not understand mercy—they are closer cousins to justice.

We stand in this quiet, staring into each other's eyes for a long moment. We understand each other, she and I. The same chill that fills me lives in her. She would do the same thing that I will—she has done it. For a few heartbeats, we are closer than I have ever been with anyone in my whole life.

Then she explodes into motion, dirk flashing toward my blade, forcing my hand. Durus's training takes over, and I lunge forward, burying my icy blade in her neck. Astrid gurgles once, falling to her knees. The snow around her grows red like it is under a blood rain. She does not look away from my eyes until the light fades from them and she sinks to the ground.

Panting with exertion, I step back to survey my handiwork. Astrid is dead. The three mega-*furia* are in pieces, scattered among the detritus like broken children's toys. Power courses through me as I refill my reserves, pulling Ancient Frost from the snow and Iron from the buried legionnaires beneath me. I am *powerful*. A madness spreads through me, an unquenchable joy at thwarting the *Argentum Consilio*'s plans at becoming what I deserve to be. Atticus's face flickers in my mind, and I grin horribly, ready to challenge him even though I still have farther to walk along my path.

"What have you done?" Felix's furious voice cuts through my euphoria like a blade, startling me enough that I release my Symbols. Pain comes crashing down on me as the numbness from my cold attunements fades. My head snaps toward Marcus's still body, heart breaking all over again. Killing his killer no longer fills the hole that he has left.

"You idiot!" Felix shouts, but I ignore him, dragging myself toward my best friend. He is dead—anyone with eyes can tell that. But I don't believe it. I won't, until I have checked for his pulse myself.

I don't remember sinking to my knees in the snow beside him, but my hands shake as they reach for his neck. They were still when I killed, but now they look like leaves in a storm. Marcus is cold—far colder than he ever was in life.

Already death has stolen the warmth that radiated from him. His face is no longer amused, just slack. He does not look peaceful, only stiff. My hands find no heartbeat, and the little ember of hope inside of me dies.

It is too cold to cry—the tears would freeze instantly—but I try anyway. I howl and beat my best friend's chest, but he does not wake up. He does not turn and mock me for my sorrow—he merely accepts it—because he is dead.

"They're going to kill you." Felix's angry voice interrupts my memorial. I turn, red-eyed and sniffling, to stare at the former plebeian. His despair manifests as rage. "You stupid, greedy fool. You did it again. You have broken your oaths. They will kill you and the rest of us for being with you."

"What are you worried about?" I demand, my own anger sparking at his interruption. "They already have tried to kill us!" I rise to my feet so that Felix cannot stare down at me any longer. He's still taller than me, but I am no longer on my knees.

"Before, you were an inconvenience—a rounding error. They dealt with you as an afterthought!"

"Now I am *dangerous*," I counter.

"Now you are *blasphemous*," he corrects, tilting his head. "They will do anything to kill you for the rules you have broken. How did you do it?"

"Which part?"

"Bind two Symbols."

Despite my irritation, I feel my eyebrows rise in surprise. None of the others put the pieces together, not even Gaius. Although maybe that was because he did not want to admit what he could see.

"I don't know."

"If you lie to me one more time, our fellowship is done." Felix's voice is colder than the remnants of Aquilo's North Wind that still whips at us. I believe him. It is one thing to seek vengeance against those who wronged us. It is another to break the foundational rule of the empire.

"I swear it," I say, holding up a hand to stop him. "It just *happened*. I think it is something the wolf-man did to me."

Felix is silent for a moment as he ponders my response. "You Ascended."

"I had to."

"You are the first *Infidelis* Iron in four hundred years."

I shudder as I realize the truth of what he is saying. For four centuries, the *electii* of the Iron Empire have faithfully followed the rule set down by the original Iron Lords: no one may attune Iron except for those in the legions, and no one may Ascend beyond Copper without the permission of the Empress.

"You have damned us all. They won't just kill us. They will erase anyone who has ever met us to make sure your secret stays buried. You are no longer a threat to a Censor, but to the empire." Felix's judgment is a scourge that bites deeper than Durus's whip. My own anger flares, given life by his condemnation.

"That's how this started," I snap, out of patience for his criticisms that are not fair. "Or have you forgotten what Atticus did, why we swore our *votum* in the first place?"

"But you have escalated it beyond—"

"And what would you have had me do?" I thunder. Subconsciously, the Symbol of Ancient Frost slips into my grasp, like a weapon eager to be used.

"They were going to kill us. THEY KILLED MARCUS!" I do not mean to shout, but the fury inside of me cannot be contained. The snow around us rumbles ominously as my emotions flail. Felix glances to the side in surprise.

"And so we trade one death for another."

"We trade one death for a chance," I correct him. "For a chance."

"For a chance to do *what?*" The former plebeian's shoulders slump. "We set out to earn our *Cor*, and the gods punished us for being cavalier with our oaths. Ten of us swore to have vengeance, and now we are two. What chance do we have, Castor?" The ground rumbles in warning, and his face pales as if he fears my anger. It hurts me to see that expression on my friend's face. I shake my head in denial.

"That was not me." His face pales even further. We are not alone. I turn away from Felix, scanning the horizon as I send my *animus* searching. My Silver senses pinpoint the source immediately as a massive *thing* burrows through the snow under our feet. My heart skips a beat as I remember the brief glimpse of what had to be a *mythus* that triggered the avalanche.

The giant blue worm coursed through the snow like it was water, and he was a fish. Tentatively, I reach out with my Ancient Frost to touch the monster as it courses along. Frozen will crushes me, knocking my *animus* away like a scolding hand. I stagger in surprise at the power, which is an order of magnitude above anything I could dream of summoning.

The thing pauses, and I sense it studying me, like a *tigris* studying a small rodent, deciding if it is worth the effort to eat. Despite my new power, I remain very, very still, trying to look as unappetizing as possible. It must work because after a moment, the thing continues on its way, ignoring me like an insect.

When it's gone, I laugh in disbelief at encountering yet another legend. Ignoring Felix and his judgment, I make a crude hand gesture at the sky and laugh. "I lived, you dead bastard!" I shout madly. "Go back to your frozen throne and rot for another four centuries."

Aquilo does not reply, but the presence of the god seems to withdraw even as the winds increase their fury, because I still have not learned my lesson about taunting dead gods.

EPILOGUE

We walk for what feels like a day. My leg begins to fail me, despite my Ascension. Even my Silver strength has limits. I have lost too much blood. I am not cold, thanks to my Symbols, but hunger gnaws at me. Thirst carves at me with its knives. I try to eat snow, but it is not enough.

The world is a white void without ending. I do not know where I am or where I am going. I try to steer us south toward Frigidus using *Sol*'s brightness, but the storm still swirls overhead, obscuring the light .

I fade in and out of conscious thought as I trudge. In my weakened state, it takes most of my concentration to put one foot in front of the other. The snow does not bar my path, which is the only reason I make it as far as I do. I can feel my spirit weakening. I cannot keep going, but I cannot stop. Eventually, even I will freeze and die in this place.

At some point, I realize that I am alone. I sweep as far as I can with my improved *animus*, but I cannot find Felix. I tell myself that the storm drove us apart, and I lost him. I cannot bear the thought that it was he who abandoned me. Maybe this is how it was always going to be. I have already cost him so much.

I am so numb.

I do not have the energy to keep this fellowship together anymore. I can barely keep walking. The sky begins to grow dark, and still I trudge, hoping for a miracle. I see the faces of my dead circling me like wolves, waiting to see if I will join them in their graves. My parents whisper in the wind, urging me to come find them in Pluto's domain. My Legion brothers watch to see if I will fail in fulfilling the *votum* of revenge we swore together. The bloody rock in my pocket weighs me down, trying to pull me into the Underworld.

Sometimes I sense the spine-tingling presence of a god. Once, I think I see a woman watching me through the snowy swirls, but when I look again, she is gone. I am plagued by despair. I know that I will not survive this place. Despite everything I have done to avenge my family and friends, the cold will claim me.

At last, my leg will go no further. I debate crawling, but I do not have the will to carry on. I settle in against the base of a tall pine and close my eyes, content to sit here for an eternity. There is no everflame here to guide my spirit once it leaves my body. It is a far cry from the warm fields of Segesta, but it is beautiful in its own way. A small smile crosses my lips as I close my eyes for the final time. Soon I will not care about gods, *vota*, or revenge. I am going home.

I am at peace when the darkness claims me.

My rest is disturbed by the sound of rattling chains and grunting oaths. I open my eyes to find myself sitting in an iron cage that rests on the back of a sled. I sit up slowly, taking stock of my surroundings. I'm still in the North, but the clear sky shows that we're heading south. Several other sleds follow in our wake, part of a train.

A few men and women eye me distrustfully from around the cage as I sit up. An iron collar rests around my neck. Not an *inhibitus*, just a collar for prisoners.

"He's awake!" a voice calls from the front of the cage.

The man nearest to me snorts in derision. "May Dead Nemesis gut snitches," he murmurs to himself as part curse, part prayer. As I come back to myself, I sit up, scanning the prisoners for Felix's lanky form. If they found me there's a chance he crossed their path as well. But I see no sign of my friend. Darkness blooms in my chest as I realize that I am well and truly alone. I am the last.

"Halt!" a strong voice calls, and our sled slows, as do the ones behind us. A rotund man lowers himself from the front seat, crunching his way through the snow to peer at me through the bars of the cage. He has a squished, mean face and bad teeth.

"Don't care what your name is or where you were goin'," he tells me without preamble. "You belong to me now. If'n you're good and don't make a fuss about it, we'll feed you and mend you." He gestures at my broken leg. "Thank the dead gods we found you at all. Storm blew us off course, and we found you sleeping in the snow."

I stare at the slaver, debating my response. It would be so easy to rip the iron bars off this cage and stab him with them. But then what? There are too many for me to fight in my current state. I need to heal before I can survive on my own, so I will play along, at least for now.

"Understood," I manage to croak with a voice that hasn't worked in a day. "Where are we going?"

"The markets in Anteforum." The obese man snorts at the expression on my face. He thinks that it is horror, but it is not. It is an opportunity. He waddles back to the front of the sled. A whip cracks, and we resume moving, sliding across the snow. "Someone get him some water!" he shouts. One of the other prisoners passes me a canteen, and I drink from it deeply.

As I swallow, I cannot stop laughing. The other prisoners stare at me warily, like they're locked in a cage with a rabid animal that might attack at any moment. But I'm not mad. I'm laughing because I am beginning to understand what I am and what I will become.

Soon, my enemies will know it too.

———

The story will continue in

IRONBOUND BOOK TWO

THANK YOU FOR READING IRONBOUND

So, how was it? I hoped you enjoyed reading *Ironbound* as much as I did writing it. If you did, the best way to help me spread the word is by leaving a review! Millions of books are published on Amazon every year. The best way to get traction and discoverability is through the reviews that readers leave. So if you enjoyed it, please let people know!

If, for some reason, you're not able to leave reviews, word of mouth is powerful! Tell your friends you think will like it. The better these books do, the more time I can spend working on them, and the more fish I can buy for my aquarium collection.

But no matter what, thanks for taking the time to read my story. I hope to find you again at the end of the next one!

- Andrew

PATREON

If you're unfamiliar, Patreon is a place where you can support your favorite authors and get access to books while they are still being worked on. You can get everything from my sincere thanks to a chance to give me feedback on the direction of the story. You can subscribe for a day, a month, or a year. It is not required by any means, but it does help me to continue this adventure!

To read the next book of Ironbound, *COLD WIND,* early, as well as my other writing projects, check out the link to the Patreon below or scan the QR code with your phone.

www.patreon.com/AndrewGivler